THE COMPLETE
CANTERBURY TALES

THE COMPLETE
CANTERBURY TALES

GEOFFREY CHAUCER
IN THE TRANSLATION BY FRANK ERNEST HILL
ILLUSTRATION BY
EDWARD BURNE-JONES AND WILLIAM MORRIS

CHARTWELL
BOOKS, INC.

Images reproduced with the permission of Dover Publications

This edition printed in 2007 by
CHARTWELL BOOKS, INC.
A Division of **BOOK SALES, INC.**
114 Northfield Avenue
Edison, New Jersey 08837

Copyright © 2007 Arcturus Publishing Limited
26/27 Bickels Yard, 151–153 Bermondsey Street,
London SE1 3HA

ISBN-13: 978-0-7858-2312-4
ISBN-10: 0-7858-2312-3

Layout: Emily Gibson

Printed in China

Contents

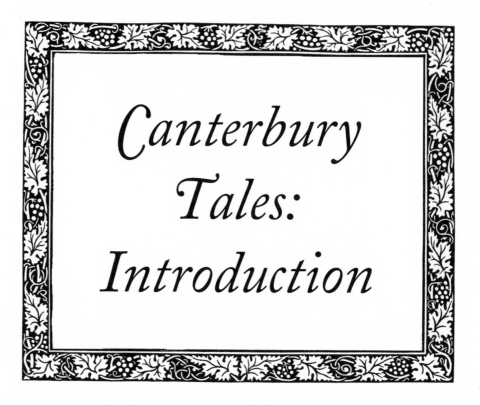

Canterbury Tales: Introduction

*M*ORE THAN THIRTY people meet by chance at an inn in London. In the morning, they will all set off on a pilgrimage to visit the shrine of Thomas à Becket in Canterbury cathedral. The inn-keeper (the Host) suggests that they hold a story-telling competition, with the winner receiving a free dinner at the inn after the return journey. And so the scene is set for *The Canterbury Tales*, the earliest and most famous collection of tales in English. The *Tales*, still popular and relevant after 600 years, is universally acclaimed as one of the greatest masterpieces of English literature.

The Canterbury Tales is far from just a collection of stories. It represents a flamboyant romp through the literary traditions of England and mainland Europe, encompassing all types of composition from the most lofty – elevated, classical love story and spiritually uplifting sermon – to the most lowly – trite, doggerel verse and bawdy comedy. The tellers present a vivid cross-section of humanity and a sparkling portrait of medieval life. Some of the stories are closely and convincingly matched to their tellers. So the Knight tells a courtly tale of battles and love, and the coarse Miller follows with a down-to-earth tale of sexual adventure and trickery. Other characters seem to be at odds with their tales, but their choice reveals much about how they see themselves. So the vain and proud Prioress tells a tale of saintly virtue, and the fat, worldly Monk recites a string of dismal tragedies. But their immediacy is undimmed by passing time and changing habits. The poet John Dryden said in 1700, 'their general Characters are still remaining in Mankind, and even in England... For Mankind is ever the same, and nothing lost out of Nature, though everything is alter'd'.

The *Tales* includes saints' legends, verse romances, fabliaux (comic, usually bawdy tales written by street entertainers in northeast France c. 13th century), moral tales, ballads and the Monk's collection of tragedies. The range of voices is just as varied. The *Tales* begins with a *General Prologue* which presents portraits of many of the pilgrims. Depicted by a naïve narrator who takes each person at face value, the character studies are often undercut by gentle comedy to satirize contemporary society. Many characters go on to present prologues of their own to introduce their tales, revealing more about their personalities. There is sometimes tension between the portrait in the *General Prologue*, a pilgrim's own prologue and the message or tenor of the tale they tell.

Collections of tales have a long history, dating back to the Arabic *Thousand and One Nights*. From Chaucer's own century, Boccaccio's *Decameron* (in Italian) presents 100 tales told over ten days by a group fleeing the Black Death. Chaucer is unique, though, in giving his tales such a vividly realized and dramatic framework. The dynamic of the group of pilgrims provides tales that generate or reflect rivalry between characters and develop themes or explore debates within the tales. The stories can be read in isolation as self-contained narratives, but much is lost by taking them out of context.

Geoffrey Chaucer, the 'father of English poetry', was the earliest great writer of English. He was a pioneer, working in English when many other British writers were still composing in either French or Latin. Even though Chaucer's 14th-century language has become increasingly remote and difficult to understand, he has had an immense influence on later writers including Shakespeare, Dryden and Tennyson. *The Canterbury Tales* is his towering achievement.

Chaucer built up the collection of stories from some time in the 1380s until shortly before his death in 1400. He may have written some of the tales before hitting on the idea of the collection and its framing narrative. He apparently did not finish the task: the plan outlined in the *General Prologue* is for each pilgrim to tell two tales on the way to Canterbury and two on the way back. Thirty-four pilgrims (including Chaucer) are introduced in the *General Prologue*, but only 24 even start a tale. Only Chaucer has more than one tale; the Host interrupts his truly terrible tale and he tells a different one, giving him one and a half tales. Some characters who are not mentioned in the *Prologue* tell tales, and some mentioned are neither fully described nor given a tale. The collection as it stands is like an unfinished symphony: a great, inspiring and inspired work that inevitably leaves us wondering what it would have been like if its creator had lived to complete it.

The text

Chaucer was writing before the invention of printing in the western world. In the 14th century, books were distributed as manuscripts, laboriously copied by hand onto paper or vellum (made of sheepskin) and hand bound into large, heavy volumes. The *Tales* was released not as a collection but in dribs and drabs. They have come down to us in more than 80 manuscripts, some containing many or all tales and some just a few. There is no finally fixed order to all the tales, no equivalent of a printed text with everything in the order which the poet intended, though some tales are clearly linked to those that follow or precede them. The tales are given here in the order in which they are most commonly printed in modern editions.

Chaucer's English (called Middle English by scholars) is very different from modern English. The tales are presented here in the modern English translation of Frank Ernest Hill, first published in America in 1935.

It is likely that spoken Middle English sounded more similar to American English than to British English. English in the 14th century had many regional variations. Modern English began to emerge with the rise of the printed book, which spread the London dialect of English around the country and standardized English spelling.

> Whan that Aprill with his shoures soote
> The droghte of March hath perced to the roote,
> And bathed every veyne in swich licour

Of which vertu engendred is the flour;

Whan Zephirus eek with his sweete breeth

Inspired hath in every holt and heeth

The tendre croppes, and the yonge sonne

Hath in the Ram his half cours yronne,

And smale foweles maken melodye,

That slepen al the nyght with open ye

(So priketh hem Nature in hir corages),

Thanne longen folk to goon on pilgrimages,

And palmeres for to seken straunge strondes,

To ferne halwes, kowthe in sondry londes;

And specially from every shires ende

Of Engelond to Caunterbury they wende,

The hooly blisful martir for to seke,

That hem hath holpen whan that they were seeke.

Opening of the *General Prologue* in Chaucer's
original (modern punctuation)

There are many recordings of extracts from *The Canterbury Tales* spoken
in the original language available online.

The Kelmscott Chaucer

Some of the manuscript sources of *The Canterbury Tales* are illustrated, but many are not. However, the *Tales* provided an inspiration for many later artists. One of the most sumptuous editions ever produced of *The Canterbury Tales* was published in 1896, the work of William Morris' private Kelmscott Press. The Kelmscott Chaucer is generally considered one of the world's finest books; the illustrations in this edition are taken from it.

Morris was a founder of the Arts and Crafts movement. Though himself an architect first and later a painter, he found fame as a designer of fabrics, wallpapers, murals, stained glass windows and furniture. He was also a writer and social reformer. With the Kelmscott Press, he aimed to recreate the quality of printing achieved by the early hand presses of the 15th and 16th centuries. The Kelmscott Chaucer – an edition of all of Chaucer's works illustrated by Morris' friend Edward Burne-Jones – was the Press's finest production. It was produced in 1896 in an edition of 486 copies. Of these, 425 copies were printed on paper and 13 copies on vellum; 48 of them were bound in white pigskin with silver clasps.

Burne-Jones' illustrations for the Kelmscott Chaucer are heavily influenced by the Pre-Raphaelite movement, with its emphasis on beauty and a romantic and – later – almost mystical bias. Burne-Jones worked closely with Dante Gabriel Rossetti, one of the founding members of the Pre-Raphaelite Brotherhood. This was a group of three painters who formed a 'brotherhood' in 1848 to promote a new style of art. They were inspired by the natural style of Italian painting from the time before the Renaissance (before Raphael) and aimed to emulate this style, rejecting the

Latine domos patrias Scithice post aspera gentis
Prelia laurigero &c.

Heere bigynneth the knyghtes tale

Whilom as olde stories tellen vs
Ther was a duc þt highte Theseus
Of Atthenes he was lord and gouernour
And in his tyme swich a conquerour
That gretter was ther noon vnder the sonne
Ful many a riche contree hadde he wonne
What with his wysdom and his chiualrie
He conquered al the regne of Femenye
That whilom was ycleped Scithia
And wedded the queene ypolita
And broghte hir hoom with hym in his contree
With muchel glorie and greet solempnytee
And eek hir faire suster Emelye
And thus with victorie and with melodye
Lete I this noble duc to Atthenes ryde
And al his hoost in armes hym bisyde
And eek if it nere to long to heere
I wolde yow haue toold fully the manere
How wonnen was the regne of Femenye
By Theseus and by his chiualrye
And of the grete bataille for the nones
Bitwixen Atthenes and Amazones
And how asseged was ypolita
The faire hardy queene of Scithia
And of the feste þt was at hir weddynge
And of the tempest at hir hoom comynge
But al that thyng I moot as now forbere
I haue god woot a large feeld to ere
And wayke been the oxen in my plough
The remenaunt of the tale is long ynough
I wol nat letten eek noon of this route
Lat euery felawe telle his tale aboute
And lat se now who shal the soper wynne
And ther I lefte I wol ayeyn bigynne
This duc of whom I make mencioun
Whan he was come almoost vn to the toun
In al his wele and in his mooste pryde
He was war as he caste his eye aside
Where that ther kneled in the weye
A compaignye of ladyes tweye and tweye

Chawat

Another beautifully illustrated version of The Canterbury Tales, *the Ellesmere Chaucer was produced c. 1400. The Knight's Tale is pictured here, featuring one of the 23 equestrian portraits of the pilgrims (including Chaucer himself) the Ellesmere Chaucer is famous for. Rich in floriated borders, most pages contain images in gold leaf. The text was written by one scribe*

formal and – as they thought – unnatural style popular in England in the mid-1800s. Burne-Jones himself leaned heavily on the work of the 15th-century Italian painters Filippino Lippi and Sandro Boticelli. The 87 illustrations in the Kelmscott Chaucer were produced by Burne-Jones as pencil sketches, then worked over by R. Catterson-Smith using Chinese white and Indian ink. The ink drawings were transferred to wooden blocks and engraved by William Harcourt Hooper. Burne-Jones worked for four years on the project, devoting every Sunday to it in the hope of completing the work before the elderly Morris died. He succeeded; Morris died the same year the edition was published.

Dr Anne Rooney, 2007

The General Prologue

IN THE GENERAL Prologue, Chaucer sets out the framework for the ensuing tales. A group of people meet at an inn in London as they prepare to set off on a pilgrimage to the shrine of Thomas à Becket at Canterbury Cathedral, the most popular shrine in England. Chaucer uses the prologue to introduce the characters who will be telling the tales. While some are vividly realized, memorable individuals, others are given only the briefest of sketches. Perhaps Chaucer would have returned to flesh them out, had he lived to complete his stated project.

THE GENERAL PROLOGUE

*Here begins the
Book of the Tales
of Canterbury*

WHEN April with his showers hath pierced the
      drought
Of March with sweetness to the very root,
And flooded every vein with liquid power
That of its strength engendereth the flower;
When Zephyr also with his fragrant breath
Hath urged to life in every holt and heath
New tender shoots of green, and the young sun
His full half course within the Ram hath run,
And little birds are making melody
That sleep the whole night through with open eye,
For in their hearts doth Nature stir them so,
Then people long on pilgrimage to go,
And palmers to be seeking foreign strands,
To distant shrines renowned in sundry lands.
And then from every English countryside
Especially to Canterbury they ride,
There to the holy sainted martyr kneeling
That in their sickness sent them help and healing.
   Now in that season it befell one day
In Southwark at the Tabard as I lay,
Ready upon my pilgrimage to start
Toward Canterbury, reverent of heart,
There came at night into that hostelry
Full nine and twenty in a company,
People of all kinds that had chanced to fall
In fellowship, and they were pilgrims all
Riding to Canterbury. The stables there

Were ample, and the chambers large and fair,
And well was all supplied us of the best,
And by the time the sun had gone to rest
I knew them and had talked with every one,
And so in fellowship had joined them soon,
Agreeing to be up and take our way
Where I have told you, early with the day.
   But none the less, while I have space and time,
Before I venture farther with my rime,
It seems to me no more than reasonable
That I should speak of each of them and tell
Their characters, as these appeared to me,
And who they were, and what was their degree,
And something likewise of their costumes write;
And I will start by telling of a knight.
   A KNIGHT there was, and that a noble man,
Who from the earliest time when he began
To ride forth, loved the way of chivalry,
Honor and faith and generosity.
Nobly he bare himself in his lord's war,
And he had ridden abroad (no man so far),
In many a Christian and a heathen land,
Well honored for his worth on every hand.
   He was at Alexandria when that town
Was won, and many times had sat him down
Foremost among the knights at feast in Prussia.
In Lithuania had he fought, and Russia,
No Christian more. Well was his worth attested
In Spain when Algeciras was invested,
And at the winning of Lyeys was he,
And Sataly, and rode in Belmarie;
And in the Great Sea he had been at hand
When many a noble host had come to land.
Of mortal battles he had known fifteen,
And jousted for our faith at Tramissene
Thrice in the lists, and always slain his foe.
And he had been in Turkey, years ago,
Lending the prince of Palaty his sword
In war against another heathen lord;
And everywhere he went his fame was high.
And though renowned, he bore him prudently;

HERE BEGINNETH THE TALES OF CANTERBURY AND FIRST THE PROLOGUE THEREOF

The tendre croppes, and the yonge sonne
Hath in the Ram his halfe cours yronne,
And smale foweles maken melodye,
That slepen al the nyght with open eye,
So priketh hem nature in hir corages;
Thanne longen folk to goon on pilgrimages,
And palmeres for to seken straunge strondes,
To ferne halwes, kowthe in sondry londes;
And specially, from every shires ende
Of Engelond, to Caunterbury they wende,
The hooly blisful martir for to seke,
That hem hath holpen whan that they were seeke.

BIFIL that in that seson on a day,
In Southwerk at the Tabard as I lay,
Redy to wenden on my pilgrymage
To Caunterbury with ful devout corage,
At nyght were come into that hostelrye
Wel nyne and twenty in a compaignye,
Of sondry folk, by aventure yfalle
In felaweshipe, and pilgrimes were they alle,
That toward Caunterbury wolden ryde.

WHAN THAT Aprille with his shoures soote
The droghte of March hath perced to the roote,
And bathed every veyne in swich licour,
Of which vertu engendred is the flour;
Whan Zephirus eek with his swete breeth
Inspired hath in every holt and heeth

Plate 1: The General Prologue (p. 16)

Meek was he in his manner as a maid.
In all his life to no man had he said
A word but what was courteous and right:
He was a very perfect noble knight.
But now to tell you what array he had –
His steeds were good, but he himself was clad
Plainly; in fustian doublet he was dressed,
Discolored where his coat of mail had pressed,
For he was lately come from his voyage,
And went at once to do his pilgrimage.

    With him there went a SQUIRE, that was his son –
A lover and soldier, full of life and fun,
With locks right-curled, as if just out of press;
His age in years was twenty, I should guess.
In stature he appeared of middle height,
And great of strength, and wondrous quick and light.
And he had gone campaigning recently
In Flanders, in Artois, and Picardy,
And in this short space bore a gallant part,
Hoping for favor in his lady's heart.
His raiment shone as if he were a mead
Broidered with flowers fresh and white and red.
Singing or fluting was he all the day;
He was as lusty as the month of May.
Short was his gown, with sleeves both long and wide,
Well could he sit a horse and fairly ride;
He could make songs, and prettily indite,
And joust and dance as well, and draw and write.
So fierce by night did love his heart assail
He slept no more than doth a nightingale.
Courteous he was, humble, willing and able,
And carved before his father at the table.

    He had a YEOMAN there, and none beside
In service, for it pleased him so to ride;
And he was clad in coat and hood of green.
He bore a sheaf of arrows, bright and keen,
And wings of peacock feathers edged the wood.
He kept his gear the way a yeoman should –
No shafts of his with feathers dragging low! –
And in his hand he bare a mighty bow.
Close-cropped his head was, and his face was brown,

He knew well all the woodcraft that was known.
Gay on his arm an archer's guard he wore;
A buckler at one side and sword he bore;
Upon the other side a dagger swung,
Sharp as a spear's point, richly wrought and hung.
Saint Christopher on his breast made silver sheen.
He bore a horn; his baldric was of green;
In truth, he was a forester, I should guess.

    Also there was a nun, a PRIORESS,
And she went smiling, innocent and coy;
The greatest oath she swore was by Saint Loy;
And she was known as Madame Eglentine.
Full well she sang the services divine,
Intoning through her nose right prettily,
And fair she spoke her French and fluently
After the school of Stratford-at-the-Bow;
(The French that Paris spoke she didn't know).
Well-taught she was at table; she would let
No food fall from her lips; she never wet
Her fingers deeply in the sauce; with care
She raised each morsel; well would she beware
Lest any drop upon her breast should fall;
In manners she delighted above all.
Always she wiped her upper lip so clean
That never a fleck of grease was to be seen
Within her cup when she had drunk. When she
Reached for her food, she did it daintily.
Pleasant she was, and loved a jest as well,
And in demeanor she was amiable.
Ever to use the ways of court she tried,
And sought to keep her manner dignified,
That all folk should be reverent of her.
But, speaking of her heart and character,
Such pity had she, and such charity
That if she saw a trapp'd mouse she would cry –
If it had died, or even if it bled;
And she had little dogs to which she fed
Fine roasted meat, or milk, or dainty bread;
How would she weep if one of them were dead,
Or any one should strike it viciously:
She was all heart and sensibility!

Her face was fair in pleated wimple draped,
Her eyes were gray as glass, her nose well-shaped,
Her mouth full small and thereto soft and red,
But of a truth she had a fair forehead,
A span in breadth or I should be surprised,
For certainly she was not undersized.
Handsome her cloak, as I was well aware;
And wrought of coral round her arm she bare
A bracelet all of beads and green gauds strung,
And down from this a golden pendant hung –
A brooch on which was written a crown'd *A*,
Followed by *Amor Vincit Omnia*.

    Another NUN rode in her retinue,
That as her chapelaine served, and THREE
    PRIESTS too.
A MONK there was, as fair as ever was born,
An out-rider, that loved the hounds and horn,
A manly man, to be an abbot able.
Full many a blooded horse he had in stable,
And when he rode ye might his bridle hear
Jingle upon the whistling wind as clear
And loud as ever the chapel bell could ring
Where this same monk and lord was governing.
The rules of Maurice and of Benedict,
These being ancient now, and rather strict,
This monk ignored, and let them go their ways,
And laid a course by rules of newer days.
He held that text worth less than a plucked hen
Which said that hunters were not holy men,
Or that a monk who follows not the rule
Is like a fish when it is out of pool –
That is to say, a monk out of his cloister.
Indeed, he held that text not worth an oyster;
And his opinion here was good, I say.
For why go mad with studying all day,
Poring over a book in some dark cell,
And with one's hands go laboring as well,
As Austin bids? How shall the world be served?
Let Austin's work for Austin be reserved!
Therefore he hunted hard and with delight;
Greyhounds he had as swift as birds in flight;

To gallop with the hounds and hunt the hare
He made his joy, and no expense would spare.
I saw his sleeves trimmed just above the hand
With soft gray fur, the finest in the land;
And fastening his hood beneath his chin,
Wrought out of gold, he wore a curious pin –
A love-knot at the larger end there was!
His head was wholly bald and shone like glass,
As did his face, as though with ointment greased;
He was full fat and sleek, this lordly priest.
His fierce bright eyes that in his head were turning
Like flames beneath a copper cauldron burning,
His supple boots, the trappings of his steed,
Showed him a prelate fine and fair indeed!
He was not pale like some tormented ghost.
He loved a fat swan best of any roast.
His palfrey was as brown as is a berry.

    There was a FRIAR, a wanton and a merry,
Licensed to beg – a gay, important fellow.
In all four orders no man was so mellow
With talk and dalliance. He had brought to pass
The marrying of many a buxom lass,
Paying himself the priest and the recorder:
He was a noble pillar to his order!
He was familiar too and well-beloved
By all the franklins everywhere he moved
And by good women of the town withal,
For he had special powers confessional
As he himself would let folk understand:
He had been licensed by the Pope's own hand!
Full sweetly would he listen to confession,
And very pleasantly absolved transgression;
He could give easy penance if he knew
There would be recompense in revenue;
For he that to some humble order hath given –
Is he not by that token all but shriven?
For if he gave, then of a certain, said he,
He knew the man was penitent already!
For many a man may be so hard of heart
He can not weep, though sore may be his smart;
Therefore his case no tears and prayers requires:

Let him give silver to the needy friars!
Always he kept his tippet stuffed with knives
And pins, that he could give to comely wives.
And of a truth he had a merry note,
For he could sing and play upon the rote –
There he would take the prize for certainty.
His neck was white as is the *fleur-de-lys*.
He was as strong as any champion.
As for the inns, he knew them every one,
Their hosts and barmaids too – much better than
He'd know a leper or a beggar-man;
For it was not for such a one as he
To seek acquaintance in the company
Of loathsome lepers – no, not for a minute!
There was no decency or profit in it.
One should avoid such trash and cultivate
Vendors of food and folk of rich estate.
And if a profit was to be expected
No courtesy or service he neglected.
There was no man so able anywhere –
As beggar he was quite beyond compare.
He paid a fee to get his hunting ground;
None of his brethren dared to come around;
For though a widow might not own a shoe,
So pleasant was his *In principio*,
That he would have a farthing ere he went;
His profits more than paid him back his rent!
And like a puppy could he romp; yet he
Could work on love days with authority,
For he was not a monk threadbare of collar,
Out of some cloister, like a half-starved scholar,
But rather like a master or a pope.
Of double worsted was his semi-cope,
And rounded like a bell hot from the press.
Somewhat he lisped his words, in playfulness,
To make his English sweet upon his tongue.
And in his harping, after he had sung,
Deep in his head his eyes would twinkle bright,
As do the stars upon a frosty night.
Hubert this begging friar was called by name.
    Next, all in motley garbed, a MERCHANT came,

With a forked beard. High on his horse he sat,
Upon his head a Flanders beaver hat;
His boots were buckled fair and modishly.
He spoke his words with great solemnity,
Having in mind his gain in pounds and pence.
He wished the sea, regardless of expense,
Kept safe from Middleburg to Orëwell.
Cunningly could he buy French crowns, or sell,
And great sagacity in all ways showed;
No man could tell of any debt he owed,
So stately was his way in everything,
His loans, his bargains, and his trafficking.
In truth, a worthy man withal was he,
And yet I know not what his name might be.
    There was a STUDENT out of Oxford town,
Indentured long to logic and the gown.
Lean as a rake the horse on which he sat,
And he himself was anything but fat,
But rather wore a hollow look and sad.
Threadbare the little outer-coat he had,
For he was still to get a benefice
And thoughts of worldly office were not his.
For he would rather have beside his bed
Twenty books arrayed in black or red
Of Aristotle and his philosophy
Than robes or fiddle or jocund psaltery.
Yet though he was philosopher, his coffer
Indeed but scanty store of gold could offer,
And any he could borrow from a friend
On books and learning straightway would he spend,
And make with prayer a constant offering
For those that helped him with his studying.
He gave to study all his care and heed,
Nor ever spoke a word beyond his need,
And that was said in form, respectfully,
And brief and quick and charged with meaning high.
Harmonious with virtue was his speech,
And gladly would he learn and gladly teach.
    A SERJEANT OF THE LAW, wise and discreet,
There was as well, who often held his seat
In the church porch; an excellent man was he,

Prudent indeed, and great of dignity –
Or so he seemed, his speeches were so wise.
Oft-times he had been justice at assize
By patent and by full commission too.
For his renown and for the law he knew
He won good fees, and fine robes many a one.
Conveyancer to match him was there none:
All turned fee simple underneath his hand;
No work of his but what was made to stand.
No busier person could ye find than he,
Yet busier than he was he seemed to be;
He knew the judgments and the cases down
From the first day King William wore his crown;
And he could write, and pen a deed in law
So in his writing none could pick a flaw,
And every statute could he say by rote.
He wore a simple, vari-colored coat,
Girt with a fine-striped sash of silken stuff:
This, as to his array, will be enough.
　　A FRANKLIN in his company appeared;
As white as any daisy shone his beard;
Sanguine was his complexion; he loved dearly
To have his sop in wine each morning early.
Always to pleasure would his custom run,
For he was Epicurus' own son,
Who held opinion that in pleasure solely
Can man find perfect bliss and have it wholly.
Householder he, a mighty and a good;
He was Saint Julian in his neighborhood;
His bread, his ale, were always prime, and none
Had better store of vintage than his own.
Within his house was never lack of pasty
Or fish or flesh – so plenteous and tasty
It seemed the place was snowing meat and drink,
All dainty food whereof a man could think.
And with the changing seasons of the year
Ever he changed his suppers and his fare.
Many fat partridges were in his mew,
And bream in pond, and pike in plenty, too.
Woe to his cook if all his gear were not
In order, or his sauce not sharp and hot!

And in his hall the plenteous platters lay
Ready upon the table all the day.
At sessions he would play the lord and sire;
He went to parliament as knight-of-shire.
A dagger and a purse of woven silk
Hung at his girdle, white as morning milk.
As sheriff he had served, and auditor;
Nowhere was any vassal worthier.
　　A HABERDASHER and a CARPENTER,
A WEAVER, DYER and UPHOLSTERER
Were with us too, clad all in livery
Of one illustrious great fraternity.
All fresh and shining their equipment was;
None of their dagger-sheaths was tipped with brass,
But all with silver, fashioned well and new;
So with their girdles and their pouches, too.
Each of them seemed a burgess proud, and fit
In guildhall on a dais high to sit;
And in discretion each was qualified
To be an alderman, and had beside
Income and goods sufficient for the station,
Which would have filled their wives with jubilation,
Or else for certain they had been to blame.
Full fair it is when one is called "Ma Dame,"
And at the vigils leads the company,
And has one's mantle carried royally.
　　They brought a COOK for this occasion, who
With marrow-bones would boil their chicken stew,
With powder-marchant tart and galingale.
Well could he judge a draught of London ale.
And he could roast and seethe and broil and fry,
And brew good soup, and well could bake a pie.
But it was pity, as it seemed to me,
That he should have a sore below his knee.
His fowl-in-cream – he made that with the best!
　　There was a SEAMAN hailing from the west,
From Dartmouth if the guess I make be good.
He rode upon his nag as best he could.
His gown of falding hung about his knee.
A dagger hanging on a slip had he,
Slung from his neck under his arm and down.

The summer heat had burned his visage brown.
He was a right good fellow; many a draught
Of wine the merry rogue had drawn and quaffed
This side of Bordeaux, the while the merchant slept.
Nice conscience was a thing he never kept.
And if he fought and had the upper hand,
By water he sent 'em home to every land.
But as to skill in reckoning the tides,
The ocean streams, the risks on divers sides;
Harbors and moons and pilotage and such –
No one from Hull to Carthage knew so much.
Bold and yet wise in what he undertook,
With many a bitter storm his beard had shook;
He knew well all the harbors as they were
From Gothland to the Cape of Finisterre,
And every creek in Brittany and Spain.
The ship he sailed was called the *Madelaine*.

A DOCTOR OF PHYSIC there was with us, too.
In all the world was not another who
Matched him in physic and in surgery,
For he was grounded in astrology.
Much could he help his patients with his powers,
Selecting well the most auspicious hours,
When the ascendant ruled, and he was sure
To prosper in the making of his cure.
He knew the cause of every malady,
Were it from Hot or Cold or Moist or Dry,
And where begun, and what its humor too;
He was a perfect doctor and a true.
The cause once known, the root of his disease,
At once he gave the patient remedies.
For he would have at call apothecaries
Ready to send him drugs and lectuaries,
For each of them from the other profit won;
Their friendship was not something just begun.
The ancient Æsculapius he knew,
Haly and Rufus and Serapion, too,
Avicenna, and great Hippocrates,
Rhasis and Galen, Dioscorides,
Averroes, Damascene, and Constantine,
Bernard and Gatisden and Gilbertine.

As for his diet, moderate was he,
And never ate to superfluity,
But for digestion and for nourishment.
Upon the scriptures little time he spent.
Sky-blue and sanguine was his whole array,
Well-lined with sarcenet and taffeta;
Yet he spent little, and with providence
Had saved his fees during the pestilence.
For gold in physic is a cordial; he
Loved gold on that account especially.

A GOOD WIFE was there dwelling near the city
Of Bath – a little deaf, which was a pity.
Such a great skill on making cloth she spent
That she surpassed the folk of Ypres and Ghent.
No parish wife would dream of such a thing
As going before her with an offering,
And if one did, so angry would she be
It put her wholly out of charity.
Her coverchiefs were woven close of ground,
And weighed, I lay an oath, at least ten pound
When of a Sunday they were on her head.
Her stockings were a splendid scarlet red
And tightly laced, with shoes supple and new.
Bold was her face, and fair and red of hue.
She was a worthy woman all her life;
Five times at church door had she been a wife,
Not counting other company in youth –
But this we need not mention here, in truth.
Thrice at Jerusalem this dame had been,
And many a foreign river she had seen,
And she had gone to Rome and to Boulogne,
To Saint James' in Galicia, and Cologne.
Much lore she had from wandering by the way;
Still, she was gap-toothed, I regret to say.
Upon a gentle, ambling nag she sat,
Well-wimpled, and upon her head a hat
As broad as is a buckler or a targe.
A mantle hung about her buttocks large
And on her feet a pair of pointed spurs.
No tongue was readier with a jest than hers.
Perhaps she knew love remedies, for she

Had danced the old game long and cunningly.
　　There was a PARSON, too, that had his cure
In a small town, a good man and a poor;
But rich he was in holy thought and work.
Also he was a learned man, a clerk,
Seeking Christ's gospel faithfully to preach;
Most piously his people would he teach.
Benign and wondrous diligent was he,
And very patient in adversity –
Often had he been tried to desperation!
He would not make an excommunication
For tithes unpaid, but rather would he give –
Helping his poor parishioners to live –
From the offerings, or his own small property;
In little he would find sufficiency.
Broad was his parish, with houses far apart,
Yet come it rain or thunder he would start
Upon his rounds, in woe or sickness too,
And reach the farthest, poor or well-to-do,
Going on foot, his staff within his hand –
Example that his sheep could understand –
Namely, that first he wrought and after taught.
These words from holy gospel he had brought,
And used to add this metaphor thereto –
That if gold rust, what then shall iron do?
For if the priest be bad, in whom we trust,
What wonder is it if a layman rust?
And shame to him – happy the priest who heeds it –
Whose flock is clean when he is soiled who leads it!
Surely a priest should good example give,
Showing by cleanness how his sheep should live.
He would not put his benefice to hire,
Leaving his sheep entangled in the mire,
While he ran off to London, to Saint Paul's,
To take an easy berth, chanting for souls,
Or with some guild a sinecure to hold,
But stayed at home and safely kept his fold
From wolves that else had sent it wandering;
He was a shepherd and no hireling.
And virtue though he loved, and holiness,
To sinful men he was not pitiless,

Nor was he stern or haughty in his speech,
But wisely and benignly would he teach.
To tempt folk unto heaven by high endeavor
And good example was his purpose ever.
But any person who was obstinate,
Whoever he was, of high or low estate,
Him on occasion would he sharply chide;
No better priest doth anywhere reside.
He had no thirst for pomp or reverence,
Nor bore too sensitive a consciënce,
But taught Christ's and his twelve apostles' creed,
And first in living of it took the lead.
　　With him his brother, a simple PLOWMAN, rode,
That in his time had carted many a load
Of dung; true toiler and a good was he,
Living in peace and perfect charity.
First he loved God, with all his heart and will,
Always, and whether life went well or ill;
And next – and as himself – he loved his neighbor.
And always for the poor he loved to labor,
And he would thresh and ditch and dyke, and take
Nothing for pay, but do it for Christ's sake.
Fairly he paid his tithes when they were due,
Upon his goods and on his produce, too.
In plowman's gown he sat astride a mare.
　　A MILLER and a REEVE were also there,
A SUMMONER, MANCIPLE, and PARDONER,
And these, beside myself, made all there were.
　　THE MILLER, big alike of bone and muscle,
Was a stout fellow, fit for any tussle,
And proved so, winning, everywhere he went,
The prize ram in the wrestling tournament.
He was thick-shouldered, knotty, broad and tough;
There was no door but he could tear it off
Its hasps, or break it, running, with his head.
His beard as any sow or fox was red,
And broad in shape as if it were a spade,
And at his nose's very tip displayed
There sat a wart, on which a tuft of hairs
Rose like the bristles on a red sow's ears;
The nostrils underneath were black and wide.

He bore a sword and buckler at his side.
Broad gaped his mouth as some great furnace door.
He would go babbling boastfully, or roar
Jests full of sin and vile scurrility.
He stole, and multiplied his toll by three,
Yet had a golden thumb, as God is true!
He wore a white coat and a hood of blue.
Upon the bagpipes he could blow a ditty,
And piped us out that morning from the city.

    There was a MANCIPLE from an inn of court,
And many a buyer might to him resort
To mark a steward's life the way he led it.
For whether he chose to pay or take on credit
Always he schemed so well and carefully,
That first in stock and well prepared was he.
Now is not that a gift of God indeed,
That one unlettered man should so exceed
The wisdom of a group of learnèd men?
For he had masters more than three times ten,
Expert in law and diligent as well,
Whereof a dozen in the house did dwell
Fit stewards for the land and revenues
Of any lord in England ye might choose,
To make him live upon the rents he had,
Debt-free with honor, if he were not mad,
Or live as plainly as he might desire;
And able to administer a shire
In all emergencies that might befall,
And yet this manciple would fool them all.

    Slender and choleric the REEVE appeared;
As close as ever he could he shaved his beard;
Around his ears the hair was closely shorn,
And docked on top, the way a priest's is worn;
His legs were long and lean, with no more calf
Than ye would find upon a walking staff.
Well could he keep a garner and a bin;
There was no auditor could do him in.
And he could estimate by drought and rain
What he would get from seed, and how much grain.
The horses, swine, and cows his lord possessed,
Stock, dairy, poultry, sheep, and all the rest –

Of all such things this Reeve had full control,
And made report by contract on the whole,
Because his lord had yet but twenty years.
No man there was could find him in arrears.
No bailiff, herd or hind but he could tell
Their shifts and trickeries – he knew them well;
These fellows feared him as they feared the death.
His dwelling stood full fair upon a heath;
Green trees made shadow there on all the sward.
He picked up money better than his lord,
Rich were the hidden stores he called his own.
And he could please his master with a loan
That came from what were justly his own goods,
Get thanks, and also get some coats and hoods!
In youth he had applied himself with care
To learn a trade; he was a carpenter.
This Reeve upon a stallion had installed him;
He was a dapple gray and Scot he called him.
A sky-blue surcoat good of length he wore,
And by his side a rusty blade he bore;
From Norfolk came this Reeve of whom I tell,
Close to a town that men call Baldeswell.
Like to a friar's his dress was tucked about,
And ever he rode the hindmost of our rout.

    There was a SUMMONER with us in that place,
That had a fiery red cherubic face,
With pimples, and his eyes were small and narrow;
As hot he was and lecherous as a sparrow;
Black scabby brows he had, and scraggly beard;
His was a face that all the children feared.
No brimstone, borax, mercury, ceruse,
White lead, or cream of tartar was of use,
Or any ointment that would cleanse or bite,
To rid him of his little pimples white,
Or of the knobs that sat upon his cheeks.
Garlic he loved, and onions, too, and leeks,
And wine as red as blood and wondrous strong.
Then like a madman would he shout ere long,
And when the wine within him held its sway,
Then not a word but Latin would he say.
He had some phrases, only two or three,

Such things as he had learned from some decree –
No wonder, for he heard it all the day;
Besides, ye know full well how any jay
Can cry his "Wat!" as well as the pope can.
But in some other matter probe the man,
Then he had spent all his philosophy:
And "*Questio quid juris*" would he cry!
He was a decent rascal and a kind;
A better fellow nowhere could ye find.
Let any man give him a quart of wine,
He might a twelve month have a concubine
Unscathed. But let him catch some fool in sin
And he would slyly fleece him to the skin.
And if he made a comrade anywhere,
Then would he teach him not to have a care
In such a case for the archdeacon's curse –
Unless, indeed, his soul were in his purse,
For in his purse his punishment should be.
"Your purse – that's the archdeacon's hell!" said he.
But here I hold it was a lie he said;
Let guilty men of curses be afraid –
They slay the soul as absolutions save it;
Also he should beware a *significavit*.
All the young people in the diocese
The man could frighten or could leave at peace,
Their secrets knew, and was their counsellor.
A monstrous garland on his head he wore,
That might have hung upon an alehouse stake.
He had made himself a buckler of a cake.

    The Summoner brought a noble PARDONER
Of Rouncyvalle, his fellow traveller
And crony, lately from the court at Rome.
Loudly he sang, "Come hither, love, O come!"
The Summoner bore him bass – a mighty voice:
Never made trumpet half so loud a noise.
This Pardoner had hair yellow as wax,
But smooth it hung, as hangs a hank of flax,
And down in strings about his neck it fell
And all about his shoulders spread as well;
Yet thin in wisps it lay there, one by one.
But hood, for jollity, the man would none,

Safe in his wallet it was packed away;
He thought he kept the fashion of the day;
Hair loose, save for his cap, his head was bared.
His bulging eyeballs like a rabbit's glared.
He had a vernicle sewed on his cap.
His wallet lay before him in his lap,
Brim full of pardons piping hot from Rome.
As small as any goat's his voice would come,
Yet no beard had he nor would ever have,
But all his face shone smooth as from a shave;
I think he was a gelding or a mare.
But at his trade, from Berwick unto Ware
There was no pardoner could go his pace.
For in his bag he kept a pillow-case
That was, he said, our Blessed Lady's veil;
He claimed to own the fragment of the sail
That Peter had the time he walked the sea
And Jesu saved him in His clemency.
He had a cross of latten set with stones,
And in a glass a handful of pig's bones.
But with these relics when he had in hand
Some humble parson dwelling in the land,
In one day he could get more revenue
Than would the parson in a month or two.
And thus with tricks and artful flattery
He fooled both flock and parson thoroughly.
But let us say, to make the truth less drastic,
In church he was a fine ecclesiastic;
Well could he read a lesson or a story,
But best of all he sang an offertory;
For well he knew that when the song was sung
Then he must preach, and smoothly file his tongue
For silver, as he could full cunningly –
Therefore he sang so loud and merrily.

    Now in few words I have rehearsed for you
Number, array, and rank, and told you too
Wherefore they came to make a company
In Southwark, at this noble hostelry,
The Tabard, standing close beside the Bell.
But now the time is come when I should tell
Of how we bore ourselves that night when we

Had all alighted at that hostelry;
Then shall I say what on the road befell,
And all else of our pilgrimage as well.
But first I pray that in your courtesy
Ye will not deem it my vulgarity
If I am wholly frank in my narration
Both of their manners and their conversation,
And give their words exactly as they fell;
For this I know – and ye must know as well –
That whoso tells a tale after a man
He must repeat as closely as he can
What has been said, and every word include,
Though much of what he writes be broad and rude;
Else must he make the tale he tells untrue,
Invent, or shape the words of it anew.
None may he spare, not though it be his brother,
Nor slight one word more than he does another.
For Christ himself speaks plain in holy writ;
Ye know well there is nothing base in it.
And Plato says, to any that can read,
The words must be the cousin of the deed.
Also I pray that ye will pardon me
That I have nowise set in their degree
The people in this tale, as they should stand;
I have but scanty wit at my command.

     Great cheer our good HOST made us every one,
And straightway to the supper set us down,
And choicest of his food before us placed;
Strong was the wine and goodly to our taste.
Our Host, a seemly man, was fit withal
To be a marshall in a banquet hall,
For he was large, with eyes that brightly shone:
In Cheapside was no fairer burgess known.
Bold of his speech he was, wise and well-taught;
In short, in ways of manhood lacked for naught.
Also he was a gladsome, merry man,
And when the meal was ended he began
To jest and speak of mirth with other things
(When we had settled all our reckonings),
And thus he said: "Lordings, for certainty
Ye have been welcome here and heartily;

For on my word, if I shall tell you true,
So merry a company I never knew
This year together in my house as now.
Fain would I please you did I know but how.
But wait – I have bethought me of a way
To give you mirth, and ye shall nothing pay.
Ye go to Canterbury – may God speed you!
With good reward the blessèd martyr heed you!
And well I know that, as ye go along
Ye shall tell tales, or turn to play and song,
For truly joy or comfort is there none
To ride along the road dumb as a stone;
And therefore I will fashion you some sport
To fill your way with pleasure of a sort.
And now if, one and all, it likes you well
To take my judgment as acceptable,
And each to do his part as I shall say,
Tomorrow, as we ride along the way,
Then by the soul of my father that is dead,
Ye shall be merry, or I will give my head!
Up with your hands now, and no more of speech!"

     Agreement took us little time to reach.
We saw no reason for an argument,
But gave at once and fully our consent,
And bade him shape his verdict as he chose.

     "Lordings," quoth he, "hear now what I propose,
But take it not, I pray you, in disdain;
This is the point, to speak both brief and plain:
Each one, to make your travelling go well,
Two tales upon this pilgrimage shall tell –
Going to Canterbury. And each of you
Journeying home shall tell another two,
Of happenings that long ago befell.
And he of us that best his tales shall tell –
That is, that telleth tales which are the best
In profit and in pleasant interest,
Shall have a supper (we to pay the cost),
Here in this place, sitting beside this post,
When we are come again from Canterbury.
And with design to make you the more merry
Myself along with you will gladly ride,

All at my own expense, and be your guide.
And whoso dares my judgment to withsay
Shall pay what we may spend along the way.
And if ye grant the matter shall be so,
Tell me without more words, that I may go
And quickly shape my plans to suit your need."

And we assented, and by oath agreed
Gladly, and also prayed our host that he
Would pledge to give his service faithfully –
That he would be our governor, and hold
In mind and judge for us the tales we told,
And set a supper at a certain price,
We to be ruled in all by his device,
In things both great and small. So to a man
We gave our full agreement to his plan.
And then the wine was fetched, and every guest
Drank of it straightway, and we went to rest,
And there was nothing further of delay.

And on the morn, with brightening of day,
Up rose our Host, and busily played the cock,
And gathered us together in a flock,
And forth we rode, just barely cantering,
Until we reached St. Thomas' Watering.
And there it was our Host at length drew rein,
And said, "Now, Lordings, hearken me again;
Here will I call your pact to memory.
If even-song and morning-song agree,
Let us see now who first begins his tale!
As I may ever drink of wine or ale
Whoso rebels at anything I say

Shall stand for all we spend along the way.
Now draw your lots before we take us hence,
And he that draws the shortest shall commence.
Sire Knight," he said, "my master and my lord,
Draw now your lot, for here ye have my word.
Come near," quoth he, "my lady Prioress,
And ye, sir Clerk, have done with bashfulness!
Don't study here! Fall to now, every man!"
Then each at once to draw his lot began,
And briefly, as to how the matter went,
Whether it were by chance or accident,
The truth is this – the lot fell to the Knight;
And all were blithe and there was much delight.
And now in reason he could hardly fail
According to the pact, to tell his tale,
As ye have heard – what more is there to say?
And when this good man saw how matters lay,
As one resolved in sense and courtesy,
His compact made, to keep it cheerfully,
He said: "Since it is I begin the game,
Come, let the cut be welcome, in God's name!
Now let us ride, and hearken what I say."
And with that word we went upon our way,
And all in merry mood this knight began
To tell his tale, and thus the story ran.

Here ends the Prologue of this Book;
and here begins the First Tale,
which is the Knight's Tale.

The Knight's Tale

THE FIRST TALE is a courtly, heroic tale of love and war. Two knights in classical Athens fall in love with the same woman, who they see from a prison window after their capture during battle. After their release, they each pray to different gods, Mars and Venus, hoping to win her hand in a tournament. The gods must honour promises to both knights, yet there is only one lady. The tale is a verse romance, but incorporates much philosophical reflection on the divine order of the universe, the reversals of fortune and the nature of human destiny.

THE KNIGHT'S TALE

Part I

Iamque domos patrias,
Scithice post aspera gentis,
Prelia, laurigero, & c.
[Statius – *Thebiad*]

ONCE, as old stories tell the tale to us,
There was a duke by name of Theseus;
Of Athens he was lord and governor
And in his time was such a conqueror
That none was greater underneath the sun.
Full many a wealthy country had he won,
And by his wisdom and his chivalry
He conquered all the realm of Femeny,
Which men in time long past called Scythia,
And wedded there the queen Hippolyta,
And to his country brought her home, with all
Glory and noble pomp and festival;
And likewise her young sister Emely;
And thus with triumph and with melody
With all his host in arms and pennons blowing,
I leave this noble duke toward Athens going.

   And were the story not too long to tell
I would relate in full for you as well
How Theseus and his knighthood valiantly
Conquered by war the realm of Femeny,
And of the battle that was fought between
The Athenians and the warriors of the queen;
Likewise how they besieged Hippolyta,
The fair and doughty queen of Scythia;
Of feasting when their wedding day was come,
And of the storm on their arrival home;
But all these things are not for telling now;
I have, God knows, an ample field to plow

And feeble oxen. The remainder of
The tale that I must tell will be enough;
Nor would I hinder any man of you,
But each should tell his tale as it is due,
And let us see who wins the supper then!
Now where I stopped will I begin again.

   This duke whereof I mention the renown –
When he had journeyed almost to the town,
All in the height of his success and pride
He saw, as suddenly he glanced aside,
How in the highway knelt by two and two,
Each after each, a doleful retinue
Of ladies, all in black, that made a cry
So loud with woe, so full of misery
That in this world no living creature is
Hath heard a lamentation like to this,
Nor would they cease their cry of woe and pain
Till they had seized Duke Theseus' bridle rein.

   "What folk are ye that with this woeful call
At my homecoming mar our festival?"
Quoth Theseus. "Be ye then so envious
Of my good fame, that cry and clamor thus?
Or who hath you insulted or offended?
And tell me if your wrong may be amended,
And why all garmented in black ye stand."

   Then spoke the eldest lady of the band,
When she had swooned with face so deathly drear
That it was pity her to see and hear,
And answered, "Lord, to whom Fortune doth give
Victory, and as conqueror to live,
Nought grieveth us your glory or success,
But we beseech you, of your nobleness,
Mercy and help; have mercy on our woe
And our distress, and from your heart let flow
Some drop of pity that may on us fall!
For truly, lord, none is there of us all
But duchess once or queen she used to be.
Now we are wretches, it is plain to see,
Thanks unto Fortune and her fickle wheel
That leaveth no estate assured of weal.
And, lord, to abide your presence, certainly,

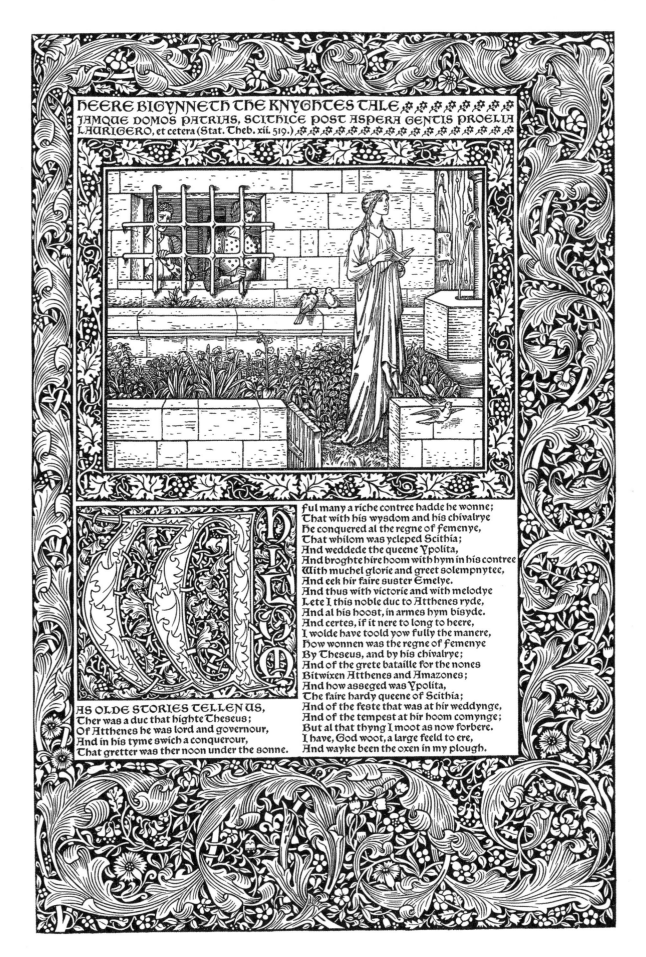

HEERE BIGYNNETH THE KNYGHTES TALE
JAMQUE DOMOS PATRIAS, SCITHICE POST ASPERA GENTIS PROELIA
LAURIGERO, et cetera (Stat. Theb. xii. 519.)

ful many a riche contree hadde he wonne;
That with his wysdom and his chivalrye
He conquered al the regne of femenye,
That whilom was ycleped Scithia;
And weddede the queene Ypolita,
And broghte hire hoom with hym in his contree
With muchel glorie and greet solempnytee,
And eek hir faire suster Emelye.
And thus with victorie and with melodye
Lete I this noble duc to Atthenes ryde,
And al his hoost, in armes hym bisyde.
And certes, if it nere to long to heere,
I wolde have toold yow fully the manere,
How wonnen was the regne of femenye
By Theseus, and by his chivalrye;
And of the grete bataille for the nones
Bitwixen Atthenes and Amazones;
And how asseged was Ypolita,
The faire hardy queene of Scithia;
And of the feste that was at hir weddynge,
And of the tempest at hir hoom comynge;
But al that thyng I moot as now forbere.
I have, God woot, a large feeld to ere,
And wayke been the oxen in my plough.

AS OLDE STORIES TELLEN US,
Ther was a duc that highte Theseus;
Of Atthenes he was lord and governour,
And in his tyme swich a conquerour,
That gretter was ther noon under the sonne.

Plate 2: The Knight's Tale (p. 30)

Here in the temple of the goddess Clemency
We have been waiting all the last fortnight;
Now help us, lord, since it is in thy might.
    "I, that bewail and weep all wretched thus,
Was once the wife of King Capaneüs
That died at Thebes (O cursèd be that day!)
And all of us that come in this array
And make this lamentation – one and all
In Thebes we lost our husbands at the wall
When under siege that wretched city lay.
And yet old Creon now – oh welaway!
That holdeth over Thebes the mastery –
He, filled with anger and iniquity,
In wicked spite and cruel tyranny,
To do their bodies shame and infamy –
The bodies of our husbands that were slain –
Hath gathered them and heaped them up amain
And now to no entreaty will agree
That they should either burned or buried be,
But giveth them in spite to dogs for prey."
And that word spoken, with no more delay
They fell face down and cried all piteously:
"Have mercy on us, wretches that we be,
And let our sorrow sink into thy heart."
    Down from his steed this noble duke did start
All full of pity when thus he heard them speak;
It seemed to him as if his heart would break
To see such piteous grief and desolate
In them that once had been of high estate.
And he embraced and raised them up, and bade
That in his good intent they should be glad,
And swore an oath, that on his truth as knight,
So well and wholly would he use his might
On tyrant Creon their revenge to wreak,
That through the whole of Greece should people
      speak
Of how King Creon was by Theseus served
As one that had his death full well deserved.
And straightway then, making no more delay,
His banner he displayed and rode away
Towards Thebes, and all his host along thereto.

No nearer Athens would he ride or go,
Nor take his ease – no, not for half a day,
But on his road that night in camp he lay,
And sent his Queen Hippolyta from there
And her young sister Emely the fair
That in the town of Athens they might dwell,
And forth he rode – there is no more to tell.
    The ruddy form of Mars with spear and targe,
Wrought against white, shines on his banner large,
That all its fields are glittering up and down;
Hard by, his pennon blazons his renown
In beaten gold, on which was worked complete
The Minotaur, that he had slain in Crete.
Thus rode this duke, thus rode this conqueror,
Leading the flower of chivalry to war,
Until at Thebes he bade his host alight
Fair in a field, where he had hope to fight.
But to speak plain and briefly of this thing,
With Creon, that was now of Thebes the king,
He fought, and slew him manly, as a knight
In open field, and put his folk to flight,
And by assault the town he won thereafter
And made a wreck of wall and beam and rafter,
And to the ladies he restored again
The bodies of their husbands that were slain
To do them obsequies, as in that day
Was custom. But too long it were to say
What clamor made these ladies at the pyre
And what lament, when upward with the fire
The bodies passed; what honors furthermore
Great Theseus did, the noble conqueror,
Unto these noble ladies when they went.
Briefly to tell my tale is my intent.
Now when this worthy duke, this Theseus,
Had Creon slain, and Thebes had conquered thus,
Still in that field all night he took his rest,
Then with the country did as pleased him best.
    Ransacking in the heap of bodies dead,
To strip them of their gear from foot to head,
The pillagers worked busily and fast
After the battle and defeat were past.

And so it fell that in the heap they found,
Torn through with many a grievous bloody wound,
Two knights together lying where they fell,
Young, and their arms the same, and fashioned well;
And of these two, Arcite was called the one;
The other knight had name of Palamon.
Not quite alive, not wholly dead were they,
But by their armour-coats and rich array
The heralds knew them, and could plainly see
That both were of the royal family
That ruled in Thebes; and were of sisters born.
The robbers from the ruck these knights have torn,
And gently thence conveyed them to the tent
Of Theseus, and he bade them both be sent
To Athens, to be kept in prison there
Forever; naught of ransom would he hear.
And this great duke, when he hath done this thing,
Homeward with all his host goes journeying,
With laurel crowned as fits a conqueror,
And liveth in honor there forevermore
A joyous life – what more is there to say?
And in a tower, from day to woeful day
This Palamon must dwell perpetually,
And Arcite too – no gold can set them free.

    And so passed year by year and day by day,
Until it fell, upon a morn in May,
That Emely, that fairer was to see
Than on his green stalk is the bright lily,
And fresh as May with blossoms born anew,
(For with the rose's color strove her hue:
I know not which was fairer of the two)
Ere it was day, as she was wont to do,
She was arisen, and garbed to greet the light.
For May will have no sluggardry by night;
The season stirreth every noble heart,
Making the sleeper from his sleep to start,
And saith, "Arise, and thine observance do!"
This brought to Emely remembrance, too,
That she should rise and honor do to May.
Now to describe her – fresh was her array;
Her yellow hair was braided in a tress

Behind her back, a yard long, I should guess,
And in the garden, as the sun uprose,
She wandered up and down, and there she chose,
Gathering now of white and now of red,
Flowers to make a garland for her head,
And like an angel sang a heavenly song.
The mighty tower, that was so thick and strong
And for the castle was the dungeon-keep
Where these two knights were held in durance deep,
Of which I told, and more shall tell withal,
This tower was close beside the garden wall
Where wandered Emely for her delight.
Clear was the morning air, the sun was bright,
And Palamon, that woeful prisoner
After his daily custom, was astir
And by his jailor's leave, paced up and down
On high where he could see the noble town,
And all the garden, green beneath him there,
Where went this Emely, so fresh and fair,
As in her walk she wandered up and down.
This woeful prisoner – this Palamon –
He paced his chamber, walking to and fro,
And to himself complaining of his woe;
Full oft that he was born he cried, Alas!
And so by chance or accident it was
That through the iron window bars that stood
Thick wrought, and square as any beam of wood,
Downward he cast his eye on Emely,
And then he started back and cried, "Ah me!"
As though the sight had stung him to the heart.
And Arcite heard the cry, that made him start
And say: "O cousin mine, what aileth thee
That art so wan and deathly pale to see?
Who hath thee done offense? Why didst thou cry?
Now for God's love take thou all patiently
Our prison; for not elsewise may it be.
Fortune hath given us this adversity;
Some wicked aspect, some unhappy station
Of Saturn doomed us so, some constellation
We never could escape, though we had sworn.
So stood the stars in heaven when we were born;

We must endure; this is brief and plain."

    Answered this Palamon and spoke again:
"Cousin, in truth, when thou dost say this thing
Thy thought is full of vain imagining.
No prison wall it was that made me cry
But that which now hath struck me through mine eye
Down to my heart; and this will be my death!
The fairness of her form who wandereth
Within the garden yonder to and fro
Is cause of all my crying and my woe;
I know not if she maid or goddess be,
But truly Venus, as I guess, is she."
And therewithal he fell upon his knees,
Saying, "Queen Venus, if it should thee please
In yonder garden in glory to appear
For me, this sorrowful, wretched creature here,
Then help us from this prison to escape!
And if it be my destiny doth shape,
By word eternal here to make me perish
Yet pity thou our race, I pray, and cherish,
That hath been brought so low by tyranny."
And with that word he looked out suddenly
Where that same lady wandered to and fro.
And with the sight her beauty hurt him so
That, if this Palamon was wounded sore,
Arcite was hurt as much as he, or more.
And with a sigh, he said all piteously:
"The fresh and sudden beauty slayeth me
Of her that wandereth in yonder place;
Unless I have her mercy and her grace,
That I may look upon her, anyway,
I am but dead; there is no more to say."

    When Palamon heard these words, all angrily
He looked on Arcite. "Sayest thou this," cried he,
"In earnest, or dost only speak in play?"

    "Now earnest; by my faith!" cried Arcite.–"Nay–
God knows I have no appetite for play!"

    Then Palamon did knit his brows and say:
"It cannot be great honor unto thee
That thou prove false, or shouldst a traitor be
To me, that am thy cousin and thy brother –

Each being deeply sworn, each pledged to other,
That never, though he perish of his pain,
Yea, to the time when death divide us twain,
Neither of us in love should cross the other,
No – nor in any matter, dear my brother;
But that thou shouldst forever further me
In every thing, and I should further thee.
This was thine oath and mine as well, I know;
Thou wilt not dare deny it standeth so.
Thus doubtless art thou pledged in secret to me,
And now all falsely goest thou to undo me,
And love my lady, whom I glorify
And serve, and always shall until I die.
Now false Arcite, thou shalt not do this thing!
I loved her first, I told my suffering
To thee, my brother pledged in secrecy,
As I have said, to aid and further me,
And therefore art thou bound, as thou art knight,
To help me, if it lies within thy might,
Or else must thou be false; I hold this plain."

    This Arcite proudly spoke to him again,
"Sooner shalt thou be false than I," said he.
"Nay, thou art false, I tell thee utterly;
For *par amour* I loved her first ere thou!
What wilt thou say? Thou knowest not even now
Whether she goddess or a woman be!
Thine is affection, born of sanctity,
And mine is love, for a human creature burning.
Wherefore to thee, my cousin and brother turning,
Plainly my hap in love did I discover.
Yet let us say thou wert the first to love her;
Knowst thou not well how runs the old clerk's saw,
That 'who shall give a lover any law?'
Now by my head, love's law is greater than
Any may be devised for earthly man;
Therefore fixed law and all such ordination
Are broke for love by men of every station.
A man he needs must love despite his head,
He may not flee from love though he be dead,
Come she as maid or widow, or as wife.
And more, thou art not likely, all thy life,

To stand within her grace – no more am I,
For well thou knowest thyself for certainty,
That thou and I are doomed in prison to rot
Perpetually; ransom avails us not,
We strive as did the two dogs for the bone;
They fought all day, and yet their share was none.
There came a kite, the while they strove all wroth,
And straightway bare the bone away from both.
So at the king's court let each man, I say,
Work for himself, there lies no other way.
Love if thou wilt; I love and always shall,
And truly, dear my brother, this is all.
Here in this prison the two of us must wait,
And as it cometh each one must take his fate."

Between the two long was the strife and great,
If only I had leisure to relate –
But to the sequel. It befell one day,
To tell you this as briefly as I may,
A worthy duke, by name Perotheüs,
That had been comrade to Duke Theseus
Since both were children in a fargone day,
Came to his comrade for a little stay,
To play about, as was his wont to do;
For in this world he loved no other so,
And him did Theseus love as tenderly;
So well they loved, as olden books agree,
That when one died, it is the truth to tell,
His friend went forth and sought him down in hell;
But of this tale I care not now to write.
This Duke Perotheüs loved Lord Arcite,
(Knowing him well in Thebes from year to year)
And he persuaded Theseus to hear
His prayer for Arcite, so that finally
Theseus without a ransom set him free
From prison, anywhere to go or dwell
But in this manner only, as I tell.

In brief, the covenant was ordered thus
Betwixt Lord Arcite and Duke Theseus:
If it befell that they should find Arcite
Ever again, either by day or night,
In any country of this Theseus,

And he were caught, it was accorded thus –
That by the stroke of sword his head should fall;
No other remedy he had at all,
But took his leave, and homeward went with speed:
His neck is under pledge; let him take heed!

How great a sorrow Arcite suffereth!
Right through his heart he feels the stroke of Death!
He weepeth, waileth, cryeth piteously;
Waiteth to slay himself in secrecy.
"Alas! the day that I was born!" he wails,
"Now have I got the worser of two jails!
Now am I doomed eternally to dwell
Not in a purgatory, but in hell!
Alas, that ever I knew Perotheus,
For elsewise had I dwelt with Theseus
Chained in his prison for evermore, and so
Had I a home in bliss, and not in woe!
Only the sight of her, the lady I serve
Though never in truth I may her grace deserve,
That would have been sufficient unto me!
O dear my cousin Palamon," quoth he,
"Thine is the victory from this event!
Thou mayst in prison stay and be content!
In prison? Truly, no – in paradise!
O well hath Fortune turned for thee the dice!
Thou hast the sight of her, while I'm denied her.
For it is possible, since thou'rt beside her,
And art a knight, well-born and bearing thee well,
That by some hap, since Fate is changeable,
Some time to thy desire thou mayst attain.
But I, that am an exile, and in vain
Seek for her grace, and so am in despair,
That naught of earth or fire or water or air,
Or any creature that created is
Can work me any help or joy in this –
Well should I die of sorrow and distress!
Farewell my life, my joy, my happiness!

"Alas, why go folk always to importune
The providence of God, or else of fortune,
That often gives to them in some disguise
Better than for themselves they could devise?

In one man lust for riches ever gnaws
That of disease or murder is the cause;
Another man from prison would be free;
At home by his own servants slain is he.
Infinite evils in such ways appear;
We know not what it is we pray for here!
We go like one as drunk as is a mouse;
A drunken man knows well he has a house,
But knoweth not the way to his abode;
And for a drunk man slippery is the road.
And truly, in this world so prosper we;
Eager and hard we hunt felicity,
Yet oft-times, of a truth, we run awry.
Thus all may say, and more than others, I,
Who had supposed, and great hope always shaped,
That when I once from prison had escaped,
Mine should be joy and perfect peace – no less;
Now am I exiled from my happiness!
Since that I may not see you, Emely,
I am but dead; there is no remedy."

    And on the other hand, when Palamon
Knew that his cousin Arcite was gone,
The mighty tower shook to its firm foundation
With grief and clamor of his lamentation.
And on his mighty shins each iron fetter
Shone with the tears he shed, all salt and bitter.
"Alas," quoth he, "Arcite, cousin mine,
Of all our strife, God knows, the fruit is thine!
Thou walkest now in Thebes, and thou art free;
Small heed thou hast for woe of mine, or me;
And manful since thou art, and also wise,
So mayst thou call on all our kin to rise,
And when in war thou hast this town attacked
Fiercely, thou mayst by accident or pact
Secure her for thy lady and thy wife
For whom I long in vain, and lose my life!
For plainly this is possibility:
Since thou art all at large, of prison free,
And a lord, thou hast advantage more than I
That here within a wretched cage must die.
For I must weep and wail the while I live

With all the woe that chains and dungeon give
And with the hurt love giveth me as well,
That makes of pain and woe a double hell."
With that the fire of jealousy upblazed
Within his breast, and gripped his heart and crazed
Him so with madness that he seemed to be
Like ashes dead and cold, or dim box-tree.
And then he cried, "O cruel gods who gird
This world with law of your eternal word,
And write upon a table of adamant
Your judgment, and your everlasting grant –
Of man what higher notion do ye hold
Than of the sheep that croucheth in the fold?
For man is slain like any other beast,
And dwells in prison, and is in arrest;
Sickness he hath and heavy punishment
Though, God knows, often he is innocent.

    "What justice lies in such a presciënce
That still tormenteth guiltless innocence?
And yet by this my pain the greater grows –
That man is bound by the respect he owes,
For the sake of God, ever to curb his will,
Whereas a beast may every lust fulfill.
And when a beast is dead his pain is ended,
But man's with tears and torment is extended,
Though in this world he suffer care and woe;
No doubt there is but that it standeth so.
Be this for holy doctors to explain;
But well I know this world is full of pain.
Alas! a serpent or a thief I see,
That worketh many a true man villainy,
Go all at large, and freely choose his way,
But I by Saturn's will in prison stay;
Also through Juno's jealousy and wrath
That well nigh all the blood destroyèd hath
Of Thebes, whose walls so wide and wasted stand;
And Venus slay'th me on the other hand,
With jealousy, and fear of him – Arcite!"

    And now no more of Palamon I write,
But let him quietly in prison dwell,
And more again of Arcite will I tell.

The summer passeth, and the nights grow long
And doubly do augment the sorrows strong
Both of the lover and the prisoner;
I know not which should be the unhappier.
For, in a word, this Palamon must be
Unto his prison damned perpetually,
In chains and cruel fetters to be dead;
And Arcite, under threat to lose his head,
Is exiled from the land he longeth for,
And he shall see his lady never more.

Now will I ask you lovers, every one,
Who hath the worse, Arcite or Palamon?
The one may see his lady day by day,
But chained in prison must forever stay;
To ride or go the other one is free,
But nevermore his lady shall he see.
Now riddle it as likes you, ye that can,
For I will go ahead as I began.

Part II

WHEN Arcite unto Thebes was come again
Full oft he swooned, and cried "Alas!" for pain,
For never more his lady should he see;
And making of his woe short summary –
Such grief no creature ever knew, for sure,
That lives, or shall live, while the world endure.
His sleep, his food, his drink he shunned, and grew
Dry as an arrow shaft, and lean thereto;
His eyes grew hollow and fearsome to behold,
His hue all sallow, and pale as ashes cold,
And solitary he was, and ever alone,
And wailing all the night, making his moan,
And if he heard a song or instrument,
Then would he weep; none might his tears prevent,
So feeble were his spirits and so low,
And altered so that nobody could know
His discourse or his voice though they should hear it.
And in his changeability of spirit
He showed, indeed, the lover's malady
Less than a mania which seemed to be

Of melancholy humors born, that lie
Forward, within the cell of phantasy.
In short, the habits and the mind were blown
About, and wholly tumbled upside down
Within this woeful lover, Dan Arcite.

But why forever of his woe indite?
When he had suffered for a year or two
This cruel torment and this pain and woe
At Thebes, in his own country, as I say,
One night it happened, as in sleep he lay,
He dreamed the shape of wingèd Mercury
Before him stood, and bade him merry be.
His staff of sleep within his hand he bare,
A hat he had upon his shining hair,
And wore such dress as he had worn that day
When watchful Argus trapped in slumber lay;
And said to him: "To Athens shalt thou go;
There shalt thou find an ending of thy woe."
Then Arcite woke and bounded from his bed.
"Now let me suffer what I may," he said,
"Yet unto Athens will I go again!
Not for the fear of death will I refrain
From seeing her I love and serve, for I
Care not if in her presence I shall die!"

And taking up a mirror with this word
He saw how grief had changed his hue and blurred
His visage till it seemed another kind.
And suddenly it ran within his mind
That, since his face was all disfigured so
With malady so long endured, and woe,
Well might he hope, if humble dress he wore,
Unknown to live in Athens evermore
And see his lady almost day by day.
And straightway then he altered his array,
And like a laborer that looked for hire,
And all alone save for a single squire
That both his secret and his suffering knew,
And wore like him a humble garb, he drew
At once to Athens by the nearest way;
And to the court he came upon a day,
And at the gate he stood and work demanded –

To drudge and draw – or what should be commanded.
And briefly of this matter now to tell,
In office with a chamberlain he fell,
One that was waiting there on Emely
(For wise this Arcite was, and quick to see
Which servants of the many served with her);
And water fetched, and was their wood-hewer,
For he was young those days and big of bone,
Mighty, and fit to see that all was done
Which any person there might bid him do.
And he had service for a year or two,
Page of the chamber of Emely the bright;
His name was "Philostratë," said Arcite.
Not half so well beloved a man as he
Ever was at the place, of his degree;
So noble his behavior was, report
Of his good name was heard throughout the court.
They said that it would be a charity
If Theseus would ennoble his degree,
And higher services for him devise
Where he might give his talents exercise;
And thus in little while his name had sprung,
Both from his deeds and courtesy of tongue,
That Theseus took him near himself, and made him
A squire of his own bedchamber, and paid him
Gold that he might maintain his new degree.
And all this time men brought him secretly
From his own country, year by year, his rent;
But worthily and wisely this he spent
And so for wonder never gave occasion.
And three years dwelt he there in such a fashion,
And bare him so in peace and so in war
There was no man beloved by Theseus more.
And in this bliss I leave him living on,
And speak a little now of Palamon.

In dark, in dungeon strong and horrible,
This seven year had Palamon to dwell.
All wasted, with his woe and great distress,
Who feeleth double wound and heaviness
But Palamon, whom love destroyeth so
That mad from out his mind he go'th for woe?

Then also his imprisonment must be
Not for a season, but perpetually.
Who hath the power in English rhyme to sing
His martyrdom and fearful suffering?
Not I; and so I pass with little stay.
    It fell that in the seventh year, in May,
The third night (say those books that, writ of old,
All of this story have more fully told),
Whether by accident or destiny,
(As, when a thing ordained is, it shall be),
That shortly after midnight Palamon,
Helped by a friend, his prison broke, and won
Beyond the city, as fast as he could flee,
For he had drugged his jailor cunningly,
Making a clarey that was mixed of wine
And subtle drugs, and Theban opium fine;
That all the night, even though men should shake him,
The man would sleep, and nothing could awake him.
And thus he fled, as fast as ever he might,
And hard the day came crowding the short night,
So of necessity he now must hide him,
And to a forest lying close beside him,
With fearful foot stealeth this Palamon.
For thus he thought: to setting of the sun
There in the forest he would hide all day,
And with the night he then would take his way
Toward Thebes, and there would make his friends
        unite
With him, against Duke Theseus to fight.
And briefly, either he would lose his life,
Or else win Emely to be his wife.
This was his thought – this his intention plain.
    Now unto Arcite will I turn again,
That little guessed how danger lay around him
Till suddenly in Fortune's snare he found him.
    The busy lark, the messenger of day,
Saluteth with her song the morning gray;
And fiery Phœbus riseth up so bright
That all the orient laugheth with the light,
And with his beams in every wood he dries
The silver dewdrop on the leaf that lies.

And Arcite, that at court with Theseus is
(Among the squires the foremost place is his),
Is risen, and looks upon the merry day.
And soon, to do observance unto May,
Remembering the end of his desire,
Upon a courser, quick as darting fire,
Unto the fields hath ridden for play and sport –
About a mile or two away from court.
So to the very wood of which I told
He chanced by accident his way to hold
Thinking to make a garland with a spray
Of woodbine leaves, or else perchance of may,
And loudly to the shining sun went singing:
"May, merry May, thy leaf and blossom bringing,
Welcome be thou! Welcome, bright budding May,
I hope to get me green to make a spray!"
And from his courser, blithe and lusty-hearted,
He leapt, and straightway through the forest started,
And on a path he wandered up and down
Where all by accident this Palamon
Crouched in the bushes, scarcely drawing breath,
For very fearful was he of his death.
That this was Arcite he in nowise knew;
Little, God knows, he would have thought it true!
But so the adage runs and has for years,
That 'fields have eyes, and every wood has ears.'
Wise man is he that holds his spirit steady –
For sudden meetings find us all unready!
Little knew Arcite of his comrade near,
That there in hiding all his speech could hear,
For in the bush he sitteth now full still.

But when of roaming Arcite had his fill,
And all his rondel had sung lustily,
He sat and fell to brooding suddenly
As lovers do, moody with their desires,
Now in the tree tops, now among the briers,
Now up, now down, like bucket in a well.
For just as Friday, always changeable,
Now shines, now soon thereafter raineth fast,
Just so can changeful Venus overcast
The spirits of her folk; even as her day

Is changeful, so she changeth her array.
Seldom indeed is Friday like the week.
Now Arcite into sighs began to break,
Having sung his song, and sat him down to mourn.
"Alas!" cried he, "the day that I was born!
How long, O cruël Juno, shall it be
That thou wilt wreak on Thebes thine enmity?
Alas! confounded is and all undone
The blood of Cadmus and of Amphion –
The royal blood of Cadmus, the first man
That builded Thebes, or first the town began,
And of the city first was crowned king.
And I am stemmed from him, and his offspring
By true line, through the royal family.
And now so wretched and enslaved am I
That he who is my mortal enemy –
I serve him as a squire of low degree.
Yet Juno works me still a greater shame:
I dare not now acknowledge mine own name!
But I that formerly was called Arcite
Am Philostratë now, not worth a mite!
Juno, alas! alas, thou dreadful Mars!
Thus have ye wrecked our kin with wrathful wars,
Save only me and wretched Palamon
That Theseus martyreth in dungeon-stone.
And more than this, Love, wholly to undo me,
Hath shot his flaming dart so fiercely through me,
Piercing my faithful heart, with care begirt,
That death was shaped for me before my shirt!
Ye slay me with your eyes, O Emely;
Ye are the cause, the cause for which I die!
On all these other things that make my care
I would not set the value of a tare
If something I could do to please you well!"
And with the word down in a trance he fell
And lay there long, and then rose up at last.

This Palamon, that crouched there all aghast,
As if he felt a cold sword through him gliding,
He shook for ire; he would not stay in hiding;
And having seen Arcite and heard his tale,
Like madman, with a visage dead and pale

He burst forth from the tangled bushes crying:
"Arcite, thou traitor base and false and lying,
Now art thou caught, that lovest my lady so,
Thou who art cause of all my pain and woe,
Who art my blood, and gave thine oath to hold thee
In faith to me, as I have often told thee,
And here hast made a dupe of Theseus,
And hast thy name all falsely altered thus;
Either I perish here, or thou shalt die!
Thou shalt not love my lady Emely;
Nay, none but I shall love her – I alone,
Who am thy mortal foe, and Palamon!
And though have I no weapon here with me,
Having from jail by fortune broken free,
This thing is sure: that either thou shalt die
Or else shalt cease to love my Emely.
Choose which thou wilt; escape me thou shalt not."

Arcite, with heart that swelled with anger hot,
When he knew Palamon, and harked his word,
As fierce as raging lion he drew a sword,
And thus he said: "By God that sits above,
Were't not that thou art sick and mad for love
And hast no weapon with thee – this I know:
Not one pace from this forest shouldst thou go,
But perish shouldst thou straightway by my sword.
For I defy the surety and the word
Which thou declarest I have pledged to thee!
O fool indeed! Know well that love is free,
And I will love her – yea, for all thy might!
But for as much as thou art worthy knight,
Seeking by arms to make thy love prevail,
Take thou my word: tomorrow without fail
Here, to no other living person known,
As I am knight, will I return alone
And armor will I bring enough for thee –
Choose thou the best and leave the worst for me.
And meat and drink this evening will I bring
Enough for thee – and clothes for thy bedding.
And, if it be that thou my lady win,
And slay me in this forest I am in,
Thou mayst well have thy lady, as for me!"

And Palamon replied: "I grant it thee."
And thus the two have parted till the morn,
Each having word of oath to other sworn.

O Cupid, stranger unto charity!
O king, that will no fellow have with thee!
For true it is, nor love nor tyranny
Ever will share his lordship willingly;
Arcite discovered this, and Palamon.
Arcite at once goes riding to the town,
And on the morn, ere yet the night had cleared
Two sets of arms in secret he prepared,
Both of a quality to test the right
When in the field the two of them should fight.
Mounted, and lone as when his mother bore him,
All of this armor carrieth he before him,
And in the wood, with time and place as set,
This Arcite and this Palamon are met.
Then straightway changed the color in each face,
Just as the huntsman in the realm of Thrace
Standing within the gap with waiting spear,
When men have roused the lion or the bear,
Hears him at length fast through the forest making,
The boughs of trees and tender branches breaking,
And thinks: "Here comes my mortal enemy:
Now without fail he must be dead, or I;
For either I must slay him at the gap,
Or he slay me, if such be my mishap–"
So went with both the changing of their hue
As soon as either one the other knew.
No salutation was there, no good-day;
With no rehearsal and no word to say
At once each went and helped to arm the other,
With friendly hand, as though he helped his brother.
And after that, with lances sharp and strong
They thrust at one another wondrous long;
And then this Palamon ye would have thought
To be a raging lion as he fought,
And like a cruel tiger was Arcite;
Like savage boars they seemed to lash and smite,
That froth like foam for maddened rage. They stood
Up to the ankle battling in their blood.

And I will leave them fighting in this way,
And something more of Theseus will I say.

    Now Destiny, that minister-at-large,
That through the world in all things doth discharge
The Providence which God hath pre-ordained –
So strong it is, that, though the world maintained
The opposite of a thing, by yea or nay,
Yet sometime shall it happen on a day
That not again within a thousand year
Shall fall; for certainly our hungers here,
Be they for war or peace or hate or love,
Wholly are governed by the Eye above.
This now I say of mighty Theseus
That for the chase is so desirous,
And most to hunt the mighty hart in May,
So that for him in bed there dawns no day
But he is clad and ready forth to ride
With hound and horn and hunter by his side;
For in his hunting hath he such delight
That it is all his joy and appetite
Himself the slayer of the hart to be,
For after Mars Diana serveth he.

    Clear was the day, as I have said ere this,
And Theseus, full of every joy and bliss,
With his Hippolyta, the lovely queen,
And Emely, all garmented in green,
Forth to the hunt went riding royally.
And to the tract of wood that lay hard by,
In which there was a hart, as he was told,
Duke Theseus soon his way direct doth hold;
And for the clearing now he sets his horse,
For thither the hart was wont to take his course,
And over a brook, as on his way he flew.
This duke will have a course at him or two,
With hounds, such as it pleased him to command.

    And when he came upon the open land
And gazed beneath the sun, he was aware
At once of Palamon and Arcite there,
Like two boars fighting, blow for raging blow;
The bright swords lunged and darted to and fro
So hideously, that with their lightest stroke

It seemed as if the blow could fell an oak;
But nothing yet he knew of what they were.
This duke he smote his courser with the spur
And "Ho!" he shouted, and a sword he drew,
And in a flash he broke between the two.
"No more," he cried, "on pain to lose your head!
By mighty Mars, I tell you he is dead
That strikes another stroke! But say to me
What kind of men the two of you may be
So bold and eager to be fighting here
Without a judge or other officer,
As in a tournament all royally?"

    Then Palamon made answer instantly
And said: "O sire, what now shall more words serve
When both of us alike our death deserve?
Two miserables, two wretches fit for gyves
Are we, that be encumbered with our lives.
And as thou art a judge and rightful lord
Mercy nor refuge do thou us accord,
But slay me first, for holy charity;
But slay my fellow too as well as me.
Or slay him first, for little though thou know,
This is Arcite, this is thy mortal foe,
Forbid thy land on pain to lose his head,
For which he well deserveth to be dead.
For this is he that to thy gateway came
And said that Philostratë was his name.
For years he fooled thee with a false belief,
Till thou didst take him for thy squire-in-chief,
And this is he that loveth Emely,
For since the day is come when I shall die
I make my plain confession: do thou know
I am that Palamon, oppressed with woe,
That won from out thy prison wickedly.
I am thy mortal foe, and I am he
That loves so fiercely Emely the bright
That I would die at once within her sight.
Therefore for death and justice do I pray –
But slay my fellow in the self-same way,
For both of us deserve well to be slain!"

    At once this worthy duke out-spake again

And loude he song ageyn the sonne shene:
MAY, with alle thy floures & thy grene,
    Welcome be thou, faire, fresshe May,
    In hope that I som grene gete may.
And from his courser with a lusty herte
Into a grove ful hastily he sterte,
And in a path he rometh up and doun,
Theras by aventure this Palamoun
Was in a bussh, that no man myghte hym se,
for soore afered of his deeth was he.
Nothyng ne knew he that it was Arcite,
God woot he wolde have trowed it ful lite.
But sooth is seyd, gon sithen many yeres,
That feeld hath eyen, & the wode hath eres;
It is ful fair a man to bere hym evene,
for al day meeteth men at unset stevene.
ful litel woot Arcite of his felawe
That was so ny to herknen al his sawe,
for in the bussh he sitteth now ful stille.
WHAN that Arcite hadde romed al his
    fille,
    And songen al the roundel lustily,
Into a studie he fil all sodeynly,
As doon thise loveres in hir queynte geres,
Now in the crope, now doun in the breres,
Now up, now doun, as boket in a welle.
Right as the friday, soothly for to telle,
Now it shyneth, and now it reyneth faste,

Right so kan geery Venus overcaste
The hertes of hir folk; right as hir day
Is gereful, right so chaungeth she array,
Selde is the friday al the wowke ylike.
Whan that Arcite had songe, he gan to sike,
And sette hym doun withouten any moore:
Allas, quod he, that day that I was bore!
How longe, Juno, thurgh thy crueltee,
Woltow werreyen Thebes the citee?
Allas, ybroght is to confusioun
The blood roial of Cadme and Amphioun,
Of Cadmus, which that was the firste man
That Thebes bulte, or first the toun bigan,
And of the citee first was crouned kyng;
Of his lynage am I, and his ofspryng
By verray ligne, as of the stok roial;
And now I am so caytyf and so thral,
That he that is my mortal enemy,
I serve hym as his squier povrely.
And yet dooth Juno me wel moore shame,
for I dar noght biknowe myn owene name,
But theras I was wont to highte Arcite,
Now highte I Philostrate, noght worth a myte.
Allas, thou felle Mars! allas, Juno!
Thus hath youre ire oure kynrede al fordo,
Save oonly me, and wrecched Palamoun,
That Theseus martireth in prisoun.
And over al this, to sleen me outrely,

Plate 3: The Knight's Tale (p. 39)

And said: "This judgment need not be delayed,
For your confession, by your own mouth made,
Hath damned you – I attest it past a doubt;
Methinks we need no rope to scourge it out;
Ye shall be dead, by mighty Mars the red!"
    At once the queen, for very womanhead,
Began to weep, and so did Emely
And all the ladies in that company.
It was great pity, so it seemed to all,
That such a misadventure should befall,
For noble men of great estate were they,
And all for love alone they fought this way;
And gazing on their wounds, red, deep and wide,
Alike the greater and the lesser cried:
"Have mercy, Lord, upon us women all!"
And on their bare knees with the word they fall,
And would have kissed his feet as there he stood,
Till softened in a little was his mood,
For quick is pity in the noble-hearted.
And though for ire at first he shook and started,
He hath considered briefly, in a word,
The offense of both, and wherefore it occurred;
And though his anger them of guilt accused,
Yet both by reason he hath soon excused,
For well he recognized that every man
Will help himself in love as best he can,
And out of prison deliver himself as well.
And also on his heart compassion fell
For the women all as one before him weeping;
And in his noble heart the thought came creeping,
And softly to himself he said, "Now fie
Upon a lord that mercy will deny,
And both in word and deed the lion be,
Alike to those that come remorsefully
And awed with fear, and to a spiteful man
That proudly holds to what he first began.
Truly that lord hath scant discerning sense
Who in such cases sees no difference,
But weighs humility and pride as one."
Thus, in a word, his anger being gone,
He looked about him with more cheerful eyes,

And pleasantly he spoke and in this wise:
    "The god of love! Ah! *benedicite*!
How mighty and how great a lord is he!
No obstacles may stand against his might,
And for his miracles shall men do right
To call him god: of every heart he maketh
In his own way what thing his fancy taketh.
Lo here! This Arcite and this Palamon,
Both from my prison free, that might have gone
To Thebes, and dwelt there well and royally,
And know I am their mortal enemy,
And that their death at my discretion lies –
And yet hath love, in spite of their two eyes,
Brought both of them together here to die.
Now look ye, is not that a folly high?
Who can a true fool be unless he love?
Behold, for the gods' sake that sit above –
See how they bleed! Are they not well arrayed?
The god of love, their lord, thus hath he paid
Their wages for their service, and their fee!
Yet very wise these lovers think they be
That give love service, let what may befall!
But this is yet the finest jest of all –
That she, for whom they have this jollity,
Can give them no more thanks than she gives me;
Of this hot work she was no more aware
By God, than is a cuckoo or a hare!
Yet they must try it all, the hot and cold,
A man must be a fool, or young or old;
This for myself I long ago proved true,
For in my time I was a servant, too.
And therefore, since I know the pain of love,
And how a man may feel the force thereof,
As one that oft hath struggled in his snare,
Full pardon for your trespass I declare
At asking of the queen that kneeleth here,
And Emely as well, my sister dear.
And ye shall swear at once your oaths to me
Never to work my country injury,
Nor wage a war against me, night or day,
But be my friends in everything ye may;

And so I pardon you this trespass wholly."
Then to his asking swore they fair and fully,
And for his judgment and his mercy prayed,
And grace he granted them, and thus he said:

"To speak of royal lineage or demesne –
Though she should be a princess or a queen,
Both of you well are worthy, I confess,
To wed when it is time; yet none the less
I speak for her, my sister Emely,
For whom ye have this strife and jealousy.
Ye know yourselves, she cannot marry two
At once, though ye eternal combat do:
One of you, be he glad or full of grief,
Must go and whistle to an ivy-leaf;
That is to say, she cannot have you both,
However jealous ye may be or wroth.
And therefore this condition I decree
For you, that each shall have his destiny
As shaped for him; hear now the way it lies –
This is your plan, this is what I devise.

"My will is this, to make a clear decision
With no discussion of it or revision;
If it shall please you, take it for the best:
That each go forth as likes him, east or west,
Free of control and all indebtedness,
And this day fifty weeks, nor more nor less,
Each of you here a hundred knights shall bring,
All armed to take the lists in everything,
Your claims on her by tournament to test;
And on my promise may ye safely rest,
Upon my truth and as I am a knight,
That unto him of you that hath the might,
That is to say, that whether he or thou
Shall with the hundred that I spoke of now
Drive from the lists or slay his adversary
To him will I give Emely to marry –
To him that Fortune yields so fair a grace.
The lists shall I have builded in this place,
And God so justly by my spirit do
As I shall be impartial judge and true.
Ye shall no other ending make for me

But one of you shall dead or taken be.
And if this seems to you to be well said,
Give your opinion and be comforted;
For this your end and your decision is."

Who now but Palamon hath joy in this?
Who leaps aloft for gladness but Arcite?
Who could in speech describe, or who could write
The joy was celebrated in that place
When Theseus hath done so fair a grace?
Then all the people there, in their degrees,
With heart and might thanked him upon their knees,
And the two Thebans most. Thus blithe of heart
And high of hope the two at length depart
Taking their leave, and straight for home they ride
To Thebes, that stands with ancient walls and wide.

Part III

I THINK that men would deem it negligence
Should I forget to tell at what expense
Duke Theseus goes about so busily
To build the lists up royally and high,
That such a noble theatre was never
Seen in this world, in any place whatever.
The circuit of it was a mile about,
And it was walled with stone and ditched without,
And like a compass they had built it round,
In tiers, and sixty yards above the ground,
So that a man set on the seat assigned him
Would hinder not the sight of one behind him.

Eastward there stood a gate of marble white,
Westward, just such another opposite,
And, in a word, there was no other place
Like it on earth within such little space;
For there was not a workman in the land,
If he arithmetic could understand,
Geometry, or carving images,
But Theseus gave him meat and princely fees
The theatre to build and to devise.
And as a place for rite and sacrifice
Eastward he made, upon the gate above,

Honoring Venus, that is queen of love,
An altar and a little oratory;
And westward, for the memory and the glory
Of Mars, he made its very counterpart
That cost him gold enough to fill a cart!
And northward, on the ramparts turreted,
Of alabaster white and coral red,
Hath Theseus wrought a temple fair to see,
Diana and the cult of chastity
With rich and noble art to celebrate.

    But still I had forgotten to relate
What pictures and what carvings nobly made,
What shape and show and figures were displayed
For sight within these oratories three.

    First in the temple of Venus mightst thou see
Wrought on the wall, full piteous to behold,
The broken slumbers and the sighings cold,
The sacred tears, the lamentations dire,
The fiery-pointed lashes of desire
That in this life love's servants must endure;
The oaths that do their covenants insure;
Pleasure and hope, desire, foolhardiness,
Beauty and youth, riches and bawdiness;
Charms, too, and force, and loss and flattery,
Spending and diligence and jealousy
(That wore of marigolds a yellow band
And had a cuckoo sitting on her hand);
Feasts also, carols, instruments and dances,
Lust and array, and all the circumstances
Of love that I can count or ever shall,
Were painted by command upon the wall,
And more than ever I can mention here.
The mount of Citheron, in truth, was there,
Where Venus hath her dwelling principal;
Well was it shown in painting on the wall,
Its garden and its amorous excess;
Nor was forgot the porter Idleness,
Nor fair Narcissus of a time far gone,
Nor yet the folly of King Solomon,
Nor yet the mighty strength of Hercules,
Nor yet Medea's magic, nor Circe's,

Nor Turnus, with his courage fierce and bold,
Nor Crœsus, rich and wretched with his gold.
Thus neither wisdom, may ye see, nor wealth,
Nor boldness yet nor beauty, strength nor stealth,
Can hold with Venus any rivalry,
For all the world at pleasure guideth she.
So meshed were all these people in her snare
Often they cried "Alas!" in their despair.
Be one or two examples here supplied,
Though I could count a thousand more beside.

    The shape of Venus, painted gloriously,
Was floating naked on the open sea,
And she was covered from the navel down
With green waves; bright as any glass they shone;
A small harp in her right hand carried she,
And on her head there rested, fair to see,
A wreath of roses, fresh and good of scent;
In fluttering flight her doves about her went.
Cupid her son was standing by her there,
And two wings on his shoulders did he bear,
And he was blind, as often represented,
And bore a bow, and arrows bright and pointed.

    But why should I not likewise tell you all
The portraiture was wrought upon the wall
Within the temple of mighty Mars the red?
The wall was painted every way it spread
Like to the bowels of that grisly place
Men call the mighty temple of Mars in Thrace,
Even in that region grim with frost and cold
Where Mars established hath his sovereign hold.

    First on the wall a wood was painted well,
Within whose bound nor man nor beast did dwell,
With knotted, gnarlèd, barren branches old
And stumps shorn off and hideous to behold,
Through which there ran a rumble and a sough
As though a storm would shatter every bough.
And downward from a hill, under a bent,
There stood the temple of Mars Armipotent,
Wrought all of burnished steel, of which the bright
High, narrow gate was ghastly to the sight;
And from it thundered such a rage and blast

That all the doors were shaken as it passed.
The northern light in through the portals shone,
For window in that iron wall was none
Through which the smallest beam of light could
        slant.
The doors were of eternal adamant,
And they were clenched across and all along
With toughest iron, and to make it strong,
Each pillar that sustained the temple there
Was iron barrel-thick, and bright and fair.

    And first I saw the dark imagining
Of felony, and its encompassing;
Rage, red as any coal, and hovering near
The Pickpurse, and the pallid face of Fear,
The Smiler with a knife beneath his cloak,
The sheepfold burning under dense black smoke,
The treason of the murdering in the bed,
And Open War, covered with wounds that bled,
Strife with a bloody knife and frowning face;
With grating noises groaned that grisly place.
The slayer of himself was also there,
His own heart's blood had matted all his hair;
The nail that pierced by night the forehead bone,
And Death himself, cold, open-mouthed, and prone.
Midway the temple darkly sat Mischance
Beside Discomfort and Sad Countenance;
Madness I saw, loud-laughing in his rage,
Outcry and Armed Complaint and fierce Outrage;
The corpse with slashed throat in the bushes lying,
A thousand slain – none of the plague were dying;
The Tyrant that by force his prey secured,
The town destroyed – nothing at all endured.
I saw the fire burn up the dancing ship,
The hunter strangled in the wild bear's grip,
The sow devour the infant from the cradle,
The cook get scalded too, despite his ladle.
Naught was forgotten: all ills ye might discover:
The carter by his own cart ridden over,–
Low on the ground beneath the wheel he lay.
And likewise Mars his temple did display
Barber and butcher and the smith that beat

Swords into sharpness in the anvil heat.
And over all, painted within a tower,
Conquest I saw, that sat enthroned in power.
And higher still, and just above his head,
A sharp sword hung, suspended by a thread.
And painted was the slaying of Juliüs,
Of mighty Nero, of Antonius;
For though at this time they were still unborn,
Yet here their deaths were pictured to adorn
The grisly walls of Mars, by form and face;
For everything was painted in that place
As it is painted in the stars above –
Who shall be slain or who shall die for love.
Of these old pictures let me one recall;
Though I might wish, I could not tell them all.

    Upon a chariot, armed, with wrath that glowed
Like madness throned, great Mars' statue rode.
Above his head two stars were shaped in flame,
These in the scriptures being called by name
The one Puella, the other Rubeüs.
The mighty god of war was pictured thus:
Low at his feet a fierce wolf crouched and glowered,
With red eyes gleaming, and a man devoured;
With skilful brush the artist showed this story,
Honoring Mars and setting forth his glory.

    Now to the temple of Diana the chaste
I turn at once, and take my way in haste
That unto you I may describe it all.
Well pictured up and down was every wall
With hunting scenes and modest chastity.
I saw unfortunate Calistophe,
And Dian's anger well depicted there
That changed her from a woman to a bear;
And later she was made the lode-star; so
Her fate was painted; nothing more I know.
Her son's a star as well, as men may see.
There I saw Danae turned into a tree;
Not goddess Dian – it was not the same,
But Penneus' daughter, Danae called by name.
There Acteon was shown, changed to a deer
Because he dared on naked Dian peer;

And his own hounds, that now no longer knew him,
Leapt on him there, and tore his flesh, and slew him!
And on the wall, along a little more,
Was Atalanta hunting the wild boar,
And Meleager, and many another too,
And him with care and woe Diana slew.
And other wondrous stories might ye see,
Which now I will not bring to memory.
High on a hart I saw this goddess sitting,
And little dogs about her feet were flitting,
And underneath her feet she had a moon,
Almost at full, yet due for waning soon.
Her image all in gladsome green was clad,
And arrow case and bow in hand she had;
Downward her eyes were looking, toward the ground
Where Pluto holds his realm in darkness bound.
A wife in labor lay before her there,
And she, because the child was hard to bear,
Turned on Lucina, piteously to call –
Crying: "Help, for thou canst the best of all!"
Well could he paint to life that had it wrought;
His paints with many a florin had he bought.

Now are these lists complete, and Theseus,
That at his great cost hath embellished thus
The lists and all the shrines of which I tell,
When it was done, he liked it wondrous well.
And now of him I stay a while to write,
And speak of Palamon and of Arcite.

The day of their return approaches now,
When each should bring, to test his cause and vow,
A hundred knights, as earlier I told.
To Athens then, his covenant to hold,
Each of the two his hundred knights hath brought,
In all ways armed for war; they lacked in naught.
And, certainly, said then full many a man,
That never, since this world of ours began,
To speak of tested knighthood truthfully,
Was there, as far as God had fashioned sea
Or land, so small yet noble a company.
For all that had a love of chivalry
And coveted an everlasting name

Had prayed for part within this knightly game,
And glad indeed was he that won a place.
And should there come tomorrow such a case
Again, ye know that every lusty knight
That hath his strength and loveth with all his might,
Were it proclaimed for England or elsewhere,
Would with full will desire to battle there,
To fight for a lady, *benedicite*!
A lusty spectacle it were to see.

And right so came they now with Palamon;
With him went knights ariding, many a one.
And some of these in coat of mail were dressed,
With doublet, and a breastplate for the breast,
And some were armed with sets of plates full large,
And some with Prussian shield would come, or targe;
And some had cased their legs from hip to heel,
And had an ax, and some a mace of steel.
Never new fashions be but they are old!
Armed were they all, and even as I have told,
According to his preference, each one.

There might'st thou see, coming with Palamon,
Ligurge himself, the mighty king of Thrace;
Black was his beard, of manly look his face;
The circlets of his eyes, deep in his head,
Glowed with a light between a yellow and red,
And like a griffin round him did he stare
From under brows where shaggy hung the hair.
His limbs were great, his muscles hard and strong,
His shoulders broad, his arms both large and long;
And as the custom was within his land,
High on a chair of gold he had his stand;
Of white bulls in the traces there were four.
No armor-coat over his gear he wore,
But, with its yellow nails as bright as gold,
A monstrous bear's skin, shaggy, black and old.
Combed was his flowing hair behind his back,
No raven's wing shone ever half so black;
A wreath of gold, arm-thick, of fearful weight,
Was on his head, and bore a shining freight
Of stones – fine rubies, glittering diamonds.
Around his car went leaping monstrous hounds,

Twenty and more, as big as any steer,
To hunt the lion with him, or the deer;
They followed now with muzzles closely bound,
With collars gold, and collar-rings filed round.
A hundred lords came riding in his rout;
Armed well they were, their hearts were stern and
     stout.
    With Arcite, as ye may in stories find,
The great Emetrius, the king of Ind,
On a bay steed with trappings iron-plated,
Covered with cloth of gold well variegated,
Came riding like the god of battle, Mars.
His armor-coat was made of cloth of Tars,
With pearls encrusted, large and round and white;
Of burnished gold his saddle, beaten bright.
A little cloak was round his shoulders spread,
Engemmed with fiery-sparkling rubies red.
Like rings upon his head curled his crisp hair,
Yellow, and glittering like sunlight fair.
High was his nose, his eyes bright citron were,
His lips full, and of sanguine character
Was his complexion, sprinkled with a few
Freckles that were a yellow-black in hue;
Like lion he his eye about him rolled;
And I would guess him twenty-five years old.
Well had his beard by now commenced to spring;
His voice was like a trumpet thundering.
Upon his head he wore of laurel bright
A garland green and goodly to the sight;
Upon his hand he bore for his delight
An eagle tame, as any lily white.
A hundred lords came riding with him there,
All fully armed, save that their heads were bare,
Richly and well, in various kinds of things,
For trust ye well that dukes and earls and kings
Were gathered in this noble company
For love and for the increase of chivalry.
And there on every side about this king
Went leopards and tame lions gamboling.
And in this way these princes, all and some,
Were on a Sunday to the city come,

At prime of day, and there they did alight.
    This Theseus then, this duke, this worthy knight,
When thus into his city he had brought them,
Lodgings for each in his degree he sought them,
And feasted them, and tendered all things to them,
And sought their ease, and courtesy to do them,
That folk were well agreed that no man's wit,
No matter what estate, could better it.
Of minstrelsy or service at the feast,
Of splendid gifts for greatest and for least,
Of Theseus' palace that in rich array is,
Of who sat first or last upon the daïs,
What ladies danced the best or were the fairest,
Or which could lightliest move or sing the clearest,
Or who could speak most feelingly of love –
What hawks were sitting on the perch above,
What dogs were lying on the floor below –
Of all this will I make no mention now;
For what came after – that seems best to me;
Now if it please you, hearken carefully –
Here comes the point. It fell on Sunday night
That Palamon heard the lark, for though the light
Showed not as yet, nor for two hours was due,
Yet the lark sang, and Palamon sang too.
And high of mood and reverent of heart
He rose, upon his mission to depart
To Cytherea, blissful and benign:
Venus I mean, well-honored and divine.
And in her hour he walketh forth a pace
Where in the lists her temple had its place,
And down he kneeleth and with a humble cheer
And a sore heart, he said as ye shall hear.
    "Fairest of fair, O lady Venus mine,
Great Vulcan's wife, daughter of Jove divine,
Thou angel of the mount of Citheron,
For that same love which bright Adonis won,
Have pity on my tears and bitter smart
And take my humble prayer to thy heart.
Alas! I have no language that can tell
The injuries or the torments of my hell;
My heart lacks strength my anguish to betray;

In my confusion nothing can I say.
But mercy, lady bright, that well dost know
My thought, and all the ills I undergo!
Think well on this; take pity on my pain
As certainly as I with might and main
Shall evermore thine own true servant be
And always wage a war on chastity –
Give me thine aid and this shall be my vow.
To vaunt of skill at arms I care not now,
Nor ask tomorrow to have the victory,
Nor even renown, nor glorious vanity
Of tourney-prize blown loudly up and down,
But ask for Emely to be mine own,
And that I serve thee, dying as a lover;
Do thou the manner and the way discover!
For I care not if it shall better be
To conquer them, or have them conquer me,
So that I have my lady in my arms;
For though great Mars may be the god of arms,
Yet thou hast power so great in heaven above
That if it please thee I shall have my love.
Thy sovereign shrine forever will I pay
Great honor, and wherever lies my way
I will make sacrifice, kindling bright fire.
And lady, if ye grant not my desire,
I pray thee well that with a spear tomorrow
Arcite may pierce my heart. For naught of sorrow
Shall I feel then, when I have lost my life,
Though he should win my lady for his wife.
The sum and point of all my prayer is here:
Give me my love, thou blessèd lady dear!"

When Palamon his prayer had wholly said,
Right afterwards his sacrifice he made
Full piteously, with all formalities;
But now I take no time to tell of these.
However, at last the statue of Venus shook
And seemed to make a sign, and this he took
To mean acceptance of his prayer that day.
For though the sign forecasted a delay,
Yet well he knew that granted was his boon,
And glad of heart for home departed soon.

The third unequal hour since Palamon
Had to the temple of Citherea gone,
Up rose the sun, and up rose Emely,
And for Diana's temple started she.
Her maidens, whom she took, at her desire
Quickly they made and with them brought the fire,
The raiment and the incense rich with spice,
And all else needed for the sacrifice;
The customary horns of mead they bore;
For sacrifice they needed nothing more.
The shrine was fair with hangings and sweet scent
When Emely, all mild and reverent,
Her body washed with water from a well.
But how she did this rite I dare not tell
Unless I speak of it in general;
Yet pleasant would it be to hear of all;
To one well-meaning it were no transgression –
Such should be free to speak at his discretion.
Her shining hair was combed and flowing down,
And there was set upon her head a crown
Of green oak leaves that glittered bright and fair.
Two flames she kindled on the altar there,
And made her ritual, as may men behold
In Stace of Thebes, and other volumes old.
And when the fire was made, with piteous cheer
Diana she addressed, as ye may hear.

"O goddess chaste of woodland and green tree,
That hast the sight of heaven and earth and sea,
Queen of the realm of Pluto, dark and low,
Goddess of maidens, that dost always know
From year to year my heart and my desire,
Keep me from thy swift vengeance and thine ire,
Which came to Acteon so cruelly!
O sovereign goddess, queen of chastity,
Thou know'st I would be maiden all my life,
And no man's lady would I be, or wife.
Thou know'st I am a maid, still holding place
Within thy crew, and love the hunt and chase,
And to be walking in the forest wild,
And would not be a wife and be with child.
Nowise I crave the company of man.

Now help me, lady, since ye may and can,
By power of those three forms thou hast in thee;
And Palamon, that hath such love for me,
And Arcite too, that loveth me so sore,
This grace I pray thee – that no trouble more
Fall on these two, but love and amity;
And likewise turn their hearts away from me,
And let their burning love and their desire,
And all their restless torment and their fire
Be quenched, or turned toward another place;
And if it come thou wilt not do me grace,
Or if by destiny it be my due
To have for husband either of the two,
Then send thou him that most desireth me.
Behold, O goddess of clean chastity,
The bitter tears upon my cheeks that fall.
Since thou art maid and keeper of us all
To keep me virgin give me now thine aid
And I will serve thee while I live a maid!"

Clear burned the fires upon the altar there
While Emely recited thus her prayer,
But suddenly she saw a wondrous sight;
For one flame sank and died, then fresh and bright
Burned up again, and soon the other one
Died in the same way and was wholly gone;
And as it died it made a whistling noise,
As when the fire a sodden brand destroys,
And beaded at the faggots' ends there stood
Many red drops that shone and dripped like blood,
At which so sore aghast was Emely
She wept aloud, for well nigh crazed was she,
And nowise knew she what it signified;
And all for fear of what she saw she cried
And wept that it was piteous to hear.
Then did Diana unto her appear,
Clad as a huntress, and her bow she bore,
And thus addressed her: "Daughter, weep no more!
Among the high gods hath it been affirmed,
By word eternal written and confirmed,
That thou shalt wedded be to one of those
That bear for thee so many cares and woes,

But unto which of them I may not say;
Farewell, for here no longer can I stay.
The fires that on my altar dim and brighten
Ere thou departest shall thee well enlighten
As to the love and fortune thou shalt face."
And with that word the arrows in her case
Began to clatter loudly and to ring,
And forth she went, and made a vanishing.
Then Emely in great astonishment:
"Alas!" she cried, "what meaneth this event?
Dian, I put myself in thy protection,
Taking the fate that comes at thy direction."
And home she went at once the nearest way;
This is what fell; no more there is to say.

At the next hour of Mars the god of war
Arcite arriveth at the temple door
Of fierce-browed Mars, his sacrifice to do,
With all the pagan rites that go thereto.
With high devotion and heart all piteous
To Mars his orison he sayeth thus:
"O mighty god, that in the regions cold
Of Thrace men honor and as lord do hold,
That hast in every realm and every land
The bridles of great armies in thy hand,
And fortune send'st them as it pleaseth thee –
Accept my piteous sacrifice of me!
And if it be my youth so much deserve,
And if the strength I have be fit to serve
Thy godhead, and thy company to gain,
I pray thee have compassion on my pain
Even for that hurt and all that scorching fire
Wherein thou once didst burn in thy desire,
And all the shining beauty drew to thee
Of the young Venus, fair and fresh and free,
And in thine arms didst have her at thy will,
Though on a time, indeed, thy luck was ill
When Vulcan slyly drew his snare around thee
And thereby lying with his lady found thee.
For that same sorrow that was in thy heart
Have pity now upon my pain and smart.
Young and unskilful am I, as thou know'st,

Two fyres on the auter gan she beete,
And dide hir thynges, as men may biholde
In Stace of Thebes, and thise bookes olde.
Whan kyndled was the fyr, with pitous cheere,
Unto Dyane she spak, as ye may heere.

CHASTE goddesse of
the wodes grene,
To whom bothe hevene
and erthe & see is sene,
Queene of the regne of
Pluto derk and lowe,
Goddesse of maydens,
that myn herte hast
knowe
ful many a yeer, and
woost what I desire,
As keepe me fro thy vengeaunce and thyn ire,
That Attheon aboughte cruelly.
Chaste goddesse, wel wostow that I
Desire to ben a mayden al my lyf,
Ne nevere wol I be no love, ne wyf.
I am, thow woost, yet of thy compaignye
A mayde, and love huntynge and venerye,
And for to walken in the wodes wilde,
And noght to ben a wyf and be with childe;
Noght wol I knowe the compaignye of man.
Now helpe me, lady, sith ye may and kan,
For tho thre formes that thou hast in thee.

And Palamon, that hast swich love to me,
And eek Arcite, that loveth me so soore,
This grace I preye thee withoute moore,
As sende love and pees bitwixe hem two,
And fro me turne awey hir hertes so,
That al hire hoote love and hir desir,
And al hir bisy torment and hir fir,
Be queynt, or turned in another place.
And if so be thou wolt do me no grace,
Or if my destynee be shapen so
That I shal nedes have oon of hem two,
As sende me hym that moost desireth me.
Bihoold, goddesse of clene chastitee,
The bittre teeres that on my chekes falle,
Syn thou art mayde, and kepere of us alle,
My maydenhede thou kepe and wel conserve,
And whil I lyve a mayde, I wol thee serve.

THE fires brenne upon the auter cleere
Whil Emelye was thus in hir preyere;
But sodeynly she saugh a sighte
queynte,
For right anon, oon of the fyres queynte
And quyked agayn, and after that, anon
That oother fyr was queynt, and al agon,
And as it queynte it made a whistelynge,
As doon thise wete brondes in hir brennynge;
And at the brondes ende out ran anoon
As it were blody dropes many oon;

Plate 4: The Knight's Tale (p. 49)

And, as I think, with love afflicted most
Of any man that life hath ever known;
Since she for whom I sigh and weep and groan
Cares not a straw whether I sink or float,
And I shall lack her mercy, well I know't,
Until by strength in yonder tourney place
I win her. Yet without thy help and grace
My strength, I know full well, will not avail me;
Then in the fight tomorrow do not fail me,
O lord, for that same fire that burned in thee
Of old, and for the flame that scorcheth me.
Make it that I tomorrow the victor be;
Mine be the toil, take thou the fame to thee!
Thy sovereign temple honor will I pay
Above all others, and strive in every way
To give thee joy and thy strong craft to ply,
And in thy temple hang my flag on high
And all the weapons of my company;
And ever more, until I die," said he,
"I will make lasting fire before thee burn;
And to this vow I bind myself in turn:
My beard and hair that now are hanging long,
And never in the past have known the wrong
Of shears or razor, I to thee will give,
And thy true servant be the while I live.
Now pity, lord, pity my grievous sorrow:
Give me but this – the victory tomorrow!"

When mighty Arcite thus his prayer had ended,
The rings that hung upon the doors suspended,
And the doors also clattered loud and fast,
Till Arcite as he listened was aghast.
And then the altar flames began to brighten,
And all the temple round about to lighten;
And from the floor breathed perfume sweet and soft.
And straightway Arcite raised his hand aloft
And incense on the fire once more he cast,
And other rites performed, and then at last
He heard the mail on Mars' statue ring,
And with that sound there came a murmuring
Low-voiced and dim, that said thus: "Victory!"
For which to Mars honor and fame gave he.

Joyful, and hoping now his bliss to win,
Arcite at once repaireth to his inn,
Glad as a bird is of the shining sun.

And instantly such battle was begun
To keep their promises in heaven above,
Between great Venus that is queen of love,
And stern-browed Mars, of arms and war the lord,
That Jupiter sought vainly an accord
Between them. Saturn then, the pale and cold,
That knew so many instances of old,
From long experience a way descried
By which the two were quickly satisfied.
Truly, great benefits in age appear,
For wisdom there and custom both inhere;
Though youth hath quicker legs, its mind runs
    slower;
Saturn, to banish strife and doubt that lower,
Though to his nature this was contrary,
For all the trouble found a remedy.

"Dear daughter Venus," Saturn said to her,
"My orbit, with its great diameter,
Holds more of power than knoweth any man;
Mine is the drowning in the ocean wan;
Mine is the prison, dark in dungeon tower;
Strangling and hanging too are in my power,
Rebellious murmurs and the churls' uprising,
Groans, and the poison-death of dark devising,
And vengeance I impose and fines as well,
What time within the lion's sign I dwell.
Mine is the wrecking, too, of high-roofed halls,
Falling of towers and tumbling down of walls
Upon the miner and the carpenter.
When Samson shook the pillars I was there
And wrought his death. Control of sickness cold,
Dark treasons and sly stratagems I hold;
My glance is father unto pestilence.
Now weep no more: I shall with diligence
Make sure that Palamon, that is thy knight,
Shall have his lady as thou saidst he might;
Though Mars shall help his knight, still there must be
Between you two a peace eventually,

Though ye be nowise of one temperament,
Which makes division thus, and discontent.
Thy grandsire I, ready to do thy will;
Cease weeping, for thy wish will I fulfill."

    Now will I cease to speak of gods above –
Of Mars, and Venus, goddess-queen of love,
And tell you as directly as I can
Of the great deeds for which I first began.

Part IV

GREAT festival made Athens on that day,
And all the lusty blossoming of May
Put folk in such a happy countenance
That all that Monday did they joust and dance
And made for Venus high festivities.
But since with morning they must all arise
Early, in readiness to see the fight,
Unto their rest they turned them with the night.
And on the morrow, when the day began,
Clatter and noise of arms for horse and man
Sounded in all the hostelries about.
And toward the palace many a troop set out
Of lords on steeds and palfreys. And therewith
Might ye have heard the armor-forging smith
At work on harness rich with many a fold
Of woven steel, embroidery and gold.
Hauberks and shields and trappings strangely
    wrought
And coats-of-arms and gold-hewn helmets caught
The light; and gay-cloaked lords went riding
    through
On coursers proud, and knights of retinue;
And squires were nailing spears and making right
The straps of shields, and buckling helmets tight,
And lacing thongs – in nothing were they idle;
And foaming steeds, each at his golden bridle,
Were champing proudly, and the armorers too
With file and hammer darted to and fro;
Yeomen and commoners with staves were out
Crowding as thick as they could move about,

Fife, trumpet sounded, clarion, kettle drum,
From which in battle bloody noises come;
All up and down the palace floors were thronged,
Three here, ten there, that great debate prolonged,
Questioning of these knights, these Thebans two;
And some said this and some said that was true;
Some held the part of him with the black beard,
Some backed the bald one, others the thick-haired;
Some said he had a grim look and would fight –
"He bears an ax is twenty pound in weight."
And thus throughout the hall they prophesy
Long after sun began to mount the sky.

    Great Theseus, that from slumber had been stirred
By minstrelsy and all the noise he heard,
Held yet the chamber of his palace splendid
Till on his will the Theban knights attended,
Each having been with equal honors greeted.
Duke Theseus was at a window seated,
Clothed like a god that sitteth on his throne,
And there at once have all the people gone
To see him and high reverence to do him,
And for his will and hest to hearken to him.

    A herald on a scaffold cried a "Ho!"
Till all the noise was quieted below
Among the crowd, and when the folk were still,
For the great duke he spoke and showed his will.

    "Of his high wisdom hath our lord decreed
It was destruction and a waste indeed
That noble blood in battle should be spent
Unto the death here in this tournament.
Wherefore, to shape it that they shall not die,
His former purpose he will modify!
Therefore let no man, lest he lose his life,
A missile or a poleax or short knife
Unto the lists have sent, or thither bring;
Nor any sword for thrusting let him swing
With cutting point, nor bear it at his side.
And no man may against his fellow ride
More than one course with sharpened spear, but he
May thrust on foot at will, defensively.
And who in peril is, his foe shall take,

And slay him not, but bring him to the stake
That shall established be on either side;
Thither shall he be forced and there abide.
And if the chief of either side shall be
Taken, or smite his rival fatally,
Then shall the tourneying no longer last.
God speed you; forth, and lay on hard and fast,
With long swords and with maces fight your fill!
Go now your ways; so saith our lord his will."

    The voice of the people knocked against the sky,
So loud they shouted and with lusty cry,
"Now God save such a lord, that is so good
He will not have a useless waste of blood!"
Up go the trumpets and the melody,
And to the lists ride all the company;
In order through the mighty town they hold,
That not with serge was draped, but cloth-of-gold.
Full lordly there did noble Theseus ride,
With the two Thebans one on either side,
After them rode the queen and Emely,
And following that another company –
This one and that, by rank from first to last.
And thus through all the city streets they passed
And at the lists were entered in good time.
The day was not yet fully come to prime
When Theseus richly sat in majesty,
Hippolyta the queen and Emely,
And other ladies in degree about.
Now to the seats go jostling all the rout,
And westward through the gate of Mars there ride
Arcite and all the hundred of his side,
With banner red uplifted to the sun.
And at the self-same moment Palamon
To eastward under Venus' gate is seen,
With banner white, and bold of face and mien.
Though ye should search the world with might and
    main
Ye would not find two companies again
Opposed so evenly as these that day.
For there was none so wise that he could say
How either side advantage might profess

In age or in estate or worthiness –
It seemed they had been picked so evenly.
Now formed in splendid rank each company,
And every name was read from off a sheet,
That in their number should be no deceit;
Then clanged the gates shut, and the cry rang loud:
"Do now your devoir, princes young and proud!"
    The heralds cease their pricking up and down,
Out peal the trumpets and the clarion,
No more now to be said – but east and west
In go the spears, couched resolute at rest;
In goes the spur, biting the charger's side;
Then see men who can joust and who can ride;
Then shiver spear shafts where the shield is thick;
On breast-bone now the rider feels the prick;
Up leap the lances twenty feet in height,
Out go the swords with flaming silver light.
Helmets they hew apart and hack and shred,
Out spurts the jetting blood in streams of red;
Now swing the mighty maces, bones they crush;
Now through the thickest press the riders push.
Strong steeds go stumbling now, and down goes all.
One rolleth underfoot as rolls a ball.
One on his feet lifts up a spear to thrust;
One with his horse goes hurtling to the dust.
One through the body is hurt, and him they take
Struggling in vain, and bring him to the stake;
And by the compact there he must abide;
Another lad stays on the other side.
And sometimes Theseus bids them take their ease
To drink or mend their strength, as they may please.
And often on that day these Thebans two
Together met, and wrought each other woe;
Each hath unhorsed the other twice that day.
No tiger in the vale of Galgafay
Robbed of her cub, more fierce or full of might
Leaps out against the huntsman than Arcite
On Palamon leapt with heart of jealousy;
No lion grim doth lair in Belmarie
That, being tracked, or wild for want of food,
Pants for his prey and thirsteth for its blood

As Palamon to slay his foe Arcite.
The jealous strokes hard on their helmets bite,
Red from their sides the blood runs fearsomely.

    Yet end of every deed at length must be
And so at last, ere setting of the sun,
Strong King Emetrius this Palamon
Seized, while with Arcite he engaged afresh,
And made his sword bite deep into his flesh,
And twenty by their strength hemmed round and
    caught him,
And so unyielding to the stake they brought him.
And seeking there to rescue Palamon
The mighty King Ligurge is smitten down,
And King Emetrius, for all his strength,
Is borne from out his saddle a sword's length,
Such fierce resistance Palamon doth make –
But all for naught: they bring him to the stake.
His bold, courageous heart availed him naught;
He must remain there, now that he is caught,
Alike by compact and by force. Which one
Lamenteth now but woeful Palamon,
He that no more may go to join the fight?
And now Duke Theseus, having seen this sight,
Raised up his voice and cried to everyone
That strove there: "Ho! No more, the fight is done!
True judge and nowise partial will I be!
Arcite of Thebes receiveth Emely
That fairly by his fortune hath her won."
At once was noise among the folk begun
For joy of this, so loud and high withal
It seemed as if the very lists would fall.

    What now can lovely Venus do above?
What says she now? What does this queen of love?
For wreck of her desire she weepeth so
Her tears come falling on the lists below.
"Now doubtless am I put to shame," she cried,
But, "Daughter, hold thy peace," Saturn replied;
"Mars hath his will, his knight hath all his boon,
And, by my head, thy comfort cometh soon."

    The minstrelsy, the trumpets pealing high,
The heralds, resonant with yell and cry,

Make merry noise for joy of Lord Arcite.
But pause and hear me well while I recite
The miracle that happened suddenly.

    This fierce Arcite, his helmet looseth he,
And on a courser through the roomy place
Goes pricking up and down to show his face,
Gazing on Emely enthroned on high;
And she on him looks down with friendly eye,
For women, speaking generally, will go
Wherever Fortune may her favor show;
And Arcite saw her and was merry-hearted.
Then from the ground a hellish fury started,
At Saturn's asking there by Pluto sent,
And Arcite's horse well mad with terror went,
And leaped aside, and stumbled as he reared;
And Arcite, all surprised and unprepared,
Was thrown, and fell, and struck upon his head;
And where he fell he lay as he were dead;
His breast was shattered by his saddle-bow.
As black he looked as any coal or crow,
For all the blood had gathered in his face.
And straightway he was carried from the place
And to the palace mournfully was borne,
And quickly of his harness was he shorn,
And fair and speedily was brought to bed,
For he was yet alive and clear of head,
And always crying after Emely.

    Duke Theseus, with all his company,
Unto his city Athens now is come,
And every pomp and joy attend him home.
For he would not, despite this accident,
That everyone should feel discouragement;
It was said also, Arcite would not die,
But they would heal him of his injury.
And in another thing they took delight –
That none of them had perished in the fight,
Though wounded were they sore, and chiefly one
Upon whose breast a spear had pierced the bone.
To use on other wounds and broken arms
Some had their salves and others worked with charms,
And sage they drank, and likewise remedies

Of herbs, for they would save their limbs with these.
Therefore the noble duke, as best he can,
Comfort and honor gives to every man,
And makes a revel lasting all the night
Unto the foreign princes, as was right.
Nor shame there was, nor any discontent,
Except as at a joust or tournament,
For no dishonoring had there been at all,
Since it was chance for any man to fall,
Or by the force of twenty knights be brought
Unto the stake, unyielding though he fought.
One person all alone with many a foe,
And haled along by arm and foot and toe,
And his steed also driven along with staves,
With men afoot, yeomen as well as knaves –
Naught of disgrace could be to him in this;
No man indeed could call it cowardice!

Wherefore Duke Theseus caused it to be cried,
Stilling all talk of bitterness and pride,
That each side stood, as much as did the other,
Victor – and each was as the other's brother,
And gave them gifts each after his degree,
And feasted them three days continuously;
And all the kings a fitting conduct showed
Out of his town a day upon their road.
And home went every man his proper way;
There was no more but "Farewell! Have good day!"
So of this battle will I cease to write,
But speak of Palamon and of Arcite.

The breast of Arcite swelled, the pain and sore
About his heart increasing more and more;
Despite the leeches all the clotted blood
Became corrupt and in his body stood,
That cupping failed, and bleeding from the vein,
And brew of herbs to help him from his pain.
The power expellant termed or animal,
Which cometh from the force called natural,
Could not throw off the venom, or expel.
The chambers of his lungs began to swell,
And poison was beginning to infest
All muscles lying downward from his breast.

Nor could he help himself, in strife to live,
By vomiting or taking laxative,
For all was broken up beyond repair,
And nature had no more dominion there.
And nature having failed, give up the search
For pills and potions: bear the man to church!
All this to say that Arcite had to die –
Wherefore he bade them send for Emely
And Palamon, that was his cousin dear,
Then thus he spake, as straightway ye shall hear.

"The woeful spirit in me cannot bring
In speech a fragment of my suffering
To you, my lady, whom I love the most;
But I bequeath the service of my ghost
To you above all other creatures, knowing
Life is in ebb, and I shall soon be going.
Alas, the woe! the agony so strong
That I for you have suffered, and so long!
Alas, O death! Alas, mine Emely,
Alas, the parting of our company!
Alas, my heart's queen! O alas, my wife,
My heart's own lady, ender of my life!
What is this world? What asketh man to have?
Now with his love, now cold within his grave –
Alone, alone, with none for company!
Farewell, sweet foe! Farewell, mine Emely.
Now gently take me in your arms, I pray,
For love of God, and hearken what I say.

"I have with Palamon, my cousin here,
Had strife and rancor lasting many a year,
For love of you, and my great jealousy.
Now Jupiter make sure the way for me
To tell you of a lover well and truly,
With every circumstance considered duly –
That is to say – truth, knighthood and estate,
Honor, humility, and kinsmen great,
Wisdom, and all such things as make the whole;
As Jupiter is living in my soul,
In all this world I know indeed of none
So worthy to be loved as Palamon,
That serves you now, and will for all his life.

And if ye ever think to be a wife,
Forget not him – this noble Palamon."
And when that word was said, his speech was done,
For from his feet crept upward to his breast
The cold of death, that shut him from the rest.
And in his two arms also came at length
The loss and vanishing of vital strength.
Only the mind, the mind and nothing more,
Within his sick and failing heart upbore;
But when the heart itself was lost to death,
Then dusk fell on his eyes, then failed his breath.
Yet on his lady still he fixed his eye:
His last word was, "Your favor, Emely!"
Then changed his spirit houses, going where
I cannot tell, since I was never there.
Therefore I stop, for no diviner I,
Nor aught of souls within my book descry,
Nor those opinions would I care to tell
Of such as write of souls and where they dwell.
Arcite is cold, Mars his protector be!
Now will I speak again of Emely.

Shrieks Emely, loud waileth Palamon,
And Theseus took his sister in a swoon
And bore her quickly from the corpse away.
What will it help to linger out the day
Telling of how she wept, both night and morrow;
For in such cases women have such sorrow,
Seeing their husbands die and from them go,
That most of them lament their losses so,
Or into such a malady are cast
That certainly they die of it at last.

Infinite were the sorrows and the tears
Of aged folk and folk of tender years
Through the whole city for this Theban's death;
Child, man, and woman for him sorroweth.
Not such a lamentation was there made
For Hector's body unto Troy conveyed,
All newly slain. Alas, the pity there!
Gashing of cheeks and rending of the hair.
"Why wouldst thou go to Death," these women cry,
"Who haddest gold enough, and Emely?"

No man might comfort Theseus then except
Ægeus, his old father, who had kept
Remembrance of this world, how wide in range
As he had seen it up and down with change,
Joy after woe, woe after happiness,
And told them parables and instances.
"Just as no man hath ever died," quoth he,
"Unless he lived on earth in some degree,
So never hath there lived a man," he said,
"In all this world, but sometime must be dead.
This earth is but a thoroughfare of woe
And we are pilgrims passing to and fro;
Death is the end of every worldly pain."
And more beside he said in such a vein;
And full of wisdom, with the people plead
That once again they should be comforted.

Duke Theseus now gives deep consideration
As to the most befitting situation
For Arcite's tomb, and asketh furthermore
What place would honor most the rank he bore.
And to this thought he came when he was done:
That there where first Arcite and Palamon
Had made for love their battle in the glade,
There where the trees were sweet and green with
    shade,
There where he had his amorous desires,
And his complaint, and scorching lover's fires,
There he would make a fire, in which they might
Accomplish fitly each funereal rite.
And Theseus then commanded men to fell
The ancient oaks, and cut them up as well,
And line them out in billets fit to burn;
And swift of foot his prompt attendants turn,
And ride at once to further his intent.
And hard upon their going Theseus sent
After a bier, and had it fully dressed
With cloth-of-gold, the richest he possessed,
And in a suit of this he clad Arcite;
But both his hands he sheathed in gloves of white,
And crowned his head with wreath of laurel green,
And laid a sword beside him, bright and keen.

And then he bared the visage on the bier,
Weeping till it was piteous to hear,
And that the folk might see it, one and all,
With day he brought the body to the hall
Where all with moaning and lament was loud.
Then clad in tear-stained black amid the crowd
This woeful Theban Palamon appeared
With ashes in his hair, and tangled beard;
And weeping most of all came Emely,
Deepest in grief of all that company.
And since he knew the funeral should be
Noble and rich for one of his degree,
Duke Theseus gave command that they should bring
Three chargers trapped in steel all glittering,
And covered with the arms of Lord Arcite.
Upon these steeds, that towered huge and white,
Were seated men. One with his shield appeared;
Another high aloft his great lance reared;
The third came carrying his Turkish bow –
With burnished gold the case and fittings glow;
And at a walk all rode with mournful cheer
Toward the grove, as later ye shall hear.
And of the Greeks the noblest that were there
Arcite's bier upon their shoulders bare,
All slack of pace, with watery eyes and red,
Down the main street that through the city led,
Where all with black was hung, that wondrous high
Covered the walls and houses toward the sky.
Aged Ægeus on the right hand rode,
Duke Theseus on the left, and richly glowed
The vessels which they bore of gold all fine,
Filled full of honey, milk, and blood and wine;
Palamon too, with a great company;
And after that came woeful Emely;
The funeral fire she carried in her hand
As was the custom in that time and land.

    Great labor went to raising of the pyre
Where should be made the service and the fire;
High into heaven itself the green top pried,
And stretched its broad arms twenty fathom wide –
That is to say, the branches had been laid

On such a space. But first was straw conveyed
And strewn about. Yet how the pyre arose
So high, and what were all the trees they chose,
As willow, plane-tree, fir, birch, alder, yew,
Poplar, elm, ash, oak (with the holm-oak too),
Maple, thorn, beech, asp, hazel, cornel-tree,
Laurel, box, linden, chestnut – shall not be
Told here, nor how the gods in agitation
Ran up and down, robbed of their habitation,
The gods that dwelt in peace and silence here –
Nymphs, fauns, and hamadryads; nor the fear
Of all the animals and birds that fled
When the green woodland was deforested,
Nor how the ground aghast was of the light
That never had known the glare of sunshine bright,
Nor how the pyre with straw at first was laid,
Then high with dry and broken limbs was made,
And then with green wood and with spicery,
And then with cloth of gold and jewelry,
And flower with flower in woven garlands blent,
And myrrh and incense breathing heavy scent,
Nor how amid all this Arcite lay,
With riches set beside him on display,
Nor how, as was the custom, Emely
Put in the funeral fire, how later she
Fell in a swoon when they had made the fire;
Nor what she said, nor what was her desire,
Nor what of jewels in the flame were cast,
When it was great of size and burning fast,
Nor how some cast the shields and spears they bore.
And some threw in the vestments that they wore,
And cups of wine and blood and milk they had
Into the fire that burned as it were mad;
Nor how the Greeks in great procession turned
Leftwards around the fire the while it burned,
Three times, and how they raised a mighty shout
And thrice their lances as they marched about
Clashed; nor of how the ladies thrice did cry,
Nor of the leading home of Emely,
Nor how to ashes cold was burned Arcite,
Nor how they held the body-wake all night

for which so soore agast was Emelye,
That she was wel ny mad, and gan to crye,
for she ne wiste what it signyfied;
But oonly for the feere thus hath she cried,
And weepe, that it was pitee for to heere.
⸿And therwithal Dyane gan appeere,
With bowe in honde, right as an hunteresse,
And seyde, Doghter, stynt thyn hevynesse.
Among the goddes hye it is affermed,
And by eterne word writt and confermed,
Thou shalt ben wedded unto oon of tho
That han for thee so muchel care and wo;
But unto which of hem I may nat telle.
farwel, for I ne may no lenger dwelle.
The fires whiche that on myn auter brenne
Shulle thee declaren, er that thou go henne,
Thyn aventure of love, as in this caas.
AND with that word the arwes in the caas
    Of the goddesse clateren faste & rynge,
    And forth she wente, and made a van-
ysshynge;
for which this Emelye astoned was,
And seyde, What amounteth this, allas!
I putte me in thy proteccioun,
Dyane, and in thy disposicioun.
⸿And hoom she goth anon the nexte weye.
This is theffect, ther is namoore to seye.

THE nexte houre of Mars folwynge this,
    Arcite unto the temple walked is
    Of fierse Mars, to doon his sacrifise,
With alle the rytes of his payen wyse.
With pitous herte and heigh devocioun,
Right thus to Mars he seyde his orisoun:
O STRONGE god, that
    in the regnes colde
    Of Trace honoured art
    and lord yholde,
    And hast in every regne
    and every lond
    Of armes al the brydel
    in thyn hond,
    And hem fortunest as
    thee lyst devyse,
Accepte of me my pitous sacrifise.
If so be that my youthe may deserve,
And that my myght be worthy for to serve
Thy godhede, that I may been oon of thyne,
Thanne preye I thee to rewe upon my pyne.
for thilke peyne, and thilke hoote fir,
In which thou whilom brendest for desir,
Whan that thou usedeste the beautee
Of faire, yonge, fresshe Venus free,
And haddest hire in armes at thy wille,
Although thee ones on a tyme mysfille,

Plate 5: The Knight's Tale (p. 50)

Unto the dawn, and how the Athenians played
The wake-plays – all of this I leave unsaid;
Nor who was entered in the wrestling test
Naked and oiled, nor who was judged the best
Will I say now – nor how they all are gone
Homeward to Athens when the sport is done –
But quickly to the point will come instead
And thereby get my long tale wholly said.

By process and by length of certain years
Stayed wholly are the mourning and the tears
Of all the Greeks, by general assent,
And then I think there was a parliament
At Athens, that for certain matters met,
Among which matters was the question set
To make with certain countries an alliance,
And get from Thebes obedience and compliance.
And royal Theseus, working to this end,
Soon after noble Palamon doth send,
And he knew not the wherefore or the why,
But in his sable raiment mournfully
Straight at the word of Theseus cometh he.
Then Theseus sent at once for Emely.
When all were seated there, and hushed the place,
And Theseus sat in silence for a space
Ere any wise word sounded from his breast,
There where he chose he fixed his eyes at rest,
And sighed with a sad visage, quietly,
And after that his will thus uttered he.

"The primal Mover and First Cause above,
When first He made the beauteous chain of love,
Great was the end, and great was His intent;
Well knew He why, well knew He what he meant.
Of that fair chain of love He made a band
Holding the air, the flame, the flood, the land
In definite boundaries, that they might not flee.
That Mover and that self-same Prince," said he,
"Hath set below here in this vile creation
Limits of certain days as a duration
For all things that are born within this place,
Beyond which day they may not go a pace
Though certainly they may their terms abridge.

Nor need we here authority allege,
For by experience we prove it well.
But let me briefly now my meaning tell –
By this arrangement, then, may all men see
Firm is this Mover, for eternity.
Now all know well, unless it be a fool,
That every part deriveth from its whole.
For surely nature never took her start
From any fragment of a thing, or part,
But something perfect, standing firm and well,
Till it became with time corruptible.
And therefore, working with a wise intent,
He hath so well ordained his government
That all progressions and all species known
In their successions shall endure alone –
Not be eternal, and no issue leave.
This ye may know and at a glance perceive.

"For lo! the oak, whose growth is always slow
From the first day when it begins to grow,
And hath so long a life, as we may see –
Yet in the end comes Death and takes the tree.

"Consider, too, the hard unyielding stone
Under our feet, where men have come and gone –
It wears to waste as by the road it lies;
And broadest river on occasion dries.
We watch great cities changing, vanishing –
So we behold an end for everything.

"Nor less of men and women is it true
That they, within one season of the two –
That is to say, in youth, or else in age –
Must die at last, the king beside the page;
One in his bed and one at sea may go,
And one in battle pass, as all men know;
Nothing avails, all take the self-same way,
And all this world must perish, I may say.
Who causeth this but Jupiter the king?
He that is prince and cause of everything,
And re-converteth all things to the source
From which, in truth, they came and took their
        course.
Against this fate no creature that hath life,

Whatever kind, makes more than futile strife.
  "Then it is wisdom, as it seems to me,
To make a virtue of necessity,
And take it well, nor shun what may befall,
Especially the things that come to all.
And who complains, he maketh but a folly,
And rebel is to Him that guides us wholly.
And honor gives that man the greatest dower
Who comes to death in excellence and flower,
When he hath certitude of goodly name;
Then hath he done nor friend nor self a shame.
And happier should his friend be in his death
When yielded up with honor goes his breath
Than when with age a withered name appears,
And all his prowess dies upon the years.
Then it is best for nobleness of fame,
That he should die when he is best of name.
To oppose this is but wilful. Why should we
Complain, why do we look so mournfully
That good Arcite, of chivalry the flower,
With honor and with duty at his hour
Hath left the wretched prison of this life?
And why lament his cousin and his wife
Whom he hath loved so well, about his lot?
What – can he thank them? God knows! – not a jot!
Since they his soul and their own selves offend,
And yet their happiness nowise amend.

  "What comes of all this lengthy argument
But I advise we turn to merriment
After our grief, and thank Jove for his grace?
And I advise, before we leave the place,
That we should fashion, of two sorrows sore,
One perfect gladness lasting evermore;
And let us see where sorrow gnaws the worst –
There will we undertake our mending first!
  "Sister," said he, "this is my whole intent,

With full accord of all my parliament –
That noble Palamon, who is your knight,
That serveth you with will and heart and might,
And ever hath, since first that ye did know him –
That ye shall now your grace and pity show him,
And take him for your husband and your lord;
Give me your hand, for this is our accord.
Now of your woman's pity let me see!
By God, a king's own brother's son is he,
And though a landless bachelor he were,
Since he hath been for years your servitor,
And such adversity for you endured,
This must be well considered, be assured;
For noble mercy ought to conquer fully."
  And then this Palamon addressing duly,
"I think a scanty sermon," he began,
"Will win us your agreement to this plan.
Come near, and take your lady's hand," he said.
And soon between them was the compact made
Called marriage, that was witnessed solemnly
By all the council and nobility.
Thus with all bliss and joyous melody
This Palamon hath wedded Emely.
And God, that all this mighty world hath wrought,
Send him his love, that hath it dearly bought.
For Palamon may count all blessings his,
Living in health and riches and in bliss,
And Emely loveth him so tenderly,
And he serves her with such nobility,
That never a word there was between the two
Of jealousy – nor other grief they knew.
And thus ended Palamon and Emely,
And God save all this goodly company. *Amen.*

Here ends the Knight's Tale

The Miller's Tale

IN STARK CONTRAST to the Knight's noble tale, the bawdy and drunken Miller recounts a tale with a similar structure – two men compete for the same woman – but a very different character. In a famously coarse and explicit tale that for many years was omitted from editions of the Tales, the Miller presents a romp set in rural medieval England that is full of trickery, antagonism and sex. It is a fabliau, a type of tale popular in 13th-century France and characterized by its socially subversive plot and characters. Typically, fabliaux show clever peasants and sexually enthusiastic wives, corrupt clergy and lustful students tricking and deceiving their social and intellectual superiors. The Miller's Tale would not have disappointed its audience's expectations.

THE MILLER'S TALE

Here follow the words between the Host and the Miller

WHEN thus the Knight his tale had fully told,
In all the company, both young and old,
Was none but praised it for nobility,
And held it fit to keep in memory,
And in particular the gentlefolk.
Then swore our Landlord, laughing as he spoke:
"This go'th aright – the bag is opened wide;
Now let us see who tells the next," he cried,
"For of a truth we prosper with our plan.
Now ye, sir Monk, come tell us if you can,
Something to pay the Knight off for his tale."
The Miller, that with drink was ghastly pale,
So it was wonder how the fellow sat –
He would not doff his hood or lift his hat,
Or wait in courtesy on any man,
But in a mighty Pilate's voice began
To swear by blood and bones in fearful fashion:
"I know a noble tale for this occasion,
With which to pay the Knight off for his tale!"

Our Host saw that the man was drowned in ale,
And said: "Hold, Robin; wait a while, dear brother;
First let some better man tell us another;
Let us work wisely; wait – be not so hot."

"No, by God's soul," he answered, "I will not.
For I will speak, or I will go my way."

"Tell on, then, in the devil's name, I say;
Thou art a fool, thy wit is sunk and gone!"

The Miller said: "Now hear me, everyone!

But first of all my protestation take:
That I am drunk – I know the sound I make;
So anything amiss ye hear me say,
Put it against the Southwark ale, I pray.
For I will tell a legend and a life
Both of a carpenter, and of his wife,
And how a certain student in this matter
Made him a fool." "Now stop thy ribald clatter,"
Spoke up the Reeve, "and drunken harlotry!
Sin and a monstrous folly it would be
That thou defame a man of any station,
Or bring to wives an evil reputation.
Thou hast enough of other things beside
To talk about." This drunken rogue replied
At once: "Dear brother Oswald," answered he,
"Who hath no wife, he can no cuckold be;
But I say not therefore that thou art one!
There are good wives, I say; yea, many a one –
A thousand good for every one that's bad;
Thou know'st it well thyself, or thou art mad.
Why art thou angry with my story now?
I have a wife, by God, as well as thou;
Yet by mine oxen, I would not take to me
More in this matter than there may be due me,
And call myself a cuckold ere I'm caught.
By God, I'd rather think that I was not!
A husband should respect, upon his life,
The privacy of God and of his wife;
So long as he may get God's plenty there,
No need to ask of what she has to spare!"

What more to say – except that he began,
And would not stop his tale for any man,
But like a churl proceeded to complete it.
And here, it seems to me, I must repeat it.
And so of every proper man I pray,
Think not, for God's sake, anything I say
Of evil intent, but that I must rehearse
All of their tales, the better with the worse,
Or falsify my matter, fact or spirit!
Then anyone that may not wish to hear it,
Turn over the leaf and choose another tale!

Among the long and short ye shall not fail
To find some story dedicated solely
To noble things, or moral ones, or holy –
If ye choose wrong, put not the blame on me.
This Miller was a churl, as ye can see;
So was the Reeve, and many another, too;
And ribaldry was all that either knew.
Beware then; blame not me when ye are done;
Nor take in earnest what is meant in fun!

Here ends the Miller's Prologue

Here the Miller begins his Tale

AT Oxford town there dwelt upon a day,
An artisan that took in guests for pay –
A wealthy wretch, a carpenter by trade.
And in his house a poor young student stayed –
One that had learned the arts, but busily
Was now devoted to astrology.
And there were certain problems and equations
That he could solve by means of calculations –
If men would ask of him at certain hours
As to a drought, or when there might be showers,
Or if they asked him what was like to fall
In other things; I cannot count them all.

  They called this student gentle Nicholas;
Skilled both in mirth and secret love he was;
And he was sly and subtle as could be,
And seemed a very maid for modesty.
There in that house he had a room alone –
None shared it with him, it was all his own –
Scented with pleasant herbs, and trim and neat;
And he himself as fragrant was and sweet
As licorice, or the odor of setwall.
His Almagest and books both great and small,
His Astrolabe, essential to his art,
His augrim-counters – all were set apart
Neatly on shelves that ran beside his bed.
He had a clothes press decked with cloth of red;
And over this there hung a psaltery

On which at night he made a melody
So sweet that all the chamber with it rang;
And *Angelus ad Virginem* he sang;
And after that he carolled the King's Note;
Often such singing blessed his merry throat.
Thus on his funds this clerk contrived to live,
With what from time to time his friends would give.

  This carpenter had newly wed a wife,
And her he loved more than he loved his life;
And she was only eighteen years of age.
Jealous he was, and kept her close in cage;
For he was old, and wild and young was she,
And much he feared a cuckold he might be.
He knew not Cato (for his wit was rude),
Who bade men wed in some similitude;
Men ought to mate with those of like condition,
For youth and age are oft in opposition;
But now, since he had fallen in the snare,
He must endure, like other men, his care.

  Fair to behold was this young wife of his,
And small and slender as a weasel is.
She wore a girdle made of stripèd silk;
And a trim apron, white as morning milk,
Over her loins, with many a cunning gore.
Of white, too, was the dainty smock she wore,
Embroidered at the collar all about
With coal-black silk, alike within and out.
On her white hood were tapes of the same hue,
And these were also silk. Her fillet, too,
Was silk, and it was broad, and worn full high.
And certainly she had a wanton eye.
Her brows were narrow – she had plucked them so –
And they were arched, and black as any sloe.
She was as gay and fair a sight to see
As any fresh young blossoming pear tree,
And soft to touch as wool of any wether.
And by her girdle hung a purse of leather,
Inlaid with bits of latten ornament,
With tassels wrought of silk. Although ye went
Through all the world, ye could not hope to meet
A darling half so gay, a wench so sweet;

She shone as clear, and had as bright a glint,
As any gold piece freshly from the mint.
And ye could hear her song as clearly ringing
As any swallow on a stable singing.
And she could be as sportive and as gay
As any suckling kid or calf at play.
Her breath was sweet as honeyed ale, or mead,
Or apples laid in hay for winter need.
Skittish she was, and frisky as a colt,
Slim as a mast, straight as a cross-bow's bolt.
Beneath her collar gleamed a brooch, as large
And bright as is the boss upon a targe.
Upon her legs her shoes were laced up high.
She was a primrose or a sweet pig's eye
For any lord that had the luck to bed her,
Or any honest yeoman who would wed her!

　　Now sirs and gentlemen, it came to pass
That on a day this gentle Nicholas
Began to wanton with this wife, and play –
Her husband having gone to Oseney –
In ways these artful students can devise;
And caught her stealthily between the thighs,
And cried: "Unless I slake my hidden thirst
And hunger for thee, sweetheart, I shall burst!"
And gripped her flanks, and pressed them hard,
　　and said:
"Come, sweetheart, love me now, or I am dead,
God save me!" As a colt, in being broke,
Leaps up and rears against the breaking-yoke,
She jumped at that, and writhed her head aside.
"I will not kiss thee, by my faith!" she cried.
"Stop it, I tell you; stop it, Nicholas!
Or I will cry, and call out, 'Help! Alas !'
Take off your hands for decency, I say!"

　　This Nicholas at once began to pray
For mercy, and he wooed so well and fast
She granted him the love he asked at last,
And she would do for him, she gave her promise,
All that he craved, and swore it by St. Thomas,
As soon as such a thing could safely be.
"My husband is so full of jealousy,

Unless ye watch and wait your time," she said,
"I know too well I am as good as dead.
In this affair ye must be sly and prudent."
　　"Nay, never worry over that! A student
Has badly used his time," he said to her,
"If he cannot deceive a carpenter."
So they agreed, and in this fashion swore
To wait a while, as I have said before.
And Nicholas, when he had done all this,
Began to stroke her thighs, and sweetly kiss
Her lips, and then he took his psaltery
And played it fast, and made sweet melody.

　　Then to the parish church, as it befell,
To honor Christ, and do his works as well,
On holidays this wife would take her way.
Her forehead always shone as bright as day,
So would she scrub it when she stopped her work.

　　Now at that church there was a parish clerk,
A young man by the name of Absalon.
His curly hair, shining like gold new-spun,
Like a great fan spread out to left and right;
The parting line showed even, straight, and white.
His cheeks were red; his eyes gray as a goose;
He had Paul's window carved upon his shoes;
His hose were red, and elegant to see.
And he was clad all tight and properly
In kirtle of the lightest watchel blue,
With laces set all fair, and thickly too;
And over this he wore a surplice gay,
As white as any bough that blooms in May.
A merry lad he was, so God me save!
And he could bleed a man, and clip and shave,
And make a deed, a charter, or a will.
And he could dance and trip with subtle skill
In twenty ways, all of the Oxford fashion,
And fling his legs out with a jolly passion;
And from the rebeck he could pluck a song,
And sing a treble as he went along,
And skilfully he played on his guitar.
In all the town was not a tavern bar
But he would give it entertainment fair

Were any lively barmaid serving there.
And yet indeed the man was far from daring
In breaking wind, and in his speech was sparing.

    This Absalon, this merry lad and gay,
Went with his censer of a holiday
Among the parish wives, and as he passed,
Full many a loving look about him cast,
And most upon this carpenter's young wife.
To look at her would be a merry life,
He thought, she was so wanton and so sweet!
If she had been a sleek mouse at his feet,
And he a cat, he would have made short work
Of seizing her!
            This Absalon, this clerk,
Hath in his heart so great a love-longing
That he would never take an offering
From any wife – he said he wanted none.
The moon at night in all its brightness shone,
And his guitar this Absalon hath taken,
With thought of lovers that his song would waken;
And forth he goes, with love and joy astir,
And reached the dwelling of this carpenter,
Just as the cocks had crowed across the land.
And by a casement window took his stand,
That in the moonlight showed against the wall.
He singeth in a gentle voice and small,
"Now lady dear, if it thy pleasure be,
I pray you well that ye will pity me,"
With music to his ditty sweetly ringing.
This carpenter awoke, and heard him singing,
And whispered to his wife, "What, Alison!
Dost thou not hear," he said, "how Absalon
Is chanting underneath our chamber wall?"
"Yes, John. God knows, indeed, I hear it all!"
Thus Alison replied when it befell.

    And thus it went. What will ye better than well?
From day to day this jolly Absalon
So wooeth her, that he is woe-begone.
He neither sleeps by night nor yet by day;
He combs his spreading locks, and dresseth gay;
He wooeth her by suit and embassage,

And swears that he will serve her as a page;
He sings with quaverings like a nightingale;
Sends her spiced wine, and mead, and honeyed ale;
And wafers from the oven, hot and brown,
And proffers money, since she lives in town.
For there are some that gold will win, and some
To boldness or to virtue will succumb.

    Sometimes, his grace and mastery to try,
He playeth Herod on a scaffold high.
But none of these will help him to succeed,
For it is Nicholas she loves, indeed,
And Absalon may go and blow the horn,
For all his labor earned him only scorn;
She makes a silly ape of Absalon,
And all his earnestness becomes her fun!
For the old proverb is a true if wry one:
"Always the nearer, if he be a sly one,
Leaveth a distant lover to be hated."
Though Absalon was madly agitated
Because he seemed but little in her sight;
This nearer Nicholas stood in his light.

    Now play it well, thou gentle Nicholas,
And Absalon may wail and sing "Alas!"

    And so it happened on a Saturday
This carpenter had gone to Oseney,
And gentle Nicholas and Alison
Agreed at last that thus it should be done:
That Nicholas a subtle plot should weave,
This simple, jealous husband to deceive,
And if the game should chance to go aright,
Then she would sleep within his arms all night,
For this was his desire and hers as well.
And soon, the story brief and straight to tell,
This Nicholas would neither wait nor tarry,
But quietly doth to his chamber carry
Both food and drink to last for several days,
And of this young wife Alison he prays
That if her husband asked for Nicholas,
She should reply she knew not where he was –
She had not seen him all that day, indeed.
She thought he must be sick; he would not heed

Her maid, though she had often gone to call;
He would not stir or answer her at all.

    So Nicholas for all that Saturday
Close and secluded in his chamber lay,
And ate or slept, or did what pleased him best,
Till Sunday, when the sun had gone to rest.

    This simple carpenter was full of wonder
At what this Nicholas might suffer under.
"St. Thomas! I am much afraid today
That something is not right with Nicholay!
Now God forbid he perish suddenly.
This world is full of instability!
Today I saw a corpse to burial borne
That I had seen at work last Monday morn.
Go up," he told his boy. "Stand there before
His room and shout, or pound upon the door;
Look in, and tell what thou canst hear or see."

    This boy obeyed. He went up sturdily,
And while he stood there, as his master bade,
He beat upon the door and cried like mad:
"What! How! What do ye, Master Nicholas!
What! Will ye sleep and let the whole day pass?"

    But all for nothing, there was not a word.
He found a hole, low down upon a board,
Through which the cat went in. There hard and fast
He set his eye and looked, and so at last
He saw the student lying there alone.
This Nicholas was staring, stretched out prone,
As if he gazed upon the crescent moon.
The boy went down, and told his master soon
In what condition he had seen the man.
"Saint Frideswide!" The carpenter began
To cross himself, a shudder running through him.
"A man knows little what may happen to him!
This man hath fallen, with all his astromy,
Into some madness or some agony.
I always guessed too well how it would be.
Men should know nothing of God's privacy.
An ignorant man is blest, that knows no more
Than his own faith. A young clerk once before
Got into trouble with his astromy.

For walking in the fields by night to see
The stars, and read the future things they tell,
Into a marble pit at last he fell.
He saw not *that*. Yet I am sad, I say,
That this should come to gentle Nicholay.
I will reprove him for his studying
If so I may, by Jesus, heaven's king.

    "Get me a staff to pry with from the floor,
While thou, good Robin, heavest up the door.
I guess he will not study longer there."
Then to the student's door the two repair.
His boy was strong; the chamber door he grasps,
And heaves it upward quickly by the hasps,
And soon upon the floor he sets it prone.
This Nicholas lay still as any stone,
Forever gazing upward into air.
This carpenter was now in great despair
And seized him by the shoulders, firm and strong,
And cried hard, as he shook him well and long,
"What! Nicholas! Stare not in such a fashion!
Awake, I say, remember Jesus' passion!
I cross thee now from spite of elves or men!"
And said the night-spell on the instant then,
In all four quarters of the house about,
And on the threshold of the door without:
Jesus Christ and holy Benedict,
Keep this house; let no ill thing afflict.
White pater-noster, *guard us till the dawn;*
St. Peter's sister, whither hast thou gone?

    At last stirred gentle Nicholas, and sighed
A long and painful sigh. "Alas!" he cried,
"Shall all the world be lost so quickly now?"

    This carpenter exclaimed: "What sayest thou?
What! Think on God, as do we working men."

    "Fetch me a drink," this student answered then,
"And later will I speak in privacy
About a matter touching me and thee.
I cannot tell it unto other men."

    This carpenter goes down, and comes again
And brings a jug of ale, a brimming quart;
And when at length each man has drunk his part,

And Nicholas has made his door all fast,
By him he sets this carpenter at last.

He said: "Now John, belovèd host and dear,
Upon thy troth I bid thee swear me here
That what I tell thou wilt betray to none,
For it is Christ's affair and his alone,
Which thou art lost indeed if thou betray;
For this would be thy punishment, I say:
Thou shouldst be struck with madness if thou did it!"
"Nay, Christ for his own sacred blood forbid it!"
This simple man declared. "I do not babble!
Nay, though I say it, I will never gabble.
Say what thou wilt; to no one will I tell
A word of it, by Him that harrowed hell!"

"John," he replied, "I will not lie to thee.
I have discovered by astrology
By gazing on the moon when it was bright,
That Monday next, a quarter through the night,
A rain shall fall, so mad and wild a spate
That Noah's flood was never half so great.
This world," he said, "beneath its hideous power,
Shall all be drowned in less time than an hour.
So shall mankind be drowned and lost to life!"

This carpenter replied, "Alas, my wife!
Alas, my Alison! And shall she drown?"
And with the thought he almost tumbled down,
And asked: "Is there no remedy for this?"

Said Nicholas: "Why yes, through God there is,
If by advice and learning thou be led;
Thou canst not hope to work by thine own head.
King Solomon the wise in words hath set it:
'Work by advice, and thou shalt not regret it!'
And if thou wilt submit from first to last
To good advice, with neither sail nor mast
I will save her along with thee and me.
Hast thou not heard how Noah rode the sea
Because God warned him, and he understood
How all the world should perish in the flood?"

"Yes," said this carpenter, "long, long ago."

"Dost thou," said Nicholas, "not also know
What trouble Noah had, and what discord,

Before he got his wife to come aboard?
I think he would have given his last black wether
If they had been apart, and not together,
She safely in her ship, and he in his!
And know'st thou then what best and needful is?
There must be haste, and with a hasty thing
There should be no delay or sermoning.
Go get for each of us a tub of wood
Or kneading trough, and let them all be good
In workmanship, and large enough to float,
So each of us can swim as in a boat;
And set in each some food and drink – a store
For one day only – we shall need no more;
The water shall subside and go away
About mid morning of the second day.
But Robin thy boy must hear no word of this,
Nor Gill thy maid; nor ask me why it is,
For though thou ask I will not answer thee;
I cannot tell what God has told to me.
Thou shouldst be grateful, if thou art not mad,
To have as great a grace as Noah had.
And I will save thy wife, too, never doubt it.
Now to thy labor, and be quick about it;
And having got for her and thee and me
These kneading tubs I spoke of, all the three,
Then thou shalt hang them near the roof, up high,
Where no man may our preparation spy.
And when thou shalt have done these things I say,
And neatly stored our food and drink away,
And also put an axe in every boat,
That each of us may cut his rope, and float,
And made a hole high up within the gable,
Off toward the garden and above the stable,
That we may freely sail forth on that day
After the great rain shall have passed away,
Then shalt thou swim as merry, I undertake,
As any white duck following her drake.
Then shall I call, 'Ho! John! Ho! Alison!
Be of good cheer, the flood will soon be done!'
And thou shalt call: 'Hail, master Nicholay!
Hail! I can see thee well, for it is day.'

And then shall we be rulers all our life
Of all the world, like Noah and his wife.

    "But I give warning to thee of one thing:
Remember this – when on that evening
Each boards his vessel, then let none of us
Whisper or call out – any one of us –
Nor cry, but each in prayer on every hand
Be diligent, for this is God's command.

    "And thou must hang thy boat far from thy wife,
That thou shalt do no sin, upon thy life,
No more in thought or look than in the deed.
This is thy full commandment. Go! God speed!
Tomorrow night, when men are all asleep,
Into our kneading tubs we three will creep,
And sit, and wait God's mercy while we pray.
Now there is no more time, so go thy way.
I must not make a sermon, by my faith.
'Say naught, but send the wise,' the prophet saith;
Thou art so wise I have no need to teach thee;
Go, save our lives, is all that I beseech thee."

    This simple carpenter now goes his way,
And often cried "Alas!" and "Well-a-day!"
And told his wife of all this secrecy.
She knew it well; and knew far more than he
What all this curious tale betokeneth;
And yet she seemed afraid, as for her death:
"Alas! Go quickly, do thy work," she said,
"And help us to escape, or we are dead.
I am thy true and loyal wedded wife;
Go, husband, go, and help to save my life."

    Lo! What a power may lie in perturbation!
A man may die of his imagination,
So deep is the impression it may make!
This simple carpenter began to shake.
He thought he saw in actuality
The flood of Noah rolling like the sea
To drown his Alison, his honey dear.
He weepeth, waileth, shuddereth with fear,
And many a heavy sigh the man blows off.
He goes at last and gets a kneading trough,
And after that a tub and kimelin,

And secretly he sent them to his inn,
And hung them in the rafters secretly;
His own hand shaped the ladders, all the three,
Which by the rungs and shafts could be ascended
Up to the beams where the tubs hung suspended.
And he provisioned both the tubs and trough
With bread and cheese, and ale to finish off –
What for a day would be an ample ration.
But first, before he made this preparation,
He sent his maid and his apprentice down
On errands for him into London town.
And then on Monday, with the falling night,
He shut his door, and lit no candle light,
And saw that all was as it ought to be.
And soon they climbed the ladders, all the three,
And sat there still, a furlong's length away.

    "Now, *pater-noster*, mum!" said Nicholay;
And "Mum!" quoth John, and "Mum!" said Alison.
This carpenter hath his devotion done,
And lies in quiet now, and says his prayer,
And waits to hear the rain, if it be there.

    But dead sleep, after all his busyness,
Fell on this carpenter, as I should guess,
At curfew time, or later, it may be;
Disturbed of heart, he groaneth grievously,
And since his head was laid an awkward way,
He snored. Then down at once stole Nicholay,
And downward Alison as softly sped,
And with no further word they went to bed
There where the carpenter was wont to be.
Then came the revel and the melody!
And so lie Nicholas and Alison;
In mirth and pleasure there they play as one
Until the bell of lauds began to ring
And in the chancel monks commenced to sing.

    This parish clerk, this amorous Absalon,
That ever is for love so woe begone,
Upon this Monday was at Oseney
With company, for pleasure and for play;
And asked by accident a cloisterer
In private of this John the carpenter.

He drew him from the church, and in his ear
He said, "I have not seen him working here
Since Saturday, and I suppose he went
For timber somewhere, by our abbot sent,
For often this is what he has to do,
Remaining at the grange a day or two;
Or he is at his house, for certainty.
Truly, I cannot tell where he may be."

    This Absalon was gay, his heart was light,
He thought: "I shall not go to bed tonight;
For certainly I have not seen the man
About his door at all since day began.
As I may thrive, at crowing of the cock,
I shall in secret at his window knock,
The one low down upon the chamber wall.
Then shall I speak to Alison of all
My longing and my love; and shall not miss
At very least, that I shall get a kiss.
I shall have comfort in some kind of way!
I had an itching at my lips all day,
And that must signify a kiss, at least.
Also I dreamed that I was at a feast.
So I will go and sleep an hour or two,
Then will I wake and play the whole night through."

    When the first cock crowed, long before the dawn,
Up rose this jolly lover Absalon,
And dressed him gay, with every artifice,
But first chewed cardamon and licorice
Before he combed his hair, for their sweet smell,
And, with the hope to be acceptable,
A "true love" leaf beneath his tongue he laid.
So to the house with languid feet he strayed,
And by her chamber window stood at rest,
The sill of which was level with his breast,
And coughed, and half aloud his suit begun:
"What do ye, honey-comb, sweet Alison?
Sweet cinnamon, my lovely bride to be,
Sweetheart, awake, I say, and speak to me.
Little, alas! ye think upon my woe,
And how I sweat for passion as I go.
No wonder that I swoon and sweat, my sweet;

I suffer like a lamb that wants the teat!
Yea, I am so consumed with longing, love,
That I am sad as any turtle dove;
I cannot eat more than a maid," he sighed.

    "Go! Leave my window, jackass," she replied.
"It will not be 'Come kiss me,' by God's name;
I love another, or else I were to blame,
Better than thee, by Jesu, Absalon.
Be off, or I will stone thee. What! Have done!
And let me sleep, in the devil's name, I say!"

    "Alas!" cried Absalon. "Alackaday!
That true love ever had so hard a debtor!
Kiss me at least, if it may be no better,
For Jesu's love and mine, I beg of thee."
"Then wilt thou go thy way?" demanded she.
"Yea, of a truth, my dear; yea, sweetheart," said he.
"Then I will come at once," she called, "make ready!"
And whispered low to Nicholas, "Lie still
And make no sound, and thou shalt laugh thy fill!"

    This Absalon kneeled down. His heart was gay.
He said: "I am a lord in every way,
Of what shall come this kiss is but the savor;
Sweetheart, thy grace! O lovely bride, thy favor!"

    Now hastily the window she undid.
"Have done! Come up, and speed thee fast," she bid,
"For fear thou shouldst attract some neighbor's eye."

    This Absalon now wiped his mouth all dry;
Like a black coal, or pitch, the darkness there
Hung dense, and out she thrust her bottom bare,
And Absalon did nothing more nor less
Than with his lips to set a sweet caress
Upon her arse, before he knew of this.
He started back, for something seemed amiss;
He knew well that a woman has no beard.
He felt a thing all rough and thickly haired,
And "Fie!" he muttered. "What is this I do?"
"Te-hee!" cried she, and clapped the window to;
And Absalon goes wretchedly away.
"A beard, a beard!" cried gentle Nicholay.
"Now by God's *corpus*, this goes well and fair!"

    This simple Absalon, that still was there,

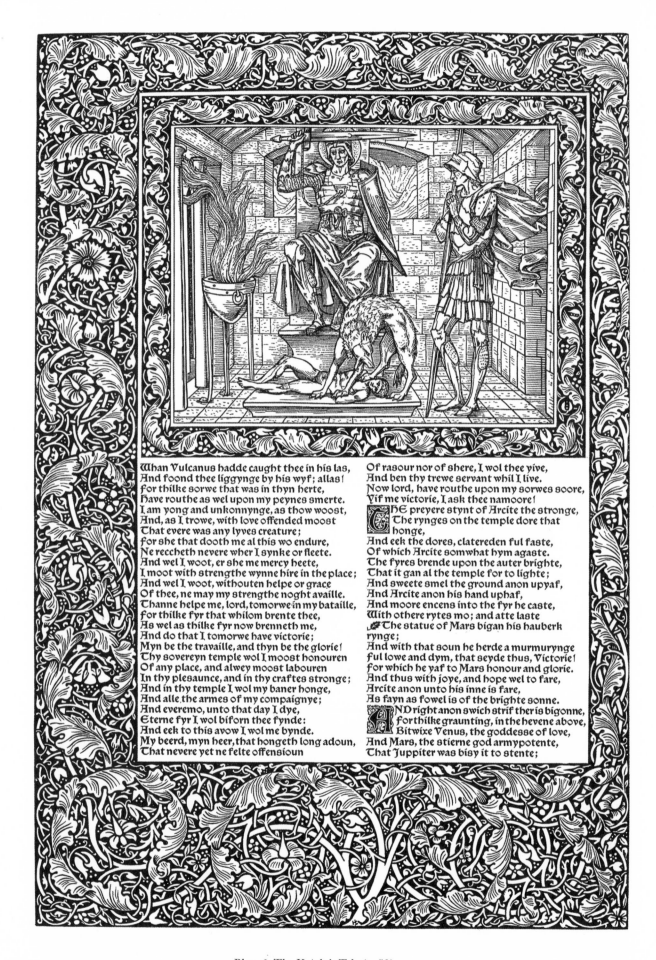

Whan Vulcanus hadde caught thee in his las,
And foond thee liggynge by his wyf; allas!
For thilke sorwe that was in thyn herte,
Have routhe as wel upon my peynes smerte.
I am yong and unkonnynge, as thow woost,
And, as I trowe, with love offended moost
That evere was any lyves creature;
For she that dooth me al this wo endure,
Ne reccheth nevere wher I synke or fleete.
And wel I woot, er she me mercy heete,
I moot with strengthe wynne hire in the place;
And wel I woot, withouten helpe or grace
Of thee, ne may my strengthe noght availle.
Thanne helpe me, lord, tomorwe in my bataille,
For thilke fyr that whilom brente thee,
As wel as thilke fyr now brenneth me,
And do that I tomorwe have victorie;
Myn be the travaille, and thyn be the glorie!
Thy sovereyn temple wol I moost honouren
Of any place, and alwey moost labouren
In thy plesaunce, and in thy craftes stronge;
And in thy temple I wol my baner honge,
And alle the armes of my compaignye;
And everemo, unto that day I dye,
Eterne fyr I wol biforn thee fynde:
And eek to this avow I wol me bynde.
My beerd, myn heer, that hongeth long adoun,
That nevere yet ne felte offensioun

Of rasour nor of shere, I wol thee yive,
And ben thy trewe servant whil I live.
Now lord, have routhe upon my sorwes soore,
Yif me victorie, I ask thee namoore!
THE preyere stynt of Arcite the stronge,
The rynges on the temple dore that honge,
And eek the dores, clatereden ful faste,
Of which Arcite somwhat hym agaste.
The fyres brende upon the auter brighte,
That it gan al the temple for to lighte;
And sweete smel the ground anon upyaf,
And Arcite anon his hand uphaf,
And moore encens into the fyr he caste,
With othere rytes mo; and atte laste
The statue of Mars bigan his hauberk rynge,
And with that soun he herde a murmurynge
Ful lowe and dym, that seyde thus, Victorie!
For which he yaf to Mars honour and glorie.
And thus with joye, and hope wel to fare,
Arcite anon unto his inne is fare,
As fayn as fowel is of the brighte sonne.
AND right anon swich strif ther is bigonne,
For thilke graunting, in the hevene above,
Bitwixe Venus, the goddesse of love,
And Mars, the stierne god armypotente,
That Juppiter was bisy it to stente;

Plate 6: The Knight's Tale (p. 52)

Heard all, and bit his lips until they bled.
"I shall repay thee!" to himself he said.

Who rubbeth now, who scours and scrubs his lips
With dust and sand and straw, with cloth, with chips,
But Absalon, who often cries, "Alas!
Now will I sell my soul to Sathanas
If rather than to hold this town in fee
I would not be revenged for this," said he.
"Fool! Fool! I lacked the sense to turn aside!"
His burning love was quenched and satisfied,
For since he gave her buttocks that caress,
He rated love not worth a piece of cress;
He was clean purged of all his malady.
He cursed all wenches long and bitterly,
And like a whipped child often sobbed and wept.
Then quietly across the street he crept,
To where Gervase, a blacksmith, had his house,
That in his forge beat out the parts of plows;
Coulters and shares he sharpened busily.
This Absalon knocked softly. "Hist!" said he,
"Come out, Gervase; undo thy door at once."

"Who art thou?" "Absalon," was the response.
"What, Absalon! By Christ upon his tree,
Why rise ye up so early, ben'cite!
What ails you, lad, I say? Some gay girl – what? –
Hath brought you out this morning at a trot;
By St. Note, boy, ye know well what I mean."

This Absalon he did not care a bean
For joking, and he would not speak or laugh.
He had more tow to spin on his distaff
Than Gervase knew, and said, "Good friend and dear,
Lend me this red hot coulter lying here
For something that I have a mind to do,
And I will shortly bring it back to you."

Gervase replied, "Of course. Why, were it gold.
Or a fat bag of nobles still untold,
It should be thine, or I be no true smith.
Eh! Foe of Christ! What will ye do therewith?"

"Let that," said Absalon, "be as it may;
I shall inform thee well when it is day,"
And caught the coulter where the steel was cool,

And softly from the smithy door he stole,
And to the carpenter's returned again.
He coughed at first, and knocked a little then
Against the window, just as he had done
Before. "Who's there?" demanded Alison,
"Who knocks? I'll warrant that some thief is here!"

"Why nay," said he, "God knows, my sweet and
    dear,
I am thine Absalon, my treasureling,
And I have brought thee here a golden ring –
My mother's, as I hope I shall be saved,
And it is fine, and cunningly engraved.
This will I give thee for another kiss."

Now Nicholas had left the bed to piss,
And thought the joke a better one to tell
If Absalon should kiss his arse as well;
And raising up the window, backed into it,
And stealthily he thrust his own arse through it,
Out past the buttocks, half way up the thigh.
This clerk, this Absalon, began to cry:
"Speak, my sweet bird; I know not where thou art."

At once this Nicholas let fly a fart,
That like a clap of thunder smote the quiet.
And Absalon was almost staggered by it,
But had the red hot iron in his hand,
And square upon the buttocks set his brand.

Off goes the skin a hand's breadth with the blow,
The red hot coulter seared his bottom so;
It smarted till he thought that he should die.
Wild as a madman he began to cry:
"Help! Water! Water! Help me, for God's sake!"

The screaming made this carpenter awake.
"Water!" was all he heard and understood.
He thought: "Alas! At last comes Noel's flood!"
He raised himself, and with no more ado
He seized his axe and cut the rope in two,
And down he went, and never stopped until
He came to rest at length beside the sill,
Upon the floor, and there aswoon he lay.

Up started Alison and Nicholay,
And ran out shouting in their agitation.

The neighbors, both of great and lesser station,
Rushed in and stared upon this fallen man,
Where he lay swooning, very pale and wan,
For he had broke his arm in his descent.
But he must still digest his accident,
For hardly had he spoke, when Alison
And Nicholas both talked him down as one;
Telling all those who came that he was mad,
Such was this fear of "Noel's flood" he had
That he had bought these tubs and troughs, all three,
Through fantasy, and in his vanity,
And hung them to the roof-beams high above,
And prayed the both of them for God's sweet love
To sit there in the roof, *pour compagnie*.

    Everyone laughed at this strange fantasy,
And in the roof began to peer and poke,
And made his injury a kind of joke.
For anything this carpenter might say
Was useless, no one listened, anyway.
With mighty oaths so many swore him down
They thought him crazy all about the town.
For every student would support the other;
They said: "The man is mad, no doubt, dear brother;"
And everyone would laugh about this strife.
Thus bedded was this carpenter's young wife
In spite of all his guard and jealousy;
And Absalon hath kissed her under eye,
And Nicholas is branded for his fun
Upon the rump. God save you; I am done!

Here the Miller ends his Tale.

The Reeve's Tale

THE REEVE (a steward who organizes the affairs of a manor) is incensed by the Miller's tale and sets out to get his own back with a tale that shows a miller in a bad light. Another fabliau, it is of a darker tone than the Miller's Tale. Lacking the *joie de vivre* characteristic of the French fabliaux, it is about manipulation, revenge and sexual exploitation. It is, no doubt, a more realistic depiction of rural life at the time, enlivened by plenty of slapstick humour and suffused with bitterness.

THE REEVE'S TALE

The Prologue of the Reeve's Tale

WHEN all had laughed about this pretty pass
Of Absalon and gentle Nicholas
Some folks said one, and some another thing,
But mostly laughed, and fell to frolicking,
And no man was offended, I believe,
Except for Oswald, possibly, the Reeve,
That was a carpenter by occupation,
He nursed at heart a little irritation
And anger, and began objecting to it.
"Well, I could tell you, if I wished to do it,
A ribald story," he began to grumble,
"Of how a haughty miller took a tumble.
But I am old, and past the years for play;
My grazing time is done; I feed on hay;
This white top shows how I am growing older.
And like my hair, my heart begins to molder.
As with the medlar, so it goes with me,
That day to day grows worse continually
Until it rots at last in trash or hay.
Yes, we old men, I fear, we go that way,
And never can be ripe until we rot.
Yet we will dance away, I doubt it not,
While the world pipes; for we are pricked to seek
A green tail with a white head, like a leek;
And though the strength we had returneth never,
Our wills are bent on foolishness forever;
For when we cannot do, then we desire
To talk: our old gray ashes hide their fire!

Four burning coals are in us, never dying:
Anger and boasting, avarice and lying.
Age always has these sparks of which I speak.
Our old limbs may be gnarled and stiff and weak,
But lust we never lose, to tell the truth.
And yet I always have the same colt's tooth,
Many as are the years now dead and done,
Since first my tap of life began to run.
For with the moment of my birth, I know,
Death drew the tap of life and let it flow;
And it has never ceased from that day on,
Till what was in the cask is all but gone.
At the staves' end the last few drops are clinging.
The foolish tongue may wail and fall to singing
Of ills endured in days now dead and cold;
Nothing is left but dotage for the old."

   After our host had heard this sermoning
He spoke at last, as lordly as a king.
"What is the sum," he cried, "of all this wit?
Why should we talk all day of holy writ?
The devil alone would set a reeve to preach,
Or from a cobbler try to make a leech.
Tell on thy tale, I say, and waste no time.
Depford is near, and it is half way prime;
Greenwich appears, the home of many a shrew;
Ramble no more – thy tale is over due."

   "Now, sires," this Reeve replied, "be not
      offended,
I beg you, if before my tale is ended,
Ye see me turn the tables on this liar;
For it is right to fight a fire with fire.

   "This drunken miller here hath told in game
Of how a carpenter was put to shame,
Perhaps in scorn of me, for I am one.
And I shall pay him off ere I am done,
And in his churl's coin, too, I undertake;
I pray God that his cursèd neck may break!
He sees too well the mote within my eye,
But in his own a beam he cannot spy!"

Here the Reeve's Tale Begins

NOT far from Cambridge, close to Trumpington,
Beneath a bridge of stone, there used to run
A brook, and there a mill stood well in view;
And everything I tell you now is true.
Here dwelt a miller many a year and day,
As proud as any peacock, and as gay.
And he could pipe and fish, wrestle and shoot,
Mend nets, and make a well-turned cup to boot,
He wore a long knife belted at his side,
A sword that had a sharp blade and a wide,
And carried in his pouch a handsome dagger.
No man durst touch him, though he boast and
     swagger.
A Sheffield dirk was hidden in his hose.
His face was round; he had a broad pug nose;
Smooth as an ape's the skull above his face.
He was a bully in the market-place.
No man dared lay a little finger on him
But he would swear to be revenged upon him.
He was indeed a thief of corn and meal,
A sly one, and his habit was to steal;
And scornful Simkin was the name he carried.
A wife of noble kindred he had married:
Her father was the parson of the town!
Many good pans of brass this priest paid down
To win this Simkin to his family!
And she was fostered in a nunnery,
For Simkin would not have a wife, he said,
That was not gently nurtured, and a maid,
To match his standing as a proper yeoman.
As pert as any magpie was this woman.
It was a sight to see them take the road
On holidays. Before her Simkin strode,
His tippet proudly wrapped about his head;
And she came after in a smock of red,
With Simkin clad in stockings of the same.
None dared to call her anything but "dame,"
And there was none that passed them on the way
So bold that he would romp with her or play,
Unless in truth he wished to lose his life
At Simkin's hand by dagger or by knife.

A jealous husband is a dangerous beast –
Or so he wants his wife to think, at least!
And since by birth a little smirched men thought her,
She was as sour of mien as stagnant water,
And haughty in her ways, and full of scorn.
She thought that, since her father was well born,
And she had got a convent education,
A distant air was suited to her station.

     A daughter had these two – a girl a score
Of years in age; and after her, no more,
Except a child a half year old they had,
Still in the cradle, and a proper lad.
This daughter was a stout and full-blown lass
With a pug nose and eyes as gray as glass,
And buttocks broad, and breasts shaped round and
     high,
And yet her hair was fair, I will not lie.

     The parson of the town, since she was fair,
Had it in mind that she should be his heir
Unto his house and goods and everything.
He was severe about her marrying.
He meant to place her in some family
Of worthy blood and lofty ancestry;
For holy church's goods must be expended
On those from holy church's blood descended;
His holy blood – he would do honor to it,
Though he devoured holy church to do it!

     This miller took great toll, ye need not doubt,
On wheat and malt from all the land about,
And from a certain college most of all,
At Cambridge, which was known there as King's Hall,
That brought their wheat and barley to his mill.
It happened once, the manciple lay ill,
And with his malady was kept a-bed,
And he was sure to die of it, men said.
Therefore this miller stole of corn and meal
A hundred times what he had dared to steal
Before; for then he took his toll discreetly,
But now the fellow was a thief completely,
Which made the warden fume and scold and swear,
Yet the bold miller did not give a tare;

But boasted loud, and swore it was not true.

    Among the Cambridge students there were two
In dwelling at the Hall of which I tell.
Headstrong they were, and quick and bold as well.
And all for lustihood and jollity
They begged the warden long and eagerly
For his permission to be gone until
They saw their grain ground at the miller's mill.
Each offered sturdily to lay his neck
The miller should not steal a half a peck
Whether by trickery or force, and so
At length the warden gave them leave to go.
One was named John, and Alan was the other;
Born in the same town both – a place called Strother –
Far to the north – I cannot tell you where.

    This Alan for the journey doth prepare,
And brought a horse to put their sack upon,
And off they go, this Alan and this John,
Each with a sword and buckler by his side.
John knew the way; they did not need a guide;
And at the mill at length the sack he lay'th.
Alan spoke first: "Hail, Simon, by my faith!
How fares thy daughter fair, and thy good wife?"

    Said Simkin: "Welcome, Alan, by my life!
And John the same! How now, what do ye here?"

    "Simon," said John, "By God, need has no peer.
Who hath no servant, as the clerks have said,
Unless a fool, must serve himself instead.
Our manciple, I fear, will soon be dead,
The poor man's jaws are waggling in his head;
So I am come, and Alan, with our sack,
To have our grain ground, and to bear it back.
I pray you, put it quickly through the mill."

    "Now by my faith," this Simkin said, "I will.
What will ye while I have the thing in hand?"

    "By God, right by the hopper will I stand,"
Said John, "and see the grain go down the maw;
For by my father's kin, I never saw
The way a hopper waggles to and fro."

    Alan replied: "What, John, and wilt thou so?
Then I will stand beneath it, by my crown,

And I will watch the meal come falling down
Into the trough; so shall I have my fun.
For, John, in faith, when all is said and done,
I am as poor a miller as are ye."

    The miller smiled at their simplicity.
"All this is but a trick of theirs," he thought.
"They think they cannot be deceived or caught;
But I shall pull the wool across their eyes
However shrewdly they philosophize.
The more involved the stratagems they make,
The more shall be the stealing when I take!
Instead of flour they shall be served with bran!
'The greatest clerk is not the wisest man,'
As the wolf heard the proverb from the mare.
I count this art of theirs not worth a tare!"

    Then when he saw his opportunity,
He slipped out through the doorway stealthily,
And looked about him when he stood outside,
And found the students' horse, which they had tied
Behind the mill, beneath an arbor there.
Then he approached it with a friendly air,
And straightway stripped the bridle from its head.
And when the horse found he was loose, he fled
Off toward the fen, where wild mares ran at play;
"We-hee!" Through thick and thin he streaked away.

    The miller then came back. No word he spoke,
But did his work, or sometimes cracked a joke,
Until the grain was well and fairly ground.
And when the meal at length was sacked and bound,
This John found that his horse had run away;
And "Help!" he shouted, and "Alackaday!
Our horse is gone! Alan, come out!" he cried,
"By God's bones, man, step lively! Come outside!
Alas! Our warden's palfrey hath been lost!"
All thought of meal and grain this Alan tossed
Into the wind, and all economy.
"What! Which way is he gone?" demanded he.

    The wife came leaping in among them then.
"Alas!" she said. "Your horse makes for the fen
With the wild mares, as fast as he can go!
Bad luck upon the hand that tied him so,

That should have bound him better with the rein!"
   "Alas!" cried John. "Now, Alan, for Christ's pain,
Off goes my sword; lay thine beside it here.
God knows I be as nimble as a deer;
He shall not get away from both of us.
Alan, thou wast a fool to tie him thus.
Why didst na' put the nag into the stable?"

   These students ran as fast as they were able
Off to the fen, this Alan and this John,
And when the miller saw that they were gone
He took a half a bushel of their flour
And bade his wife go knead it up that hour
Into a cake. "These students were a-feared!
A miller still can trim a student's beard
For all his art! Now let them go their way!
Look where they run! Yea, let the children play;
They will not get him quickly, by my crown!"

   These simple students scurried up and down
With "Whoa there, whoa!" "Hold hard!" "Look to
      the rear!"
"Go whistle to him while I keep him here!"
But, to be brief, until the edge of night
They could not, though they strove with all their
      might,
Capture their horse, he ran away so fast,
Till in a ditch they cornered him at last.

   Like cattle in the rain, wet through and through,
And wearied out, they plodded back, the two.
"Alas!" cried John, "the day that I was born!
Now we are brought to mockery and scorn!
Our grain is stolen; each will be called a fool
Both by the warden and our friends at school,
And by the miller most. Alackaday!"

   Thus John came back, complaining all the way,
With Bayard's rope in hand, through brush and mire.
He found the miller sitting by the fire,
For it was night. Return they did not dare,
And begged him he would give them lodging there,
For love of God, and they would pay their penny.

   The miller answered: "Yea, if there be any,
Such as it is, that will I share with you.

My house is small; but ye are schooled, ye two,
And by your arguments can make a place
A mile in breadth from twenty feet of space!
Let us see now if this will hold us all,
Or talk it larger, if it be too small!"

   "Now by St. Cuthbert, Simon, shrewdly spoke!"
This John replied. "Always thou hast thy joke!
They say a man must choose between two things:
Take what he finds, or do with what he brings.
But specially I pray thee, landlord dear,
Get us some meat and drink, and make good cheer,
And we will pay in full upon demand.
No one can lure a hawk with empty hand;
Lo! – here our silver ready to be spent."

   This miller to the town his daughter sent
For ale and bread, and roasted them a goose,
And tied their horse so it should not get loose –
And in his own room laid them out a bed
With sheets and blankets well and fairly spread,
Not more than ten or twelve feet from his own.
His daughter had one for herself alone,
In the same chamber, in its proper place.
Better it might not be – the little space
Within the house had made it necessary.
They sat and supped and talked and made them merry
And drank strong ale, and so the evening sped.
At midnight, or about, they went to bed.

   Well was this miller varnished in the head:
So pale with drink his face was drained of red.
He hiccoughs, and his voice comes through his nose
As if he had a cold. To bed he goes,
And by his side the good wife goes her way.
She was as light and saucy as a jay,
So well her merry whistle had been wet.
At the bed's foot the baby's crib they set,
To rock it, and to give the child the dug.
And when the ale was emptied from the jug
The daughter followed with no more ado;
And then to bed went John and Alan too.
No need of drugs to send them off to sleep;
This miller of the ale had drunk so deep

He snorted like a horse, nor had a mind
For any noises from his tail behind.
His wife sang with him – such a lusty singing
Two furlongs off ye might have heard it ringing;
The wench snored loudly, too, *pour compagnie*.

   Alan the student heard this melody,
And nudging John he whispered: "Sleepest thou?
Heardst ever such a song as this ere now?
Lo! what an evening liturgy they make!
May wild fire all their cursèd bodies take!
Who ever heard so weird a chant ascending?
Yea, they deserve the flower of all bad ending!
All this long night I shall not get my rest.
No matter – all shall happen for the best.
For John, as I have hope to thrive," he said,
"I shall go lay that wench in yonder bed.
The law allows some easement unto us:
For, John, there is a law that puts it thus:
That if a man in one point shall be grieved,
Then in another he shall be relieved!
Our grain is stolen – there is no saying nay,
Ill luck hath dogged us all this livelong day.
Now since for this I get no compensation,
I mean to salve my loss with consolation.
By God's soul, this shall be the way, I swear!"

   This John replied, "Nay, Alan, have a care.
This miller is a dangerous man," he said,
"And if ye wake him as he lies in bed,
He might do both of us an injury."

   Alan replied: "I count him not a fly,"
And rose, and to the wench's bed he crept.
The girl lay on her back and soundly slept.
Before she knew what Alan was about
It was too late for her to cry or shout,
And, to be brief, the two were soon as one.
Now, Alan, play! for I will speak of John.

   John lay in silence while a man might go
A furlong, and he moaned for very woe.
"Alas! This is a wicked jest," cried he.
"Plainly it makes a clumsy ape of me.
My comrade gets some pay for all his harms;

He holds the miller's daughter in his arms;
He hath adventured, and his quest hath sped,
And I lie like a sack of bran in bed.
And when this prank of ours is told at school,
I shall be held a milk-sop and a fool!
I will arise and risk it, by my faith!
'No pluck, no luck,' is what the proverb saith."
And up he rose, and with a noiseless tread
Stole to the cradle, and bore it to his bed,
And at the foot he set it on the flooring.

   Soon after this the wife left off her snoring,
Rose and relieved herself, and came again,
But by her bed she missed the cradle then,
And in the darkness groped about and sought.
"Alas! I almost went amiss," she thought,
"I would have climbed into the students' bed!
Eh, *ben'cite*! That would be bad!" she said.
And groped, and found the cradle, and went past
With hand outstretched, and reached the bed at last.
And had no thought but everything was good
Because the baby's cradle by it stood,
And in the dark she knew not where she went.
So she crept in, relieved and well content,
And there lay still, and would have gone to sleep.
But soon this John the student with a leap
Was on this wife, at work with all his might;
So merry she had not been for many a night;
He pricketh hard and deep, as he were mad.
And thus a jolly life these students had
Until at length the third cock started crowing.

   Alan, with dawn a little weary growing,
For all night he had labored hard and well:
"Sweetheart, dear Malin, I must say farewell.
Day comes; I cannot stay beyond this kiss;
But always, as my soul may win to bliss,
I am thy student, where I go or ride."

   "So then, dear love, farewell," the wench replied.
"But one thing, while thou lie beside me still –
When thou art going homeward by the mill –
Right at the entry door – look thou behind;
A loaf of half a bushel wilt thou find,

Kneaded and baked it was from thine own meal
Which yesterday I helped my father steal.
Now, sweetheart, may God save thee well, and keep."
And with that word almost began to weep.

Alan arose. "Before the night shall end,
I will go creep in bed beside my friend,"
And touched the cradle as he groped along.
"By God," he muttered, "I am going wrong;
My head is dizzy from my work this night
And hath confused me, so I go not right,
For by the cradle I can surely tell;
Here lie the miller and his wife as well."
By twenty devils, forth he goes his way,
And found the bed in which the miller lay,
And crawled in softly where his comrade slept,
As he supposed, and to the miller crept,
And caught him by the neck, and softly spake,
Saying: "Thou, John, thou swine's head! What! Awake!
And hear, for Christ's soul, of this noble sport;
For by St. James, although this night was short,
Thrice have I laid the miller's daughter flat
Upon her back, and had her, and all that
While like a coward thou hast lain in bed."

"Yea, hast thou, lecherous rogue?" the miller said.
"Ha! thou false student, traitor false!" cried he.
"Thou shalt be dead, yea, by God's dignity!
Who dare disgrace," he cried in fearful rage,
"My daughter, come of such a lineage?"
And caught this Alan by the Adam's apple,
And choked him as the two began to grapple,
And smote him with his fist full on the nose.
Down on his breast the warm blood spurting flows,
And on the floor; his nose and mouth were broke.
They wallow like two pigs tied in a poke,
And up they go, then down again are thrown,
Until the miller on a paving stone
Stumbled, and fell down backward on his wife,
That lay there dead to all this crazy strife,
For she began a little sleep to take
By John, that all night long had been awake,
And started from her slumber when he fell.

"Help, cross of Bromholm!" she began to yell.
"*In manus tuas*! Lord, I call on thee!
Simon, awake! The fiend hath fallen on me;
My heart is cracked! Help! I am all but dead!
One on my belly, one upon my head!
Help, Simon! for these lying students fight!"
This John jumped up as quickly as he might,
And back and forth along the wall he flew
To find a staff, and she had jumped up too,
And knew the room much better than he knew it,
And where a staff was, and went quickly to it,
And saw a little shimmering of light,
For through a hole the moon was shining bright,
And by the light in struggle saw the two,
But did not know for certain who was who,
But saw a glimmer there of something white,
And with this white thing dancing in her sight,
She thought, because she could not see it clearer,
It was a student's night-cap, and drew nearer,
And would have hit this Alan, but instead
She struck the bald spot on the miller's head,
And down he went, and cried out: "Help, I die!"
These students beat him well and let him lie,
And dressed themselves, and got their horse and meal,
And on their homeward journey off they steal.
And at the mill they got the loaf of bread –
Of half a bushel – and away they sped.

Thus was the haughty miller roundly beat,
And got no pay for grinding all their wheat,
And paid for supper ere the game was through
For Alan and John, that thrashed him soundly, too.
His wife and daughter are both of them disgraced;
So fares a miller that is double-faced
And false: the proverb tells the honest truth:
"Let him not look for good that evil do'th;"
He that deceives, himself deceived shall be.
And God, that sits aloft in majesty,
Save you, both great and humble, without fail!
Thus I pay off the miller with my tale!

Here the Reeve's Tale is Ended

The Cook's Tale

Continuing the lowered tone of the Tales, the Cook's tale promises to be the bawdiest yet, but is unfinished. The Cook's prologue sets out his intention to tell a lewd tale, and the truncated story ends with the revelation that the character, Perkin, has a friend whose wife is a whore. This ends a group of tales held together by structural echoes and rivalry between the tellers of the tales.

THE COOK'S TALE

*The Prologue of the
Cook's Tale*

WHILE the Reeve spoke, the Cook of London clawed
        him –
For very glee upon the back he pawed him.
"Ha! ha!" he cried, "I tell you, by Christ's passion,
This miller got it in a lively fashion
In that affair of lodging for the night!
Solomon had the tongue to put it right:
'Bring ye not every man,' his words run thus,
'Into thine house.' Such things are dangerous.
It pays a man to study carefully
Whom he shall welcome to his privacy.
I pray God that he give me grief and care
If ever, since my name was Hodge of Ware,
I heard of miller tricked a neater way.
They fooled him badly in the dark, I say.
But God forbid that we should stop with this.
And therefore, if ye take it not amiss
That I should speak, who am a plain, rude man,
I will relate as fairly as I can
A jest that happened in our town," said he.
    Our Host replied, and said: "I grant it thee.
Now tell on, Roger – look that it be good.
For many a pasty hast thou drawn the blood,
And many a Jack o' Dover hast thou sold
That hath been two times hot and two times cold.
From many a pilgrim hast thou had Christ's curse,
That after eating knew he fared the worse
For parsley on a fat goose of thy warming;

For in thy shop the flies are fairly swarming.
Tell on now, by thy name, for I am done;
And be not angry for a little fun;
A man may say true things in play and jest."
    "Thou say'st right, by my troth," the Cook
        confessed;
"But, 'True play, bad play,' as the Fleming saith,
And therefore, Harry Bailly, by thy faith,
Be thou not wroth if something I relate
About a Host, before we separate.
I will not tell it now, and yet I say
Before I leave thee, thou shalt have thy pay."
With this he laughed, and all in jollity
He told his tale, as follows presently.

Thus ends the Prologue of the Cook's Tale

Here begins the Cook's Tale

ONCE an apprentice dwelt within our town,
By guild a victualer. And he was brown
As is a berry, of figure short and good,
As gay as any goldfinch in the wood,
With black locks always combed with elegance.
He moved so well and merry in a dance
That he was known as Perkin Reveller.
Lucky the wench that had this lad with her!
He was as full of love-making and love
As any hive is with its honey-trove.
At every wedding he would sing and hop;
He loved the tavern better than the shop!
    For if through Cheapside some procession passed,
Out of the shop this Perkin leapt full fast;
Till he had seen the sights in full, and then
Jigged for a spell, he would not come again.
And he had gathered up a following
Of such as he, that loved to dance and sing,
And by appointment they would plan to meet
And play at dice upon a certain street.
For there was no apprentice anywhere
Could cast a pair of dice with better air

Than Perkin could; and he was generous, too,
In spending, in some places that he knew.
Of that his master came to be aware,
For many a time he found his cash-box bare;
For an apprentice busied constantly
At dice, and making love, and revelry,
Will always make his master suffer by it,
Though he, poor man, have no part in the riot.
For theft and riot – of a kind they are,
Though the thief play the rebeck or guitar.

   This gay apprentice with his master stayed
Till he had almost served his time of trade,
Though he was reprimanded early and late,
And sometimes piped by minstrels to Newgate.
But in the end his master called to mind,
When once he asked to have his quittance signed,
A proverb that this word of warning bore:
"Better take one bad apple from the store
Than let it rot the rest." And this is true

Of a bad servant and his fellows, too;
It is the lesser harm to let him fare
Than ruin all the other servants there.
Therefore his master gave him his discharge,
And with a curse he bade him go at large;
Thus jolly Perkin came by his release.
Now let him revel all the night – or cease.

   And since there is no thief without a crony
To help him eat or drink or waste the money
That he can get by borrowing or theft,
He sent his bed and clothing when he left
Unto a friend who loved, like him, a life
Of revel, dice, and pleasure, and whose wife
For mere appearance feigned to keep a store,
But really got her living as a whore.

*   *   *   *   *   *

Of this Cook's Tale Chaucer wrote no more

The Lawyer's Tale

THE LAWYER TELLS a tale of a virtuous woman, whose patience and faith are tried by an extravagant series of unwarranted misfortunes. It is something of a secular saint's life, or a Christian, rather than courtly, romance. The lawyer pleads eloquently to engage our sympathy for his heroine, whose unusually unlucky life leaves a trail of murder and destruction from Syria to Northumberland and finally Rome. Constance is far from dynamic, but her stoicism, virtue and Christian faith save her from numerous unpleasant fates in a tale that endorses the role of providence in human affairs.

The Lawyer's Tale

*The words of the Host
to the Company*

OUR Host saw clearly that the shining sun
The arc of the artificial day had run
The fourth part, and a half an hour and more,
And though not deeply expert in such lore,
He understood it was the eighteenth day
Of April, that is messenger to May,
And saw well that the shadow of every tree
Had reached in length as great a quantity
As was the upright body's causing it.
And therefore by the shadow he had the wit
To know that Phœbus, shining clear and bright,
Had climbed to forty-five degrees in height,
So it was ten o'clock, he must conclude,
Considering the day and latitude;
And turned his horse, and pulled up suddenly.

 "Lordings, I warn you, all this company,"
He said, "The fourth part of the day is gone;
For love of God, I pray you, and St. John,
Lose ye no needless time now in delay.
For, lordings, time goes wasting night and day,
And steals from us, forever slyly taking
In sleep, and through our negligence when
 waking,
As the stream does, that never turns again,
Descending from the mountain to the plain.
Thus Seneca, and such philosophers
Say well, who say that loss of time is worse
Than loss of gold, for loss of property

May be repaired, but loss of time must be
A shame to us; nor comes again," he said,
"No more in truth than Malkin's maidenhead
When she has lost it in her wantonness.
Let us not molder thus in idleness.
Sir lawyer," said he, "as ye hope for bliss,
Tell us a tale, as our agreement is.
Ye have submitted by your free consent
To take my judgment, without argument;
Then keep your promise, and discharge it now:
So shall ye do your duty, anyhow."

 "Host," he replied, "By God's grace I assent.
To break a contract is not mine intent.
Promise is debt, and I will gladly pay
My promises: no better can I say.
'What law a man another man shall give,
By that law he himself should rightly live –'
The proverb runs. However, this is true:
I have no profitable tale for you;
For Chaucer, though half ignorant at times
Of meter, and unskilled in making rhymes,
Has told them in such English as he can
Already, as is known to every man.
And if he has not told them, dear my brother,
In one book, he has told them in another.
For here or there he tells more tales of lovers
Than ever Ovid wrote between the covers
Of his Epistles, that were writ of old.
Why should I tell them then, since they are told?
He wrote of Ceys and of Alcyone
In youth, and since hath spoken of all that be
Of noble women and of lovers, too.
Whoso will read his lengthy volume through –
"Legends of Cupid's Saints –" so runs the title –
Shall witness there the wounds, gaping and vital,
Of Babylonian Thisbe and Lucrece;
And Dejanira's and Hermione's
Laments; the sword on which Queen Dido
 died;
And how Hypsipyle in anguish cried,
And Phyllis hung for love upon a tree,

And Ariadne's island in the sea,
And drowned Leander for his Hero dying;
The tears of Helen and the woeful crying
Of Briseis, and of thee, Laodamia;
The cruelty that thou didst, O queen Medea,
Who by the neck thy little children hung
Because of Jason's falseness. But among
All wives, Penelope, he holds you best,
With you, O Hypermnestra and Alceste.

   "But neither word nor syllable writes he
About the wicked case of Canacee,
She that was lost in sin and loved her brother;
Fie on that story, and fie on every other
Like it; or that of Apollonius
Of Tyre, and how the vile Antiochus
Bereft his daughter of her maidenhead –
So horrible a tale I never read –
How on the paving stones he threw her down!
And he, with purpose, to his good renown,
Would never write in one of his relations
Of such unnatural abominations;
Neither will I rehearse them, if I may.

   But for my tale – what shall I tell today?
I should be loath to seem like one of these
False muses that men call Pierides –
The *Metamorphoses* knows what I mean –
But none the less, I do not care a bean
Though with baked haws I follow in my time;
I speak in prose, and let him speak in rhyme."
And with that word, and with a sober cheer,
He told his tale, as ye shall read it here.

The Prologue of the Lawyer's Tale

O HATEFUL ill! O state of poverty,
By thirst, by cold, by hunger so confounded!
To ask for help is heart-felt shame to thee;
If none thou ask, with need must thou be wounded;
True need lays bare thine every secret wound hid;
Despite thyself, thou must against thy good
Steal, beg, or borrow for thy livelihood!

Thou blam'st Christ, saying bitterly that He
Has misdivided riches temporal;
Or else thou blam'st thy neighbor sinfully,
And sayst thou hast too little, and he hath all.
"In faith," thou criest, "sometime shall payment fall,
When in the red hot coals his rump shall bleed
Who never helps the needy in their need."

Consider well this judgment of the wise:
"Better to die than live in penury";
Thy very neighbor will thy lot despise;
If thou art poor, farewell thy dignity!
Take from the wise man this philosophy:
"Unto the poor man all his days are evil";
Beware then, lest thy want become thy devil!

If thou art poor, thy brother hateth thee,
And all thy friends shall flee from thee, alas!
O wealthy merchants, happy may ye be,
O noble prudent people of that class!
Your bags are never filled with *ambes as*,
But with *sis cink*; then run and seize your chance;
In Christmas weather merry may ye dance!

Ye search the land and sea to get your winnings,
As wise folk, know ye well the whole estate
Of realms; news hath with you its first beginnings,
And tales of peace and struggle ye relate;
And I of tales should now be desolate
Save that a merchant in a byegone year
Taught me a tale, and this ye soon shall hear.

Here the Lawyer begins his Tale

IN Syria once there dwelt a company
Of merchants that were rich, discreet, and true,
That far and wide sent forth their spicery,
And cloths of gold, and satins rich of hue,
And always offered wares so cheap and new
That all men liked to trade with them right well,
And also bring them merchandise to sell.

It happened that the masters of this guild
Had shaped their plans for Rome, to travel there,
Whether with hope of trade or pleasure filled;
And they would send no message, but repair
To Rome themselves – thus ended this affair –
And take their lodging in such neighborhood
As seemed most like to do their purpose good.

These merchants made their sojourn in that town
For such a time as they had liking for;
And so it happened that the high renown
Of Constance, daughter of the emperor,
With every circumstance was set before
These Syrian merchants, coming day by day
In such a fashion as I now shall say.

This was the common voice of every man:
"Our emperor of Rome, blest may he be!
A daughter hath that, since the world began,
If goodness count with beauty equally,
There never was another such as she!
I pray that God in honor her sustain;
And would as queen of Europe she could reign!

"High beauty dwells in her, unspoiled by pride;
Youth without greenness or frivolity;
In every action virtue is her guide;
Her meekness slays all hint of tyranny;
She is the mirror of perfect courtesy;
True chamber is her heart of holy living;
Her hand the minister of all almsgiving."

And all this voice was truth, as God is true.
But from our purpose let us not depart;
These merchants bade their ships be freighted new,
And having seen this maiden, home they start,
And back to Syria journey, blithe of heart,
And ply their business as they did before,
And prosper well; I cannot tell you more.

It happened that these merchants stood in grace
With him that was their sultan, so that he,
When they were come from any foreign place,
Would always, in benignant courtesy,
Make them good cheer, and search out busily
Tidings of sundry realms, to have their word
Of wonders that they might have seen or heard.

Above all other things, especially
Of Constance have these merchants to recite
So much in praise, with such fidelity,
That soon this sultan has a great delight
To keep her in his mind, and all his might
And all his will and busy care are cast
That he may love her while his life shall last.

And peradventure in their skyey book
The stars had written it should come to pass
Even at his time of birth, that he must look
To have his death because of love, alas!
For in the stars, clearer than any glass,
Is writ, God knows, for anyone to scan
Its meaning there, the death of every man.

The stars did Hector and Achilles warn,
Long winters ere their deaths, that they should die;
Pompey's and Julius' deaths, ere they were born,
The strife of Thebes, were mirrored in the sky.
Socrates, Samson – both were doomed on high,
Turnus and Hercules. But men are dull;
None has the wit to read these things in full.

This sultan for his privy council sent,
And, of this thing the fewest words to say,
He made his mind and feeling evident,
And told them plain: "Unless he found a way
To have Dame Constance, and with scant delay,
He was but dead," and charged them speedily
That for his life they shape some remedy.

Then different men said different things in season;
Argued, and made proposals what to do,
And cast their thought in many a subtle reason,
And spoke of magic and deception, too;
But after all their words, when they are through,
They cannot see advantage there, and own
That marriage seems the way, and that alone.

Then they perceived how doubtful this would be,
And all in reason, since when truth was said,
In the two lands the great diversity
Between their laws to this opinion led:
They held: "No Christian prince his child would wed
Knowing that she by those sweet laws must dwell
Which Mahmout our great prophet taught so well."

"Rather," he said, "than I should Constance lose
I will be christened – know that this is true.
I must be hers, nor otherwise can choose.
Then hold your arguments, I beg of you,
And save my life. Do what is need to do;
Only get her that hath my life in cure,
For in this woe I cannot long endure."

What need is there to lengthen this narration?
I say, by treaty and by embassy,
And through the Pope, that worked by mediation,
And all the church, and the nobility,
That – for destruction of idolatry,
And Christ's increase, whose law they held so dear –
They were agreed at last, as ye shall hear:

This sultan and his barons should be led,
And all their lieges, to the font, and be
Christened, and Constance should be his to wed,
And gold, I know not what the quantity;
And all was bound with pledges solemnly;
This same accord was sworn on either side;
Almighty God, fair Constance, be thy guide!

Now, as I guess, some will expect of me
That I should tell of all the preparation
Which th'emperor in his great nobility
Made for his daughter at her embarcation.
Yet all men know that such great ordination
As was arranged so high a cause to grace
No man could hope to tell in little space.

Bishops prepare themselves to go with her;
Ladies and lords and knights of high renown,
And many folk of other sorts there were;
And it is well proclaimed throughout the town
That everyone should piously kneel down
And pray of Christ this marriage to receive
With grace, and speed their voyage when they leave.

The day is come at last for their departing;
I say, the woeful, fatal day is there;
No longer may they linger out their starting,
But one and all for setting forth prepare;
All pale and spent with sorrowing and care,
Constance arose, preparing for the day;
For she must go – she sees no other way.

Alas! What wonder is it though she wept,
That to a foreign nation now must go
From friends, that her so tenderly have kept,
There is subjection to be set below
The will of one whose ways she did not know.
Husbands are always good, and were of yore;
Wives know it well – now I dare say no more!

"Father, thy Constance in her wretched plight,
Thy daughter, fostered tenderly by thee,
And thou, my mother, the supreme delight
Above all else save only Christ to me –
Constance, your child, commends her constantly
Unto your grace; my way to Syria lies
Where I shall never see you with mine eyes.

"Alas! for Barbary, that heathen nation,
I must depart at once, as is your will;
But Christ, who died to bring our soul's salvation,
Give me the grace his high commands to fill.
O wretch! What matter though I end in ill?
Women were born to serve and suffer pain,
And bow to men, that hold the right to reign."

Never at Troy when Pyrrhus broke the wall,
Or Ilion burned, neither at Thebes could be,
Nor yet at Rome, for fear of Hannibal,
Who three times vanquished Roman armies three –
Such tender weeping, sounding piteously,
As in that chamber rang at her departing;
But weep or sing, the time was come for starting.

O thou first moving, cruël firmament,
That crowdest ever with thy diurnal sway,
And hurlest all from East to Occident
That naturally would hold another way,
Thy crowding set the heavens in such array
For this dark voyage, that its cruël master,
Fierce Mars, hath brought this marriage to disaster.

Unfortunate ascendant tortuous!
The lord of which hath helpless fallen from place,
Out of his angle into darkness thus –
O Mars, O Atazir, as in this case!
O moon, thou go'st with sad and feeble pace;
Where thou hast joined it is not favorable,
And thou hast left the place where thou wast well.

Imprudent emperor of Rome, alas!
Hadst thou no man that knew astrology?
Is there no choice of times in such a case?
No choice of when a ship should go to sea? –
Especially for folk of high degree,
Or when a horoscope is plain to know?
Alas! We be too ignorant or too slow.

To ship was brought this fair and woeful maid;
With pomp and circumstance they led her there;
"Now Jesus Christ be with you all," she said;
There was no more but "Farewell, Constance fair!"
Bravely she strove to keep a cheerful air,
And in this fashion forth I let her sail,
And once again return to tell my tale.

The mother of the sultan, well of vices,
Perceived the course on which her son was bent –
How he would cease his olden sacrifices;
And for her council speedily she sent;
And they appeared, to know of her intent,
And when they had assembled at her call,
She sat, and spoke as I shall tell you all:

"My lords," said she, "ye know now every man
My son has willed, and cannot be deterred,
To leave the holy law of Al Koran,
Which, brought by Mahmout, speaks God's holy word.
But let my vow to mighty God be heard:
The life shall rather from my body part
Than Mahmout's law be riven from my heart!

"What should we gain to take this new, strange faith,
Save pain upon our slavish bodies laid?
And afterwards in hell to know the scathe
Of souls to Mahmout's teaching renegade?
But, lords, will ye assure and swear your aid,
As I shall say, assenting to my plan,
If I forever save you, every man?"

They swore and made agreement, every one,
To live with her and die, and by her stand,
And each to do the most that could be done
To aid her with his friends throughout the land,
And so she takes this enterprise in hand,
Which, as I tell the tale, will soon be plain,
Then spoke like this to all of them again:

"First shall we feign the Christian faith to take;
Cold water will not burn us much, or bite,
And I shall such a feast and revel make,
As will, I trust, repay the sultan quite,
For though his wife be christened never so white,
And bring a font of water with her here,
She shall not wash the red away, I fear."

O Sultaness, root of iniquity,
Virago, second-born Semiramis,
O serpent coiled in femininity,
Like to the snake bound deep in hell's abyss,
All that to truth and virtue deadly is,
Breedeth in thee, thou feigning woman-devil,
Where malice makes a nest for every evil!

O Satan! steeped in envy since the day
That thou from out our heritage wast harried;
To women know'st thou well the olden way!
Through Eva into bondage were we carried;
Thou wouldst not have this Christian couple married;
And when upon deception thou art bent,
Of woman dost thou make thine instrument!

This sultaness on whom I heap these curses
Let secretly her council go its way;
Why lengthen out this tale with further verses?
She rides to see the sultan on a day,
And tells him she would put her faith away
And take the Christian creed; her grief was strong
That she had lived a heathen for so long.

And for the honor of a feast she pled,
To give the Christians when they came to land;
"To please them will I labor well," she said.
He answered: "I will do as ye command,"
And kneeling, gave her thanks for what she planned.
So glad he was he knew not what to say;
She kissed her son, and home she went her way.

Part II

THIS Christian folk are come to land at last,
In Syria, with a great and festive rout;
This sultan sent his messengers full fast,
First to his mother, then to the realm about,
And said, his wife was come, beyond a doubt,
And begged the sultaness to meet the queen
To keep the honor of his high demesne.

Great was the crowd and splendid the array
Of Syrians and Romans meeting there.
The sultan's mother, richly dressed and gay,
Receiveth Constance with as glad an air
As mother might for well-loved daughter wear;
And to the nearest city, close at hand,
They rode slow-paced and stately through the land.

I think not even the triumph of Julius,
Which Lucan has described with such a boast,
Shone forth more royal or more sumptuous
Than the assembly of that joyous host.
But this old scorpion, this wicked ghost,
The sultaness, for all her flattering,
Planned under this to plant her deadly sting.

The sultan comes himself soon after this,
So royally, that wonder is to tell,
And welcomes her with every joy and bliss,
And thus in mirth and joy I let them dwell.
The fruit of all this pomp is yet to tell.
When the time came, it seemed that it was best
The revel cease, and all go to their rest.

And the time came when this old sultaness
Had fixed to have this feast of which I told;
And to the feast the Christian people press
In general – yea, both the young and old.
And men may feast, and royalty behold,
And dainties more than I can tell you here;
Yet ere they rose, the cost was all too dear.

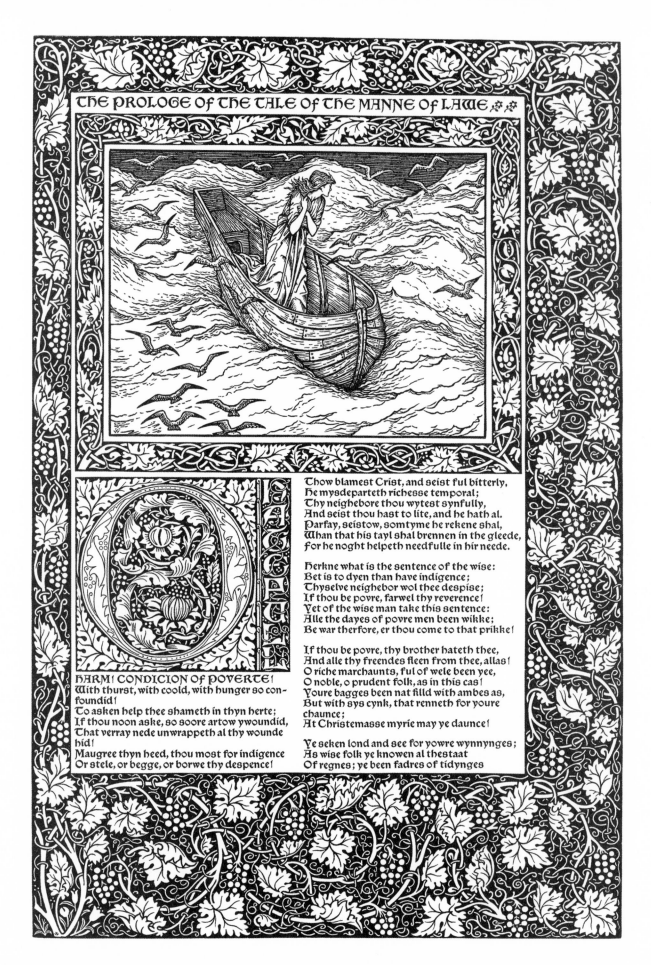

THE PROLOGE OF THE TALE OF THE MANNE OF LAWE

HARM! CONDICION OF POVERTE!
With thurst, with coold, with hunger so confoundid!
To asken help thee shameth in thyn herte;
If thou noon aske, so soore artow ywoundid,
That verray nede unwrappeth al thy wounde hid!
Maugree thyn heed, thou most for indigence
Or stele, or begge, or borwe thy despence!

Thow blamest Crist, and seist ful bitterly,
He mysdeparteth richesse temporal;
Thy neighebore thou wytest synfully,
And seist thou hast to lite, and he hath al.
Parfay, seistow, somtyme he rekene shal,
Whan that his tayl shal brennen in the gleede,
For he noght helpeth needfulle in hir neede.

Herkne what is the sentence of the wise:
Bet is to dyen than have indigence;
Thyselve neighebor wol thee despise;
If thou be povre, farwel thy reverence!
Yet of the wise man take this sentence:
Alle the dayes of povre men been wikke;
Be war therfore, er thou come to that prikke!

If thou be povre, thy brother hateth thee,
And alle thy freendes fleen from thee, allas!
O riche marchaunts, ful of wele been yee,
O noble, o prudent folk, as in this cas!
Youre bagges been nat filld with ambes as,
But with sys cynk, that renneth for youre chaunce;
At Christemasse myrie may ye daunce!

Ye seken lond and see for yowre wynnynges;
As wise folk ye knowen al thestaat
Of regnes; ye been fadres of tidynges

Plate 7: The Lawyer's Tale (p. 89)

O sudden woe, that ever art the neighbor
To worldly bliss, still poisoned more or less
With pain! O end of all our worldly labor!
Woe sets a term to all our happiness!
Attend these words of wisdom, and possess:
Reflect, even on thy day of joy and laughter,
Of unknown woe and ill that follow after!

To tell this matter briefly, in a word,
The sultan and the Christians every one
Were stabbed and hewn to pieces at that board,
Save for Dame Constance – she was spared alone.
This agèd sultaness, accursèd crone,
Had brought this deed to cursèd consummation,
Hoping to rule alone in all that nation.

There was no Syrian that had been converted,
That of the counsel of the sultan knew,
But he was slain as from his seat he started;
And forth with Constance hastily they flew,
And to a ship without a rudder drew,
And set her there, and bade her sail the sea
From Syria back again to Italy.

A certain treasure that was with her sent,
And a great store of food and drink they brought her,
And clothes she had for her habiliment,
And forth she sails upon the salty water;
Ah, Constance mine, O emperor's young daughter,
Beloved and fair, with goodness sanctified,
He that is lord of fortune be thy guide!

She crossed herself, and thus began to falter
Unto the cross of Christ full piteously:
"O holy cross, O bright and blessèd altar,
Red with the Lamb's blood that was shed to free
And wash the world from old iniquity,
From the fiend's claws protect me well, and keep,
That day when I sink drowning in the deep!

"Victorious Tree, Thou to the faithful given
For refuge, that alone wast fit to bear
The gaping gashes of the King of Heaven,
The white Lamb, that was wounded with the spear,
Scourger of fiends from all that hold Thee dear,
Above whose heads Thy sheltering arms extend,
Keep me, and give me strength my life to amend!"

For years and days this hapless creature floated,
Drifting from Greece to the Moroccan strait
As Fortune willed; and many a time devoted
Her thoughts to death, yet never found her fate;
And many a sorry meal this woman ate
Before the driving waves that ship would cast
Unto the place where she should come at last.

But men might ask me: Why was she not slain?
And at the feast who might her body save?
To that demand will I demand again,
Who guarded Daniel in the horrible cave
Where every man save he, master or knave,
Went down the lion's jaws, and was no more?
No one but God, that in his heart he bore.

God pleased this wondrous miracle to give
Through her, that we his mighty works should see;
Christ, that to every ill is curative,
Can, as clerks know, by certain agency
Do something for a purpose that may be
Dark to man's wit; our clouded human sense
Can never know his larger providence.

Now since she was not slain, what man or law
Kept her from drowning later in the sea?
But who kept Jonah in the fish's maw
Till he was spouted up at Nineveh?
Well may men know that it was none but He
That led the Hebrews in escape from slaughter
With dry feet through the walls of ocean water.

Whence might this woman drink and victual have?
How could her food three years and more endure?
Who fed St. Mary the Egyptian in her cave,
Or in the desert? None but Christ, for sure.
With a few loaves and fish to feed the poor –
Five thousand – was as marvellous a deed.
God sent his plenty to her in her need.

Into our English ocean thus she came,
Drifting its savage length, until at last
Under a fortress that I cannot name,
Far in Northumberland, her ship was cast
Upon a bar of sand, and stuck there fast;
All of an hour it would not wash away;
The will of Christ was clear that she should stay.

The constable came from the castle there
To see this wreck, and through the ship he sought,
And found this woman, worn and full of care,
And also found the treasure that she brought;
And in her language mercy she besought:
That he her life and flesh at once should sever,
And her from woe long lasting thus deliver.

Her language was a Latin of a kind –
Corrupt, yet such as he could understand,
And seeing there was nothing more to find,
He brought this woeful woman to the land;
Thankful to God, she knelt upon the sand,
But what she was, she would to none discover
For foul or fair – nor threat of death could move her.

She said that on the sea her toil and horror
Had mazed her, and destroyed her memory;
The constable had such great pity for her,
As had his wife, they wept for sympathy;
So free of sloth she worked, so busily,
To serve and please all persons in that place,
All loved her well that looked upon her face.

The constable and Hermengild his wife
Were pagans, and that country everywhere;
But Hermengild loved Constance as her life,
And Constance hath so long resided there
With orisons and bitter tears, and prayer,
That Jesus hath converted through His grace
Dame Hermengild, the lady of that place.

In all that land no Christians dared be found
In groups; for they had long since had to flee
From pagans that had conquered all around
The regions of the north, by land and sea;
To Wales had fled the Christianity
Of the old Britons dwelling in that island;
There was their refuge – in that rocky highland.

But Christian Britons were not so exiled
But there were some that still, in secrecy,
Honored their Christ, and heathen folk beguiled;
Of such close to the castle there were three.
And one of them was blind, and could not see,
Save with the inward vision of the mind,
Which men can see with after they are blind.

Bright was the sun upon a summer's day,
Which made the constable disposed to go
With Constance and his wife the shortest way
Down to the sea, a furlong off or so;
To play there and to wander to and fro;
And in their walk they met, and would have passed,
This gnarled old blind man with his eyes shut fast.

"In the name of Christ," this blind old Briton said,
"Dame Hermengild, give me my sight again!"
This lady at his words was sore afraid,
Thinking her husband, to be brief and plain,
Might for her love of Jesus have her slain,
Till Constance made her bold, and quickly brought her
To do Christ's will, as should His Church's daughter.

The constable, abashed to see this sight,
Demanded, "What is all this mummery?"
Constance replied: "Sire, it is Christ's own might,
That from the devil's snare can make men free;"
And so explained our faith so cogently
Before the evening, that her words sufficed
To make him convert, and believe in Christ.

This constable was not lord of this place
Where he had found Dame Constance by the strand,
But kept it well for many a winter's space
For Aella, king of all Northumberland,
A prudent prince, that bore a heavy hand
Against the Scots, as he who will may learn:
But to my story I will now return.

Satan, our ever-waiting arch-betrayer,
Beheld in Constance all her perfect good,
And schemed how in his time he might repay her;
And made a young knight of that neighborhood
Love her so foully, with so hot a blood,
It seemed to him that he must satisfy
His lust for once at least, or he would die!

He wooeth her, but this availeth naught,
For she will do no sin, try what he may;
And so he schemed with a revengeful thought
To bring her death about in shameful way;
So, when this constable had gone one day,
By night in secret to the room he crept
Of Hermengild, the while this lady slept.

Weary and worn with making many prayers
Lay Hermengild asleep, and Constance too.
This knight, entangled deep in Satan's snares,
Unto their bed with stealthy footsteps drew
And cut the throat of Hermengild clean through,
And by Dame Constance laid the bloody knife,
And went his way – may God destroy his life!

Soon now this constable came home again,
With Aella, king of all the land around;
And saw his wife so pitilessly slain,
And wrung his hands, and wept with fearful sound;
And by Dame Constance in her bed he found
The bloody knife! Alas! What could she say?
For very woe her wit was fled away!

To Aella king was told this fearful horror,
Also the time, and place, and in what way
Constance had come, and of the ship that bore her,
As ye that listen here have heard me say;
And in his heart compassion held its sway
To see such mildness and benignity
Fall on misfortune, grief, and misery.

For as a lamb that to its death is brought,
So stood this innocent before the king,
And the false knight that this vile treason wrought
Under his oath swore that she did this thing;
But all the people stood there sorrowing,
And murmured, for they said, "they could not guess
That she had done so great a wickedness.

"For they had always seen her virtuous,
And loving as her life Dame Hermengild."
All persons in that house bore witness thus,
Save he that with the knife that lady killed.
This noble king was with suspicion filled
As to this witness, and resolved to go
Deeper into this deed, the truth to know.

Constance, alas! No champion is thine;
Thou hast no way to fight, alackaday!
May He who saved us with His death divine,
And Satan bound (who lies yet where he lay),
Be thy strong champion upon this day!
For Christ today must show a wonder plain,
Or thou, despite thine innocence, be slain!

Down on her knees she dropped, and thus she prayed:
"Immortal God, thou who didst save Susanna
From a false charge, and thou, benignant maid,
Mary I mean, the daughter of St. Anna,
Before whose child the angels sing Hosanna –
If I am innocent of this felony,
Be thou my help, for otherwise I die!"

Have ye not seen some time a pallid face
Among a crowd – the face of one that go'th
Unto his death, and past all hope of grace,
And such a color in his visage show'th
That men might know his face and peril both
From all the other faces streaming past?
So Constance stood, so looked around aghast.

O queens that live in high prosperity,
And duchesses, and ladies every one,
Have pity now on her adversity;
The daughter of an emperor stands alone;
And she hath none to whom to make her moan.
O royal blood, standing in jeopardy,
In thy great need thy friends are far from thee!

Aella this king such great compassion knew –
For noble hearts are full of sympathy –
That from his eyes the tears like water flew.
"Now go and fetch a book at once," said he;
"And if this knight will swear on it that she
This woman slew, then must we straightway face
The choice of judge for trying of this case."

A book of gospels, in fair British written,
Was fetched, and soon upon this book he swore
That she was guilty. Meanwhile he was smitten
Upon the neck, and fell upon the floor
Like stone, and lay as if to move no more,
And both his eyes burst outward from his face
In sight of every person in that place.

And then a voice was heard by everyone
Which said: "Thou hast defamed the innocent
Daughter of Holy Church. This hast thou done
In royal presence, and yet am I content
To hold my peace!" All in astonishment
And dread of wrath, stunned as if turned to stone
The people stood, save Constance there alone.

Great was the fear and deep-repenting mood
Of those who had believed the accusation
Against Dame Constance, innocent and good,
And by this miracle and revelation
Constance converted, through her mediation,
The king and many another in that place
To Christian faith, thank be to Jesu's grace!

Then was this false knight punished for his lying
By instant death, at Aella's just decree,
And yet had Constance pity for his dying;
And Jesus after this most mercifully
Made Aella wed with all festivity
This holy maid, the fairest to be seen;
And thus has Christ of Constance made a queen.

But who was wroth this wedding rite to see
But Donegild, to tell the story true,
The king's own mother, full of tyranny?
She thought her cursèd heart had burst in two.
This was no thing she wished her son to do –
It seemed dishonor he should celebrate
Marriage with such strange creature for his mate!

To lengthen out this tale with chaff and straw
Is less my liking than to use the corn;
Why tell of all the royalty men saw
Come to this wedding, or what course was borne
First to the board, or who blew fife or horn?
The fruit of every tale should be essayed:
They ate, they drank, they danced, they sang and
played.

They go to bed, as reason is and right,
For though a wife be never so holy a thing,
Still she must take with patience in the night
What may be needful for the pleasuring
Of him that may have wed her with a ring,
And lay her holiness aside a bit
At such a time; for this is only fit.

Soon of a boy-child did the queen conceive;
And Aella put her in a bishop's care,
And in his constable's, for he must leave
For Scotland now, to seek his foemen there;
Now Constance, amiable and mild and fair,
Unto her chamber keeps, in quiet still,
Being long with child, and there awaits Christ's will.

The time is come, a boy is born to her;
They named him Maurice at the christening;
This constable calls forth a messenger,
And writes a letter unto Aella the king,
Telling him of this joyous happening,
And other urgent news that he would say;
He takes the letter, and rides upon his way.

This messenger, his profit slyly seeking,
To the king's mother rideth speedily,
And gives her salutation, fairly speaking:
"Madam, be glad; and in your jollity
Thank God a hundred thousand times," said he;
"My lady queen hath child, without a doubt,
To joy and bliss of all this realm about.

"Lo, sealed here are the letters on this thing,
Which I must bear with all the haste I may;
If ye have something for your son the king,
I am your servant, both by night and day."
Donegild answered: "Not at this time – nay;
But here all night it is my will thou tarry;
To-morrow will I say what thou shalt carry."

This messenger drank deep of ale and wine;
His letters from his box were secretly
Stolen as he lay there sleeping like a swine;
And then they wrought with sly iniquity
Another, counterfeited sinfully,
Unto the king as from his constable
About this matter, as I soon shall tell.

"The queen delivered hath," this letter ran,
"A child so fiendlike and so horrible,
That in the castle even the bravest man
Hath not the heart for any time to dwell;
The mother was an elf, by magic spell
Or charm, or accident cast from the sea,
And everyone abhors her company."

Sad was the king, having this letter read;
But in his sorrow none for counsel took,
But once more wrote, by his own hand, and said:
"Welcome the word of Christ to me, that look
Unto His will, and read now in His book;
Lord, welcome be Thy pleasure and Thy will;
My pleasure lies beneath Thy judgment still.

"Keep ye the child, if it be foul or fair,
Also my wife, till I return and see;
Christ when it pleases Him may send an heir
More to my liking than this first may be."
He seals the letter, weeping secretly;
Which to the messenger is given anew,
And forth he goes – there is no more to do.

O messenger, in drunken stupor gone!
Thy strong breath reeks, thy feeble limbs give way,
Thou must reveal thy secrets everyone;
Thy mind is lost, thou chatterest like a jay;
Thy face is changed, and wears a new array!
In any crowd where drunkenness may reign
There is no counsel hidden – that is plain.

O Donegild, I have no fitting English
To paint thy malice and thy tyranny!
Unto the fiend I must my task relinquish;
Let him describe thy hideous treachery!
Fie, coarse and mannish – Nay, by God, I lie! –
Fie, *fiendish* spirit, for I know too well
Though thou walk here, thy spirit is in hell!

Again this messenger came from the king,
And at the mother's court drew reign once more;
And she was glad, nor failed in anything
To do him pleasure. Drink he got in store,
And food to stretch the girdle that he wore.
And so he slept, and snored thus all the night,
Until the sun rose, and the day shone bright.

His letters, one and all, were stolen again,
And false new letters in this manner made:
"The King commands the constable, on pain
Of hanging, and severest sentence laid,
That Constance leave his realm, nor be delayed –
Let him not fail in this who has the power –
Beyond three days, and a quarter of an hour.

"But in the self-same ship in which he found her,
Set her and her young son and all her gear,
And push her out till open sea surround her,
And charge her that again she come not here."
O Constance, well thy heart may freeze with fear,
And sorrow in thy sleep press hard upon thee
When Donegild hath set this sentence on thee.

This messenger, awaking with the morrow,
Unto the castle took the nearest way;
The constable was filled with deepest sorrow
To read the thing this letter had to say.
"Alas !" he cried, and then, "Alackaday!
Lord Christ, how can this world we suffer in
Endure, with many a man so full of sin?

"O mighty God, if this shall be Thy will,
Since Thou art rightful judge, how can it be
That Thou wilt let the innocent perish still,
And wicked men reign in prosperity?
Alas! good Constance, what a woe for me
That I must die, or else tormentor play
To thee and thine – there is no other way!"

Now wept the young and old in all that place
Because the king that cursèd letter sent,
And Constance, with a pale and death-like face,
On the fourth day down to the vessel went,
And with a brave heart took this punishment
As will of Christ, and kneeled upon the shore;
"Welcome Thy word, O Lord, forevermore!

"He that preserved me from false accusation
While I was dwelling with you on the land,
Will shield me now from harm and defamation
At sea, though how I cannot understand.
All strength he ever had is in His hand;
In Him I trust, and trust His mother dear,
That shall be sail to me, and pilot here.

Her little child lay weeping on her arm;
And kneeling, piteously to him she said:
"Peace, little son, I will not do thee harm;"
And then she drew the kerchief from her head,
And over his little eyes the cloth she spread,
And in her arms she sang him lullabies,
While upward unto heaven she turned her eyes.

"Mary," she said, "O maid and mother bright,
Lost was mankind, it cannot be denied,
Through woman – damned to everlasting night;
And for this cause thy child was crucified.
Thine eyes beheld his pain, and how he died;
Then all comparison is worse than vain
Between thy woe, and woe that men sustain.

"Thou sawest thy child before thine own eyes dying;
And yet my little child still lives, *par fay*!
O thou to whom all suffering souls are crying,
Maiden of fairness, shining star of day,
Glory of women, refuge in dismay,
Pity my child, that, in thy nobleness
Pitiest all the pitiful in distress!

"O little child, alas! what guilt hast thou,
That never wrought a sin, as God can see;
Why will thy ruthless father slay thee now?
O mercy, O dear constable!" cried she,
"And let my little child dwell here with thee;
And if thou dar'st not save him, fearing blame,
Give him one kiss now in his father's name!"

With that she gave a last look at the land.
"Farewell, O pitiless husband," then she cried;
And up she rose, and walketh down the strand
Toward the ship, the people at her side;
And ever she hushed her infant as it cried,
And took her leave; and all devoutly bent
And crossed herself, and to the ship she went.

No doubt there is, this ship was stored with victual
Abundantly, for length of many days,
And all things needful, be they big or little,
She had enough – to God be thanks and praise!
Almighty God the wind and weather raise
To bring her home – no better can I say;
Across the sea she drives upon her way.

Part III

SOON after this, the king comes home from war
Unto his castle, the same of which I told,
And asketh where his wife and baby are.
About his heart this constable went cold,
And all that had occurred he plainly told
As ye have heard – I cannot tell it better –
And showed the king his seal, and showed the letter,

And said, "O lord, these your commandments were
On pain of death; thus surely have I done."
To torture then they put this messenger,
Until he told the places, one by one,
Where he had lain each night. And they begun
By wit and subtle inquiry to guess
Who was the source of all this wickedness.

The hand that wrote the letter thus they show,
And all the venom of this cursèd deed;
But how they worked it out, I do not know.
At length the end was this, as men may read:
That Aella slew his mother, and with speed,
As traitor to her duty. So was killed –
May she be cursed! – this vile old Donegild.

Now Aella in his sorrow night and day
Wept for his wife and child, and mourned them so
No human tongue could half his grief convey;
But now again to Constance will I go,
That drifts upon the sea, in pain and woe,
As Christ ordained, for five long years and more,
Before her ship at length approached a shore.

Beneath a heathen castle's walls at last,
For which no name within my text I find,
The child and Constance by the waves were cast;
Almighty God, that saveth all mankind,
Keep Constance and her child now in thy mind,
That in a heathen land must soon draw breath,
And know, as I shall tell, the fear of death.

Down from the hold come trooping knight and vassal
On Constance and her stranded ship to stare;
But soon at night came stealing from the castle
The steward – God his evil end prepare! –
A thief, and recreant to the faith we swear.
Unto the ship this wretch alone doth go
To be her leman, if she would or no.

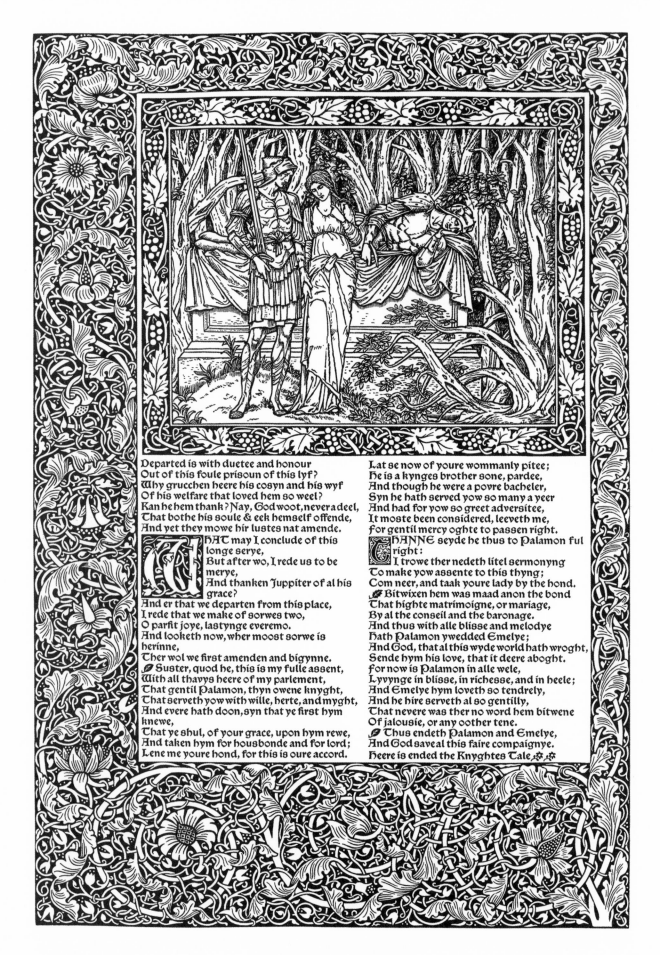

Departed is with duetee and honour
Out of this foule prisoun of this lyf?
Why grucchen heere his cosyn and his wyf
Of his welfare that loved hem so weel?
Kan he hem thank? Nay, God woot, never a deel,
That bothe his soule & eek hemself offende,
And yet they mowe hir lustes nat amende.

WHAT may I conclude of this longe serye,
But after wo, I rede us to be merye,
And thanken Juppiter of al his grace?
And er that we departen from this place,
I rede that we make of sorwes two,
O parfit joye, lastynge everemo.
And looketh now, wher moost sorwe is herinne,
Ther wol we first amenden and bigynne.
Suster, quod he, this is my fulle assent,
With all thavys heere of my parlement,
That gentil Palamon, thyn owene knyght,
That serveth yow with wille, herte, and myght,
And evere hath doon, syn that ye first hym knewe,
That ye shul, of your grace, upon hym rewe,
And taken hym for housbonde and for lord;
Lene me youre hond, for this is oure accord.

Lat se now of youre wommanly pitee;
He is a kynges brother sone, pardee,
And though he were a povre bacheler,
Syn he hath served yow so many a yeer,
And had for yow so greet adversitee,
It moste been considered, leeveth me,
For gentil mercy oghte to passen right.
THANNE seyde he thus to Palamon ful right:
I trowe ther nedeth litel sermonyng
To make yow assente to this thyng;
Com neer, and taak youre lady by the hond.
Bitwixen hem was maad anon the bond
That highte matrimoigne, or mariage,
By al the conseil and the baronage,
And thus with alle blisse and melodye
Hath Palamon ywedded Emelye;
And God, that al this wyde world hath wroght,
Sende hym his love, that it deere aboght.
For now is Palamon in alle wele,
Lyvynge in blisse, in richesse, and in heele;
And Emelye hym loveth so tendrely,
And he hire serveth al so gentilly,
That nevere was ther no word hem bitwene
Of jalousie, or any oother tene.
Thus endeth Palamon and Emelye,
And God save al this faire compaignye.
Heere is ended the Knyghtes Tale.

Plate 8: The Knight's Tale (p. 61)

Then were her woe and danger great indeed;
Her child cried, and with piteous voice cried she,
But holy Mary helped her in her need,
For struggling there with Constance violently,
This thief fell overboard into the sea,
And there he drowned, and all his plot was vain;
So Christ kept Constance pure of any stain.

Foul lust of lechery! Lo, here thine end!
Not only dost thou poison a man's mind,
But wilt his body to corruption send!
The fruit of all thy work and passions blind
Is grief alone; how many a man shall find
That not for any deed, but for the plain
Intent to sin, he shall be shamed or slain.

How could this feeble woman find the might
To save her virtue from this renegade?
O great Goliath, measureless in height,
How could thy length so low in death be laid
By David – young, unarmored, unafraid?
How dared he look upon thy dreadful face?
Well may men see, he did it by God's grace.

Where was it Judith found the bravery
For slaying Holofernes in his tent,
Delivering out of wretched slavery
The people of God? And this is evident –
That just as God the spirit of vigor sent
To save that people in their evil hour,
So came to Constance such a will and power.

Her ship goes plunging through the narrow mouth
Of Ceuta and Gibraltar, driving fast,
Now turning West and now to North and South,
Or East, while day on weary day went past;
Until Christ's blessèd mother planned at last,
In her eternal goodness, how to bring
An end to all her care and suffering.

Now let us cease of Constance for a space,
And of the emperor speak, that got by water
Letters from Syria, which disclosed the place
And manner of the Christians' fearful slaughter,
And of the great dishonor done his daughter
By this vile sultaness, this wicked traitor,
That slew them at the feast, the less and greater.

Because of this the emperor hath sent
His senator, with royal preparation,
And other lords – God knows that many went –
To take high vengeance on the Syrian nation;
They sweep the land with sword and conflagration
For many a day; but done with war and burning,
They thought of Rome, and planned for their
        returning.

This senator embarked for Rome in glory,
Sailing victorious and royally,
And met the very ship, as says the story,
In which Dame Constance sat in misery.
They knew her not, nor how she chanced to be
In such array, for she will make reply
To nothing that they ask her, though she die.

He brought her back to Rome, and to his wife
This woman and her little child he bore,
And with the senator she lived her life;
So can our lady out of woe restore
Constance to peace, and many another more.
A long time she was dwelling in that place,
And wrought at holy works, as was her grace.

The lady of this senator was her aunt,
And yet her niece she could not recognize;
But I will turn again – my time is scant –
To Aella, who bewails his wife with sighs
And bitter tears that often fill his eyes;
And I will leave Dame Constance dwelling there
Beside this senator, and in his care.

Aella, who caused his mother to be slain,
With time had come so deeply to repent
That, if I make my story brief and plain,
He went to Rome, on prayer and penance bent,
And asked the Pope to give him government
In high and low, and Jesus Christ besought
Forgiveness for the wicked deeds he wrought.

The news is quickly flown to Rome before him,
How he will make a pilgrimage, this king;
For men had come to choose his lodgings for him.
The senator, on hearing of this thing,
Rode out to meet him with a following,
As much to show his high magnificence
As to salute a king with reverence.

Aella was fêted by this senator,
And he by him in turn, ye need not doubt;
Each paid the other honor more and more;
So in a day or two it came about
This senator for Aella's house set out
To feast, and with him took, in verity,
The son of Constance in his company.

And some men say that Constance made a prayer
The senator should take him to this feast;
I cannot tell you all that happened there,
But this is true: the child appeared, at least.
At her request, before the dinner ceased,
This boy drew close to Aella in that place,
And stood before him, looking in his face.

And Aella gazed upon him with great wonder,
And to the senator said presently:
"Whose is that fair child that is standing yonder?"
"Now by St. John, I cannot say," said he.
"Mother he hath, but who his sire may be
I know not –" but the talk soon going round,
He told King Aella how the child was found.

"But God knows," said he, as a final word,
"So virtuous a one in all my life
I never saw, nor more of praise have heard
For any worldly woman, maid, or wife;
To sin – No, she would rather plunge a knife
Clean through her breast, I swear, than think to do it;
There is no man alive could bring her to it."

More like to Constance ye could never find
A living thing, than seemed this child to be;
And Aella hath her visage well in mind,
And mused upon the possibility
That the child's mother might indeed be she;
And secretly he sighed, and left the table
With a sick heart as soon as he was able.

"God's faith!" he thought, "my mind is fantasy;
For this by sense and truth is evident:
My wife was lost upon the salty sea."
But afterwards he made this argument:
"How do I know but she was hither sent,
As to my country she was sent before,
By Christ Himself, and from as far a shore?"

And with this hope of wonder running through him,
He seeks the senator that afternoon;
This senator doth every honor to him,
And afterwards he sent for Constance soon.
Less wish she had to dance then than to swoon,
When she perceived the cause of this command;
Upon her feet she scarce had strength to stand.

Fair when they met did Aella give her greeting,
And wept so it was pitiful to see;
For at the very instant of their meeting
He knew beyond a doubt that it was she.
And she stood dumb with grief as any tree,
So fast her heart was shut in her distress
When she remembered all his ruthlessness.

Two times she swooned before his very eyes;
He wept, and pled his innocence piteously:
"God in His shining hall of paradise
So look in mercy on my soul," said he,
"And know me innocent of harm to thee
As Maurice my own son is like thy face;
Else may the devil seize me in this place!"

Long was the pain they knew, and bitter crying,
Before their woeful hearts might find relief;
Most piteous it was to hear them sighing;
Each lamentation multiplied their grief;
I pray you, let my labor now be brief –
I cannot sing their woe until tomorrow,
For I am weary speaking of their sorrow.

But when she knew what ye have known before –
That Aella in her woe had had no share,
They must have kissed a hundred times or more,
And such a gladness fell upon them there
That none hath known a joy that might compare
With what it was – nor any can there be,
Save for the bliss that lasts eternally.

Then, as a balm for all her time of sorrow,
Humbly her husband does she ask and pray
That he would ask the emperor tomorrow
If he would come and dine with them some day;
And asked this too – that Aella in no way –
As he might have regard for her, and love her,
Should give her father any tidings of her.

Some men have said that the boy Maurice went
To take this message at a certain hour;
But Aella, I should think, would not have sent
A child to him that had the sovereign power
Of Christian folk, and was their head and flower;
Better it is that I should tell you here
He went himself, and so it might appear.

This emperor in high nobility
Agreed to come and dine, as Aella prayed him;
And saw this child, and he thought suddenly
About his daughter, as the likeness made him;
Aella then sought his inn, and there arrayed him
With all his skill in raiment fair and good
Against this feast, as it was fit he should.

And on the morrow Aella dressed him fair,
And his wife too, this emperor to meet,
And forth they ride with glad and happy air,
And when she saw her father in the street
She got down, and she fell before his feet:
"Father," she cried, "your daughter Constance
          vanished
Long since, and from your memory is banished;

"I am your daughter Constance – lo, in me
Your child that long ago to Syria went,
And it is I that on the salty sea
Was set alone, and so to death was sent;
Now mercy, father! Let you be content,
And send me now to no more heathen lands,
But thank my kind lord, that before you stands."

Who can describe the piteous joy they know –
These three that meet together as I say?
But to the ending of my tale I go;
I will not lag, for swiftly runs the day;
These happy folk to dinner take their way,
And now at meat enjoy a thousand fold
All joy and bliss that can by tongue be told.

Maurice the child became the emperor
By the Pope's hand, Christian to live and die;
And did the Church great honor evermore,
But I must stop, and pass his story by;
With Constance chiefly doth my story lie;
In olden Roman legends ye may find
Maurice's life – I keep it not in mind.

King Aella, when he saw the fitting day,
With Constance, sweet, and rich in piety,
Came back to England by the shortest way,
And lived in quiet there, and joyously;
But little time, I promise you, can be
Joy of this world, for time abideth never,
But like the tide goes on in change forever.

Who ever lived in such delight one day
That conscience never moved him, or his pride,
Envy, ambition, or some blood affray,
Insult or wrath, or lust unsatisfied?
And so this joy and pleasure might abide –
As all this signifies – this happy life,
But a short time for Aella and his wife.

For death, that takes his toll of high and low,
Before a year had passed, as I should guess,
Called forth King Aella from this world we know,
For which Dame Constance knew a great distress.
Now let us pray that God his spirit bless!

And after this my final word to say
Is, that to Rome Dame Constance took her way.

At Rome again this holy wife doth find her,
And all her friends are there, and whole and sound,
And her adventures now are all behind her,
And once again her father she hath found;
And on her knees she falleth to the ground,
Weeping the tender joy her heart confesses;
A hundred thousand times high God she blesses!

In piety and virtuous alms-giving,
No more to part, their busy lives they spend –
Till death divides them, in this fashion living.
Now fare you well, my tale is at an end;
And Jesus Christ, that in His might can send
Joy after woe, still rule us in His grace,
And keep us all that tarry in this place.

*Here ends the Tale of the Lawyer; and
next follows the Seaman's Prologue.*

The Seaman's Tale

THIS TALE IS another fabliau, rather simpler and more straightforward than the earlier examples. It seems it was originally supposed to have been told by a woman, and may initially have been intended for the Wife of Bath. It offers a new twist on an old tale, in which a trickster cheats a man out of his money and sleeps with his wife. In Chaucer's version, though, the woman is also wily and deceives her husband to her own benefit.

THE SEAMAN'S TALE

*Here the Seaman's
Prologue Begins*

OUR Host upon his stirrups stood up high.
"Good men, attention!" he began to cry;
"That was a profitable tale to hear!
Now by God's bones, sir Parish Priest, come near!
Tell us a tale," he said, "as ye agreed.
For all ye learnèd men, I see indeed,
Know much of profit, by God's dignity!"

    The Parson made him answer: "*Ben'cite!*
What ails the man, so sinfully to swear?"

    Our Host replied: "Ho, Jankin, are ye there?
I smell a Lollard in the wind," said he.
"Good men," our Host cried, "lend an ear to me!
Now by the holy passion of our Lord,
Wait – we shall have a sermon, on my word;
This Lollard here will preach to us a little!"

    "Nay, by my father's soul – no jot nor tittle,"
The Seaman said. "Here shall he do no preaching,
Nor gloze a gospel here, nor fall to teaching.
We all believe in one great God," said he.
"He would begin to sow perplexity,
Or drop his cockle into our clean grain;
And therefore, Host, I warn thee, true and plain,
This jolly fellow shall a story tell!
And I will clink you such a merry bell
That I will waken all this company.
But it shall not be of philosophy,
Nor physics, nor of cunning terms of law;
There is but little Latin in my maw."

Here the Seaman ends his Prologue

Here begins the Seaman's Tale

THERE dwelt a merchant once at St. Denis;
And he was rich, and so was thought to be
Wise also; and his wife was fair to see,
Good company, and fond of revelry,
Which is a thing that causes more expense
Than all the pleasure and experience
That men may find at festivals and dances;
For all such play of talk and countenances
Passes as shadows do upon a wall.
But woe to him that payeth for it all!
The simple husband always has to pay,
To clothe us and to set us rich array,
And, for his honor, do it handsomely;
In which array we dance in jollity.
And if he cannot pay, or to be sure,
Likes not to bear such great expenditure,
Thinking it something gone to waste, and lost –
Then someone else will have to pay the cost,
Or lend us gold, although the risk is bad.

    A worthy house this noble merchant had;
And such great crowds were always gathered there,
Since he was lavish and his wife was fair,
That it was wonder. But attend my story.
Among his guests, of great or little glory,
There was a monk, a fair man and a bold,
And I should guess him thirty winters old,
One who would often visit at that place.
This monk, that was so young and fair of face,
Had such an old acquaintance with this man
(Since first their friendly intercourse began)
That in his house as much at home was he
As it is possible a friend could be.
And since it happened that this worthy man,
And this monk, too, of whom my tale began,
Were born in the same town, the monk had claimed him
As cousin, and as such had always named him;
And he to that had never once said Nay,

But as a bird is glad of dawning day,
So did it fill his heart with a great joyance.
Thus they are knitted in a firm alliance,
And each assured the other of a fast
And tender brotherhood, while life should last.
Sir John was generous in what he spent
Within that house; and always diligent
In giving pleasure, and with gifts the same.
None was forgotten by him when he came –
Not the least page; to all in their degree –
The lord, his wife, and all the company,
He gave, upon his coming, some good thing;
Which made them happy in his visiting
As any bird is when the sun upriseth.
But now no more of this, for it sufficeth.

    It came about upon a certain day
This merchant makes his plans to go his way
Toward the town of Bruges, for there he buys
A certain quantity of merchandise.
Wherefore he soon hath sent a runner on
To Paris, and he prays his cousin John
That he will come to St. Denis, and play
With him and with his wife there for a day
Before he goes to Bruges – it must not fail.

    This noble monk, of whom I tell my tale,
Had always of his abbot a permission –
Being a man of prudent disposition,
And bailiff, to ride out when he might please
And see their barns and spacious granaries;
And soon to St. Denis he rideth on.
Who was so welcome as my lord Sir John,
Our courteous cousin, loved so heartily?
With him he brought a jug of Malvesy,
Another of Vernage, of fine bouquet,
And fowls as well, as always was his way.
So monk and merchant pledge their love anew
With feast and drink and play, a day or two.

    But on the third this merchant as he rises
Considers soberly his enterprises,
And seeks his counting house, this worthy man,
To calculate as clearly as he can

His status for the year – for he would see
How he had used his gold and property,
And if he had a gain to show, or none.
His money bags and ledgers, many a one,
He laid upon the board to read and measure;
Rich were his hoarded savings and his treasure;
So he had shut the door and barred it, too,
To work with his accounts till he was through,
And no one should disturb him for that time.
And thus he sat at work till after prime.

    Sir John had risen some little time ago,
And in the garden sauntered to and fro,
And now hath duly said his office through.

    This good wife quietly came strolling too
Into the yard, where he was softly walking,
And she saluted him, and fell to talking.
A child, her maid, was with her, that was still
Beneath the rod, and pliant to her will,
And thus could easily be ruled or led.
"O cousin mine, O dear Sir John," she said,
"What ails you to be getting up so early?"
"Niece," he replied, "five hours are ample, clearly,
To spend in sleep at night upon a pillow,
Unless it were for some old languid fellow
Such as these wedded men, that make a habit
Of dozing like some poor distracted rabbit
All wearied out by dogs. But by my head,
Dear niece, ye look too pale to-day," he said.
"I think for certainty our worthy man
Hath worked upon you since the night began,
So that ye snatched your sleep in haste," said he.
And with that word he laughed out merrily,
And at his own thought waxed a rosy red.

    This fair young wife began to shake her head,
And answered thus: "Well, God knows all," said she.
"No, cousin, that is not the way with me.
For by that God that gave me soul and life,
In all the realm of France is not a wife
That hath less pleasure in that sorry play.
For I may sing Alas! and Well-a-way!
That I was born, but there is none," said she,

"To whom I dare tell how it stands with me.
And so sometimes I think to leave this land,
Or else to end myself with mine own hand,
So full of fear and trouble is my life!"

    The monk began to stare upon this wife.
"Alas! my niece! Now God forbid," he said,
"That ye, for any sorrow or any dread,
Should harm yourself. But tell me what may grieve
    you,
And I, perhaps, can help you and relieve you,
Or else advise. Therefore unfold to me
All your distress; all shall be secrecy;
For on my breviary I make my oath
That never in my life, for lief or loath,
Will I betray your trust in any way."

    "To you, dear John, the same again I say;
By God and by this breviary I swear,
Though into pieces men my body tear,
That never, though I run the risk of hell,
Will I betray a word of what ye tell;
And not for kinship nor alliance, surely,
But out of love and high affection purely."
Thus sworn, they kissed, and by this compact eased,
Each of them told the other what he pleased.

    "Cousin, if I had time enough," said she,
"As I have not, and here especially,
Then would I tell a legend of my life –
My suffering since I became a wife,
Although it be your cousin I have wed."

    "Now by St. Martin and by God," he said,
"He is no more a cousin unto me
Than is the leaf that hangs on yonder tree!
By St. Denis, I call him that," he swore,
"Only, dear niece, that I may be the more
With you, whom I have loved especially
Above all women, of a certainty!
Upon my very calling do I swear it.
But tell me all your grief while I may share it,
Lest he come down; and quickly then be gone."

    "O my dear love," she said, "O my Sir John,
Fain would I keep this hidden were I stronger;

But it must out – I cannot hold it longer.
My husband is to me the cruellest man
That ever was, since first the world began.
But I, that am his wife, should not be free
To speak to others of our privacy,
Whether a-bed, or any other place.
Nay, God forbid I do it, by His grace!
No wife, I know it well, should take upon her
To speak about her husband but with honor;
Only to you this much I have to say:
God knows he is not worth in any way
More than the value of a fly to me.
But most I hate that he is niggardly.
And women crave six things, as well ye know –
And all like me, for nature shapes us so:
We would have husbands that are wise and bold,
And rich, and open-handed with their gold,
Indulgent to their wives, and fresh in bed for us!
But by that Lord whose sacred blood was shed for us,
Next Sunday, for the cost of such array
As only fits his honor, I must pay
A hundred francs, or I am lost for sure.
Yet I would rather perish than endure
To have my name in scandal tossed about.
And also, if my husband found it out,
I should be lost! So dear Sir John," she said,
"Lend me that sum, I pray, or I am dead!
Sir John, I say, lend me these hundred francs.
By God, I will not fail to give you thanks,
If ye will deign to help me as I pray you.
For on a certain day I will repay you,
And do you all the service that I can,
And pleasure, too – whatever ye may plan;
Or else God give such punishment to me
As France gave Ganelon for his treachery!"

    This monk made answer as I tell you here:
"Now of a truth, my own fair lady dear,
I have such love and pity for you – both,
That here I swear to you, and give my troth,
That when your husband shall to Flanders go,
I will deliver you from all this woe,

For I will bring you then a hundred francs."

  And with that word he caught her by the flanks,
And kissed her often, and embraced her hard.
"And now," he said, "go softly through the yard,
And let us dine as quickly as we may;
My dial shows past prime. Then go your way,
And be as true in this as I shall be."

  "Now God forbid it otherwise," said she,
And off she runs as merry as a pie,
And saw the cooks, and bade them all be spry,
And get the dinner soon. And after that
She went to seek her husband where he sat,
And on his door knocked boldly. He inside
Cried out, "*Qui la*?" "By Peter, I!" she cried.
"What, sire, how long then will ye sit there fasting
And doing sums, and all this ever-lasting
Business with books and bags and other things?
The devil take charge of all such reckonings!
Ye have enough with that which God hath sent.
Let your bags stand, come out, and be content.
Are ye not shamed to have your cousin John
Half slain with fasting while the day runs on?
What! Let us hear a mass and go and dine."

  "Wife," said this man, "thou canst not well divine
The strange affairs I have in preparation.
For of us merchants, may I have salvation!
And by that holy lord men call St. Ive,
Among a dozen, scarcely ten will thrive
Unto old age, through all our change and chance.
Well may we smile and make good countenance,
And take our luck, whatever it may be,
And keep our true estate in secrecy
Until we die; or for relief some day
Start on a pilgrimage; or go away.
And so I have great need to study hard
This curious world, and be upon my guard;
For always in our trading we must fear
Things that with chance or fortune may appear.

  "I go to-morrow early, as I plan,
To Flanders, and as quickly as I can
I will return. Until I come again

Be courteous, I beseech you, to all men,
And keep good watch upon our property,
And rule our household well and honestly.
Thou hast enough of everything, indeed,
That any sober house is like to need;
Food and array, and neither shalt thou lack
Silver to line thy purse till I come back."
And with that word he shut and locked the door,
And down he went, for he would stay no more,
But heard a mass as soon as he was able,
And had his servants quickly lay the table;
And so to eat and drink at once they fell;
The monk was feasted by the merchant well.

  And afterwards, Sir John with gravity
Drew him aside, and speaking privately
Said to him thus: "Now, cousin, I perceive
Ye will be off for Bruges, and when ye leave
God and St. Austin prosper you and guide!
I pray you, though, be prudent as ye ride,
And have a care as well in what ye eat;
Be moderate, especially in this heat.
We need no ceremonious words, we two:
Cousin, farewell! God keep and prosper you!
If there is anything by day or night,
If it is in my power or in my might,
That ye would have me do in any way,
It shall be done, exactly as ye say.

  "One thing before ye go, if it may be,
I would request: will ye not lend to me
A hundred francs, just for a week or more,
For certain cattle I must buy and store
Within a place of ours not far from here?
Would God that it were yours, my cousin dear!
Be sure I will not fail to keep my day –
Not for a thousand francs! But let me pray
Ye pay this gold to me in no man's sight,
For I must buy these beasts this very night.
Farewell, dear cousin, I say, and *grand merci*
For all your trouble and hospitality."

  This noble merchant answered him at once.
"O cousin mine, Sir John," he made response,

"Now certainly this is a small request.
My gold is yours, whenever suits you best,
And like my gold, my goods are for your sharing –
Take what ye like, by God, and be not sparing.

   "But one thing I will mention to you now –
Ye know in trade that money is our plough.
We may have credit while we have a name,
But not to have our gold – it spoils the game.
Therefore repay it when ye can, I say;
I want to please you well in every way."

   These hundred francs he brought forth instantly,
And paid them to Sir John in secrecy;
No person in the world knew of this loan
Except this merchant and Sir John alone.

   They drink, they talk, they wander to and fro,
Until Sir John must to his abbey go.

   And off for Flanders, with the break of day,
This merchant went; his 'prentice showed the way
And rode in merrily to Bruges at last.
And there he labored busily and fast –
Bought, or procured on credit, as it chanced,
But never sat to play at dice, nor danced;
But rather as a merchant, so to say,
He led his life, and there I let him stay.

   On the first Sunday after he was gone,
To St. Denis rode back the monk, Sir John,
All fresh and newly shorn of crown and beard.
And all the house was glad when he appeared;
No boy so small, none of the maids or men,
But they were glad Sir John was come again.
And, to the point directly and with speed,
This buxom wife with good Sir John agreed
That for these hundred francs he should of right
Have her within his arms the live-long night;
And this agreement was performed, indeed.
In mirth all night a jolly life they lead
Until the morning, when he goes his way,
Bidding the household, "Now farewell – good day!"
For none of these, that honor him and love him,
Nor of the townfolk, have suspicion of him.
Off to his abbey then, or where he chose,

He rode – and I will leave him as he goes.

   This merchant, when the market closed at last,
To St. Denis rode homeward gay and fast,
And with his wife made feast and merry cheer.
He tells her, merchandise is now so dear
He must arrange a loan to meet his need,
Being by contract bounden and agreed
For twenty thousand crowns. So in a day
To Paris must this merchant take his way,
And borrow there a sum of francs among
Some friends of his – the rest he brought along.
And first, arriving in the town, he went
To find Sir John, for joy and merriment,
And all because he did so greatly love him,
And not to ask or borrow money of him,
But to learn how he throve in everything,
And tell him all about his trafficking,
As friends will do in meeting one another.
Sir John received and dined him like a brother;
And then this merchant told about his buying,
And how his merchandise, thank God, was lying
All purchased, whole, and in a good condition.
Yet it was needful now for his position
That he should borrow something, he confessed.
Then would his mind be happy, and at rest.

   "I am well pleased," Sir John made answer then,
"To see you home so sound and well again.
And were I rich, as I have hope of heaven,
Ye should have twenty thousand crowns times seven;
For ye so kindly but the other day
Lent me that gold; and as I can and may,
By God and by St. James I thank you for it.
But none the less, to your good wife I bore it.
There on your counter did I pay that gold,
And she, by certain tokens she must hold,
Knows it, as I could tell her … But today,
Asking your leave, I cannot longer stay.
Our abbot shapes his plans to leave the city,
And I must go along – the more the pity –
Give our good dame, my own sweet niece,
      my greeting;

Cousin, farewell, until another meeting!"
    This merchant, being cautious and discreet,
Procures his credit, and is prompt to meet
His bond at Paris, which some Lombards hold;
Into their hands he pays the sum of gold;
And home he goes, merry as a popinjay,
For well he knew he stood in such a way
That he was bound to gain at all events
A thousand francs above his whole expense.

    His wife was ready at the gate to greet him,
For so by habit she would always meet him,
And all that night in mirth and joy they met,
For he was rich and clearly out of debt.
But with the day, this merchant turned anew
And clasped his wife, and often kissed her, too,
And up he go'th, and worketh hard and fast.

    "No more! Ye have enough!" she cried at last,
And wantonly again began to play,
Until at length she heard this merchant say:
"By God, I am a little vexed," said he,
"With you, wife, though I do not like to be.
And know ye why? Because, as I should guess,
Ye have occasioned some unfriendliness
Between my cousin, good Sir John, and me.
Ye should have told me, of a certainty,
That he had paid a hundred francs to you
By ready token. He was angry, too,
Because I chanced to speak to him of credit;
I thought so by his manner when I said it,
Though by that God that rules in heaven as king,
I never meant to ask for anything.
Wife, let it not occur again, I pray,
But always tell me, when I go away,
If thou hast taken something from a debtor,
Lest through thy negligence I know no better,
And ask him for a debt that he has paid."

    This wife was neither flustered nor afraid,
But answered, prompt and bold: "False monk! How
        dare he?
Now I defy and scorn him, by St. Mary!
I care not for his tokens – not a jot!
He brought some money – I deny it not.
Bad luck, I say, upon his monkish snout!
God knows it well, I never had a doubt
It was a gift – made me because of you,
For me to spend, as something only due
In cousinship, and for the pleasant cheer
That he has often had and relished here.
But since I see I stand in such position,
I speak straight to the point, without condition:
Sir, ye have slacker debtors than I be.
For I will pay you well and readily
From day to day, and if ye find I fail –
I am your wife – score it upon my tale,
And when I can, I promise I will pay.
For, by my faith, all for mine own array,
And not a franc for waste or folly went it.
And since so wisely and so well I spent it,
To do you credit – for God's sake, I say,
Be not displeased, but let us laugh and play.
My jolly body is your pledge," she said;
"By God, I will not pay you save in bed!
Forgive me now, my spouse and husband dear;
Come, turn this way, and be of better cheer."

    The merchant saw there was no remedy –
To scold was only acting foolishly;
The thing was done, although he might deplore it.
"Well, wife," he answered, "I forgive thee for it;
But be no more so liberal, on thy life;
Keep our wealth better: this I charge thee, wife."
So ends my tale. I pray God that He send
Tales to suffice us till our lives shall end.

Here ends the Seaman's Tale

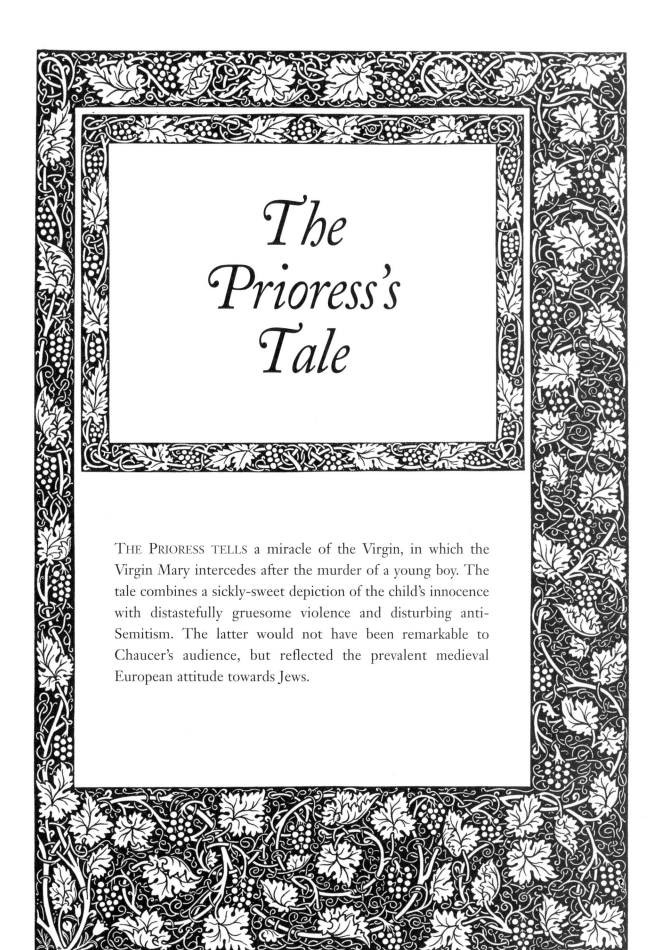

The Prioress's Tale

THE PRIORESS TELLS a miracle of the Virgin, in which the Virgin Mary intercedes after the murder of a young boy. The tale combines a sickly-sweet depiction of the child's innocence with distastefully gruesome violence and disturbing anti-Semitism. The latter would not have been remarkable to Chaucer's audience, but reflected the prevalent medieval European attitude towards Jews.

THE PRIORESS'S TALE

*Behold the merry words of
the Host to the Seaman and
to the lady Prioress*

"WELL said, by *corpus dominus*," cried our Host;
"Long mayst thou sail thy ship along the coast,
Sir noble mariner and noble master!
God give this monk a thousand years' disaster!
Fellows! Aha! Beware of jests like that!
He stuck an ape beneath the merchant's hat,
And, by St. Austin, made his wife one, too!
Bring in no monks to share your house with you!
    "But pass that now, and let us rather see
Who shall tell first, of all this company,
Another tale." And with that word he said,
As courteously as any modest maid:
"Now by your leave, my lady Prioress,
If I should give you no unpleasantness,
Then would I rule that ye were next to tell
A tale for us, if that would please you well.
Now will ye deign to do so, lady dear?"
    "Gladly," said she; and spoke as ye shall hear.

The Prologue of the Prioress's Tale

O LORD our Lord, how far across the ways
Of this wide world Thy name is spread – said she;
Not only is Thy high and precious praise
Performed by men of lofty dignity,
But from the mouths of children hailing Thee
It comes; for they, while suckling at the breast
Thy glory and Thy good sometimes attest.

Therefore in praise of Thee, as best I may
Or can, and of the fair white lily flower
That bore thee, and remained a maid alway,
To tell a tale will I devote my power;
Not that I can increase her honor's dower,
For she is honor, and next her Son, for sure,
The root of goodness and of souls the cure.

O mother-maid! O maiden-mother free!
O bush unburned, burning in Moses' sight,
That down didst draw, with thine humility,
The spirit of God within thee to alight,
Out of whose virtue, when His will made bright
Thine heart, the Father's wisdom came to birth –
Now help my tale to honor thee on earth!

Lady, thy goodness and thy shining glory,
Thy virtue and thy great humility,
No learnèd tongue can ever put in story,
For sometimes, lady, ere we pray to thee,
Thou hast foreseen, in thy benignity,
And by thine intercession gett'st us light
That to thy dear Son guides our feet aright.

O blessèd queen, so feeble is my wit
To utter thy surpassing worthiness,
I cannot well sustain the weight of it,
But like a child twelve months of age or less,
That scarce a word or two can well express,
So am I now; therefore I pray of you,
Guide well my song that I shall say of you.

Here begins the Prioress's Tale

THERE was in Asia, in a city great,
Mid Christian folk, a Jewish colony,
Protected by a lord who ruled that state,
For wicked gain and foulest usury,
Hateful to Christ and to His company;
And through the street all men could walk or ride;
For it was free, with both ends open wide.

A little school of Christian people stood
Down at the farther end, in which there were
Children full many come of Christian blood
That studied in that school from year to year
The kind of lessons taught to students there –
Singing, that is to say, and reading too,
Such things as children in their childhood do.

Among these children was a widow's son –
A little chorister but seven years old;
Who day by day to school had always gone;
And any time he might the form behold
Of Jesu's mother, then, as he was schooled,
It was his custom down to kneel and say
His *Ave Maria* as he went his way.

The widow thus her little son had taught
Always to worship Christ's own mother dear,
Lady of bliss; and nowise he forgot,
For a good child is quick of eye and ear,
But when I call to mind this story here,
St. Nicholas himself appears to me,
For he when young served Christ so reverently.

This little child, while studying among
The others in the school was soon aware
Of *Alma Redemptoris* being sung
By children that were learning anthems there;
And ever he edged as close as he might dare,
And listened to the singing, word and note,
Until he had the whole first verse by rote.

Nothing he knew of what this Latin said,
Being too tender in his years, and young,
But with a comrade on a day he plead
To explain this song to him in his own tongue,
Or tell him wherefore it was being sung;
To know the words and what was meant by these
Eager and oft he prayed him on bare knees.

His comrade was an older boy than he,
And answered thus: "This song, I hear folk say,
Was made about our blissful Lady free,
To hail and give her greeting, and to pray
Her help and grace when we shall pass away.
No more about the matter can I tell;
Singing I learn, but grammar not so well."

"And is this song made then in reverence
Of Christ's dear mother?" cried this innocent;
"Now truly, I will make great diligence
To know it all, ere Christmastide be spent,
Though in my work I suffer punishment
And thrice an hour be beaten for it," said he,
"Yet will I learn it, honoring our Lady."

Each day his fellow taught him privately
While going home, until he knew by rote
The whole, and sang it well and lustily
From word to word, according to the note,
And twice a day the song would pass his throat,
Once when to school and once when home he went;
On Christ's dear mother was his whole intent.

This child passed through the Jewish colony,
As I have said, in going to and fro,
And there full merry would he sing, and cry
"*O Alma Redemptoris!*" for the glow
And sweetness pierced his little spirit so
Of Christ's dear mother, that he could not stay
His song to pray to her along the way.

Satan, that serpent and our ancient foe,
That hath in Jewish heart his hornet's nest,
Swelled up and cried, "Woe, Hebrew people, woe!
In such dishonor do ye dwell at rest?
Must ye endure these accents ye detest,
Hearing this boy that goes with evil cause
To desecrate by song your faith and laws?"

HEERE BIGYNNETH THE PRIORESSES TALE ✿✿✿✿✿

A litel scole of cristen folk ther stood
Doun at the ferther ende, in which ther were
Children an heepe, ycomen of cristen blood,
That lerned in that scole yeer by yere
Swich manere doctrine as men used there,
This is to seyn, to syngen and to rede,
As smale children doon in hire childhede.

AMONG thise children was a wydwes
sone,
A litel clergeon, seven yeer of age,
That day by day to scole was his wone,
And eek also, whereas he saugh thymage
Of Cristes mooder, hadde he in usage,
As hym was taught, to knele adoun and seye
His Ave Marie, as he goth by the weye.

Thus hath this wydwe hir litel sone ytaught
Oure blisful lady, Cristes mooder deere,
To worshipe ay, and he forgate it naught,
For sely child wol alday soone leere;
But ay, whan I remembre on this mateere,
Seint Nicholas stant evere in my presence,
For he so yong to Crist dide reverence.

This litel child, his litel book lernynge,
As he sat in the scole at his prymer,

WAS IN ASYE, IN A GREET CITEE,
Amonges cristene folk, a Jewerye,
Sustened by a lord of that contree
For foule usure, and lucre of vileynye,
Hateful to Crist and to his compaignye;
And thurgh the strete men myghte ride or
wende,
For it was free, and open at eyther ende.

Plate 9: The Prioress's Tale (p. 116)

And from that day the wicked Jews conspired
How they could bring this innocent to die,
And to this end a homicide they hired
That had his dwelling in an alley nigh,
And as the little child was going by,
This Jew leapt forth and seized him fast, and slit
His throat, and cast his body in a pit.

Into a privy they his body threw,
Where all these Jews had purged them commonly,
O cursèd folk, O Herods born anew,
What shall avail you all your infamy?
Murder will out; yea, this is certainty;
And where God's honor lifteth voice to plead,
Loud cries the blood against your cursèd deed!

O martyr wedded to virginity
Now mayst thou sing indeed, and follow on
After the white celestial Lamb (cried she);
Of thee the great evangelist, St. John
In Patmos wrote, saying of martyrs gone
Before the Lamb, and singing songs all new,
That never women in the flesh they knew!

This widow sat awaiting all the night
Her little child, and yet he cometh not;
So when the day drew once again to light,
Her face all pale with fear and heavy thought
At school and every place about she sought,
Until thus much she learned at length – that he
Was seen last in the Jewish colony.

With mother's pity burning in her breast,
She goes as if she had but half her mind,
To every place where there could be the least
Of likelihood her little child to find;
And ever on Christ's mother meek and kind
She called, and so at length, and long distraught,
Among the cursèd Jews her child she sought.

She asketh and she prayeth piteously
Of all the Jews that dwelt within that place,
To tell her if they saw her child go by,
And they said "No." But Jesu, of His grace,
This impulse gave her in a little space:
That for her little son she stood and cried
Where he within the pit lay close beside.

O mighty God, who let'st Thy praise be called
By mouths of innocents, lo, here Thy might!
This gem of chastity, this emerald
Of martyrdom, this blessèd ruby bright,
There where he lay with throat all gashed and white,
"*O Alma Redemptoris*;" clearly sang –
So loud that all the place about him rang.

The Christians on the street, that came and went,
Rushed up with wonder as they heard him sing,
And for the provost hastily they sent;
Who came with no delay or tarrying;
And Christ he praised that is of heaven the King,
And His dear mother, glory of mankind;
And after that, the Jews he bade them bind.

This little child with piteous lamentation
Was lifted up the while he sang his song,
And, honored by a mighty congregation,
Unto the nearest abbey borne along;
There by the bier his mother swooning hung,
And scarcely could the people that were there
This second Rachel from his body tear.

This provost bade at once that every Jew
With torture and by shameful death should die
That anything about this murder knew;
He would not tolerate such iniquity;
Evil to them where evil ought to lie!
So first he had them dragged behind wild horses,
Then hanged: the judgment which the law enforces.

Upon his bier still lay this innocent
By the chief altar while the mass was said
And after that, the priests and abbot went
With all dispatch to burial of the dead;
But sprinkling holy water on his head,
They heard him speak, at sprinkling of the water,
And sing – "*O Alma Redemptoris Mater*!"

Now this good abbot was a holy man,
As all monks are (or leastwise ought to be!)
And so to conjure this young child began,
And said, "Beloved child, I ask of thee,
By virtue of the Holy Trinity,
Tell me the reason why, though it appear
Thy throat is cut, thou singest still so clear."

"My throat is cut, yea, to the very bone,"
Answered this child, "and following nature's way,
Long time ago I should have died and gone,
But Jesu Christ, as find ye books to say,
Wills that His glory be in mind, and stay,
And so for honor of His mother dear,
Still may I sing *O Alma* loud and clear.

"Always I loved Christ's Mother, well of grace,
My wit and knowledge wholly thus applying,
And when they threw my body in that place,
She came to me and spoke as I was lying,
And bade me sing this song when I was dying,
As ye have heard, and, after I had sung,
I thought she laid a grain upon my tongue.

"Therefore I sing, and sing I must indeed,
In honor of that sainted maiden free,

Till from my tongue ye take away the seed;
And afterwards these words she said to me:
'My little child, I will come back for thee
When from thy tongue the grain at last is taken;
Be not dismayed, thou shalt not be forsaken.' "

This holy monk, this abbot, instantly
Drew out the tongue and took away the grain,
And he gave up his spirit quietly;
And when the abbot saw this wonder plain,
His salt tears trickled down his cheeks like rain,
Face down he fell all flat upon the ground,
And lay there still as he with cords were bound.

And all the convent on the pavement lay
Weeping and praising Christ's own mother dear,
And after that they rose and went away
Taking this blessed martyr from his bier
And made for him a tomb of marble clear,
And in it closed his little body sweet;
Where he is now, pray God we all shall meet!

O Hugh of Lincoln, slain in youth also
By cursèd Jews, as all the world knows well,
For it was but a little time ago,
Pray too for us, sinful and changeable,
That God, in whom abounding mercies dwell,
May multiply His grace on us, and thence
Do to His mother Mary reverence!

Here ends the Prioress's Tale

Chaucer's Tale of Sir Thopas

CHAUCER IS PRESENT in the General Prologue as a pilgrim. The Host later comments on the good and virtuous poems that Chaucer has written. Here he presents himself telling a tale, and it is pretty appalling – but enjoyably so. The Tale of Sir Thopas is a parody of a verse romance, told in terrible doggerel. The Host interrupts the tale as it is too awful. Chaucer has said from the start that he was only writing down what others said on the pilgrimage, and by showing his own character in the Tales to be quite exceptionally incompetent he maintains the conceit.

CHAUCER'S TALE OF SIR THOPAS

Behold the merry words of the Host to Chaucer

WHEN she had told this miracle, every man
Was sober – it was wonderful to see –
Until our Host some mirth or jest began,
And for the first time then he looked at me,
And thus – "What man art thou?" demanded he.
"Say now – how many rabbits hast thou found? –
For ever I see thee staring at the ground.

"Approach, came near, and look up pleasantly.
Now, sirs, make way, and give this man a place;
Look ye: he hath a well-shaped waist, like me;
A doll that any woman might embrace –
A pleasant armful, small and fair of face!
But by his look he seems an elfish one,
For of us all the fellow talks with none.

"Tell something now – others have said their say;
Some merry tale – one neither dull nor slow."
"Host," I replied, "be not displeased, I pray;
But this is true – the only tale I know
Is a poor rhyme I learned once long ago."
"Yea, good! For judging by his face," said he,
"We shall hear something rare, it seems to me."

Here begins Chaucer's Tale of Thopas

Now listen, lordings, with delight,
And I will tell you true and right
    Of mirth and merry game;
All of a fair and noble knight,
Alike in tournament and fight;
    Sir Thopas was his name.

In distant country born was he –
In Flanders, far beyond the sea;
    Popering was the place;
His father stood in high degree,
Holding the land in sovereignty,
    As was God's will and grace.

A doughty life Sir Thopas led;
White was his face as wheaten bread,
    His lips as red as rose;
His skin like scarlet dye was red,
And if the simple truth be said,
    He had a comely nose.

His beard and hair, of saffron shade,
Down to his girdle gently swayed;
    Cordovan were his shoes;
His robe was of a fine brocade –
Full many pence for that he paid –
    His stockings came from Bruges.

And he could hunt the fleet wild deer,
And hawk by riverside or mere,
    Holding a goshawk gray;
Good archer was he, as I hear,
And none at wrestling was his peer
    To bear the ram away.

In bower was many a maiden bright
That mourned for love of him by night
    When better were repose;
But he was chaste, no lecherous wight,
And sweet alike of smell and sight
    As is the wild red rose.

And so it happened on a day,
And this is true, as I can say,
   Forth would Sir Thopas ride;
He climbed upon a charger gray,
Within his hand a lance did sway;
   A sword was at his side.

He pricks along through forest fair
Where many a wild beast had its lair,
   Yea, bucks and hares as well;
And north and east as he did bear
He almost met a mishap there
   As I shall straightway tell.

Herbs great and small grew in that dale;
Ginger nor licorice did fail,
   Nor cloves among the rest;
And nutmeg fit to put in ale,
(Whether the draft be new or stale)
   Or lay aside in chest.

Birds sang, I cannot tell you Nay:
The sparrowhawk and popinjay,
   Till it was joy to hear.
The throstle-cock made merry lay,
The wood dove sitting on the spray
   Sang very loud and clear.

When Thopas heard the throstle sing
Love-longing in his heart did spring;
   Like madman off he rides;
His fair steed from the galloping
Sweats like a rag that ye could wring;
   All bloody are his sides.

Thopas was weary too at last,
Over the soft grass pricking fast
   With heart at fiery heat,
And on the ground himself he cast,
To rest his steed; and good repast
   To give him there to eat.

"O holy Mary, *ben'cité*!
What ails this love to fetter me
   And thus in thralldom keep?
By God, all night I dreamed," said he,
"An elf-queen should my sweetheart be,
   Beneath my robe to sleep.

"An elf-queen will I love, indeed;
No woman of an earthly breed
   Were wife for me to take in town;
All other women I forsake,
And to an elf-queen will I make
   My way by dale and down!"

To saddle with alacrity
He climbed – past stile and stone spurred he,
   Seeking this queen to marry;
Till riding long and constantly,
He found in hidden secrecy
   The countryland of Faery so wild;
For in that land would none agree
To ride with him for company –
   No, neither wife nor child.

Until a mighty giant came;
That bore Sir Elephant for name,
   A man of dangerous deed;
"By Termagant," did he exclaim,
"Young knight, spur hence, or I will maim
   And quickly slay thy steed with mace.
Here lives of Faeryland the queen;
With harp and pipe and tambourine
   She dwelleth in this place."

"As I may thrive," replied the knight,
"Tomorrow, armored for the fight,
   I swear to meet with thee;
And *par ma foi*, I hope and swear,
By grace of this good lance I bear,
   To pay thee bitterly; thy head
Or belly, ere the prime of day

This point shall pierce, for if I may
   Here will I leave thee dead!"

Back then Sir Thopas drew full fast,
And stones at him this giant cast
   Out of a cruel staff-sling;
But Thopas safely from that place
Escaped, and all through God's good grace,
   And deft maneuvering.

Still listen, lords, unto my tale –
As merry as any nightingale –
   And I will whisper plain
How, pricking over hill and dale
Lean-shanked Sir Thopas did not fail
   To come to town again.

His merry men commanded he
Great sport to make for him, and glee,
   For he must needs go fight
A giant fierce whose heads were three
For love and joyous ecstasy
   Of one that shone full bright.

"Bring in my minstrels!" rang his call,
"To sing me ballads, one and all,
   While quickly now I arm me;
And let me hear romances fall
Of king and pope and cardinal,
   And love-sick lays to charm me!"

They fetched him wine was sweet and good,
And mead in bowl of maplewood,
   And royal spicery;
And finest gingerbread for food;
And licorice and cummin stood
   All sugared, fair to see.

And next his white flesh he put on,
Of finest woven, clearest lawn,
   Some breeches and a shirt;

A quilted tunic next he wore,
And then a coat of mail, the more
   To keep his heart from hurt.

And over that a hawberk fine,
All wrought by Jews with rich design,
   Of strong plate forged aright;
And then his surcoat did he wear,
As white as any lily fair,
   In which he meant to fight.

His shield was gold, all shining red,
And on it showed a great boar's head
   And a carbuncle as well;
And there he swore, by ale and bread,
The giant now should soon be dead,
   No matter what befell.

Boiled leather were his greaves beneath,
Of ivory his longsword's sheath,
   His helm of latten bright;
His saddle of a fine whale bone;
His bridle like the sunshine shone,
   Or like the fair moonlight.

His spear of finest cypress wrought
Boded hard battles to be fought,
   The head was sharply ground;
His horse was all a dapple gray,
And ambled gently on the way,
   And would not jerk or pound around.
Lo now, my lords, I end a fit;
If ye will any more of it
   To tell it I am bound.

[The Second Fit]

Now hold your tongues, *par charitee*,
Both knight and gracious lady free,
   And listen to my story;
For I will tell of chivalry,

Of ladies sighing grievously,
    Of knights and battles gory.

Men speak of high romance to read –
Horn Child and Ypotis, indeed,
    Of Bevis and Sir Guy;
Of Sir Libeux and Pleyndamour,
And yet Sir Thopas bears the flower
    For royal knighthood high.

His good steed now this knight bestrode,
And forth upon his way he glowed
    Like spark cast from the flame;
Upon his crest he bore a tower,
And in it stuck a lily flower;
    God keep his flesh from shame.

And, being an adventurous knight,
At no house would he deign t'alight,
    But slept within his hood;
His helm was pillow for his head,
And close at hand his charger fed
    On herbage green and good.

Himself drank water of the well,
As did the knight Sir Percivel,
    So worthy neath his garb,
Till on a day –

Here the Host stops Chaucer's Tale of Sir Thopas

The Tale of Melibeus

CHAUCER'S SECOND ATTEMPT at telling a tale to the pilgrims is scarcely better than his first (his tale of Sir Thopas). *The Tale of Melibeus* is a long prose tale, full of allegory, moralizing and cited authorities. It addresses issues of political interest including war and peace, national honour, armament and disarmament, and policy-making. The Host is greatly pleased with the tale; it is difficult to tell now whether a medieval audience would have been equally impressed, but it seems unlikely that it would have been received with much enthusiasm.

THE TALE OF MELIBEUS

"No more of this, sir, for God's dignity!"
Shouted our Landlord, "for thou makest me
So weary with thine utter silliness
That, as I hope that God my soul will bless,
Mine ears are aching with thy worthless drivel!
Cast all such cursèd rhyming to the devil!
Well may men call it doggerel!" cried he.

　"Why so?" said I. "Why wilt thou hinder me,
And stop my tale and let the others go,
Since I recite the best rhyme that I know?"

　"Because, by God, to tell thee in a word,
Thy filthy rhyming is not worth a turd;
I tell thee thou dost waste our time," he swore.
"Sir, in conclusion, thou shalt rhyme no more!
But let us see if thou canst tell instead
Some lay, or something cast in prose," he said,
"That gives us mirth or doctrine in some fashion."

　"Gladly," I made reply, "by God's sweet passion!
I will relate a little thing in prose
That ought to please you well, as I suppose,
Or ye are hard to suit, for certainty.
It is a moral, virtuous homily,
Though various men give various versions, too,
That tell it, as I shall explain to you.
As thus: ye know how each evangelist
That tells us of the pain of Jesus Christ
Writes not in all things as the others do;

Yet none the less, all of their tales are true,
And as to meaning, all of them agree,
Though in detail they show diversity.
For when they tell the piteous pain He bore
Some will write less, and some of them write more –
Matthew, I mean, and Mark and Luke and John –
Yet doubtless in their meaning they are one.
And therefore, sirs, as to my speech I say
That if ye think I veer in any way –
That is, if I shall tell you somewhat more
Of proverbs than ye may have heard before
Included in this little treatise here,
To make what I shall say more strong and clear –
And though the words I use are not the same
As ye have heard, yet put me not in blame
Too much for that, for ye shall find, indeed,
My meaning and the meaning ye may read
Within the treatise whence I draw this merry
Tale that I tell you, will not greatly vary.
And therefore listen well to what I say.
And let me tell my tale in full, I pray.

Here begins Chaucer's Tale of Melibeus

A YOUNG man called Melibeus, powerful and rich, begat upon his wife, named Prudence, a daughter that was called Sophia.

　One day it happened that for his pleasure he went into the fields to roam about. He left his wife and daughter within his house, the doors of which were shut fast. Three of his old enemies saw this, and they set ladders against the walls of the house, and entered it by the windows; and they beat his wife, and wounded his daughter with five mortal wounds in various places – that is, in her feet, hands, ears, nose and mouth; and they left her for dead and went away.

　When Melibeus came back to his house and saw all this evil, he was like a madman; and rent his clothes and began to weep and cry.

　Prudence his wife as much as she dared begged him

to cease his weeping, but at that he cried and lamented the more.

This noble wife Prudence recalled the opinion of Ovid, in his book that is called *The Remedy of Love*, where he says: "He is a fool that restrains a mother from weeping for the death of her child, for a time, until she has wept her fill; and then he should make every effort to comfort her with loving words, and beg her to stop her weeping." For this reason this noble wife Prudence permitted her husband to weep and cry for a certain while; and when she saw that the time was ripe for it, she spoke to him in this fashion. "Alas, my lord," said she, "why do ye play the fool? For indeed it is not fitting for a wise man to sorrow so. Your daughter, with the help of God, shall be healed and escape death. And even were she already dead, ye ought not to destroy yourself. Seneca says: 'The wise man should not be too greatly distressed for the death of his children, but should suffer it in patience, as firmly as he awaits his own death.' "

Melibeus answered her quickly, and said: "What man should stop his weeping that has so great a cause to weep? Jesus Christ, our Lord, Himself wept for the death of Lazarus His friend." Prudence replied: "Indeed, I know well that moderate weeping is not forbidden to one that is sorrowful, among those that are in sorrow; rather it is permitted to him to weep. The apostle Paul writes to the Romans: 'A man shall rejoice with those that have joy, and weep with such as weep.' But though moderate weeping is permitted, excessive weeping is surely forbidden. A temperance in weeping should be considered, according to the wisdom that Seneca teaches us. 'When thy friend is dead,' said he, 'let not thine eyes be too wet with tears, nor too dry; though the tears come to thine eyes, do not let them fall.' And when thou hast lost thy friend, seek diligently for another; there is more wisdom in this than to weep for the friend thou hast lost, for there is no help in that. Therefore, if ye rule yourself with wisdom, put sorrow from your heart. Remember that

Jesus the son of Sirach says: 'If a man is joyous and glad of heart it preserves him and lets him flourish when he is old, but truly a sorrowful heart makes his bones dry.' Also he said this: 'A sorrowful heart slays many a man.' Solomon says: 'Just as moths in the sheep's wool injure the clothes, and small worms a tree, just so does sorrow harm the heart.' And so we should have patience, as much at the death of our children as at the loss of our worldly goods.

"Recall the patience of Job. When he had lost his children and his property, and received and endured many a grievous harm in his body, yet he spoke thus: 'Our Lord hath given it to me, and our Lord hath taken it from me; as our Lord hath willed, so is it done; blessèd be the name of our Lord.' "

To these things Melibeus replied to Prudence his wife: "All thy words," he said, "are true, and profitable also; but indeed my heart is so greatly troubled with this sorrow that I know not what to do." Said Prudence: "Let all thy true friends be called in, and thy wise relatives, and tell them thy situation; and listen to what advice they give thee, and be guided by their opinion. Solomon says: 'Act in all thine affairs by counsel, and thou shalt never repent.' "

Then according to the advice of his wife Prudence, Melibeus summoned a great gathering of people, such as surgeons, physicians, old folk and young, and some of his old enemies that were apparently reconciled, and taken into his love and grace; and there came as well some of his neighbors that gave him respect more in fear than in love, as often happens. There came also a number of subtle flatterers, and wise advocates versed in the law.

And when these people were assembled together, Melibeus in a sorrowful manner explained his situation to them. And from his way of speaking it seemed that he had in his heart a cruel anger, and was ready to wreak vengeance upon his foes, and desired that the war should begin quickly. Yet none the less he asked their advice in the matter. A surgeon, by the permission and agreement of such as were wise, arose and spoke to Melibeus as ye shall hear.

"Sir," he said, "since it is the practice of us surgeons, that we do for every man what we can, when we are retained by him, and do no injury to our patients, and it often happens, that when two men have wounded each other, one surgeon heals both of them – therefore it does not accord with our art to promote war, or to support factions. But in truth, as to the healing of your daughter, though she is so dangerously wounded, we shall work diligently from day to night, so that by the grace of God, she shall be sound and whole as soon as possible." The physicians answered Melibeus almost in the same manner, except that they said a few words more – "that, just as sicknesses are cured by their opposites, so shall men cure strife with vengeance." His neighbors, full of envy, and his feigned friends that seemed reconciled to him, made a pretense of weeping, and much aggravated and made worse this matter, by greatly praising Melibeus for his might, his power, his wealth, and his friends; and by disparaging the power of his adversaries. They said plainly that he should revenge himself upon his foes at once, and begin a war with them.

Then there arose an advocate that was wise, with the permission and by the advice of others that were wise, and said: "Lordings, the cause for which we are gathered in this place is a thing most grave, and an important matter. This is so because of the wrong and wickedness that has been done, and also because of the great losses that in time to come may possibly be suffered on this account; and also by reason of the great wealth and power of both the parties. And for these reasons it would be great peril to err in this affair. Therefore, Melibeus, this is our opinion: we counsel you above all things that for the present ye be diligent in keeping your person, in such a way that ye shall lack neither spy nor sentinel to save your body. And after that, we advise that ye set a sufficient garrison in your house, so that it may protect your body as well as your house. But indeed, to begin a war, or suddenly to take vengeance, we cannot judge that it would be expedient in so short a time. Therefore we ask space and leisure to deliberate before we judge finally as to that. For the common proverb runs: 'He that judges quickly, quickly repents.' And also, men say that a judge is wise that quickly informs himself about a matter, but makes his decision at leisure. For although all delay is annoying, nevertheless it is not to be scorned in the rendering of a judgment, when it is sufficient and reasonable, nor in taking vengeance. And that our Lord Jesus Christ showed us by His example. For when the woman that was taken in adultery was brought before Him, to ask Him what should be done with her, although He knew well Himself what He would answer, yet He would not answer suddenly, but wished to deliberate; and He wrote twice upon the ground. And for this reason we ask time for deliberation; and we will then, by the grace of God, advise thee the thing that will be profitable."

And then the young people sprang up quickly, and the greater part of the crowd that scorned the wise old men. And they began to make a clamor, and said that just as men should strike while the iron is hot, so they should right their wrongs while they were fresh and new. And with a loud voice they cried, "War! War!"

Then one of these old wise men arose, and signed with his hand that they should be still and give him a hearing. "Lordings," said he, "there is many a man that cries 'War! War!' that knows little what war means. War, at its beginning, has an entry-way so great, that everyone may enter it that will, and easily find war. But in truth, the result that shall ensue is not easy to know. For indeed, when war is once begun, there is many a child still unborn that shall die young because of that war, or else live in sorrow and die in wretchedness. And therefore, before any war is begun, men should deliberate and advise much." And when this old man began to enforce his utterance by reasons, almost all of those there began to rise to break up his speech, and told him often to shorten his words. For truly, he that preaches to those that do not wish to hear his words, annoys them with his sermon. For Jesus the son of Sirach says that "music is an annoying thing to weeping" – that is, it is of as much use for one to speak to those whom his speech annoys, as to sing to a man that weeps. And when this wise man saw that he lacked an audience, he sat down again, shamed. For Solomon says: "Where thou canst not get a hearing, do not insist on speaking." "I see well," said this wise man, "that the common proverb is truth; that 'good advice fails where there is most need.' "

Yet there were many that in private advised Melibeus to a certain effect, and said the opposite in public.

When Melibeus saw that the greater part of his counsellors agreed that he should make war, he at once agreed to their advice, and approved their opinion. Then Dame Prudence, when she saw how her husband prepared to avenge himself upon his foes, and begin war, humbly said these words to him, when she saw her time: "My lord, I beseech you as earnestly as I dare and can, go not too fast; by all the services that give me a right to be heard. For Petrus Alphonsus says: 'Whoever does to another good or harm, be not in haste to repay it; for in this way thy friend shall safely abide, while thine enemy shall live the longer in fear.' The proverb says: 'He makes haste well that can wisely wait,' and in wicked haste lies no profit."

Melibeus replied to his wife Prudence: "I do not propose to act by thine advice, for many causes and reasons. For then every man would hold me a fool; that is to say, if by thy counsel I should change things that have been ordained and affirmed by so many wise counsellors. In the second place, I say that all women are wicked, and none among them good. For, 'Among a thousand men,' says Solomon, 'I found one good man; but truly, among all women I never found a good one.' And again, if I should be governed by thine advice, it would seem that I had given thee the mastery over me; and God forbid that it should be so. For Jesus the son of Sirach says: 'If a wife have the mastery, she is in opposition to her husband.' And Solomon says: 'Never in thy life, neither to thy wife, nor to thy child, nor to thy friend, give anyone power over thee. For it is better that thy children ask of thee things that are needful for them, than that thou see thyself in the hands of thy children.' And also, if I go by thine advice, of a truth though my counselling must often be secret, until the time comes when it must be known, this cannot be. For it is written that 'the gossipping of women can conceal only things that they do not know.' Furthermore, the philosopher says: 'In bad advice women vanquish men,' and for these reasons I ought not to follow your advice."

When Dame Prudence, pleasantly and with great patience, had heard all her husband wished to say, then she asked leave to speak, and answered in this manner. "My lord," said she, "as to your first reason, surely it may easily be answered. For I say that it is no folly to change a decision when the thing in question is changed, or when it seems otherwise than it seemed before. And moreover I say, that though ye may have sworn and pledged yourself to an undertaking, and nevertheless ye fail, for just cause, to carry it out, men should not therefore say that ye are a liar, or forsworn. For the Book says: 'The wise man suffers no loss when he turns his heart to something better.' And although your enterprise may be decided upon and ordained by a great multitude of people, yet ye need not carry out that decision unless it may please you. For the truth and profit of things are found rather in a few that are wise and full of reason, than in a great multitude, where every man cries out and jabbers what may please him. Indeed, such a multitude is not a seemly thing. As to the second reason, when ye say that 'all women are bad;' saving your grace, in speaking thus ye despise all women; and 'he that despises all, displeases all,' as the Book says. And Seneca declares that 'whoever desires wisdom, shall disparage no man; but he shall gladly teach what knowledge he knows, without presumption

WITH torment, and with shameful deeth echon,
This provost dooth these Jewes for to sterve
That of this mordre wiste, and that anon;
He nolde no swich cursednesse observe,
Yvele shal have, that yvele wol deserve,
Therfore with wilde hors he dide hem drawe,
And after that he heng hem, by the lawe.

UPON his beere ay lith this innocent
Biforn the chief auter, whil masse laste,
And after that, the abbot with his covent
Han sped hem for to burien hym ful faste;
And whan they hooly water on hym caste,
Yet spak this child whan spreynd was hooly water,
And song, O Alma redemptoris mater!

This abbot, which that was an hooly man,
As monkes been, or elles oghten be,
This yonge child to conjure he bigan,
And seyde, O deere child, I halse thee,
In vertu of the hooly Trinitee,
Tel me what is thy cause for to synge,
Sith that thy throte is kut, to my semynge?

My throte is kut unto my nekke boon,
Seyde this child, and, as by wey of kynde,
I sholde have deyed, ye, longe tyme agon;
But Jhesu Crist, as ye in bookes fynde,
Wil that his glorie laste and be in mynde,
And, for the worship of his mooder deere,
Yet may I synge O Alma, loude and cleere.

This welle of mercy, Cristes mooder sweete,
I loved alwey, as after my konnynge,
And whan that I my lyf sholde forlete,
To me she cam, and bad me for to synge
This anthem verraily in my deyynge,
As ye han herd, and whan that I hadde songe,
Me thoughte she leyde a greyn upon my tonge:

Wherfore I synge, and synge I moot certeyn
In honour of that blisful mayden free,
Til fro my tonge oftaken is the greyn;
And afterward thus seyde she to me,
My litel child, now wol I fecche thee
Whan that the greyn is fro thy tonge ytake;
Be nat agast, I wol thee nat forsake.

THIS hooly monk, this abbot, hym meene I,
His tonge outcaughte, and took awey the greyn,

Plate 10: The Prioress's Tale (p. 120)

or pride. And such things as he does not know, he shall not be ashamed to learn them, or ask about them from those of less importance than himself.' And sir, that there has been many a good woman may easily be proved. For truly, sir, our Lord Jesus Christ would never have descended to be born of a woman if all women had been wicked. And later, because of the great goodness that lies in women, our Lord Jesus Christ, when He was risen from death to life, appeared rather to a woman than to his apostles. And though Solomon says that 'he never found a good woman,' it does not therefore follow that all women are bad. For though he never found a good woman, many another man has found many a woman very good and true. Or else perhaps the meaning of Solomon was this: that, as to supreme goodness, he found no woman good; that is to say, that there is no person that has supreme goodness save God alone, as He Himself records in his gospel. For there is no creature so good that he does not lack something of the perfection of God, that is his creator. Your third reason is this: ye say that 'if ye follow my advice, it will seem that ye have given me the mastery and lordship over your person.' Sir, saving your grace, it is not so. For if it were so – that no man should be advised except by those that had lordship and mastery over his person – men would not be counselled so often. For truly, the man that asks advice regarding a purpose has none the less a free choice whether he will act by that advice or not. And as to your fourth reason, when ye say that 'the gossipping of women can only conceal things that they do not know,' as one would say, 'A woman cannot hide what she knows;' sir, these words apply to women that are babblers and wicked. Of such women, men say that 'three things drive a man out of his house – that is to say, smoke, the dripping of rain, and wicked wives.' And of such women Solomon says, 'It is better to dwell in a desert, than with a clamoring woman.' And, sir, by your leave, I am not of that kind; for ye have often tested my silence and my patience, and also how well I can hide and conceal what should be secret. And indeed, as to your fifth reason, when ye say that 'in bad advice women vanquish men,' God knows, that reason does not apply in this case. For understand this now – ye ask advice to do wickedness; and if ye seek to do wickedness, and your wife restrains this wicked purpose, and overcomes you by reason and good counsel, your wife should of a truth be praised rather than blamed. Thus should ye interpret the philosopher that says, 'in bad advice women vanquish their husbands.' And as to your blaming all women and their reasoning, I shall show you by many examples that many a woman has been good, and is today; and that their advice has been wholesome and profitable. Also some men have said, that 'the advice of women is either too dear, or else is of too little value.' Yet though many a woman is evil, and her counsel vile and nothing worth, yet men have found many a good woman, and discreet and wise in counsel. Lo, Jacob – that by the advice of his mother Rebecca won the blessing of his father and the lordship over all his brothers. Judith, by her good counsel, delivered the city of Bethulia, in which she dwelt, from the hands of Holofernes, who had besieged it and would have destroyed it entirely. Abigail delivered Nabal her husband from David the king, who would have slain him, and appeased the anger of the king by her wit and her good advice. Esther by her good counsel greatly advanced the condition of the people of God during the reign of Ahasuerus the king. And men can tell the same virtue in good counselling of many a good woman. And moreover, when our Lord had created Adam our first father, he said thus: 'It is not good that the man should be alone; let us make him an helpmeet for him, like to himself.' Here ye may see, that if women were not good, and their counsels good and profitable, our Lord God of heaven would never have wrought them, nor called them the help of man, but rather the confusion of man. And a scholar once said in two verses: 'What is better than gold? Jasper. What is better than jasper?

Wisdom. What is better than wisdom? Woman. And what is better than a good woman? Nothing.' And sir, by many other reasons ye can see that many women are good, and their advice good and profitable. And therefore, sir, if ye will put trust in my advice, I will restore your daughter to you whole and sound. And also, I will so act for you, that ye shall have honor in this matter."

When Melibeus had heard the words of his wife Prudence, he spoke thus: "I see well that the word of Solomon is truth. He says, that 'words that are spoken discreetly, with consideration, are honeycombs; for they give sweetness to the soul and wholesomeness to the body.' And, wife, because of thy sweet words, and also because I have assayed and proved thy great wisdom and truth, I will be governed by thine advice in all things."

"Now, sir," said Dame Prudence, "since ye deign to be governed by my counsel, I will inform you how ye shall govern yourself in choosing your advisers. Ye shall first, in all your acts, humbly beseech high God that He will be your counsellor, and conduct yourself in such a manner that He will give you counsel and comfort, as Tobias taught his son. 'At all times thou shalt bless God, and pray Him to direct thy ways;' and see that all thine advice is drawn from Him forever more. Saint James says also: 'If any of you have need of wisdom, ask it of God.' And then afterwards ye shall take counsel of yourself, and examine well your thoughts, seeking the thing that seems most to your profit. And then ye shall drive from your heart three things that are hostile to good counsel – that is to say, anger, covetousness, and haste.

"First, he that asks advice of himself must certainly be without anger, for many reasons. The first is this: He that has great anger and wrath within him always thinks that he can do that which he cannot do. And secondly, he that is wrathful and angry, cannot judge well; and he that cannot judge well cannot well advise. The third is this: that 'he that is wrathful and angry,' as

Seneca says, 'cannot speak without giving blame,' and with his vicious words he stirs up other men to anger and wrath. And also, sir, ye must drive covetousness from your heart. For the apostle says that 'covetousness is the root of all evils.' And trust well that a covetous man can judge or think only to effect his covetous ends; and certainly that can never be accomplished, for the greater store of wealth that he has, the more he desires. And, sir, ye must also drive haste from your heart, for indeed, ye cannot approve as best a sudden thought that falls into your heart, but ye must rather consider it often. For as ye have heard before, the common proverb is this – that 'he that decides quickly repents quickly.'

"Sir, ye will not always be in the same state of mind; for in truth, a thing that sometimes seems good to you to do, at another time may seem the opposite.

"When ye have advised with yourself, and have decided through good deliberation upon the thing that seems best to you, then I advise you that ye keep it secret. Betray your counsel to no person, unless ye know surely that, by revealing it, ye shall better your condition. For Jesus the son of Sirach says: 'Neither to thy foe nor to thy friend reveal thy secrets nor thy folly; for they will give thee hearing and attention and approval in thy presence, and scorn thee in thine absence.' Another writer says that 'thou canst scarcely find any person that can keep counsel secret.' The Book says: 'While thou keepest thy counsel in thine heart, thou keepest it in thy prison; and when thou dost betray thy counsel to any man, he holds thee in his snare.' And therefore it is better for thee to hide thy counsel in thine heart, rather than to pray him to whom thou hast revealed it that he will keep it close and silent. For Seneca says: 'If thou canst not keep thine own counsel, how shalt thou dare to beg another to keep it secret?' But none the less, if thou thinkest surely that by revealing thy counsel to someone thy condition shall thereby be improved, then shalt thou tell it to him in this manner. First, thou shalt in no way show by thine appearance whether peace or war is more pleasing to thee, or this or that, nor show him thy desire nor thine intention. For trust well that in general these counsellors are flatterers – that is, the counsellors of great lords. For they seek always to speak pleasant words, inclining to the lord's desire, rather than words which are true and profitable. And therefore men say: 'The rich man seldom gets good counsel unless he gets it from himself.' And after that, thou shalt consider thy friends and thine enemies. And with regard to thy friends, thou shalt consider which of them are most faithful and wise, and oldest, and most respected for their advice. And of them thou shalt ask thine advice, as the case requires.

"I say that first ye shall call to your confidence those of your friends that are true. For Solomon says that 'just as the heart of a man delights in a taste that is sweet, so does the advice of true friends give sweetness to the soul.' He says also: 'Nothing can compare with a true friend.' For truly, neither gold nor silver is so valuable as the good will of a true friend. And again he says that 'a true friend is a strong defense; whoever finds it, finds indeed a great treasure.' Then ye shall consider also if your true friends are discreet and wise. For the Book says: 'Always ask thine advice of those that are wise.' And for that same reason ye shall call to counsel, among your friends that are of fitting years, such as have spoken on and are expert in many matters, and have been admired for their advice. For the Book says: 'In old men is the wisdom, and in long experience the prudence.' And Tully says that 'great things are not accomplished by strength, nor by dexterity of the body, but by good advice, by the authority of men, and by knowledge; and these three things are not enfeebled by age, but indeed increase and grow stronger day by day.' And then ye shall keep this for a general rule. First shall ye call to counsel a few of your particular friends, for Solomon says: 'Many friends thou hast, but from a thousand choose one to be thy counsellor.' For although at first thou tell thy counsel to a few, thou canst afterward tell it to more people, if there is need. But look always that thy counsellors have the three qualities that I have mentioned before; that is to say, that they are true, wise, and of long experience. And act not always in every emergency by the advice of one adviser only, for sometimes it is good to be counselled by many. For Solomon says: 'Security lies in having many counsellors.'

"Now since I have told you by which persons ye should be counselled, now I will teach you what advice ye should avoid. First, ye shall reject the advice of fools, for Solomon says: 'Take no advice from a fool, for he can only advise after his own desire and liking.' The Book says that 'the character of a fool is this: he easily believes harm of every man, and easily believes all good of himself.' Ye shall also shun the advice of all flatterers, such as seek rather to praise you by flattery than to tell you the truth.

"Concerning this Tully says: 'Among all the ills attending friendship, the greatest is flattery.' And therefore there is greater need that thou avoid and fear flatterers than any others. The Book says: 'Thou shalt rather fear and flee from the sweet words of those that praise flatteringly, than from the sharp words of a friend that tells thee the truth.' Solomon says that 'the words of a flatterer are a snare with which to catch those that are innocent.' And Cato says: 'Be well advised, and avoid the words of sweetness and pleasure.' And in like way thou shalt reject the advice of thine old enemies that are reconciled. The Book says that 'no man returns safely into the grace of his old enemy.' And Æsop says: 'Trust not to those with whom thou hast sometime been at war or enmity, neither tell them thy counsel.' And Seneca tells the reason for this. 'It cannot be,' he says, 'that where great fire has long endured there will not be some breath of heat.' And therefore Solomon says: 'In thine old enemy trust never.' For surely, though thine enemy may be reconciled and make a show of humility, and bow to thee with his head, never trust him. For indeed he shows that feigned humility more for his profit than for any love of thy person, for he thinks that by such a false countenance he will gain the victory over thee, that he could not win by strife or war. And Peter Alphonsus says: 'Take not the companionship of thine old enemies; for if thou do them good, they will pervert it into wickedness.' And again, thou must avoid the advice of those that are thy servants, and have great reverence for thee; for perhaps they will advise more in fear than in love. And therefore a philosopher speaks in this manner: 'There is no person perfectly true to one that he too greatly dreads.' And Tully says: 'There is no emperor has a power so great that it can long endure, unless he has more love from his people than fear.' Thou shalt also avoid the advice of drunken men, for they can hold no confidences. For Solomon says: 'There is no privacy where drunkenness reigns.' Ye shall also be suspicious of the advice of such people as advise you one thing privately, and advise another in public. For Cassiodorus says that 'it is a kind of trick to hinder you, when one pretends to do a thing openly and works the opposite in secret.' Thou shalt also be suspicious of the advice of wicked men. For the Book says: 'The advice of wicked ones is always full of fraud.' And David says: 'Happy is that man who has not followed the counsel of evil folk.' Thou shalt also shun the advice of the young, for they are not yet ripe in counsel.

"Now, sir, since I have shown you from what people ye should take advice, and those whose counsel ye should follow, I will now teach you how ye shall examine advice, after the doctrine of Tully. In the examining of your counsellor, ye shall consider many things. First of all, thou shalt make certain that in the thing thou wilt undertake, and concerning which thou wilt have advice, that truth shall be said and heeded; that is to say, tell thy tale truly. For he that speaks falsely cannot be well advised as to his situation. And after this, thou shalt consider the things said by thine advisers that agree with what thou hast a purpose to do, if there is reason in them. And also, thou shalt consider

if thy power can attain to it, and if the greater and better part of thy counsellors agree to that, or no. Then thou shalt reflect as to what thing will follow from that advice, as hate, peace, war, profit, or harm, and many other things. And in all these things thou shalt choose the best, and reject all other things. Then shalt thou inquire from what root the substance of thine advice springs, and what fruit it may conceive and bring forth. Thou shalt also consider all these causes – from what they spring. And when thou hast examined thy counsel as I have said, and which part is the better and more profitable, and hast had it approved by many wise men and old, then shalt thou consider, if thou canst execute it and get from it a good result. For indeed, it is not reason that any man should begin a thing, unless he can carry it through as he should. Nor should any man take upon himself so heavy a burden that he cannot bear it. For the proverb says: 'He that takes too much can hold little.' And Cato says: 'Attempt what thou hast power to do, lest the effort try thee so sorely that it behooves thee to abandon what thou hast begun.' And if thou art in doubt as to whether thou canst perform a thing or no, choose rather to endure than to begin. And Peter Alphonsus says: 'If thou hast power to do something of which thou must repent, it is better to say "Nay" than "Yea,"' that is to say, that it is better for thee to hold thy tongue, than to speak. Then thou canst understand by stronger reason, that if thou hast power to do something of which thou shalt repent, it is better that thou wait rather than begin. Well do they say, that forbid every man to attempt anything of which he doubts his ability to do it. And afterwards, when ye have examined your advice as I have said before, and know well that ye can carry out your undertaking, stand to it resolutely then until it be completed.

"Now it is reasonable, and the proper time, that I show you when and why ye can change your decision without reproach. Truly, a man can change his purpose and his decision if the cause for it ceases to exist, or if a new cause should develop. For the law says that 'for things that have newly occurred new advice is fitting.' And Seneca says: 'If thy decision come to the ear of thine enemy, change thy decision.' Thou mayst also change what thou hast determined if thou discover that, by reason or error, or some other cause, injury or damage will come of it. Also, if thy decision is dishonest, or comes from a dishonest source, change it. For the laws say that 'all commands that are dishonest have no value.' And also, change it if it should be impossible, or can not well be carried out or followed.

"And take this for a general rule, that every decision that is affirmed so strongly that it cannot be changed, by any circumstances that may arise, I say that such a decision is wicked."

This Melibeus, when he had heard the teaching of his wife Prudence, answered in this manner. "Dame," said he, "as yet, up to this time, ye have taught me well and suitably how in general I shall act in choosing and rejecting of my counsellors. But I would be glad if ye would condescend to tell me in particular how ye like, or how appear to you, the counsellors that we have made choice of in our present need."

"My lord," said she, "I beseech you in all humbleness, that ye will not reply willfully to my reasons, nor be disturbed in heart though I may say what shall displease you.

"For God knows well that, as to my purpose, I say it for your best interest, and for your honor and your profit, too. And indeed, I hope that your goodness will receive it with patience. Trust me well," said she, "that your decision in this instance should not, to speak properly, be called a decision; but rather a gesture or motion of folly; in which ye have erred in many different ways.

"First and foremost, ye have erred in assembling your advisers. For ye should first have called a few people to your counsel, and later, ye might have lain the matter before more, if there had been need. But indeed, ye called suddenly to your advisement a great multitude of people, very changeable and disagreeable to hear.

Also, ye have erred, in that when ye should have called into counsel your true friends, old and wise, ye called strange people, and young folk, false flatterers, and enemies reconciled to you, and such as give you reverence without love. And again ye have erred, for ye brought to your deliberations anger, covetousness, and haste, three things which are hostile to all honest and profitable deliberation.

"These three things ye destroyed and eradicated neither in yourself nor in your advisers, as ye should have done. Ye have erred again, for ye showed your advisers your wish and inclination to make war at once, and take vengeance. They perceived from your words how ye were inclined. And therefore they counselled you after your desire rather than to your profit. Ye have erred also, for it was evident that it satisfied you to be advised by these advisers only, and with little advice; while in so great and high a need, more advisers were required, and more deliberation to perform your undertaking. Again ye have erred, for ye did not examine your decision in the aforesaid manner, nor in such due fashion as the case demands. Ye have erred also, for ye made no distinction between your advisers; that is to say, between your true friends and your false counsellors. Nor have ye learned the wish of your true friends, old and wise; but ye cast all their words into a hodgepodge, and turned your heart to the larger part and the greater number, and were pleased to consider their opinion. And since ye know well that men will always find a greater number of fools than wise men; for that reason in the advice offered at gatherings and multitudes of people, where men take more regard for the number than the wisdom of persons, ye can see well that the fools have the mastery." Melibeus answered again and said: "I grant freely that I have erred; but since thou hast told me before that he is not to blame that changes his advisers in certain cases and for just causes, I am ready to change my advisers just as thou wilt suggest. The prophet says that 'to do sin is human but indeed to persevere long in sin is the work of the devil.' "

To this opinion Dame Prudence answered soon and said: "Examine," said she, "your advice and let us see which of them spoke most reasonably and gave you the best counsel, and inasmuch as examination is necessary, let us begin with the surgeons and with the physicians, that were the first to speak in this affair. I tell you that the surgeons and physicians spoke to you discreetly in their conference, as they should; and in their speech they said wisely, that it was the part of their profession to do honor and profit to every person and to injure none. And they said that according to their art they made every effort for the cure of those to whom they gave their supervision. And, sir, just as they spoke wisely and discreetly, so I advise that they be highly and nobly rewarded for their noble speech; and also because they will give the more attentive care in the curing of your dear daughter. For although they are your friends ye should not, on that account, permit them to serve you for nothing; but ye ought rather to reward them and show them your generosity. And concerning the opinion which the physicians gave in this case, that is to say that in sickness one evil is overcome by another I would be glad to know how ye understand that sentiment and what is your opinion." "Truly," said Melibeus, "I understand it in this way: that, just as they have done me an injury so I should do them another. For just as they have revenged themselves on me and done me wrong, just so I shall revenge myself upon them and do them wrong; and then I will have cured one evil by another."

"Lo! Lo!" said Dame Prudence, "how easily is every man inclined to his own desire and to his own pleasure! Truly," said she, "the words of the physicians should not have been understood in this sense. For, indeed, wickedness is not the opposite of wickedness, nor vengeance of vengeance, nor wrong of wrong, but rather they are alike, and therefore one vengeance is not healed by another vengeance nor one wrong by another wrong, but each of them increases and aggravates the other. But, in truth, the words of the physicians should have been understood in this manner: that good and wickedness are two opposites, and peace and war, vengeance and patience, discord and harmony, and many other things. And, indeed, wickedness shall be healed by goodness, discord by harmony, war by peace, and so forth as to other things. And Saint Paul the Apostle gives his agreement to this in many places. He says: 'Give not injury for injury, nor wicked words for wicked words; but do well to him that does thee harm and bless him that speaks evil to thee.' And in many other places he admonishes us to peace and harmony. But now I will speak to you of the counsel which was given to you by the men of law and the wise folk that said all of one accord as ye have heard before: that, above all things ye should make every effort to protect your person and fortify your house. And they said also, that in such a case ye ought to work carefully and with great deliberation. And, sir, as to the first point that touches the keeping of your person; ye shall understand that he that hath war at hand shall ever more meekly and devoutly pray above all things, that Jesus Christ of His great mercy will keep him in His protection, and be his sovereign help in his need. For, indeed, in this world there is no person that can be advised or preserved sufficiently without the help of our Lord Jesus Christ. To this opinion the Prophet David agrees. He says: 'If God does not keep the city, he that guards it stays awake in vain.' Now, sir, ye shall accordingly commit the keeping of your person to your true friends that are proved and known; and of them shall ye ask help to keep your person. For Cato says: 'If thou hast need of help, ask it of thy friends; for there is none that is so good a physician as thy true friend.' And after this, then shall ye avoid all strange people, and liars also, and be suspicious always when in their company. For Peter Alphonsus says: 'Do not take up company along the way with a strange man, unless it be that thou hast known him in a former time. And if he should by accident fall into thy company without thy

THE TALE OF MELIBEUS

consent, then inquire as subtly as thou canst, of his habits and his previous life, and speak in a feigned manner as to thy journey; say that thou goest where thou wilt not go; and if he bears a spear, keep on his right side, and if he bears a sword, keep on his left.' And after this, then, shall ye wisely keep from all such people, as I have said before, and reject them and their advice. And then ye shall protect yourself in such manner that in any presumption of your strength ye shall not despise or account as so little the power of your adversary that ye forego the protection of your person in your presumption; for every wise man is fearful of his enemy. And Solomon says: 'Happy is he that is fearful of all; for, in truth, he that through the boldness of his heart and his confidence in himself has too great presumption, him shall evil befall.' Then ye shall always be on your guard against ambushes and all kinds of spies. For Seneca says: 'The wise man that is in fear of evil avoids evil; nor does he fall into dangers who avoids them.' And although it may seem that thou art in a safe place, yet thou shalt always try to protect thy person; that is to say, to be careful in guarding thy person, not only against thy greatest enemies, but also against thy least enemy. Seneca says: 'A man that is well advised fears his least enemy.' Ovid says: 'The smallest weasel can slay the greatest bull and the wild hart.' And the Book says: 'A little thorn may prick a great king sorely; and a dog will hurt a wild boar.' But nevertheless, I say not that thou shalt be so cowardly as to be fearful where there is no need for fear. The Book says: 'Some people have a great eagerness to deceive, yet fear to be deceived.' Yet shalt thou fear to be poisoned and keep thyself from the company of scorners. For the Book says: 'Join not the company of scorners, but flee from their words as from venom.'

"Now as to the second point, in which your wise counsellors advised you to fortify your house with great diligence, I would gladly know how ye understand these words and what is your opinion."

Melibeus answered and said: "Truly, I understand it

in this way – that I shall fortify my house with towers such as castles and other like edifices have, and with defensive armor and artillery, by which things I may so keep and defend my person and my house that my enemies shall be in fear to approach my dwelling."

To this opinion Prudence answered soon: "The fortifying of high towers and great edifices," said she, "sometimes is associated with pride; and also men make high towers and great edifices at great expense and with great labor. And when they have been constructed, they may not be worth a straw unless they are defended by true friends that are old and wise. And understand well that the greatest and strongest garrison that a rich man can have not only to keep his person but also his goods is that he be beloved among his subjects and his neighbors. For thus says Tully: 'There is a kind of garrison that no man can vanquish or discomfit, and that is when a lord is beloved by his fellow-citizens and by his people.'

"Now, sir, as to the third point; when your old and wise counsellor said that you ought not to proceed suddenly and hastily in this need, but that ye should provide and prepare in this case with great diligence and deliberation, I believe, indeed, that they said wisely and truly. For Tully says: 'In every danger before thou begin to act, prepare thee with great diligence.' Then I say, that in taking vengeance in war, in battle, and in fortifying, ere thou begin thou shouldst prepare for it and do it with great deliberation. For Tully says that 'long preparation before the battle makes the road to victory short.' And Cassiodorus says: 'A garrison is stronger when it has been a long time prepared.'

"But now let us speak of the counsel that was agreed upon by your neighbors such as do you reverence without loving you, your old enemies reconciled, and your flatterers that counsel you certain things privately and publicly counsel you to revenge yourself and make war at once. And truly, sir, as I have said before, ye have greatly erred to have called such people to be your advisers; for such counsellors are sufficiently reproached by reasons given above. But none the less, let us now come to the particular point. Ye shall first proceed after the teaching of Tully. Certainly the truth of this matter or of this advice need not be diligently inquired into, for it is well known who they are that have done you harm and injury; and how many of them there were, and in what manner they have done all this wrong and evil to you. And after this then shall ye examine the second condition which Tully adds in this connection. For Tully speaks of a thing which he calls 'consenting,' that is to say, who they are and how many and what they are that consented to the resolve which thou didst wilfully take to do hasty vengeance. And let us also consider who they are and how many they are and what they are that lend support to your adversaries. And indeed, as to the first point, it is well known what people they were that agreed with your hasty wilfulness; for truly, none of them that advised you to make sudden war were your friends. Let us now consider who they are whom ye hold so greatly your friends as to your person. For although ye are mighty and rich, surely ye are alone. For indeed, ye have no child but a daughter, and ye have no brothers nor cousins germane, and no other near kindred, on whose account your enemies should forebear in fear to dispute with you or to destroy your person. Ye know also that your wealth may be divided among various persons and when every man has his part he will give but little attention to avenging your death. But your enemies are three and they have many children, brothers, cousins and their kindred; and though ye should slay two or three of them, yet there would remain enough to avenge their death and slay thee. And although your kinsmen are more stable and steadfast than the kinsmen of your adversaries, yet nevertheless your kindred is only a remote kindred; and the kin of your enemies are very close to them. And in truth, in that respect their condition is better than yours. Then let us consider also if the advice of those that counsel you to take sudden vengeance is in accord with reason. And certainly, ye

know well it is not. For by right and reason no man can take vengeance upon another except the judge that has jurisdiction over the dispute, when it is permitted him to take that vengeance swiftly or with deliberation as the law requires. And in addition, with regard to that word which Tully terms 'consenting,' thou shalt consider if thy strength and power may consent and suffice to thy wilfulness and thy advisers. And indeed, thou mayst well say 'No' to that. For surely, to speak properly we can do only such things as we can do rightly. And indeed, rightfully ye can take no vengeance on your own authority. Then ye may see that your power does not consent or accord with your determination. Let us now examine the third point that Tully calls 'sequent' to the others. Thou shalt understand that the vengeance that thou hast purposed to take is this 'sequent,' and from this there will ensue another vengeance, peril, and war, and other injuries without number, all of which we are not aware of at this time. And regarding the fourth point which Tully calls the 'product,' thou shalt consider that this wrong that is done to thee is produced from hate of thine enemies; and from taking vengeance on that account shall come another vengeance and much sorrow and wasting of wealth, as I say.

"Now, sir, as to the point that Tully calls 'causes' which is the last point, thou shalt understand that the wrong that thou hast received hath certain causes, which clerks call *Oriens* and *Efficiens*, and *Causa longinqua* and *Causa propinqua*; that is to say, the remote cause and the near cause. The remote cause is Almighty God that is the cause of all things. The near cause is thy three enemies. The accidental cause was hate. The material cause were the five wounds of thy daughter. The formal cause is the manner of their working who brought ladders and climbed in at thy windows. The final cause was the attempt to slay thy daughter. And they were not stayed in this more than they could help. But to speak of the remote cause, as to what results shall come, or what shall finally happen to them in this

HEERE BIGYNNETH THE TALE OF THE CLERK OF OXENFORD ❦❦❦ PRIMA PARS ❦❦❦❦❦❦❦❦

A markys whilom lord was of that londe,
As were his worthy eldres hym bifore;
And obeisant and redy to his honde
Were alle his liges, bothe lasse and moore.
Thus in delit he lyveth, and hath doon yoore,
Biloved and drad, thurgh favour of fortune,
Bothe of his lordes and of his commune.

Therwith he was, to speke as of lynage,
The gentilleste yborn of Lumbardye;
A fair persone, and strong, and yong of age,
And ful of honour and of curteisye;
Discreet ynogh his contree for to gye,
Save in somme thynges that he was to blame,
And Walter was this yonge lordes name.

I BLAME him thus, that he considereth noght
In tyme comynge what hym myghte bityde;
But in his lust present was al his thoght,
As for to hauke and hunte on every syde;
Wel ny alle othere cures leet he slyde;
And eek he nolde, and that was worst of alle,
Wedde no wyf, for noght that may bifalle.

Oonly that point his peple bar so soore,

THER IS, AT THE WEST SYDE OF YTAILLE,
Doun at the roote of Vesulus the colde,
A lusty playne, habundant of vitaille,
Where many a tour & toun thou mayst biholde,
That founded were in time of fadres olde,
And many another delitable sighte,
And Saluces this noble contree highte.

Plate 11: The Student's Tale (p. 237)

case, I can only judge by conjecture and supposition. For we may suppose that they will come to a wicked end, for the Book of Decrees says: 'Seldom or with great difficulty are actions brought to a good end when they are badly begun.'

Now, sir, if men should ask me why God suffered these people to do you this injury, certainly I cannot in truth answer well. For the Apostle says, that 'the knowledge and judgments of our Lord God Almighty are deep; no man may comprehend or conceive them sufficiently.' Nevertheless, by certain presumptions and conjectures I hold and believe that God, who is full of justice and righteousness, has permitted this for just and reasonable ends.

"Thy name is Melibeus, that is to say, 'a man that drinks honey.' Thou hast drunk so much honey of sweet temporal wealth and delights and honors of this world that thou art drunk and hast forgotten Jesus Christ thy Creator; thou hast not done Him such honor and reverence as thou shouldst have done. Neither hast thou taken good heed to the words of Ovid who says: 'Under the honey of the gods of the body is hidden the venom that slays the soul.' And Solomon says: 'If thou hast found honey, eat what suffices of it; for if thou eat of it beyond measure, thou shalt cast it up,' and be needy and poor. And perhaps thou art in ill-favor with Christ and He has turned from thee His face and His merciful ear; and also has suffered that thou shouldst be punished in the manner in which thou hast sinned. Thou hast committed a sin against our Lord Christ, for indeed, the three enemies of mankind, that is to say, the flesh, the devil and the world, thou hast wilfully permitted to enter thy heart by the windows of thy body and hast not defended thyself sufficiently against their assaults and their temptations, so that they have wounded thy soul in five places, that is to say, the deadly sins that entered into thy heart by thy five senses. And in the same manner our Lord Christ has willed and permitted that thy three enemies should enter thy house by the windows and

wound thy daughter in the aforesaid manner."

"Indeed," said Melibeus, "I see well that ye speak strongly to overcome me in such a way that I shall not revenge myself upon my enemies; showing me the perils and the dangers which might ensue from this vengeance. But whoever should consider in all cases of vengeance the perils and evils that might come from revenge would never take vengeance, and that were an evil. For by vengeance are wicked men set apart from good men. And they that have a will to do evil restrain their wicked purpose when they see the punishing and chastising of offenders."

And to this Dame Prudence replied: "Truly," said she, "I grant freely that much evil and much good come from vengeance; but the taking of vengeance belongs properly not to everyone, but only to judges and to those that have jurisdiction over the offenders. And again I say further that just as a single person sins in taking vengeance upon another man, just so the judge sins if he takes no vengeance upon those that have deserved it. For Seneca says thus: 'That judge,' he says, 'is good that punishes the evil.' And as Cassiodorus says: 'A man fears to do injuries when he knows that it is displeasing to judges and sovereigns.' And another says: 'The judge that fears to do right makes men evil.' And Saint Paul the Apostle says in his Epistle when he writes to the Romans that 'judges do not bear the spear without cause;' but they carry it to punish evil ones and wrong-doers and to protect good men. If ye will then take vengeance upon your enemies ye should bring your grievance to the judge that has jurisdiction over them and he shall punish them as the law asks and requires."

"Ah," said Melibeus, "this vengeance I like not at all. I recollect now and consider, how Fortune has nourished me from my childhood and has helped me through many a greater difficulty. Now I will test her, believing with God's help that she will help me to avenge my shame."

"Indeed," said Prudence, "if ye will work by my

advice, ye will not test Fortune in any way. Nor shall ye bend or bow unto her, according to the opinion of Seneca, for 'things that have been foolishly done and done in hope of Fortune will never come to a good end.' And as the same Seneca says: 'The more clear and shining Fortune is, the more brittle and sooner broken.' Do not trust in her, for she is not steadfast or stable; for when ye believe yourself to be most sure or certain of her help, she will fail you and deceive you. And as to the saying that Fortune has nourished you from your childhood, I say that on that account shall ye trust and believe in her the less. For Seneca says: 'Whatever man is nourished by fortune she will make a great fool of.' Now then, since ye desire and ask vengeance and the vengeance that is done according to the law and by the judge does not please you, and the vengeance that is done in hope of fortune is dangerous and uncertain, then ye shall have no other remedy but recourse to the Sovereign Judge that avenges all injuries and wrongs. And He shall avenge you in the way in which He testifies Himself, when He says: 'Leave vengeance to me, and I shall do it.' "

Melibeus answered: "If I do not avenge myself for the wrong that men have done me, I summon or warn them that have done that wrong to me, and all others also, to do me another injury. For it is written: 'If thou take no vengeance for an old wrong, thou summonest thy adversaries to do thee a new wrong.' And also, on account of my patience, men would do me so much wrong that I could neither bear it nor sustain it, and so I should be considered contemptible. For men say: 'Through too much suffering shall many things happen to thee which thou shalt not be able to endure.' "

"Truly," said Prudence, "I grant you that too much patience is not good. Yet it does not follow on that account that every person to whom men do an injury takes vengeance for it. For that relates and belongs solely to the judges, for they shall punish wrongs and injuries. And therefore the two authorities that ye have quoted above speak only with regard to the judges, for

when they permit too many wrongs and villainies to be done without punishment, they not only summon men to do new wrongs, but they command it. Also a wise man says, that 'the judge that does not correct a sinner commands and bids him to sin.' And the judges and sovereigns might permit so much on the part of evil men and wrong-doers in their land that these might by such sufferance, with process of time, grow to such power and might that they should put the judges and sovereigns from their places and at last make them lose their authority.

"But let us now suppose that ye have permission to avenge yourself. I say ye have not at present the power and might to do it. For if ye will make comparison with the power of your adversaries, ye shall find that in many things which I have explained to you before, their condition is better than yours. And therefore I say that for the present it is good that ye suffer and be patient.

"Furthermore, ye know well that according to the common proverb: 'It is madness for a man to strive with a stronger or a mightier man than he is himself; and for him to strive with a man of the same strength, that is to say, with as strong a man as he, is a danger; and to strive with a weaker man is a folly.' And therefore a man should avoid strife as much as he can. For Solomon says: 'It is a great honor to a man to keep himself from noise and strife.' And if it should happen that a man of greater strength than thou art should do thee an injury, study and busy thyself rather to quiet this grievance than to be avenged for it. For Seneca says: 'He puts himself in great peril that strives with a greater man than he himself is,' and Cato says: 'If a man of high station or degree, or more mighty than thou, does thee injury or annoyance, permit him to do so; for he that once injures thee may another time relieve thee and help.' Yet I will put the case that ye have both power and permission to avenge yourself. I say that there are many things that should restrain you from taking vengeance and make you inclined to be patient and to endure the things that have been done to you.

First and foremost, ye must consider the faults that have been in your own person, for which God has permitted you to have this suffering, as I said to you before. For the poet says that 'we ought to take patiently the tribulations that come to us, when we think and consider that we have deserved to have them.' And Saint Gregory says: 'When a man considers well the number of his defects and sins, the pains and tribulations that he suffers seem the less to him; and insofar as he considers his sins the more heavy and grievous, to that degree his pain seems the lighter and easier to him.' Also ye ought to incline and bow your heart to take the patience of our Lord Jesus Christ, as Saint Peter says in his epistles. 'Jesus Christ,' he says, 'has suffered for us and given example to every man to follow and be like him. For he never did a sin nor did there ever come an evil word from his mouth. When men cursed him, he cursed them not; and when men beat him, he threatened them not.' Also the great patience which the saints that dwell in Paradise had in the tribulations which they suffered without desert or guilt ought to incite you greatly to patience. Furthermore, ye should strive to have patience, considering that the tribulations of this world endure but a little while and soon are past and gone. And the joy that a man seeks to have by patience in tribulations is imperishable, according to what the Apostle says in his epistle: 'the joy of God,' he says, 'is imperishable.' That is to say, everlasting. Also hold and believe steadfastly that he is neither well-nourished nor well-taught that cannot have patience or will not accept patience. For Solomon says that 'the doctrine and the wit of a man is known by patience.' And in another place he says: 'He that is patient rules himself with great prudence.' And the same Solomon says: 'The angry and wrathful man makes noises and the patient man moderates them and is quiet.' He says also: 'It is of more value to be patient than to be very strong; and he that has the lordship of his own heart is more to be praised than he that by his force or strength takes great cities.' And therefore says Saint James in his epistle that 'patience is a great virtue.'"

"Surely," said Melibeus, "I grant you, Dame Prudence, that patience is a great virtue looking towards perfection; but every man cannot have the perfection that ye seek; nor am I of the number of very perfect men, for my heart can never be at peace until the time that it is avenged. And although it was a great peril to my enemies to do me an injury in taking vengeance upon me, yet they took no heed of that peril but carried out their wicked will and spirit. And therefore, it seems to me men ought not to reproach me though I should put myself to some peril for vengeance, and even though I do a great excess, that is to say, that I avenge one outrage by another."

"Ah," said Dame Prudence, "ye speak your will as it pleases you, but in no case in this world should a man do outrage or excess in order to avenge himself. For Cassiodorus says: 'He that avenges himself by an outrage does as illy as he that does the outrage.' And therefore ye shall avenge yourself according to right, that is to say, by the law; and not by excess or outrage. And also if ye will avenge yourself for the outrage done by your adversaries in another manner than that which right commands, ye sin. And on this account Seneca says: 'A man shall never avenge great evil with great evil.' And if ye say that right requires a man to oppose violence with violence and fighting with fighting, indeed ye say truly, when his action is taken at once without interval or without tarrying or delay and to defend himself and not to avenge himself. And it is proper that a man should defend himself with such moderation that men have no cause or ground to reproach him with excess and cruelty; for otherwise it would be against reason. By God, ye know well that ye are taking no action now to defend yourself but rather to avenge yourself; and therefore it follows that ye have no will to do this action temperately. And therefore it seems to me that patience is good. For Solomon says: 'A man that is not patient shall come to great evil.'"

"Surely," said Melibeus, "I grant you that when a man is impatient and angry concerning that which touches him not and does not belong to him though it harm him, it is no wonder. For the law says: 'He is culpable that interferes or meddles with a thing that does not pertain to him.' And Solomon says: 'He that interferes in the strife of another man is like to one that takes a dog by the ears.' For just as he that takes a strange dog by the ears is sometimes bitten by the dog, just in the same way is it reasonable that he should have harm that by his impatience meddles with the trouble of another man when it does not affect him. But ye know well that this matter, that is to say, my grief and my suffering, touches me closely. And therefore, though I am angry and impatient, it is no wonder. And saving your grace, I cannot see that it might greatly harm me though I should take vengeance, for I am richer and more mighty than my enemies are. And ye know well that by money and by having great possessions all things of this world are governed. And Solomon says: 'All things submit to money.' "

When Prudence had heard her husband boast of his wealth and of his money, dispraising the power of his adversaries, she spoke in this manner: "Indeed, dear sir, I grant you that ye are rich and mighty and that the riches are useful to such as have got them well and can well use them. For just as the body of a man cannot live without the soul, no more can it live without temporal goods. And through riches a man may get himself great friends. And therefore says Pamphilus: 'If a netherd's daughter,' he says, 'is rich, she may choose from a thousand men which one she will take for her husband. For out of a thousand men, not one will forsake her or refuse her.' And this Pamphilus says also: 'If thou art very happy, that is to say, if thou art very rich, thou shalt find a great number of friends and companions. And if thy fortune change and thou grow poor, farewell friendship and fellowship; for thou shalt be alone without any companions unless it be the companionship of poor folk.' And again this Pamphilus

says: 'They that are thralls and bond-servants by lineage shall be made worthy and noble by wealth.' And just as by wealth there come many good things, just so with poverty there come many harms and evils. For great poverty constrains a man to do many ill things, and therefore Cassiodorus calls poverty the 'mother of ruin,' that is to say, the mother of overthrowing or disaster. And therefore says Peter Alphonsus: 'One of the greatest adversaries to be found in this world is when a free man by nature or by birth is forced by poverty to feed on the charity of his enemy.' And the same says Innocent in one of his books. He says: 'Sorrowful and unhappy is the condition of a poor beggar, for if he does not beg his meat he dies for hunger, and if he beg he dies for shame, and in any case necessity constrains him to beg.' And therefore Solomon says: 'It is better to die than to have such poverty.' And the same Solomon says: 'It is better to die a bitter death than to live in such a manner.' For these reasons that I have told you, and for many other reasons that I could cite, I grant that riches have been good for those that have got them well and for those that have well used them. And therefore I will show you how ye shall behave and bear yourself in the gathering of riches and in what manner ye shall use them.

"First, ye shall get them without great desire, by good leisure, – gradually, and not too hastily. For a man who is too desirous to get wealth surrenders himself first to theft and then to all other evils. And therefore Solomon says: 'He that exerts himself too busily to grow rich shall not be innocent.' He also says that 'the riches that come quickly to a man pass from him soon and easily; but riches that come little by little always grow and multiply.' And, sir, ye shall gain riches by your wit and by your labor for your profit; and that without wrong or harm-doing to any other person. For the law says that 'no man makes himself rich if he does harm to another person.' That is to say, that nature forbids in accordance with right that any man make himself rich through harm to another person. And

Tully says that 'no sorrow or dread of death nor any thing that may happen to a man is so much against nature as a man's increasing his own means through harm to another man. And though the great men and mighty men may get wealth more easily than thou, yet thou shalt not be idle or slow to make profit for thyself, for thou shalt in every manner avoid idleness.' For Solomon says that 'idleness teaches a man to work many evils.' And the same Solomon says: 'He that labors and busies himself to till his land shall eat bread, but he that is idle and puts himself to no business or occupation, shall die of hunger.' And he that is idle and slow can never find a suitable time to serve his profit. For there is a versifier that says: 'The idle man excuses himself in winter because of the great cold and in summer by reason of the heat.' For this cause Cato says: 'Be wakeful, and do not give thyself to sleep very much; for too much repose nourishes and causes many vices.' And therefore says Saint Jerome: 'Do some good deeds, that the devil who is our enemy shall not find you unoccupied. For the devil does not take easily into his service such as he finds occupied in good works!'

"Thus in acquiring wealth ye must avoid idleness and afterwards ye shall use the wealth which ye have got by your wit and your industry in such a manner that men consider you neither too parsimonious, nor too sparing, nor too foolishly generous, that is to say, very free as a spender. For just as men blame an avaricious man because of his parsimoniousness and niggardliness, in the same way he is to blame that spends too freely. And therefore says Cato: 'Use,' he says, 'thy wealth that thou hast in such a manner that men have no ground or cause to call thee mean or niggardly; for it is a great shame to a man to have a poor heart and a rich purse.' He says also: 'The goods that thou hast acquired, use them in measure,' that is to say, spend them in reason; for they that foolishly waste and expend the goods that they have, when they have no more goods of their own, they plan to take the goods of another man. I say then that ye shall flee avarice, using your wealth in such manner that men shall not say that your riches are buried, but that ye have them in your power and under your government. For a wise man reproves the avaricious man and says thus in two verses: 'To what end and wherefore does a man bury his goods through his great avarice, knowing well that he needs must die; for death is the end of every man as regards this present life?' And for what cause or action does he knit himself so fast to his goods that all his wits cannot part him or sever him from them; when he knows well, or ought to know, that when he is dead he shall bear nothing with him out of this world? And therefore Saint Augustine says: 'The avaricious man is like unto hell; the more it swallows the more desire it has to swallow and devour.' And just as ye would avoid being called an avaricious or parsimonious man, just so ye should keep and govern you in such a manner that men shall not call you foolishly generous. On this account Tully says: 'The goods of thy house shall not be hidden nor kept so closely, that they cannot be opened by pity and graciousness;' that is to say, to give part to them that have great need; 'nor shall thy goods be so free as to be every man's goods.' Afterwards, in the getting and using of your wealth ye shall always have three things in your heart; that is to say, our Lord God, conscience, and your good name. First, ye shall have God in your heart; and for no wealth shall ye do anything which may in any manner displease God, that is your Creator and Maker. For according to the word of Solomon, 'It is better to have a small property with the love of God, than to have a great property and treasure, and lose the love of God.' And the Prophet says that 'it is better to be a good man and have little property and treasure than to be considered an evil man and have great wealth.' And yet I say that ye should always exert yourself to get wealth, so long as ye get it with a good conscience. And the Apostle says: 'There is nothing in this world in which we should have such great joy as when our conscience bears us good witness.' And the wise man says: 'The possessions of a man are good when sin is not in his conscience.' Afterwards, in acquiring your riches and in using them, ye must exert yourself diligently that your good name shall be always kept and preserved. For Solomon says: 'It is better for a man to have a good name than to have great riches.' And therefore he says in another place: 'Exert thyself greatly to keep thy friends and thy good name, for these shall abide longer with thee than any treasure, be it never so precious. And surely he should not be called a noble man that, in accord with God and with a good conscience, does not make an effort to keep his good name. And Cassiodorus says that 'it is a sign of a noble heart when a man loves and desires to have a good name.' And therefore says Saint Augustine that 'there are two things that are necessary and needful, and these are good conscience and good renown; that is to say, good conscience within thine own person, and good renown among thy neighbors outside. And he that trusts himself so much in his good conscience that he affronts and sets at naught his good name or renown and does not care to keep his good name is but a cruel churl.'

"Sire, now have I shown you how ye shall go about the acquiring of riches, and how ye shall use them. And I see plainly that because of the trust ye put in your wealth, ye will begin war and battle. I advise you that ye begin no war confiding in your riches, for they do not suffice to maintain war. And therefore a philosopher said: 'That man who desires war and will have it in any case shall never have sufficiency; for the richer he is, the greater expenditures he must make, if he will win honor and victory.' And Solomon says that 'the more wealth a man has, the more spenders of it he shall find.' And, dear sire, although ye can command a multitude of people with your wealth, yet it is neither fitting nor good to begin war, when ye might in other ways have peace, to your honor and profit. For victories by battle in this world are not won by great numbers of people or by the bravery of man, but they lie in the will and hand of the Lord God Almighty. And therefore Judas Maccabeus, who was God's knight, when he fought with an adversary that had a greater number, and a greater multitude of people and stronger than the people of Maccabee, comforted his little company, and spoke in this manner: 'Our Lord God Almighty,' he said, 'may as easily give victory to a few as to many. For victory in battle comes not because of a great number of people, but it comes from the Lord God in heaven.' And, dear sir, since there is no man certain if he is worthy that God should give him victory, no more than he is certain that he is worthy of the love of God, according to what Solomon says, therefore every man should fear greatly to begin wars. And he should fear also, because many perils occur in battle, and it often happens that the great man is slain as often as the little man, and, as it is written in the Second Book of Kings, 'the happenings of battle are adventurous and nothing sure,' for one is hurt as easily with a spear as another. And because there is great peril in war, a man should turn from it and avoid it, as much as he properly can. For Solomon says: 'He that loves peril shall fall in peril.' "

After Dame Prudence had thus spoken, Melibeus answered and said: "I see well, Dame Prudence, by your fair words and your reasons ye have shown me, that ye like war not at all. But I have not heard your advice as to how I shall act in this extremity."

"Truly," said she, "I advise you that ye reach an accord with your adversaries, and make peace with them. For St. James says in his Epistles, that 'by concord and peace the smallest riches grow great, and by dispute and discord great wealth diminishes.' And ye know well that one of the greatest and most sovereign things in the world is unity and peace. And therefore our Lord Jesus Christ spoke to his apostles in this fashion: 'Happy and blessed are they that love and promote peace; for they shall be called the children of God.'

"Ah!" cried Melibeus, "now I see well that ye love

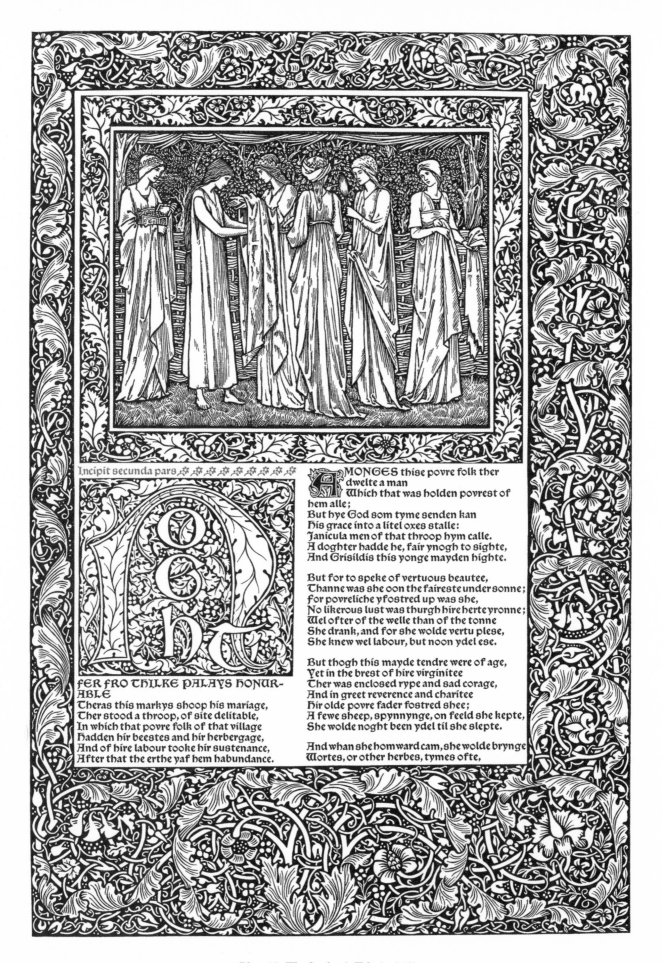

Incipit secunda pars

AMONGES thise povre folk ther
dwelte a man
Which that was holden povrest of
hem alle;
But hye God som tyme senden kan
His grace into a litel oxes stalle:
Janicula men of that throop hym calle.
A doghter hadde he, fair ynogh to sighte,
And Grisildis this yonge mayden highte.

But for to speke of vertuous beautee,
Thanne was she oon the faireste under sonne;
For povreliche yfostred up was she,
No likerous lust was thurgh hire herte yronne;
Wel ofter of the welle than of the tonne
She drank, and for she wolde vertu plese,
She knew wel labour, but noon ydel ese.

But thogh this mayde tendre were of age,
Yet in the brest of hire virginitee
Ther was enclosed rype and sad corage,
And in greet reverence and charitee
Hir olde povre fader fostred shee;
A fewe sheep, spynnynge, on feeld she kepte,
She wolde noght been ydel til she slepte.

And whan she homward cam, she wolde brynge
Wortes, or other herbes, tymes ofte,

FER FRO THILKE PALAYS HONUR-
ABLE
Theras this markys shoop his mariage,
Ther stood a throop, of site delitable,
In which that povre folk of that village
Hadden hir beestes and hir herbergage,
And of hire labour tooke hir sustenance,
After that the erthe yaf hem habundance.

Plate 12: The Student's Tale (p. 240)

not mine honor and reputation. Ye know well that my adversaries have begun this dispute and contention by their outrage; and ye see clearly that they do not pray or require peace of me, nor do they ask to be reconciled. Will ye then have me go humble myself and obey them, and cry mercy of them? In truth, that were not to mine honor. For just as men say that 'over-great familiarity causes contempt,' so is it also with too great humility and meekness."

Then Dame Prudence began to pretend anger, and said: "Indeed, sir, saving your grace, I love your honor and profit as I do mine own, and always have done so; nor have ye or any others seen ever the contrary. And yet, if I had said that ye should promote peace and reconciliation, I had not been much mistaken, or said amiss. For the wise man says: 'Let another man begin dissension, and begin reconciliation thyself.' And the prophet says: 'Turn from wickedness, and do good; seek peace and follow it as much as thou canst.' Yet I do not say that ye should seek your adversaries for peace more than that they should seek you; for I know well that ye are so hard-hearted ye will do nothing for me. And Solomon says: 'He that has a heart over hard shall at last suffer mischance.' "

When Melibeus heard Dame Prudence make this appearance of anger, he spoke in this manner: "Dame, I pray you that ye be not displeased at things that I say; for ye know well that I am angry and wrathful, and that it is no wonder, and they that are angry do not know well what they do or say. Therefore spoke the prophet: 'A troubled eye has no clear sight.' But speak and counsel me as ye please, for I am ready to do right according to your desire. And if ye reprove me for my folly I am the more constrained to love you and praise you. For Solomon says that 'he that reproves another for folly shall find better grace than he that deceiveth him with sweet words.' "

Then spoke Dame Prudence: "I make no appearance of wrath or anger except for your profit. For Solomon says: 'He is of more worth that reproves or scolds a fool for his folly, making a pretence of anger, than he that supports him and praises him in his wrong doing, and laughs at his folly.' And this same Solomon says afterward that 'by the sorrowful visage of a man,' that is to say, by the sorry and sad countenance of a man, 'the fool corrects and improves himself.' "

Then said Melibeus: "I shall not be able to answer so many fair reasons as ye have set before me. Tell me briefly your will and your advice, and I am all ready to fulfill and perform them."

Then Dame Prudence showed him all her will, and said: "I advise you above all things that ye make peace between God and you, and be reconciled to Him and His grace. For as I have said to you before, God has permitted you to have this trouble and affliction because of your sins. And if ye do as I tell you, God will send your adversaries to you, and make them fall at your feet, ready to do your will and your commandments. For Solomon says: 'When the state of a man is pleasing to God, He changes the hearts of the man's adversaries, and constrains them to ask peace and grace of him.' And I pray you, let me speak with your adversaries in a private place; for they shall not know that it is with your will and assent. And then, when I know their will and purpose, I can advise you more surely."

"Dame," said Melibeus, "do your will and liking, for I put myself wholly at your disposition and government."

Then Dame Prudence, when she saw the good will of her husband, deliberated and took advice with herself, thinking how she could bring this extremity to a good end. And when she saw her time, she sent for these adversaries to come to her in a secret place, and showed wisely to them the great goods that come of peace, and the great harms and perils that lie in war; and said to them in a fair manner that they should greatly repent the injury and wrong that they had done to Melibeus her lord, and to her, and to her daughter.

And when they had heard the goodly words of

Dame Prudence, they were surprised and pleased, and had such great joy because of her that it was wonder. "Ah, lady!" cried they, "ye have shown to us 'the blessings of sweetness,' according to the proverb of David the prophet. For the reconciliation which we are not in any manner worthy to have, unless we beg it with great contrition and humility, ye in your great goodness have presented to us. Now we see well that the wisdom and cunning of Solomon is true; for he says that 'sweet words multiply and increase friends, and make evil persons gentle and meek.'

"Indeed," said they, "we put our action and all our affair and cause wholly at your good will, and are ready to obey the speech and commands of the lord Melibeus. And therefore, dear and benign lady, we pray you and beseech you as meekly as we can, that it please your great goodness to fulfill in deeds your good words. For we know that we have offended Lord Melibeus out of all measure, so greatly, that we lack the power to make him amends. And therefore we obligate and bind ourselves and our friends to do entirely his will and commands. But perhaps he has such resentment and wrath toward us because of our offense that he will lay such a penalty upon us as we are not able to sustain. And therefore, noble lady, we beseech your womanly pity to take such counsel in this extremity that we shall not be disinherited or destroyed because of our folly."

"Surely," said Prudence, "it is a difficult and dangerous thing that a man should put himself utterly under the arbitration and judgment, and in the might and power of his enemies. For Solomon says: 'Believe me, and trust what I shall say; I declare,' said he, 'ye people, folk, and governors of Holy Church, that ye shall not give power over your bodies while ye live to your sons, or wives, or friends, or brothers.' Now since he forbade that a man give his brother or his friend power over his body, by a stronger reason he forbids a man to give himself to his enemy. And none the less I advise you that ye distrust not my lord. For I know well and truly that he is gentle and meek, generous,

courteous, and not covetous of goods or wealth. There is nothing in this world that he desires except honor and reputation. In addition I know well, and am sure, that he will do nothing in this emergency without my advice. And I shall so work in this matter that by the grace of our Lord God, ye shall be reconciled to us."

Then they said with one voice: "Worshipful lady, we put ourselves and our goods fully at your will and disposition, and are ready to come on whatever day it pleases your nobleness to assign to us, to make our obligation and bond as strong as your goodness wishes, that we may fulfill the will of you and the Lord Melibeus."

When Dame Prudence had heard the reply of these men, she told them to be gone secretly, and she returned to her lord Melibeus, and told him how she had found his adversaries very repentant, humbly acknowledging their sins and their offense, and how they were ready to suffer all penalty, asking and praying of him mercy and pity.

Then Melibeus said: "He is worthy to have pardon and forgiveness for his sin that does not excuse it, but acknowledges it and repents, asking indulgence. For Seneca says: 'There is remission and forgiveness where there is confession.' For confession is the neighbor of innocence. And he says in another place: 'He that has shame for his sin and acknowledges it, is worthy to have it remitted.' And therefore I assent and agree to have peace, but it is good that we should not do it without the assent and willingness of our friends."

Then Dame Prudence was very glad and joyful, and said: "Surely, sir, ye have answered well. For just as by the advice, assent, and help of your friends, ye have been stirred to avenge yourself and make war, just so without their advice ye ought not to be reconciled now, or make peace with your adversaries. For the law says: 'There is nothing so good by way of nature, as for a thing to be undone by him who did it.'"

And then Dame Prudence, without delay or tarrying, at once sent messages for their kin, and for their old friends who were true and wise, and told them by command, in the presence of Melibeus, all this matter as above described, and begged them that they would give their advice and counsel as to what was best to do in this extremity. And when Melibeus' friends had advised and deliberated upon the aforesaid matter, and had examined it with great diligence and care, they gave unanimous advice to have peace and concord, and that Melibeus should receive with a good heart his adversaries, and grant them forgiveness and mercy.

And when Dame Prudence had heard the assent of her lord Melibeus, and the advice of these friends, and saw that both accorded with her own will and intention, she was wondrously glad in her heart, and said: "There is an old proverb that 'the goodness that thou canst do this day, do it; and wait not or delay until the morrow.' And therefore I advise you that ye send your messengers, such as are wise and discreet, to your adversaries, telling them, on your behalf, that if they will discuss peace and accord, they prepare themselves without delay to come to us." And this thing was done. And when these offenders and repenters of their follies, that is, the adversaries of Melibeus, heard what these messengers said to them, they were glad and joyful, and answered meekly and benignly, giving courtesy and thanks to their Lord Melibeus and all his company; and they prepared themselves without delay to go with the messengers, and obey the command of their lord Melibeus.

And soon they took their way to the court of Melibeus, and took with them some of their true friends, to swear faith for them and be their pledges. And when they had come into the presence of Melibeus, he spoke these words to them: "It stands thus, and is true that ye, without cause or reason, have done great injuries and wrongs to me and my wife Prudence and my daughter as well. For ye have entered my house by violence, and have done such an outrageous deed, that all men know well that ye have deserved death. And therefore will I know and require of you, whether ye will put the punishing and chastising and vengeance for this outrage at the will of me and my wife Prudence, or whether ye will not."

Then the wisest of the three answered for them all, and said: "Sire, we know well that we are unworthy to come into the court of so great a lord and so worthy as ye are. For we have erred so greatly, and have offended and been guilty in such a way against your high lordship, that indeed we have deserved death. But yet, because of the great goodness and gentleness to which all the world testifies of you, we submit ourselves to the excellence and benignity of your gracious lordship, and are ready to obey all your commands, beseeching you that in your merciful pity ye will consider our great repentance and lowly submission, and grant us forgiveness for this outrageous injury and offense. For well we know that your liberal grace and mercy reach farther into goodness than do our outrageous sins and offenses into wickedness, although most cursedly and damnably we have sinned against your high lordship."

Then Melibeus lifted them up from the ground most gently, and received their bonds and promises by their oaths and upon their pledges and sureties, and assigned them a certain day to return to his court, to accept and receive the sentence and judgment that Melibeus would command to be executed upon them for the causes previously told. And these things done, every man returned to his house.

And when Dame Prudence saw her time, she asked her lord Melibeus what vengeance he thought to take on his adversaries.

To which Melibeus answered: "Truly, I think and have purpose fully to disinherit them of all that they have, and put them in exile forever."

"Surely," said Dame Prudence, "this would be a cruel judgment, and much against reason. For ye are rich enough, and have no need of other men's property; and ye might easily in this way get yourself a name for being covetous, which is a vicious thing, and ought to be avoided by every good man. For according to the proverb of the apostle: 'Covetousness is the root of all evils.' And therefore, it were better for you to lose as much property of your own than to take from them in this manner. For it is better to lose property with honor, than it is to win property by wickedness and shame. And every man ought to work diligently to get himself a good name. And yet he should not only busy himself in keeping his good name, but he should strive always to do something by which he may renew his good name. For it is written: 'The former good praise or good name of a man is soon passed and gone, when it is not freshly renewed.' And with reference to what ye say of exiling your adversaries, that again seems to me much against reason, and out of moderation, considering the power over themselves that they have given to you. And it is written: 'He is worthy of losing his privilege that misuses the power that is given him.' And I set the case that though ye might enforce that penalty by right and law, which I believe ye cannot do, ye could not perhaps put it into execution, and then the war would be likely to return as before. And therefore, if ye would that men did you honor, ye must judge more courteously – that is, give easier sentences. For it is written: 'He that commands most courteously, him will men most obey.' And therefore, I pray you that in this need ye seek to overcome your heart. For Seneca says: 'He that overcomes his heart is twice a victor.' And Tully says: 'There is nothing so commendable in a great lord as when he is gentle and meek, and easily appeased.' And I pray you that ye will forbear to do vengeance, in such a way that your good name may be conserved, and that men shall have cause to praise you for pity and mercy, and that ye shall have no cause to repent of what ye have done. For Seneca says: 'He is a poor victor that repents of his victory.' Therefore I pray you, let mercy be in your mind and heart, to the end and purpose that God Almighty have mercy on you in his last Judgment. For St. James says in his epistle: 'Judgment without mercy shall be done him, that has no mercy on another.' "

When Melibeus had heard the great causes and reasons of Dame Prudence, and her wise teachings, his heart began to incline to the will of his wife, considering her true purpose, and soon made him conform, and agree fully to act by her advice. And he thanked God, from whom all virtue and goodness proceeds, that he had sent him a wife of such discretion. And when the day came on which these adversaries should appear, he spoke fairly to them, and said: "Although in your pride and presumption and folly, and your thoughtlessness and ignorance, ye have borne yourselves amiss and injured me, yet since I behold your great humility, and see that ye are sorry and repent your offenses, I am constrained to give you grace and mercy. Therefore I receive you into my grace, and forgive you freely all the offenses, injuries, and wrongs that ye have done against me and mine, to the end that God in His endless mercy will at our deaths forgive us our wrongs to Him in this wretched world. For doubtless, if we are sorry and repentant of our sins in the sight of our Lord God, He is so generous and merciful, that He will forgive us our sins, and bring us to His bliss that has no end. Amen."

Here ends Chaucer's Tale of Melibeus and Dame Prudence

The Monk's Tale

THE MONK'S TALE is a collection within a collection, comprising a string of dismal tragedies. In the Middle Ages, a tragedy could be simply a tale of the reversal of fortune, with a character first raised up and then dashed down. The Monk's message is that the vagaries of Fortune should lead us to eschew worldly benefits and fix our sights on God – a suitable message for his profession, though his own personality, as revealed in the General Prologue, suggests he is not entirely enthusiastic in his own adherence to the principle. The Knight puts an early stop to the depressing sequence of narratives.

THE MONK'S TALE

*The Merry Words
of the Host to
the Monk*

WHEN I had told my tale of Melibee,
And Prudence and her great benignity,
Our Host cried: "As I am a faithful man,
And by the precious *corpus Madrian*,
Rather than have a barrelful of ale,
I would my love and wife had heard that tale!
For she knows nothing of the patient life
That showed in Prudence, Melibeus' wife.
By God's bones! When I give my lads a thrashing,
Out with the cudgels comes my dame a-dashing;
"Slay them!" she cries; "slay the dogs, every one!
Beat them until ye break them, back and bone!"
Or if perhaps some neighbor at the mass
Make not a reverence to her as he pass,
Or rashly should offend her in that place,
When she comes home she flyeth in my face
Crying: "False coward, go avenge thy wife!
By *corpus* bones! Here, I will take thy knife,
While at the distaff thou shalt set to spinning!"
From dawn to night she makes some such beginning:
"Alas!" she cries, "that I should not escape
This marriage with a milksop or an ape
That every wretch can shame! Thou dost not dare
Defend thy wife's rights!" This is how I fare –
Unless I choose to fight, as she would make me.
And out of doors at once I have to take me
Or I am lost – unless, indeed, I fly on
These quarrels like some wild and crazy lion!

I know well she will some day work on me
To slay some neighbor for her, and then flee;
For I am dangerous with a knife in hand,
Though she is one I never dare withstand;
For, by my faith, she has a mighty arm,
As he shall find that dares to do her harm
Either by word or deed. But let it be.
    "My lord Sir Monk, be merry now," said he,
"For ye shall tell a tale at my command.
Lo! Rochester is lying near at hand.
Ride up, my lord, and do not spoil our game!
But, by my truth, I do not know your name,
Whether, in hailing you, to call upon
Sir Thomas, or Sir Alban, or Sir John.
From what house come ye, by your father's kin?
I vow to God, thou hast a fair-hued skin;
There is good pasture everywhere thou go'st;
Thou art not like a penitent or ghost!
Upon my faith, thou art some officer,
Some worthy sacristan, or cellarer;
Yea, by my father's spirit, I would swear
When thou art home, thou art the master there;
No cloister-monk, no novice treading shyly,
But one that governs, ever wise and wily;
A fine, up-standing figure, too – I own –
Well-fleshed, and good alike of brawn and bone.
May God confuse the wretched man, I say,
That brought thee to religion, anyway!
Thou wouldst have made a brave cock in thine hour!
Had thou had freedom, as thou hast the power,
And from thy lusty manhood procreated,
Full many a creature hadst thou generated!
Alas! Why dost thou wear so wide a cope?
God give me grief unless, were I a pope,
Not only thou, but all men strong and great,
Though they were shorn high up upon the pate,
Should have their wives. The world is lost, indeed!
Religion has the best of all the seed
From treading – lo! what shrimps we lay-folk be!
But feeble shoots come from a feeble tree.
This makes the heirs we bear so weak and slender

They lack the strength to properly engender!
This makes our wives eager to make assay
Of you religious men, that better pay
The debts of Venus than we can, alas!
God knows, no counterfeited coin ye pass!
But be not angry if I jest, my lord;
I have heard truth in many a sportive word."
This worthy monk in patience heard him through.
"Now I will do the best that I can do,
So far as virtue may be served," said he,
"To tell a tale for you, or two, or three.
And if your pleasure be to give me ear,
St. Edward's life I will relate you here;
Or first, perhaps, some tragedies will tell,
Of which I have a hundred in my cell.
By tragedy I mean a kind of story,
Of him that lived at first in wealth and glory,
As ancient books remind us frequently,
And from his height falls into misery,
And comes upon a wretched end at last.
The verses of these tragedies are cast
In six feet, and are called hexameters.
And they are done in prose as well as verse,
And wrought in various kinds of meters, too.
Lo! this description should suffice for you.
    "Now hear me, if indeed ye think it best.
But first in this I make you one request:
Though I set not the order of these things,
Whether of popes or emperors or kings,
All in their proper times, as ye may read,
But some too soon and some too late, indeed,
As I can best remember them, by chance;
I pray, excuse me for mine ignorance."

*Here begins the Monk's Tale of the cases of
illustrious persons*

I WILL lament in manner tragical
The woe of them that stood in high degree,
And fell, and had no remedy at all
To lift them out of their adversity.

For once let Fortune set herself to flee,
None then can check the thing she wills to do;
Let no man trust in blind prosperity;
Be warned by these examples old and true.

LUCIFER

With Lucifer, though he was not a man,
But angel of the Lord, I will begin;
For he (though Fortune never did nor can
Harm any angel) fell because of sin
Down into hell, and lieth still therein.
O Lucifer, angel most bright of all,
Now thou art Satan, that canst never win
From misery that followed on thy fall.

ADAM

Lo, Adam! in Damascus that was wrought
By God's own finger in the garden free,
And not by unclean sperm of man begot;
And ruled all Paradise, except one tree!
Never had worldly man such high degree,
Till for misconduct in the end he fell,
And so was driven from high prosperity
To labor, and misfortune, and to hell.

SAMSON

Lo, Samson, he whose birth was celebrated
By th' angel, long ere his nativity,
And unto mighty God was consecrated,
And stood in honor while he still could see –
There never was another such as he,
To speak of strength and of courageousness,
But to his wives his secret foolishly
He told, and slew himself in great distress.

Samson, this hero strong and great of heart,
All weaponless save for his hands that day,
The dreadful lion slew and tore apart,

As to his wedding forth he went his way.
His false wife could so subtly please and pray,
That thus she won his secret; then, untrue,
Turned to his foes his counsel to betray,
And she forsook him, and was wed anew.

Three hundred foxes Samson caught in ire,
And bound by two's the tails of all that band,
And then he set the foxes' tails on fire,
To every pair he tied a burning brand;
And they burned all the grain within that land,
And vines and olives; he slew, it came to pass,
A thousand men with nothing in his hand
For weapon but the jaw bone of an ass.

He had so great a thirst when they were slain
He was nigh lost; and he began to pray
That God would have some pity on his pain,
And send him drink, or he must pass away;
Then from the dry bone of the ass that day,
Out of a molar, gushed a spring, indeed,
From which he drank his fill. Thus God, I say,
Succored him, as in *Judges* ye may read.

By Gaza once at night, despite the bands
Of Philistines that called him enemy,
He tore the city gates off with his hands,
And bore them off upon his back, and he
Set them upon a hill for all to see!
All-mighty Samson, noble, loved, and dear,
Hadst thou not told thy secrets foolishly
To women, none had ever been thy peer!

This Samson never drank a drop of wine,
Nor razor ever touched his head, nor shear,
By precept of a messenger divine,
For in his locks did all his strength inhere;
And fully twenty winters, year by year,
In Israel he had the rule of all;
But he shall shed full many a bitter tear,
For women now shall bring about his fall.

He let Delilah, his beloved, persuade him
To tell how in his hair his puissance lay,
And falsely to his foemen she betrayed him;
And while he slept upon her breast one day
She clipped or sheared his tresses all away,
And let his foemen thus his strength apprize,
And when they found him in this sad array,
They bound him fast, and put out both his eyes.

Before the shears had shorn his locks away
There were no bonds could fetter him or bind;
Now in a prison-cave he had to stay,
And turn a mill, his foemen's grain to grind;
O noble Samson, strongest of mankind,
Once thou wast judge, and dwelt in wealth and glory;
Now thou must weep with eyes gone dark and blind,
Since all thy fortune proved but transitory.

This wretch's end at length was of the sort
That I shall tell: his foes at feast one day
Within a splendid temple, for their sport,
Brought him before them there, the fool to play;
But havoc there he wrought, and foul dismay;
He shook two pillars that sustained the hall,
And down the temple fell, and there it lay,
And slew him and his foemen, one and all.

That is to say – the princes, every one,
And other bodies, full three thousand, fell,
Crushed by that mighty temple's roof of stone;
No more now of this Samson will I tell.
From this clear case and old take warning well
That none should share his counsel with his wife
About such things as should in secret dwell
If they affect his body or his life.

HERCULES

Of Hercules the sovereign conqueror,
Sing now his works – their praise and rumor wide;
He was the flower of strength in peace and war;

He slew the lion, and bore away its hide;
He brought to dust the Centaur's boast and pride;
He slew the Harpies, and he stole as well
The golden apples from the dragon's side;
He brought out Cerberus, the hound of hell;

Busiris, harsh and tyrannous, he slew,
And let his horses eat him, flesh and bone;
He killed the fiery, venomous serpent, too;
Of fierce Achelous' horns, he shattered one;
He slaughtered Cacus in his cave of stone;
He killed Antaeus, that great giant high,
The grisly boar he conquered all alone;
And long upon his neck he bore the sky.

None ever lived, since first the world began,
That slew so many monsters as did he;
Throughout the world his name on rumor ran,
Both for his strength and high integrity;
And every realm of earth he went to see.
He was so strong no man could bar his way;
At the world's ends, instead of boundary,
He set a pillar up, doth Trophee say.

A mistress had this noble champion,
Called Dejanira, and as fresh as May;
And as these scholars tell us every one,
She sent a shirt to him, all fresh and gay.
Alas, this shirt, alas, and welaway!
So cunningly with poison had been filled
That ere he wore it more than half a day
His flesh fell from his bones, and he was killed.

But none the less, some writers would excuse her,
Saying one Nessus schemed this vile attack;
Be as it may – I will not here abuse her;
He wore this shirt upon his naked back
Till with the poison all his flesh was black;
And when he saw no other cure to try,
Hot coals about his body did he pack,
For by no poison would he deign to die.

Thus died this strong and noble Hercules!
Who dares to trust in Fortune for a day?
For he who leads the world as he may please
Before he knows it, goes the downward way.
Wise is the man that knows himself, I say;
Beware! When Fortune wishes to deceive
She waits her time to strike, and takes her prey
In such a way as he would least believe.

NEBUCHADNEZZAR

The precious treasure and the mighty throne,
The glorious sceptre, royal majesty
That Nebuchadnezzar wielded as his own –
The tongue can scarce describe them fittingly.
Twice conqueror of Jerusalem was he,
And took the temple vessels when he went.
At Babylon, with pomp and revelry,
He kept his sovereign seat of government.

The fairest children of the Jewish race,
Of royal blood, were gelded one and all
And made his servants; and within that place
Daniel among the others was his thrall;
He was the wisest youth within that hall,
For he the visions of the king expounded,
Though no Chaldaeans versed in magical
Learning could read them, but were all confounded.

This proud king had a statue made of gold,
In cubits sixty long and seven wide,
And gave command that men both young and old
Should bow to it, and hold it sanctified;
Or in a furnace filled from side to side
With flame, be burned if they should disobey;
But Daniel with two friends of his defied
This law, and would not yield in any way.

This king of kings, in pride and high elation,
Thought now that God, who sits in majesty,
Could not bereave him of his lofty station;

But soon he lost his reason suddenly,
And like a very beast appeared to be,
And ate hay like an ox, and slept outside,
And in the rain with wild beasts wandered he,
Until a time that God had specified.

Like to an eagle's feathers grew his hair;
His nails like wild bird's talons did appear;
Until at last God was resolved to spare
This king, and gave him wit; and many a tear
He shed in thanks; and lived his life in fear
To trespass more, or sin against the right;
And till the time they laid him on his bier
He knew that God was full of grace and might.

BELSHAZZAR

His son, Belshazzar, came to be the king,
And held the reign after his father's day,
Yet from his father's fate could learn no thing,
For proud of heart he was, and of display;
Ever to heathen idols would he pray;
His high position made him strong in pride;
But Fortune cast him down, and there he lay,
With all his realm beginning to divide.

He made a feast to all the lords about
Once on a time, and bade them merry be;
And to his officers began to shout:
"Go now, and bring the vessels forth," said he,
"Which once my father, in prosperity,
Took from the temple in Jerusalem;
And thank our gods for honor valiantly
Won by our elders, which we got from them."

His wife, his nobles, and his concubines,
Drank till their appetite was quenched at last
Out of these noble vessels – various wines;
And on a wall this king his eyes upcast,
And saw an armless hand there, writing fast;
And fearing this, he shook and sighed full sore;

The hand, that struck Belshazzar so aghast,
Wrote *mene, techel, phares,* and no more.

No man of magic was there in that land
That could inform him what these letters meant,
But Daniel made them clear to understand,
Saying, "O king, God to thy father lent
Glory and honor, treasure, rank, and rent,
And he was proud, and held God in disdain;
Therefore a fearful punishment God sent,
And from his hands he took away the reign.

"Cast wholly from man's company away,
With asses must he take his habitation,
Beast-like in sun or rain to feed on hay,
Until at last he knew by revelation
And by his mind, that God has domination
Over all realms and every living thing;
Then God had mercy, and his former station
Restored, and the appearance of a king.

"Thou too, that art his son, art filled with pride,
And all these things thou know'st for certainty,
Art foe to God, and hast Him now defied,
And drunk here of His vessels brazenly;
Thy wife, too, and thy harlots sinfully
Have drunk wines from them. In thy cursèd fanes
Thou sett'st false gods, to praise them wickedly:
Therefore for thee great sorrow God ordains.

"This hand was sent from God, that on the wall
Wrote *mene, techel, phares,* trust ye me.
Thy reign is done, thou hast no weight at all;
Thy realm is now divided, and shall be
Given to the Medes and Persians," ended he.
And it befell the king was slain that night,
And great Darius took the sovereignty,
Though it was his neither by law nor right.

Lordings, here by example ye perceive
How in a lordship is no steadiness;

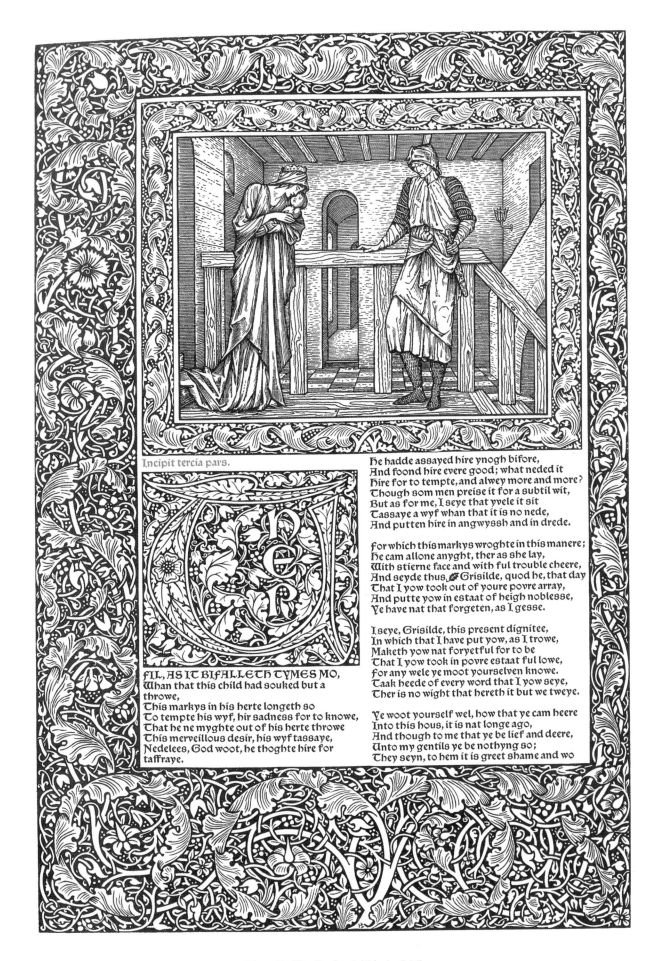

Incipit tercia pars.

He hadde assayed hire ynogh bifore,
And foond hire evere good; what neded it
Hire for to tempte, and alwey more and more?
Though som men preise it for a subtil wit,
But as for me, I seye that yvele it sit
Tassaye a wyf whan that it is no nede,
And putten hire in angwyssh and in drede.

For which this markys wroghte in this manere;
He cam allone anyght, ther as she lay,
With stierne face and with ful trouble cheere,
And seyde thus, Grisilde, quod he, that day
That I yow took out of youre povre array,
And putte yow in estaat of heigh noblesse,
Ye have nat that forgeten, as I gesse.

I seye, Grisilde, this present dignitee,
In which that I have put yow, as I trowe,
Maketh yow nat foryetful for to be
That I yow took in povre estaat ful lowe,
For any wele ye moot yourselven knowe.
Taak heede of every word that I yow seye,
Ther is no wight that hereth it but we tweye.

Ye woot yourself wel, how that ye cam heere
Into this hous, it is nat longe ago,
And though to me that ye be lief and deere,
Unto my gentils ye be nothyng so;
They seyn, to hem it is greet shame and wo

FIL, AS IT BIFALLETH TYMES MO,
Whan that this child had souked but a
    throwe,
This markys in his herte longeth so
To tempte his wyf, hir sadness for to knowe,
That he ne myghte out of his herte throwe
This merveillous desir, his wyf tassaye,
Nedelees, God woot, he thoghte hire for
    taffraye.

Plate 13: The Student's Tale (p. 244)

For Fortune, when she once decides to leave,
Takes from a man wealth, kingdom, and success,
And friends as well, the greater with the less;
For all the friends that Fortune gathers to one,
Turn foes beneath disaster, I should guess;
This proverb is a common and a true one.

ZENOBIA

Zenobia, of great Palmyra queen,
As Persians write of her nobility,
So valiant was in battle, and so keen,
That there was none fought more courageously;
And none had gentler ways, or ancestry.
From royal Persian kings she was descended;
I say not none have been more fair than she,
And yet her form could not have been amended.

Even from her childhood, as I find, she fled
The ways of women; and many a fair wild hart
Through forest ways she tracked, and shot it dead
As from her bow she sent a broad-winged dart;
After the fleetest quarry she would start
And catch it, and when older she would kill
Lions and bears, and rend their limbs apart,
And with her hands subdue them to her will.

She dared to seek the wild beast in his lair,
Or through the mountains run the livelong night,
And sleep beneath a bush; and she would dare
To wrestle with main strength, and match her might
With any youth, however strong or light;
And in her arms was none could ever stand;
She kept her maiden state untouched and bright;
To no man would she deign to give her hand.

Her friends at last contrived to have her married
To Odenatus, prince in that same land,
Though long she made them linger while she tarried.
And Odenatus, ye must understand
Had fancies like to hers. But hand to hand

When they were knit at last, it would appear
That theirs were joy and rapture to command,
For each to other was beloved and dear.

Save for one thing – that she would not consent
In any way, that he should with her lie
But once, for she had set her clear intent
To have a child, the world to multiply;
And just as soon as she could well espy
That she was not with child from that one act,
Then she would quickly let him gratify
His passion, and more times than one, in fact.

And if she were with child at the first cast,
Then he should play no further at that game
Until the space of forty days had passed;
Then she would grant him once to do the same;
And be this Odenatus wild or tame,
He got no more of her, for thus she said:
"Otherwise were it lechery and shame
For wives, if men should play with them in bed."

Two sons this queen by Odenatus bore,
And reared them well in books and virtuous ways;
But to our story let us turn once more;
I say, a creature so deserving praise,
And wise, and nobly generous all her days,
And vigilant in war, and courteous too,
And fitter for the toil that battles raise,
Could never have been found the whole world
        through.

The richness of her state could not be told,
Whether as to her garments, or her store
Of vessels; she was clad in gems and gold;
And when she lay at leisure, free from war,
Not to the hunt, but rather to explore
And learn new tongues she turned, and found
        delight
In reading books, and learning more and more
How she might live by virtue and by right.

And, to be brief in telling you this story,
So doughty was her husband, as was she,
That in the orient soon they swelled their glory
With lands they won, and cities fair to see,
That all had bowed beneath the majesty
Of Rome. And strong of hand they held them fast,
And never could their foemen make them flee
Till Odenatus' days were done at last.

He who would read of battles that she made
Against great Sapor king, and many more,
How these events fell out, why she essayed
Her conquests, and what right to them she bore;
Of her misfortune later, and the war
In which she was besieged and captured, too,
Let him my master Petrarch's book explore,
That wrote enough of this, I promise you.

When Odenatus died, she valiantly
Held all the realm, and with a mighty hand
Fought all her foes with such ferocity
That not a king or prince was in that land
But he was glad such mercy to command
That she would not attack him; in this way
Was many a treaty and alliance planned
To give them peace, and let her ride and play.

Not Claudius, the Roman emperor,
Nor Gallienus, who had held the throne
Before him, had such appetite for war,
Nor was Armenian or Egyptian known,
Or Syrian or Arabian, that had shown
A heart to take the field with her and fight,
Lest with her hands this queen should strike them
        prone,
Or with her armies scatter them in flight.

In kingly dress her sons would ride with her,
As heirs to whom their father's realms would fall;
And Thymalaë and Hermanno were
Their names, as Persians called them, one and all.

But Fortune's honey ever hides its gall;
For no great time endured this queen's success;
Down from her kingdom Fortune made her fall
Into mischance and woe and wretchedness.

Aurelian, when at length the government
Of Rome was in his hands, prepared one day
For vengeance on this queen, and forth he went,
And with his legions soon he took his way
Unto her realm. What more is there to say?
He put to rout and captured her at last,
And chained her sons and her with no delay,
And won the land, and home to Rome he passed.

Among the other trophies that he won
Her chair, of gold and gems wrought splendidly,
This mighty Roman, this Aurelian,
Brought back to Rome, for everyone to see.
And in this emperor's triumph walketh she,
With gilded chains about her neck, and crowned
In token of her former sovereignty,
And all in jewelled garments richly gowned.

Alas! she that was feared and held in honor
By kings and emperors in other hours,
Stands now where all the crowd may stare upon her;
And she that helmed in steel displayed her powers
In bitter war, and stormed strong towns and towers
Shall wear a helm of glass upon her head,
And for the victor's sceptre wreathed in flowers,
Take up a distaff now, to earn her bread.

OF PEDRO, KING OF SPAIN

O noble, O worthy Pedro, glory of Spain,
Whom Fortune held so high in majesty,
Well ought men for thy piteous death complain!
Out of thy land thy brother made thee flee,
And later, at a siege, insidiously
Thou wast betrayed, and to his tent wast led,
And by his own hand there he murdered thee,

And got thy realm and rents when thou wast dead.
He that for arms bore on a field of snow
An eagle by a flame-hued rod ensnared,
He brewed this deed of cursedness and woe;
The "wicked nest" in this vile ambush shared –
No Charles' Oliver, that ever cared
For truth and honor, but a Ganelon
Of Olivers, that for a bribe prepared
The snare by which this good king was undone.

OF PETER, KING OF CYPRUS

O worthy Peter, that wast Cyprus' king,
And Alexandria won by strategy,
Full many a heathen wrought'st thou suffering,
For which thy very lieges envied thee;
And only for thy skill in chivalry
They slew thee in thy bed upon a morrow;
Thus Fortune guides her wheel, and suddenly
From happiness brings men to woe and sorrow.

OF BERNABO OF LOMBARDY

O great Bernabo, viscount of Milan,
The god of pleasure, scourge of Lombardy,
Why not recount thy fortune, that began
With high ascent, and closed disastrously?
Thy brother's son, two times allied to thee,
For he was son-in-law and nephew to thee,
In prison made thee die in misery,
But I know neither how nor why he slew thee.

OF UGELINO, COUNT OF PISA

Of Ugelino hath no tongue the power,
For pity, to relate the misery;
A little out of Pisa stands a tower,
And in this tower in prison languished he,
And with him were his little children three,
The oldest of them scarce five years of age.
Fortune, alas! It was great cruelty

To put such little birds in such a cage!
In dungeon there he was condemned to die,
For Roger, bishop of the town, had spread
A rumor of this earl, which, though a lie,
Among the people a rebellion bred,
And they imprisoned him, as I have said.
And in that tower the meat and drink they had
So meagre were, they scarcely could be fed,
And it was likewise very coarse and bad.

One day it came to pass that, at the hour
When food and drink by custom were supplied,
The jailor shut the two doors of the tower.
He spoke not, though he heard them clang outside
But through his heart the thought began to glide
That they would let him die of hunger there;
"Alas! Alas! that I was born," he cried,
And from his eyes the tears fell in despair.

His young son, three years old, spoke to him thus:
"Father," he asked, "why sit ye weeping there?
When will the jailor bring our food to us?
Is there no crust of bread ye hide somewhere?
I cannot sleep for hunger that I bear.
Would God I might forever sleep," he said;
"Then would no hunger at my belly tear;
There is no thing I want so much as bread."

Thus day by day this little child would cry,
Till in his father's lap he laid his head,
And whispered: "Farewell, father, I must die,"
And kissed him, and that very day was dead.
And when the father saw that life had fled
He bit his arms for sorrow, and exclaimed:
"Alas, O Fortune! Now, O day of dread!
For all my woe can thy false wheel be blamed!"

His children thought it was for want of bread
He gnawed his arms; and not for any woe.
"Alas, O father! Do not thus!" they said;
"But rather eat our flesh, for well ye know

Ye gave it to us; take it from us now
And eat enough;" thus both his children cried;
And after that, within a day or so,
They laid themselves upon his lap, and died.

He, in despair, perished of hunger, too;
So died this Earl of Pisa wretchedly,
Whom Fortune from high station overthrew;
This should suffice now for this tragedy.
And he that would a longer version see,
Let him go read in Dante, as they call
The great Italian poet; faithfully
From point to point in full he tells it all.

NERO

Though Nero was as vicious in his ways
As any fiend that lies in deepest hell,
Yet all this wide world, as Suetonius says,
Under his rule did in subjection dwell,
Both East and West, and North and South as well.
With rubies, sapphires, and with pearls moon-white
Were all his garments wrought, for truth to tell,
In jewels took this Nero great delight.

More delicate, more pompous in array,
More proud was never emperor than he;
The clothing he had worn a single day,
After that time he never wished to see.
And nets of gold he had – a quantity –
To fish the Tiber when he wished to play;
His passions all were law by his decree,
For Fortune was his friend, and would obey.

He burned Rome for the pleasure of his eye;
He bade the senators be slain one day
That he might hear how men would weep and cry;
He killed his brother, and by his sister lay.
How piteously did he his mother slay –
He slit her womb, for this cause and no other:
To see whence he was born! Ah, welaway!

That he should feel so little for his mother!
No tear fell from his eyes to see this sight.
He only said: "A fair woman was she!"
It is great wonder how he could or might
Judge her dead beauty so dispassionately.
He bade them bring him wine, and presently
He drank. No other sign of woe he made.
When cruel heart joins with authority,
Too deep, alas! the poison will invade!

In youth a master taught this emperor
The ways of learning and of courtesy,
And if the books speak true, no man was more
The flower of moral virtue then than he.
And while this master had authority
He made him gentle and intelligent,
So it was long indeed ere tyranny
Marked him, or other vice was evident.

This Seneca, of whom I tell you here,
Because this Nero held him in such dread;
For he would scourge all vice that might appear,
And not by act, but by wise words instead –
"An emperor, sire, must for his good," he said,
"Be virtuous, and hate all tyranny –"
He bade that in his bath he should be bled
In both arms, till he perish finally.

This Nero in his youth by custom, too,
Before his master always used to rise,
Which afterwards he thought a shame to do;
Therefore he made him perish in this wise.
But none the less this Seneca the wise
Chose in a bath to die, than face the fear
Of other torment Nero might devise;
And thus hath Nero slain his master dear.

It fell at last that Fortune pleased no longer
This Nero's soaring pride to tolerate,
For though he might be strong, yet she was stronger;
She thought: "By God, my folly is too great

To set on high so vile a reprobate
And let men call him emperor, one and all.
By God, now will I pull him from his seat!
When least expecting, soonest shall he fall!"

The people rose against his rule one night,
Hating his crimes, and when he was aware
Of what they did, he left his house in flight,
To friends, with hope of refuge, to repair;
And fast he knocked, and always, everywhere,
The more he cried the faster shut each door.
He knew himself deceived, and in despair
He went his way, and dared to call no more.

The people cried and muttered all about;
He heard the thing they said, and was dismayed:
"Where is this tyrant Nero?" ran the shout,
And all but crazed he listened, sore afraid.
And piteously to all his gods he prayed,
But never got the help for which he cried;
Almost he died for fear. Then he essayed
Within a garden near at hand to hide.

Two churls were sitting in the garden there
Before a fire that flickered great and red;
And he began to pray them in despair
That they would slay him, cutting off his head,
So that his body, after he was dead,
Might not be marred by men, and put to shame.
But he was forced to slay himself instead,
And Fortune laughed at this, and made her game.

HOLOFERNES

Never was captain under any a king
That brought more realms by conquest to his
    crown,
Or showed more strength at war in everything,
In all his age, or had such great renown,
Or more with pomp and lofty pride was blown
Than Holofernes. Fortune spurred him to it,

Bawdily kissed and led him up and down,
Until his head was off before he knew it!

Not only must men give him worldly awe
For fear they lose their wealth or liberty,
But likewise must deny their holy law.
"Nebuchadnezzar was a god," said he;
"Ye shall adore no other deity."
All men to this command of his bowed down
Save in Bethulia, where there chanced to be
Eliachim, a priest of that same town.

But let the death of Holofernes warn!
One night he drowsed after his drunken play
Within his tent, as large as any barn;
And there, despite his pomp and proud array,
Judith, a woman, slew him as he lay,
Smiting his head off, and she left his tent
Unknown to all, and took a secret way,
And with his head back to her city went.

OF THE ILLUSTRIOUS KING ANTIOCHUS

What need to tell of King Antiochus –
His high estate and royal majesty,
His lofty pride, his actions infamous?
There never was another such as he.
Read of him in the book of Maccabee,
And there behold his words of insolent pride,
And why he fell from high prosperity,
And how all wretched on a hill he died.

Fortune had so increased his vaunting pride
He thought in very truth he could attain
Unto the stars, spreading on every side,
Weigh mountains in the balance, and restrain
The tides, and all the waters of the main;
And God's own people most he held in hate,
And all of them in torment would have slain,
Thinking that God could not his pride abate.

And since the Jews had put to rout in war
His captains two, Nichanor and Timothy,
So high a hate against that race he bore,
His chariot on the instant ordered he,
And with an oath he swore most pitilessly
To seek Jerusalem and wreck his ire
Upon that place with every cruelty,
But soon this king was balked of his desire.

God for this threat so heavily did smite him
With hidden wound impossible to cure,
That in his entrails did so cut and bite him
He suffered pain impossible to endure.
And this revenge was justice, to be sure;
For others' entrails had he wounded sore,
But from his purpose cursèd and impure
He would not turn, but held to it the more.

And soon he bade them marshal out his host;
But suddenly, before he was aware,
God daunted all his pride and all his boast;
For from his chariot he tumbled there,
And skin and limb with many a bruise and tear
So hurt that he could neither walk nor ride,
But men were forced to bear him in a chair,
Bruised badly on the back and on the side.

The wrath of God fell with such cruelty
That loathsome worms within his body crept;
And more than this, he stank so horribly
That none of those that tended him or kept,
Alike in waking hours, or when he slept,
Could bear the fearful stench of this great king;
In this misfortune then he wailed and wept,
And knew God lord of every living thing.

To all his army and to him as well
His carrion's stench was loathsome as could be.
None could endure to lift him for the smell.
And in this stench and fearful agony
Upon a hill he perished wretchedly.

Thus did this robber and this homicide
That brought so many to calamity
Receive such guerdon as belongs to pride.

OF ALEXANDER

So widely known is Alexander's story
That every man of any education
Has heard a part, at least, or all his glory;
And, to be brief, all of this world's creation
He won by force, and had such reputation
That kings to sue for peace were well content,
For man and beast he held in subjugation
To the world's ends, whatever way he went.

No conqueror ever lived that could resemble
Or be compared with him in fame and power;
For all this world with fear of him did tremble;
Of knighthood and of freedom was he flower,
And Fortune gave her honor as his dower.
Save wine and women, nothing could assuage
His lust for arms and toil of battle-hour,
So like a lion did his spirit rage.

How could I praise him then, although I told
Of Darius and a hundred thousand more,
Of kings and dukes, of earls and princes bold
He conquered, and what woe through him they bore?
The world was his, as I have said before,
As far as any man could walk or ride;
To tell or write his knightly strength in war
I could not, though forever more I tried.

Twelve years he reigned, as says the *Maccabees*,
And he was Philip's son, that rose in place
From Macedon, as the first king of Greece;
O noble Alexander, what disgrace
That thou shouldst ever stand in such a case!
By thine own people poisoned must thou be;
False Fortune turned thy six into an ace,
And yet she never shed a tear for thee.

Who now shall give me tears for my lament
Over his high estate and nobleness
That swayed the world, and yet was not content
With what could be no more, but still must press
In lofty spirit flamed for high success?
Alas, who now will help me execrate
That poison, and false Fortune none the less –
Those two on whom I blame his woeful fate?

OF JULIUS CÆSAR

By wisdom, manhood, and high work in war,
From humble bed to royal majesty
Julius uprose, the mighty conqueror,
That won the occident by land and sea
With force, or treaties fashioned skilfully,
And thus to Rome made it all tributary;
And later, emperor of Rome was he
Till Fortune turned at length his adversary.

O mighty Cæsar, that in Thessaly
Against thy father-in-law, great Pompey, drew,
Who brought from all the East the chivalry
As far as where the day dawns in the blue –
Thou through thy knighthood took them all,
        or slew,
Save for a remnant that with Pompey fled,
Thus didst thou awe the Orient, and subdue;
Thank Fortune, that so prospered thee and sped!

But now a little while will I lament
Pompey, of Rome the noble governor
That forth in flight after this battle went;
One of his men, a false conspirator,
Smote off his head, and this to Julius bore,
Hoping to win great favor as his friend.
Pompey, alas! the Orient's conqueror,
That Fortune brought thee thus to such an end!

To Rome again went marching Julius,
Laurelled, and riding in a triumph high,

But on a time one Brutus Cassius,
That saw his high estate with jealous eye,
Formed a conspiracy full dark and sly
Against this Julius, in a subtle way,
And fixed the very place where he should die,
Struck down by daggers, as I soon shall say.

Unto the capitol this Julius passed
One day, for there by habit would he go,
And in the capitol they seized him fast,
This Brutus false, and many another foe,
And with their daggers many a grievous blow
They dealt him, and they left him where he fell,
And only once or twice he groaned for woe,
If it is not a lie the legends tell.

So manly was the heart this Julius bore,
And so he loved a noble modesty,
That, though his deadly gashes hurt him sore,
Across his thighs his mantle quietly
He cast, that none his nakedness should see,
And in his dying swoon as he reclined,
And knew his death a certain thing to be,
The thought of modesty was in his mind.

Lucan, to thee this story I commend,
And to Valerian and Suetonius,
That set it down, its substance and its end:
How Fortune with these conquerors did thus
Begin as friend, and then was traitorous.
Let none put trust upon her favor long,
But watch her always. For so teacheth us
The fate of all these conquerors so strong!

CRŒSUS

Rich Crœsus, Lydia's king in byegone day,
By Cyrus that was greatly held in dread,
Amid his pride saw fortune snatched away,
And to be burned towards the fire was led.
But such a rain the heavens above him shed

It quenched the fire, and thereby let him flee;
But still he had no wisdom in his head
Till Fortune brought him to the gallows tree.

When he was free, then nothing could prevent
His making war on Cyrus once again;
He thought that Fortune sent this accident,
And showed, by his escaping through the rain,
That by his foemen he should not be slain;
Also, there came a dream to him one night
Which made this monarch both so glad and vain
He planned for vengeance now with all his might.

He saw himself upon a tree, he thought,
With Jupiter to wash him, back and side,
And a fair towel Phœbus to him brought,
With which to dry himself. And full of pride,
Unto his daughter by his side he cried,
Since she for noble learning was renowned,
And bade her tell him what it signified,
And she began his vision to expound.

"The tree is for a gallows meant," said she;
"The sun and rain betoken Jupiter;
And Phœbus and his towel I take to be
The sun's beams that shall fall upon you, sir;
Father, thou shalt be hanged, I must infer;
And rain shall wash thee, and the sun shall dry."
Thus flat and plain was Crœsus warned by her;
And Phania was the name they called her by.

Thus in his pride was Crœsus hanged, this king;
His royal throne could prove of no avail;
Tragedy is no other kind of thing,
And in its singing cannot help bewail
That Fortune waits forever to assail
With unexpected strokes great kingdoms proud,
For when men trust her, always will she fail,
And mask her shining visage in a cloud.

Here the Knight stops the Monk in his Tale

The Nun's Priest's Tale

THE NUN'S PRIEST is not present in the General Prologue, yet he tells a brilliant tale. His traditional animal fable becomes a mock heroic tragedy about a cockerel pursued by a fox. The tale is packed with literary and classical references, and relates to many of the other tales and their themes. It ends with a cluster of possible morals that could be drawn from it. It is one of the finest of the tales.

THE NUN'S PRIEST'S TALE

The Prologue to the Nun's Priest's Tale

"Ho!" cried the Knight, "no more, sir, of this stuff!
What ye have said is certainly enough
And more besides; a little heaviness
Will do for most of us, as I should guess.
For me, it is a thing that cannot please
To hear how men that dwelt in wealth and ease
Are fallen on days that strip them or destroy!
Rather I find the opposite a joy
And comfort – when a man of poor estate
Rises in life, and grows more fortunate,
And there stays on in his prosperity;
That is a happy thing, it seems to me,
And of such matters it is good to tell."
"Yea," said our Landlord. "Now by St. Paul's bell,
Ye speak the truth. This Monk, he jabbers loud:
He told how Fortune 'covered with a cloud'
I know not what – and of a 'tragedy'
Just now ye heard. By God, what good can be
For any one to wail so or complain
For what is done? Also, it gives us pain,
As ye have said, to hear of sorrow thus.
God bless you, Monk, no more of that for us!
Your tale distresses all this company;
Such talking is not worth a butterfly!
What pleasure can it give, or chance for game?
Wherefore, Sir Monk, or else, to use your name,
Sir Piers, I pray you, tell us something else;
For to be sure, but for those jingling bells

That deck your bridle there on every side,
By heaven's King, that for us bled and died,
I should long since have tumbled off in sleep,
Although the slough beneath were never so deep;
And then your tale had all been told in vain,
For truly, as these writers make it plain:
'When a man cannot find an audience,
To speak his mind is neither help nor sense.'
And if a man speak something well, I know
I have the stuff within that tells me so.
Give us a tale of hunting, sir, I pray."
"No," said the Monk, "I have no will for play;
Go bid another tell – my tale is told."
Then spoke our Landlord, rude of speech and bold,
And to the Nun's priest called out quick and clear:
"Thou Priest, come hither; thou Sir John, come here!
Gladden our hearts with some gay escapade –
Be jolly, though thou ride upon a jade!
Although thy horse may be both foul and lean,
So that he serve thee, care thou not a bean,
But let thy heart be merry ever more!"
"Yes, sir," this Priest replied, "Yes, Host," he swore,
"Unless ye find me merry, then scold me well!"
And soon his tale this Priest began to tell,
And in this way to all of us spoke on –
This goodly man, this sweet priest, this Sir John.

*Here begins the Nun's Priest's Tale of the Cock and
the Hen, Chanticleer and Pertelote*

ONCE, long ago, set close beside a wood,
Meagre of look, a little cottage stood
Where dwelt a poor old widow in a dale.
This widow, she of whom I tell my tale,
Even since the day when she was last a wife
All patiently had led a simple life;
Small were her earnings and her property,
But what God sent she used with husbandry,
And kept two daughters and herself. Of sows
Three and no more she had about the house,
Also a sheep called Molly, and three kine.

Her sooty hall and bower were nothing fine,
And there full many a slender meal she ate.
No poignant sauce was needed for her plate;
No dainty morsel passed her throat; her fare
Accorded with the clothes she had to wear.
With surfeit she was never sick, but in
A temperate diet was her medicine,
And busy labor, and a heart's content.
Gout never kept her from a dance; nor bent
With stroke of apoplexy was her head.
Of wine none drank she, neither white nor red;
Her board was mostly served with white and black:
Milk and brown bread; of these she found no lack;
And bacon, or an egg, was not uncommon,
For in her way she was a dairywoman.

    She had a yard, that was enclosed about
By sticks, and a dry ditch that ran without,
And there she kept a cock named Chanticleer;
None in the land at crowing was his peer.
His voice was merrier than the organ's tone
That loud on mass-days in the church is blown,
And surer from his lodge his crowing fell
Than stroke of any clock or abbey bell.
He knew by nature each ascension of
The equinoxial circle arched above,
For when fifteen degrees had been ascended,
He crowed, so that it could not be amended.
Redder than coral was his comb, and all
Crested with notches, like a castle wall;
His bill was black – like jet it seemed to glow –
Like azure shone each leg and every toe,
His nails were white – the lily flower is duller;
And gold all burnished was his body's color.
This noble cock had under goverance
Seven hens, to do all wholly his pleasance;
Which were his paramours and sisters dear
And in their colors matched him wondrous near;
Of whom she that was fairest hued of throat
Fairly was called, Damoselle Pertelote.
Courteous she was, discreet and debonaire,
Companionable, and bore herself so fair

Even since the day that she was seven nights old,
She hath the heart of Chanticleer in hold –
Locked in each motion, in each graceful limb;
He loved her so, that this was well with him.
But what a joy it was to hear them sing
In sweet accord: "My Love's Gone Journeying"
While the bright sun uprose from out the land,
For this was in the time, I understand,
When all the birds and beasts could sing and speak.

    So once it fell, as day began to break,
And Chanticleer with his wives one and all
Was sitting on his perch within the hall,
And next him sat this fair Dame Pertelote,
That Chanticleer groaned deeply in his throat,
Like one that in his dream sore troubled is.
And when she heard this roaring groan of his,
Pertelote was aghast, and cried: "Dear heart,
What aileth you, that thus ye groan and start?
What a fine sleeper! Fie now, fie for shame!"
But Chanticleer replied: "I pray you, Dame,
Take it not so amiss; by God, I seemed
Just now in such a danger as I dreamed
That still my heart is strangely terrified.
God bring my dream to something good!" he cried,
"And out of prison foul my body keep!
Now I was roaming (so I dreamed in sleep)
Within our yard, and there I saw a beast
Was like a dog, and would have made arrest
Upon my body, and would have had me dead.
His color was between a yellow and red,
And tipped his tail was, likewise both his ears,
With black, quite different from his other hairs.
His snout was small between two glowing eyes;
Even now my heart with terror almost dies;
And doubtless it was this which made me start."

    "For shame!" quoth she. "Fie on you, small of heart!
Alas!" she cried, "for, by the God above,
Now have ye lost my heart and all my love:
I cannot love a coward, by my faith.
For truly, what so any woman saith,
We all desire, if such a thing can be,

Husbands that shall be sturdy, wise, and free,
Trusty, and not a fool, nor one to hoard,
Nor such as stands aghast to see a sword,
Nor yet a boaster, by the God above:
How durst ye say for shame unto your love
That there was anything on earth ye feared?
Have ye no man's heart, though ye have a beard?
And was it dreams that brought this melancholy?
God knows that nothing is in dreams but folly.
Dreams are engendered out of gluttony,
And drink, and from complexions, it may be,
That show of humors more than should be right.
Surely this vision which ye dreamed last night
Comes of the too great superfluity
Ye have of your red *colera*, pardee,
Which makes folk in their dreams to have great dread
Of arrows, or of fire with tongues of red,
Of great beasts, that will bite them, and of all
Struggle and strife, and dogs both great and small –
Just as the humor of melancholy will make
Full many a man within his sleep to break
Out crying with fear of black bears or black bulls
Or else of some black devil that at him pulls.
Of other humors I could tell you still
That work on many a sleeping man much ill,
But I will pass as quickly as I can.

"Lo, Cato, he that was so wise a man,
Said he not thus: Take no account of dreams?
Now, sire," she said, "when we fly from the beams
For God's love take a little laxative;
Upon my soul, and as I hope to live,
My counsel is the best, and it is wholly
The truth: for choler and for melancholy
Purge yourself now and, since ye must not tarry,
And in this town is no apothecary,
I will myself to certain herbs direct you
That shall be profit to you, and correct you;
And in our very yard such herbs should be
Which of their nature have the property
To purge you wholly, under and above.
Forget this not, I say, for God's own love!

Ye are too choleric of complexion;
Then take good heed lest the ascending sun
Shall find you all replete with humors hot;
For if it do, I dare to lay a groat
That ye shall straightway have a tertian fever
Or ague, that may be your bane forever.
A day or two ye shall your diet make
On worms, and then your laxatives shall take:
Spurge-laurel, for example, and centaury
And fumitory, or hellebore, may be,
With caper-spurge, too, or the gaytree berry,
And herb-ive, with the taste that makes you merry.
Just peck them where they grow, and eat. But make
Good cheer now, husband, for your fathers' sake.
Fear ye no dream; now can I say no more."

"Madam," quoth he, "*grand merci* for your lore
Yet touching this Lord Cato who, I own,
Hath for his wisdom such a great renown,
Though he adviseth us to take no heed
Of dreams – by God, in old books can ye read
Of many a man, more in authority
Than ever Cato was, God prosper me,
That say just the reverse of what he says,
And by experience in many ways
Find that our dreams may be prophetic things
Alike for joys and woeful happenings
That in this present life all folk endure.
This needs no argument to make it sure,
For the full proof is shown in many a deed.

"One of the greatest authors that men read
Says thus: that on a time two friends set out
On pilgrimage, and they were both devout;
And it befell they came unto a town
Where were such crowds of people up and down
And in the hostelries so little space
There was not even a cottage in the place
Wherein the both of them might harbored be.
So they were forced, of sheer necessity,
For that night's sleeping to part company,
And each of them goes to his hostelry
To take his lodging as it might befall.

Enformed of his wyl, sente his message,
Comaundynge hem swiche bulles to devyse
As to his crueel purpos may suffyse,
How that the pope, as for his peples reste,
Bad hym to wedde another, if hym leste.

I seye, he bad they sholde countrefete
The popes bulles, makynge mencioun
That he hath leve his firste wyf to lete,
As by the popes dispensacioun,
To stynte rancour and dissencioun
Bitwixe his peple and hym; thus seyde the
bulle,
The which they han publiced atte fulle.

The rude peple, as it no wonder is,
Wenden ful wel that it hadde be right so;
But whan thise tidynges cam to Grisildis,
I deeme that hire herte was ful wo.
But she, ylike sad for everemo,
Disposed was, this humble creature,
Thadversitee of fortune al tendure,

Abidynge evere his lust and his plesance
To whom that she was yeven, herte and al,
As to hire verray worldly suffisance;
But shortly if this storie I tellen shal,
This markys writen hath in special
A lettre in which he sheweth his entente,

And secreely he to Boloigne it sente.

To the erl of Panyk, which that hadde tho
Wedded his suster, preyde he specially
To bryngen hoom agayn his children two
In honurable estaat al openly.
But o thyng he hym preyde outrely,
That he to no wight, though men wolde en-
quere,
Sholde nat telle, whos children that they
were,

But seye, the mayden sholde ywedded be
Unto the markys of Saluce anon.
And as this erl was preyed, so dide he;
For at day set he on his wey is goon
Toward Saluce, and lordes many oon
In riche array, this mayden for to gyde,
Hir yonge brother ridynge hire bisyde.

Arrayed was toward hir mariage
This fresshe mayde, ful of gemmes cleere;
Hir brother, which that seven yeer was of age,
Arrayed eek ful fressh in his manere.
And thus in greet noblesse and with glad
cheere,
Toward Saluces shapynge hir journey,
Fro day to day they ryden in hir wey.

Explicit quarta pars.

Plate 14: The Student's Tale (p. 249)

The one of them was bedded in a stall
Out in a yard with oxen of the plow;
The other got a proper place somehow,
As was his chance, or fortune, it may be,
That governs all lives universally.
    "And it befell that, long before the day,
This man, as dreaming in his bed he lay,
Thought that he heard his friend begin him call,
Crying: 'Alas! for in an ox's stall
This night shall I be murdered as I lie.
Now help me, dear my brother, ere I die.
Arise! in all haste come to me!' he said.
His comrade started from his sleep in dread,
But when he was awakened from his dreaming
He turned, and gave no notice to it, deeming
That all his dream was but a vanity!
And twice as he was sleeping thus dreamed he.
And then he thought he saw his friend again
A third time, and he said, 'Now am I slain.
Behold my wounds, bloody and deep and wide!
Arise up early on the morrow-tide
And at the west gate of the town,' quoth he,
'A cart with dung full laden shalt thou see,
In which my body is hidden secretly;
Then boldly stop that dung-cart instantly.
My gold did cause my murder, to say truly.'
Then all the slaying did he tell him duly,
With a full piteous face and pale of hue.
And ye may trust, his dream he found full true.
For on the morrow, with the break of day,
Unto his comrade's inn he took his way,
And when he came upon the ox's stall
To his companion he began to call.
    "The landlord spoke and answered him anon
After this fashion: 'Sir, your friend is gone;
He went from out the town when day first broke.'
Then straightway in this man suspicion woke,
For he remembered what he dreamed, and he
Would stay no more, but went forth instantly
Unto the west gate of the town, and found
A dung-cart, set as if to dung the ground,

That was arrayed exactly in the way
As in his dream he heard the dead man say.
Then with a bold heart he began to cry
Justice and vengeance on this villainy:
'My friend was slain last night, and in this cart
Lies staring with a wound above his heart!
I cry upon the officers,' quoth he,
'That should keep rule here, and security!
Help! Help! Alas, here lies my comrade slain!'
What should I add to make the tale more plain?
The folk rushed out and cast the cart to ground,
And in the middle of the dung they found
The body of the man, murdered all new.
    "O blissful God, that art so just and true!
Lo! always thus murder dost thou betray!
Murder will out, we see it day by day.
So loathsome is it, and such cursèd treason
To God, the soul of justice and of reason,
That never will He let it hidden be;
Though it should stay a year or two or three,
Murder will out – this is my whole opinion.
Straightway the officers that had dominion
Over the city, seized and tortured so
The carter, and the landlord with him, too,
That soon they both confessed their villainy
And by the neck were hanged. So men may see
From such examples, dreams are to be feared.
And truly, in the same book there appeared,
Right in the chapter following on this
(I lie not, as I hope for joy or bliss)
A tale of two that would have left the strand
To cross the sea and reach a far-off land
If the wind's motion had not been contrary,
But in a city this had made them tarry
That stood full pleasant by a harbor-side.
But finally, one day, toward eventide,
The wind made change; right as they wished it blew,
Then happy to their slumber went the two
With hope full early to be voyaging.
But unto one befell a marvellous thing,
For, in his sleep, almost at break of day,

He had a wondrous vision as he lay.
It seemed to him a man stood at his side
Warning him in that city to abide,
Saying: 'If thou tomorrow go thy way
Thou shalt be drowned; I have no more to say.'
He woke, and told his vision to his friend,
And prayed him, lest the dream some ill portend,
To put the voyage off beyond that morn.
At that his friend began to laugh in scorn
Lying the while near by within his bed,
'No dream shall ruin my affairs,' he said,
'Stirring my fears with fancies wild and teeming.
I wouldn't give a straw for all thy dreaming.
Vain tricks are dreams wherethrough the mind escapes
To fashion fantasies of owls or apes,
And many a maze. By God, for certainty,
Men dream what never was and cannot be.
But since I see that thou art bent on staying,
Wasting thy time with visions and delaying,
God knows I am sorry for it – so good day.'
And thus he took his leave and went his way.
But it befell ere half his course was sailed,
I know not why, nor what it was that failed,
By accident his vessel's hull was rent,
And ship and man beneath the water went
In sight of other ships not far away
That at the same time sailed with them that day.
Therefore, my fair, belovèd Pertelote,
From such old stories mayst thou clearly note
That no man should too greatly scoff about
His dreams; indeed, I tell thee, out of doubt
Full many a dream deserveth well our dread.
    "Lo, lately in Saint Kenelm's life I read –
That was Kenulphus' son, the noble king
Of Mercia, how young Kenelm dreamed a thing.
One night, a little time ere he was slain,
His murder in a dream was shown him plain.
His nurse explained this vision well unto him,
And warned him of the treason men might do him.
And bade him be on guard; yet having but seven
Years only, and a heart all fixed on heaven,

To any vision little heed gave he.
By God, but it were worth my shirt to me
If thou hadst read this, Madam, as have I.
Dame Pertelote, this truth I certify:
Macrobeus, that wrote down long ago
In Africa the dream of Scipio,
Commendeth dreams, and says they often be
Warnings of things that afterwards men see.
    "And furthermore, I pray you notice well
In the Old Testament, if Daniël
Believed that dreams were any vanity,
And read of Joseph too, and ye shall see
Whether some dreams may be (I say not all)
Warnings of things that afterwards befall.
Consider Egypt's King, Dan Pharao,
And let his baker and his butler show
Whether of dreams they felt not the result.
Whoso will divers histories consult
May read of dreams full many a wondrous thing.
    "Lo, Crœsus, that in Lydia was king, –
Did he not dream he sat upon a tree,
Which signified his hanging that should be?
And lo, Andromache, Dan Hector's wife –
Before the day that Hector lost his life
Dreams gave her warning that should Hector go
With day to join the fight against the foe,
The life of Hector would be lost, and she
Warned him of this, but unsuccessfully.
He went to fight, holding her vision vain,
And so was shortly by Achilles slain.
But this tale is too long to tell, and dawn
Draws near already; I may not go on.
In brief, and for conclusion, I assert
That of this vision I shall have some hurt.
And, Madam, I will tell you furthermore
That on these laxatives I set no store,
For they are venomous, I'll never try them;
I love them never a jot, and I defy them!
    "Now let us speak of mirth, and stop all this;
Dame Pertelote, as I have hope of bliss,
In one thing God hath richly sent me grace,

For when I see the beauty of your face
Ye be so scarlet red about the eyes
That as I gaze all dread within me dies,
For sure as gospel I would have you know,
Mulier est hominis confusio;
Madam, the meaning of this Latin is –
Woman's the joy of man and all his bliss.
For when at night I feel your fluffy side,
Although I may not then upon you ride,
Because our perch, alas, is made so narrow,
Such joy and solace pierce me to the marrow
That then do I defy both vision and dream."
And with that word he flew down from the beam –
For it was day – and his hens one and all;
And with a chucking he commenced to call,
For in the yard he had found a grain of corn.
His fear he scorned now with a royal scorn;
He feathered Pertelote full twenty time,
And trod as often, ere that it was prime.
All like unto a lion grim he goes,
And strutteth up and down upon his toes.
Scarcely he deigned with foot to touch the ground,
And chucked all proudly when a corn he found,
And then his wives ran to him, one and all.
Thus royal, like a prince within his hall,
Here of this Chanticleer I take farewell,
And after of his danger will I tell.

Now when the month in which the world began,
That March is called, when God first fashioned man,
Was ended; yea, and in addition too
(Since March began) thirty more days and two,
It fell that Chanticleer, in all his pride,
His wives all seven walking by his side,
Cast his eye upward to the shining sun
That in the sign of Taurus now had run
Twenty and one degrees and somewhat more,
And knew by nature (and no other lore)
That it was prime, and crew out lustily.
And, "Now the sun has climbed the heaven," said he,
"Forty degrees and one, and more for sure;
Dame Pertelote, my bliss and paramour,

Hearken these birds how joyfully they sing,
And see the flowers, how fresh and bright they spring;
Full is my heart of joy and revelling."
But suddenly befell a grievous thing,
For ever the farther end of joy is woe.
God know'th that joys of earth are soon to go,
And if an orator could write this well,
He might embed it in a chronicle
As a fact of sovereign notability.
Let every wise man listen unto me;
This story is just as true, I undertake,
As is the book of Launcelot of the Lake,
Whereof are ladies reverent and fain;
Now to my theme will I return again.

A black-marked fox, wicked and very sly,
Had lurked for three years in the wood near by,
And by a fine, premeditated plot
That same night, breaking through the hedge, had got
Into the yard where Chanticleer the fair
Was with his wives accustomed to repair;
And in a bed of herbs stone-still he lay
Till onward to eleven went the day,
Waiting his time on Chanticleer to fall
As do the murderers gladly – one and all –
That low in ambush crouch to murder men.
O treacherous murderer, lurking in thy den!
O new Iscariot! O new Ganilon!
O false dissembler, O thou Greek Sinon
That broughtest Troy all utterly to sorrow!
O Chanticleer, accursèd be that morrow
That thou into the yard flew from the beams.
Thou hadst been well admonished in thy dreams
That this same day was perilous to thee.
But that which God foreknows must surely be
As certain scholars make the matter work.
This ye will learn from any well-trained clerk:
Upon that point has been great altercation
Within the schools, and lengthy disputation
Among a hundred thousand if a man!
But I could never sift it to the bran
As could the holy doctor Augustine,

Or Boëthius, or Bishop Bradwardine
To say if God's divine forewitnessing
Compelleth me of need to do a thing
(By need I mean simple necessity)
Or whether a free choice be granted me
To do that same thing or to do it not,
Though God foreknew it ere that it was wrought;
Or if his knowing binds me not a whit,
Save on condition, to accomplish it!
In no such matters will I interfere;
My tale is of a cock, as ye may hear,
That from his wife took counsel, to his sorrow,
To walk within the yard upon that morrow
That he had dreamed the dream I have related.
Women's advice is oftentimes ill-fated!
Counsel of woman brought us first to woe
And out of Paradise made Adam go
Though he was merry there, and well at ease.
But since I know not whom it might displease
Should I the advice of women hold to blame –
Forget it, for I said it but in game.
Read authors where they treat of such affairs
And hear of women in these books of theirs;
These are the cock's words only, none of mine,
For in no woman can I harm divine!

  Fair in the sand, to bathe her merrily
Lieth Pertelote, with all her sisters nigh
In the warm sun, and Chanticleer so free,
Sung merrier than the mermaid in the sea;
(*Physiologus* says for certainty
That they sing very well and merrily).
And so it fell that, as he cast his eye
Among the worts, upon a butterfly,
He saw this fox before him, crouching low.
Nowise it pleased him then to strut or crow,
But quick "Cok, Cok," he cried, and up he started
Like one fear striketh suddenly weak-hearted.
For any creature will desire to flee
If suddenly his enemy he see,
Though never before he saw it with his eye.
  This Chanticleer, when he the fox did spy,

He would have fled, but that the fox anon
Said, "Noble sire, alas! will ye be gone?
Be ye afraid of me that am your friend?
Now truly, I were worse than any fiend
If I should plan you hurt or villainy.
I came not to disturb your privacy;
Surely, the one and only reason bringing
Me here – it was to listen to your singing.
For certainly ye have as merry a steven
As any angel hath that sings in heaven;
There is more feeling in your music than
Boëthius had, or any singing man.
My lord your father (God him sanctify)
Likewise your mother (in her great courtesy)
Have been within my house, to my great ease,
And truly, sire, full fain I would you please.
But with respect to singing, in this wise
I say: that as I hope to keep my eyes
I never heard such singing from a man
As from your father when the day began –
Truly, it was full lusty, all his song;
And that his voice might ring more clear and strong
He used to strain until his eyes would close,
So loudly would he cry; and he uprose
Upon his toe tips as he crowed withal,
And stretched his neck out very long and small.
He was of such discretion, too, that there
Was none in any country anywhere
That him in song or wisdom might surpass.
True, I have read in *Sir Burnell the Ass*,
Among his verse, how that there was a cock
Who, all because a priest's son gave a knock
Unto his leg when he was young, – for this
Schemed that he later lost his benefice;
But certainly, no man can well compare
The high discretion and the wisdom rare
Your father had, with that cock's trickery.
But sing, sire, sing for holy charity;
Try now, can ye your father counterfeit?"
This Chanticleer his wings began to beat
As one that could no treachery descry –

So was he ravished by this flattery.

    Alas! ye lords, how many a rogue resides
Within your courts, and flatterers besides,
That are in faith more popular with you,
Than he who tells you plainly what is true.
Go read Ecclesiasticus, and see;
Beware, ye lordings, of their treachery!

    This Chanticleer stood high upon his toes,
He stretched his neck, he made his eyes to close,
And thus began to make a mighty cry.
Sir Russell Fox up-bounded instantly
And by the throat he seized this Chanticleer,
And flung him on his back, and sped from there
Off toward the wood, and no man saw him run.
O Destiny, that none of us may shun!
Alas! that Chanticleer flew from the beams!
Alas! that Pertelote recked not of dreams!
And on a Friday fell all this mischance!
O Venus, that art goddess of pleasance,
Since Chanticleer was servant unto thee
And spent himself to serve thee faithfully,
More for delight than the world to multiply,
Why wouldst thou suffer him on thy day to die?
O Geoffrey, master dear, supreme, and skilled,
That when King Richard was with arrow killed
Made for thy noble lord complaint so sore,
Why do I lack thy meaning and thy lore,
Friday to chide with singing, as did ye?
(For truly, on a Friday slain was he).
Then would I raise my sorrowful refrain
For Chanticleer's affright, and for his pain.

    Not such a lamentation and great crying
Did Trojan ladies make for Ilium dying,
When fire and Pyrrhus' naked sword they feared,
Who seized the aged Priam by the beard
And slew him (so the *Æneid* tells the tale)
As did these hens that in the yard made wail
To see their Chanticleer in fearsome plight.
But Pertelote shrieked with surpassing might;
Louder she cried than did Hasdrubal's wife
What time she saw Hasdrubal lose his life

And Carthage burned by Roman torches. She
Was filled with grief and torment utterly,
And in the fire she flung herself, and so
Steadfast of heart in flames to death did go.
O woeful hens, your cry was like the cry
When Nero sent Rome City to the sky
And there was fearful wailing from the wives
Of Roman senators that lost their lives;
All guiltless, wicked Nero had them slain!
Now to my tale will I return again.

    This simple widow and her daughters two
Heard all these hens lament with great to-do,
And rushing out of doors at once, they see
The fox make toward the forest hastily
Bearing the cock away upon his back.
They cried: "Out!" "Harrow!" "Weladay!" "Alack!"
"Ha! Ha! the fox!" and after him they ran,
And with them waving sticks came many a man;
And Collie our dog and Talbot and Gerland,
And Malkin, with a distaff in her hand;
The cows and calves ran, and the very hogs,
Crazed as they were with the barking of the dogs
And men and women making great halloo;
Their hearts with running all but burst in two.
They yelled like fiends in hell – who could have stilled
    them?
And the ducks cried as someone would have killed
    them.
The geese for fear went flying over trees,
Out of the hive there poured a swarm of bees;
Ah! *Benedicite*! such wild noise rang
In truth, that Jack Straw ramping with his gang
In search of some poor Fleming they could kill
Never made shouting that was half so shrill
As on that day was made about this fox.
They came with trumpets made of brass and box,
Of horn and bone on which they blew and tooted,
And therewithal they shrieked and whooped and
    hooted
Until it seemed that heaven itself would fall.
And now, good men, I pray you hearken all!

Look now how Fortune turneth suddenly
The hope and triumph of their enemy.
This cock, upon the fox's back that lay,
Despite his fear, still found a voice to say
Thus to the fox: "Now, sire, were I as ye,
God help me, I would shout defiantly:
'Turn once again, proud churls, turn one and all!
A very pestilence upon you fall!
Look ye, at last I stand within the wood!
Now do your worst, the cock is mine for good,
For I will eat him up, and quickly, too.' "
The fox replied: "In faith, that will I do!" –
But as he spoke the word, the cock broke free
Out of his open mouth full dextrously
And flew high up and perched upon a limb.
And the fox saw him there and called to him:
"Alas! O Chanticleer, alas!" quoth he,
"I fear that I have done you injury!
I frightened you by seizing you so hard
And rushing with you hither from your yard;
But, sire, I did it with no ill intent –
Come down, and I will tell you what I meant.
God help me, I will speak you fair and true."
"Nay, then," quoth he, "my curse upon us two,
And first I'll curse myself, both blood and bones,
If thou shalt fool me oftener than once!
Thou shalt no more with crafty flatteries
Make me to sing for thee and close my eyes.
For he who shuts his eyes when he should see –
God give no good to any such as he!"
"Nay," quoth the fox, "but God give him mischance
That is so indiscreet of governance
That jabbers when he ought to hold his tongue!"

So of the negligent my tale is sung,
That reckless are, and trust in flattery.

But if ye deem this naught but vanity,
As of a fox, or of a cock and hen,
Take ye the moral that it hath, good men.
For Saint Paul, saith he not that all things writ
Can point our doctrine and embellish it?
Then take the grain and let the chaff lie still.
And now, good God, if it shall be Thy will
As saith my lord, so make us all good men
And bring us into holy bliss. *Amen.*

Here the Nun's Priest's Tale ends

The lines which follow appear in only three manuscripts, and are generally regarded as having been discarded by Chaucer. Note the resemblance which they bear to a passage in The Monk's Prologue.

Epilogue to the Nun's Priest's Tale

"SIR Nun's Priest," soon our Host Sir John addressed,
"Now may thy breech and every stone be blessed!
That was a merry tale of Chanticleer.
Wert thou a layman, who could have a fear
But thou wouldst be a tread-fowl strong and fair?
If thine ambition matched the power that's there
I think thou wouldst have need of hens, by heaven,
Yea, more indeed than seventeen times seven!
See the great muscles on this priest," he cried,
"His great neck, and his breast so deep and wide!
And like a sparrow-hawk he darts his eye!
He has a ruddy hue that needs no dye –
Brasilin, or the red of Portingale!
Now, sire," he said, "good luck for this your tale I"
    And after that, he turned with merry cheer,
And to another spoke, as ye shall hear.

The Physician's Tale

THE PHYSICIAN TELLS an affecting tale of domestic tragedy which tenderly draws on the relationship between father and daughter. Chaucer was the earliest English writer to develop this type of domestic interest. The Physician's Tale works with the tales of the Lawyer, the Prioress, the Clerk, and part of the Monk's Tale, to develop a recurring theme of parent and child relations. The Physician adds an inappropriate moral to his tale of the abuse of power and its tragic consequences.

THE PHYSICIAN'S TALE

*Here follows the
Physician's Tale*

ONCE, as we learn from Titus Livius,
There was a knight men called Virginius;
Rich both in honor and nobility,
And strong in friends, and great in wealth was he.
    One daughter had Virginius by his wife,
Nor other children had he all his life.
This maid was of a loveliness that shone
Above all other maidens men had known.
For Nature, with a sovereign diligence,
Had formed her with such passing excellence
It seemed as if she said: "Lo! I, great Nature,
Thus have the skill to shape and paint a creature
When I desire. Who then can counterfeit
My work? Pygmalion cannot equal it,
Though he forever forge or carve or stain;
Zeuxis, Apelles – both would work in vain,
By forge or paint or chisel to create,
Should they presume my work to imitate.
For He that is the chief creator, He
Hath taken me for his general deputy
To give all earthly things their hue and feature.
At pleasure then I supervise each creature
Under the moon, growing or perishing.
And for my work I never ask a thing.
My Lord and I are in a full accord;
I made her in the honor of my Lord;
And thus I work with other creatures, too,
Whatever figure they may have, or hue."

So Nature would have said, it seems to me.
    Twelve years and two this maiden grew to be
In whom Dame Nature had such great delight.
For just as she can paint a lily white
And a rose red, so on each gracious part
Of this fair creature had she laid with art
Her colors where such colors ought to be.
And Phœbus with his shining archery
Had dyed her ample tresses with a hue
Like to the burnished streams of light he threw.
If she was unexcelled in beauty thus,
She was a thousand times more virtuous.
There lacked in her no elements that meet
To make a woman thoughtful and discreet.
As chaste in spirit as in flesh was she,
And so she blossomed in virginity
With meekness, patience, and abstemiousness,
And temperate ways. In bearing and in dress
She showed a proper sense of moderation.
She was discreet in all her conversation.
Though she was wise as Pallas, I dare say,
And had a womanly and simple way,
She used no terms of artificial grace
For show, but in accordance with her place
Spoke always, and with something to express
At one with virtue and with nobleness.
Modest in maiden's modesty was she,
Constant of heart, and full of industry
That drove away all sluggish ways and idle.
Her mouth was not subdued to Bacchus' bridle,
For wine and youth make Venus rise the higher,
As oil and grease when cast upon a fire.
And in her own clear virtue, unconstrained,
Many a time a sickness hath she feigned,
Wishing to leave some crowd that, growing jolly,
Was more and more disposed to talk of folly,
As at these feasts and dances where excess
Grows fast and often ends in wantonness.
Such things make children turn too suddenly
Mature and bold, as it is plain to see –
This is a peril, and always has been so.

For all too soon the innocent will know
The ways of boldness, being made a wife.
    And ye dames in your later years of life,
That have the daughters of a lord in care,
Take no offense at what I now declare;
Ye have this government ye exercise
For reasons, and but one of two applies:
Either that ye have kept your honesty,
Or fell once from the ways of constancy
And know the old dance fully, and have shaken
Such ill ways from you wholly, and forsaken
Them finally. For Christ's sake then, I say,
Shirk not to teach them virtue day by day.
One that has been a thief of venison,
But with his evil skill and ways is done,
Protects a forest best of any man.
Then keep them well, for if ye will, ye can.
Wink at no faults they show, lest ye should find
That ye are censured for your evil mind;
For he that winks at evil must betray
His trust. And heed well what I have to say:
Of treasons, none so sovereign pestilent
As falseness that betrays the innocent.
    Likewise, ye parents, it devolves on you,
That have your children, though but one or two,
To keep them in your charge, and give them
        schooling
For the full time they stay beneath your ruling.
Look then, that by the lives that ye present,
Or by your negligence in chastisement,
They perish not. For I will tell you clearly
That if they do, then it will cost you dearly.
Under a careless shepherd, though no coward,
The wolf hath many a sheep and lamb devoured.
Let this one instance make the matter plain;
Now to my story I must turn again.
    This maid of whom I tell did not require –
She kept herself so well – a woman by her;
For in her life might any maiden read,
As in a book, every good word and deed
A virtuous maiden rightly should possess,

Such prudence had she and such graciousness.
Thus of her goodness and her beauty, too,
On every side the rumor sprang and flew,
And through the land all praised her character
That virtue loved, save those that envied her,
Hating to see one living prosperously,
And glad of sickness and calamity
(Well hath the doctor set this matter down).
This maid one day was going through the town
Toward a temple, her mother at her side,
As is the way of maidens far and wide.
    Now in the town that day there chanced to stand
A justice, that was governor of that land;
And as this maid was meekly going by,
It happened that this justice cast his eye
Upon her; and he saw her with a start;
And in a little all his mood and heart
Were altered by the beauty of this maid.
And to himself in secrecy he said,
"She shall be mine, in spite of any man."
    Into his heart the fiend leapt with a plan,
Teaching him quickly how with cunning skill
He might constrain this maiden to his will.
For not by force, nor any bribe, he thought,
Would he attain the purpose that he sought;
For she was strong in friends; and fixed as well
In a firm goodness so incomparable,
That well he knew that he could never win
Her own assent to yield herself to sin.
And therefore, after great deliberation,
He sent for one that had a reputation
Within the town for cunning ways and bold.
Unto this man the judge his story told
In secrecy, the man his promise giving
That he would tell it to no creature living,
And if he did, that he should lose his head.
And when the shaping of this plan had sped,
This judge was glad, and made him merry cheer,
And gave him many presents rich and dear.
    When he had shaped all this conspiracy
From point to point, so that his lechery

Should be accomplished in a subtle way,
As later ye shall hear me plainly say,
Home goes this churl, whose name was Claudius.
This false judge Appius, for men called him thus –
Such was his name (for this is no mere fable,
But something both historical and stable,
The substance of it true, beyond a doubt) –
This false judge with all speed now set about
To hasten his delight in every way.
And soon it happened, on a certain day,
This false judge, as these olden tales report,
Sat, as his custom was, within his court,
Giving his judgment there in case on case.
In came this Claudius at a rapid pace,
And said: "O lord, if it may be your will,
Do justice by me on this piteous bill
Against Virginius, that I bring to you.
And if he shall declare my bill untrue,
Then I will prove it, and by witness show
That what is set therein is right and so."

  "On this, and he not here," the judge replied,
"I cannot give a judgment. Go outside
And have him called, and I will gladly hear it;
Here thou shalt have full justice; do not fear it."

  Virginius came, to know the judge's will,
And then at once was read this cursèd bill,
The gist of which was what ye now shall hear.

  "To you, my lord, Sire Appius so dear,
Shows Claudius, your humble servant, thus:
How that a knight, by name Virginius,
Against the law, against all equity,
And most against my will, withholds from me
My servant, one that is my thrall by right,
That from my house was stolen away one night
While she was young; and I will prove this, too,
By witnesses, if it seem good to you.
His daughter she is not, whatever he say;
Therefore to you, my lord the judge, I pray
Give me my servant, if it be your will."
Lo, this was the full substance of the bill.

  Virginius on this churl had set his eye,

But in a flash, before he could reply,
And prove, as he was able, as a knight,
By witnesses that would have shown his right
And all the falseness of his adversary,
This false judge, that would not a moment tarry,
Nor hear a word more from Virginius,
Spoke up and gave his judgment, saying thus:

  "My sentence is, this churl shall have his thrall;
Thou shalt not keep her longer in thy hall.
Go bring her here and put her in our care;
The churl shall have his servant, I declare."

  And when this worthy knight Virginius,
By sentence of this Appius, rendered thus,
By force must yield his daughter speedily
Unto the judge, to live in lechery,
Homeward he went, and there sat down appalled;
And gave command his daughter should be called,
And with a face like ashes cold and dead
Gazed on her humble countenance, and said,
His heart with father's pity deeply shaken,
Though firm he held the purpose he had taken:

  "Daughter," he cried, "Virginia – by thy name
There are two ways, for it is death or shame
Thou must endure. Why was I born, alas!
Thou never didst deserve like this to pass
By any stroke of fatal sword or knife!
O my dear daughter, ender of my life,
Whom I have fostered with a care so pleasant
That in my mind thou wast forever present –
O daughter, thou who art my final woe,
And the last joy, alas! my life shall know,
O gem of chastity, take patiently
Thy death, for this is what I now decree.
For love, and not for hate, thou must be dead;
These piteous hands of mine must take thine head.
Alas! that Appius ever gazed upon thee!
Thus hath he falsely passed his sentence on thee –"
And told her all as ye have heard before –
How the case went – no need to tell you more.

  "O mercy, O dear father!" cried this maid;
And as she said this word her two arms laid

About his neck, as she had often done;
Forth from her eyes the tears began to run.
"Good father, tell me, must I die?" said she;
"Is there no grace, is there no remedy?"

   "No, truly, none, my daughter," he replied.

   "Then give me but a little time," she cried,
"That I may sorrow for my death a space;
For Jepthah, truly, gave his daughter grace
Ere slaying her, in which to make her moan.
And God knows that her sin was this alone –
That she was first of those who ran to see
And welcome him with great festivity."
And saying this, she swooned away at last.
And in a little, when her swoon was passed,
She rose again, and to her father said:
"Blessèd be God that I shall die a maid!
Give me my death before I come to shame;
Work on your child your purpose, in God's name!"

   And with that word she begged of him and prayed
That he would smite her gently with the blade,
And swooning with that word, lay pale and still.
Her father, with a woeful heart and will,
Smote off her head, and took it by the hair,
And bore it to the judge, still sitting there,
Giving his judgments, in consistory.
And Appius, when he saw it, instantly
Bade them lead forth Virginius to his doom.
But now a thousand people stormed the room
In pity and compassion, to save this knight.
For all this baseness now was come to light.
And they had been suspicious of this thing,
And from the churl's address in challenging,
They thought it was the wish of Appius,
For well they knew that he was lecherous.
Therefore against this Appius they have risen,
And seized him, and have cast him into prison,
Where soon he slew himself, and Claudius,
The tool of Appius, they have treated thus:
They doomed him to be hanged upon a tree.
But good Virginius, in his clemency,
So prayed, they gave him banishment instead,

Or else for certainty had he been dead.
The rest were hanged, the lesser and the greater,
That had connived in this to help this traitor.

   Here men may see how sin receives its pay!
Beware, for no man knows in any way
Where God will strike, nor how the worm within
Will gnaw and shudder at a life of sin,
However secret it may be, or dim.
For no man knows of that but God and him.
For be he ignorant or be he wise,
He cannot know when terror will surprise
And conquer him. This counsel then I make you:
Forsake your sin before your sin forsake you!

Here ends the Physician's Tale

THE WORDS OF THE HOST

The words of the Host to the Physician and the Pardoner

OUR Host began to swear like mad. He cried:
"Now by the nails and blood of Him who died,
That judge was false, and so too was his man!
As ill a death as any heart can plan
Come to such judge, and to his advocate!
But the poor maid, alas! she met her fate –
She paid too dearly for her loveliness!
Wherefore I say that men must still confess
Gifts that from Chance or Nature may descend
Bring many a luckless creature to his end.
Her beauty was her death, I hold it plain.
Alas! How piteously the maid was slain.
From both these gifts of which I spoke but now
Men get more hurt than profit, anyhow.
But of a truth, my worthy master dear,
That was a piteous tale for one to hear.
Yet none the less, no matter – let it go –
I pray God save thy body, even so,
Thy chamberpots and medicated greases,
And all thy Galens and Hippocrateses,
And every box full of thy lectuaries –

God's blessing on them, and our Holy Mary's!
As I may thrive, thou art a proper man,
And like a prelate, by St. Ronian!
Said I not well? By terms I cannot speak.
But thou hast almost made my heart to break –
I all but had a spasm, as I live.
By Corpus bones! I need a purgative,
Or else a draught of new or malty ale;
Or if I cannot hear a merry tale,
My heart will melt with pity for this maid.
Thou *belle ami*, thou Pardoner," he said,

"Give us some mirth or jesting instantly."
"Now by St. Ronian, that I will," said he.
"But first," he said, "here by this ale-house stake
I mean to drink, and eat a bit of cake."
    But all the noble folk began to cry,
"Nay! Let him tell no kind of ribaldry,
But something moral, to improve the spirit
And store the mind – then we will gladly hear it."
"Surely; I will," he said. "But I must think
About some virtuous story while I drink."
[Ends]

The Pardoner's Tale

THE PARDONER BEGINS with a prologue in which he boasts of how he has cheated people of their money by selling false pardons for sins and fake saints' relics. His tale is a well-told story of three greedy men whose quest to find the character Death leads them into trouble. The brilliantly realised scenes of the drunken men contribute to an accomplished sermon against greed, but the Pardoner has not given up his own greedy ambitions.

THE PARDONER'S TALE

Here follows the Prologue to the Pardoner's Tale

Radix malorum est Cupiditas: ad Thimotheum, sexto

"LORDINGS," he said, "in churches when I preach
I try to have a high-resounding speech,
And ring it out as round as any bell;
I know by heart all of the things I tell;
My theme is always one, and ever was:
Radix malorum est Cupiditas.

   "The place that I have come from first I call,
And then my bulls I show them, one and all;
My letter, with our liege lord's signature,
I show them first, my body to secure,
That none may be so daring, priest or clerk,
As to disturb me in Christ's holy work.
And after that I say my say, and then
Show bulls from popes and cardinals again,
And patriarchs and bishops – not a few;
And then in Latin say a word or two
To give a flourish to my sermonizing,
And set the piety in men to rising.
I show my boxes, made of crystal stone,
Crammed full of bits of cloth and broken bone;
And all think these are relics. And I keep
A shoulder-bone in latten, from a sheep
In ancient times owned by a holy Jew.
"Good men, take heed," I tell them, "all of you;
For if this bone be washed in any well,
And cow, or calf, or sheep, or ox shall swell
Because a snake hath bitten it, or hath stung,
Take water from that well, and wash its tongue,

And it will soon be whole! And furthermore,
From pox or scab or any kind of sore
Shall any sheep be healed that of this well
May drink a draught; take heed of what I tell.
And if the husbandman that owns the flock
Shall every week, ere crowing of the cock,
Fasting, drink from this well, I tell you, sirs,
As that same Jew did teach our ancestors,
He will increase in flocks and property.
And, sirs, it is a cure for jealousy;
For though a man fall into raging dotage
Of jealousy; if ye will make his pottage
With this same water, he will then mistrust
His wife no more, although he know her lust,
And she of priests had taken two or three.
   "Here is a mitten, too, that ye may see.
He that will put this mitten on his hand,
Shall have the grain grow thick upon his land
When he hath sown it, be it wheat or oats –
If he will pay his pennies here, and groats.
   "Good men and women, one fair word of warning:
If there be one within this church this morning
Hath done a sin so horrible to name
That he dare not be shriven of it, for shame,
Or a young woman, or an old and staid,
That of her husband hath a cuckold made,
Such people shall not have the power or grace
To pay me for my relics in this place.
And he that knows him free of all such blame,
May come and make his offering in God's name,
While I absolve him by the authority
Which has by bull been granted unto me."
   By such tricks I have gathered, year by year,
A hundred marks since I was Pardoner.
There in my pulpit like a clerk I stand,
And see the lay folk sit on every hand,
And preach, as ye have heard, and tell a store
Of other yarns besides – a hundred more.
I take good pains to stretch my neck far out,
And east and west I thrust and nod about
As doth a dove upon a stable sitting.

So busily my hands and tongue go flitting
It is joy to see me work like this!
Of all such cursed things as avarice
My preaching ever is, to make them free
In giving pence – especially to me!
For all my interest is in what I win,
And not in saving people from their sin.
When they are buried, why should I be worrying
Whether or not their souls have gone blackberrying?
For often preachments, if the truth be told,
Grow out of ill intentions men may hold.
Some, pleasing folk by wit and flattery,
Seek an advancement through hypocrisy;
Some spring from vanity, and some from hate.
For should I need thus to retaliate,
Then in my preaching I will lash a man
So he shall never – do the best he can –
Escape, if he have done some injury
To any of my brethren, or to me.
For though I never speak his proper name
Yet men shall recognize him just the same,
By many a hint or other sly allusion.
And thus I bring our foes to their confusion,
Thus I spit out my venom under hue
Of holiness, and seem devout and true.

   But briefly, my intention it is this:
I preach of nothing but of avarice;
Therefore my theme is this, and always was,
Radix malorum est Cupiditas.
Thus I can preach against the very vice
I have myself, and that is avarice.
And yet though I myself am guilty of it,
I can discourage other folk that love it
From avarice, and make them sore repent.
But that is not my principal intent.
I do no preaching but for avarice;
Now this, as to that matter, should suffice.

   And then I tell them instances I know
From ancient stories many years ago,
For ignorant people love old stories well;
Such things they can remember and re-tell.

What? Do ye think while I am busy preaching,
And win good gold and silver from my teaching,
That I will gladly live in poverty?
Nay, nay, I never thought it, certainly.
For I will preach and beg in various lands,
And I will do no labor with my hands,
As, making baskets, that I need not go
In idleness a-begging, to and fro.
No poor apostle will I imitate;
I will have money, wool, and cheese, and meat,
Though from the poorest page I get my pillage,
Or from the poorest widow in a village,
Although her children from starvation pine,
Nay! I will drink good liquor of the vine,
And have a jolly wench in every town.
But lordings, if the end of this be shown,
Your liking is that I shall tell a tale.
And having drunk a draught of new-brewed ale,
I hope, by God, I have a thing to tell
That will, and that with reason, please you well.
For though a vicious man in much I do,
Yet I can tell a moral tale for you
Which I have preached, some profit thereby winning.
Now hold your peace, my tale is now beginning.

Here begins the Pardoner's Tale

IN Flanders once there dwelt a company
Of young folk, steeped in foolish revelry –
Who haunted brothels, feasts and games of chance;
And to the harp and lute they used to dance,
And they would cast at dice both day and night,
And also eat and drink beyond their night,
And in the devil's temple in this evil
Manner make sacrifices to the devil
By their abominable superfluity.
They swore so loudly and so damnably
It was a grisly thing to hear them swear.
They rent our blessèd Savior's body there,
As if the Jews had not enough defiled
Those limbs, and at each other's sins they smiled.

And dancing girls would come, graceful and slender,
And after them, fruit-wenches, young and tender,
Singers with harps, bawds, and confectioners,
"That are the very devil's officers
To kindle and fan the fire of lechery
That is so near allied to gluttony.
Let holy scripture witness that excess
And lust are born of wine and drunkenness.

    Lo, against nature did not drunken Lot
Lie with his daughters two, and knew it not?
He was too drunk to be responsible.

    And Herod, let him look it up who will,
When wine had made him sodden and unstable,
Gave his command, sitting at his own table,
That guiltless John the Baptist should be slain.

    Seneca says a word both wise and sane.
He says there is no difference he can find
Between a man that may have lost his mind
And one that's lost in drink, save that insanity,
Uniting with the evil in humanity,
Will persevere longer than drunkenness.
O gluttony, full of such vile excess,
The primal source of all our degradation,
The very origin of our damnation
Till Christ redeemed us with His blood again!
To put it in a word, how dearly then
This cursèd sin was paid for, when ye see
That all the world was lost through gluttony!

    Adam our father for that very vice
Was scourged to woe and toil from Paradise,
And Eve as well – there is no doubt, indeed;
For Adam, while he fasted, as I read,
Remained in Paradise; but instantly
When he had eaten of the forbidden tree,
He was cast out to pain and degradation.
Thou dost deserve our bitter accusation,
O gluttony! Ah, if a man could guess
The maladies that follow on excess
He would take care to be more moderate,
Sitting at table, in the things he ate.
Alas! The short throat and the tender mouth

They rule men East and West and North and South,
And make them slave in water, earth, and air
To get a glutton dainty drink and fare.
Of this, O Paul, the word thou sayst is good:
"Food unto belly, and belly unto food –"
As Paul has said, "God shall destroy them both!"
Alas, it is a foul thing, on mine oath,
More in the act, but foul when merely said,
When a man drinks so of the white and red
That of his throat, accursed with that excess,
He makes a privy in his wantonness.

    The apostle, weeping, cried out piteously:
"Many there go, described for you by me,
And now with piteous voice I say of these
That they of Christ's cross are the enemies,
And Belly is their god, their end is death."
O Belly, O thou bag of stinking breath,
Where dung and vile corruption do offend,
Foul is the sound of thee at either end!
What great expense for thee, what toilsome pain!
These cooks – see how they pound and grind and
      strain,
And thus turn "substance" into "accident,"
To make thy lecherous appetite content!
They crack the hard bones, taking out the marrow,
For they discard no thing that through the narrow
Mouth of the gullet soft and sweet can go;
With leaf and root and bark and spice they sow
The glutton's sauce, prepared for his delight,
To give him still a fresher appetite.
And yet the man whom such delight entices
Is dead while he is living in those vices.

    Wine leads to lechery; drinking to excess
Promotes contentious ways and wretchedness.
O drunkard, all distorted is thy face,
Thy breath is sour, thou'rt loathsome to embrace;
And through thy drunken nose the sound comes
      playing
As "Samson, Samson!" thou wert always saying.
Yet Samson never tasted wine, God knows!
Like a stuck pig, thou tumblest on thy nose;

Thy tongue is lost, thy seemly ways forgot,
For drunkenness is the true burying plot
For man's discretion, wit, and moderation;
For he in whom drink has its domination
Can never, surely, hold a secret tight.
Then keep yourselves far from the red and white,
Especially from the white wine of Lepe
They have for sale in Fish Street or in Cheape.
This grape of Spain has such a subtle spirit
It creeps through others that are growing near it,
And from this mingling such strong fumes proceed
That when a man has had three drinks, indeed,
And thinks that he is still at home in Cheape,
He is in Spain, within the town of Lepe –
Not at Rochelle, in truth, nor at Bordeaux;
Then "Samson, Samson," will the fellow go.

But, lordings, listen to one word, I pray:
All of the sovereign acts, I dare to say,
Of victories in the Old Testament,
Through grace of God that is omnipotent
Were done in perfect abstinence and prayer.
Look in the Bible, ye shall find it there.

Look at the conqueror, Attila the great –
He died in sleep, meeting a shameful fate
Of nosebleed, caused by drinking to excess.
Let a great captain live in soberness.
And more than this, consider long and well
That was commanded unto Lemuel;
Not Samuel, but Lemuel, I say –
Read in the Bible, and find it plain as day –
That giving wine to judges was a vice.
But now no more, for this will well suffice.

And now that I have preached of gluttony,
I will forbid you gambling equally.
Gambling is mother of deceitful scheming,
Cursèd forswearing, lies, and Christ's blaspheming,
And homicide. There comes great waste through it
Of gold and time. It is the opposite
Of honor – nay, its shame and degradation,
To have a common gamester's reputation.
The higher that a man is in degree,

The more abandoned is he held to be,
For if a prince will play at games of chance,
In public policy and temperance
He will be held, by general opinion,
The less deserving of his high dominion.

Stilbon, the wise ambassador, was sent
With great pomp by the Spartan government
To Corinth, an alliance there to bind.
When he arrived, he came by chance to find
All of the greatest men within that land
Playing at hazard there on every hand.
And for that cause, as soon as it could be,
He stole home to his country quietly,
And said: "I will not thus lose my good name,
Nor will I dare so greatly to defame
Your honor as with gamblers to ally you.
Send other envoys who may satisfy you;
For by my troth I would prefer to die
Than see you take such gamesters for ally.
Your honor stands so glorious and so fine,
Ye shall not thus be bound by will of mine,
Nor any treaty in which I concur."
Thus spoke to them this wise philosopher.

See also how to King Demetrius,
The king of Parthians, as is writ for us,
Dispatched in scorn a pair of golden dice;
For gambling heretofore had been his vice,
For which the Parthians held his reputation
And glory at but little valuation.
Lords can discover other kinds of play
Honest enough to drive the time away.

Now of false oaths and great I speak to you,
As old books deal with such, a word or two.
Great swearing is a plain abomination,
And to swear false more worthy reprobation.
High God forbade all swearing, as ye see
In Matthew, and still more particularly
The holy Jeremy speaks thus of swearing:
"Swear true oaths only, false oaths never daring,
And swear with judgment and in righteousness."
But idle swearing is a vile excess.

See in the table unto man first handed
Of all the noble things high God commanded,
How in the second rule He wrote this plain:
"Take ye my name not idly or in vain."
Lo, swearing thus is earlier denied
Than many a cursèd thing like homicide.
I say that, as to order, it stands so.
They understand, who God's commandments know,
The second one commands us as I say.
Further, I tell thee in the plainest way
That vengeance shall not leave his house that dares
To make his oaths outrageous when he swears.
"By God's own precious heart, and by his nails,
And by the blood of Christ, that is in Hales,
My chance is seven and thine is five and three;
By God's arms, if thou play it false with me
This dagger shall go through thy heart at once;"
This is the fruit grown from the bitchèd bones:
False swearing, anger, falseness, homicide.
Now for the love of Christ that for us died,
Leave off your oaths, I pray, both great and small;
But, sirs, I tell my tale – let this be all.

Now these three rioters of whom I tell,
Long yet ere prime was rung by any bell,
Were seated in a tavern at their drinking.
And as they sat, they heard a death-bell clinking
Before a body going to its grave.
Then roused the one and shouted to his knave –
"Be off at once!" he cried. "Run out and spy
Whose body it may be that passeth by;
And look thou get his name aright," he cried.
    "No, need, sir – none at all," this boy replied.
"They told me that before ye came, two hours;
He was, God's name, an old fellow of yours.
By night, it seems, and sudden was his dying;
Flat on his bench, all drunken, was he lying,
When up there crept a thief that men call Death
(Who in this country all the people slay'th)
And smote his heart asunder with his spear
And all in silence went his way from here.

During the plague he hath a thousand slain,
And, master, ere ye meet him this is plain:
That it is wise and very necessary
To be prepared for such an adversary,
Have readiness to meet him evermore;
So taught my mother – now I say no more."
"Yea, by Saint Mary," said the taverner,
"The boy speaks true, for he hath slain this year
Woman and child and man in yonder town,
And page and villain he hath smitten down.
I hold his habitation must be there.
Great wisdom were it that a man beware –
Lest he some fearful injury incur."
"Yea, by God's arms," replied this rioter,
"Is he so perilous a knave to meet?
Now will I seek him both by way and street,
Upon the bones of God I make a vow!
Fellows, we three are one – then hear me now:
Let each of us hold up his hand to th' other,
And each of us become the other's brother;
And we will slay this faithless traitor Death –
He shall be slain, he that so many slay'th,
Yea, by God's dignity, ere it be night!"
    And so all three together made their plight
To live and die each one of them for other,
As though he had been born the other's brother.
And in this drunken passion forth they started,
And toward that very village they departed
Of which the tavern-keeper spoke before.
And then full many a grisly oath they swore,
And rent the Saviour's body limb from limb –
Death should be dead if they discovered him!
When they had travelled hardly half a mile,
Just as they would have stepped across a stile,
They chanced to meet a poor and agèd man.
This old man meekly spake, and thus began
To greet them: "May God look upon you, sirs!"
    The greatest braggart of these rioters
Replied: "Now curse thee, churl! What, where apace?
Why all wrapped up and hidden save thy face?
How darest thou live so long in Death's defy?"

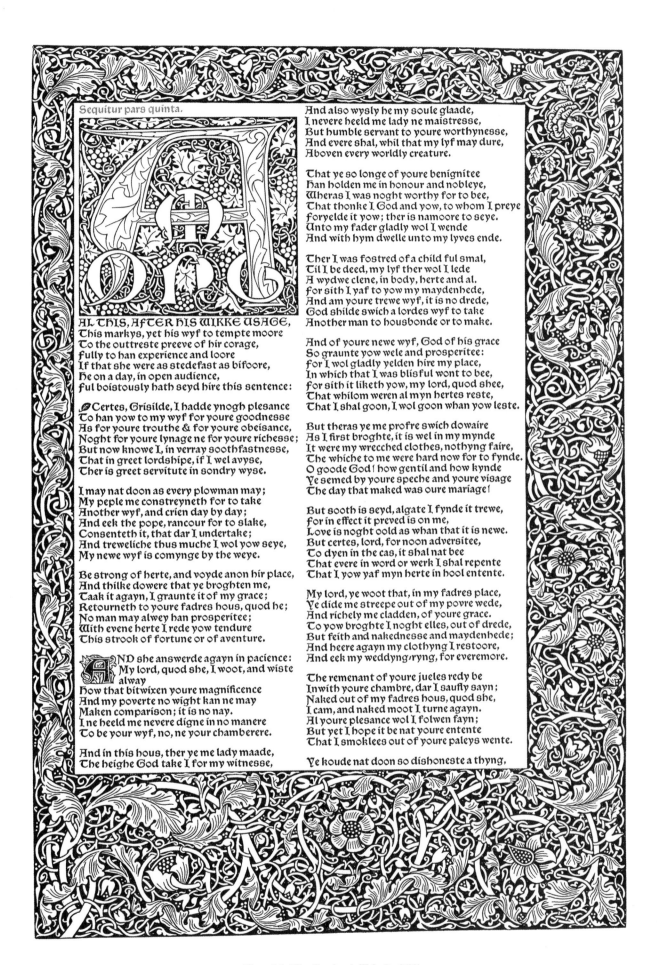

A ONE

AL THIS, AFTER HIS WIKKE USAGE,
This markys, yet his wyf to tempte moore
To the outtreste preeve of hir corage,
Fully to han experience and loore
If that she were as stedefast as bifoore,
He on a day, in open audience,
Ful boistously hath seyd hire this sentence:

Certes, Grisilde, I hadde ynogh plesance
To han yow to my wyf for youre goodnesse
As for youre trouthe & for youre obeisance,
Noght for youre lynage ne for youre richesse;
But now knowe I, in verray soothfastnesse,
That in greet lordshipe, if I wel avyse,
Ther is greet servitute in sondry wyse.

I may nat doon as every plowman may;
My peple me constreyneth for to take
Another wyf, and crien day by day;
And eek the pope, rancour for to slake,
Consenteth it, that dar I undertake;
And treweliche thus muche I wol yow seye,
My newe wyf is comynge by the weye.

Be strong of herte, and voyde anon hir place,
And thilke dowere that ye broghten me,
Taak it agayn, I graunte it of my grace;
Retourneth to youre fadres hous, quod he;
No man may alwey han prosperitee;
With evene herte I rede yow tendure
This strook of fortune or of aventure.

AND she answerde agayn in pacience:
My lord, quod she, I woot, and wiste
alway
How that bitwixen youre magnificence
And my poverte no wight kan ne may
Maken comparison; it is no nay.
I ne heeld me nevere digne in no manere
To be your wyf, no, ne your chamberere.

And in this hous, ther ye me lady maade,
The heighe God take I for my witnesse,
And also wysly he my soule glaade,
I nevere heeld me lady ne maistresse,
But humble servant to youre worthynesse,
And evere shal, whil that my lyf may dure,
Aboven every worldly creature.

That ye so longe of youre benignitee
Han holden me in honour and nobleye,
Wheras I was noght worthy for to bee,
That thonke I God and yow, to whom I preye
Foryelde it yow; ther is namoore to seye.
Unto my fader gladly wol I wende
And with hym dwelle unto my lyves ende.

Ther I was fostred of a child ful smal,
Til I be deed, my lyf ther wol I lede
A wydwe clene, in body, herte and al.
For sith I yaf to yow my maydenhede,
And am youre trewe wyf, it is no drede,
God shilde swich a lordes wyf to take
Another man to housbonde or to make.

And of youre newe wyf, God of his grace
So graunte yow wele and prosperitee:
For I wol gladly yelden hire my place,
In which that I was blisful wont to bee,
For sith it liketh yow, my lord, quod shee,
That whilom weren al myn hertes reste,
That I shal goon, I wol goon whan yow leste.

But theras ye me profre swich dowaire
As I first broghte, it is wel in my mynde
It were my wrecched clothes, nothyng faire,
The whiche to me were hard now for to fynde.
O goode God! how gentil and how kynde
Ye semed by youre speche and youre visage
The day that maked was oure mariage!

But sooth is seyd, algate I fynde it trewe,
For in effect it preved is on me,
Love is noght oold as whan that it is newe.
But certes, lord, for noon adversitee,
To dyen in the cas, it shal nat bee
That evere in word or werk I shal repente
That I yow yaf myn herte in hool entente.

My lord, ye woot that, in my fadres place,
Ye dide me streepe out of my povre wede,
And richely me cladden, of youre grace.
To yow broghte I noght elles, out of drede,
But feith and nakednesse and maydenhede;
And heere agayn my clothyng I restoore,
And eek my weddyng/ryng, for everemore.

The remenant of youre jueles redy be
Inwith youre chambre, dar I saufly sayn;
Naked out of my fadres hous, quod she,
I cam, and naked moot I turne agayn.
Al youre plesance wol I folwen fayn;
But yet I hope it be nat youre entente
That I smoklees out of youre paleys wente.

Ye koude nat doon so dishoneste a thyng,

Plate 15: The Student's Tale (p. 250)

Straightway this old man looked him in the eye
And answered thus: "Because I cannot meet
A man, by country way or city street,
Though unto Ind I made a pilgrimage,
Willing to give his youth and take my age!
So must I have my age in keeping still,
As long a time, indeed, as God shall will.

"Nor Death, alas! will have my life from me;
So like a wretch I wander restlessly
And on the ground, which is my mother's gate,
Knock with my staff and cry both early and late,
'Mother, belovèd mother, let me in!
See how I wither, flesh and blood and skin;
Alas, my bones! When shall they be at rest?
Mother, how gladly would I change my chest
That in my room so long a time hath been –
Yea, for a hair-cloth I could wrap me in!'
But yet she will not do me this poor grace:
Wherefore all pale and withered is my face.

"But, sirs, ye lack in common courtesy
That to an agèd man speak villainy
When he hath sinned neither in word nor deed.
For well in holy writings may ye read,
'Before an agèd man, whose hair is gray,
Ye should arise'; and therefore thus I say:
To an old man no hurt or evil do,
No more than ye would have men do to you
In your old age, if ye so long abide.
And God be with you, where ye walk or ride –
I must be gone where I have need to go."

"Nay now, old rogue! By God, thou shalt not so!"
Answered another rioter anon;
"Thou partest not so lightly, by Saint John!
Thou spake right now of that same traitor Death
That in this country all our comrades slay'th;
Have here my word: thou art a spy of his!
Then take the worst, or tell us where he is,
By God and by the Holy Sacrament!
For truly, thou art of his covenant,
To slay young folk like us, thou false intriguer!"

"Now, sirs," he answered, "since ye be so eager

To find this Death, turn up that crooked way;
There in yon wood I left him, sooth to say,
Under a tree, and there he will abide.
Not for your boasting will he run and hide.
See ye that oak tree? Ye shall find him there.
God, that redeemed mankind, save you and spare,
And better you!" Thus spoke this agèd man;
And toward the tree these drunken rascals ran
All three, and there, about its roots, they found
Of golden florins, minted fine and round,
Well nigh eight bushels lying, as they thought.
No longer then the traitor Death they sought,
But each was made so happy by the sight
Of all those florins shining fair and bright
That down they sat beside the precious hoard.
The worst of them was first to speak his word.

"Brothers," he said, "take heed of what I say;
My wit is great, although I jest and play!
Fortune hath found it fit to give this treasure
That we may live our lives in lust and pleasure;
Lightly it comes – so shall it melt away!
God's dignity! Who would have dreamed today
That we should have so fine and fair a grace?
But could the gold be carried from this place
Home to my house, or else to one of yours –
For well we know that all this gold is ours –
Then were we in a high felicity!
But such a thing by day could never be;
Men would proclaim us thieves and cause our seizure;
Might even make us hang for our own treasure!
This gold must then be carried hence by night
With secrecy and cautious oversight.
Wherefore I say, draw lot among us all,
And let us mark the way the lot shall fall;
And he that draws it shall with willing heart
And nimble pace toward the town depart,
And fetch in secret wine and bread, and we
That stay behind shall guard full carefully
This gold; and if our comrade does not tarry,
When it is night we will this treasure carry
Wherever by agreement shall be planned."

The one held out the lots within his hand,
And bade them draw, and look where it would fall;
And it fell on the youngest of them all,
And so by compact toward the town he started.
And scarce a moment after he departed
The one of them spoke slyly to the other:
"Thou know'st well thou art sworn to be my brother;
Now something to thy profit will I say.
Thou see'st our fellow takes himself away;
And here is gold, and that great quantity,
That shall be portioned out among us three.
Nevertheless, if I could shape it so
That we should share it all between us two,
Had I not done a comrade's turn by thee?"

The other said: "But that could never be!
He knows we two are here and guard the gold;
What could we do? What wouldst thou have him
            told?"

"Shall what I say be secret?" asked the first;
"Then shortly shall the method be rehearsed
Whereby I think to bring it well about."
"Agreed," replied the other, "out of doubt
I will betray thee not, as God is true."

"Now," said the first, "thou know'st that we are
            two,
And two of us are mightier than one.
Watch when he sits, then go as if in fun –
As thou wouldst play about with him, and grip him,
And with my dagger through his sides I'll rip him,
While thou art struggling with him, as in play;
And see thou use thy knife the self-same way.
Then all this treasure shall belong to none,
My dearest friend, but me and thee alone!
Then may we sate our lusts until we tire
And play at dice whenever we desire!"
And thus these rascals have devised a way
To slay the third, as ye have heard me say.

This youngest, he that journeyed to the town,
Within his heart rolled often up and down
The beauty of these florins new and bright.
"O Lord!" quoth he, "if it were so I might

Have all this treasure to myself alone,
There liveth no man underneath the throne
Of God, that might exist more merrily
Than I!" And so the fiend, our enemy,
Put in his head that he should poison buy
Wherewith to make his two companions die;
Because the fiend found him in such a state
That he had leave his fall to consummate,
For it was out of doubt his full intent
To slay them both, and never to repent!
So forth he goes – no longer will he tarry –
Unto the town, to an apothecary,
And prays for poison to exterminate
Some rats, and pole-cats that had robbed of late
His roosts – and he would wreak him, if he might,
On vermin that tormented him by night.

Then this apothecary, answering:
"God save my soul, but thou shalt have a thing
That, let a living creature drink or eat
No bigger portion than a grain of wheat,
And he shall die, and that in shorter while,
By God, than thou wouldst take to walk a mile –
This poison is so strong and violent."

All on his cursèd wickedness intent,
This rascal ran as fast as he could fly,
Bearing the poison, to a street near by,
And got three bottles of a man he knew;
And then he poured his poison in the two,
But in the third, his own, put none at all.
For all the night he thought to heave and haul
Carrying gold – then would he slake his thirst.
And so this rascal (may he be accurst!)
Filled all his bottles full of wine; and then
Back to his fellows he repaired again.

What need is there to sermon of it more?
For just as they had planned his death before,
They slew him now, and quickly. Then the one
Spoke to the other after it was done:
"Now let us eat and drink and make us merry,
And afterwards we will his body bury."
And so by chance he drank, that very minute,

Out of a bottle with the poison in it,
And gave his comrade drink when he was through,
From which in little while they died, the two.
    But truly Avicenna, I suppose,
Wrote never in his canons of such throes
And wondrous agonies of poisoning
As these two wretches had in perishing.
Thus died these murderers of whom I tell,
And he who falsely poisoned them as well.

O cursèd sin, too evil to express!
O treacherous homicide, O wickedness!
O gluttony, O lechery and gaming!
O thou blasphemer, Christ forever shaming
With insult, with habitual oaths and proud!
Alas, mankind! How can it be allowed
That to thy Maker, that of clay did knead thee,
And with His own dear precious heart's blood freed
    thee,
Thou art so false, and so unnatural!
    Good men, may God forgive you, one and all,
And guard you from the sin of avarice!
My holy pardon cures you all of this,
If sterling coin make up your offerings,
Or nobles, silver brooches, spoons, or rings.
Come, bow your head beneath this holy bull!
Come up, ye wives, and give your yarn or wool;
See, here I enter your name upon my roll;
Right to the bliss of heaven ascends your soul!
I will assoil you by my sovereign power
As clear and clean as at the very hour
When ye were born (this is the way I preach);
And Jesus Christ, that is our soul's true leech,
Graciously grant you pardon and receive you,
For that is best, sirs; I will not deceive you.
    But I forgot one word, sirs, it is clear;
I have indulgences and relics here
As fair as any man's on English land,
And these were given me by the pope's own hand.
If any of you would come up piously,
Make offering, and be absolved by me,

Come up at once, and kneel, and meekly take
The pardon that I give you for Christ's sake;
Or, if ye like, receive it as ye ride,
At every town's end, newly sanctified,
If every time ye offer me anew
Nobles and pence, each ringing fair and true.
It is an honor to you, it is clear,
That, riding in the lonely country here,
Where accidents are likely to occur,
Ye can be served by such a pardoner!
For ye might tumble, one or more of you,
Off of your horses, and break your necks in two.
How fortunate, what great security
For all that I have joined your company,
Who can absolve you, be ye low or high,
What time the soul shall from the body fly.
And I advise our Host here shall begin,
For he is most of all enmeshed in sin.
Come up, Sir Host, and make thine offering,
And thou shalt kiss the relics – everything –
Yea, for a groat! Come up, unlock thy purse!"
    "No," he replied; "first may I have Christ's curse!
Not I, as I may thrive in health or riches!
For thou wouldst make me kiss thy mouldy breeches
Swearing the rag upon some saint had hung,
Though it were all discolored with thy dung!
But by the cross, St. Helen's sanctuary,
I would I had thy testicles to carry
Instead of relic or of halidom!
Let's cut them off! I'll help thee keep them – come!
We will enshrine them – yea, in a pig's turd!"
    This Pardoner he answered never a word;
He was so angry, no word could he say.
    "Now," said our Host, "I will no longer play
With thee, or any other angry man."
But all at once the worthy Knight began –
Seeing the people laugh on every side –
"No more of this! It is enough!" he cried.
"Sir Pardoner, be glad – cheer up," said he;
"And ye, Sir Host, that are so dear to me.
I pray you, cease, and kiss the Pardoner.

And Pardoner, come here, I pray you, sir,
And let us, as before, all laugh and play."
And soon they kissed, and rode upon their way.

Here ends the Pardoner's Tale

The Wife of Bath's Tale

THE LUSTY, MIDDLE-AGED, much-married Wife of Bath is one of the most famous characters in English literature. Her prologue establishes her earthy character in an extended confession of her many misdeeds. It draws on traditions of satirical depiction of women which are hostile to this type of character, yet she is engaging and largely sympathetic. The message of her tale, when it finally comes, is that women should be afforded a degree of control in their lives. This is quite in keeping with her personality. However, the form of her tale – courtly romance – comes as something of a surprise.

THE WIFE OF BATH'S TALE

The Prologue of the Wife of Bath's Tale

"EXPERIENCE would be quite enough for me,
Even though this world gave no authority,
To speak of woe that marriage has in store,
For, thanks to God that lives forevermore,
At the church door, since I was twelve years old,
Five husbands have I sworn to have and hold;
So often have I been a wedded wife.
And each was worthy in his way of life.
But it was told me not so long ago
That since Christ only went once, as we know,
To any wedding – at Cana in Galilee –
That He by this example teaches me
I should have wed but once. And ye have heard
How by the well a sharp reproving word
Was spoken by this Jesus, God and man,
The time He talked with the Samaritan:
'Five husbands hast thou had ere now,' said he,
'And he – the man that liveth now with thee –
Is not thine husband.' Sure he spoke this way,
But what His meaning was I cannot say.
But I would ask you, why was this fifth man
No husband unto the Samaritan?
Unto what number could she be a wife?
I never heard a soul in all my life
Make any definition of that point.
They argue till their jaws are out of joint;
But by express command, to tell no lie,
God told us we should wax and multiply,

That noble text I fully understand.
And to my husband this is his command:
To leave his father and mother and cleave to me.
But mention of no number maketh he –
Whether two times or eight we married be –
Why is it worse then than monogamy?
    Lo, the wise king, the lordly Solomon –
I know well that he had more wives than one.
Now would to God it were permitted me
To be refreshed but half as much as he!
Ah, what a gift of God for every wife!
No man today could match it, for his life!
God knows, this noble king – I have no doubt –
On the first night had many a merry bout
With each, so glad he was to be alive.
Blessed be God that I have wedded five!
[In which I took good care to pick the best
For under-purse as well as treasure chest.
Diet of different schools makes perfect clerks;
And different practices in different works
Help make a perfect workman, certainly.
The pupil of the five appears in me!]*
Welcome the sixth, however and whenever;
In truth, I will not keep me chaste forever;
For when my husband from the world is passed
Some Christian man shall marry me at last.
For then the apostle says that I am free
To wed, in God's name, where it pleases me.
He says it is no sin for us to wed;
Better be wedded than to burn instead!
What do I care if folk speak villainy
Of wicked Lamech and his bigamy?
I know that Abraham was a holy man,
And Jacob too – as clearly as I can;
Both wedded several wives ere they were through;
And many a holy man was like them, too.
In what age – have ye ever seen or read –
Did high God, by one word expressly said,
Prohibit marriage? Pray you, show it me.

* *Genuine lines, but probably rejected by Chaucer*

Or where did he command virginity?
I know that doubtless th' apostle said,
When in his speech he spoke on maidenhead,
How in that matter, precept had he none.
Men may advise a woman to live alone,
But counselling is not commanding, surely;
He left it to our own discretion purely.
Had God commanded us to stay unwedded
He had condemned all marriage when he said it,
And if indeed no seed were ever sown
From what then should virginity be grown?
Ye may be sure Paul would not dare command
A thing on which his Master took no stand.
The prize is posted for virginity:
Race then, and see who wins the victory!

 Yet every man should not receive this word,
But only those by whom God wants it heard.
A virgin life Paul the apostle led;
Yet none the less, although he wrote and said
He wished all men were like him – this could be
Only advice to keep virginity;
For certainly he gave me leave to wed,
And if I marry when my mate is dead
My marriage cannot be reproach to me,
Or be regarded as a bigamy.
To touch a woman is a sin, he said,
But on a couch, he meant, or in a bed.
For it is danger touching flint to tow –
What that comparison suggests, ye know.
And all this means he held virginity
A better state than wedded frailty.
I call it frailty if a man and wife
Do not live chastely in their wedded life.

 I say, they do not give offense to me
That praise a chaste life more than bigamy;
They would be clean in body and in spirit:
My state of life – I boast not of its merit.
For ye know well, a lord in his household
Will not have all his dishes made of gold;
Some are of wood, and serve him well, I say.
God calls us to Him in no single way.

Each has a special gift within his range –
Some this, some that, as He may please to change.

 Virginity, indeed, is great perfection,
And continence, that keeps in high subjection
The flesh; but Christ, that was perfection's well,
Did not command all men to go and sell
All that they had, and give it to the poor,
And follow Him. He spoke, I hold it sure,
Only to those that would live perfectly;
And, sirs, with your permission, not to me!
I will bestow the flower of all my life
In acts and fruit that make a wedded wife!

 And tell me also, why was there creation
Of organs to be used for generation,
And why were men created, anyway?
They were not made for nothing, I dare say.
Come, smoothe it over, and say in explanation
That they were merely made for urination,
And that our little things are no avail
Except to tell a female from a male,
And for no other cause: do ye say No?
Experience shows us that it is not so.
And if the scholars will not be offended,
I say that it is clear they were intended
For both: for use, and for our pleasure, too,
If we displease not God by what we do.
For otherwise, I ask why scholars set
These words in books: *A man should pay his debt
Unto his wife*? What could these words have meant
But that he pay her with his instrument?
Then they were made that we might make purgation
Of urine, and as well for procreation.

 But I say not that all are obligated,
Who have such apparatus as I stated,
To go and use it getting progeny.
That were to take no heed of chastity.
For Christ was chaste, yet shaped like any man,
And many saints were, since the world began;
Yet always lived as chaste as man could be.
I will not quarrel with virginity;
Let them be loaves of finest wheaten bread,

And we wives be hot barley loaf instead;
And yet with barley bread, doth Mark record,
Was many a man refreshed by Christ our Lord.
I am resolved to live in such a state
As God assigned – I am not delicate.
And all as freely as my maker sent
It to me, I will use my instrument;
If I am niggardly, God bring me sorrow!
My husband shall enjoy it night and morrow
When he shall please to come and pay his debt.
And such a husband will I surely get
As shall be both my servant and my debtor.
I will collect my tribute to the letter
Upon his flesh, while I remain his wife.
I have the power as long as I have life
Over my husband's body, and not he.
For so th' apostle gave the text to me,
Telling our husbands they should love us well.
I like that judgment, every syllable–"

    Here on a sudden spoke the Pardoner:
"By God and by St. John," he said to her,
"Ye make a noble preacher for your creed.
I was about to wed a wife, indeed,
But shall I pay with flesh, and pay so dear?
I think I'll wed no wife at all, this year!"

    "Wait, now," she said, "my tale is not begun.
Nay, thou shalt drink yet from another tun
Before I stop, of a worse taste than ale.
And when I finish telling you my tale
Of tribulations known to married life,
Where I am expert more than any wife –
That is to say, I held and used the whip –
Then mayst thou tell me whether thou wilt sip
Of what is in that cask that I shall broach.
Beware, I say, ere thou too near approach,
For I shall give examples more than ten!
And he who will not learn from other men –
By him shall other men corrected be;
These are the very words of Ptolemy;
Look in his Almagest, and find them there."

    "Dame, I would pray you," said this Pardoner,
"That, if ye like, ye speak as ye began;
Tell us your tale, nor stint for any man,
And let us young men learn of practice through you."

    "Gladly," she said, "if it be pleasing to you.
But first I pray of all this company,
That if my fancy run away with me,
Ye take offense at nothing that I say;
For all my inclination is to play."

    Now, sires, I shall proceed to tell my tale.
As I may ever drink of wine or ale,
This is the truth – the husbands I have had –
Three of the lot were good and two were bad.
The three good men were rich, and they were old
And scarcely found it possible to hold
The law that bound them to me. Ye know well
What I mean there, by God – I need not tell.
So help me God, I laugh about it yet
To think how hard a-night I made them sweat –
For little credit, if the truth be told.
For they had given me all their goods and gold;
I had no longer need of diligence
To win their love or do them reverence.
So well they loved me that by God above,
I took but little pleasure in their love!
A woman who is wise will set about it
To get love, when she finds herself without it.
But since I had them wholly in my hand,
And they had deeded over all their land,
Why should I try to please them, why take heed
Save for my profit and my joy indeed?
In faith, I made a labor of their play,
And many a night they sang "Alackaday!"
The bacon was not fat for them, I know,
As for a few in Essex at Dunmow.
So well I ruled them by the law I had
That all of them full joyous were and glad
To bring me gay things from the market place,
And happy if I showed a pleasant face –
For God alone knows how I used to scold them!

    Now hear how well and firmly I controlled them –
Ye women wise enough to understand!

Thus shall ye scold and keep the game in hand;
For there is not, and never was a man
Can swear as boldly as a woman can;
Or lie. (This that I say is necessary
Not for wise wives, but those whose plans miscarry.)
A shrewd wife, if she knows where lies her gain,
Will take her oath the crow has gone insane,
And find a witness for it in her maid
To back her up – but hear now what I said.

"What now, old dotard – what! is this thy way?
Why is my neighbor's wife so fine and gay?
Why is she honored everywhere she goes
While here at home I hide in rags, God knows?
Why always at her house? Why hovering thus?
Is she so fair? Art thou so amorous?
Why whisper with our maid so? *Ben'cite!*
Sir graybeard lecher, let such antics be!
And if I have a gossip or a friend
Thou scoldest like the devil, without end,
If I walk out or visit at his house.
Thou com'st home here as drunk as any mouse,
To sit upon thy bench and preach at me.
Thou sayst it is a great calamity
To wed a poor wife, with the cost so great;
Or if she have high kin or rich estate,
Then thou wilt call it torment and a folly
To suffer from her pride and melancholy;
And if she's fair, thou sayst, thou very cur,
She will be prey to any adulterer –
She cannot long in chastity abide
That is assailed so much on every side.

"Thou sayst again, our wealth attracts a man,
Or that our figures or our beauty can;
Or else a woman's dancing or her singing,
Or playfulness, or birth and good up-bringing,
Or hands and arms shaped smooth and soft and small;
So, by thy tale, the devil wins it all.
Thou call'st a wall impossible to guard
Assailed so many places and so hard.

"And if she's ugly, thou wilt sayst that she
Lusts after every man that she may see;

For like a spaniel she will leap and fawn
Until she gets some man to prey upon.
Thou sayst – no goose upon the lake so gray
But she will get a mate as best she may.
And it is hard to curb – thou sayst again –
What of his own free will none would retain.
Thus say'st, thou rascal, when thou go'st to bed,
And no wise man is in need to wed,
Nor any with his hopes on heaven's wonder.
With fiery lightning flash and clap of thunder
May that old withered neck of thine be broke!

"Thou sayst that falling beams and sight of smoke
And ranting wives are things that make men flee
From their own houses. Villain. *Ben'cite!*
What ails so old a man to sit and rail?

"Thou sayst we hide the things in which we fail
Till we are wed, then show them when too late.
That is the proverb of a reprobate!

"Thou sayst that oxen, horses, dogs, and asses
Are tested out at times, and so with brasses,
And pans and basins, too, before men buy them,
And spoons and chairs – they have a chance to try
    them –
Kettles and clothes, and all habiliment,
But with their wives they can't experiment
Until the wedding day has come and passed,
And then, thou say'st we show our faults at last.

"Also thou sayst thou fearest my displeasure
Unless thou praise my beauty out of measure,
And always gaze with longing on my face,
And call me 'fair madame' in every place,
And make a feast to celebrate the day
That I was born, and clothe me fresh and gay,
And always look that honor shall be paid
Unto my nurse, and to my chambermaid,
And all my father's relatives likewise –
Thus sayst thou, thou old barrel full of lies!

"And Jankin our apprentice, since his hair
Is curling gold, that gleameth fine and fair;
And since he squires me somewhat through the town,
Thou dost suspect him – falsely, vile old clown!

I should not want him, though thou died tomorrow!
    "But tell me this: why hide – God give thee sorrow–
The keys that lock thy chest away from me?
By God, thou knowst it is my property
As well as thine! Wouldst make an idiot
Out of thy wife? I tell thee thou shalt not,
By St. James, though thou rave and rage at me,
Have both my body and my property!
One shalt thou yield, despite thine eyes, I say;
Why must thou spy upon me, anyway?
Yea, thou wouldst lock me in thy chest, I know.
Thou shouldst say, 'Wife, go where thou please to go;
I will believe no tales told me in malice;
Go play; I know thee for a true wife, Alice!'
We love no man that spies or gives us charge
Where we shall go – we want to be at large.

    "Among all men, most blessed may he be –
The wise astrologer, Lord Ptolemy,
That gives this proverb in his Almagest:
'Of all mankind his wisdom is the best
That never cares who has the world in hand.'
And by this proverb thou shalt understand
That if thou have enough, why vex or care
How merrily that other people fare?
For, by thy leave, thou stingy dotard white,
Thou shalt have all thou ask of me by night.
He is a niggard that will not permit
A candle from his lantern to be lit;
He has no less if all his light remain;
And thou, with plenty – thou shouldst not complain.

    "Thou sayst again that if we deck us gay
With clothing and with other rich array,
It is a peril to our chastity;
And to support thy words – bad luck to thee! –
Thou sayst this in the good apostle's name:
'In garments made with modesty and shame
Ye women shall apparel you,' he said,
'And not with wealth of gems and plaited head,
Nor ropes of pearls nor gold nor costly clothing.'
That text and gloss I look upon with loathing,
And will not follow them more than a gnat!

And thou saidst this: that I was like a cat;
For if ye catch the cat and singe her skin,
Then will she not go out, but stay within;
But if her fur be sleek and rich and gay,
She will not keep the house for half a day,
But out she runs, as soon as night is falling,
To show her coat, and go a caterwauling!
That is to say, that I will hurry out
If gayly dressed, to show myself about!

    "Sir graybeard fool, whom hopst thou to surprise?
Though thou asked Argus, with his hundred eyes,
To be my bodyguard, as best he could,
He should not keep me close unless I would;
As I may thrive, I'd trim his whiskers well!

    "There are three things, as thou wilt also tell,
That trouble all the earth, from south to north,
And that no person can endure the fourth.
Sir Ranter, Jesus shorten thy vile life!
Yea, thou dost preach, and sayst a hateful wife
Among these evils should be held as one.
Are there not things fit for comparison
Besides a simple wife, which ye could use
To make your parable, if ye would choose?

    "Thou dost compare a woman's love to hell,
To barren land that has no spring or well;
And thou dost liken it to raging fire –
The more it burns, the stronger its desire
Is to consume all things insatiably.
And just as worms, thou sayst, destroy a tree,
A woman will destroy her husband's life –
This any man knows well that serves a wife!"

    Lordings, just so, as ye have well perceived,
I swore, to these old husbands, who believed
That thus they spoke in their intoxication;
And all was false; but my corroboration
Was Jankin's word, and what my niece would swear.
O Lord! The suffering I made them bear!
And by God's pain, without a ghost of right!
For like a filly I could whine and bite,
And rant like mad, though I were in the wrong;
Or many a time I had not lasted long!

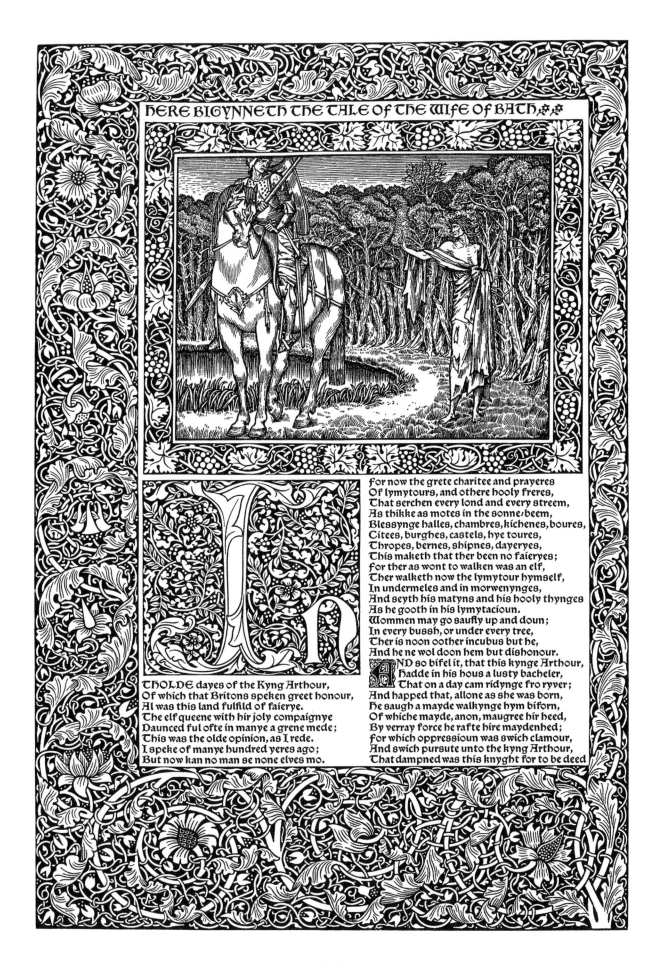

HERE BIGYNNETH THE TALE OF THE WIFE OF BATH.

IN THOLDE dayes of the Kyng Arthour,
Of which that Britons speken greet honour,
Al was this land fulfild of faierye.
The elf queene with hir joly compaignye
Daunced ful ofte in manye a grene mede;
This was the olde opinion, as I rede.
I speke of manye hundred yeres ago;
But now kan no man se none elves mo.

For now the grete charitee and prayeres
Of lymytours, and othere hooly freres,
That serchen every lond and every streem,
As thikke as motes in the sonne-beem,
Blessynge halles, chambres, kichenes, boures,
Citees, burghes, castels, hye toures,
Thropes, bernes, shipnes, dayeryes,
This maketh that ther been no faieryes;
For ther as wont to walken was an elf,
Ther walketh now the lymytour hymself,
In undermeles and in morwenynges,
And seyth his matyns and his hooly thynges
As he gooth in his lymytacioun.
Wommen may go saufly up and doun;
In every bussh, or under every tree,
Ther is noon oother incubus but he,
And he ne wol doon hem but dishonour.

AND so bifel it, that this kynge Arthour,
Hadde in his hous a lusty bacheler,
That on a day cam ridynge fro ryver;
And happed that, allone as she was born,
He saugh a mayde walkynge hym biforn,
Of whiche mayde, anon, maugree hir heed,
By verray force he rafte hire maydenhed;
For which oppressioun was swich clamour,
And swich pursute unto the kyng Arthour,
That dampned was this knyght for to be deed

Plate 16: The Wife of Bath's Tale (p. 200)

First to the mill, first get your grinding done!
I scolded first, and soon the war was won.
For they were quick and eager to repent,
Though they might be completely innocent.
　　Sometimes, though one was quite too drunk to
　　　　stand,
I swore that he had had a wench in hand;
And yet it pleased him, though I overbore him.
He thought it showed a great affection for him.
I swore I walked at night, instead of sleeping,
Only to find what wenches he was keeping;
And on that pretext often had my mirth.
For all such cunning comes to us at birth –
Weeping, deceit, and lying doth God give
Abundantly to women, while they live.
And thus of one thing I can boast – to wit,
That I would always have the best of it,
By trickery or force or in some fashion –
By constant nagging or pretended passion.
And most in bed I had my way with them;
For I would scold, and never play with them –
And if I felt an arm across me laid,
I would not stay in bed till he had paid
His ransom to me, and in proper measure,
And then indeed I let him have his pleasure.
And so to every man I tell this tale –
Win he who can, everything is for sale.
Men catch no hawks unless they have a lure;
When I had won, his lust I would endure,
And would pretend to have an appetite;
And yet in truth I never took delight
In play with these old fools that made me chide them.
For though the pope himself had sat beside them,
I would not spare them – not at their own board;
For by my faith, I paid them word for word.
So help me God, true and omnipotent,
Though I sat now to make my testament,
I should not owe a word I did not pay,
For with my wit I managed in such way
That they surrendered, knowing it was best –
Or else we never should have been at rest.

For let him be a lion breathing fire,
Yet he would always fail of his desire!
　　Then I would say to him, "Look, sweetheart dear,
How patient stands our good sheep Wilkin here;
Husband, come here and let me pat thy cheek;
Ye should be patient too," I'd say, "and meek,
And have a conscience sweet and delicate,
That of Job's patience love so much to prate.
Since ye can preach it – suffer and endure;
If not, then we will teach you well, be sure,
That it is sweet to have a wife at peace.
One of us two must yield before we cease,
And since a man is much more reasonable
Than woman, ye must learn to bear it well.
What ails you to complain so much, and groan?
Ye want my *quoniam* to yourself alone?
Why, take it all, I say; yea, every bit.
Curse you if ye have not great love for it;
For if I wished to barter my *belle chose*,
I could walk forth as fresh as any rose.
But I will keep that sweet for your own tooth;
Ye are to blame, by God, to tell the truth!"
　　Such words I had always, and brought them forth
For these three husbands. Now about the fourth.
　　This fourth one was a mighty reveller;
He kept a wench, and he was fond of her.
Lively and young and passionate was I.
Stubborn and strong, and jolly as a pie.
I danced well to the harp, to tell no tale,
And sang indeed like any nightingale
When I had drunk a draught of good sweet wine.
Metellius, foul churl, the cursèd swine,
That beat his wife until she lost her life –
Because she drank – if I had been his wife,
He never should have hindered me from drinking.
And after wine, to Venus runs my thinking –
For just as sure as cold produces hail,
A lecherous mouth begets a lecherous tail!
A woman fired with wine has no defense –
All lechers know it by experience.
　　But Lord Christ, when I call to memory

My youth, and think on all my jollity,
It tickles all the roots about my heart!
It does me good to think I bore my part
And had my day when I could take my fling!
But age, alas! that poisons everything,
Hath stolen the strength and beauty that I knew;
Go, then, farewell! The devil go with it too!
The flour is gone – there is no more to say –
And I must sell the bran as best I may.
Yet I will find a merry life somehow.
Of my fourth husband will I tell you now.

   I say, at heart I bore it bitterly
That he rejoiced in anyone but me.
But by St. Joyce and God above, I paid him!
Of the same wood a bitter stick I made him.
Not with my body, through sin of any sort;
But made with others so much game and sport,
That in his own grease he fried merrily
For anger and for very jealousy.
By God, I was his earthly purgatory,
Through which, I hope, his soul has gone to glory.
Often, God knows, the man would sit and sing,
When the shoe pinched, for very suffering.
Yea, there was none but God, I think, beside him,
That knew the many ways in which I tried him.
He died when I returned from Palestine,
And though his tomb shows not the rich design
That hath the king Darius' sepulcher,
Wrought by Apelles, the artificer,
In church beneath the rood I had it placed.
A lavish burial were only waste.
Farewell, God rest his soul, I pray it often
Now that he lies entombed and in his coffin.

   Now of the fifth at length I come to tell.
I pray God that his soul went not to hell!
Yet I must say that he, more than the rest,
Was harsh to me, as all my ribs attest,
And shall indeed until my dying day.
But in our bed he was so fresh and gay,
And flattered me so subtly, as God knows,
When he was bent on having my *belle chose*,

That, had he beaten me all black and blue,
He quickly could have won my love anew.
I loved him best because he used to be
So much a niggard in his love with me.
We women, if I tell you truly there,
Are strangely fanciful in that affair;
For something not too easy to be had,
We always crave and cry for it like mad.
Forbid us something – that seems precious to us;
But we will flee if anyone pursue us.
Scorn us – we offer all with open hand.
For things are dear when there is great demand,
And what is cheap, that will we all despise;
And every woman knows it who is wise.

   Now my fifth husband, may he reach God's throne!
I wed him not for wealth, but love alone.
He was a student once at Oxford town,
But he had left his college and come down
To board in our town with my gossip – one
I pray God save! Her name was Alison.
She knew my heart, and all my secrets, too, –
More than our parish priest, to tell you true.
I kept back nothing – nay, I told her all,
For had my husband pissed against a wall,
Or done a thing that might have cost his life,
To her, and to another worthy wife,
And to my niece, whom I loved passing well,
I would have told them all there was to tell!
And so I often did, as God doth know!
And this would make his face go hot, and glow
For shame, and he would blame himself that he
Had told so great a secret unto me.

   And so it happened on a day in Lent
(For often to my gossip's house I went;
For I was always eager to be gay,
And walk – in March, in April, and in May,
From house to house, where various tales were spun)
This student Jankin and Dame Alison
And I myself, out in the meadow went.
My husband was in London all that Lent;
I had the greater leisure thus for sport,

And seeing people of a jolly sort,
And being seen; how could I tell which spot
Was like to bring me luck, and which was not?
And so I made my visits to confessions,
To various pilgrimages and processions,
To plays of miracles and marriage, too,
And heard full many a solemn preachment through,
In dresses made of gallant scarlet cloth.
And never a worm, and never a mite or moth
Upon my peril, marred them with a touch.
And know ye why? They were in use too much!

Now I will tell what happened there to me.
I say, we walked forth in the fields, we three,
Until I told this student in flirtation –
With foresight for my future situation –
That if the time should ever come to be
When I were widowed, he should marry me.
For, not to boast about myself unduly,
I always have a proper foresight, truly,
In marriage, and in other things I seek.
I hold that mouse's heart not worth a leek
That only has one hole where it can run,
And if that fail, then all the dance is done.

I told him he had cast a spell on me;
My mother schooled me in such subtlety.
And I had dreamed of him all night, I said:
He would have slain me as I lay abed;
And all the bed was swimming with my blood;
But yet I hoped that he would do me good,
For I was taught that blood meant gold. But all
Was false: I had not dreamed of him at all.
I did as I had heard my mother tell
In this, and so in other things as well.

But now, sir, let me see – where am I then?
Aha! By God, I have my tale again.

When my fourth husband lay upon his bier
I made great sorrow, weeping many a tear,
As every wife should do in such a case,
And with my kerchief covered up my face.
But for the husband that was now at hand
I wept but little, ye can understand.

Upon the morrow to the church they bore him,
With many neighbors making sorrow for him,
Our student Jankin with them in the throng.
God help me, as I saw him walk along
After the bier, I thought he had a pair
Of legs and feet shaped all so clean and fair
That all my heart was his to have and hold.
He was, I think, but twenty winters old,
And I was forty, if I tell the truth.
But I had always had a young colt's tooth.
Gat-toothed I was; and that sat well upon me;
St. Venus' seal had left its imprint on me.
So help me God, I was a lusty one,
And fair, and rich, and young, and full of fun.
And truly, as my husbands said to me,
I had the choicest *quoniam* that could be.
My feelings spring from Venus, by the stars!
But all my spirit comes from warlike Mars.
From Venus comes my lust and amorousness,
From Mars my sturdy will and hardiness.
Taur my ascendant was, and Mars therein.
Alas! alas! that love was ever sin!
I always acted on my inclination,
And this by virtue of my constellation,
And so to no good fellow could deny
My gate of Venus! Yet I know that I
Bear the clear mark of Mars upon my face,
As well as on another secret place.
For, as I pray to God for my salvation,
I never practiced a love with hesitation,
But followed hot upon my appetite,
Let him be short or long, or black or white –
I never cared, so he was fond of me,
How poor he was, or what his pedigree!

What should I say, but, when a month had passed,
This jolly Jankin wedded me at last,
With celebration that was good to see.
And then I gave him all my land and fee –
All that I had been given – every bit;
But bitterly in time repented it.
Of nothing that might please me would he hear.

By God, he struck me once upon the ear
Because I tore some pages from a book,
And all that ear was deafened from the stroke.
I was as stubborn as a lioness,
And with my tongue a very shrew, I guess,
And I would walk, as I had done before,
From house to house, although indeed he swore
I should not. He would often preach to me,
From ancient Roman tales, and teach to me
How one Simplicius Gallus left his wife,
Forsaking her indeed for all his life
Because one day he saw her at the door
Bare-headed, looking out, and nothing more!

He told me once another Roman's name
That, when his wife went to some summer's game
Without his knowledge, he forsook her too.
And he would sometimes thumb his Bible through
To find Ecclesiastes' admonition,
Which bids a man by solemn prohibition
Not to permit his wife to gad about.
Then he would always turn to me and shout:
"Whoever builds his whole house out of sallows,
And whips his blind old horse across the fallows,
And lets his wife go seeking saints and hallows
Is worthy to be hanged upon the gallows!"
But all for naught. I didn't give a haw
For his old proverb or his mouldy saw,
Nor at his hand would I corrected be.
I hate whoever tells my faults to me,
And so do more of us, God knows, than I.
This made him mad with anger by and by;
I would not give him any peace, I promise.

Now I will tell you truly, by St. Thomas,
Why from that book of his I tore a leaf,
And how he smote me so that I was deaf.

He had a book that, for his great delight,
He always loved to read, both day and night.
He called it "Theophraste and Valerie,"
And when he read it, laughed uproariously.
And also there was once a clerk at Rome,
A cardinal, by name of St. Jerome,

That wrote a book against Jovinian;
And in this book too were Tertullian,
Crysippus, Trotula, and Heloïse,
An abbess, close to Paris, if you please;
Also the parables of Solomon,
And *Ovid's* Art, and many books in one
Bound in a single volume in this way.
It was his custom, every night and day,
When he had leisure and was on vacation
From other and more worldly occupation,
Out of this book to read of wicked wives.
He knew more legends of them, and more lives
Than ye could find of good wives in the Bible.
And trust ye well, a clerk is never liable
To speak the smallest word in praise of wives –
Unless he write a book about Saints' lives –
Of others not. Tell me, if ye are able
Who painted Æsop's lion in the fable?
By God, if women set to writing stories,
As do these scholars in their oratories,
They would have told more wickedness of men
Than all of Adam's race could right again.
Children of Venus and of Mercury
Will never work at all in harmony,
For Mercury loves science and great learning,
Venus for revel and display is yearning;
And from these differences in inclination,
Each falleth in the other's exaltation;
And thus, when Mercury sinks desolate
In Pisces, Venus soars in shining state,
And Venus falls when Mercury is raised;
And so no woman by a clerk is praised.
The clerk, when he is old, and cannot do
More work for Venus than his worn-out shoe –
Then he sits down in dotage to disparage
Our sex, and says we cannot keep a marriage!
But now to tell you, as I undertook,
By God, how I was beaten for a book.
One night it fell that Jankin, our good sire,
Read in his book, while sitting by the fire,
Of Eva first, who in her wickedness,

Brought all mankind to evil and distress,
For which Lord Jesus Christ Himself was slain,
And so redeemed us with His blood again.
Lo, here of woman ye expressly find
That woman was the bane of all mankind!

And then he read how Sampson lost his hair
In sleep; his sweetheart came and sheared it there,
And through this treason made him lose his sight.
And then he read me, if I tell you right,
Of Hercules, and of his Dejanire,
And how through her he set himself a-fire.

He did not skip the woes of Socrates,
Or the two wives that were the cause of these;
Xantippe throwing urine on his head;
The poor man sat as still as he were dead,
And wiped his head, and did not dare complain:
"Before the thunder stops, there comes a rain."
He thought the wickedness of Pasiphaë,
The queen of Crete, as sweet as it could be –
Fie, speak no more of that abomination –
Her horrible lust and her infatuation!

Of Clytemnestra that, for lechery,
Murdered her husband in foul treachery,
Devotedly he read the story through.

And he would tell on what occasion, too,
Amphiaraus lost at Thebes his life.
My husband had the legend of his wife –
Eriphyle – how to the Greeks she told
In secrecy, to gain an ounce of gold,
Where was her husband's hiding place, and he
Fared ill at Thebes through this her treachery.

Of Livia and Lucilia yet again
He read, that caused their husbands to be slain,
One through her love, the other in her hate.
For Livia, when the night was dark and late,
Poisoned her husband, whom she held her foe.
Lucilia, amorous, loved her husband so
That she attempted, through a lover's potion,
To win and hold forever his devotion;
And he, before the day had dawned, was dead.
So husbands always come to grief, he said.

And then he told me how Latumius
Complained to his companion Arrius
How in the garden grew a certain tree
On which, he said, because of jealousy
His wives had hanged themselves – three perished
     thus.
"O my dear brother," said this Arrius,
"Give me one blessèd slip, I beg of you,
And in my garden I will plant it, too!"

Of other wives in later times he read;
One of them slew her husband in his bed,
And let her lover lie with her all night,
While on the floor the body lay in sight.
And some, he read, drove great spikes through the
     brain,
And thus their husbands while they slept were slain;
And some would poison what they bade them drink of,
He told more evil than the mind can think of,
And in addition knew more proverbs, too,
Than all the grass or herbs that ever grew.
"Better," he said, "for house-mate to rely on
A dragon foul, or take a raging lion,
Than wed a woman that is always chiding."
"Better," he said, "high in the roof be hiding,
Than dwell below beside an angry wife.
Adverse and wicked are they all their life,
And what their husbands love, they hate and mock."
He said, "A woman casting off her smock
Casts off her modesty." One more I tell:
"A comely wife that is not chaste as well,
Is like a golden ring in a sow's nose."
Who would believe, who could indeed suppose,
What pain was in my heart, what wrath and woe?

And when I saw he would not stop, but go
On reading all night from this cursèd book,
Three pages of it suddenly I took,
Even as he read, and tore them from their place,
And with my fist I struck him in the face,
So that he tumbled backward on the fire.
And up he leaped, as raging wild for ire
As any lion, and smote me on the head;

And down upon the floor I fell, as dead.
And when he saw how motionless I lay,
He was aghast, and would have fled away,
Until at length half in my swoon I sighed!
"False thief! And hast thou slain me thus?" I cried,
"And murdered me to get my land, I say?
Yet will I kiss thee, ere I pass away."

    And he came close, and courteously knelt down,
And said to me, "Dear Sister Alison,
I will not ever strike thee, sweetheart mine!
For that which I have done, the blame is thine;
Forgive me, I beseech, and hear me speak –"
But all at once I struck him on the cheek:
"I am revenged that much," I made reply.
"Now I can speak no more, and I will die."
But in end, with care and trouble thus,
We made a peace between the two of us.
He put the bridle wholly in my hand,
To have the rule alike of house and land,
And of his acts and all that he might say.
I made him burn his book then, right away,
And when at last I gathered unto me
By victory, the total sovereignty,
And he had said to me, "My own true wife,
Do as may please thee all thy live-long life,
Keep all thine honor, and hold my property –"
After that day no argument had we;
And I, as God may bless me, was as kind
As any wife from Denmark unto Ind,
And true as well, and so was he to me.
I pray that God, who sits in majesty,
May bless his soul in heavenly mercy dear.
Now will I tell my tale, if ye will hear.

Behold the words between the Summoner and the Friar

THE Friar began to laugh on hearing this,
"Now, dame," he cried, "as I have hope of bliss,
This is a long preamble to a tale!"
    The Summoner heard him, "Yea, it cannot fail,"
He cried, "by God's two arms, our Lord and King!

A friar will stick his nose in everything!
Lo, sirs, a fly will tumble, and a friar
In every dish and every heap of mire!
What sayst thou of preambling?" with a frown,
"Amble, or trot, or walk, or go sit down;
Thou dost destroy our sport, I tell thee, sir."
    "Yea?" said the Friar. "Wilt thou, Sir Summoner?
Now by my faith, I shall ere I am through
Tell of a summoner such a tale or two
That every one shall laugh about this place."
    "Now, friar, I tell thee I will curse thy face,"
This Summoner said, "and curse myself as well,
Unless I find a tale or two to tell,
Of friars before I come to Sittingbourne,
For which thy rascal's soul shall writhe and mourn;
For well I know thy patience is all fled."
    "Peace now, at once, I say!" our Landlord said;
And added, "Let the woman tell her tale.
Ye act like drunken fellows drowned in ale.
Dame, tell your tale," he said, "for that is best."
    "All ready, sir," said she, "as ye request,
If this good friar will grant his leave to me."
    "Yes, dame; tell on, and I will hear," said he.

Here the Wife of Bath ends her Prologue

Here begins the Tale of the Wife of Bath

IN olden days, when Arthur was the king,
Whom all the Britons join in honoring,
All of this land was full of fairy power.
Often the elf-queen made a merry hour
Dancing with all her band on bright green mead.
This was the old opinion, as I read.
I speak of many hundred years gone by;
Today no man can any elves espy.
For now the charity and high desires
Of limiters and other worthy friars
That haunt the lands and rivers every one,
As thick as motes that crowd a beam of sun,
Blessing all halls and chambers, kitchens, bowers,

Boroughs and cities, castles and high towers,
And villages and stables, barns and dairies –
These make it that we see no more of fairies!

    For where in other days there walked an elf,
Today there goes the limiter himself,
From morn till eve busy with his affairs,
And says his holy offices and prayers,
As in his begging-ground he roams about.
Women with safety now may wander out,
For under any bush or shady tree
The only incubus to fear is he,
And he will do no harm – except in sport
To ruin them!

    Now at King Arthur's court
There dwelt a knight, a lusty one and gay;
And from the river as he rode one day
He saw a maid, and felt great longing for her.
She was alone as when her mother bore her;
And soon this maid, despite her very head,
By force he ravished of her maidenhead.
But there was such a clamorous protestation
Unto the king about this violation
That soon the knight was sentenced to be dead
By course of law, and would have lost his head,
Perhaps, for this by statute was his due,
But that the queen and other ladies, too,
For mercy never ceased to make their prayer,
Until his life King Arthur granted there,
And gave him to the queen to work her will,
And at her choice to spare him or to kill.

    The queen then thanked the king as best she might,
And after this she spoke thus to the knight
When she perceived her proper time one day.
She said: "Thou standest yet in such a way
That of thy life thou hast no certainty.
But I will grant it if thou answer me
What thing by women is most coveted?
Beware, and save thy neck from iron!" she said.
"And if this be a thing thou dost not know,
Then none the less I give thee leave to go
Abroad a year and day, to bring to me

An answer that is satisfactory.
And pledge me surety, ere thou disappear,
That on the day thou yield thy body here."

    This knight was sad; he sighed beyond all measure;
But what! This business lay not at his pleasure,
And so he chose to travel forth at last,
And come again, when the full year had passed,
Trusting that God might show him what to say.
And takes his leave and goes upon his way.

    He visits every house and every place
Where he had any hope to get his grace,
And learn what thing all women loved the best.
But he could not discover, he confessed,
Seek as he might, two creatures anywhere
That would agree regarding this affair.

    Some said that wealth gave women most content;
Others that honor would, or merriment;
Some said rich clothing; others, lust in bed,
And to be widowed often, and re-wed.

    Some said of us, the thing that chiefly mattered
Was, that we should be pleased, and also flattered.
He strikes close to the truth, I will not lie;
A man will win us best by flattery;
Attentions, too, will snare us, I should guess,
And diligence in courting, more or less.
And some said that we covet more than these
Freedom to do exactly as we please,
And have none scold us for our faults, but grant
That we are wise, and no way ignorant.
To tell the truth, who is there that will not –
If some one scratch him in a tender spot –
Kick when he hears the truth – so why deny it?
This he will find that has a mind to try it.
For we desire, though never so vile within,
To be considered wise, and free of sin.

    And some say that we find it passing sweet
That men should think us stable and discreet,
And steadfast to the purpose that we hold,
And not betray a thing that we are told.
That is not worth the handle of a rake!
We cannot hold a thing, I undertake.

Midas, for instance – will ye hear his story?

King Midas, notwithstanding all his glory,
Says Ovid among other tales, had growing
Two ass's ears, beneath his long and flowing
Tresses. This fault he hid as best he might,
Slyly concealing it from all men's sight,
So that his wife alone knew of the thing:
He loved her most, and trusted her, this king;
And prayed her that of this disgraceful feature
She breathe no word to any living creature.

She swore that "No! Although she stood to win
The wide world, she would never do that sin,
Making her husband have so foul a name –
She would not tell it for her own great shame!"
And yet at length she thought that she would perish,
Having this thing in secrecy to cherish;
It swelled so in her heart, she feared some word
Would burst out from her sometime, and be heard;
And since she dared reveal it to no man,
Down to a near-by marsh one day she ran,
And reached the edge, her very heart a-fire,
And as a bittern bumbles in the mire,
She bent and laid her lips close to the ground:
"Betray me not, thou water, with a sound;
I tell this thing to thee alone," she said;
"Two ass's ears grow on my husband's head!
Now it is out; my heart is whole, and stronger;
I know well I could not have kept it longer."
Ye see, though something for a while we hold,
Out it will come – the secret must be told!
If ye would know the rest of this affair,
Go read in Ovid: ye shall find it there.

This knight, of whom in chief I tell this tale,
When he perceived that he must surely fail
To find this thing that women loved the best –
His heart was full of sorrow in his breast;
But home he went, no longer could he stay.
The day was come to take the homeward way,
And on his road by chance he came to ride,
Lost in his care, beneath a forest-side,
Where in a dance upon the woodland floor

He saw some ladies, twenty-four and more;
And toward that dance, with hope to hear some word
Of wisdom from them, eagerly he spurred.
And yet before this knight was fully there,
The dance had disappeared; he knew not where.
No creature could he see there bearing life,
Save, sitting on the green, an agèd wife.
None could imagine a more loathsome sight.
And this old woman rose to meet the knight,
Saying, "Sir Knight, here shall ye find no way.
What seek ye? Tell me, by your faith, I say;
And ye may profit by it, possibly;
Old folk are wise in many things," said she.

"Dear mother, of a truth," replied this knight,
"I shall be dead unless I say aright
What women most desire; if ye could tell
What that thing is, I would reward you well."

"Plight me your troth, here in my hand," said she,
"Whatever thing I first require of thee
Thou wilt perform, if it is in thy might,
And I will tell you that before this night."
"Take here my pledge; for I agree," he cried.

"Then I will dare to boast," this wife replied,
"Thy life is safe, for I will stand thereby
Upon my life, the queen will say as I.
Let me behold the proudest of them all
That wears at court a coverchief or caul,
That dares say Nay to that which I shall teach.
Let us go forward then, without more speech."
And then she whispered softly in his ear,
And told him to be glad, and have no fear.

When they were come to court, this knight averred
That "he had kept his day, as was his word,
And had his answer ready –" so he said.
And many a noble wife, and many a maid,
And widows (they were wise for this affair),
With the queen's self sitting in judgment there,
Were gathered that they might his answer hear;
And afterwards they bade this knight appear.

Then silence was proclaimed, and he was told
Before this great assemblage to unfold

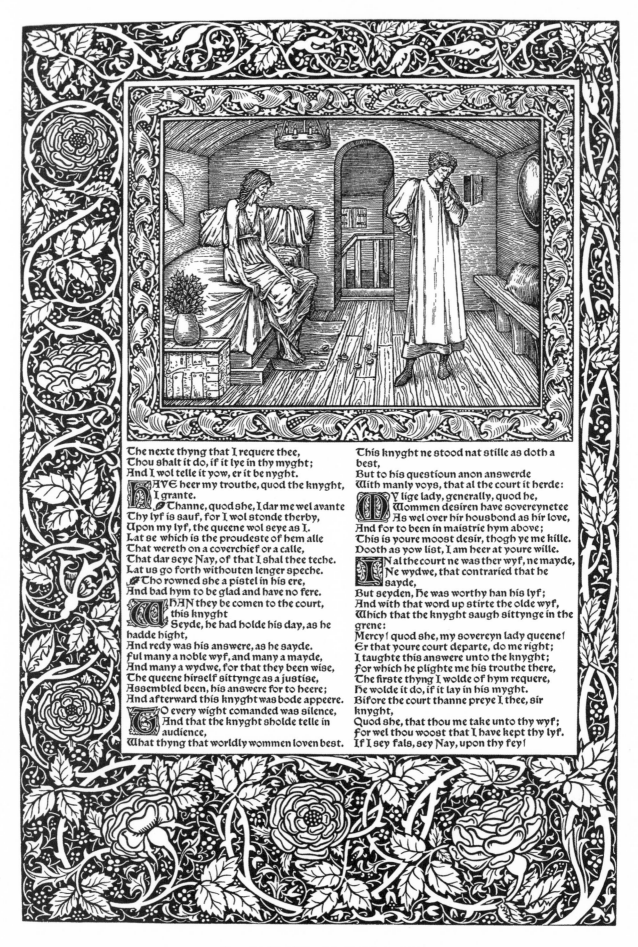

The nexte thyng that I requere thee,
Thou shalt it do, if it lye in thy myght;
And I wol telle it yow, er it be nyght.
HAVE heer my trouthe, quod the knyght,
  I grante.
    Thanne, quod she, I dar me wel avante
Thy lyf is sauf, for I wol stonde therby,
Upon my lyf, the queene wol seye as I.
Lat se which is the proudeste of hem alle
That wereth on a coverchief or a calle,
That dar seye Nay, of that I shal thee teche.
Lat us go forth withouten lenger speche.
    Tho rowned she a pistel in his ere,
And bad hym to be glad and have no fere.
WHAN they be comen to the court,
  this knyght
    Seyde, he had holde his day, as he
hadde hight,
And redy was his answere, as he sayde.
Ful many a noble wyf, and many a mayde,
And many a wydwe, for that they been wise,
The queene hirself sittynge as a justise,
Assembled been, his answere for to heere;
And afterward this knyght was bode appeere.
TO every wight comanded was silence,
  And that the knyght sholde telle in
  audience,
What thyng that worldly wommen loven best.

This knyght ne stood nat stille as doth a
best,
But to his questioun anon answerde
With manly voys, that al the court it herde:
MY lige lady, generally, quod he,
  Wommen desiren have sovereynetee
  As wel over hir housbond as hir love,
And for to been in maistrie hym above;
This is youre moost desir, thogh ye me kille.
Dooth as yow list, I am heer at youre wille.
IN al the court ne was ther wyf, ne mayde,
  Ne wydwe, that contraried that he
  sayde,
But seyden, He was worthy han his lyf;
And with that word up stirte the olde wyf,
Which that the knyght saugh sittynge in the
grene:
Mercy! quod she, my sovereyn lady queene!
Er that youre court departe, do me right;
I taughte this answere unto the knyght;
For which he plighte me his trouthe there,
The firste thyng I wolde of hym requere,
He wolde it do, if it lay in his myght.
Bifore the court thanne preye I thee, sir
knyght,
Quod she, that thou me take unto thy wyf;
For wel thou woost that I have kept thy lyf.
If I sey fals, sey Nay, upon thy fey!

Plate 17: The Wife of Bath's Tale (p. 213)

What thing was most a woman's worldly will.
Not like a beast he faced them, dumb and still,
But to the question spoke with ready spirit
And manly voice, that all the court could hear it.

"My lady liege, through all the world," said he,
"Women desire to have the sovereignty
Over their husbands, or of such as love them,
And ever live in mastery above them.
This is your chief desire, though ye may slay me;
Do as ye please; under your will I lay me."

In all the court there was no wife or maid
Or widow, that this speech of his gainsaid,
But cried "that he deserved to have his life."

And with that word up started this old wife
Whom he had met there sitting on the green.
"Mercy," she cried, "my sovereign lady queen!
Before your court dissolve, defend my right!
I taught this answer unto yonder knight;
For which he swore to me, at my desire,
That the first thing I should of him require
He would perform, if it were in his might.
Before the court I pray thee then, Sir Knight,"
She said, "that thou wilt take me for thy wife,
For well thou knowst that I have saved thy life.
If I speak false, now by thy faith, say Nay!"

This knight replied: "Alas! Alackaday!
This was mine oath, I know it and attest;
For God's love change, and choose a new request;
Take all my goods, and let my body go."

"First will I curse us both," she answered. "No –
For though I stand here poor and foul and old,
Rather than all the ore and all the gold
Buried in earth, or lying here above,
I will prefer to be thy wife and love !"

"My love?" he cried. "No, rather my damnation!
Alas, indeed! that such a degradation
Should fall on any of my family!"
But all for nothing – it could only be
That in the end he was constrained to wed,
And take his agèd wife, and go to bed.

Now some men, it may be, will take offense,
That I omit, in what seems negligence,
To tell you all the joy and great array
With which they held the feast upon that day.
To this let short and simple answer fall:
I say, there was no joy or feast at all.
There was no thing but heaviness and sorrow,
For privately he wedded her one morrow,
And stayed all day in hiding, like an owl –
Such woe he felt – his wife appeared so foul.

And dismal thoughts went racing through his head
When with his wife at last he went to bed.
He tossed and turned about in deep despair.
His old wife all the time lay smiling there,
And said to him: "Dear husband, *ben'cite*!
Doth every knight act with his wife as ye?
Is this the law," she asked, "your king decrees?
Is every knight of his so hard to please?
I am your love, I am your wedded wife;
I am the one to whom ye owe your life;
I never did you anything but right;
Why should ye treat me thus on this first night?
Ye act like someone who hath lost his wit.
What is my guilt? For God's sake out with it!
I will amend it if I can," she cried.

"Amend it! No, alas!" this knight replied;
"It will not be amended, cannot be.
Thou art so old, and art so foul to see,
And of a low degree that I must spurn,
It is small wonder that I toss and turn.
I would to God my heart would burst in two!"

"And is it this," she asked, "that troubles you?"
"Yea, surely; and no wonder," he replied.

"Now, sire, that could be quickly rectified –
Yea, if I wished, ere three days passed, if ye
Would only show some courtesy to me.

"But since ye speak of such nobility
As comes from olden wealth, and say to me
Ye knights because of this are noble men,
I find such arrogance not worth a hen.
Look rather who may show an inclination,
Public or private, and without cessation,

To virtue, doing all such deeds he can,
And choose him as the greatest nobleman.
Christ wishes us to seek nobility
Through him, and not through wealth or ancestry.
Our sires may give us all things that were theirs,
And we may claim high station as their heirs,
Yet none of us inherits through their giving
The virtue of the lives that they were living,
That earned for them the name of noble men,
And, as they acted, bids us act again.

 "Ripe with his wisdom, speaks the Florentine,
The poet Dante, in his lofty line;
Lo, thus ye see the rime of Dante flowing:
'Seldom from its own little branches growing
Rises the worth of man; God wills that we
Should turn to Him to win nobility.'
For from our fathers nothing can we claim
But temporal things, that men can hurt and maim.

 "And this as well as I know'th every creature –
That if nobility were some fixed feature
Given by Nature to a family,
Then always, secretly or openly,
They would express the good that lay within
And could not do a villainy or sin.

 "Take fire, and hide it in the darkest room
From here to Caucasus, yet in the gloom
Though men may shut the doors and leave it there,
The fire will lie and burn as bright and fair
As if some twenty thousand saw it burning.
It holds its natural office, never turning
From that, as I may live, until it die.

 "Here ye may well perceive, gentility
Is not associated with possession,
Since human nature does not give expression,
Like fire, that never varies as to kind.
For God knows well that men will often find
A lord's son doing shame and villainy.
And he that boasts of his gentility
Because his family was illustrious,
And all his forbears noble and virtuous,
But will not follow them when they are dead,

But turns away from noble deeds instead –
He is not noble, though a duke or earl,
For low and wicked actions make a churl.
For nobleness is only the renown
Thy fathers had, which their good deeds pass down,
And this is strange to thee, and not thine own.
Thy nobleness must come from God alone;
Then true nobility is born of merit,
And nothing that with rank we may inherit.

 "Recall how noble, as saith Valerius,
Was that great Tullius Hostilius,
That rose from poverty to his high station.
Read Seneca, or read the *Consolation*;
There beyond doubt ye shall expressly read
The noble man is one of noble deed.
Therefore, dear husband, I must thus conclude:
That though my ancestry might be but rude,
High God, and so I hope that it will be,
May of His grace let me live virtuously;
And then shall I be noble, that begin
To live by virtue and to turn from sin.

 "And since my poverty has made you grieve,
High God himself, in whom we all believe,
Chose here in poverty to live his life.
And every man, and every maid, or wife
Can understand that Jesus, heaven's king,
Would choose no vicious life. It is a thing –
This poverty – most honorable to bear,
As Seneca and other clerks declare.
A man content to live in poverty –
I hold him rich, though not a shirt hath he.
The one that covets is the one that's poor,
For he would have what he has not, for sure.
He that has nothing, and that craves no more,
Is rich, though ye consider him a boor.

 "True poverty may sing in jollity.
Juvenal says of it full merrily:
'The poor man, as he goes along the way,
May laugh at thieves, and freely sing and play.'
It is a hateful good, as I should guess,
A sovereign curative for all distress;

And, for a man that takes it patiently,
A great improver of sagacity;
Though it seem worthless, this at least is true:
For its possession none will challenge you!
Through poverty a man may come to know
Himself and God, when he is fallen low;
It is an eye-glass, for a man to see
Who are his true friends, as it seems to me.
And therefore, since I give you no offense,
Speak no more, sire, about my indigence.

   "Age, sire, ye say, is a reproach to me;
But not to speak of such authority
As books, ye gentlemen yourselves, I find,
Say that good breeding asks you to be kind
To an old man, and call him 'father,' too;
And books, I think, will hold this to be true.

   "And since ye call me old and foul of hue,
Ye need not fear that men will cuckold you;
For filth and age, as God may prosper me,
Are mighty wardens of our chastity.
But since I know in what ye take delight,
I shall appease your worldly appetite.

   "Choose now," said she, "which of these things
     to try –
To have me foul and old until I die,
And always be your true and humble wife,
Giving you no offense throughout my life,
Or, if ye like, to have me young and fair,
And take your chance how many shall repair
Unto your house, attracted there by me,
Or to some other place, it well may be.
Choose for yourself now, which will please you best."

  He thought, and sighed, and lay there much
     distressed,
But spoke at last as I shall tell you here.
"My lady and my love, my wife so dear,

Under your wise rule will I gladly rest;
Choose for yourself that which will please you best,
And honor you the most, and me as well.
As for these two, I cannot care or tell;
What pleases you is good enough for me."

   "Then have I got the mastery," said she,
"Since I may choose, and rule as I suggest?"

     "Yea, surely, wife," he said, "I think it best."

     "Kiss me," she said, "we are no longer wroth.
And, by my faith now, ye shall find me both –
That is, both good, and comely to the eye.
I pray God that in madness I may die
Unless I be to you as good and true
As ever wife was, since the world was new.
And if with morning I am not as fair
As lady, queen, or empress anywhere
Between the boundaries of East and West,
Do with my life and death as suits you best.
Lift up the curtain, look ye how it is!"

   And when this knight beheld this wife of his
Lying there young, indeed, and fair to sight;
He clasped her in his arms for sheer delight,
And all his heart was bathed in very bliss.
A thousand times seemed not too much to kiss.
And she obeyed him well in everything
That could promote his will or pleasuring.

   And thus they lived their lives out to the end
In perfect joy; and may Christ Jesus send
Husbands as young and meek and fresh a-bed,
And let us all survive the ones we wed!
Also may Jesus shorten all the lives
Of husbands that submit not to their wives,
And sour old niggards, wary of expense;
God send them soon a very pestilence!

Here ends the Wife of Bath's Tale

The Friar's Tale

THE FRIAR'S TALE is an attack on the Summoner in the party. It tells of an arrogant summoner who meets a fiend and foolishly engages in a competition with him. A summoner was an official who called people accused of crimes to court. He was, understandably, an unpopular figure. The summoner in the Friar's Tale is also spiteful and greedy; traits which anger the Summoner in the company and goad him to take revenge on the Friar with his own tale.

THE FRIAR'S TALE

*The Prologue to the
Friar's Tale*

THIS worthy limiter, this noble Friar,
Had all the time been glowering in ire
Upon the Summoner, but for manners' sake
Up to this time no rude word to him spake.
At last, however, he addressed the Wife:
"Now, Dame," he said, "God give you right good life!
For as I hope to thrive, ye here advance
Scholastic matters of significance,
And many a thing have told right well, I say.
But, Dame, as we are riding on our way,
We need to speak of nothing save in game,
And leave authorities, in God's good name,
To those who preach or read divinity.
And now, if it may please this company,
A jest about a summoner I will tell.
Of summoners, as the name will show you well,
There's nothing to be said that's good or pleasant
I pray that I offend no person present!
For these are fellows that by occupation
Run up and down with writs for fornication
And get well thrashed at every village end!"

   Our Host spoke up: "Ye should be courteous, friend,
As to your station is appropriate.
Here will we have no brawl or loud debate.
Then tell your tale, and let the Summoner be."

   "Nay," said the Summoner, "let him say to me
Whatever he likes, and when it falls my lot,
By God, I will repay him every jot.

For I shall tell what honor it confers
To serve among these flattering limiters,
And I shall paint his business for him, too."

   Our Host replied with "Peace now! This will do!"
Then to the Friar once more he turned his head.
"Dear master mine, on with your tale," he said.

Here begins the Friar's Tale

ONCE an archdeacon dwelt within my land –
A man of eminence, and hard of hand
In laying punishment on perpetrators
Of witchcraft, and upon all fornicators,
Defamers, and corrupt church officers,
And panders also, and adulterers,
Breakers of contracts, those who gave offense
Through wills, or through neglect of sacraments,
And also many another kind of crime
That needs not to be listed at this time.
With simony, he dealt, and usury,
But hardest was his hand on lechery:
He gave it to the lechers till they bleated!
And tithe-defaulters, too, were roughly treated.
Just let some parson name one – he would see
The wretch escaped no fine in penalty!
For petty unpaid tithe or offering
How piteously he made the people sing!
For ere the bishop caught them with his hook,
This bold archdeacon wrote them in his book,
Then had he power, by right of jurisdiction,
To lay a fine for every dereliction.
He had a summoner always close at hand,
No lad so sly as he in all the land;
For skilfully he spread his band of spies
That told him much that he could utilize.
A pair of lechers he could well ignore
If they would tell of four-and-twenty more;
For though he was as crazy as a rabbit,
Yet will I tell of every filthy habit
This summoner had: he cannot make conviction
On us, because he hath no jurisdiction

Over our ways, no friar can he abuse!
   "Peter! Just as the women of the stews
Are out of my control," the Summoner said.
   "Peace now, I say, and curses on thy head,"
Our Host spoke up, "and let him tell his tale.
Tell on, no matter how the Summoner rail,
Dear master mine, and neither spare nor tire!"
   This lying thief, this summoner, (said the Friar)
Always had bawds, obedient one and all
As any hawk is to the hunter's call,
To tell him what they had of secret news.
They were informers he would slyly use –
Their friendship was not something of the minute.
And thus his labor had great profit in it:
His master knew not always of his winning.
For he would call some foolish man for sinning,
Using no writ, and threaten Christ's own curse;
And such were more than glad to fill his purse,
And feast him at the ale-house well and high.
And just as Judas kept upon the sly
A purse, and was a thief – so was he, too.
His master got no more than half his due.
He was, to praise him rightly and applaud,
A thief, a summoner also, and a bawd!
And in his service were some wenches, too,
That, were the man Sir Robert or Sir Hugh,
Or Jack or Ralph – whoever it chanced to be
That lay with them, they told him secretly:
The wench and he thus had their understanding.
Then would he bring a bogus writ commanding
Both to the chapter-house immediately,
And skin the man and let the girl go free!
Then he would say: "Friend, since I hold thee dear,
In our black books this wench shall not appear:
Trouble thyself no more – this case shall end;
When I can serve thee I will be thy friend."
More kinds of robbery this summoner knew
Than I could tell of in a year or two;
For in this world was never a hunter's hound
Knew a hurt deer from one without a wound
Better than could this summoner tell for sure

Lecher, adulterer, or paramour.
And since this knowledge sent his income higher
He gave it all his mind and whole desire.
   So it befell that on a certain day,
This summoner, ever eager for his prey,
Rode out to summon a poor old widow, bent
On robbing her, for she was innocent.
And soon beneath the trees he saw before him
A yeoman on a horse, that gayly bore him;
A bow he had, and arrows bright and keen,
And wore a little jacket all of green,
And hat with fringes black upon his head.
   "Hail, sir, and all good health!" this summoner said.
   "Well met," he cried, "and all good fellows like you!
Where through this greenwood riding? Whither strike
    you?"
This yeoman answered. "Wilt thou far today?"
   The summoner answered promptly with a "Nay;
Hard by I go," he said, "where I am bent
To see about the payment of some rent –
A part of that belonging to my lord."
   "Art thou a bailiff then?" "Yea," was his word.
He dared not say "a summoner," for shame,
And utter infamy – such was the name!
   "*Depardieux*!" said this yeoman, "dear my brother,
As thou art bailiff, so am I another!
I am a stranger here, and sir, I pray
Acquaintance with thee – come, what dost thou say?
And brotherhood as well, if thou art willing.
With golden sovereign and with silver shilling
My chest is filled, and com'st thou to our shire
All shall be thine, just as thou shalt desire!"
   "*Gra'mercy*! by my faith!" this summoner said.
So each his hand within the other's laid,
Swearing true brotherhood till death; and so
In merry talk upon their way they go.
   This summoner, full of gab and curiosity
As are these butcher-birds of animosity,
Now asking of one thing, now of another –
   "Where is your dwelling?" said he. "Tell me,
    brother,

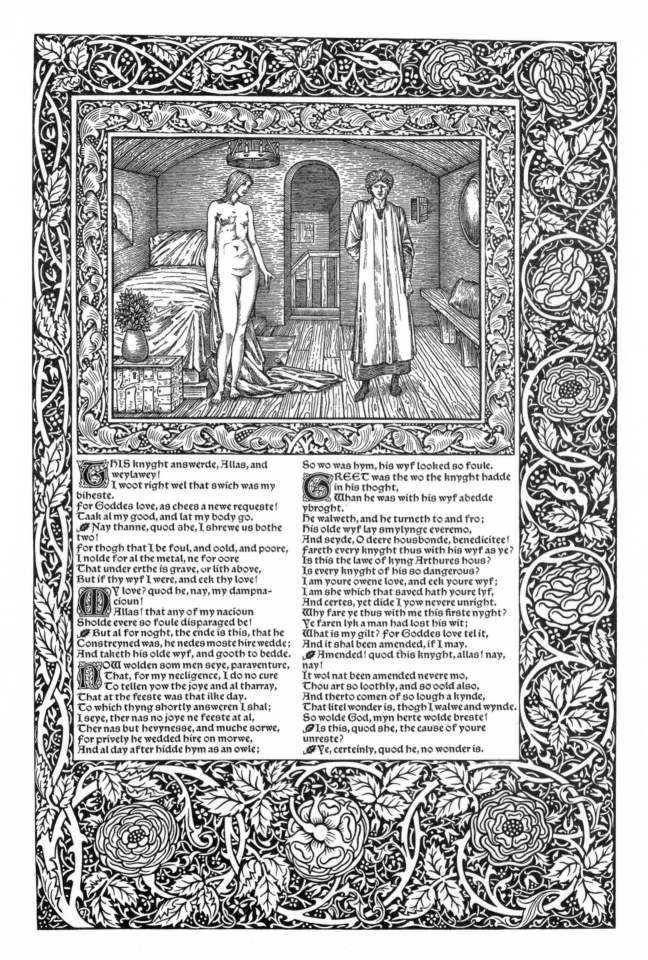

THIS knyght answerde, Allas, and weylawey!
I woot right wel that swich was my biheste.
For Goddes love, as chees a newe requeste!
Taak al my good, and lat my body go.
Nay thanne, quod she, I shrewe us bothe two!
For thogh that I be foul, and oold, and poore,
I nolde for al the metal, ne for oore
That under erthe is grave, or lith above,
But if thy wyf I were, and eek thy love!
MY love? quod he, nay, my dampnacioun!
Allas! that any of my nacioun
Sholde evere so foule disparaged be!
But al for noght, the ende is this, that he
Constreyned was, he nedes moste hire wedde;
And taketh his olde wyf, and gooth to bedde.
NOW wolden som men seye, paraventure,
That, for my necligence, I do no cure
To tellen yow the joye and al tharray,
That at the feeste was that ilke day.
To which thyng shortly answeren I shal;
I seye, ther nas no joye ne feeste at al,
Ther nas but hevynesse, and muche sorwe,
For prively he wedded hire on morwe,
And al day after hidde hym as an owle;

So wo was hym, his wyf looked so foule.
GREET was the wo the knyght hadde in his thoght,
Whan he was with his wyf abedde ybroght.
He walweth, and he turneth to and fro;
His olde wyf lay smylynge everemo,
And seyde, O deere housbonde, benedicitee!
Fareth every knyght thus with his wyf as ye?
Is this the lawe of kyng Arthures hous?
Is every knyght of his so dangerous?
I am youre owene love, and eek youre wyf;
I am she which that saved hath youre lyf,
And certes, yet dide I yow nevere unright.
Why fare ye thus with me this firste nyght?
Ye faren lyk a man had lost his wit;
What is my gilt? For Goddes love tel it,
And it shal been amended, if I may.
Amended! quod this knyght, allas! nay, nay!
It wol nat been amended nevere mo,
Thou art so loothly, and so oold also,
And therto comen of so lough a kynde,
That litel wonder is, thogh I walwe and wynde.
So wolde God, myn herte wolde breste!
Is this, quod she, the cause of youre unreste?
Ye, certeinly, quod he, no wonder is.

Plate 18: The Wife of Bath's Tale (p. 215)

In case some future day I come a-seeking."
    This yeoman made him answer, softly speaking:
    "Brother," he said, "far northward lies my way,
Where I have hope to see thee come some day.
Before we part, thou shalt have preparation
Will never let thee miss my habitation."
    "Now, brother," said this summoner, "I pray
Teach me, as we are riding on our way,
Since ye too are a bailiff, just like me,
Some of your skill. And tell me truthfully
How shall I make the most from what I do?
And let not sin or conscience hinder you,
But as my brother tell me of your practice."
    "Now by the truth, my brother dear, the fact is,
As I shall tell a story true in all,
My wages are but limited and small.
My lord is haughty and severe with me,
My work demandeth endless industry,
And by extortions therefore must I live.
I take from men all I can make them give,
Whether by trick or violence, and so
From year to year I manage as I go –
No truer could I tell were Truth my name."
    "For sure!" this summoner cried. "I do the same.
God knows I take it all – no matter what –
Unless it be too heavy or too hot!
What I can get by shift or sly endeavor
It troubles not my conscience whatsoever:
But for extortion I were not alive.
Such tricks as these are not for priests to shrive.
Of pity or of conscience I have none:
Father-confessors curse I every one!
By God and by St. James, well met we were!
But, dear my brother," said this summoner,
    "Tell me thy name, then."
                    For a little while
This yeoman smiled the shadow of a smile.
"Brother," he said, "and wilt thou I shall tell?
I am a fiend: my dwelling is in hell.
And here I go about my trafficking
To see where men will give me anything.

And what I win this way is all I get.
Look how thou ridest for the same thing set:
Something to gain – no thought thou hast of how;
Just so with me – I will go riding now
To the world's end, if I can get my prey."
    "Ah!" cried this summoner, "what is that ye say!
In truth, ye seemed a yeoman to my eye.
Ye have as good a man's shape as have I.
Have ye some fixed appearance in addition
In hell, when ye assume your true position?"
    "Nay, certainly," he said, "there have we none.
Yet at our pleasure we can take us one.
Or we can make you think we have a shape,
Now sometimes seem a man, sometimes an ape –
Or like an angel we can ride or go.
This is no wonder, though the thing be so;
A wretched juggler plays his tricks on thee,
And I, by God, know much more craft than he."
    "Why," asked this summoner, "do ye ride or run
In various shapes – not always in the one?"
    "Because," he said, "we seek from day to day
The forms that help us most to take our prey."
    "What is the cause for all this work ye do?"
    "More causes, dear sir summoner, than a few,"
Replied this fiend. "But all things have their time.
The day is short, and it is more than prime,
Yet I have won no profit all this day.
Now I intend to get it if I may,
And of our secrets shall no further speak.
For, brother mine, thy wit is all too weak
To understand, though I explained to thee.
But, since thou askest why our industry –
Sometimes as instruments in God's own hands
We are the means of doing His commands,
When it shall please Him, on His creatures here.
In various ways and figures we appear;
Surely no power were ours unless He chose us,
At least, if it should please Him to oppose us.
Sometimes, at our petition, we have leave
Only the body, and not the soul to grieve –
As witness Job, to whom we brought such woe.

And sometimes we have power upon the two –
That is to say, the body and the soul.
And sometimes we have power to lay our toll
Upon the spirit, and do it great unrest,
But not the body – yet all is for the best.
For if the man withstandeth our temptation,
This shall become the cause of his salvation
Though it was not our will indeed to save him,
But rather for the pains of hell to have him.
And sometimes we are servants unto men,
For instance, to St. Dunstan. And again
Unto the apostles was I servant, too."

    Then said this summoner, "Yet tell me true –
Devise ye these new shapes in which ye go
Of elements?" The fiend responded: "No;
Sometimes we feign, and sometimes we will raise
The bodies of the dead in various ways
And through them speak as reasonably and well
As unto Endor's witch did Samuel.
Yet there are men who say it was not he!
I have no use for your divinity!
Yet I forewarn thee: thou shalt not be fooled;
Thou hast at all cost longing to be schooled
As to our shapes: hereafter shalt thou be
Where thou shalt have no need to learn of me;
Thine own experience shall fit thee there
To lecture on this matter from a chair
Better than Virgil could before he died
Or Dante. But along, and let us ride!
For I will still hold company with thee
Until the time that thou abandon me."

    "That," said this summoner, "shall be seen by no
      man.
Both far and wide men know me for a yeoman;
And I will keep my faith for good or evil.
For though thou shouldst be Sathanas the devil
Still will I hold my compact with my brother
As I am sworn, and each of us to other,
To be true brother to thee, by my troth.
So go we now to get our profit both.
Take thou thy part, whatever men will give;

I shall take mine: so both of us shall live.
Should either one have more than hath the other,
Let him be true and share it with his brother."

    "Now by my faith," the fiend said, "I agree."
So on their way they rode forth speedily,
And as they reached the edges of the village
Whither this summoner was bent on pillage,
They came upon a cart heaped high with hay,
And watched the carter drive it on its way.
The ruts beneath the cart were deep and bad;
The carter whipped and cried, as he were mad:
    "Come, Brock! Hi! Scot! What! Stop ye for th
      stones?
Now the fiend take you, body, blood and bones
As clean as ever I helped to rid the mare of you!
God knows the way I suffer from the pair of you!
The devil take all now, horse and cart and hay!"
    This summoner said, "Now shall we have some
      play!"
And all as not a thought were going through him.
He edged towards the fiend and whispered to him:
    "Listen, my brother; listen, upon my faith!
Dost thou not hear this thing the carter saith?
Seize it at once, for he hath given it thee –
The hay and cart and horses – all the three."

    "Nay," said the devil, "God knows – never a jot!
The fellow says it, but he means it not.
Ask him thyself if thou hast doubt of me,
Or wait a little while and thou shalt see."

    This carter pats his horses till again
They lean against the tugs and draw and strain.
    "Hi there!" cries he, "Christ bless you now, and all
The creatures he hath made, both great and small!
That was well-pulled and true, mine own gray boy!
I pray God that he save you, and Saint Loy!
By God, my cart is safely through the slough!"

    "What said I, brother – was my word not true?"
Questioned the fiend. "Here may ye see, dear brother,
The fellow said one thing but thought another.
Let us along now with no more delay;
Here win I nothing I can cart away."

When they were somewhat out of town again,
This summoner to his brother whispered then:
"Here, brother," said he, "doth an old hag live
Would almost lose her neck ere she would give
A penny from her store. Yet will I sever
Full twelve pence from her, be she mad as never,
Or I will summon her to our chapter hall;
And yet I know no fault in her at all!
But since in these parts it is hard for thee
To get thy profit, take a look at me!"

The summoner knocketh at the widow's gate.
"Come out," he cried. "Come out, thou old gray-pate;
Art thou within there with some priest or friar?"

"Who knocks?" this widow cried. "God save you,
    sire!
Ben'cite! Pray, sir, what is your sweet will?"

"I have," said he, "of summons here a bill;
On penalty of curse, look that thou be
Tomorrow morn at the archdeacon's knee
To answer to the court for certain things."

"Now, lord," said she, "Christ Jesu, King of Kings,
Give me His help who have no other way.
I have been sick, and that for many a day.
I cannot go so far," she said, "nor ride,
But I shall die, such pain is in my side.
May I not have a brief, sir summoner,
And by my proctor make my answer there
Unto such things as men may say of me?"

He said, "Yes. Pay at once – now let me see –
Twelve pence to me – and thou shalt have acquittal.
My profit in the matter will be little;
My master gets it – nothing comes to me.
Pay up, and let me ride off speedily;
Give me twelve pence: I cannot longer tarry."

"Twelve pence!" she cried. "Now as our holy Mary
May help me out of sorrow and of sin,
Though all this wide world I should thereby win,
I could not find twelve pence inside my door!
Ye know it well that I am old and poor –
Then show to me, poor wretch, your charity!"

"Nay, may the foul fiend fetch me," answered he,

"If I excuse thee, though thou fall down dead."

"Alas! God knows I have no guilt," she said.

"Pay me," cried he, "or by the sweet St. Anne,
I shall bear off with me thy newest pan
For debt, which thou hast owed me since the time
Thou mad'st thy husband cuckold – for that crime
I paid thy fine and saved thy reputation."

"Thou liest," she said, "as I may win salvation!
Never was I, as widow or as wife,
Summoned unto your court in all my life
Till now, nor with my body was untrue.
Unto the devil, rough and black of hue,
May both my pan and thy vile body go!"

And when the fiend heard how she cursed him so
Upon her knees, as hard as she was able,
He said to her: "Mine own dear mother Mabel,
Is this your will in earnest, what ye cry?"

"The devil," said she, "fetch him before he die
And pan and all, unless he shall repent!"

"Nay then, old mare, that is not mine intent,"
This summoner said, "repenting of success
I win from thee. I would I had thy dress
And every rag thou hast – yes, the last shred."

"Now, brother, be not wroth," the devil said.
"Thy body and this pan are mine by right,
And thou shalt go to hell with me tonight,
Where thou shalt know of our deep privacy
More than a master of divinity!"
And with that word the foul fiend gripped him strong;
Body and soul; so went this wretch along
To where indeed all summoners may find
Their heritage. And God, who made mankind
In his own image, save us, as he can,
And let this summoner change to a good man!

Lordings, I could have told you – if I were
To speak at leisure of this summoner –
After the text of Christ and John and Paul,
And of our other doctors one and all,
Such pains as would have made your souls to shake
And yet no mortal tongue can undertake –
Though for a thousand winters I should tell –

To paint the torments of that house of hell.
To save ourselves from that accursed place,
Let us awake and pray for Jesu's grace,
To keep us still from Satan and temptation.
Hear, and beware in such a situation.
The lion sits ever with a dark intent,
Waiting his chance to slay the innocent;
Then always set your hearts that they may save you

From the fiend that seeks to bind you and enslave you.
He cannot tempt you past your power and might,
For Christ will be your champion and knight.
And pray these summoners may repent, and break
    them
Of their ill ways before the fiend shall take them.

Here ends the Friar's Tale

The Summoner's Tale

TO GET BACK at the Friar for his tale about an iniquitous summoner, the Summoner tells a base, comic fabliau about a sinful and hypocritical friar. While preaching against lust, greed and anger, the friar in the tale demonstrates all these sins in his own behaviour. He is finally outwitted and humiliated by an intellectual inferior when a coarse trick is played on him.

THE SUMMONER'S TALE

The Prologue to the Summoner's Tale

The Summoner in his stirrups rises high,
Such rage and madness glittering in his eye
That like an aspen leaf he shakes for ire.
"Lordings, one thing alone do I desire;
I ask you as a courtesy," he cries,
"That since this Friar has filled you with his lies,
Ye let me tell the tale that I shall tell.
This friar hath boasted that he knoweth hell;
And God knows too that it is little wonder;
Your friars and fiends are not so far asunder.
For often times, by God, have ye heard tell
How once a friar was snatched away to hell
In spirit as he dreamed. An angel there
Led him about, and showed him everywhere
The torments that were wrought in smoke and fire.
And yet in all the place he saw no friar,
Although enough of other suffering men.
Unto this angel spoke the friar then.

   "Now, sir,' he asked, 'have friars so large a grace
That none of them are coming to this place?"

   "Yes, many a million come," said he, replying,
And led him down where Sathanas was lying.
"Satan," he told him, "hath a tail as large
As any sail that flies upon a barge.
Hold up thy tail, thou Sathanas!" said he;
"Show us thine arse, so that the friar may see
Where all the friars are nesting in this place!"
Before a man could walk a furlong's space,

As from a hive a swarm of bees comes pouring,
Out of the devil's arse there tumbled roaring
Some twenty thousand friars in a crowd,
And up and down through hell went swarming loud,
And, hurrying back as fast as they could run,
Into his arse went creeping every one.
Then down he clapped his tail, and lay there still.
This friar, when he had looked, and seen his fill
Of all the torments in that hellish hole –
God in his grace again restored his soul
Back to his body, and so he woke at last.
And yet for fear he lay and shook, aghast –
The devil's arse forever in his mind,
The natural heritage of all his kind.
God save you all now, save this cursèd friar;
No more of prologue doth my tale require.

Here the Summoner begins his Tale

Lordings, there is in Yorkshire, as I guess,
A marshy country men call Holderness,
In which a limiter once went about
And preached, and also begged, there is no doubt.
This friar, it seems, appeared in church one day
And preached a sermon in his usual way,
And in his preaching put great emphasis,
And stirred the people up with things like this:
As, masses for the dead, and that they give
Toward houses where religious men should live,
And holy mass be fitly sung each day,
And not devoured or idly thrown away
Nor where indeed there was no need for giving,
As unto those endowed, that have their living,
Thank God, and fare well and abundantly,
"Trentals deliver the souls of friends," said he,
"From penance, whether they be old or young;
That is, when they are well and promptly sung,
And do not keep some jolly priest and gay
That will not sing above a mass a day.
Deliver the souls, and that at once!" he cried;
"O it is hard when flesh-hooks tear the side,

Or in the flames the body burn or bake!
Hasten, make speed, I bid you, for Christ's sake!"
　　And when this friar his eloquence had spent,
With *Qui Cum Patre* on his way he went.
　　When those at church had given him what they
　　　　would,
He would not tarry in the neighborhood,
But went with scrip and staff, gown tucked up high.
At every house he stopped to peer and pry,
And beg for meal and cheese, or else for corn.
A staff his comrade carried, tipped with horn,
And tablets fashioned all of ivory,
And stylus polished smooth and handsomely;
And always wrote the names down, as he stood,
Of all who gave him any of their good,
As if to pray for them. And he would cry:
"Give us a bushel of wheat or malt or rye,
A God's cake, or a little piece of cheese,
We cannot choose – let it be what ye please –
God's ha'penny, or else for mass a penny;
Or let us have some brawn, if ye have any;
A strip of blanket give us then, good dame;
See, my dear sister – here I write your name;
Bacon or beef, whatever thing ye find."
　　A sturdy lout came following behind –
That served their convent's guests. He bore a sack,
And what men gave them, put it on his back.
And hardly would this friar have left the door
When he would stop, and with a knife he bore
Shave off the names that he had written there;
He served them all with tricks and empty air!
　　"Nay," cried the friar, "stop, Summoner, there
　　　　thou liest!"
　　"Peace!" said our Host, "for Christ's sake, the
　　　　All-highest:
Tell on thy tale; and spare it not at all."
　　"Yea, as I thrive," this summoner said, "I shall."
　　He went from house to house, and came at last
To one that had received him in the past
Better than any hundred in that town.
He found the master ill, and lying down;

Bed-ridden, low upon a couch he lay.
"*Deus hic*," cried he. "Thomas, good friend, good day!"
So spoke this friar, and made his voice to soften.
"Thomas, God bring you health again; full often
Here on this bench have I fared well," he said,
"With many a merry meal before me spread,"
And from the bench he drove away the cat,
And then he laid his staff down, and his hat,
And his bag, too, and softly sat him down.
His fellow had gone before him to the town,
And the man too, seeking the hostelry
Where it had been his plan that night to be.
　　"O my dear master," murmured this sick man,
"How have things gone with you since March began?
I have not seen you these two weeks or more."
"God knows," he said, "that I have labored sore,
For thy salvation more than anyone's,
Praying for thee, with precious orisons,
And other friends, God bless them all, I pray!
And in your church I preached at mass to-day
A sermon fashioned from my simple wit,
And not entirely from holy writ,
For that alone would leave you at a loss;
And therefore will I teach you all the gloss.
Glossing is glorious; glossing much repays us;
The clerics have a saw: *The letter slays us.*
So I have taught men to be charitable,
And spend their wealth where it is reasonable.
Our dame was there. Where is she now, I wonder?"
　　"Within the yard I think she is – out yonder;
She will be coming soon," this man replied.
　　"Ah, master, welcome!" this good housewife cried;
"By St. John, welcome! Fare ye well?" said she.
　　The friar rose up, the pink of courtesy,
And with his arms embraced and held her tightly,
And chirping like a sparrow kissed her lightly
With a sweet kiss: "Right well, dame," answered he,
"As one that is your servant utterly!
Thanks to the God that gave you soul and life,
For nowhere did I see so fair a wife,
God save my soul, in all the church to-day."

"Yea? God amend my failings! Any way
There is good welcome in this house for you."
"*Grand merci*; I have always found it true.
But of your goodness, now, and by your leave,
I pray you that ye neither fret nor grieve –
With Thomas will I have a word or so.
These curates are too negligent and slow
To search a conscience in the proper fashion.
Shriving and preaching: these things be my passion,
And studying Peter's words, and those of Paul.
I fish for souls of men, to make my haul
And render Jesus Christ His proper rent.
To spread His word – that is my whole intent."
    "Dear sir, with your permission," answered she,
"Scold him, for love of holy Trinity.
He is as full of wrath as any ant,
Though he has all that he could ever want.
For though at night I cover him all warm,
And lay my leg upon him or my arm,
He groaneth like our boar there, in our sty.
I get naught else, however I may try;
I cannot please him, what I do or promise!"
    "O Thomas, *Je vous dis*, O Thomas! Thomas!
The fiend works here – this must be cured and
        chidden!
Wrath is a thing by holy God forbidden;
On that I will pronounce a word or so."
    "Now, master," said the wife, "before I go,
What will ye dine on? I will set it out."
    "Now, dame," he answered, "*Je vous dis sans doute*
If ye will give me but a capon's liver,
And of your soft white bread the thinnest sliver,
And then a roast pig's head – though I should be
Much grieved that any beast should die for me –
This plain and homely meal were my delight.
I am a man of little appetite.
The Bible gives my soul its sustenance;
My flesh is so inured to vigilance
And fasting, that my stomach is destroyed.
I pray you, dame, in no way be annoyed
That I explain my habits thus to you;

God knows that I would speak of them with few."
    "Now, sir, one word before I go," she said,
"It is not yet two weeks my child is dead;
He died soon after your last visit here."
    This friar replied: "I saw his death appear
By revelation, at our dormitory;
And, dame, I say I saw him born to glory
Within a half hour after he had died;
For so I dreamed, as God may be my guide.
And our infirmarer and sexton too
Both dreamed the same, that fifty long years through
Were both true friars; by God's great clemency
They walk alone now, in their jubilee.
And I arose, and all within the place,
And many a tear went trickling down my face;
There came no noise, nor clattering of bells,
Te deum was our song and nothing else,
Save that I gave our thanks to Christ in prayer,
That sent His revelation to me there.
For, sir and dame, believe me here in all –
Our orisons are more effectual,
And we see more of Christ's mysterious things
Than any laymen do, though they be kings.
We live in poverty and abstinence,
And they in richness and magnificence
Of meat and drink, and fleshly appetite.
This world's lusts are as nothing in our sight.
Dives and Lazarus diversely spent
Their lives, and their rewards were different.
He who would pray must first fast, and be clean,
Fatten his soul and make his body lean.
We go as said th'apostle – clothes and food
Suffice us, though they may not be too good.
We friars by fasting and by purity
Make Christ accept our prayers more willingly.
    "Lo, Moses fasted forty days and nights
Before high God at length from Sinai's heights
Spoke forth in power and told him of the way.
Hollow of belly from fasting many a day
Thus he received the law that God's own finger
Had writ; and long Elias had to linger

On Horeb, fasting, to perform his mission
Of speech with God that is our lives' physician;
He fasted long and dwelt in contemplation.

　"Aaron, that kept in his administration
The temple, and all the priests that served him there,
When going to the temple to make a prayer
For people, or hold a service – they would never
Partake of any kind of drink whatever
Which of its nature could intoxicate,
But, lest they die, would always pray and wait
In abstinence – take heed of what I say.
If they should not be sober that dare to pray
For people's souls – beware! But this will do.
And, as the scripture says, Lord Jesus too
By fast and prayer a holy way inspires.
Therefore we mendicants, we simple friars,
Are wed to poverty and continence,
Charity, humbleness, and abstinence,
To persecution for our righteous ways,
To mercy, tears, and cleanness all our days,
And so our prayers – ye see it must be thus –
We friars, we mendicants, I speak of us –
Come to high God as more acceptable
Than yours, that sit at table feasting well.
From Paradise, if I shall tell no lie,
Was man first chased by God for gluttony;
Yet he had dwelt there chaste until that day.

　"But, Thomas, give an ear to what I say.
I have no text that gives it, I suppose,
And yet I find it in a kind of gloze;
And it is this, that Jesus, our sweet Lord,
Had friars in mind when He pronounced this word:
'Blessèd be they that are the poor in spirit.'
And judge if all the gospel, as ye hear it,
Is closer, word for word, to our professions,
Or unto theirs, that swim in their possessions.
Fie on their pomp and gluttony, say I;
I curse them for their ignorance, and defy!

　"For they, I think, are like Jovinian,
Fat as a whale, and waddling like a swan;
As full of wine as is the bottle there

Within the buttery. Reverent is their prayer;
But when for souls they sing the psalm of David,
Lo, 'Buf!' they belch, '*cor meum eructavit!*'
Who go the way of Christ and live his creed
But we – so chaste, so humble, so in need,
Doers of God's word, not mere listeners?
As with a soaring flight a hawk upwhirs,
Cleaving the air, just so the prayers that we
Send in our chaste and busy charity
Soar up to God, and reach his ears at length.
O Thomas, Thomas, as I hope for strength,
And by that lord, I tell you, called St. Ive,
If thou wert not our brother, thou shouldst not thrive!
But all our chapter prays now day and night
To Christ, that he will send thee health and might,
To fight the flesh and get control of it."

　"God knows," he said, "I get no benefit.
In a few years, as Christ may be my aid,
To various kinds of friars my purse hath paid
Full many a pound, yet no good have I tasted.
My property, for sure, is all but wasted.
Farewell, my gold! It is all gone!" he cried.

　"Is that the way ye do?" this friar replied.
"Why change about, why seek so many friars?
What man that has a perfect leech desires
To hunt for other doctors in the town?
Your own inconstancy hath put you down!
Think ye that I and all my brethren too
Are insufficient aid in prayer for you?
Thomas, that trick is worth nor jot nor tittle;
Your sickness comes because we get too little.
'Ah, give that order a half a quarter of oats!'
'Ah, give this order four and twenty groats!'
'Ah, give that friar a penny and let him go!'
Nay, Thomas, ye will profit nothing so.
The twelfth part of a farthing, by my soul,
What is it worth? A thing when it is whole
Is strong, but loses all its strength when scattered.
Thomas, I will not have thee duped or flattered:
Thou hop'st to have our labor all for naught.
But the high God, that all this world hath wrought,

That thilke wombe in which youre children leye
Sholde, biforn the peple, in my walkyng,
Be seyn al bare; wherfore I yow preye,
Lat me nat lyk a worm go by the weye:
Remembre yow, myn owene lord so deere,
I was youre wyf, though I unworthy weere.

Wherfore, in guerdon of my maydenhede,
Which that I broghte,and noght agayn I bere,
As voucheth sauf to yeve me, to my meede,
But swich a smok as I was wont to were,
That I therwith may wrye the wombe of here
That was youre wyf; and heer take I my leeve
Of yow, myn owene lord, lest I yow greve.

THE smok, quod he, that thou hast on thy bak,
    Lat it be stille, and bere it forth with thee.
But wel unnethes thilke word he spak,
But wente his wey for routhe and for pitee.
Biforn the folk hirselven strepeth she,
And in hir smok, with heed and foot al bare,
Toward hir fader hous forth is she fare.

THE folk hire folwe wepynge in hir weye,
    And fortune ay they cursen as they goon;
But she fro wepyng kepte hire eyen dreye,
Ne in this tyme word ne spak she noon.
Hir fader, that this tidynge herde anoon,
Curseth the day and tyme that nature
Shoop hym to been a lyves creature.

for out of doute this olde povre man
Was evere in suspect of hir mariage;
for evere he demed, sith that it bigan,
That whan the lord fulfild hadde his corage,

FRO
BOLOIGNE IS THIS ERL OF PANYK COME,
Of which the fame up sprang to moore and lesse,
And in the peples eres alle and some

Hym wolde thynke it were a disparage
To his estaat so lowe for talighte,
And voyden hire as soone as ever he myghte.

AGAYNS his doghter hastiliche goth he,
    for he by noyse of folk knew hire comynge,
And with hire olde coote, as it myghte be,
He covered hire, ful sorwefully wepynge;
But on hire body myghte he it nat brynge,
for rude was the clooth, and moore of age
By dayes fele than at hire mariage.

Thus with hire fader, for a certeyn space,
Dwelleth this flour of wyfly pacience,
That neither by hire wordes ne hire face
Biforn the folk, ne eek in hire absence,
Ne shewed she that hire was doon offence;
Ne of hire heighe estaat no remembraunce
Ne hadde she, as by hire contenaunce.

No wonder is, for in hire grete estaat
Hire goost was evere in pleyn humylitee;
No tendre mouth, noon herte delicaat,
No pompe, no semblant of roialtee;
But ful of pacient benyngnytee,
Discreet and pridelees, ay honurable,
And to hire housbonde evere meke &stable.

Men speke of Job, and moost for his humblesse,
As clerkes, whan hem list, konne wel endite,
Namely of men, but as in soothfastnesse,
Though clerkes preise wommen but a lite,
Ther kan no man in humblesse hym acquite
As womman kan, ne kan been half so trewe
As wommen been, but it be falle of newe.
Explicit quinta pars. Sequitur pars sexta.

Was kouth eek, that a newe markysesse
He with hym broghte, in swich pompe and richesse,
That nevere was ther seyn with mannes eye
So noble array in al West Lumbardye.

The markys, which that shoop and knew al this,
Er that this erl was come, sente his message
for thilke sely povre Grisildis;
And she with humble herte and glad visage,
Nat with no swollen thoght in hire corage,
Cam at his heste, and on hire knees hire sette,
And reverently and wisely she hym grette.

GRISILDE, quod he, my wyl is outrely
    This mayden that shal wedded been to me,
Received be tomorwe as roially
As it possible is in myn hous to be,
And eek that every wight in his degree
Have his estaat in sittyng and servyse
And heigh plesaunce, as I kan best devyse.

Plate 19: The Student's Tale (p. 252)

Declares the laborer worthy of his hire.
None of your treasure, Thomas, I desire
For my own self, but that our house may pray
For you, as they desire to, night and day;
And to build Christ's own church. O Thomas,
    Thomas!
Of building churches ye may find, I promise,
If it be good, as Thomas wrote it fair,
Who went to India and labored there.
Ye lie here full of anger and of ire,
With which the devil sets your heart afire,
And scold your wife, this simple innocent,
As meek and patient as was ever sent!
Thomas, believe me, if ye love your life,
For your own good, contend not with your wife.
And bear this word away now, by my faith:
Touching this matter, thus the wise man saith:
'Within thy house no wrathful lion be,
Nor with thy subjects deal oppressively,
Nor cause thy friends to flee from thee in fear.'
And, Thomas, I will charge thee, now and here,
Beware of her that in thy bosom sleepeth;
Take warning of the snake that slyly creepeth
Under the grass, to sting thee secretly.
Beware, and listen patiently to me:
For twenty thousand men have lost their lives
By striving with their mistresses or wives.
Now since ye have so meek and holy a wife,
Why, Thomas, will ye kindle all this strife?
There is no snake so cruel, so worth your dread,
If anyone upon his tail should tread,
As woman is, when kindled once to ire;
Vengeance is then the whole of their desire.
Anger is sin, and great among the seven,
Abominable to God that sits in heaven,
Ruin to all that harbor it or show it.
All ignorant vicars or rude parsons know it
To be the certain cause of homicide.
Anger is the executor of pride.
I could speak on in sorrow and in warning
Of anger, talking until tomorrow morning.

By night and day, I pray God every hour
He will not put a wrathful man in power –
Great harm and pity that will always be,
To give a man of wrath authority.
    "For once there lived a choleric potentate
Says Seneca, that, while he ruled the state,
It fell two knights went riding forth one day.
By Fortune's will the matter fell this way –
One of the two returned, the other not.
This judge declared, to whom the knight was brought,
'Thy comrade hast thou murdered, it is plain;
For this my judgment is that thou be slain,'
And to another knight near by he saith:
'I charge thee now, go lead him to his death.'
But as they went upon their way again
Unto the place where he should soon be slain,
They met the knight that men supposed was dead.
Then it seemed best, when all was thought and said,
To take them both before the judge again.
They said: 'O lord, this knight here hath not slain
His comrade, for he standeth here alive.'
'Ye shall be dead,' he cried, 'as I may thrive!
That is to say, both one and two and three!'
Then to the first he said: 'I sentenced thee,
Therefore in any case must thou be dead.
And thou,' he cried, 'must also lose thy head,
Since it is thou for whom thy fellow dieth.'
Then to the third knight angrily he crieth,
'Thou hast not done what I commanded thee.'
And thus he caused them to be slain, all three.
    "Wrathful Cambyses loved both drink and revel,
And had delight to play the fiend and devil.
A lord belonging to his company
That loved both virtue and morality,
When once they sat alone, spoke to him thus:
'A lord is lost that is not virtuous;
And drunkenness is but a shameful thing
In any man, and chiefly in a king.
Against a king are many an eye and ear
Set, though he knows not where, to see and hear.
For God's love then, drink ye more temperately;

For wine makes men lose the control,' said he,
'In shameful fashion, both of mind and limb.'
   " 'The opposite,' Cambyses said to him,
'Is true, and thou shalt have the proof direct
That wine on men hath no such ill effect.
There is no wine that can destroy my might
Of hand or foot,' he said, 'or dim my sight.'
And in his arrogance he drank much more –
A hundred times – than he had drunk before;
And soon this angry, cursèd king, this sot,
Commanded that this knight's own son be brought
Before him; there he ordered him to stand.
And suddenly he took his bow in hand,
And pulled the string back swiftly to the ear,
And with an arrow slew the child right there.
'Now is my hand unsure or not?' he said.
'And is my strength, or are my senses fled,
Or hath this wine bereft me of my sight?'
   "Why should I tell the answer of the knight?
His son was slain, there is no more to say.
Therefore beware before ye start to play
With lords. *Placebo* sing; and if I can
I shall – unless it be some humble man.
To tell a poor man of his faults is well;
But not a lord, though he be bound for hell.
   "Lo, wrathful Cyrus, king of Persia, hath
Destroyed the River Gyndes in his wrath,
For, as he marched on Babylon, to win it,
It happened that his horse was drowned within it.
When he was done so small a stream was there
A woman could wade through it anywhere.
Lo, the great teacher – thus his saying ran:
'Be no companion to an angry man,
Nor with a madman go along the way,
Lest thou repent.' There is no more to say.
   "Now, Thomas, leave thine anger at my prayer.
Thou'll find that I am straight as any square.
Hold not the devil's knife against thy heart;
Thine anger gives thee only pain and smart;
Make thy confession to me, full and free."
   "Nay, by St. Simon," quickly answered he.

"My curate gave me shrift this very day,
And I have cleansed myself in every way;
There is no need to speak of it," said he,
"Unless I choose, of my humility."
   "Then give me of thy gold, to build our cloister,"
Said he, "for many a mussel and many an oyster,
When other men have dined in pleasant halls,
Have been our food, that we might raise our walls.
And yet God knows, that gives us our salvation,
We have not more than finished the foundation,
Nor set a paving tile upon the ground,
Yet owe a debt for stones of forty pound.
Now, Thomas, help! by Him that harrowed hell,
Or we shall have to bring our books to sell;
And if it come to pass ye lack our preaching,
The world shall perish then for want of teaching.
For were we gone, the world, with your permission,
God save my soul, were in a worse condition
Than if the sun itself were taken away.
For who can teach like us, or work, or pray?
And this is not a thing of short duration,
For friars have done their holy ministration
Before Elijah's or Elisha's days,
And all for charity, God have the praise!
Now, Thomas, help, for holy charity!"
And with the word he dropped upon his knee.
   This sick man, all but crazy now with ire,
Wished that the friar might be consumed by fire
For all his whining words and false profession.
"Something," he said, "that is in my possession –
That I can give away – that and no other.
Have ye not said thus – that I am your brother?"
   "Yea," said the friar, "as sure as thou hast life;
I took our seal and letter to thy wife."
   "Now, well," he said; "and something I shall give
Unto your holy order while I live;
And thou shalt have it soon within thy hand;
But on condition, thou must understand,
That thou divide it, my beloved brother,
So every friar have equal share with other.
This on thine oath thou first must swear to me,

With no evasion or duplicity."

    "I swear it, by my faith," the friar cried,

And gave his hand; and he was satisfied.

"Lo! here mine oath. In me shall be no lack."

    "Then with thy hand," he said, "reach down my
       back

And feel about till thou art well behind;

Beneath my buttocks something thou shalt find

That I have hidden for thee secretly."

    "Ha!" thought the friar. "Here lies good luck for
       me!"

And quickly thrust his hand below the rift,

All full of hope that he would find his gift.

And when the sick man felt this greedy friar

Groping about, all eager with desire,

Into the Friar's hand he let a fart.

No cart-horse, tugging strongly at his cart,

Could ever let a fart that louder sounded.

    Up like a maddened lion the friar bounded.

"Ha! thou false churl! By God's own bones and might,

This thou hast done to shame me, and for spite!

Thou shalt pay well for this, by God!" he swore.

    The servants, that were listening at the door,

Came leaping in, and chased the friar away.

So off he went. Black anger on him lay.

He sought his comrade out, that kept their store.

He looked as fearsome as a savage boar;

He ground his teeth with rage. With rapid pace

He strode down to the castle in that place.

A man of high degree was the possessor,

Whom he had always served as a confessor.

This worthy man was lord of all the town.

The friar could hardly keep his fury down,

But entered while this noble lord was eating,

And for a time could give no word of greeting,

But in a while, "God save you!" muttered he.

    This lord sat looking at him. "*Ben'cite!*

Come, friar John, what kind of world is this?

It's plain to see that something runs amiss.

Ye look as if a band of thieves had seized you.

Sit down, and say whatever hath displeased you,

And I will have it righted if I may."

    "I was," he said, "insulted so today

Within your village here, that I am sure

There is not in the world a page so poor

But would abominate the vile disgrace

That I received today within this place.

But most of all I hate with all my might

That this old rascal, with his locks of white,

Blasphemed our great and holy order too."

    "Now, master," said this lord, "I beg of you –"

    "No master, sire," he said, "but servitor;

Though once in school, indeed, that rank I bore.

God liketh not such names for us at all,

Neither in market place nor in your hall."

    "No matter; what hath grieved you? Tell me, pray."

    "Sire," he replied, "there did befall this day

An odious insult to my order and me,

And so *per consequens* to each degree

Of Holy Church. May God avenge it, too."

    "Sir," said this lord, "ye know well what to do.

Ye are my priest. What is this tempest worth?

Ye are the salt and savor of the earth.

Be patient, then," he urged him, "and unfold

All of your wrong." And quickly it was told,

As ye have heard; for ye know everything.

    The lady of the house sat listening

Till she had heard the friar tell out his story.

"Mother of God," she cried, "thou Maid of Glory!

Is there some more? Now tell me faithfully."

    "Madame, what do ye think of this?" said he.

    "What do I think? God be my help in need!

I say, a churl hath done a churl's own deed.

Bad luck to him! What answer can there be?

The man is sick and full of fantasy;

He hath a kind of frenzy in his head."

    "Madame, unless in other ways," he said,

"I may achieve the vengeance that I seek,

I shall denounce him everywhere I speak –

This false blasphemer, that commanded me

That I divide among us equally

What no one can divide! God send him ill!"

The lord as in a trance sat long and still,
And in his mind reviewed the situation:
"How had this fellow the imagination
To show the friar this problem, anyhow?
I never heard of such a thing ere now;
The devil, I think, hath put it in his mind.
For no man in arithmetic can find
A problem like to this, nor an equation.
And who indeed could make a demonstration
Of how each man could have an equal part
Both of the sound and odor of a fart?
Curse him – he is a cunning rascal, clearly.
Lo, gentlemen," the lord declared severely,
"Who ever heard of such a thing ere now?
To every man alike! Come, tell me how!
It is impossible, it cannot be!
Ah, cunning churl, God never prosper thee!
The rumbling of a fart, and all its sound,
It is the noise of air that moves around,
And little by little doth waste itself away.
What man can make a judgment, who can say
If it had been divided equally?
So much for that! Yet what a subtlety
The fellow showed to set this riddle out!
He is a lunatic, beyond a doubt!
Now eat your meat, and let the churl go play,
And hang himself, and go to hell, I say."

Now the lord's squire was standing by the board,
And carved his meat, and listened, word by word,
To everything as I have set it down.
"If I might have the cloth to make a gown,
My lord, I could explain to you, Sir Friar,"
He said, "if it would nowise stir your ire,
How to divide this fart exact and true
Among your order, if it pleased me to."

The lord said: "Tell us, and the cloth is thine,
By God's grace, and by St. John the divine!"

"My lord," he answered, "when the weather is fair,
Without a wind, or movement of the air,
Order a cart-wheel carried to this hall.
See that its spokes are in it, one and all –

Within a proper wheel, twelve spokes should lie.
And bring me then twelve friars; and know ye why?
Thirteen will make a convent, I should guess.
And our confessor, in his worthiness,
He shall complete the number by the wheel.
Then by agreement all of them shall kneel,
And every friar lay firmly, as he bends,
His nose exactly where a wheel-spoke ends.
But your confessor, God him bless and protect,
Beneath the hub shall hold his nose erect.
Then shall this churl, with belly stiff and taut
As any drum, into the hall be brought,
And set upon this wheel from off a cart,
Upon the hub, and made to let a fart.
Then by my life ye shall perceive it well,
By proof both certain and demonstrable,
That this device in equal parts will send
The sound and stink to every wheelspoke's end;
But your confessor, as the worthiest,
Standing in honor well above the rest,
Shall have the first fruit, as is only reason –
This is the way of friars for many a season –
The worthiest ones must first of all be served.
And certainly, he hath it well deserved.
For he hath taught today so much of good,
As in the pulpit he a-preaching stood,
That he shall have first smell, for all of me,
Not of the first fart only, but of three;
And surely all his convent would agree –
He bears himself so fair and holily."

The lord, the lady, and everyone agreed,
Except the friar, that Jankin spoke indeed
As well as Euclid could, or Ptolemy.
As for the churl, they said his subtlety
And shrewd wit made him shape this cunning plan.
He was no fool, nor yet a crazy man.
And Jankin in this fashion won his gown.
My tale is done; now we are close to town.

Here ends the Summoner's Tale

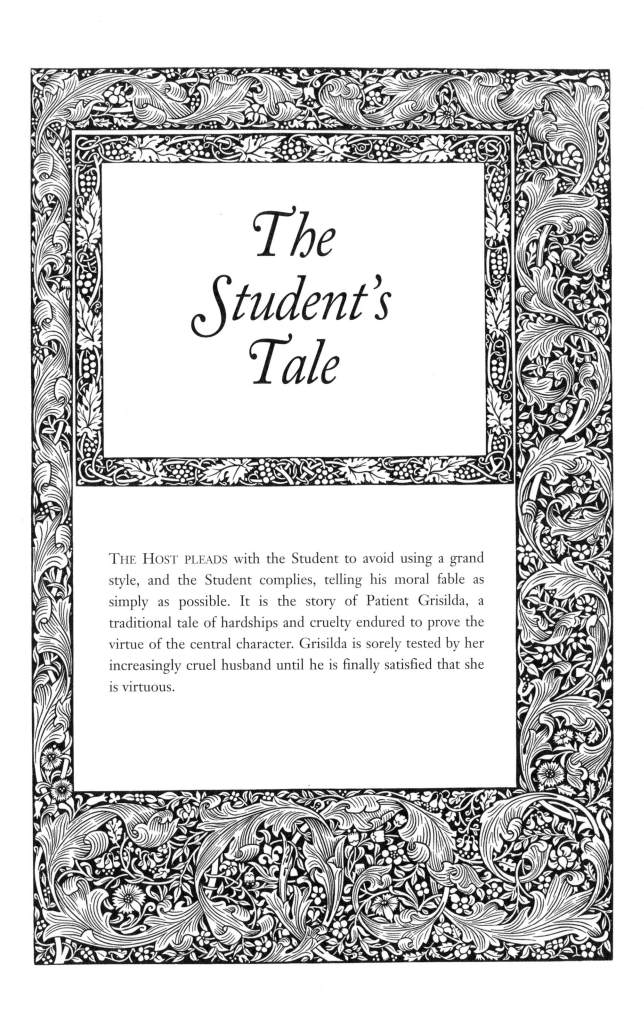

The Student's Tale

THE HOST PLEADS with the Student to avoid using a grand style, and the Student complies, telling his moral fable as simply as possible. It is the story of Patient Grisilda, a traditional tale of hardships and cruelty endured to prove the virtue of the central character. Grisilda is sorely tested by her increasingly cruel husband until he is finally satisfied that she is virtuous.

THE STUDENT'S TALE

Here follows the Prologue to the Oxford Student's Tale

"SIR Oxford student, riding coy and staid,
Ye sit there," said our Host, "as might a maid
Sitting at table, newly wed and young.
All day I hear no word fall from your tongue;
I think ye toy with logic or with rime.
But Solomon says that 'all things have their time.'

"For God's sake, therefore, be of better cheer.
This is no time to fall a-studying here.
Tell us some merry tale, then, by your faith;
For when a man hath joined a game, and play'th,
Then he must give the game his full assent.
But preach not, as the friars do in Lent,
About forgotten sins, to make us weep;
Nor tell a tale that sends us all asleep.

"Tell some adventurous tale to make us smile.
Your colors, metaphors, and lofty style –
Keep them until ye write of higher things,
As men may do that fashion tales for kings.
Speak in plain language to us now, I pray,
That we may understand the things ye say."

This student answered, courteous and pleasant:
"Your rod, Host, is above me for the present.
Ye govern here, and no man may gainsay you;
And therefore in this matter I obey you,
As far, indeed as reason will permit it.
This tale I tell, by chance I came to get it –
At Padua, from a worthy scholar there –
As all his words and works alike declare.

Now he is dead, and buried in his chest.
I pray God give his soul eternal rest.
    Francis Petrarch, the poet, laurel-crowned,
They call him, and his rhetoric, of sweet
    sound,
Lighted all Italy with poetry,
As Linius did with his philosophy,
Or law, or special work in other sphere.
But death, that lets us have our dwelling here
No longer than the twinkling of an eye,
Has slain them both! Thus all of us shall die.

"But to inform you of this worthy man
From whom I learned this tale – as I began:
First, ere he writes the body of his story,
He shapes a Proem, telling Piedmont's glory,
And of Saluzzo, which they call that land;
And speaks about the Apennines, that stand
In high hills, bounding western Lombardy;
And of Mount Vesulus especially
Is it his labor in this place to sing –
Where the great Po bursts from a little spring,
And has his first beginning and his source,
Enlarging always as he takes his course
To Emilia and Ferrara on his way
To Venice. But all this were long to say;
And, if I give my own opinion now,
I think it unessential, anyhow,
Except to introduce and make more clear
His tale, which if ye listen ye shall hear."

Here begins the Tale of the Student from Oxford

THERE is, at the west side of Italy,
Down at the roots of Vesulus the cold,
A fertile plain, that bears abundantly,
Where many a tower and town mayst thou
    behold,
That in our father's time were built, of old;
And other fair sights lie about in legion.
Saluzzo is the name they give this region.

A marquis once was lord of all that land,
As had his fathers been since long ago;
Obedient and ready to his hand
Were all his lieges, both the high and low;
Thus in delight he lived, long dwelling so;
Beloved and feared – for Fortune called him hers –
Both by his lords and by his commoners.

With this he was, to speak of lineage,
The noblest born in all of Lombardy;
And fair in form, and strong, and young in age,
And full of honor and of courtesy.
Discreet enough in government was he,
Save for some things in which he was to blame;
And Walter was this fair young marquis' name.

I blame him that he gave no careful thought
To any need that coming years might hide,
But let his mind by passing sport be caught –
To hawk and hunt, for instance, or to ride;
As for most other things, he let them slide,
And he would not – and that was worst of all –
Marry a wife, whatever might befall.

This point his people bore with such unrest
That to him one day in a flock they went,
And one of them, perhaps in learning best,
Or one from whom the lord would least resent
That he should tell him what his people meant,
Or else that he could make such things appear
To best advantage, spoke as ye shall hear.

"O noble marquis, your humanity
Assures us and must make our fear the less
In times like this when necessarily
We have a grievous sorrow to express.
Then, lord, permit us in your nobleness
That we may speak our hearts, for they are painful;
Of these my words, I pray, be not disdainful.

"I have no greater cause for being here
Than any other man has in this place;
Yet since in all these days, my sovereign dear,
Ye ever have shown me favor and good grace,
I dare the more to ask of you a space
Of audience, and to show you our request,
Which ye shall deal with as ye think is best.

"For certainly we love you, lord, so well,
And all your work, and always have, that we
Could not among ourselves devise or tell
How we might live in more felicity,
Save for one thing alone. If it could be
Your pleasure, lord, to take the wedded state,
Then should we feel relieved and fortunate.

"Then take that yoke, so happy and so holy,
That is no servitude, but sovereignty,
Which men call wedlock, lord. And ponder fully
In your wise thought, how all our days must flee
In varying ways, on to eternity;
For sleep or wake, in spite of all endeavor,
Time waits for none of us, but flees forever.

"And though your green youth still may shine in
        flower,
Age creeps upon it, silent as a stone;
Death threatens every age, and lays his power
On every rank; all yield to him alone;
And just as surely as to all is known
That we shall die, as surely none can say
How death shall cut him down, or name the day.

"Then look with favor on our true petition,
Who never yet rejected your command;
And if ye please to alter your condition,
We will, if ye permit us, take in hand
To choose a wife for you – in all the land
Noblest and best, and fit in our opinion
To honor God and you and your dominion.

"Deliver us then from all this restless doubt,
And take a wife, for the sake of God on high,
For if, as God forbid, it come about
That with your death your lineage should die,
And some strange prince should win your throne
    thereby,
That were as woeful as unnecessary!
Therefore we pray you speedily to marry!"

Their meek prayer, their concern that showed so
    clearly,
Worked in his heart and moved him tenderly;
"Ye ask, O people whom I love so dearly,
What once I told myself should never be.
I have rejoiced to have my liberty,
Which seldom may in marriage be pursued;
Where I was free, I take to servitude.

"Yet none the less, I see your true intent,
And trust your wisdom, as hath been my way,
Wherefore of my free will, I do consent
To marry, and as quickly as I may.
But for the offer that ye make today
To choose my wife yourselves, I would not take it,
And pray you well that ye no longer make it.

"Children may be, God knows, for ill or good,
Unlike their parents that have gone before them;
Gifts are of God, indeed, not of the blood
In which they were engendered, and which bore them;
I trust God's gifts, and being thankful for them,
My marriage and estate and all my ease
I leave to God, to do with as he please.

"Leave then to me the choosing of my wife;
I take that burden on my back alone;
And this I pray and charge you on your life –
The wife that I shall take to share my throne,
While ye may live, honor her, everyone,
In word and work alike, as much or more
As she were daughter of an emperor.

"And furthermore, this ye shall swear: that ye
Against my choice will grumble not, nor strive,
For since I shall forgo my liberty
At your request – as I shall hope to thrive,
Where I have set my heart, there will I wive;
And if ye will not make this promise to me,
About this marriage, pray, no longer sue me."

And they agreed, and swore, all happy-hearted,
To everything – no person there said nay;
Beseeching him, of grace, ere they departed,
That he appoint for them a certain day
For marriage, and as soon as ever he may;
For all the time the people somewhat dreaded
That this young marquis never would be wedded.

He named a day, as suited him the best,
On which he would be wed for certainty,
And said, he did all this at their request,
And they with humble hearts, submissively,
Proffered their thanks to him on bended knee
With reverence, and being well content
To win their suit, dispersed, and homeward went.

And all his officers he now requires
To make provision for the festival,
And gives to all his knights and all his squires
Such charges as he likes, and one and all
At his commandment to their labor fall,
And each is diligent with preparation,
To make that fête a fitting celebration.

Part II

NOT far from that same stately palace bright,
At which this marquis fixed his wedding day,
There lay a village, on a pleasant site,
Where the poor peasants had their stores of hay,
And cattle, and the huts in which they lay;
And, after earth had blessed them with her giving,
From their own labor took their simple living.

Among these humble people dwelt a man
Who was considered poorest of them all;
But high God, in accordance with His plan,
Can send his glory to an ox's stall.
Janicula the peasants used to call
This man; and in his family was a daughter
By name Grisilda – fair enough men thought her.

But were it virtuous beauty ye might seek,
Few were more fair to find beneath the sun;
For poverty had reared her, so to speak,
And let no lecherous fevers in her run;
She drank more from the well than from the tun;
And since her whole wish virtue was to please,
She knew much labor, but no idle ease.

But though this maiden was of tender age,
Yet in the breast of her virginity
There was enclosed a spirit ripe and sage;
With a great kindness and all reverently
Her poor and aging father tended she;
Some sheep for spinning in the fields she kept,
And never would be idle till she slept.

And homeward as she came from field or wood,
She stopped to gather herbs of many a kind,
Which she would cut and seethe and use for food.
Hard was her bed as any ye could find.
She kept her father's happiness in mind,
With all the service and obedience
A child may do to show its reverence.

Upon Grisilda, this poor maid and lowly,
The marquis oftentimes had set his eye
When riding to the hunt, and saw her wholly –
On these occasions when he passed her by –
Not with a wanton look, but with a high
And grave regard. Often with such a glance
He fixed his eyes upon her countenance;

And of her virtue thought with satisfaction,
As of her womanhood, that they were great
In one so young, as well in look as action;
For though most people have no delicate
Insight in virtue, yet he saw each trait
That she possessed, and to himself he said
That he would wed her only, if he wed.

The day arrived, yet still must all men wonder
Who was the woman that his bride might be.
The town indeed was all but torn asunder
To know, and many whispered secretly:
"Will not our lord forsake this vanity?
Will he not wed? Alas! Who could believe
He would himself and us alike deceive?"

Nevertheless he bade his jewellers make
Of gems, and set in azure and in gold,
Rich rings and brooches for Grisilda's sake,
And had rich clothing fashioned in a mold
After a maiden like her to behold;
And other ornaments he had them fashion
As should be fit for such a great occasion.

Now was the time mid-morning of that day
On which this wedding had been set to be;
And all the palace was in good array,
Both hall and chamber, each in its degree;
And rooms for serving shone with quantity
Of dainties, richly spread on every hand,
From all the length of the Italian land.

This royal marquis, all in rich array,
With lords and ladies in his company
Invited to the festival that day,
And youths in training for their chivalry,
With many a sound of varied melody,
In this array straight to the little town
That I have told you of, came riding down.

Grisilda, ignorant that any sought her,
Or had prepared for her all this array,
Was going to the well to fetch some water,
And hasten home as soon as ever she may,
For she had heard it said, how on this day
The marquis would be wed, and thought it good
To see that celebration, if she could.

She thought: "With other maidens such as I,
Here at our doorway will I stand, and see
The marchioness, perhaps; so I will try
To do at home as quickly as may be
Whatever labor there may fall to me,
So I may have the sight of her today
If toward the castle she should pass this way."

But just as she was passing through the door,
The marquis came, and soon she heard him call;
She set her water pot upon the floor
Beside the threshold, in an ox's stall,
And down upon her knees made haste to fall;
And grave of countenance she knelt all still
Until she heard her lord declare his will.

The thoughtful marquis spoke then to this maid,
Sober of face. "Grisilda," was his word,
"Where is your father?" She in answer said,
Humbly, and with a reverent accord:
"He is all ready – here at hand, my lord,"
And rose and went within as she replied,
And fetched her father to the marquis' side.

He took his hand, and leading him apart,
Said to him gravely, while they stood aside,
"Janicula, the pleasure of my heart
I can no longer, and I will not hide.
For I will take thy daughter for my bride
Before I go, if thy consent thou give,
To be my wife as long as she shall live.

"Thou lovest me, I know for certainty;
Thou art my vassal born, faithful and true,
And I dare say that that which pleases me
Will thus please you. Yet thou must tell me, too,
About this thing that I have hope to do –
If to that purpose thou hast mind to draw –
And wilt accept me as thy son-in-law?"

This man, astounded at the thing he heard,
Turned red, and all abashed and trembling stood,
And scarcely could he say another word,
Save this: "O lord, whatever ye hold good
Is good to me; no thing at all I would
That ye would not; ye be my master dear:
Act as may please you in this matter here."

"Yet," said this marquis quietly, "would I
That in thy chamber I and thou and she
Should have a conference. And knowst thou why?
I will inquire if she would willingly
Become my wife and take her rule from me;
But all this in thy presence, do not doubt me;
I will not speak a word to her without thee."

And in the chamber while these three were talking,
And to an end that I shall soon declare,
The people gathered, many of them walking
About the house, and marvelled at the care
And thrift with which she kept her father there;
And yet Grisilda might have wondered more,
For such a sight she had not seen before.

No wonder she was all astonishment
To see so great a guest come to that place;
For she had never known a like event,
And a strange pallor settled on her face;
But not to let this story lag in pace,
These are the words with which the marquis laid
His will before this good and faithful maid.

"Grisilda, it is well that ye should know
It seems good to your father and to me
That I should wed you. Therefore stands it so,
As I suppose, that ye too will agree.
But I will ask these questions first," said he:
"That, since this thing has been precipitate,
Will ye consent, or ponder it and wait?

"And are ye well prepared, I ask again,
To do my will, and promise that I may –
As best may please me – cause you joy or pain,
And ye will not resent it, night or day,
And when I say a 'Yea,' not answer 'Nay,'
Neither by word, or frown, or mute defiance?
Swear this, and here I swear my firm alliance."

Trembling for fear, and wondering at his word,
She answered: "Both in worth and dignity
I am unfit for what ye ask me, lord;
But what ye will, that same is will to me.
And here I swear that never willingly,
Though I should die, will I by act or breath
Fail you, though I were loath to suffer death."

"That is enough, Grisilda mine," he told her;
Then to the door he passed with sober cheer,
And she appeared behind him at his shoulder,
And he addressed the people waiting there.
"This is my wife," he said, "that standeth here.
Honor her then, and love her well, I pray,
Whoso loves me; there is no more to say."

And since it was not meet that she should wear
Her present raiment to his house, he bade
That certain women should undress her there,
Of which these ladies were not over-glad
To touch the clothes in which they found her clad;
But none the less this maiden bright of hue
They clothed again from head to foot all new.

They combed her hair, that lay there all untressed,
And with their fingers delicate and small
Upon her head a golden crown they pressed;
And on her raiment jewels great and small.
Why should I linger here to tell it all?
Folk scarcely knew her for her loveliness,
Translated as she was with costly dress.

This marquis with a ring brought for the rite
Hath wedded her, and after they were married
He set her on a charger, snowy white,
And to the palace went, and never tarried,
By joyful throngs of people were they carried;
And all that day they spent in feast and revel
Until the sun sank to his western level.

And if I tell my tale in briefest space,
I say, that to this new-made marchioness,
God of his goodness sent surpassing grace,
And there was none who saw her that would guess
She had been born and bred in lowliness,
Such as a cottage or an ox's stall,
But nurtured rather in an emperor's hall.

And she was honored so, and held so dear,
That even the folk that dwelt where he had sought her,
And from her birth had known her, year by year,
Scarcely believed her this Janicula's daughter,
But would have sworn she was not, for they thought her –
By their conjecture – quite another creature,
For so she seemed in manner, form, and feature.

For though she had been virtuous before,
Now she was so increased in excellence,
With gifts of goodness set, that shone the more
For modesty of speech and eloquence;
So kind and so deserving reverence;
And could so well the people's heart discover,
That all who looked upon her face must love her.

Not by Saluzzo's citizens alone
Was sent abroad the goodness of her name;
In many another region not her own,
If one said well, another said the same;
So did her goodness spread and grow in fame,
That men and women, the younger with the older,
Would journey to Saluzzo to behold her.

Thus Walter humbly, yet all royally
Wedded with true and honest happiness,
And lived God's peace in all tranquillity
At home, and had abroad enough success;
And since he saw that under humble dress
There might be virtue, he was thought to be
A prudent man, and such is rare to see.

Grisilda knew indeed by native wit
All kinds of work a proper woman knows;
And also, if the case required it,
She could the public happiness compose;
There were no rancors, discords, griefs or woes
In all that land that she could not appease,
And wisely shape them all to rest and ease.

And though her husband left her now and then,
If nobles, or the folk of less degree
Quarrelled, then would she make them friends again;
Such wise and understanding speech had she
And judgments charged so clear with equity,
It seemed to men that heaven had sent her there
To save the people, and every wrong repair.

Grisilda had not been a long time wed
When she conceived, and soon a daughter bore –
Though rather had she borne a son instead;
Glad were the people, and the marquis more,
For though a maid child thus had come before,
Yet she could bear a boy child, none the less,
Since there was now no fear of barrenness.

Part III

IT happened, as it would again, indeed,
That when this child had suckled but a spell,
This marquis was possessed of such a need
To tempt his wife, and try her patience well,
That he could no way from his heart dispel
This marvellous desire to test her out.
Needless he thought to frighten her, no doubt.

She had been tested quite enough before,
And he had proved her good. Why should he find
A need to tempt her always more and more?
Some men have praised him for a subtle mind,
But as for me, I say it is not kind
To try a wife that shows no fault or error
And put her thus in anguish and in terror.

Which in this way the marquis brought about:
He came at night when she was in her bed,
With a stern, troubled face, and full of doubt,
And told her thus: "Grisilda mine," he said,
"Ye will remember well the day we wed,
And how I took you from your rude condition,
And set you here in such a high position.

"I say, Grisilda, in your present station,
In which my hand hath set you, it is sure,
Ye should not all forget the occupation
And life I took you from when ye were poor,
For any happiness ye may procure.
Take heed of every word I say to you.
There is none by to hear it but us two.

"For ye yourself know well how ye came here
Into this house – it was not long ago;
And though to me ye be beloved and dear,
Unto my nobles ye are nothing so.
They call it a dishonor and great woe
That they are subjects, and in servitude
To thee, born in a village small and rude.

"Especially since ye your daughter bore
They speak like this – I cannot more deny it.
But I desire, as I have done before,
To live my life with them in peace and quiet,
And not be reckless – nay, I dare not try it;
Thy daughter I must deal with for the best,
Not what I wish, but what my folk suggest.

"And yet, God knows, this is a grief to me;
But none the less I do not think to do it
Without your knowledge – yet I wish," said he,
"That ye will give me your agreement to it;
This thing is hard, yet show your patience through it,
As in your village once ye swore to do –
Upon the morning when I married you."

She heard all this, and yet she did not stir,
Nor spoke, nor changed expression of her face;
For, as it seemed, this had not troubled her.
"Lord, all is at your liking in this case.
My child and I bow humbly to your grace;
For we are yours, and ye may waste or treasure
Your own possession: do as is your pleasure.

"There is no thing, as God my soul may bless,
That ye may like, but I will like it too,
And there is nothing that I would possess,
Or fear to lose, O lord, save only you.
And this shall be my will my whole life through;
No length of days, nor death, can make me falter,
Or can my heart in any fashion alter."

Glad was the marquis hearing this reply,
And yet, indeed, pretended not to be,
But left the chamber with a troubled eye,
And face of sadness and perplexity.
A furlong's space he went, or two or three,
And secretly explained his whole intent
Unto a man, that to his wife he sent.

A sergeant was this confidential man,
Whom he had often found discreet and true
In things important; and such people can
Be counted on in evil matters, too.
The sergeant loved and dreaded him, he knew;
And when this man his master's purpose found,
Into her room he strode without a sound.

"Madam," he said, "ye must forgive it me
If I fulfill my duty to your pain;
I know that ye are wise enough to see
That to dispute a lord's command is vain.
One may bewail against it, or complain,
But when a man is told, he must obey;
And so will I; there is no more to say.

"It is commanded that I take this child –"
And spoke no more, but seized the innocent
With ruthless hands, and with a look as wild
As if he would have slain it ere he went.
Grisilda must endure it and consent;
And like a lamb she sat there meek and still
And let this cruel sergeant work his will.

Ill was the reputation of this man,
His very look and word suspicious were;
Strange was the hour at which this work began;
Alas! her daughter, dear as life to her –
She feared this man would be its murderer;
And yet she did not weep, and was not daunted,
But gave assent to what the marquis wanted.

But in the end Grisilda thus began,
And meekly to this sergeant made her plea
That as he was a true and worthy man,
He let her kiss the child, ere it should be
Killed, and she pressed it to her tenderly,
With a sad countenance, and softly kissed it,
And lulled it tenderly, and then she blessed it;

And in benign voice said amid her loss,
"Farewell, my child, whom I no more shall see;
But since my lord hath marked thee with the cross,
By that same Father may thou blessèd be
That died for us upon a cross of tree;
To Him, my child, thy spirit I commend,
Since thou for me tonight shalt meet thine end."

I think that for a nurse in such a pass
This piteous sight would have been hard to see;
And well a mother might have cried, "Alas!"
But none the less, she stood so steadfastly
That she endured all this adversity,
And meek of manner to the sergeant said,
"Now take again your tender little maid.

"Do now the thing for which my lord hath sent you;
But of your mercy hear me speak one word;
If some command of his does not prevent you,
See that this little body is interred
Safe from the claws of prying beast or bird."
But no word of his purpose would he say,
But took the child again, and went his way.

This sergeant, soon returning to his lord,
Reported of Grisilda, as was due him;
And all she said he told him word for word,
And then his daughter dear presented to him;
This marquis felt some pity stealing through him,
But none the less held to his purpose still,
As lords are wont to do who seek their will.

And bade the sergeant go in secrecy
Wrapping the child with gentle hand, he said,
And using it in all ways tenderly,
And in a sling or chest to make its bed;
And, if he had no wish to lose his head,
Let no man know at all of his intent,
Or whence he came, or to what place he went;

And to Bologna, to his sister dear,
Then countess of Panigo, he should go,
And give the child, and make this matter clear,
And beg her all her diligence to show
To rear it as a noble child should grow,
But tell no man, the marquis asked of her,
Whose child it was, whatever might occur.

This sergeant goes, and has performed this thing;
But of the marquis let our story be,
For evermore he went imagining
If by his wife's behavior he could see,
Or by her words have evidence that she
Was changed; but though he watched, he could not find
That she was anything but grave and kind.

As glad, as meek, as busy day by day
In work and love as she had used to be,
Was she to him in every kind of way;
Nor of her daughter any word spoke she.
No strange behavior in adversity
Appeared in her, and nothing ever brought her
In earnestness or jest to name her daughter.

Part IV

SO in this way went by four years or more,
And she conceived; and God, that heard her prayer,
Willed that by Walter now a boy she bore,
Gracious to look upon, and very fair.
And when his father knew he had this heir,
He and his land made merry cheer for days
Over this child, and gave God thanks and praise.

When it was two years old, nor any longer
Went to the nurse's breast to get its food,
This marquis had a wish, and ever stronger,
Once more to tempt Grisilda if he could.
O this was needless now, and nothing good!
But married men will never use in measure
One that is patient underneath their pleasure.

And whos child that it was he bad hir hyde
From every wight, for oght that may bityde.

℣ The sergeant gooth, and hath fulfild this
thyng;
But to this markys now retourne we;
For now gooth he ful faste ymagínyng
If by his wyves cheere he myghte se,
Or by hire word aperceyve that she
Were chaunged; but he nevere hire koude fynde

But evere in oon ylike sad and kynde.

As glad, as humble, as bisy in servyse,
And eek in love, as she was wont to be,
Was she to hym in every maner wyse;
Ne of hir doghter noght a word spak she.
Noon accident for noon adversitee
Was seyn in hire, ne nevere hir doghter name
Ne nempned she, in ernest nor in game.
Explicit tercia pars. Sequitur pars quarta.

IN THIS ESTAAT ther passed been foure yeer
Er she with childe was; but, as God wolde,
A knave child she bar by this Walter,
Ful gracious and fair for to biholde.
And whan that folk it to his fader tolde,
Nat oonly he, but al his contree, merye
Was for this child, and God they thanke and
herye.

Whan it was two yeer old, and fro the brest
Departed of his norice, on a day
This markys caughte yet another lest
To tempte his wyf yet ofter, if he may.
O nedelees was she tempted in assay!
But wedded men ne knowe no mesure,
Whan that they fynde a pacient creature.

℣ Wyf, quod this markys, ye han herd er this,
My peple sikly berth oure mariage,

Plate 20: The Student's Tale (p. 246)

"Wife," said this marquis, "ye have heard before
Of how my people bear our marriage ill,
But since my son is born, I hear it more;
Now is it worse than ever it was, until
The murmur slays my courage and my will;
For to my ears it comes so sharp and plain
That almost it destroys my heart with pain.

"Now they say thus: 'When Walter shall be gone,
Then shall Janicula supply the seed
That rules us, for of other is there none.'
Such are the words my people speak, indeed.
I hear the talk; I ought to give it heed;
For such a sentiment is worth my fearing,
Although they speak not plainly in my hearing.

"Well would I live in quiet, if I might;
And so my mind is fixed that this must be:
That, as I served his sister once by night,
So must I serve him too, in secrecy;
And so I warn you, do not suddenly
Start from yourself in woe for what I do.
Be patient in this thing, I pray of you."

She answered: "This I said, and ever shall:
Nothing I wish, nor would from aught refrain,
But as ye please. I shall not grieve at all
Although my daughter and my son be slain
At your commandment, lord; for of these twain
This is indeed the sum of all I know:
Sickness, and after sickness pain and woe.

"Ye be our lord; with what is yours, therefore,
Do as ye please; ask no advice from me;
For as I left at home the clothes I wore,
When first I came to you, just so," said she,
"I left my will and all my liberty,
And took your clothing; therefore, lord, I pray you
Do what your pleasure is – I will obey you.

"And truly, could I know what will was hidden
Within your heart, my lord, before ye told it,
I would be quick to pleasure you unbidden;
And since I know it now, as ye unfold it,
All firm and stable in my heart I hold it;
For had I knowledge that my death would ease you,
I would be glad to die, and thereby please you.

"Death cannot hope to make comparison
Unto your love." Before this constancy
The marquis was abashed; and he cast down
His eyes, and wondered what his wife might be
To suffer all he did so patiently.
And he went forth with heavy countenance,
Yet felt his heart with a great pleasure dance.

This ugly sergeant, in the same rude way
In which he took her daughter formerly,
Or worse, if that were possible to say,
Now seized her son, so beautiful to see.
Steadfast in patience, naught in agony
She spoke; nor would by any look confess it,
But kissed her child, and then began to bless it;

Save this: she prayed of him, if that might be,
He would her little son in earth inter,
To save his limbs, so delicate to see,
From any birds or beasts that prowling were,
No word of answer would he give to her.
He went his way with hard indifferent stare,
But brought it to Bologna with all care.

This marquis fell to wonder more and more
About her patience, and indeed if he
Had not had certain knowledge long before
That she had loved her children perfectly,
He would have thought it was a subtlety,
Or malice, or a cruelty of spirit
That with so calm a visage she could bear it.

But next to him – and this he knew was so –
She loved her children most in every way;
But from you women now I wish to know,
Were not these tests enough? What more, I say,
Could a harsh husband plan to put in play
To prove her wifehood and her constancy
And he continuing ever in cruelty?

But there are those of such a character,
That, let them once a certain purpose take,
Nothing can ever stop them or deter,
But, as if chains had bound them to a stake,
They will not from their first fixed purpose slake.
Just so this marquis kept his purpose still
To tempt his wife, as first had been his will.

He waited, if by word or countenance,
Her love might seem to change or be arrested,
But never found the slightest variance;
Both heart and face her constancy attested;
The more she lived, the more she manifested
Her truth in love, if that were possible,
And greater eagerness to serve him well.

Therefore it seemed there was between these two
One will; for any wish he might suggest
At once became the pleasure that she knew;
And God be thanked, all happened for the best.
She clearly showed, no wife should manifest,
In restlessness, or of her own desire,
A will, but as her husband may require.

Ill rumor now of Walter widely spread,
That he with cruel heart and wickedly,
Because he had a lowly woman wed,
Had murdered both his children secretly.
A common thing this rumor came to be –
Nor was it strange, for in the people's ear
No word but of this murder could they hear.

And so, though they had loved him heretofore,
And well, the growing breath of this ill-fame,
Now made them hate him ever more and more;
The name of murderer is a hateful name.
Yet none the less, for earnest or for game,
He would not stay his cruel intent, for still
To tempt his wife was all his wish and will.

And when his daughter grew to twelve years old,
Unto the court of Rome, with subtle skill,
Already of his secret purpose told,
He sent his messenger; and bade them fill
Such bulls out as would work his cruel will,
Saying the pope, all for his land's repose,
Bade him to wed another if he chose.

I say, he told them they should counterfeit
The pope's bulls, which should make the explanation
That he was free, if he desired it,
To leave his wife, by the pope's dispensation,
And thus allay the strife and agitation
Between him and his folk – thus read the bull,
Which soon was published through the land in full.

The simple people, as no wonder is,
Had not a doubt but all of this was so;
But when at last Grisilda heard of this,
I think her heart was heavy with her woe;
But she, that ever only calm would show,
Was still disposed, humble and meek and pure,
All adverse brunt of fortune to endure;

Submitting to his liking and his pleasure
To whom her heart and all were dedicated,
As to her sole and only earthly treasure.
But that this story now may be related
With brevity, this marquis clearly stated
Within a letter, what was his intent,
Which to Bologna secretly he sent;

Praying the earl of Panigo, who had wed
His sister, that he would in courtesy
Prepare and have his children homeward led,
In honorable estate, all openly,
But one thing asked of him especially –
That to no person, though it might occur
That men should ask, he answer who they were;

But that they went, indeed, to wed the maid
Unto Saluzzo's marquis, he should say;
And the earl did in all as he was prayed,
For with the dawn he started on his way,
With many lords riding in rich array
On toward Saluzzo, as her retinue;
And her young brother rode beside her, too.

Fair was the dress this fresh young maiden had
Against her wedding, bright with jewels fair;
Her brother, now of seven years, was clad
In like array to grace this rich affair;
And thus with noble pomp and gladsome air
On toward Saluzzo, day by happy day
They shape their course, and ride upon their way.

Part V

BUT meanwhile, after all his wickedness,
To tempt his wife to the extremity
By the last proof that he could find to press,
And so by full experience to see
If she were still as true as formerly,
This marquis in a place where all men heard
With a rough manner spoke to her this word:

"Grisilda, I have had enough of pleasure
From the great goodness that I find in you.
And though ye brought no lineage or treasure,
Ye gave me truth, and all obedience, too;
But now I know that this is only true:
If I consider well, I must conclude
Great lordship always brings great servitude.

"I may not do as every plowman may.
My people are demanding that I wed
Another wife, and clamor day by day,
Also the pope, to see them quieted,
Consents to have it done – this may be said;
And thus much to you of a truth I say –
My new wife is already on the way.

"Be strong of heart, I say, and quit her place;
And that same dower that ye first brought to
    me,
Take it again – I grant it of my grace;
Return now to your father's house," said he;
"No man can always have prosperity;
And take with constant spirit, I advise you,
The stroke of fortune that so shrewdly tries you."

She answered in her calm and patient way:
"My lord," she said, "I know and always knew
That no man can compare my poor array
With the magnificence that hedges you.
There is no doubt of this: it is too true.
I never thought me fit, as I have said,
To be your wife, or even your serving maid.

"And in this house where ye a lady made me,
With high God for my witness I profess,
As He may ever bless my soul and aid me –
I never held me lady or mistress,
But humble servant to your worthiness;
And ever shall, for all my will is yours
Above all others', while my life endures.

"That ye so long in your benignity
Have held me here in honor and array,
Where I had never the worthiness to be,
I thank both you and God, who will, I pray,
Reward you. There is nothing more to say.
Now to my father I go cheerfully,
To dwell with him as long as life shall be.

"There from a child I had my fostering;
There will I lead my life till I am dead,
In body clean, and heart, and everything.
For since I yielded you my maidenhead,
I am your wife. God let it not be said
That such a lord's wife ever changed her state
To take another husband or a mate.

"And from your new wife, God now in His grace
Grant you well-being and prosperity;
For I will gladly render her my place,
Where I have always dwelt full happily;
For since it is your pleasure, lord," said she,
"That were in other days my whole heart's ease,
That I shall go, I will go when ye please.

"But since ye offer me again the dower
I first brought, it is clearly in my mind
It was my wretched clothes which, at this hour,
It would be hard indeed for me to find.
Good God above! how gentle and how kind
Ye seemed to me in speech and face and carriage
The day on which was solemnized our marriage.

"But truth is said – at least I find it true –
For by effect it proves itself on me –
That love grown old is not the same as new;
Yet, lord, though I shall have adversity
To death itself in this – ye shall not see
That I repent by any deed or word
That my whole heart on you was thus conferred.

"My lord, ye know that, in my father's place
Ye bade them strip my humble clothes from me,
And had me clad all richly, of your grace,
So that I brought you nothing, certainly,
But nakedness and my virginity;
And here again my clothing I restore,
And wedding ring as well, forevermore.

"Your other jewels, ye will find them laid
Within your chamber, I can safely say;
Naked from out my father's house," she said,
"I came, and naked I return today;
For I would do your will in every way.
And yet I hope ye spare me the distress
To leave your palace here without a dress.

"Ye could not do me such a shameful thing –
That the same womb in which your children lay
Should go all bare before the wondering
Eyes of the people, and for this I pray
Let me not like a worm crawl by the way.
Remember, O my lord, as I do love you,
I was your wife, though all unworthy of you.

"And so, in guerdon of my maidenhead,
Which I brought here, but cannot ever bear
Again, deign now to give me in its stead
The kind of dress that once I used to wear,
That with it I may hide the womb of her
That used to be your wife. And here I leave you,
My own dear lord, lest I perchance should grieve you."

"The smock upon thy back, then – let it stay,"
Was his reply, "And carry it out with thee."
Yet found this almost more than he could say,
And in compassion left her suddenly.
Then she disrobed, with all the crowd to see,
And in her smock, and bare of head and feet,
Toward her father's house went down the street.

The people followed her with tearful cries;
Cursing Dame Fortune that this thing occurred;
But she wept not at all – dry were her eyes –
And all the while she did not speak a word.
Her father soon these dismal tidings heard,
And cursed alike the day and hour that nature
Had ever shaped him as a living creature.

For out of doubt this agèd, lowly man
Had viewed Grisilda's marriage with suspicion,
And always had believed, since it began,
His lord at last would have a disposition –
His lust fulfilled, to think that his condition
Would suffer from so low a choice, and try,
When he esteemed it safe, to put her by.

He went to meet his daughter hastily,
For by the people's noise he knew she came;
With her old coat, as well as this might be,
Weeping, he tried to cover up her shame;
But could not, for the cloth was not the same
As when she wed, being crude, and – truth to tell –
Older than then by many days as well.

Thus with her father for a certain space
This flower of wifely patience made her dwelling;
Nor with the people, by her words or face,
Nor in their absence, was there any telling
That any sense of wrong was in her swelling;
And of her high estate no memory,
To judge her by her countenance, had she.

No wonder – for amid her high estate,
Her spirit had dwelt in plain humility;
No tender taste, no heart too delicate,
No pomp or royal ways affected she;
She always went benign and patiently,
Discreet and honorable and free of pride,
And firm and humble by her husband's side.

Men talk of Job and his humility,
As scholars, when it pleases them, can write,
And most of men. But, speaking honestly,
Though scholars make their praise of women slight,
No man in meekness ever holds a light
To women, or can be one half so true,
Or if he can, then it is something new.

Part VI

THIS great earl from Bologna now is there,
And soon his fame is known to high and low,
While out among the people, everywhere,
Of a new marchioness the tidings go
Whom he has brought with such great wealth and show
That there was never eye of man to see
Such noble state in all West Lombardy.

The marquis, who had planned and knew it all,
Ere the earl came dispatched his messenger
And summoned poor Grisilda to the hall,
And she, with humble mind in which there were
No prideful thoughts, gladly prepareth her,
And came, and kneeling down where he was seated,
Discreetly and with reverence him greeted.

"My will, Grisilda, is in certainty
To have this maid with whom I soon shall wed
Received tomorrow here as royally
As in my house is possible," he said;
"And have all here, as may be merited
By rank, receive their due in fullest measure
In seating and in service and high pleasure.

"I have no women able to prepare
The chambers as my liking would command;
Therefore it pleases me to have thy care,
And put such matters wholly in thy hand.
My pleasure thou didst fully understand
Of old; and though thy raiment hath no beauty
And is but mean, still thou canst do thy duty."

"Not only, lord, shall I be glad," said she,
"To do your will, but in my proper station
I seek to serve you all unfeignedly,
And please, and always shall, without cessation;
And neither happiness nor tribulation
Shall turn my heart from seeking, lord, forever
To love you best with all my true endeavor."

And to prepare the house, even with this word,
She went about, for there were beds to make
And tables to be set, and fast she stirred,
And prayed the chambermaids, for God's sweet sake,
They would make haste, and quickly sweep and shake,
And she, the most industrious of all,
Put in array each chamber and his hall.

This earl and these two children did alight
When it was middle morning of that day,
And all the people ran to see the sight,
So rich to gaze upon, of their array;
And then at first among themselves they say,
No fool was Walter, it was manifest,
To change his wife, for it was for the best.

For fairer than Grisilda was, indeed,
And younger she appeared, they all declare,
And therefore from these two there should proceed,
Through better blood, a far more pleasing heir.
Also they found her brother's face so fair
That all the folk were glad, and with one voice
They now began to praise the marquis' choice.

Author. "O stormy people, shifting and untrue,
Unwise, and always changing like a vane,
Taking delight in rumor that is new,
For like the moon ye ever wax and wane;
Dear at a penny, full of noise inane;
False is your mind, your constancy deceives,
He is a great fool that in you believes!"

Thus sober men declared, when they could see
The people ever gazing up and down,
All filled with gladness, just for novelty,
To have another lady for their town;
But now this matter I will let alone,
And to Grisilda turn once more, to tell
Her busy care and constancy as well.

Busy Grisilda was, neglecting nothing
That to the festival was pertinent;
She was abashed in no way by her clothing,
Though it was rude and also somewhat rent;
But forth to greet the marchioness she went
With others, with as glad a face as theirs,
And then returned again to her affairs.

And she received his guests with such good cheer,
Greeting each one by rank so tactfully
That none saw any fault in her appear,
But who – they wondered – might this woman be,
Clad in apparel that was poor to see,
Yet so well knowing fine and reverent ways?
And her discretion moved them all to praise.

Meanwhile she never ceased to do her part
To praise this maiden, and her brother too,
With a good purpose and with all her heart,
That no man there could any better do.
But when at last these many lords withdrew
To sit at meat, Walter began to call
Grisilda, busy still within his hall.

He said, "Grisilda," as it were in play,
"How seems the beauty of my wife to thee?"
"Right well, my lord, for by my faith I say
I never saw a fairer one than she.
I pray God give her all prosperity,
And hope that He to both of you will send
Pleasure enough until your days shall end.

"One thing I warn you of, and beg of you:
That ye will not torment with cruëlty
This maiden, as with me ye used to do,
For she was fostered far more tenderly
In her upbringing, and it seems to me,
Could not the same adversity endure
As one whose fostering was mean and poor."

And when he saw her stand so patiently,
Cheerful and free of malice through it all,
Though he had often done her injury,
And staid and steadfast ever as a wall,
Still innocent whatever might befall,
Through Walter's sternness welled a deep emotion
Of pity for that wifely, true devotion.

"This is enough, Grisilda mine," said he,
"Be now aghast no more, nor more dismayed;
I have thy faith and thy benignity,
As much as woman's ever was, assayed,
Both in high state, and wretchedly arrayed.
And now I know thy constancy." With this,
He took Grisilda in his arms to kiss.

And she for wonder could not, it would seem,
Take heed of this, nor hear what thing he cried;
It was as if she started from a dream
And had not cast the daze of sleep aside.
"Grisilda, by the God that for us died,
Thou art my wife, no other wife I have,
Nor ever had, as God my soul may save.

"This is thy daughter whom thou hast supposed
To be my wife; the other one shall be
Mine heir, as I have ever more proposed;
Thou in thy body bore him, certainly.
I kept them at Bologne in secrecy;
Take them again, for now thou canst not say
That either has been lost or put away.

"And those that otherwise have said of me,
I warn them well that nothing that I did
Was done in malice or in cruelty,
But to assay thy woman's virtue hid,
And not to slay my children, God forbid!
But to preserve them secret and apart
Until I knew thy purpose and thy heart."

And hearing this, down in a swoon she falleth
For piteous joy, and when the swoon had passed,
Her two young children unto her she calleth,
And then her arms, with piteous sobbing, cast
About them both, and kissed and held them fast
In tenderness, like any mother there,
And her tears bathed their faces and their hair.

O what a piteous thing it was to see
Her swooning, and her humble voice to hear!
"*Graunt merci*, lord; I thank you now," said she,
"That ye have saved me thus my children dear.
I care not now though I should die right here!
For since my heart your love and favor knows,
Death matters not, nor when my spirit goes!

"O my dear children, young and newly flowered,
Your woeful mother feared that it must be
That cruel dogs or vermin had devoured
Your bodies both; but God, in clemency,
And your dear father, acting lovingly,
Hath kept you well;" and with that word once more
All suddenly she swooned upon the floor.

And in her swoon with such tenacity
She held her children in her firm embrace,
That they must labor long and skilfully
From her tight clutch the children to unlace.
O many a tear on many a pitying face
Fell down the cheeks of those that stood and eyed her;
Scarcely could they endure to stay beside her.

Now Walter cheered her and her grief grew less,
And all abashed she rose up from the floor,
And all there strove to give her happiness,
Till she recovered countenance once more;
And Walter sought to gladden and restore
Her heart, so faithfully that it was rare
To see their joy, once more together there.

The ladies, when they saw their chance occur.
Into a chamber took her off alone,
And of her rude array divested her;
And in a cloth of gold that brightly shone,
And on her head a crown with many a stone
Of price, once more they brought her to the hall,
Where she was fitly honored by them all.

Thus had this piteous day a happy ending,
For man and woman, each with all his might,
The livelong day in mirth and revel spending,
Rejoiced until the stars in heaven were bright;
This day was far more splendid in men's sight
And greater in expense and preparation
Than that which saw her marriage celebration.

For many a year in high prosperity
These two lived on, in quiet concord blest;
His daughter he hath married splendidly
Unto a lord, one of the worthiest
In Italy; and then in peace and rest
The father of his wife at court he kept
Until the soul out of his body crept.

His son succeeded him in his estate
In rest and peace, after his father's day,
And he in marriage too was fortunate,
But tested not his wife in such a way.
This world is not so strong, say what ye may,
As once in older times of which ye heard,
And therefore listen to this author's word.

This tale is told, not to suggest that wives
Follow Grisilda in humility;
For they could not endure it, for their lives;
But to incite each person in degree
To steadfastness beneath adversity
Like to Grisilda's – therefore Petrarch writes
This story, which with high style he indites.

For since a woman was so patient
Unto a mortal man, the more we ought
Receive with meekness all that God hath sent;
For it is sure, He testeth what He wrought.
But any He hath saved, He tempteth not,
As doth Saint James in his epistle say;
Although no doubt He tests men every day;

And thus provides that we be exercised
With the sharp scourges of adversity
In various ways, that we may be chastised;
Not to discern our will, for certainly
Ere we were born, He knew our frailty;
And for the best is all His ordination –
Then let us live in virtuous resignation.

But one word ere I leave you finally –
It would be hard today, though ye should pass
Through all a town, to find even two or three
Grisildas, for in such assays, alas!
Their gold, so badly now alloyed with brass,
Though in the coin it might be fair to view,
Before it bend, would surely break in two!

And therefore, for the Wife of Bath's sweet sake,
Whose life and all her tribe may God support
In dominance, or it were a sad mistake,
With a fresh heart and green, to give you sport,
I sing a song now, of a lusty sort;
And let us leave all earnestness, and hear
My song, which goes as shortly shall appear.

L'Envoy de Chaucer

Grisilda and her patience both are dead,
And buried deep in some Italian vale;
And so from me to all men be it said:
Let no man have the daring to assail
The patience of his wife in hope to find
Grisilda's, since for certain he shall fail!

O noble wives, of prudent heart and head,
Let no humility your sharp tongues nail,
And let no scholar's diligence be fed
To write of you as marvellous a tale
As was Grisilda's, patient, meek, and kind,
Lest Chivevache attack you, and prevail!

But be like Echo, never quieted,
That always answers from the hill or dale;
Let not your innocence be cause of dread,
But sharply for the mastery assail;
Imprint this lesson well upon your mind
For profit; ye may find it of avail.

Archwives, as strong as any camel bred,
Stand in defense, and never flinch or pale;
Let no man harm you – punish him instead;
And slender wives, for battle weak and frail,

Be keen as any tiger in far Ind,
And clatter like a windmill in a gale!

Do them no reverence, be not in dread,
For though thy husband should be armed in mail,
Thy crabbèd eloquence like arrows sped
Would pierce his breast and break his aventail;
With jealousy thou mayst him also bind,
And thou shalt make him cringe like any quail.

If thou art fair, where crowds are gatherèd
Display thy raiment, and thy face unveil;
If thou be foul, then let thy gold be spread
And work for friends until thou dost prevail;
Be gay as any linden leaf in wind,
And let him weep and wring his hands and wail!

Here the Student of Oxford ends his Tale

The Merchant's Tale

THE MERCHANT HAS recently made an unhappy marriage and his tale reflects this in its theme. In his story, a beautiful young woman married to an aged and repulsive man plans an adulterous interlude with a virile young man. Although the plot is from the fabliau tradition, the merchant tells it in a lofty and courtly style with ornate description and classical reference. The tale echoes elements of the Student's Tale which precedes it.

The Merchant's Tale

The Prologue to the Merchant's Tale

"WEEPING and wailing, care and other sorrow
I know enough, by even-tide and morrow,"
This merchant said, "and so do others, too,
Among the married – yea, I hold it true,
For well I know it goes like that with me.
I have a wife – the worst that there could be –
For though the devil and she were made to pair it,
Yet she would get the best of him, I swear it!
Why should I tell you here the mean and small ways
Her malice has? She is a shrew in all ways!
There is a difference large as it is long
Between Grisilda's patience and the strong
And unexampled cruelty of my wife!
If I were free, as I may thrive in life,
I would not ever again endure the snare!
We wedded men – we live in grief and care;
Try it who will, and he shall find, I promise,
The truth of what I tell you, by St. Thomas –
As to most cases, not indeed in all –
Nay, God forbid that *that* should ever fall!
    "Sir Host, by God, it is a two months' span –
No more – since I became a married man;
And yet I know that one who hath been wifeless
For all his days, though ye should strike him lifeless,
Rending his heart, could not describe such woe
As I could of the cursedness I know,
If something of my wedded life I gave you."
    "Now," cried our Host, "Merchant, as God may save you,

Since ye have learned so well the art of it,
Tell us, I pray you well, some part of it!"
    "Gladly; and yet I cannot, for distress,
Speak further of mine own unhappiness."

Here begins the Merchant's Tale

ONCE on a time a knight of high degree,
Though born in Pavia, dwelt in Lombardy,
And there he lived a rich and prosperous life.
For sixty years this knight had had no wife,
But ever fed his bodily delight
On women, where he had an appetite,
As foolish laymen do. But when at last
With course of time his sixtieth year was passed,
In dotage, or in fear for his salvation
I know not which, a great determination
Fell on this knight to be a wedded man,
And day and night he labors all he can
To find where he might marry fittingly,
Praying our Lord to grant him clemency
That he for once might know the blissful life
Shared always by a husband and his wife,
Living beneath the bond God gave to man
And women when their common life began.
"No other life is worth a bean, for sure,
For wedlock is so easy and so pure,
That here on earth it is a paradise!"
Thus said this knight, who thought himself so wise.
    And certainly, as sure as God is king,
To take a wife, it is a glorious thing,
Especially when a man is old and hoary.
Then of his treasure is she fruit and glory.
Then should he take a young wife and a fair,
On whom he can beget himself an heir,
And live his life in joy and merriment
While bachelors go sing their discontent
When they encounter some adversity
In love, which is but childish vanity.
And truly it is well that this is so –
That bachelors should often have their woe.

Building on sand, they look for surety,
And find no thing but insecurity.
They live their lives like any beast or bird,
In liberty, by no restraint deterred,
Whereas a married man lives with his wife
A blissful and a regulated life,
Bound underneath the yoke of wedded bliss;
Well may his heart laugh and rejoice in this.
For who can be so humble and so true
As is a wife? And so attentive, too,
Whether her mate be whole, or sickness take him?
For weal or woe, she never will forsake him.
She never tires to love him and attend,
Though he may lie bedridden to his end.
And yet some clerks deny it and oppose –
This Theophrastus – he is one of those.
What matter, though, if Theophrastus lie?
"Take not a wife," he said, "and save thereby
That which would cost thy household much expense;
A faithful servant shows more diligence
To save thy property than thine own wife.
For she will claim her half part all her life;
And, God so save me, if thou shouldst be ill,
A faithful boy will show a better will
To nurse thee – or thy friends – than she who waits,
And long has, for thy goods and thine estates.
And she thou tak'st, in hope that she will love thee,
Can all too easy make a cuckold of thee."
These things, and hundreds worse in every way,
The fellow writes. God curse his bones, I say!
But give no heed to all such vanity –
Spurn Theophrastus; listen now to me.

A wife is God's gift, utterly and purely,
For other gifts, as ye must know too surely –
Estates and rents, pasture or common land,
Or furniture, these come from Fortune's hand,
And pass like any shadow on a wall;
But, doubtless, speaking frankly to you all,
A wife will last, and in your house endure –
Longer than it may please you, to be sure.

High sacrament is marriage justly named;

A man that has no wife – I hold him shamed;
Helpless he lives and wholly desolate –
I speak of men of secular estate.
And hear why, for not idly is this stated:
To be man's helpmate woman was created.
When high God, shaping Adam from the clay,
Saw him alone, and naked as the day,
In His great goodness God divulged His plan:
"Let us now make a helper for this man
Like to himself," and then created Eve.
Here ye may see, and thus the proof receive
That in a wife man's help and solace lies,
His pleasure and terrestrial paradise.
So good and so obedient is she,
They cannot help but live in unity.
One flesh they are, and one flesh, I should guess,
Has but one heart, in woe or happiness.

A wife! Ah, by St. Mary – *ben'cité*!
How could a man have any adversity
That has a wife? Indeed, I cannot say.
The bliss that binds their union, day by day,
No heart can dream of, and no tongue can tell.
If he is poor, she labors with him well;
She keeps his goods, and never wastes a mite;
Her husband's will is always her delight;
When he says, "Yes," then never a "No" will be;
"Do this," he cries; "All ready, sir," says she.
O precious wedlock! blissful, ordered state,
Thou art so pleasant, thy virtues are so great,
And so approved wherever men may speak,
That any man that holds him worth a leek
Should on his bare knees, all his live-long life,
Give God his thanks for sending him a wife,
Or pray to God that He will quickly send
A wife, to last him till his life shall end.
For then his life will be a thing secure;
He cannot be deceived, I hold it sure,
If he have her advice to guide him by;
Then can he boldly hold his head up high,
So wise are wives in all ways, and so true;
Therefore, if thou wouldst do as wise men do,

By woman's counsel always shape thy deed.

Lo, see how Jacob, as these scholars read,
Did what his dame, Rebecca, had advised him,
And with a kid's skin on his neck disguised him,
And won his father's blessing in this way.

Lo, Judith, likewise, as the legends say,
By her wise counsel God's own people kept,
And slew great Holofernes as he slept.

Lo, Abigail, whose wisdom, it is plain,
Saved Nabal, who had otherwise been slain;
And think of Esther, too, that, as ye know,
By wise advice delivered from their woe
The people of God, and worked so Mordecai
Was by Ahasuerus set on high.

Nothing is more superlative in life,
As Seneca tells us, than a humble wife.

Bear thy wife's tongue, as Cato bids thee do;
She shall command, and thou permit her to;
She will obey at times, in courtesy!
A wife will keep thy household frugally;
Well may the sick man lift his voice, and weep,
Who has no wife about, his house to keep.
I warn thee, if thou wouldst with wisdom work,
Love thy wife well, just as Christ does his kirk.
Love but thyself, and thou must love thy wife;
No man can hate his flesh, but all his life
He fosters it; so, while thou art alive,
Cherish thy wife, or thou shalt never thrive.
Husband and wife – let people jest and play –
Among the worldly hold the safest way.
They are so knit that no adversity
Can harm them – through the wife, especially.
Therefore this January, of whom I told,
Considered well, as he was growing old,
The lusty life, the virtuous peace replete,
That seemed to lie in marriage honey-sweet;
And sent a summons to his friends one day
To tell them all where his intention lay.

With a grave countenance his tale he told:
He said: "Friends, I am growing hoar and old,
Close to the grave, God knows – yea, near the brink;

So of my soul a little I must think;
My body I have foolishly expended –
Blessèd be God, that it shall be amended!
For I will be, indeed, a wedded man,
And that, too, with the utmost speed I can,
Seeking some maid of tender years, and fair.
I pray you then, work quickly to prepare
My marriage, for I will no longer tarry.
And I myself shall look for one to marry
Promptly, if such a maid I can espy.
But since ye are so many more than I,
Ye should the rather look for this alliance
Than I, and tell me whom I should affiance.

"But this, dear friends, in warning let me say:
I will have no old wife in any way;
For more than twenty years she must not be;
Old fish, young fowl, shall be the dish for me.
Better a pike than pickerel," he said,
"And no old beef, but tender veal instead;
No wife of thirty years – let that be law;
They are coarse fodder only, and bean-straw.
And these old widows, too, as God doth know,
Have such a craft for making Wade's boat go,
So many cunning dodges when they please,
That I could never live with them in ease.
Clerks taught at several schools do subtle work;
A woman doubly schooled is half a clerk;
But a young girl, indeed, responds to leading,
As warm wax in the hands will shape with kneading.
And therefore, for the reasons ye have heard,
I say, I want no old wife, in a word.
For if, unhappily, it should occur
That I could have no kind of joy in her,
Then I should sink to an adulterer's level,
And when I died, go straightway to the devil!
Nor might she bear me children, to complete me –
And yet I should prefer that dogs should eat me
Than that the heritage I have should fall
Into strange hands, and this I tell you all.
I do not dote, for I can plainly tell
Why men should marry, and I know as well

The prologe of the Marchantes Tale ❧❧

WEPYNG and waylyng, care and oother sorwe
I knowe ynogh, on even and a morwe,
Quod the Marchant, and so doon othere mo
That wedded been, I trowe that it be so;
for wel I woot, it fareth so with me.
I have a wyf, the worste that may be;
for thogh the feend to hire ycoupled were,
She wolde hym overmacche, I dar wel swere.
What sholde I yow reherce in special
Hir hye malice? She is a shrewe at al.
Ther is a long and large difference
Bitwix Grisildis grete pacience
And of my wyf the passyng crueltee.
Were I unbounden, al so moot I thee!
I wolde nevere eft comen in the snare.
We wedded men lyve in sorwe and care.
Assaye whoso wole, and he shal fynde
I seye sooth, by Seint Thomas of Ynde,
As for the moore part, I sey nat alle;
God shilde that it sholde so bifalle!
A! good sir Hoost! I have ywedded bee
Thise monthes two, and moore nat, pardee!
And yet, I trowe, he that al his lyve
Wyflees hath been, though that men wolde him ryve
Unto the herte, ne koude in no manere
Tellen so muchel sorwe, as I now heere
Koude tellen of my wyves cursednesse!
❧ Now, quod our Hoost, Marchant, so God yow blesse!
Syn ye so muchel knowen of that art,
ful hertely I pray yow telle us part.
❧ Gladly, quod he, but of myn owene soore,
for soory herte, I telle may namoore.

HEERE BIGYNNETH THE MARCHANTES TALE ❧❧

WHER was dwellynge in Lumbardye
A worthy knyght, that born was of Pavye,
In which he lyved in greet prosperitee;
And sixty yeer a wyflees man was hee,
And folwed ay his bodily delyt
On wommen, theras was his appetyt,
As doon thise fooles that been seculeer,
And whan that he was passed sixty yeer,
Were it for hoolynesse or for dotage
I kan nat seye, but swich a greet corage
Hadde this knyght to been a wedded man,
That day and nyght he dooth al that he kan
Tespien where he myghte wedded be;
Preyinge oure Lord to granten him, that he
Mighte ones knowe of thilke blisful lyf
That is bitwixe an housbonde and his wyf;
And for to lyve under that hooly bond
With which that first God man and womman bond.
❧ Noon oother lyf, seyde he, is worth a bene;
for wedlok is so esy and so clene,
That in this world it is a paradys.❧
Thus seyde this olde knyght, that was so wys.

AND certeinly, as sooth as God is kyng,
To take a wyf, it is a glorious thyng;
And namely whan a man is oold and hoor,
Thanne is a wyf the fruyt of his tresor.
Thanne sholde he take a yong wyf and a feir,
On which he myghte engendren hym an heir,
And lede his lyf in joye and in solas;
Wheras thise bacheleres synge Allas!
Whan that they fynden any adversitee
In love, which nys but childyssh vanytee.
And trewely it sit wel to be so,
That bacheleres have often peyne and wo;
On brotel ground they buylde, & brotelnesse
They fynde, whan they wene sikernesse.
They lyve but as a bryd or as a beest,
In libertee, and under noon arreest,
Theras a wedded man in his estaat
Lyveth a lyf blisful and ordinaat,
Under the yok of mariage ybounde.
Wel may his herte in joye & blisse habounde;
for who kan be so buxom as a wyf?
Who is so trewe, and eek so ententyf
To kepe hym, syk and hool, as is his make?
for wele or wo she wole hym nat forsake.
She nys nat wery hym to love and serve,
Thogh that he lye bedrede til he sterve.

AND yet somme clerkes seyn it nys nat so,
Of whiche he, Theofraste, is oon of tho.
What force though Theofraste liste lye?
❧ Ne take no wyf, quod he, for housbond-rye,
As for to spare in houshold thy dispence;
A trewe servant dooth moore diligence
Thy good to kepe, than thyn owene wyf,

Plate 21: The Merchant's Tale (p. 258)

That many a man will talk of marrying,
Though like my page he hardly knows a thing
Of why a man should think to take a wife.
If he cannot live chastely all his life
Let him then take a wife, with piety,
And lawfully beget his progeny
In honor of the God that sits above,
And not alone for paramours or love;
And thus the snares of lechery eschew,
And promptly pay his debt when it is due;
Or that the one of them can help the other
In ill days, as a sister will a brother,
And live a holy life in chastity;
But such, sirs, by your leave, is not for me.
For, God be thanked, I will not hesitate
To say my limbs are strong and adequate
For everything a man should carry through;
And I myself know best what I can do.
For I, though white of hair, am like a tree
That blooms before the fruit shall come to be;
A blossoming tree is neither dry nor dead,
And I am hoary only on my head.
My heart is green, and all my limbs are, too,
As any laurel fresh the whole year through.
And having heard my purpose in this way,
Agree, I pray, with what I have to say."

    Then various men in various ways related
Old instances of marriage consummated.
Some blamed it, and indeed some praised it, too;
But in the end, to make no more ado,
As any day will come an altercation
When friends engage themselves in conversation,
His own two brothers to a quarrel came;
And one of these Placebo was by name;
Justinus, of a truth, men called the other.

    Placebo said: "O January, my brother,
Small need had ye, belovèd lord and dear,
To ask advice of any that is here;
But ye are filled with such a high discretion
That ye are disinclined to make transgression
Of that good word spoken by Solomon.

This good advice he gave us, every one:
'Act in all things by counsel,' was his sentence,
'And thou shalt have no reason for repentance.'
And yet, though Solomon spoke such a word,
My own belovèd brother and my lord,
May God as surely bring my soul to rest
As I approve your counsel as the best.
For, dear my brother, let this thought sink in:
All of my life a courtier have I been,
And though I never merited such grace,
Yet by my fortune I have had a place
Close unto lords that were of lofty station,
And yet with none have had an altercation.
I never would oppose them or deny:
I knew well that my lord knew more than I.
For what he said I held was true and stable,
And said the same, or as near as I was able;
For he is but a fool, it seems to me,
Who serves with any lord of high degree,
And dares presume (or even dream of it)
His counsel may exceed his master's wit.
Nay, by my faith, lords are not fools, I say.
For ye yourself have shown us here today
Wisdom so holy, high, and well-expressed,
That I agree throughout, and well attest
The truth of all your words, and what ye plan.
By God, in all this town is not a man
Could speak so well, no, nor in Italy.
Christ with this counsel gladly will agree.
Truly, it is a noble soul appears
In any man so well advanced in years
To take a young wife! By my father's kin,
I say your heart hangs on a jolly pin!
Do as it pleases you in this affair,
For, in conclusion, that is best, I swear."

    Justinus, that in silence sat and heard,
Made answer to Placebo with this word:
"Now brother mine, sit patiently, I pray,
Since ye have spoken, and hear what I shall say.
Seneca says, among his other saws,
A man should ponder well, and with good cause,

To whom he gives his land or property.
And since I should consider carefully
To whom I give the goods I have in store,
I think I should consider even more
To whom I give my body, for I say –
To warn you well – that it is no child's play
To take a wife except on long reflection.
A man must ask, before he makes selection,
If she is wise, or staid, or given to drink,
Or proud, or bad in other ways, I think;
If she is wasteful, or will scold or rant,
Is rich or poor, or is a termagant.
And though in all the world no man shall see
One that in all these ways trots perfectly,
As he would wish – Nay, neither man nor beast –
Nevertheless, it should suffice at least
With any wife, if she is better stored
With virtues than with traits to be deplored;
And all this needs some searching to appear.
For God knows I have shed full many a tear
In secret since the time I took a wife.
Let him who will extol a husband's life –
I find it nothing but expense and care,
And watching, and its joys but thin and bare.
And yet, God knows, my neighbors next to me,
And droves of women, sir, especially,
Say that I have a firm and steadfast wife,
The meekest, too, that lives this earthly life;
But I know where the pinch is in my shoe.
For all of me, do as ye like to do.
Ye are a man of years – then hesitate
Before ye enter on the married state,
Especially with a young wife and a fair.
By Him that made the water, earth, and air,
The youngest man in all this company
Will labor hard to have the certainty
That he enjoys his wife alone, I say.
Ye will not please her three years, anyway –
That is to say, win her full approbation.
A wife needs much in careful ministration.
Be not aggrieved at what I say to you."

"Well," said this January, "and art thou through?
A straw for Seneca and all his laws!
I would not give a basket-ful of haws
For all thy school-terms; wiser men than thou,
As thou hast heard, are in agreement now
About my purpose; Placebo, what say ye?"
   "I say, it is a cursèd man," said he,
"That would prevent a marriage, or oppose."
And with that word they suddenly arose,
And all are in agreement that he should
Be wedded when he pleased and where he would.
   Now careful thoughts of how he ought to marry
Mingled within the soul of January
Day after day, with visions high and rare.
Many fair forms, and many a face as fair
Went passing through his heart, night after night
As one who takes a mirror burnished bright,
And sets it in the general market place,
Shall there behold full many a figure pace
Within his mirror – so in the same way
The thoughts of January began to play
Among the maidens that were dwelling by him.
He could not tell which best would satisfy him.
For if one had a loveliness of face
Another stood so well in people's grace
For sober ways and kindness, that these gave her
The greatest voice to have the people's favor.
Though rich, some had a name not of the best.
But in the end, through earnestness and jest,
He found one maiden that he set apart,
And let the others vanish from his heart,
And chose her, on his own authority,
For love is always blind, and cannot see.
At night, as in his bed he lay reclining,
He saw in heart and mind fair visions shining
Of her fresh beauty and her youth so tender,
Her little waist, her arms so long and slender,
And thought her wise and staid as he had seen her,
Of gentle ways and womanly demeanor.
And once his fancy by this maid was caught,
His choice could not have been improved, he thought;

For having pleased himself, the man was sure
That others' wit and judgment were so poor
That none could by a possibility
Challenge his choice: this was his fantasy.
He sent then for his friends without delay,
Urging them all his pleasure to obey,
And come at once in answer to his call;
For he would end their labors, one and all.
No need to walk or ride another day
On his account; he knew where he would stay.

    Placebo came; his friends, too, followed soon;
And first of all he craved of them a boon:
That none of them an argument would make
Against the course that he proposed to take,
"Which was a course pleasing to God," said he,
"And a sure ground for his prosperity."

    He said, there was a maiden in the town
That for her beauty had a great renown,
Although she was a maid of low degree;
Her youth and beauty were sufficiency
For him. And her he wanted for his wife,
To lead a pleasant and a holy life;
And thanked God he could have her all alone,
Sharing with none the bliss to be his own;
And prayed them all to labor in this need,
And by their help assure him to succeed,
For then, he said, his mind would be at rest.
"And then for nothing shall I be distressed,
Save that my conscience has a prick or two
For one thing I shall now explain to you."

    "I have long since," he said, "heard men say this:
No man can twice attain a perfect bliss –
That is to say, on earth and then in heaven.
For though he keep from sin, yea, all the seven,
And every branch of that accursèd tree,
Yet married life is such an ecstasy,
In such a peace and perfect rapture passed,
That in my age I find myself aghast
To think that I shall live so merry a life,
So ravishing, so free from woe and strife,
That I shall have my heaven on earth thereby.

For since true heaven is always priced so high,
Being bought with penance, pain, and tribulation,
How then should I, that live the consummation
Of joy, that all men know who wed like me,
Come to the bliss of Christ's eternity?
This is my fear, and ye, my brothers two,
Resolve this question now, I beg of you."

    Justinus, with a mocking voice and eye –
For he despised his folly – made reply,
Citing no learned books for what he said,
Since he would make his story brief instead.
"Sire, if this obstacle of which ye tell
Is all, then God may work his miracle,
And in His mercy so may deal with you,
That, ere of Holy Church ye get your due,
Ye may repent you of this wedded life
In which ye say there is no woe or strife.
And God forbid that grace should not be sent
A wedded man, through which he may repent,
More often than to any single man!
And, to advise you now as best I can,
Despair not, sire, of your eternal glory,
For she, perhaps, may be your purgatory.
Yes, she may be God's instrument and whip;
Then up to heaven, through her, your soul shall skip
Swifter than any arrow from a bow!
I hope to God, hereafter ye shall know
That there is no such great felicity
In marriage, and indeed shall never be,
That it will prove a bar to your salvation,
If you enjoy your wife in moderation –
And this is only just and reasonable –
And as a lover please her not too well,
And also keep yourself from other sin.
My tale is done; my wit is weak and thin.
Be not disturbed by this, my brother dear."
(But let us wade through all this matter here;
The Wife of Bath, if ye have understood,
Has told us well of marriage, ill and good –
Which is our subject – in a little space.)
"Fare well now, and God keep you in His grace!"

And with this word Justinus and his brother
Have taken their leave, each of them of the other.
For when they saw at last that it must be,
By contract they arranged it skilfully,
With prudence, that this maid, whose name was May,
Should with the shortest possible delay
Be bound in wedlock to this January.
I think it were too long for you to tarry
If I should tell what bonds and bills they planned,
By which she was enfeoffed with all his land,
Or tell of all this maiden's rich array
Against the wedding. Finally the day
Arrived, and to the church this couple went
There to receive the holy sacrament.
His stole about his neck, the priest appeared.
Like Sarah and Rebecca be revered,
He told her, as a wise wife and a true;
And prayed, as it is usual to do,
And asked God's grace, and with the cross he signed
     them,
And went through holy rites enough to bind them.

Thus they are married ceremoniously,
And at the feast are seated, he and she,
And other worthies on the dais there;
And joy was in the palace everywhere;
And music; and fair victual stood revealed,
The daintiest all Italy could yield.
And there were instruments to play upon,
So fine that Orpheus or Amphion
Never made melody so fine and proud.

With every course came minstrelsy so loud
That Joab's trumpet never rang more cheerly,
Nor did Theodamus play half so clearly
At Thebes, when there was peril in that land.
And Bacchus poured his wine on every hand,
And laughing Venus filled them with delight.
For January had now become her knight,
And he would doubly prove his spirit now,
In freedom, and beneath the marriage vow,
And torch in hand, she dances merrily
Before the bride, and all the company.

And of a certainty, I dare say this:
That Hymen, that the god of weddings is,
Never had seen so merry a wedded man.
Now hold thy peace, thou poet Martian,
That tell'st us of the rites that merrily
United Hermes and Philology,
And of the songs made by the muses then.
Thy language is too feeble, and thy pen,
To paint this marriage on a written page.
When tender youth has wedded stooping age
There is such mirth that none may write about it.
Try it yourself, and see then, if ye doubt it,
Whether I lie or not in this affair.

May sat there with so ravishing an air
It was as if she cast a faery spell.
Queen Esther never let her eyes so dwell
Upon Ahasuerus, with a glance
So meek. I cannot paint her radiance
In full for you, but thus much I can say:
That she was bright as morning is in May,
And full of all sweet beauty and delight.

Each time he fed his eyes upon this sight
Old January sat ravished in a trance.
And in his heart the threat began to dance
That he would clasp her soon with such an ardor
That Paris never strained Queen Helen harder
Against his breast. And yet his mood was tender
To think how with the night he must offend her.
"Alas!" he thought, "O tender thing and pure,
I would to God that ye could well endure
All of my love! So it is sharp and strong
I fear ye cannot well sustain it long!
Yet God forbid I work with all my power …
I would that it were night this very hour,
And that the night forever more would stay.
I wish these people all were gone away!"
And finally, as well as he can plan,
Saving his honor, he does the best he can
To speed them from the feast in shortest season.

The time came when to rise was only reason,
And then to dance and drink the people fall,

And spices strew about by room and hall,
And full of joy and bliss was every man –
All but a squire, a youth called Damian,
Who carved before the knight on many a day.
He was so ravished with his lady May
Pain all but drove his reason from its seat;
Almost he swooned and fainted on his feet,
So sorely Venus hurt him with her brand
As she went dancing by him, torch in hand;
And to his bed in haste he stole away.
Now for the time no more of him I say,
But leave him there to weep and to complain
Till lovely May has pity on his pain.

Author: O perilous fire that in the bedstraw lurks!
O household foe, eager for evil works!
O traitor-servant, truthful still of mien,
O adder in the bosom, false, unseen,
God from acquaintance with you shield us all!
O January, drunk with the festival
Of marriage, see now how thy Damian,
Thine own squire, that was born thy very man,
Is scheming in his heart to bring thee woe.
God grant thou mayst espy thine household foe,
For in this world no worse a plague can try thee
Than such a foe forever dwelling by thee.
    The sun had traversed his diurnal arc;
His body could no longer hold the dark
From the horizon, in that latitude.
Night came, and spread his mantle dark and rude,
The hemisphere about to overcloud.
And so departed all this lusty crowd
From January, with thanks on every side.
Home to their houses merrily they ride,
Each busy there with that which pleased him best,
And when their time had come, they went to rest.
Soon after that this eager January
Must go to bed, no longer would he tarry;
But first drank claret to increase his spirit,
And spiced vernage as strong as he could bear it
And many a fortifying syrop fine,

Such as the cursèd monk Sir Constantine
Describes well in his book, *De Coitu*;
He took them all, omitting none he knew,
And to his close friends whispered urgently,
"For love of God, as soon as it may be,
In courteous fashion get them to retire!"
And soon they managed after his desire;
Men drank, then forth to draw the curtain sped;
Still as a stone, the bride was brought to bed.
Then came the priest, the bed was duly blessed,
Forth from the room departed every guest,
And January with May in rapture lies,
Clasping his fresh young mate, his paradise.
He lulled and kissed her, and her cheek was speared
With bristles of his thick and prickly beard,
Sharp as the skin of dogfish, or a briar,
For he was newly shorn. Hot with desire
He rubbed her tender face, and said to her:
"Alas! Now must I be a trespasser
On you, my wife, and I may much offend
Before the time shall come when I descend.
Yet none the less, consider this," said he;
"There is no workman, whosoever he be,
That works in haste, whose work will bear inspection;
And this needs leisure to attain perfection.
It matters not how long we lie at play;
We two are joined in wedlock from this day,
And blessèd be the yoke that we are in,
For nothing that we do can be a sin.
A man can do no sin with his own wife;
He cannot hurt himself with his own knife,
For by the law we have full leave to play."
And so he labored till the break of day,
Then in fine clarey dipped a sop of bread,
And ate, and then he sat erect in bed,
And fell to singing in a loud, clear strain,
And kissed his wife, and played with her again.
Coltish he was, riding his passion high,
And full of chatter as a speckled pie.
And while he sang the slack skin at his throat
Shook, and he chanted with a croaking note.

God knows what thoughts this fair May had to hide
While in his shirt he sat there by her side,
With night-cap, and his neck all loose and lean;
She did not think his capers worth a bean!
"The day is come," he said, "and I will take
My rest; for now I cannot stay awake;"
And so lay down, and slept till it was prime.
Then somewhat later, when he thought it time,
This January arose; but fresh young May
Kept to her chamber unto the fourth day,
As wives still do by custom, for the best.
For every labor must be crowned with rest,
Or he that labors cannot long endure;
That is, no living creature can, for sure,
Be it a fish, or bird, or beast, or man.

    Now will I speak of woeful Damian,
That languishes for love, as ye shall hear;
And I address him as will now appear.
I say: "O hapless Damian, alas!
Answer to what I ask thee in this pass!
How shalt thou tell thy lovely lady May
The woe thou hast? For she will answer, 'Nay;'
And also, if thou speak, she will betray thee;
All I can say is, May God help and stay thee."

    This fevered Damian in Venus' fire
So burns, he all but dies of his desire.
And so he puts his life on the assay;
He could not suffer longer in this way.
In secrecy a pen-case did he borrow,
And in a letter wrote out all his sorrow,
Giving it form of a complaint or lay
Unto his fresh and lovely lady May,
And put it in a silken purse, and strung it
Over his shirt; against his heart he hung it.

    The moon, that at the noontide of that day
When January had wedded fresh young May,
In Taurus hung, had into Cancer passed –
So long had May kept to her chamber fast,
As do these noble ladies, one and all.
A bride must never eat within the hall
Until four days go by, or three at least;

Then let her go, indeed, and join the feast.
From noon to noon the fourth day now was sped,
And so, the high mass being duly said,
This January sits in his hall, and May,
As fresh as any shining summer's day.
And now it happened that this worthy man
Called to his memory this Damian.
"St. Mary!" he exclaimed, "how can it be
That Damian is not here to wait on me?
What is the cause? Is he still sick?" he cried.
His squires, that stood in waiting at his side,
Excused him; for his sickness, as they said,
Hindered his duty; were he not a-bed
No other cause, indeed, could make him tarry.

    "That grieves me greatly," said this January;
"For by my faith, a gentle squire is he;
If he should die, it were calamity;
He is as wise, as subtle, and discreet
In his degree as any ye may meet,
Ready to serve, and ever manly, too,
And like to prosper ere his days are through.
But after meat I shall not long delay
To visit him myself, and so shall May,
To give him all the comfort that I can."
And for that word they blessed him, every man,
That had in noble kindness this desire
To go and bring such comfort to his squire
That lay there sick. It was a noble deed.
"Dame," said this January, "take good heed
That after meat, ye and your women all,
Returning to your chamber from this hall,
Go all of you to see this Damian;
And cheer him up; he is a gentle man;
And tell him I will visit him as well
When I have rested but a little spell.
And do it quickly; I will wait for you
To come and sleep by me when ye are through."
And with that word he raised his voice to call
A squire, one that was marshal of his hall,
And told him certain things he wished to say.

    Then with her women fresh and lovely May

Went straight to Damian's chamber after that,
And close beside his bed this lady sat,
And gave him all she could of happy cheer.
This Damian, when he saw his time appear,
In secret slipped the purse, in which reposed
The rhyme in which his passion was disclosed,
Into the hand of May, and did no more,
Save that he sighed then wondrous deep and sore,
And in a whisper said, "Mercy, I pray thee!
And for the love of God, do not betray me,
For I am dead if this should come to light!"
She slipped it in her bosom out of sight,
And went her way; ye get no more from me.
Back to this January repaireth she,
Who sat upon his bed and waited for her.
He took her, and with kisses overbore her,
And then lay down, and soon he slept, indeed.
And she pretended she must go of need
Where all folk must, as ye are well aware.
When she had read the note she carried there,
She tore it into little bits at last,
And in the privy all the pieces cast.

Who ponders now but fresh and lovely May?
Down by this aged January she lay,
Who slept until awakened by his cough.
He prayed her then to take her garments off,
For he would have, he said, some pleasure of her,
And clothes were an encumbrance to a lover;
And like the thing or not, she must obey.
Some nice folk might be angry should I say
How he performed, and so I dare not tell,
Or whether she thought it paradise or hell;
But at their work the afternoon they passed
Till evensong, when they must rise at last.

Now were it chance or destiny began it,
Or nature, by the working of some planet
Or constellations shaping such a state
Within the skies, that it was fortunate
To slip a billet of Venus on that day
(For all things have their times, as scholars say)
To any woman, with hope to win her love,

I cannot say; but the great God above
Who knows that cause and act can never cease –
Let Him decide, for I will hold my peace.
But this is true, that what occurred that day
Made such impression on this fresh young May,
Rousing her pity for sick Damian,
That in her heart, let her do what she can,
The wish to heal this lover haunts her still.
She thought: "Let this displease whomever it will –
Here I assure him, all my promise giving,
To love him best of any creature living,
Although his shirt were all that he possessed."
Ah, swift is pity in a noble breast!

Here ye may see the generosity
Of women, when they ponder carefully.
Some tyrant (and indeed, there's many a one!)
That has a heart as hard as any stone,
Might have preferred to be his murderer
Than grant the grace he begged so hard of her,
Would have rejoiced in cruel, unyielding pride,
And cared not though she were a homicide!

This gentle May, with pity sorely smitten,
A letter with her own fair hand hath written,
In which she fully granted him her grace;
Only the day was lacking, and the place,
Where pain and passion both should be appeased;
For all should be, she wrote him, as he pleased.

And when she saw her time, upon a day,
To visit Damian goes lovely May,
And slipped beneath his pillow, soft and still,
Her letter. Let him read it if he will!
She took his hand, and hard she wrung and pressed it.
So secretly, that there was none that guessed it,
And bade him soon be whole, and forth she went
To January, when after her he sent.

And Damian arises on the morrow;
All vanished are his sickness and his sorrow.
He preens and pranks himself, and combs his hair,
And does his lady's liking well and fair,
And unto January he is as docile
As any dog is to the bowman's whistle;

And speaks to all in such a pleasant way
(If one can use it, tact will always pay)
None has a word to say of him but good;
And fully in his lady's grace he stood.
Now let him do the things he has to do
While I proceed to tell my tale to you.
　　Some writers say he wins the fullest measure
Of happiness who gets the greatest pleasure;
And so this January, with all his might,
And honorably, as well befits a knight,
Had planned his life to live in happiness.
His house was wrought, his furnishings and dress,
As nobly for his station as a king's.
And there he fashioned, among other things,
A garden, that was walled about with stone;
Nowhere was any fairer garden known.
For past all doubt, I must indeed suppose,
That he who wrote the Romance of the Rose
Could not describe the beauty of it well;
Nor would Priapus have the tongue to tell,
Though God of gardens and their flowering,
The beauty of the place, or of the spring
Beneath a laurel that was always green.
There many a time had Pluto and his queen
Prosperina, and all their company
Of fairies, it was said, with melody
Danced by the spring in sport, and made them merry.
　　This noble knight, this agèd January,
Loved so to walk and play within the wall
That he would trust the key to none at all
Except himself; for he would constantly
Bear for a gate a little silver key
With which he would unlock it when it pleased him.
And there in summer, when the longing seized him,
To pay his wife the debt that was her due,
With May his wife, and none beside the two,
He went, and things that were not done a-bed
There in the garden were performed and sped.
Thus in this way, for many a day full merry,
Lived lovely May and this old January.
But worldly joy, alas! endureth never

Neither for him, nor any man whatever.

Author: O chance, O Fortune, false and fickle one!
Dyed in deception, like the scorpion!
What words of flattery lie upon thy lip
While strikes thy tail, death poised upon the tip!
O brittle joy! O venom sweet and strange!
O monster, that canst paint a subtle change
Upon thy gifts, that seem so all-enduring
That high and low are victims of thy luring!
Why, having been his friend, as he believed,
Hast thou poor January thus deceived?
And now of both his eyes hast thou bereft him,
Until he cries that death alone is left him.
　　Alas! this generous, noble January,
So prosperous, so lusty, and so merry!
All suddenly goes blind – his eyesight fails!
How piteously he sighs and weeps and wails,
While fire of jealousy so rages through him,
With fear of folly that his wife might do him,
Searing his heart, that he were nothing loath
If someone with a sword had slain them both.
For while he lived and after he was buried
He wished her neither to be loved nor married,
But all in black to keep a widow's state,
Lone as the turtle that has lost its mate.
But in the end, after a month or two,
A little less at length his sorrow grew;
For when he knew that nothing else could be,
He took in patience his adversity;
Save that from this he never could recover:
That he continued to be jealous of her;
Which jealousy was so inordinate
That neither in his room, nor when he ate,
Nor in another place, if she went out,
Would he permit his wife to go about
Unless her hand in his he safely kept.
And lovely May for this cause often wept,
For now so sweetly she had come to cherish
Her Damian, that she thought that she must perish
Or have him at her will, to love and take.

She waited for her very heart to break.
   And on his part this lover Damian
Is sunk in sorrow more than any man
That ever was, for neither night nor day
Could he address a word to lovely May
Or speak his purpose with a lover's spirit,
But January would be sure to hear it,
That always had a hand upon her fast.
And yet by writing to and fro at last
He knew her meaning, and by secret signs;
And she too knew the end of his designs.

Author: O January, what profit or avail,
Though thou couldst see as far as ships can sail?
As well be blind and bear such treachery,
As be deceived, alack! when thou canst see.
Lo, what could Argus do, the hundred-eyed?
It made no difference how he peered or pried,
He was deceived – and others, too, God knows,
Not half so wise as often they suppose.
But skipping this is pleasure, so no more.
   This lovely May, of whom I spoke before,
Has pressed in wax the key which January
Had for the little gate, and used to carry,
And with it to his garden often went.
And Damian, that knew her full intent,
In secret had another like it made.
Now there is nothing more to be conveyed,
Except that if ye wait, there shall appear
A marvel through this key, which ye shall hear.

Author: O noble Ovid, God knowst thou sayst truly
There is no trick a lover will not duly
Unravel, long and hard though it may be.
Of Pyramus and Thisbe men may see
How, though so strictly guarded, after all
They spoke together, whispering through a wall;
Who could detect a ruse so strange and sly?
   But to my tale. Before eight days went by –
Before July – urged by his fair wife May,
This January was so possessed one day

To play about within his garden fair –
They two alone, with no attendants there –
That on a morning to this May he cries:
"Rise up, my wife, my noble lady, rise;
Sweet dove, the turtle in the sun is singing;
Winter is gone, and all his cold and stinging
Rains are no more; O dove-eyed sweetheart mine,
Come forth; thy breasts are lovelier than wine!
Walled is the garden safely, all about.
Come forth, my fair white spouse; ah, never a doubt
But thou hast pierced my very heart, O wife!
I've known no blemish in thee all my life.
Come, then, and let us go and take our pleasure;
I chose thee for my comfort, wife, and treasure!"
   Such lewd old words he spoke, this doting man;
And she has made a sign to Damian
That he should go before them with his key.
This Damian for the gate made instantly
And went inside, but took great pains to bear him
That none about should either see or hear him;
And crouched beneath a bush there, all alone.
   This January, as blind as any stone,
Holding May's hand, with no one else around,
Seeks the fresh beauty of the garden ground,
And claps the gate behind him suddenly.
"Now none is here," he said, "but thee and me,
Thee, wife, whom best of all the world I love.
For, by the Lord that sits in heaven above,
Far rather would I die upon a knife
Than to offend thee, dear and faithful wife!
For God's sake, give a little thought to this:
The way I chose thee – not for avarice,
But only for the love I had for thee.
And even if I am old and cannot see,
Be true to me, and I will tell thee why.
Three things for certain shall ye win thereby;
First, love of Christ; and for yourself great dower
Of honor; and my holdings, town and tower;
I give them to you – draw then as ye please
The deeds; tomorrow we shall finish these
Before the sun sets, as I hope for bliss!

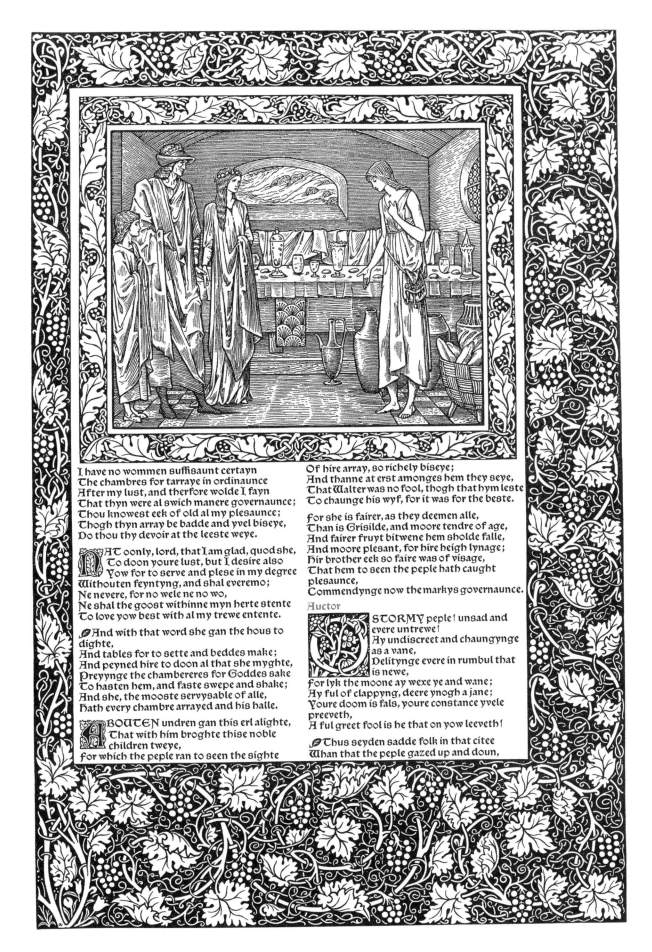

I have no wommen suffisaunt certayn
The chambres for tarraye in ordinaunce
After my lust, and therfore wolde I fayn
That thyn were al swich manere governaunce;
Thou knowest eek of old al my plesaunce;
Thogh thyn array be badde and yvel biseye,
Do thou thy devoir at the leeste weye.

NAT oonly, lord, that I am glad, quod she,
To doon youre lust, but I desire also
Yow for to serve and plese in my degree
Withouten feyntyng, and shal everemo;
Ne nevere, for no wele ne no wo,
Ne shal the goost withinne myn herte stente
To love yow best with al my trewe entente.

And with that word she gan the hous to
dighte,
And tables for to sette and beddes make;
And peyned hire to doon al that she myghte,
Preyynge the chambereres for Goddes sake
To hasten hem, and faste swepe and shake;
And she, the mooste servysable of alle,
Hath every chambre arrayed and his halle.

ABOUTEN undren gan this erl alighte,
That with him broghte thise noble
children tweye,
For which the peple ran to seen the sighte

Of hire array, so richely biseye;
And thanne at erst amonges hem they seye,
That Walter was no fool, thogh that hym leste
To chaunge his wyf, for it was for the beste.

For she is fairer, as they deemen alle,
Than is Grisilde, and moore tendre of age,
And fairer fruyt bitwene hem sholde falle,
And moore plesant, for hire heigh lynage;
Hir brother eek so faire was of visage,
That hem to seen the peple hath caught
plesaunce,
Commendynge now the markys governaunce.

Auctor

STORMY peple! unsad and
evere untrewe!
Ay undiscreet and chaungynge
as a vane,
Delitynge evere in rumbul that
is newe,
For lyk the moone ay wexe ye and wane;
Ay ful of clappyng, deere ynogh a jane;
Youre doom is fals, youre constance yvele
preeveth,
A ful greet fool is he that on yow leeveth!

Thus seyden sadde folk in that citee
Whan that the peple gazed up and doun,

Plate 22: The Student's Tale (p. 252)

And first, in covenant, I ask a kiss.
And though I may be jealous, yet be kind;
Ye are so deeply graven in my mind
That, when your beauty in my thought appears,
And I remember my unfitting years,
I cannot, though it were the death of me,
Bear any parting of our company
For very love; lo, this is past all doubt.
Now kiss me, wife, and let us roam about."

    This fair May, having heard these words he cried
All mild and kind to January replied,
But first, before she spoke, began to weep.
"I have," she said to him, "a soul to keep
As well as ye, and have mine honor, too,
And tender flower of wifehood, fresh and new,
Set in your hands, my lord, as justly due you
With the priest's words that bound my body to you.
Then by your leave, my lord I love so dear,
Thus will I speak in answer to you here:
I pray God there shall never dawn the day
I shall not die, as foul as woman may,
If I shall do my kin so great a shame
And so besmirch the honor of my name
As to be false; and if I do that sin,
Strip me, and get a sack to put me in,
And in the nearest river let me die.
A gentlewoman and no wench am I!
Why do ye speak like this? But falseness taints
You men – ye greet us still with fresh complaints!
Ye have no other pretext, I should guess,
But talk about reproof and faithlessness."

    And with that word she saw where Damian
Sat underneath the bush, and she began
To cough, and then made signals urgently
That Damian at once should climb a tree
Laden with fruit, and up this lover went,
For of a truth he knew well what she meant,
And all the meaning that her signs might carry
Better than did her husband, January.
For in a letter she had made it clear
How he should go about this matter here.

And thus I leave him sitting in the tree
While January and May roam merrily.
    Bright was the day and blue the firmament,
And Phœbus down his streams of gold hath sent
And with his bright warmth gladdened every flower.
He was, I think, in Gemini at that hour,
But close to Cancer and his declination,
Which brings to Jupiter his exaltation.
And so it fell, on that bright morning-tide,
That in the garden, at the farther side,
Pluto, that is the king of Fairyland,
With many a fairy lady in his band
All following his wife, Queen Proserpine,
Each after each, as straight as any line –
While she was gathering flowers in the mead,
Ye may in Claudian the story read
How off he bore her in his chariot grim –
This king of Fairyland now seated him
Upon a bench of turves all fresh and green,
And in this manner soon addressed his queen:
    "My wife," he said, "no one can say this Nay:
Experience keeps proving every day
The treason that ye women do to men.
Of your untruth and fickleness, again,
Ten hundred thousand stories could be told.
O Solomon, so shrewd, so rich in gold,
So full of worldly glory, and so wise,
Thy words are worthy ones to keep and prize
For all who value wit and reason well.
The good that lies in men now hear him tell:
'Among a thousand men I found but one;
Among all living women I found none.'
    "Thus says the king that knows your wickedness;
And Jesus, son of Sirach, as I guess,
Can seldom speak of you with reverence.
A wild fire and corrupting pestilence
This very evening on your bodies light!
Do ye not see this honorable knight
That his own man will shame here in his fold
Because, alas! he is both blind and old?
Lo, there he sits, the lecher, in the tree!

Now I will promise, of my majesty,
To this old blind and honorable knight
That he shall once more wholly have his sight
When his wife wrongs him. So then shall he see
And know the sum of all her harlotry
To the reproach of her and others, too."

His queen replied: "Is this what ye will do?
I swear now by my mother's father's soul
That she shall have an answer, good and whole,
And women ever after, for her sake;
Though found in guilt, they shall have wit to make
A bold defense that always will excuse them
And bear down any men that shall accuse them.
None shall be slain for want of good replies.
For though a man shall see with both his eyes
Yet shall we women boldly face it out,
So subtly scold, so weep and swear and shout,
That men shall be as ignorant as geese.
What do I care for your authorities?

"This Solomon ye tell about, this Jew,
Found many women fools, I know it true.
Yet though he never found one that was good,
Others found many a woman (as they should)
With goodness, truth, and virtue that sufficed.
Think of the women in the house of Christ,
That proved with martyrdom their constancy.
The Roman legends bring to memory
Many a true and constant woman, too.
Nor, sire, be ye aggrieved though it be true
He said he found no good wife anywhere.
I pray you, seek the meaning hidden there:
He meant, in sovereign goodness there can be
No one but God, that sits in Trinity.

"Ah, for the love of God, the true and one,
Why do ye make so much of Solomon?
What though he made a temple, the house of God?
What though his wealth and fame were spread abroad?
He also built false gods a fane, this king –
How could he do a more forbidden thing?
Plaster his name however fairly, sir,
He was a lecher and idolater,

And left the one true God when he was old.
Had God not spared him, as the Book hath told,
For David's sake, He would have rent away
His kingdom sooner than He did, I say.
For all ye write to blame us and decry
I care no more than for a butterfly.
I am a woman: therefore I must speak
Or swell with wrong until my heart will break.
And since he says that we are termagants,
As I may keep my hair, at every chance
I shall not hesitate for courtesy
To speak him ill that plans our injury."

"Dame," Pluto said, "be angry now no more.
I give it up. And yet, because I swore
That I would let him have his sight again,
My word must stand. That much is clear and plain.
I am a king; it fits me not to lie."

Said she: "The queen of Fairyland am I,
And she shall have her answer, too – I swear.
But let us talk no more of this affair;
I would no longer play your adversary."

Now let us turn again to January,
That in the garden, with his lovely May,
Goes singing merrier than a popinjay,
"I love you best, none will I love but you!"
Thus many a garden path he wandered through,
Until at length he reached the very tree
Where Damian sat above him merrily
High up, among green leaves and many a pear.

This lovely May, that looked so bright and fair,
Began to sigh, and said: "Alas! my side!
Whatever happens, this is sure," she cried,
"Sir, I must taste these pears that I can see
Or I shall die, such longing comes to me
To eat these pears, so small and sweet and green.
Now help me, for the love of heaven's queen!
I tell you that a woman in my plight
May long for fruit with such an appetite
That she may die if she must go without."

"Alas!" said he, "had I a boy about
That might climb up! Alas! Alas!" cried he,

"That I am blind!" "No matter, sir," said she.
"But for God's sake, I beg of you, draw near,
And put your arms about the pear tree here
(For well I know ye are suspicious of me);
Then I could climb up by these limbs above me,
If I could set my foot upon your back."

    "Truly," he answered, "there ye shall not lack;
Would I could help you with my own heart's blood!"
Then he stooped down, and on his back she stood,
And pulled herself up quickly by a bough.
Ladies, I pray you, be not angry now;
I cannot gloss it – I am a rough man.
All in a flash this lover Damian
Pulled up the smock, and he was in ere long.

    At once when Pluto saw this monstrous wrong,
He gave his sight to January once more,
And made him see as well as ever before.
And when he found himself restored to sight,
No man was ever filled with such delight;
But always thinking of his wife, he raised
His eyes aloft, and in the tree he gazed,
And saw how Damian, that was hard at play,
So held his wife as I could never say
If with a courteous tongue I tell my tale.
At once he raised a mighty roar and wail
As does a mother that fears her child will die.
"Alas! Help! Harrow!" he began to cry,
"O bold, bad woman, what is this ye do?"

    But she replied: "Sir, what is wrong with you?
Have patience; and let reason rule your mind!
I have restored your eyes, that both were blind!
For by my soul's rest, let me tell no lies:
Thus was I taught – if I would heal your eyes,
There was no better way to make you see
Than struggling with a man within a tree;
God knows, I did a good, sire, and no sin!"

    "Struggle!" he cried. "I saw it going in!
God give you both a shameful death to die!
He laid thee – yea, I saw it with mine eye,
Let them go hang me if it be not true!"

    "Why then, my medicine is bad for you,"

She said, "for certainly, if ye could see
Then ye would speak no words like these to me;
Your sight is but a glimmer, not yet good."

    "I see," cried he, "as well as ever I could,
Thanks be to God, with both mine eyes, I know;
And by my truth, I thought he had thee so."

    "Ye are confused, good sire, confused," said she.
"This is my thanks for having made you see.
Alas!" she cried, "that I was ever so kind."

    "Now, Dame," he answered, "put it out of mind.
Come down, my love; if I have spoken amiss
I am sorry for it, as God may give me bliss.
But by my father's soul, it seemed to me
That Damian was lying there with thee,
And that thy smock upon his breast was lying."

    "Yea, sire, think as ye please," she said, replying.
"But, sire, a man when first awakening
Out of his sleep, may not behold a thing
All of a sudden in any perfect way
Until he grow accustomed to the day.
And so a man that hath been blind for long,
He sees not suddenly so well and strong
The first time that he hath his sight anew,
As one that has it for a day or two.
Until ye grow accustomed to your sight
Ye may not see full many a thing aright.
Beware, I pray you; for by heaven's King,
Full many a man thinks that he sees a thing
That in reality is otherwise.
His judgment then will err, as did his eyes."
And with that word she leapt down from the tree.

    This January – who now is glad but he?
He kissed her, and embraced her with sweet sighs,
And stroked her softly in between her thighs,
And led her to his palace happily.
And now, good men, I pray you merry be.
Thus I end here my tale of January;
God bless you, and his holy mother Mary!

Here ends the Merchant's Tale of January

Epilogue to the Merchant's Tale

"EH!" cried our Host, "God's mercy on my life!
I pray He keep me safe from such a wife!
Lo, what a bag of tricks and subtleties
These women hold! As busily as bees
They fly about, deceiving simple men!
And from the truth again and yet again
They veer: this Merchant's story proves it so.
I have a wife as staunch as steel, I know,
Though she is poor. Yet it is all too true
That with her tongue she is a blabbing shrew,

And has a pack of faults besides – a store.
No matter – let us talk of that no more.
But know ye what? I say in secrecy
I sore repent that she is tied to me.
Yet I should be a fool now if I chose
To count up all the vices that she shows –
And for this reason, that it soon would be
Told her by people in this company;
By whom, is no occasion to declare –
Women know how to manage that affair;
Also I lack the wit that might uncover
All of her faults – therefore my tale is over."

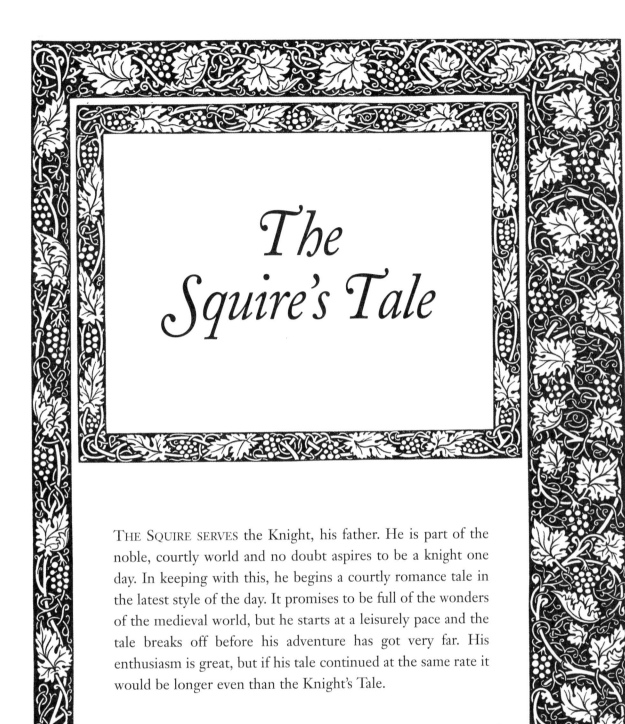

The Squire's Tale

THE SQUIRE SERVES the Knight, his father. He is part of the noble, courtly world and no doubt aspires to be a knight one day. In keeping with this, he begins a courtly romance tale in the latest style of the day. It promises to be full of the wonders of the medieval world, but he starts at a leisurely pace and the tale breaks off before his adventure has got very far. His enthusiasm is great, but if his tale continued at the same rate it would be longer even than the Knight's Tale.

THE SQUIRE'S TALE

The Squire's Prologue

"SQUIRE, if it please you," said our Host, "come
    here,
And something tell of love, for it is clear
Ye know as much of that as any man."
"Nay, sir; but I will tell you what I can
With a good will, for I will not rebel
Against your wish. My tale, sir, I will tell.
Excuse me if in any way I fail;
My will is good; and lo, this is my tale.

Here begins the Squire's Tale

AT Sarray, in the land of Tartary,
There dwelt a king, that warred on Muscovy;
And many a brave man perished in this war.
Cambuscan was the name this monarch bore,
Who in his time was of repute so fair
That there was in no region anywhere
So excellent a lord in every thing;
He lacked for nothing that befits a king.
As to the faith to which he had been born,
He kept it loyally, as he had sworn,
And he was rich and brave, prudent of mind,
Merciful, just, and honorable and kind,
Faithful to any pact that he might enter,
Steadfast of nature as is any center,
And young and strong, and eager in the sport
Of arms as any young knight at his court.

Fair of his mien he was, and fortunate,
And always kept so well his high estate
That no man was his like in everything.
This Tartar, this Cambuscan, this good king,
Had had two sons by Élpheta his wife,
Of which the elder's name was Algarsyf;
Cambal they called the other of the two.
A daughter had this worthy king and true,
The youngest of them all, called Canacee.
It lies not in my ingenuity
Or language to describe her loveliness –
I dare not undertake, as I confess,
So high a thing – my English is too weak;
It needs some rhetorician, skilled to speak
With all the colors that adorn his art
If he describe her well in every part.
I am not such, and I must tell my story
As best I can.

                        So when his kingly glory
Cambuscan had for twenty years maintained,
After his yearly custom he ordained
By crier, that his birthday festival
In Sarray be observed, his capital,
On the last Ides of March, as ran the year.
Phœbus the sun was shining glad and clear,
For he had now approached his exaltation
In Mars' face, and therefore had his station
In Aries, in the hot and choleric sign.
The days were beaming lusty and benign,
And all the birds about were gaily singing
For gladness of the shining sun, and springing
Of tender green, and all the season's cheer.
It seemed to them they had protection here
Against the sword of winter, sharp and cold.
  Cambuscan, of whose glory I have told,
Within his palace, clad in robe and crown,
With pomp upon his daïs sat him down,
And held his festival so rich and fair
The world could not have matched it anywhere.
If I began to tell all that array
I should be occupied a summer's day;

Ye maze, maze, goode sire, quod she;
This thank have I for I have maad yow see;
Allas! quod she, that evere I was so kynde!
Now, dame, quod he, lat al passe out of mynde.
Com doun, my lief, and if I have myssayd,
God help me so, as I am yvele apayd.
But, by my fader soule! I wende han seyn,
How that this Damyan had by thee leyn,
And that thy smok had leyn upon his brest.
Ye, sire, quod she, ye may wene as yow lest;
But, sire, a man that waketh out of his sleep,
He may nat sodeynly wel taken keep
Upon a thyng, ne seen it parfitly,
Til that he be adawed verraily;
Right so a man, that longe hath blynd ybe,
Ne may nat sodeynly so wel yse,
First whan his sighte is newe come ageyn,
As he that hath a day or two yseyn.
Til that youre sighte ysatled be a while,
Ther may ful many a sighte yow bigile.
Beth war, I prey yow; for, by hevene kyng,
Ful many a man weneth to seen a thyng,
And it is al another than it semeth.
He that mysconceyveth, he mysdemeth.
And with that word she leep doun fro the
tree.
This Januarie, who is glad but he?
He kisseth hire, and clippeth hire ful ofte,
And on hire wombe he stroketh hire ful
softe;
And to his palays hoom he hath hire lad.
Now, goode men, I pray yow to be glad.
Thus endeth heere my tale of Januarie;
God blesse us, and his mooder Seinte Marie!
Heere is ended the Marchantes Tale of
Januarie.

Words of the Host to the Squire

Y! Goddes mercy!
seyde oure Hoost tho,
Now swich a wyf I
pray God kepe me fro!
Lo, whiche sleightes
and subtilitees
In wommen been! for
ay as bisy as bees
Been they, us sely men
for to deceyve;
And from a sothe evere wol they weyve.
By this Marchauntes tale it preveth weel.
But doutelees, as trewe as any steel
I have a wyf, though that she povre be;
But of hir tonge a labbyng shrewe is she,
And yet she hath an heep of vices mo;
Therof no fors, lat alle swiche thynges go.
But wyte ye what? In conseil be it seyd,
Me reweth soore I am unto hire teyd;
For, and I sholde rekenen every vice
Which that she hath, ywis, I were to nyce,
And cause why; it sholde reported be
And toold to hire of somme of this meynee;
Of whom, it nedeth nat for to declare,
Syn wommen konnen outen swich chaffare;
And eek my wit suffiseth nat therto
To tellen al; wherfore my tale is do.
SQUIER, come neer, if it youre wille be,
And sey somwhat of love; for certes, ye
Konnen theron as muche as any man.
Nay, sir, quod he, but I wol seye as I kan
With hertly wyl; for I wol nat rebelle
Agayn youre lust; a tale wol I telle.
Have me excused, if I speke amys,
My wyl is good; and lo, my tale is this.

HEERE BIGYNNETH THE SQUIERES TALE

Incipit prima pars

SARRAY, IN THE LAND OF Tartarye,
Ther dwelte a kyng, that werreyed Russye,
Thurgh which ther deyde many a doughty
man.
This noble kyng was cleped Cambynskan,
Which in his tyme was of so greet renoun
That ther was nowher in no regioun
So excellent a lord in alle thyng;
Hym lakked noght that longeth to a kyng.
As of the secte of which that he was born
He kepte his lay, to which that he was
sworn;
And therto he was hardy, wys, and riche,
And pietous and just, alwey yliche;
Sooth of his word, benigne and honurable,
Of his corage as any centre stable;
Yong, fressh, and strong, in armes desirous
As any bacheler of al his hous.
A fair persone he was, and fortunat,
And kepte alwey so wel roial estat
That ther was nowher swich another man.
This noble kyng, this Tartre Cambynskan
Hadde two sones on Elpheta his wyf,
Of whiche the eldeste highte Algarsyf,

Plate 23: The Squire's Tale (p. 278)

Also it were a needless thing observing
For every course the order of the serving.
I will not tell you of their curious stews,
Nor of their heron or their swan ragouts;
And in that land, as old knights say, some meat
Is held to be a dainty thing to eat,
While here they hold its virtue to be small.
There is no man that can report it all.
I will not linger, then, for it is prime,
And no fruit to be won but loss of time;
Unto my tale I turn again at last.

    It came about, when the third course was past,
While in his state the king was sitting thus,
And minstrels with their lays melodious
Made at the board delicious harmony,
Through the hall door there entered suddenly
A knight that rode upon a steed of brass,
And bore a mirror, broad and made of glass.
Upon his thumb a golden ring he wore,
And by his side a naked sword he bore.
And to the highest table took his way.
None in the hall had any word to say
For wonder of this knight; both young and old
Paused as he rode to watch him and behold.

    This knight that came thus, sudden and unknown,
All richly armed save for his head alone,
Saluted now in order, one and all,
The king, and queen, and nobles in the hall,
With such a deferential elegance
Alike in language and in countenance,
That Gawain, come again from Fairyland,
His ancient courtesy at his command,
Could never have improved it with a word.
And after that, before the highest board,
In the best usage of his speech prepared,
With manly voice his message he declared,
Without a fault of syllable or letter;
And that his message might appear the better,
Unto his words he shaped his manner, too,
As those that study speaking learn to do.
And though I cannot imitate his style,

Nor ever hope to mount so high a stile,
As to its purport, this I can convey,
Which will amount to what he had to say
If I still have it well in memory.

    He said: "The King of Ind and Araby,
That is my lord, on this momentous day
Salutes you, sire, as best he can and may,
And sends, to honor well your feast and land,
By me, that wait to do your least command,
This steed of brass, that easily and fast
Can in the space a natural day will last,
That is to say, in four and twenty hours,
Whereso ye please, whether in drought or showers,
Transport your body unto every spot
Your heart may long to see, and harm you not
In any way at all, through foul or fair.
Or would ye fly as high upon the air
As any eagle when he deigns to soar,
This steed will then convey you evermore,
Unharmed, where ye may please, though as he goes
Ye sit at rest, or else in sleep repose;
And when ye twirl a pin, he will return.
The one that wrought it set himself to learn
Full many a craft; and many a constellation
He watched for ere he did this operation,
And many a magic learned to understand.

    "This mirror that I hold within my hand
Hath such a power that in it ye can see
When there shall happen any adversity
To you, or to the land in which ye reign;
And friend and foeman it will show you plain.
And more than this, if any lady bright
By chance have set her heart on any knight,
And he is false, his falseness shall appear,
His new love and his guile be mirrored here
So clearly, she shall know in full his treason.
Therefore, against this lusty summer season,
This mirror and this ring, that ye can see,
He sendeth to my lady Canacee,
Your daughter excellent, beside you here.

    "The virtue of the ring, if ye will hear,

Is this: that if she shall be pleased to wear it
Upon her thumb, or in her purse to bear it,
There is no bird that under heaven flies
But she through this shall understand his cries
And clearly know the thing that he is crying,
And give him answer, in his speech replying.
And she shall know all grasses that may be,
And who from each can find a remedy,
Although his wounds be never so deep and wide.

   "This naked sword, that hangs here by my side,
Has such a virtue, that what man ye smite,
Clean through his armor it will shear and bite,
Though it were thick as any strong-branched oak.
And any man so wounded with that stroke
Shall never heal, unless ye, of your grace,
Vouchsafe to strike him in the wounded place
With the flat blade. This is indeed to say
That if ye please to touch the wound this way
With the flat sword, then it will quickly close.
This is the truth, without a word of gloze;
While it is in your hand it will not fail."

   And when this knight had thus rehearsed his tale,
He rode out, and proceeded to alight.
His steed, that like the sun was shining bright,
Stood in the court, as still as any stone.
And soon this knight is to his chamber shown,
Unarmed there, and conducted to the board.
The gifts – that is, the mirror and the sword,
With royal circumstance to suit the hour,
Are borne forth soon, into a lofty tower,
By officers ordained to do this thing;
And unto Canacee they bore the ring
With ceremony, as she sat at table.
But of a certainty, to tell no fable,
The horse of brass, that would not move around,
Stood there, like something glued fast to the ground.
None could have drawn it thence, though he should
     fully
Apply the force of windlass or of pulley,
Because, indeed, none understood the art.
So in the place they let it stand apart,

Until the knight, as ye shall later hear,
Had made the trick of his removal clear.

   Great was the rabble swarming to and fro
To stare upon this horse that standeth so.
That was so great of height and breadth and length,
With all proportions shaped to give it strength,
It might have been a steed of Lombardy;
And was so quick of eye, and perfectly
Shaped like a horse, that it appeared indeed
Like a fine courser of Apulian breed.
From ear to tail men said there was no part
That nature could improve upon, or art.
But most they wondered how this came to pass:
That it could move, and yet was wrought of brass;
The people thought it was the work of fays;
And various ones would judge in various ways –
For many heads, as many fantasies!
They buzzed and murmured like a swarm of bees,
Each reasoning by his imagination.
Talk of old poems filled their conversation:
It was like Pegasus, some men went crying –
The fabled horse that had great wings for flying;
Or like the horse that Sinon built at Troy,
The crafty Greek, the city to destroy,
As in these ancient legends men may read.
"My heart is full of fear," one said, indeed.
"I think armed men may well be hidden in it,
That reached the city thus, and plot to win it;
Good if all things like that were known and clear."
Another whispered in his fellow's ear,
Saying: "He lies, for it is rather like
An image some magician's skill might strike,
When jugglers at great feasts their tricks display."
Thus various fears they uttered in this way,
As ignorant people by their habit will,
Of things that have been fashioned with a skill
That in their ignorance they cannot trace –
Always they fear the worst in such a case.

   And some were moved with wonder at the power
Of that strange mirror carried to the tower –
And of the things that it would let men see.

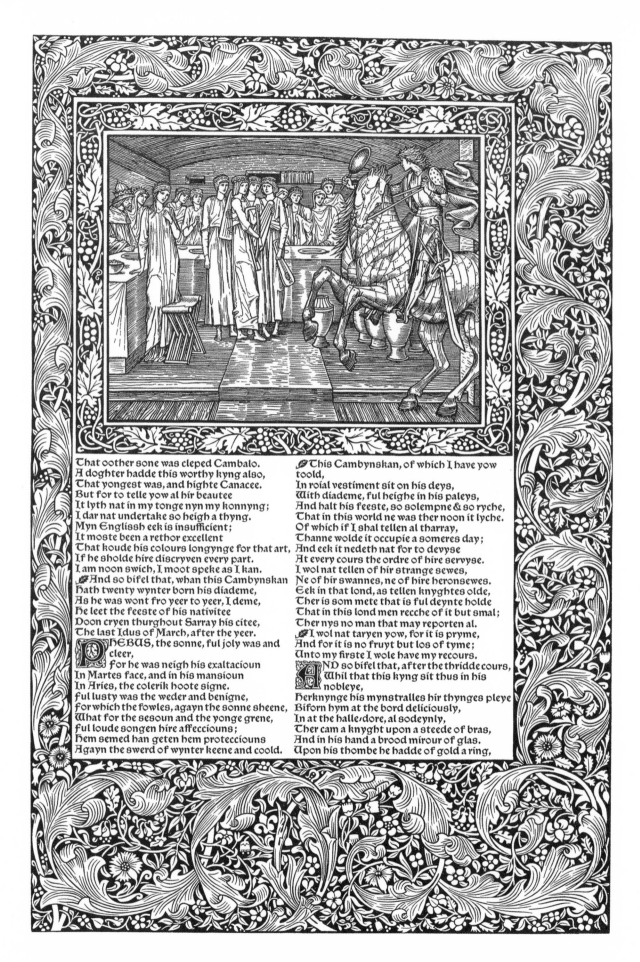

That oother sone was cleped Cambalo.
A doghter hadde this worthy kyng also,
That yongest was, and highte Canacee.
But for to telle yow al hir beautee
It lyth nat in my tonge nyn my konnyng;
I dar nat undertake so heigh a thyng.
Myn Englissh eek is insufficient;
It moste been a rethor excellent
That koude his colours longynge for that art,
If he sholde hire discryven every part.
I am noon swich, I moot speke as I kan.
And so bifel that, whan this Cambynskan
Hath twenty wynter born his diademe,
As he was wont fro yeer to yeer, I deme,
He leet the feeste of his nativitee
Doon cryen thurghout Sarray his citee,
The last Idus of March, after the yeer.
PHEBUS, the sonne, ful joly was and cleer,
For he was neigh his exaltacioun
In Martes face, and in his mansioun
In Aries, the colerik hoote signe.
Ful lusty was the weder and benigne,
For which the fowles, agayn the sonne sheene,
What for the sesoun and the yonge grene,
Ful loude songen hire affecciouns;
Hem semed han geten hem protecciouns
Agayn the swerd of wynter keene and coold.

This Cambynskan, of which I have yow
toold,
In roial vestiment sit on his deys,
With diademe, ful heighe in his paleys,
And halt his feeste, so solempne & so ryche,
That in this world ne was ther noon it lyche.
Of which if I shal tellen al tharray,
Thanne wolde it occupie a someres day;
And eek it nedeth nat for to devyse
At every cours the ordre of hire servyse.
I wol nat tellen of hir strange sewes,
Ne of hir swannes, ne of hire heronsewes.
Eek in that lond, as tellen knyghtes olde,
Ther is som mete that is ful deynte holde
That in this lond men recche of it but smal;
Ther nys no man that may reporten al.
I wol nat taryen yow, for it is pryme,
And for it is no fruyt but los of tyme;
Unto my firste I wole have my recours.
AND so bifel that, after the thridde cours,
Whil that this kyng sit thus in his
nobleye,
Herknynge his mynstralles hir thynges pleye
Biforn hym at the bord deliciously,
In at the halle-dore, al sodeynly,
Ther cam a knyght upon a steede of bras,
And in his hand a brood mirour of glas.
Upon his thombe he hadde of gold a ring,

Plate 24: The Squire's Tale (p. 278)

Another answered that it well might be
Through nature, by adjusting the directions
Of angles, thus producing strange reflections;
In Rome, they said, was one that was its fellow.
They spoke too of Alhazen and Vitello,
And Aristotle, that all of mirrors tell,
And of perspective glasses write as well,
As all men know that have their works explored.

    And other people wondered at the sword
That had a strength to pierce through everything;
And fell in speech of Telephus the king,
And of the wondrous spear Achilles bore;
For he could wound, or heal the wound once more,
Just as was possible with this sword as well
Of which but now yourselves have heard me tell.
They spoke of methods used for hardening
Metals, and drugs men used to do this thing,
And how and when to harden properly;
But this is all unknown, at least to me.

    They spoke of Canacee then, and her ring;
And all agreed that such a wondrous thing
In rings was never known by anyone,
Except that Moses and King Solomon
Had had the name of cunning in that art.
And thus they spoke, gathered in groups apart.
Some said it was a wonder come to pass
When men could make fern ashes into glass;
Glass is not like fern ashes, but since men
Have known and seen it done time and again,
Now they have ceased their clamor and their wonder.
Others will marvel at the cause of thunder,
Gossamer, mist, or ebb and flow of tide,
And all things, till the cause is clarified.
Thus they pronounce and speculate and gabble
Until the king has risen from the table.

    Phœbus had left the high meridian,
While in the sky, along with Aldiran,
Leo ascended still, the royal beast,
When from his lofty daïs at the feast
Up rose Cambuscan, this great Tartar king.
The minstrelsy, full loudly carolling,

Before him to his presence chamber went,
And there drew sound from many an instrument,
Until it seemed like heaven itself to hear it.
Now Venus' children dance with lusty spirit,
For in the Fish their lady sits on high
And looks upon them with a friendly eye.

    This noble king sits on his throne of might.
Before him soon they fetch the stranger knight,
And in the dance he goes with Canacee.
Here there was revelling and jollity
That no dull man could ever hope to tell.
Love and his service he must savor well,
And be a festive man as fresh as May
That should describe their merriment that day.

    For who could tell the forms of all the dances,
The strange and fresh and merry countenances,
The secret glancing and dissimulation
That masked themselves from jealous observation?
No man but Lancelot, and he is dead!
I will not try, but turn away instead,
And say no more, leaving them at their play
Till supper calls them with the fading day.

    The steward called, amid this music fine,
That spices should be brought at once, and wine;
The squires and ushers go at his command,
And spice and wine alike are soon at hand.
They eat and drink; and after, in due season,
Toward the temple they go, as was but reason.

    The service done, they supped – and still by day.
What need to tell you all that great array?
Ye know well that the guests, at a king's feast,
Have plenty, both the greatest and the least,
And dainties more than I have means of knowing.
The supper done, the king is bent on going
To view the horse of brass, and all the rout
Of lords and ladies follow him about.

    Such wonder was there at this horse of brass
That since the siege of Troy had come to pass,
When a horse, too, was wonder of all men,
There never was such marvelling as then.
The king made question of this knight at length

As to the horse's uses and his strength,
And prayed him tell about its governance.

   At once the horse began to trip and dance
When the knight laid a hand upon its rein,
Saying: "Sir, there is nothing to explain,
Except that when it pleases you to ride,
Ye twirl a pin, set in his ear, inside,
As I shall tell to no one else but you.
And ye must name the country for him, too,
Or place therein to which ye wish to go,
And when ye see it lying there below,
Bid him descend, and twirl another pin
(The root of this contrivance lies therein),
And he will take you down, and do your will,
And stay there as ye leave him, standing still.
Or, if it please you bid him to depart,
Then turn the pin again, and he will start,
And in an instant vanish from the sight
Of all; and come again, by day or night,
When ye may wish to call him back again
After a way which I shall soon explain
When none is by to hear me speak but you.
Ride where ye please, there is no more to do."

   And having been instructed by the knight,
And got an understanding, clear and right,
As to the form and manner of this thing,
Then glad and gay this brave and noble king
Returns to keep his revel as before.
The bridle to the lofty tower they bore,
And stored it with his dearest gems away.
Then the horse vanished – how I cannot say –
Out of men's sight – ye get no more from me.
Thus in their lustihood and jollity
I leave Cambuscan and his lords at play
Almost until the dawning of the day.

Part II

SLUMBER, that is the nurse of good digestion,
Blinked at them now, and made his sly suggestion
That after drink and labor sleep must fall;

And with a yawning mouth he kissed them all,
And told them, "It was time they went to bed,
For blood was in his dominance," he said;
"Cherish the friend of nature, blood," said he.
They yawned and gave him thanks, now two, now
      three,
And every person turned to take his rest
As Sleep advised, accepting it as best.
The dreams they dreamed shall not be told by me;
Their heads were full of fumes, that commonly
Are cause of dreams that have no rule or rime.
They lay asleep till it was fully prime,
The most of them – except for Canacee.
For she was temperate, as generally
Are women, and had taken her farewell
To go to rest soon after evening fell.
She had no liking to look pale and faded,
Nor to be listless with the day, and jaded,
And slept her first sleep, after which she woke.
For on her heart so great a gladness broke
For her strange ring, and for the mirror, too,
That twenty times or more she changed her hue,
And in her mind this mirror still was gleaming
The while she slept, and made her fall to dreaming.
Therefore, before the sun announced the day,
She called her woman that beside her lay,
And said it was her pleasure to arise.

   This chamber-woman, proud of being wise,
As are old women, answered from the bed:
"Madame, where do ye think to go?" she said,
"Thus early, for the folk are sleeping still."
"I will arise; for now I have no will
To sleep, but wish to roam about," said she.
   The woman then called out a company
Of ladies, ten or twelve, and up they rose,
And Canacee was up as soon as those,
As bright and ruddy as the new-born sun
That in the Ram but four degrees has run;
He was no higher before she left the place,
And set out walking at an easy pace,
Arrayed to suit the sweet and lusty day,

Lightly – that she might walk about and play,
With only five or six for company.
Down through an alley in the park went she.
The vapor breathing upward from the ground
Made the sun glimmer ruddy, broad, and round;
Yet with so fair an aspect, none the less,
Their hearts were dancing, light with happiness,
What with the season and the sun upspringing,
And all the birds she heard about her, singing,
For she could tell the things they said ere long,
And all about their feeling, from their song.

   The end and point for which a tale is told,
If left until the appetite is cold
In those that long have listened, will at length
Little by little lose its salt and strength,
In fulsomeness of such prolixity.
And for this reason it appears to me
I should not spoil my point by too much talking,
And make a quick conclusion of her walking.

   As Canacee went playing in her walk,
In a dry, withered tree, as white as chalk,
Above her head, a falcon sat on high,
That with a piteous voice made such a cry
That all the wood resounded with her woe;
And beat herself with many a fearful blow
From both her wings, till blood ran down the tree
On which she perched and cried so fearsomely.
Never she ceased to cry her cry, and shriek,
And tore herself so fiercely with her beak
That no harsh beast or tiger that may dwell
In any forest shade or wooded dell
Could help but weep, if he could weep at all,
For pity of her loud, incessant call.
For there was never a man that earth might walk on,
If only I could well describe a falcon,
That heard of any other fair as she
For plumage or for noble symmetry
Of form, and all good points that might be seen.
She seemed to be a falcon peregrine
From a strange land; and always as she perched,
She swooned for loss of blood, and swayed and lurched

Till she was close to falling from the tree.
   This daughter of a king, this Canacee,
That on her finger wore this curious ring
Through which she comprehended everything
That any bird might in his language cry,
And in his language, too, could make reply,
Hath comprehended all this falcon said,
And pity for it all but struck her dead.
At once she took her stand beneath the tree,
Gazing upon the bird compassionately,
And held her dress out, being certain now
The falcon soon must tumble from the bough,
When it should swoon again for loss of blood.
A long time waiting for it thus she stood,
Until she spoke unto the hawk at last
As ye shall hear ere little time is passed.
   "What is the cause, if ye are free to tell,
Ye suffer thus these furious pains of Hell?"
This Canacee asked of the hawk above.
"Is it for grief at death, or loss of love?
For, as I think, these causes are the twain
That most afflict a noble heart with pain.
What need to speak of other hurtful thing?
For ye yourself now wreak this suffering
Upon yourself; which proves that love must be,
Or fear, the cause of all this cruelty,
Since I perceive none other to pursue you.
For love of God, show ye some pity to you,
Or what help can ye find? For west or east
I never saw till now a bird or beast
That used himself in such a fearful fashion.
Your sorrow makes me have such great compassion.
Ye slay me, truly, with the pain thereof.
Then come down from the tree, for God's own love,
And as I am the daughter of a king,
If I could learn about your suffering,
And know the cause, and it were in my might,
Then I would cure it for you ere 'twere night,
May the great god of nature be mine aid!
And I will seek for herbs now, to be laid
Upon your wounds, and make them whole again."

Then shrieked this falcon as with greater pain
Then ever before, and to the ground like lead
She fell, and like a stone lay there as dead,
And in her lap fair Canacee hath taken
This hawk, to hold her till she should awaken;
And when at length out of her swoon she woke,
Soon in the speech of falcons thus she spoke:
"That pity in a noble heart will spring
Swiftly to see its own kind suffering
Is each day manifest, as men may see,
As well by deed as by authority,
For noble hearts act out their nobleness.
And I perceive ye have for my distress
A great compassion, my fair Canacee,
Born of a woman's true benignity
Ingrained by Nature in your character.
Yet, with no hope to be the happier,
But to repay your generosity,
And let the world be warned, knowing of me,
As lions learn from a dog's chastisement –
For this cause, and with this as my intent,
While I have time to tell about my woe
I will confess it here before I go."
And ever, while the bird its sorrow taught her,
The other wept, as she would turn to water,
Until the falcon bade her to be still,
And with a sigh, in this way spoke her will:
    "Where I was bred (Alas! Unhappy day!)
And fostered on a rock of marble gray,
So tenderly no harm could come to me,
I had no knowledge of adversity
Till I could soar far up beneath the sky.
There was a tercelet that lived near by,
Who seemed the well of all nobility.
Though he was full of treason and falsity,
They were so masked beneath a humble bearing,
And hue of truth forever well-appearing,
And glad devotion in all things he did,
None could have guessed the feigning ways he hid,
So deep he dyed his colors in the grain.
Just as some serpent in the flowers hath lain

Until at last he saw his time, and bit –
Just so this god of love, this hypocrite,
Made all his ceremonious ritual,
And gave attentions that conformed in all,
And were in harmony with noble love.
As in a tomb that seems all fair above,
But hides the corpse beneath, such as ye know,
In hot and cold, this hypocrite would show
A fair face, while he shaped what he designed;
Except the fiend, none ever knew his mind.
Until so long lamenting and complaining,
Year in and out devotion to me feigning,
He so besieged my heart, all innocent
Of his crowned malice, and to pity bent,
That on his oaths and other surety,
And lest he die, as it appeared to me,
I granted him my love, on this condition –
That evermore my honor and position,
Public and private both, should be preserved.
That is, in guerdon for the way he served,
I gave him all my heart and all my mind –
God knows, and he, that naught else I resigned –
And took his heart for mine, forevermore.
But truth was said these many years before:
'A true man and a thief think not the same.'
And when he saw the progress of the game –
That I had fully granted him my love
In such a way as I have said above,
And given him my true heart, as generously
As he swore he had given his heart to me,
This tiger then, full of dissimulation,
Upon his knees made humble protestation
With such high reverence, and, by his bearing,
Like lover of the noblest heart appearing,
So ravished, as it seemed, for very joy,
That never Jason – Nay, nor Paris of Troy –
Jason? Why, no, nor any other man
Since Lamech lived, the first of all began
A twofold love, as olden books have stated,
Nor none, indeed, since man was first created,
Could, by the twenty-thousandth of a part,

Approach the feignèd cunning of his art,
And, as to making what was false seem true,
Be worthy even to unlace his shoe,
Nor thank a person as that wretch thanked me.
His manner would have been a heaven to see
For any woman, were she never so wise,
So did he smooth and paint his words with lies,
While like his words his countenance he dressed.
And I so loved him for his faith professed,
And the deep truth I thought his heart contained,
That, when he seemed in any fashion pained,
Even slightly, and I knew his suffering,
It seemed to me that death my heart would wring.
And, to be brief, so far at length this went,
That my will soon was his will's instrument;
That is to say, my will obeyed his will
In all things, though in bounds of reason still,
Keeping the safety of mine honor ever.
A thing so dear, or dearer, knew I never
Than he – nor ever shall: God knows it true.

"This lasted longer than a year or two,
That I had thought no thing of him but good.
And yet with time at length the matter stood
That by the will of Fortune he must go
Away from me. No question of the woe
I suffered at the prospect of his leaving;
I have no language to describe my grieving;
For one thing I will tell you – from that woe
The pain of dying is a thing I know,
Such grief I felt that he must go away.
And so he took his leave upon a day;
And I supposed, to hear him plain and sigh,
That he had felt as great a grief as I,
For so his words said, and his manner, too.
But none the less, I thought he was so true,
And hoped as well that in a little season
He would return; then, too, it stood in reason,
I thought, that for his honor he must go,
As oftentimes indeed it happened so –
I made a virtue of necessity,
And took it well, because it had to be.

As best I could I hid my sorrow sore,
And took his hand, and by St. John I swore,
And said, 'I am all yours. Now be as true
As I have been, and shall be now, to you.'
What he replied I need not here rehearse.
Who can speak better than he, or who do worse?
When he had spoken all fair, he wrought his deeds.
'Who takes a dinner with a friend, he needs
A long spoon, truly.' Thus I hear them say.
So in the end he had to go his way,
And forth he flew until he came to where
He wished to go. And when he settled there,
I think he must have had this text in mind,
That 'Every one is glad at length to find
His own true nature.' So men say, I guess;
For men by nature love newfangledness,
As birds do that ye keep in cages fair.
For though by night and day ye give them care,
And line their cages fair and soft as silk,
And give them honey, sugar, bread, and milk,
Yet on the instant that his door is up,
With a swift foot the creature spills his cup,
And seeks the wood to hunt for worms to eat.
Thus so newfangled are they as to meat,
And by their nature long for novelties –
No nobleness of blood controlleth these.
So with this tercelet, alas the day!
Though he was nobly born, and fresh and gay,
Generous, meek, and goodly to the eye,
Yet soon he saw a kite go soaring by,
And suddenly so loved her and revered;
The love he had for me quite disappeared,
And thus the truth he pledged was falsified.
She hath my love in service by her side,
And I am lost, lost without remedy!"
And with that word she cried out piteously,
And in the princess' lap she swooned again.

Great was the sorrow for this falcon's pain
That Canacee and all her women had.
They knew not how to make the falcon glad.
But Canacee hath taken her in her lap,

And soft with bandages began to wrap
The wounds the bird had made with her own beak.
Now Canacee can do no more than seek
Herbs in the ground, compounding ointments new
Out of rare plants, and fine of scent and hue,
To heal this hawk with; and by day and night
She labors busily with all her might.
And at her bed's head she installed a mew,
And covered it with velvet, soft and blue,
Symbolic of the truth in women seen.
Outside, the mew was painted all in green,
And there were painted all deceitful fowls –
Such as are tidifs, tercelets, and owls,
And all in scorn of them were wrought near by
Magpies, to mock them with their scolding cry.

    Thus Canacee I leave now with her hawk,
And of her ring no further will I talk,
Till later; but the story tells you then
Of how this falcon got her love again,
And his repentance, as the tale doth go,
Through mediation of this Cambalo,
The king's son, that I told you of before.
So to my purpose will I hold once more,
To speak of chances and of battle thunders
So great that never were there known such wonders.

    First of Cambuscan shall the tale be spun,
That in his season many a city won,
And later will I speak of Algarsyf,
How he won Theodora for his wife,
And would have come to many a dangerous pass
Without assistance from the steed of brass;
And I will speak of Cambalo 'mid others,
That in the lists encountered both the brothers
Of Canacee, before he won her then.
And where I stopped I will begin again.

Part III

APOLLO whirled his chariot up so high,
Until the house of Mercury, the sly,
[*Unfinished*]

Here follow the words of the Franklin to the Squire,
and the words of the Host to the Franklin

"SQUIRE, in faith, thou hast thyself well quit;
And to be frank I highly praise thy wit,"
The Franklin said, "considering thy youth.
I must applaud thee, if I tell the truth.
And in my judgment there is no man here
May hope in eloquence to be thy peer
If thou shalt live; God give thee luck, I say,
And keep the virtue thou hast shown today;
Thy speaking is a great delight to me.
I have a son; and by the Trinity,
Though it were possible to close my hand
Upon the worth of twenty pound of land,
I would prefer that he should show discretion
Such as ye have. Now fie upon possession
Unless a man have virtue with his holdings!
I chide my son, and still shall give him scoldings,
Because he shows no will to make a friend
Of virtue; nay, to play at dice, and spend,
And lose all that he has – such is his way.
For he will gossip with a page, I say,
Rather than one of nobler rank address,
Where he could rightly learn of gentleness."

    "Straw for your gentleness!" exclaimed our Host.
"Come, Franklin! What, sir! Now by God, thou
      know'st
That each of you must tell a tale or more
Or else ye break the compact that ye swore."

    "Yes, sir, I know it well, by God above me.
And yet I pray you, be not scornful of me
If to this man I speak a word or two."

    "Tell on thy tale, and make no more ado!"

    "Gladly, Sir Host," he said. "I will obey you.
Now listen well to what I say, I pray you.
For, if the wit I carry will permit,
I promise to oppose you not a whit.
I hope to God it please you, for I know
It will be good enough, if that is so."
[*Ends*]

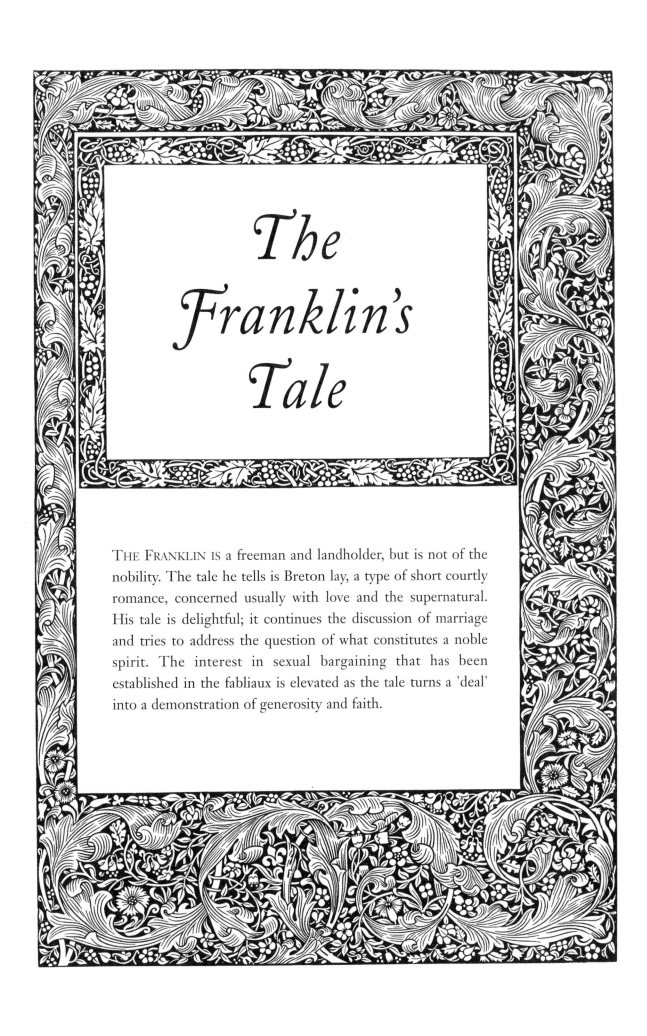

The Franklin's Tale

THE FRANKLIN IS a freeman and landholder, but is not of the nobility. The tale he tells is Breton lay, a type of short courtly romance, concerned usually with love and the supernatural. His tale is delightful; it continues the discussion of marriage and tries to address the question of what constitutes a noble spirit. The interest in sexual bargaining that has been established in the fabliaux is elevated as the tale turns a 'deal' into a demonstration of generosity and faith.

THE FRANKLIN'S TALE

The Prologue to the Franklin's Tale

THESE noble Bretons in the ancient days
Of various adventures made their lays,
Metered and rimed in the first Breton tongue;
Which lays unto their instruments they sung,
Or read them for their pleasure, possibly.
And one of these I have in memory
Which I will gladly tell as best I can.
But since I am a plain, unlettered man,
As I begin, I pray you all and each
That ye excuse the rudeness of my speech;
I never studied rhetoric, indeed,
And what I say is bare and plain, of need.
I never slept on Mount Parnassus – No
Nor studied Marcus Tullius Cicero;
And as for colors, never learned a thing,
Except of those in meadows blossoming,
Or those for dyes or painting, it may be.
Colors of rhetoric – those are strange to me:
For such queer matters never pricked my spirit.
But I will tell my tale, if ye will hear it.

Here begins the Franklin's Tale

ONCE in Armorica, called Brittany,
There lived a knight that loved, and manfully
Labored for favor in his lady's eyes;
And many a work and noble enterprise
He undertook for her, ere she was won.

For she was fairest underneath the sun,
And, in addition, of so high a station
That scarcely did he dare, for trepidation,
To plead his woe, his pain, and his distress.
But in the end she saw his worthiness,
And deferential ways in everything,
And felt such pity for his suffering
That privately she came to an accord
To take him for her husband and her lord –
Such lordship as men have over their wives –
And, that the more in bliss they lead their lives,
Of his free will he swore that, as a knight,
Never in all his life, by day or night,
Would he take on himself authority
Against her will, or show her jealousy,
But would obey her always, and fulfill
Her pleasure, as a faithful lover will;
Except that he would have the reputation
Of sovereignty, for honor of his station.

She thanked him; and with great humility
She said: "Sire, since in your nobility
Ye make me proffer of so free a rein,
God grant there never come between us twain,
Through fault of mine, hostility or strife.
Sir, I will be your true and humble wife,
I pledge you, till the heart break in my breast."
Thus both of them were now at peace and rest.

For one thing, sires, I hold it safe to say:
That friends must be considerate, and obey
Each other, if they would stay in company.
Love will not be constrained by tyranny.
For when it comes, the god of love will rise
And beat his wings: Farewell! and off he flies!
For love, like any spirit, must be free.
Women by nature want their liberty,
And not to live like thralls within a pen;
And if I tell the truth, why, so do men.
The patient lover, all things said and done,
Has his advantage over everyone.
Patience is high among the virtues, clearly,
For it will win things that with rigor merely,

As scholars say, ye never could attain.
Men should not fall to scolding, or complain
At every word; learn to endure your lot,
Or ye will have to, if ye will or not.
For no one in this world so perfect is
That he has never done or said amiss.
Sickness or anger or his constellation,
Or changing humors, or intoxication
Will often make him err in act or speech.
A man can never be revenged for each
And every wrong. According to the occasion
All prudent men must practice moderation.
And so this wise knight, seeking harmony,
Promised forbearance to her faithfully,
And she to him as faithfully did swear
That she too never would be lacking there.

    Here men may see a humble, wise accord;
Thus did she take her servant and her lord:
In wedlock, lord; in love, at her direction;
Then was he both in lordship and subjection.
Subjection? Nay, but high his lordship is,
Since lady now and love alike are his;
His lady she, but wife the none less truly,
Who to that law of love assented duly.
And having found this prosperous content,
Home to his country with his wife he went,
Not far from Penmark, where he had his dwelling,
And lived in joy and peace beyond the telling.

    For what unwedded man could ever guess
The joy and the repose and happiness
Shared by a wedded husband with his wife?
A year or more endured this blissful life,
Until this knight of whom I tell you thus,
Of Kayr-rud, and by name Arveragus,
Prepared to go and dwell a year or two
In England, that as Britain some men knew,
At arms to seek a fame and reputation,
For all his joy was in such occupation;
And dwelt there for two years – the book says thus.

    But now no more of this Arveragus,
For I will speak of Dorigen his wife,

That loves her husband as her heart's own life.
She mourns for him with tears and agonies,
As do these noble ladies when they please.
She mourneth, waileth, fasteth, crieth, waketh;
Her longing for him such a frenzy taketh
That all this wide world is as nothing to her.
Her friends, that know what heavy thoughts pursue
    her,
Console her in it all as best they may.
They preach to her, they tell her night and day
She kills herself with causeless lamentation;
And everything by way of consolation
That they can find, they press upon her there,
Hoping to draw her from this dark despair.

    With time, as all of you have seen and known,
Men can, by constant graving on a stone,
Imprint some shape upon it finally.
And they have solaced her so long, that she,
Through reason and a hopeful expectation
Has felt the imprint of their consolation,
So her great sorrow was assuaged at length;
It could not hold at such a raging strength.

    Also Arveragus, through all these cares,
Had sent home letters full of his affairs,
And word that he would quickly come again –
Else were her heart with very sorrow slain.

    Her friends saw how her sorrow, by degrees,
Grew less and less, and prayed her on their knees
To come and roam with them for company,
To drive away her gloomy fantasy.
And in the end she granted that request,
For well she saw that it was for the best.

    High stood her castle close beside the sea,
And there with friends she wandered frequently
To take her pleasure, on the rocky height.
There ships and barges passed before her sight,
Sailing their courses – where they pleased to go;
But that was part and parcel of her woe.
For often to herself, "Alas!" cried she,
"Is there no ship of all the ships I see
Will bring my lord home? Then my bitter pain

Were healed, and all my heart were whole again."
    Another time she would sit there and think,
And let her eyes go downward from the brink.
But when she saw black, grisly rocks appear,
Then would her heart so quake for very fear
That she could scarcely stand upon her feet.
Then on the green grass she would take her seat,
And gaze upon the sea with piteous eyes,
And murmur thus, with cold and woeful sighs:
    "O God, eternal, wise, and provident,
Guiding the world by Thy sure government,
Men say that idly Ye have fashioned nothing;
But these black rocks, that fill me full of loathing,
That rather seem some horrid desecration
Of labor, Lord, than any fair creation
Of a wise God, stable in everything –
Why wrought Ye so unreasonable a thing?
For by this work – south, north, or west or east
There is no living man or bird or beast
That gets a good thing from it, to my mind.
See Ye not, Lord, how it destroys mankind?
There must have been a hundred thousand men
Destroyed by rocks, though I forget just when;
Men, that so fair among Thy works are rated
That in Thine image they have been created.
Then it appeared Thou hadst great charity
For mankind, Lord; but how then can it be
That ye take such devices to destroy it,
Which do no good, but injure and annoy it?
I know that scholars make it manifest
By arguments, that all is for the best,
Though still I find their reasons hard to know.
But may that God that made the wind to blow
Preserve my husband! That is my conclusion;
I leave to scholars all their fine confusion
Of arguments. For his sake would I well
That all these black rocks might be sunk in hell!
These rocks destroy my very heart with fear."
So she would say, with many a piteous tear.
    Her friends soon saw it was no pleasure for her
To wander by the sea, but pain and horror,

And planned for other games and wanderings.
They led her off by rivers or by springs,
Or other places rich in loveliness.
They played backgammon, danced, or sat at chess.
    So once when morning lay upon the land,
Unto a garden that was close at hand,
In which they planned to have a celebration
With food and various other preparation,
They go for play and pleasure all the day.
And this had fallen upon the sixth of May;
Which May had painted with his gentle showers
This garden full of leaves and shining flowers;
And craft of man's hand had so curiously
Arrayed this garden, that for certainty
Its like was never seen for loveliness
Unless in paradise itself, I guess.
The odor of flowers and all the gay, fresh sight
Would have made any heavy heart more light
That ever was born, unless too much distressed
With sickness, or with too great grief oppressed;
It was so full of joy and radiance.
After the dinner go they forth to dance
And also sing, save Dorigen alone,
Who always made her sorrow and her moan.
For in the dance she did not see him move
Who was her mate – and also was her love.
But none the less, she must a while abide,
And have good hope, and let her sorrow slide.
    And as they danced, among the other men
There danced a squire before this Dorigen,
That fresher was, and jollier of array,
In my opinion, than the month of May.
He sang and danced better than any man
That lives, or has lived, since the world began.
And to describe him – as I hope to thrive,
He seemed the best appearing man alive;
Young, strong, and wise, and rich, and high in station
And well beloved, and good in reputation.
And briefly, if the truth must be confessed,
Though Dorigen had never known nor guessed,
This lusty squire, by name Aurelius,

Servant of Venus, loved her; and had thus,
As was his fate, adored her for two years;
But never dared, besieged by doubts and fears,
To tell her how his love and suffering went;
Without a cup he drank his punishment.
Despairing, not a word he dared to say,
Save in his songs a little to betray
His woe, and in a general way complain;
He said he loved, but was not loved again.
Of such material made he many lays –
Songs and complaints, roundels and virelays –
How he could never dare his sorrow tell,
And languished like a fury down in hell;
And he must die, he said, as Echo did,
That sought Narcissus' love, yet always hid
Her woe from him. In any other way
He did not dare discover or betray
His woe to her, except that at some dance
Where young folk met in mirth and dalliance,
It may well be he looked upon her face
As a man gazes when he begs for grace,
But nothing did she know of what he meant.
Yet now it happened, that before they went,
Because he was her neighbor, and, she knew,
A man of consequence and honor, too,
And she had known him since some time before,
They fell in speech, and ever more and more
Toward his purpose drew Aurelius,
And when he saw his time, spoke to her thus:

    "Madam, by God that made this world," said he,
"If I had known that ye might happier be
Of heart, I would, when your Arveragus
Went over the sea, that I, Aurelius,
Had gone too, and had never come again,
For well I know my service is in vain.
My only guerdon is a breaking heart.
Madam, have pity on my pain and smart,
For ye can slay me with a word, or save;
Here at your feet would God I had my grave!
Now can I speak no further than to cry:
'Have mercy on me, sweet, or else I die!' "

    Dorigen stared at this Aurelius;
"Is this your will," she asked, "and say ye thus?
I never guessed," she told him, "what ye meant.
But now that I perceive your plain intent,
By that same God that gave me soul and life,
I will not ever be a faithless wife
In word or work, so far as I have wit;
I will be his to whom my heart is knit;
Then take this as your final word from me."

    But after that she told him playfully:
"Aurelius," she said, "by God above,
I would indeed that I could be your love,
Since I have heard you moan so piteously;
And when from all the shores of Brittany
Ye shall remove the rocks, yes, stone by stone,
That ships that sail there find the sea alone,
I say, when ye have made the coast so clean
Of rocks that never a stone is to be seen,
Then will I love you best of any man;
This will I swear, and this is all I can!"

    "Is there no other grace in you?" said he.
    "No, by that Lord that hath created me!
For such a thing could never be, I know.
Hold then to no such follies – let them go.
What pleasure should a man have in his life
To set his love upon another's wife,
That at his pleasure takes her body to him?"

    Aurelius felt an utter grief go through him
To hear these words; often and hard he sighs,
And with a heart all sorrow he replies:
    "Madam, this were impossible," he saith;
"Now may I die a sudden, fearful death!"
And with that word at once he turned away.
Then other friends appeared, to talk and play,
And in the pathways up and down they went,
But never knew a thing of this event;
And they began their revel all anew,
Until the shining sun had lost his hue,
For the horizon had stolen away his light –
Which is as much as saying it was night.
And home in joy and peace they went their way

Save poor Aurelius, alackaday!
He seeks his house with sorrow and with sighing.
He sees no way is left for him but dying.
It seemed to him his heart began to freeze;
He knelt down on the floor on his bare knees,
And raised his hands to heaven, and kneeling there,
Raving in frenzied fashion said his prayer.
For very woe he went out of his head;
He knew not what he spoke, but thus he said;
Out of his piteous heart his protest burst
Unto the gods, and to the sun the first:

   He said, "Apollo, god and governing power
Of every plant and herb, of tree and flower,
That givest, according to thy declination,
To each of them his season and duration
As thy position shifts from low to high –
Lord Phœbus, in thy mercy cast an eye
On poor Aurelius, who am lost indeed.
Lo, Lord! My lady hath my death decreed
Without a cause; may thy benignity
Look on my dying heart and pity me.
For well I know, Lord Phœbus, if ye would,
Ye could do more for me than any could
Except my lady; let me tell you then
How ye may help to make me whole again.

   "Your holy sister, Lord, Lucina bright,
Is goddess of the sea, and queen, of right;
Though Neptune has a godship in the sea,
Yet empress and above him ruleth she.
Ye know well, lord, that just as her desire
Is to be sped and lighted by your fire,
For which she followeth you full busily,
Just so it is the yearning of the sea
To follow her, high goddess, both of all
The sea, and of the rivers, great and small,
Therefore, lord Phœbus, this request I make;
Work thou this miracle, or wholly break
My heart – that now, at the next opposition
When in the Lion thou shalt take position,
Pray her to cause so great a flood to sweep
That it will cover full five fathom deep

The highest rock in all of Brittany;
Let it endure two years continuously.
Then surely to my lady I can say:
'Now keep your oath; the rocks are all away!'

   "Lord Phœbus, work this miracle for me;
Pray her to go no faster than do ye.
I say, persuade your sister she shall go
No faster course than yours a year or so.
At full then for that season shall she stay,
And spring flood last forever, night and day.
And if in this way she will not agree
To bring my sovereign lady's love to me,
Then pray her to submerge each rock and stone
Under the ground, where Pluto holds his throne,
In her own region, dim and cold and shady;
Else never can I hope to win my lady.
Thy shrine in Delphi barefoot will I seek;
Lord Phœbus, see the tears upon my cheek,
And have compassion on my pain, I pray."
And with that word he fell, and swooned away,
And it was long before he woke again.

   His brother, that had known about his pain,
Lifted him up and brought him to his bed.
With this despair and torment in his head,
I turn, and leave this woeful creature lying;
Let him decide on living or on dying!

   Arveragus, with health and fame and power,
As one that was of chivalry the flower,
Has now come home, with other worthy men.
And happy art thou now, O Dorigen,
That hast thy lusty husband in thine arms,
The fresh young knight, the worthy man at arms,
Who loves thee as he loves his own heart's life.
He had no wish to wonder if his wife
Had spoke with any man while he was gone
Of love – for this he never thought upon,
Nor had a doubt, nor any kind of fear.
He jousted, danced, and made her merry cheer;
And thus in joy and bliss I let them dwell,
And of the sick Aurelius will I tell.

   In languor and in torment furious

Two years and more lay poor Aurelius
Before he set a foot on earth again;
And got no help for his enduring pain
Save from a clerk, his brother, who well knew
About his labor, and his anguish too;
For to no other creature would he dare
To breathe the barest word of this affair,
But hid it in his breast more secretly
Than Pamphilus his love for Galatee.
Seen from without, his breast was sound and whole,
But the sharp arrow festered in his soul;
And wounds that heal without, but still endure
Within, ye know are difficult of cure,
Unless the surgeon find the arrow there,
And take it out. His brother, in despair,
Secretly wept and wailed, until by chance
He thought how once in Orleans, in France,
Like most of these young clerks, that have a liking
To study arts unusual and striking,
Poking in every corner to discover
Some occult science they can marvel over,
Upon a certain day – he called to mind –
While he was studying, he had chanced to find
A book on natural magic, as he saw –
One that his friend, a bachelor of law,
Though then he learned another craft, indeed,
Had left upon his desk for him to read.
This volume had much matter to relate
About the moon, and of her twenty-eight
Mansions, and when they worked, and in what way –
Folly that is not worth a fly today,
For Holy Church's faith in our belief
Lets no illusion harm, or bring us grief.
And having called this book to mind by chance,
His heart for happiness began to dance,
And to himself he whispered, well assured:
"Now shall my brother's sickness soon be cured!
For I am certain that, with right conditions,
Men can by science summon apparitions
Such as these subtle jugglers make appear;
For many times at banquets, as I hear,

Will these magicians, in a chamber large,
Make water flow, and on its breast a barge,
That in the hall goes rowing to and fro.
Or else a savage lion they will show;
Or flowers and grass will flourish there instead;
Or else a vine, with grapes both white and red,
Or a high castle, all of lime and stone;
And when they will, lo – all of it hath flown!
So hath it seemed to everybody there.
    "Now then, if I to Orleans repair,
And there might come on some old comrade soon,
That understands these mansions of the moon,
Or if not such a magic, then another,
Could he not win this lady for my brother?
For he, by some illusion, it is clear,
Could make the black rocks seem to disappear
From Brittany, and none show any more;
And ships would come and go beside the shore;
And this appearance last a day or so;
So he would heal my brother of his woe;
For she would have to keep her oath, and pay,
Or he would shame her for it, anyway."
    Why make a longer story of this thing?
Off to his brother's chamber hastening,
Such comfort soon of Orleans he said,
That this Aurelius leaps up from his bed,
And goes upon his way with eagerness
And hope to be relieved of his distress.
    When they had journeyed almost to that place,
Having to go but several furlongs' space,
They met a young clerk walking all alone,
Who spoke in Latin in a courteous tone,
Greeting them. Then he said a wondrous thing:
"I know the purpose of your travelling."
And so before they moved another pace
He told them all their business in that place.
    This Breton clerk now questioned him, to know
Of comrades that had lived there long ago,
And he replied that all of them were dead,
And many a tear on hearing this he shed.
    Aurelius now alighted from his horse,

And forth with this magician took his course
Home to his house. He made them well at ease.
They had whatever victual they might please;
So well-arrayed a house as here was shown
Aurelius in his life had never known.

This clerk, before their supper, made appear
Forests, and parks with herds of running deer;
And harts he saw with horns that towered high –
The greatest ever seen by human eye.
He saw a hundred of them slain by hounds,
And some with arrows bled from bitter wounds;
Then the deer vanished, and he saw instead
Some falconers that on a river sped;
And with their hawks a heron they have slain.

Then saw he jousting knights upon a plain;
And after this he had a greater pleasure:
He saw his lady as she trod a measure,
And he himself was dancing there, he thought.
And when the master, that this magic wrought,
Saw it was time, he clapped his hands, and lo!
Farewell! The revel vanished with the blow.
Yet while they saw this, strange and marvellous,
They never left the house, but watched it thus
There in his study, sitting quietly
With all his books about them – just the three.

At length this master called his squire, and said:
"Is supper ready? When shall we be fed?
Almost an hour has passed away, I swear it,
Since I commanded you to go prepare it –
When these good gentlemen first came with me
Among my books, here in the library."

"Sire, when it pleases you," replied this squire.
"It is all ready – now, if ye desire."

"Then let us sup," he said, "for that is best –
These lovers have to have some time for rest."

The supper done, they talked about the fee
That might reward this master fittingly,
If he removed the last rock that had lain
From the Gironde east to the mouth of Seine.

He said that it was hard. By God, he swore,
He must receive a thousand pounds or more,

And even for that he would not try it gladly.

Aurelius' heart for joy was beating madly,
And he replied, "Fie on a thousand pound!
This whole wide world, which men declare is round,
I would bestow, were I its lord, indeed.
This is a bargain: we are well agreed.
And by my faith, ye shall be promptly paid.
But look – this matter must not be delayed;
After tomorrow let us set to work!"

"Nay, have my faith as pledge," replied this clerk.

Aurelius when it pleased him went to sleep,
And almost all that night his rest was deep;
What with his work and hope of happiness
His heart was lightened of its deep distress.

And in the morning, after it was day,
To Brittany they took the shortest way,
The sorcerer and Aurelius as well,
And they dismounted where they chose to dwell.
And this was – from my reading I remember –
The cold and frosty season of December.

Phœbus grew old, and latten-hued and dull,
That had been burnished gold and beautiful
In his declension hot, with shining rays;
But he had sunk in Capricorn these days,
And, as I tell you, shone but dim and pale.
The bitter frost had come, and rain and hail,
And the last green in yards had disappeared.
Janus sat by the fire, with double beard,
And from his bugle horn he drank the wine.
Before him stood the brawn of tuskèd swine,
And "Noël" was the cry of every man.

Aurelius now, in every way he can,
Makes cheer, and does his master reverence;
And prays him he will use all diligence
To help him lose his pain, and be restored,
Or he will slit his heart upon a sword.

The clerk hath so much pity for this man
That night and day he hurries all he can
To find the time for bringing to conclusion
His task – that is, to make a great illusion
By apparitions and by jugglery –

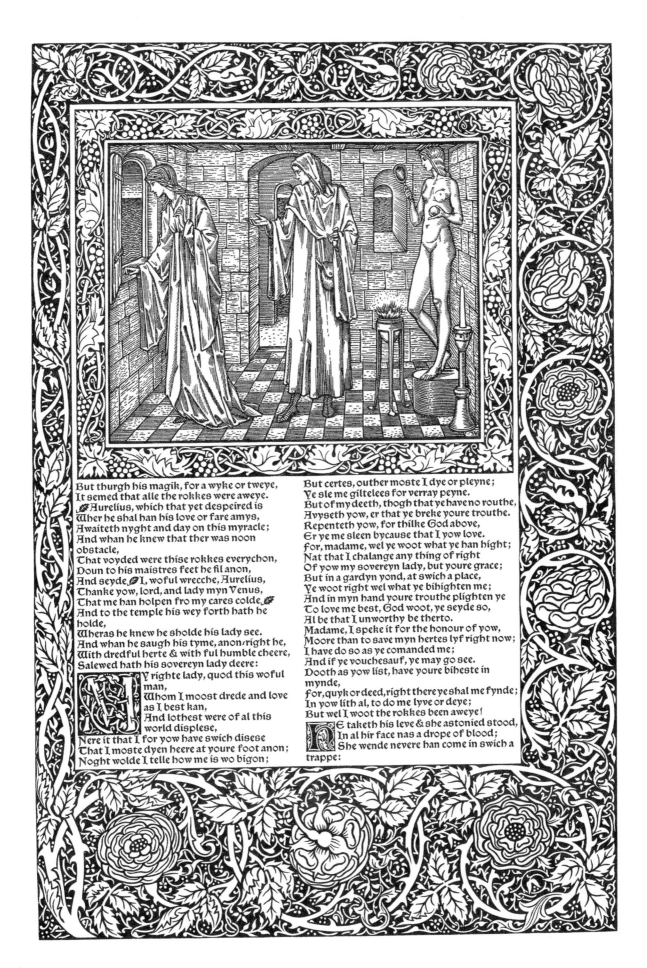

But thurgh his magik, for a wyke or tweye,
It semed that alle the rokkes were aweye.
Aurelius, which that yet despeired is
Wher he shal han his love or fare amys,
Awaiteth nyght and day on this myracle;
And whan he knew that ther was noon
obstacle,
That voyded were thise rokkes everychon,
Doun to his maistres feet he fil anon,
And seyde I, woful wrecche, Aurelius,
Thanke yow, lord, and lady myn Venus,
That me han holpen fro my cares colde.
And to the temple his wey forth hath he
holde,
Wheras he knew he sholde his lady see.
And whan he saugh his tyme, anon right he,
With dredful herte & with ful humble cheere,
Salewed hath his sovereyn lady deere:

Y righte lady, quod this woful
man,
Whom I moost drede and love
as I best kan,
And lothest were of al this
world displese,
Nere it that I for yow have swich disese
That I moste dyen heere at youre foot anon;
Noght wolde I telle how me is wo bigon;

But certes, outher moste I dye or pleyne;
Ye sle me gilteless for verray peyne.
But of my deeth, thogh that ye have no routhe,
Avyseth yow, er that ye breke youre trouthe.
Repenteth yow, for thilke God above,
Er ye me sleen bycause that I yow love.
For, madame, wel ye woot what ye han hight;
Nat that I chalange any thing of right
Of yow my sovereyn lady, but youre grace;
But in a gardyn yond, at swich a place,
Ye woot right wel what ye bihighten me;
And in myn hand youre trouthe plighten ye
To love me best, God woot, ye seyde so,
Al be that I unworthy be therto.
Madame, I speke it for the honour of yow,
Moore than to save myn hertes lyf right now;
I have do so as ye comanded me;
And if ye vouchesauf, ye may go see.
Dooth as yow list, have youre biheste in
mynde,
For, quyk or deed, right there ye shal me fynde;
In yow lith al, to do me lyve or deye;
But wel I woot the rokkes been aweye!

E taketh his leve & she astonied stood,
In al hir face nas a drope of blood;
She wende nevere han come in swich a
trappe:

I know no phrases from astrology –
That she and everyone would think and say
That all the rocks at last had gone away
From Brittany, or sunk beneath the ground.
And so at length his proper time he found
To work his tricks and raise this supposition
Spun by his sorry, cursèd superstition.
He had Toledo tables, well corrected;
Also his tables for his years collected
And single years were set in order there,
Also his roots, and all his other ware,
Such as his centers and his arguments,
And tables of proportional elements
For his equations of whatever kind.
Now by his calculations he could find
How Alnath in the eighth sphere had been shoved
By Aries' head above, that never moved,
And dwelleth in the ninth, by estimation;
Shrewdly he found all this by calculation.

　　When the first mansion in this way he knew,
Then by proportion all the others too
He learned; and the moon's rising he knew well,
And in what planet's face and term it fell;
And knew the mansion that the moon was in
Favored this matter that he would begin,
And knew as well the various other things
For such illusions and such magickings
As heathen people practised in those days.
And so at last he made no more delays,
And by his magic, for a week or more,
It seemed the rocks were gone from all the shore.

　　Aurelius, still in half-despairing woe,
Doubtful if he should have his love or no,
By night and day waits for this miracle;
And when at last he saw that all was well,
And the rocks gone, and all the work complete,
He fell down quickly at his master's feet,
And said, "I, woeful wretch Aurelius,
Thank you, my lord, and Lady Venus thus,
That both have helped me from my cold despair;"
And toward the temple took his way from there,

Where he knew well that he would see his lady.
And when he saw his time, no whit delayed he,
But humbly, with a heart that shook with fear,
Saluted there his sovereign lady dear.

　　"My lady," said this woeful man, "whom now
I fear, and love the best that I know how,
And were most loath to cause uneasiness,
Did I not have through you such great distress
That at your feet I think that I must die –
I would not tell you of my misery
Except that I must die or else complain –
Ye slay me innocent for very pain.
But though ye have no pity for my death,
Yet be advised before ye break your faith.
Repent, I pray you, by the God above you,
Before ye slay me now because I love you.
For, madam, well ye know the pledge ye made.
I challenge not that anything be paid
Except, my sovereign lady, of your grace;
But in yon garden, in a certain place,
Ye know well what it was ye promised me;
Your hand in mine, ye promised solemnly
To love me best, God knows that sits above,
Though I am all unworthy of your love.
I say this not to save my heart's life merely,
But for your honor, madam, all as clearly;
For I have done what ye commanded me;
And if ye will, why, ye may go and see.
Do what ye will, but think what ye did swear;
For dead or living, ye shall find me there;
All lies with you, to save me or to slay,
But well I know, the rocks are gone away!"

　　He took his leave, and all aghast she stood;
And in her face was not a drop of blood.
She had not dreamed of such a trap. "Alas!"
She cried, "that this should ever come to pass!
Never, by any possibility,
Did I suppose this monstrous thing could be!
It is not nature, it is past belief!"
And home she goes all stricken with her grief,
And in her fear scarce had the strength to go.

She wept and wailed all of a day or so,
And swooned: till it was pitiful to see.
But why it was she kept in secrecy,
For out of town was this Arveragus.
But to herself she spoke, and often thus,
With a pale face and a despairing spirit,
Made her complaint, as ye shall quickly hear it:
    "Fortune," she cried, "against thee I complain,
That wrapped me unsuspecting in thy chain,
From which I know no way of breaking free
Except to die, or to dishonor me.
One of these two I shall be forced to choose.
But none the less, far rather would I lose
My life than lend my body to a shame,
Or know that I am false, or lose my name.
And I can win release by death, I know.
Has many a noble wife, long years ago,
And many a maid not slain herself, for sure,
To escape from sin, and keep her body pure ?
    "Yes, of a truth, these stories testify:
When thirty tyrants, ripe with villainy,
Slew Phido once at Athens, as he feasted,
And gave command his daughters be arrested
And brought before them naked in the palace
That they might sate their lewd delight and malice
And made them dance there in their father's gore –
God curse them – on the paving of the floor –
These maidens then, despairing and afraid,
Each with a high resolve to die a maid,
Ran secretly and jumped into a well,
And drowned themselves thus, as the stories tell.
    "They of Mycenae sought and gave command
For fifty maidens from the Spartan land,
Whom they would use for lust and lechery.
But there was none in all that company
That was not slain, and, firm in courage steeled,
Preferred to perish rather than to yield
Her maidenhead; why then should I be sighing
And hesitate, and be in fear of dying?
    "And lo! the tyrant Aristoclides
Who loved a maiden called Stimphalides –

One night he caused her father to be slain;
And she fled straightway to Diana's fane,
And with her two hands seized the image there,
And would not let it go. No one could tear
Her arms apart, locked in that fast embrace,
Until at length they slew her in that place.
Since maidens thus refuse with scorn and fright
To be defouled by men for lewd delight,
A wife should surely slay herself than be
Defouled in such a way, it seems to me.
    "What shall I say of that Hasdrubal's wife
Who robbed herself at Carthage of her life?
For when she saw that Rome had won the town,
She took her children, and went skipping down
Into the fire, and rather chose to die
Than let a Roman do her villainy.
    "Hath not Lucrece by her own hand escaped
Through death at Rome, the time that she was raped
By Tarquin, since she held it but a shame
Longer to live when she had lost her name?
    "The seven maidens of Miletus slew
Themselves because of fear and anguish, too,
To save their honor from the men of Gaul.
A thousand stories I could tell in all
Relating to this matter, I suppose.
    "When Abradates fell before his foes,
His dear wife slew herself, and let her blood
Fall in his deep, wide wounds in gushing flood,
Saying: 'This body of mine, at any rate,
While I have life, no man shall desecrate.'
    "What more of such examples should I need,
When all these women slew themselves, indeed,
Rather than to be fouled by lechery?
I will conclude that it is best for me
To slay myself than be dishonored thus.
I will be true to my Arveragus,
Or like Demotion's well-belovèd daughter
I will obey the virtuous pride that taught her
Rather to die than yield to shameful passion.
    "O Scédasus! It fills me with compassion
To read the tale of how thy daughters died,

That for like cause committed suicide.

"It was as great a pity, or a greater,
That, when Nicanor tried to violate her,
The Theban maiden slew herself; and so
Another girl of Thebes, for a like woe,
When one of Macedon had done her shame,
With death redressed her chastity and name.

"What shall I say of Niceratus' wife,
That for such provocation took her life?

"And lo! how true to Alcibiades
His love was, that would risk the agonies
Of death to bury him when he was dead:
And such a wife Alceste was, too," she said.

"And what says Homer of Penelope?
Through all of Greece they knew her chastity.

"So of Laodamia it is written,
That when Protesilaus had been smitten
At Troy, she would not live beyond his day.

"The same of noble Portia can I say;
When Brutus died her life was terminated;
For all her heart to him was dedicated.

"And Artemisia's perfect wifehood stands
In honor everywhere through heathen lands.

"Queen Teuta! To thy chastity may wives
Hold up a mirror that might shape their lives.
The same thing I can say of Bilia,
Of Rhodogune, and of Valeria."

Thus Dorigen a day or two went sighing,
With all her heart and purpose fixed on dying.

But when at last the third day grew to night,
Home came Arveragus, this worthy knight,
And asked what made her weep so sore, and cry;
And she wept all the harder in reply.

"Alas!" she cried, "that I was ever born!
Thus did I speak," she said, "thus have I sworn –"
And told him all that ye have heard before –
No need now to repeat it any more.

With friendly word and nothing save good cheer
This husband spoke as I shall tell you here:
"Dorigen, is there more than this to tell?"

"Nay, nay," said she; "God help me, who knows well;

This is too much, though it were God's own will."

"Yea, wife," he said. "Let sleeping dogs lie still.
Perhaps this thing may yet go well today.
Ye shall be true and keep your oath, I say.
May God as surely grant His mercy to me,
As I would rather have a sword run through me,
Yea, for the very love I hold for you,
Than ye should fail in what ye pledged to do!
Truth is the highest thing man has in keeping."
But with that word at once he burst out weeping,
And said, "I charge you now, on pain of death,
That never, while ye have your life and breath,
Ye breathe a word of this to any man.
I will endure my woe as best I can,
And never show a heavy countenance,
To make men doubt or look at you askance."

Then instantly he called a squire and maid:
"Go out with Dorigen at once," he said,
"And lead her to the place that I shall say."
They take their leave, and go upon their way,
But never knew why she was going there;
With no man would this knight his purpose share.

Many of you, perhaps, in listening,
Will think this knight did but a foolish thing
To put his wife in danger in this way;
But hear the tale and save your tears, I say;
She may have better luck than you suppose;
Judge when ye hear the way the story goes.

This squire Aurelius who, I say again,
Was filled with such a love for Dorigen,
Now came upon her, as by accident,
As through the busiest street of town she went
Toward the garden, by the shortest way,
To keep the promise she had made that day.
And he was going to the garden, too,
For well he kept his watch, and always knew
When she would leave her house for any place.
And so they met, by accident or grace.
He greeted her, his face with gladness glowing,
And after that he asked where she was going.

And she responded, half like one gone mad,

"Unto the garden, as my husband bade,
Alas! Alas! To keep my promise there!"
    Aurelius wondered at her wild despair,
And through his heart there surged a great compassion
To see how she lamented in this fashion,
And for that worthy knight, Arveragus,
Who bade her keep her promise to him thus,
So loath was he his wife should break her word.
Thus such a pity in him strongly stirred,
Considering what was best from every side,
That he preferred to go unsatisfied
Rather than do so base an infamy
To noble faith and generosity;
And therefore with few words he answered thus:
    "Madam, say to your lord Arveragus
That since I see his lofty nobleness
Toward you, and see as plainly your distress –
That he (and that is pity!) has preferred
To bear this shame than have you break your word,
I choose now ever more to bear my pain
Rather than break the love betwixt you twain.
Madam, here cancelled I return to you
All bonds and pledges that were ever due
From you to me – to the last promise sworn
Even from the very day that ye were born.
I plight my troth that I will never grieve you
For any promise made; and here I leave you,
And leave, I say, the best and truest wife
That I have ever known in all my life.
But let all wives beware, and think again,
Before they give their faith, of Dorigen.
And thus a squire can do a noble deed
As well as any knight, as ye may heed."
    On her bare knees she thanked him, and arose;
And homeward to her husband quickly goes,
And told him all that ye have heard me say;
And be ye sure, he was so glad that day
That I could never write the joy he knew.
What further is there I can say to you?
    Arveragus and Dorigen his wife
In sovereign bliss lived on through all their life;

Never between them more was anger seen;
He cherished her as though she were a queen,
And she forever loved him faithfully.
Now of these two ye get no more from me.
    Aurelius, losing all that he has spent,
Curses the birth that brought such punishment.
"Alas!" he cried, "alas! that I agreed
To pay this thousand pounds of gold, indeed,
To this philosopher! What shall I do?
I shall be ruined if I see it through!
I shall be beggared, I shall have to sell
My heritage! And here I cannot dwell,
Shaming my kindred all about the place,
Unless I get of him some better grace.
But I will beg him that he let me pay
From year to year, upon a certain day,
And I will thank him for his courtesy.
But I will keep my compact faithfully."
    He goes with heavy heart and seeks his coffer,
And took a sum of gold that he would offer –
Five hundred pounds in value, as I guess.
And begged the man that, of his nobleness,
He give him time until the rest was due.
"Master," he said, "I dare well boast to you
I never failed to keep my promise yet.
And this is sure: I will discharge the debt
I owe you, whatsoever be my hurt,
Though I should beg, clad only in my shirt.
But will ye not, upon security,
Extend my time for two years more, or three;
Then I can do it; else I have to sell
My heritage – there is no more to tell."
    Then this philosopher, with sober eye,
When he had heard these words, made his reply:
"Have I not kept my covenant with thee?"
"Yea, surely – well and true," responded he.
"Hast thou not had thy lady, as was thy will?"
"No, no," he said, and sighed, and stood there still.
"What was the cause, then? Tell me if thou can."
At once Aurelius his tale began,
And told him all as ye have heard before –

No need that I rehearse it any more.
 He said, "Arveragus, in his nobleness,
Preferred to die in sorrow and distress
Than have his wife to any oath untrue."
The grief of Dorigen he told him, too,
How loath she was to be a wicked wife,
And would that day rather have lost her life;
And made in innocence that strange condition.
"She never heard of such an apparition.
This sent a wave of such great pity through me,
That just as freely as he sent her to me,
So did I send her freely on her way.
And this is all – there is no more to say."
 Then this philosopher replied, "Dear brother,
Each of you acted nobly toward the other.
Thou art a squire, and he, thou say'st, a knight;
Now God forbid it, in His holy might,

That a clerk could not do a noble deed
As well as any of you, when there is need.
 "Sire, I release thee of thy thousand pound,
As though thou hadst just crept from out the ground,
And never before had seen or heard of me.
For, sire, I will not take a penny of thee
For all my skill, nor for my labor thence.
For thou hast paid me well for my expense:
It is enough. Farewell, and have good day!"
And so he took his horse and rode his way.
 Now, lordings, answer this, and tell me true:
Which was most generous, as it seems to you?
Tell me, before we ride along – which one?
And now I know no more – my tale is done.

Here ends the Franklin's Tale

The Second Nun's Tale

THE SECOND NUN tells a saint's life, an appropriate choice for a nun. It is a tale of the persecution and martyrdom of early Christians. The virtuous Cecilia is miraculously preserved when the Romans try to burn her. The Second Nun contrasts Cecilia's faith with the beliefs of the philosopher, Almachius, who is shown to be ineffectual and deluded.

THE SECOND NUN'S TALE

*The Prologue of the
Second Nun's Tale*

THE minister and nurse of all our vices,
In English, Idleness, that keeps the gate
To sensuous delight that man entices,
We ought to shun and seek to extirpate
By good activity, which, so to state,
Is opposite to her, and from her frees us –
Lest through our idleness the fiend should seize us.

For with a thousand hidden cords he lies,
Always in wait to take us unaware,
And when some man in idleness he spies,
So easily can he catch him in his snare
That, till the fiend has seized his garment there,
He knows not he is in the devil's hand!
Thus idleness is something to withstand.

And though men never feared at all to die,
Yet they can see, unless their reason cease,
That Idleness is rotten sluggardry
From which there never comes a good increase;
And see that Sloth still holds her in a lease,
To let her eat, drink, slumber, and devour
All that which others sweat for many an hour.

And to divorce us from such idleness,
That is the cause of so great degradation,
I have worked well to render with success,
According to the legend, in translation,

Thy glorious life and painful sublimation –
Thou, Saint Cecilia, on whose brow reposes
The garland wrought of lilies and of roses.
[*Invocacio ad Mariam*]

AND thou that art the flower of virgins all,
Of whom Bernard has such a love to write,
To thee now in beginning first I call!
Comfort of wretched us, help me recite
Thy maiden's death, who, through her merit bright,
Won life eternal, vanquishing with glory
The fiend, as men can read here in her story.

Thou daughter of thy son, mother and maid,
Thou well of mercy, sinful souls' physician,
In whom for goodness God to dwell essayed,
Thou humble, yet enthroned in high position,
So didst thou lift our nature with thy mission
That He that made all nature thus was won
To clothe in flesh and blood His only Son.

Within the blissful cloister of thy side
To man's shape grew the eternal Love and Peace,
Lord of the three-fold universe, and Guide,
Whom earth and heaven and ocean never cease
To praise. Thou, spotless virgin, for a space,
Bore in thee, maiden still in every feature,
He that Creator was of every creature.

In thee are mercy and magnificence,
Goodness and pity in such unity
That thou, that art the sun of excellence,
Not only helpest those that pray to thee,
But often times, in thy benignity,
Freely, before men any help petition,
Thou dost appear, and art their lives' physician.

Help me, thou lovely, meek, and blessèd maid,
Who banished now in bitterness must dwell;
Think on the wife of Canaan, she who said
That dogs would feed upon the crumbs that fell

Down from their master's table. I know well
That I am sinful, wretched son of Eve,
And yet accept my faith, for I believe.

And since all faith, when lacking works, is dead,
So give me now for work both wit and space,
That I from darkness be deliverèd!
O thou that art so fair and full of grace,
Be advocate for me in that high place
Where there is endless singing of "Hosannah!"
Mother of Christ, dear daughter of St. Anna!

And from thy light my soul in prison light,
Where it is troubled by contamination
Of this my body, and the heavy weight
Of earthly lust, and all false inclination;
O heaven of refuge for us, O salvation
Of all souls whom distress and sorrow neighbor,
Help me, for I will now attempt my labor!

And yet of you that read my tale, I pray
Forgive me that I make no effort here
To set it forth in any subtle way;
For I have both the words and meaning clear
Of him that wrote this story to revere
The saint; and seek to write that legend true;
I pray you then, correct what I shall do.
[*Interpretacio nominis Cecilie, quam ponit frater
Iacobus Ianuensis in Legenda Aurea*]

AND first the name Cecilia I distinguish,
As men may find it in her history;
And "lily of heaven" it denotes in English,
For the pure chasteness of virginity;
Or, for the pallor of her modesty
And fresh green of her conscience, and good fame
Sweet in its savor, "lily" was her name.

Or else Cecilia means, "path of the blind,"
Since through good teaching she example bore,
Or, as in certain written works I find,

Cecilia is a linking up, once more,
Of "heaven" and "Leah," and here, by metaphor
"Heaven" stands for the thought of sanctity,
And "Leah" means her constant industry.

Also, Cecilia may be thus expressed:
"The lack of blindness," for her shining flame
Of wisdom, and the virtues she possessed;
Or else this maiden drew her lustrous name
From "heaven" and "leos," and, if thus it came,
She might be called "the heaven of people" then,
Symbol of wise and holy works for men.

For "leos," set in English, signifies
"People," and just as men on all sides see
The sun and moon, and planets in the skies,
So in this maid the magnanimity
Of faith appears when sought for spiritually,
And perfect clearness, too, of sapience,
And various works of shining excellence.

And as philosophers will often write
That heaven is swift and round and burning ever,
In such a way Cecilia, fair and white,
In good works sped, and stayed her action never,
And she was round and whole in good endeavor,
And ever in shining charity she flamed;
Thus have I told you well what she was named.

Here begins the Second Nun's Tale of the Life of Saint Cecilia

CECILIA, this bright maiden, was a Roman,
Her life declares, and of a noble kind,
And from her cradle fostered was this woman
In Christ's faith, and his gospel bore in mind,
And never ceased her prayers, in books I find,
And to love God and fear, and supplicate
That He preserve her in her maiden state.

And when this maid was plighted to a man
Whom she should wed, one that had not yet passed

His tender years, by name Valerian,
And when her marriage day was come at last,
She, humble, and in piety steadfast,
Under her robe of gold, that glittered fair,
Next to her flesh had set a shirt of hair.

And while the organ forth its music poured,
To God alone within her heart sang she:
"Direct my soul and body both, O Lord,
And keep me clean, lest I confounded be;"
And for His love that died upon a tree,
She spent in fasting every day or two,
And piously her orisons said through.

The night came on, and she must go to bed,
She and her husband, as folk often do;
And soon to him in secrecy she said,
"O my sweet husband, well belov'd and true,
I have a secret to impart to you,
And gladly will, if ye will hear me say it,
And swear to me that ye will not betray it."

Valerian with a solemn oath then swore
Whatever cause or reason there might be,
He would betray her secret never more;
And only then she spoke to him. Said she:
"I have an angel hath great love for me,
Who, whether I am waking or am sleeping,
Forever has my body in his keeping.

"And if that angel feel, I doubt it not,
That ye impurely love or with me lie,
He instantly will slay you on the spot,
And in your very youth thus should ye die;
But if your love for me is clean and high,
He for your cleanness will love you as me,
And show his joy and his effulgency."

Valerian, by God's chastening will controlled,
Replied: "If I shall put my trust in thee,
Then let me see that angel and behold,

And judge if it an angel really be;
Then will I do as thou hast prayed of me.
And if another have thy love and troth,
Right with this sword then I will slay you both."

Cecilia answered soon, and thus advised:
"And if ye wish, that angel ye shall see,
So ye believe in Christ and be baptized.
Go forth to Via Appia," said she,
"That from this town stands but two miles or three,
And to the poor folk that are dwelling there
Speak in the fashion I shall now declare.

"Tell them that I, Cecilia, sent you to them,
To take you unto Urban, good and old,
For secret need and purpose working through them;
And when the holy Urban ye behold,
Then tell again to him what I have told,
And when from sin Urban has purged your heart,
That angel shall ye see, ere ye depart."

Unto the place Valerian quickly sped,
And just as she had taught him of this thing,
Among the grave stones of the sainted dead
He found this holy Urban wandering;
And on the instant, without tarrying,
Gave him the message there, and when he gave it,
Urban raised up his hands in joy to have it.

And from his eyes the tears began to fall;
"Almighty Lord, O Jesus Christ," cried he,
"Sower of chaste advice, Shepherd of all,
Receive thou now the seed of chastity
That in Cecilia once was sown by Thee!
Lo, like a busy bee, guileless in all,
Cecilia ever serves thee, thine own thrall!

"That husband whom she lately took, and who
Was like a fierce wild lion, she sends here
As meek as ever walked a lamb, to you!"
And with that word, Valerian saw appear

In swich a gyse as I shal to yow seyn
Bitwixe yow and me, and that ful soone.
Ride whan yow list, ther is namoore to doone.
ENfORMED whan the kyng was of
that knyght,
And hath conceyved in his wit aright
The manere and the forme of al this thyng,
ful glad and blithe, this noble doughty kyng
Repeireth to his revel as biform.

THE brydel is unto the tour yborn
And kept among his jueles leeve and
deere,
The hors vanysshed, I noot in what manere,
Out of hir sighte; ye gete namoore of me;
But thus I lete in lust and jolitee
This Cambynskan his lordes festeyinge,
Til that wel ny the day bigan to sprynge.
Explicit prima pars. Sequitur pars secunda.

NORICE OF DIGESTIOUN, the sleepe,
Gan on hem wynke, & bad hem taken keepe,
That muchel drynke & labour wolde han reste;
And with a galpyng mouth hem alle he keste,
And seyde, it was tyme to lye adoun,
for blood was in his domynacioun.
Cherisseth blood, natures freend, quod
he.
They thanken hym galpynge, by two, by thre,
And every wight gan drawe hym to his reste
As sleep hem bad; they tooke it for the beste.

HIRE dremes shal nat been ytoold for
me;
ful were hire heddes of fumositee,
That causeth dreem, of which ther nys no
charge.
They slepen til that it was pryme large,
The mooste part, but it were Canacee.

Plate 26: The Squire's Tale (p. 284)

An old man, with white garments shining clear,
With a gold-lettered book within his hand;
Before Valerian he took his stand.

Valerian like one dead fell down for fear
To see this man, and he upraised him then,
And from his book read as I set it here:
"One Lord, one faith, one world of Christian men,
One God, one Father of us all again,
Above all, over all things everywhere;"
And all in gold these words were written there.

When this was read, then spoke this agèd man:
"Believest thou this thing? Say Yes or No."
"Yea, I believe it," said Valerian,
"For truer thing than this no man below
High heaven could think: I dare to hold it so."
Then the old man was gone, he knew not where,
And the Pope Urban christened him right there.

Valerian went home, and there he found
Cecilia, and he saw an angel stand
Beside her. And he held, of lilies wound
And roses, two crowns, one in either hand;
First to Cecilia, as I understand,
He gave the one; the other, as they state,
He carried to Valerian, her mate.

"With a clean body and unsullied thought
Forever keep these garlands well," said he;
"For these from Paradise to you I brought,
And they shall never more corrupted be,
Nor lose their fragrant odor, trust ye me;
And they alone shall see them with their eyes
That live chaste lives, and all base ways despise.

"And thou, Valerian, since thou didst so soon
Give thine assent to good advice, again,
Say what thou wouldst, and thou shalt have thy boon."
"I have a brother," said Valerian then,
"And him I love above all earthly men;

I pray you that my brother may have grace
To know the truth, as I do in this place."

"God," he replied, "is pleased with your request,
And both of you the martyr's palm shall bear,
And come before Him at the blessèd feast."
And then he saw Tiburce, his brother, there;
And of the fragrance he was soon aware
Which both the lilies and the roses shed,
And marvelled greatly in his heart, and said:

"I wonder, at this season of the year,
What brings this fragrance drifting pleasantly
Of roses and of lilies to me here.
For though I held them in my hands," said he,
"The perfume could no deeper sink in me;
And the sweet smell that in my heart I find
Has changed and made me all another kind."

Valerian answered him: "Two crowns have we,
Snow-white and rose-red, shining bright and clear,
Which thine eyes have not yet the power to see.
As by my prayer thou knowst their fragrance here,
So shalt thou see them also, brother dear,
If setting sloth aside thou wilt receive
The truth itself, and rightly wilt believe."

Tiburce replied: "Dost thou say this to me
In truth, or in a vision do I hear it?"
"In visions," said Valerian, "certainly
We have lived, brother, till this time, I fear it.
But now our dwelling is in truth and spirit."
"How know'st this?" Tiburce asked. "In what
    way?"
Valerian answered: "That I soon shall say.

"This truth by God's own angel I was taught;
Thou too shalt see it if thou put from sight
Thine idols and be clean – otherwise not."
And of these crowns by miracle made bright
St. Ambrose in his preface deigns to write.

This dear and noble doctor solemnly
Commends it, and in this way speaketh he:

To take the palm of martyrdom instead,
Cecilia, filled with God's own gift, put by
The world, and also shunned her marriage bed;
To this Valerian's faith can testify,
Tiburce's too; for God, in goodness high,
Granted them crowns of flowers of fragrant scent;
Bearing these crowns God's very angel went.

The maid brought both these men to bliss above;
The world learned thus how precious is the gain
When chastity is served by pious love;
And then Cecilia showed him, clear and plain,
That idols all are wretched things and vain,
For they are dumb, and deaf as well, and she
Charged him to leave his idols instantly.

"He that believes not this is but a beast,"
Tiburce said then, "if I shall tell no lie."
And she that heard began to kiss his breast,
Filled with delight that he could truth espy.
"This day I take thee now as mine ally,"
Said this belov'd and fair and blessèd maid,
And after that, as ye shall hear, she said:

"Lo! even as the love of Christ," said she,
"My wedding with thy brother solemnized,
So now I take thee mine ally to be,
Since thou thy heathen idols hast despised.
Go with thy brother now, and be baptized,
And make thee clean, so that thou mayst behold
The angel's face of which thy brother told."

Tiburce replied and said, "O brother dear,
First tell me where to go, and to what man?"
"To whom?" cried he. "Come, start we gladly
   here
And I will find thee Urban if I can."
"Urban? Ah, brother mine, Valerian,"

Tiburce said then, "To him shall we proceed?
That seems to me a wondrous thing indeed.

"Dost thou not mean that Urban," he said then,
"Condemned by law so often to be dead,
Living from nook to nook unknown to men,
And never daring once to show his head?
To the red flames his body would be fed
If men could find him, or indeed espy him;
And we too, if they chanced to find us by him.

"And while we seek divinity to know
That in the heaven is veiled in secrecy,
We shall in any case be burned below!"
To which Cecilia answered fearlessly:
"Men might indeed have fear, and reasonably,
To lose existence here, mine own dear brother,
If this life stood alone, without another.

"But better life waits in another place,
That never shall be lost, have thou no fear,
Of which God's Son has told us through His
   grace –
That Father's Son that fashioned all things here;
And all his creatures in which minds appear,
To such the Holy Spirit that went out
From God the Father giveth souls, no doubt.

"God's Son by spoken word and miracle,
When he was in this world, assured us here
There was another life where men can dwell."
To whom Tiburce replied, "O sister dear,
Didst thou not just now seek to make it clear
There is but one God, Lord in verity?
How canst thou now bear witness unto three?"

"That, ere I go, shall have interpretation.
Just as a man has three wise faculties:
Memory, intellect, imagination,
So in one Being, the Divinity's,
Three separate persons may exist with ease."

Then she began industriously to preach
Of how Christ came, and all His woes to teach,

And many a point about His passion high –
How God's Son to this world was relegated
A full remission for mankind to buy,
In sorrows cold and sin incarcerated;
All this Cecilia to Tiburce related,
And he soon after, sober of intent,
Unto Pope Urban with Valerian went;

Who thanked God, and with heart all glad and light,
Christened him then, and made him in that place
Perfect in Christian knowledge, and God's knight.
And after that Tiburce received such grace
That every day he saw, in time and space,
Th'angel of God; and every kind of boon
He asked of God was granted to him soon.

Hard would it be in order to report
How many wonders Jesus for them wrought,
But in the end, to make my story short,
The Roman sergeants these two brothers sought,
And to the prefect Almachius brought
Both of them; and he learned soon what they were,
And sent them to the shrine of Jupiter;

"Who will not sacrifice," he said, irate,
"Strike off his head; this judgment I declare."
These martyrs then, whose story I relate,
One Maximus hath taken in his care,
The prefect's officer and chief clerk there;
And when he led these saints out through the city
This captain could not help but weep for pity.

When Maximus had heard them talk and pray,
He from the executioners got leave,
And took them to his house without delay,
And by their preaching, ere it grew to eve,
They made these executioners receive,
And Maximus, and all his people there,

The God and true belief that they declare.

Cecilia came, when it had grown to night,
With priests, and christened them together there,
And afterwards, when day had grown to light,
She said to them with grave and sober air:
"Now, knights of Christ, beloved and dear and fair,
The works of darkness wholly cast away
And arm yourselves in armor bright as day.

"For ye indeed have waged a mighty strife,
Your course is done, your faith preserved," she said.
"Go now to take the unfading crown of life;
The righteous Judge, whose service ye have sped,
Shall give it to you, nobly merited."
And when this thing was spoken as I say,
To sacrifice men led them all away.

But when they were conducted to the spot
To sacrifice – briefly the thing to tell –
Or offer incense, truly they would not,
But on their knees instead these brothers fell,
With humble hearts and steadfast faith as well;
And by the axe the lives of both were ended.
Their spirits to the King of Grace ascended.

And Maximus, who witnessed all this thing,
Soon told with piteous tears how in his sight
The souls of both to heaven rose triumphing,
With angels clothed in clear and radiant light;
And with his word converted many a wight;
And he for this was flogged with whips of lead,
As Almachius bade, till he was dead.

Within a burial place that was her own
Cecilia buried him in secrecy,
Beside the brothers, underneath the stone.
And Almachius ordered now that she
Be brought to him for judgment publicly,
That in his presence he might ask of her
Incense and sacrifice for Jupiter.

But soon his ministers, when they had heard
Her wise instruction, wept most grievously,
And often cried, believing in her word:
"Christ, Son of God in all equality,
That has so good a servant, surely He
Is very God, this with one voice we cry,
This is our judgment truly, though we die."

And Almachius, hearing of this thing,
Sent for Cecilia, that he might her see,
And first of all thus went his questioning:
"What kind of woman art thou?" then said he.
"I am a gentlewoman born," said she.
"I ask thee, though that may be to thy grief,
Of thy religion and of thy belief."

"Ye have begun your question foolishly,"
Said she, "that seek two answers to include
In one demand; ye have asked ignorantly."
And Almachius to that similitude
Replied: "Whence comes thine answering so
    rude?"
"Whence?" said Cecilia, when she understood;
"From conscience and a faith unfeigned and good."

"Hast thou no heed," this Almachius said,
"As to my power?" And thus she made reply:
"Your power is but a little thing to dread;
The power of any man beneath the sky
Is like a bladder wind makes round and high.
For all its boast, when it is proudly blown,
Can with a needle's point be levelled down."

"Thou hast begun most wrongfully," said he,
"And yet in wrong I see thee persevere.
Knowst not our mighty princes by decree
And ordinance proclaimed have made it clear
That every Christian shall be punished here
Unless he shall forswear the Christian creed;
But if he will renounce it, shall be freed?"

"Your princes err, even as your nobles do,"
Cecilia said, "and with a mad decree
Ye make us guilty, and it is not true;
For ye, that know how innocent we be,
Since we in reverence do our fealty
To Christ – because we bear the Christian name,
Ye put a crime upon us, and great blame.

"But we who know that name which ye abuse
Is virtuous, we cannot put it by."
He said: "Between these two I bid thee choose:
Do sacrifice, or Christian faith deny,
That thou mayst now escape thy death thereby."
At which the holy, fair, and blessèd maid
Began to laugh, and to the justice said:

"O judge, confused in folly," answered she,
"Shall I abandon innocence and salvation
And be a wretch lost in iniquity?
Lo! All may witness his dissimulation,
And how he madly stares in perturbation!"
Said Almachius: "Thou unhappy wretch,
Dost thou not know how far my power can
    stretch?

"Did not our mighty princes to me give
Yea, both the power and the authority
To order men to die or let them live?
Why speakest thou then so proudly unto me?"
"I only speak in steadfastness," said she,
"Not proudly, for I tell thee, on my side,
We Christians hate this deadly sin of pride.

"And if to know a truth thou dost not fear,
Then just and open reason will I give
To show a falsehood thou hast uttered here.
Thou sayest thy princes gave prerogative
To thee to slay a man or make him live;
Thou, that canst only take life for an hour,
Thou hast no warrant more than this, nor power.

"But thou canst say, thy princes have decreed
Thee minister of death; if thou say more
It is a lie – thy power is bare indeed."
"Leave off thy boldness," Almachius swore,
"And make our gods a sacrifice before
Thou go: for me, I mind not any slur;
I can bear all like a philosopher;

"But all these insults which thou hast applied
Unto our gods I cannot bear," said he.
"O foolish creature!" she in turn replied,
"There is no word that thou hast said to me
But showed the folly that resides in thee,
And proved in every manner that thou were
A vain judge and an ignorant officer.

"And in thy fleshly eyes thou art but blind,
For something that we all can understand
Is stone, as men can plainly see and find,
That stone becomes a god at thy command.
I do advise thee, touch it with thine hand
And feel it well, and thou shalt find it stone,
Since to thy blind eyes this could not be shown.

"It is a shame that people scorn thee so,
And at thy folly laugh with mocking eye;
For this is something that all creatures know:
That mighty God sits on His throne on high;
And images, as thou canst well espy,
Profit thee not, nor give to Him delight,
For, in effect, they are not worth a mite."

These words and others like them uttered she.
And he grew wroth, and bade that she be led
Homeward. "And burn her in her house" said he,
"Within a bath of fire all flaming red."
And this was carried out as he had said;
For in a bath they shut her, and they light
A fire beneath, and feed it day and night.

All the long night and all next day again,
In spite of all the bath's heat and the fire,
She sat quite cold, and felt no kind of pain,
Nor did the flames make her a drop perspire.
Yet in that bath at last she must expire,
For Almachius in his wicked wrath
Ordered that they should slay her in the bath.

Three strokes the executioner delivered
Upon her neck, but by no kind of chance
Could strike so that her neck was wholly severed;
And since in that day, by an ordinance,
None was allowed a man's pain to enhance
By a fourth stroke, however light or sore,
This executioner dared do no more;

But with her mangled neck, half murdered lying,
He left her there, and went upon his way.
The Christians, gathered there as she was dying,
Caught all the blood in sheets; and there she lay
Living in torment unto the third day,
And never ceased to show the faith by teaching;
To those whom she had taught she went on preaching,

And gave them her effects and property,
And then committed them to Urban's care;
"This I beseeched of heaven's King," said she –
"My life for three days and no more to spare,
To recommend, ere I for death prepare,
These souls to you, and make my house secure,
Here as a church perpetually to endure."

Saint Urban with his deacons secretly
The body fetched, and buried it by night
Beside his other saints, with dignity.
Her house "The Church of Saint Cecilia" hight;
Saint Urban hallowed it, as well he might,
And there in noble fashion to this day
To Christ and to his saint men service pay.

Here ends the Second Nun's Tale

The Canon's Yeoman's Tale

THE CANON'S YEOMAN is a servant who serves a canon, an officer of the church. He joins the pilgrimage part way through, and leaves it again, so fracturing the closed world of the pilgrims. His tale falls into two parts. The first is an exposition of the trickery practised by alchemists, the second a tale of a canon who tricks a greedy priest. Alchemy was quite new at the time when Chaucer was writing. The vivid depiction of the alchemist's laboratory and his repeated, fruitless attempts to turn base metal into gold, endorse the message of the Second Nun's Tale that faith is more reliable and virtuous than scientific knowledge.

THE CANON'S YEOMAN'S TALE

The Prologue of the Canon's Yeoman's Tale

WHEN Saint Cecilia's life had thus been said,
And we had not yet jogged five miles ahead,
At Boughton-under-Blean, from farther back,
A man rode up all clothed in clothes of black,
And under those, of white, a surplice lay.
His hackney, that was all a dapple gray,
Sweated so hard that wonder was to see;
He must have spurred three miles, it seemed to me.
Also, his yeoman's horse was sweating so
It seemed as if the beast could hardly go;
The foam about the breastband frothed up high;
The horse was speckled with it, like a pie.
A folded bag upon his crupper lay;
He carried little clothing, I would say.
All light for summer rode this worthy man,
And in my heart a wonderment began
What he could be. And then I saw his hood
Was all sewn to his cloak, and understood
Through this, when I had turned it in my mind
A while, he was a canon of some kind.
His hat, held by a string, hung down his back,
For more than walk or pace had gone his hack;
He must have spurred along like one gone mad.
A burdock leaf beneath his hood he had,
To stay the sweat, and shield him from the heat.
It was a joy indeed to see him sweat!
His forehead dripped with all that fearful hurry
Like a still with plantain and with pellitory.

And as he came he cried out instantly:
"God save," he said, "this merry company!
I have spurred fast," he told us, "for your sake,
Because of my desire to overtake
And ride with all this pleasant company!"
His yeoman, too, was full of courtesy.
"This morning, sires, not long ago," he cried,
"Out of your hostelry I saw you ride,
And warned at once my lord and sovereign, too,
Who much desired to ride along with you;
He loves good talk and sport upon the way."

  "Friend," said our Host, "God give thee luck, I say,
For warning him! Thy master, it would seem,
Is a good judge, as I may justly deem,
And jolly also, I dare wager you.
Can he not tell a merry tale or two
To cheer this company along the way?"

  "Who, sire? My lord? Why, to be sure – yea, yea,
He knows enough of mirth and jollity –
More than enough. Believe it, sir, from me;
And sir, if ye could know him as I do,
To see how well he works, and shrewdly, too,
In various ways, were wonder for your eyes.
He undertakes full many an enterprise
Which any here would find it hard, no doubt,
Unless they learned of him, to bring about.
And homely though he seem to you that view him,
Ye would have great advantage if ye knew him.
Ye would prefer to lose much gold, I say,
Rather than lose acquaintance with him. Yea,
I wager all I have in my possession.
He is a man of very high discretion;
I warn you, far superior to most."

  "Well! Then I pray thee: tell me," said our Host,
"Is he a clerk? What kind of man is he?"

  "Nay, greater than a clerk, assuredly,"
This yeoman said, "and in a word or two,
Host, I will somewhat show his craft to you.

  "I say, my lord knows so much subtlety
(But all his art ye cannot know through me,
Though in his practice I assist somewhat)

Though all this ground beneath on which we trot
Until we come to Canterbury town,
He hath the power to turn clean up-side-down,
And pave it all with silver and with gold."

And when the yeoman had this story told
Unto our Host, he answered, "*Ben'cité*!
But this is passing marvellous to me:
That since thy lord has such high skill and wit,
And men should reverence him because of it,
His heed for his own honor is so slight
The cloak he wears is hardly worth a mite,
As I may thrive, for such a man as he!
For it is foul, and torn in half, I see.
Why is thy lord so sluttish, then, I pray,
When he could well afford a good array
If his performance tally with thy speech?
Now tell me that – so much will I beseech."

"Why?" said this yeoman. "Wherefore ask ye me?
Because he'll never win prosperity!
(Yet I would not acknowledge what I say,
And therefore keep it secret, sir, I pray).
As I believe, he is too wise, indeed;
For what is overdone will not succeed;
It is a fault, as scholars freely grant,
And he is silly there, and ignorant.
For when a man harbors too great a wit
Often it happens he misuses it;
So with my lord, and that thing grieves me sore.
May God amend it! I can say no more."

"Then let it go, good yeoman," said our Host.
"Since all the cunning of thy lord thou know'st,
Tell how he works, right heartily I pray,
Since he has such a subtle, skilful way.
Where do ye dwell, if thou can tell it me?"

"Out in the suburbs of a town," said he,
"Lurking in corners and in alleys blind,
Where in their fearful residence ye find
Such as are thieves and robbers by their nature,
Like men that daren't be seen by any creature,
Just so live we, to tell you truthfully."

Our Host said: "Let me talk some more with thee.

Why is thy face discolored in this way?"

"Peter!" he cried. "Bad luck to it, I say;
I have to blow the fire so much, God knows,
That it has changed my color, I suppose.
Ye seldom see me in a mirror prying;
I labor hard, and learn this multiplying.
Ever we grope and pore above the fire,
Yet for all that, we fail of our desire,
For what we seek comes never to conclusion.
In many folk we foster an illusion,
And borrow gold – a pound or two may come,
Or ten or twelve, perhaps a larger sum –
And make them think the least that we shall do
With every pound will be to make it two.
Yet it is false, but always we are hoping
To do the thing, and after it keep groping.
But still that knowledge flees as we pursue it,
So that we cannot, though we swore to do it,
Catch it; it always slips away so fast.
The thing will make us beggars yet, at last."

While he spoke thus, the canon stole up near,
And listening to the two, he soon could hear
All that was said; for none could say a word
But some suspicion in this canon stirred.
For Cato says a guilty man will be
Certain all things refer to him; and he
For this cause had drawn near, and listened well
To everything his yeoman had to tell.
And soon he said to him of what he heard:
"Now hold thy peace, and speak not another word,
For if thou do, then it will cost thee dear.
Thou slanderest me to all these people here,
And dost reveal what thou shouldst rather hide."

"Tell on, whatever comes!" our Host replied;
"Care not a mite how he may threaten thee!"

"Little enough I do, in faith!" said he.
And when he saw the yeoman would explain
His secrets, and that further talk was vain,
For grief and shame the canon fled away.

"Now," cried the yeoman, "for some merry play!
Now I shall tell you everything I know!

The prologe of the frankeleyns Tale

THISE olde gentil Britons in hir dayes
Of diverse aventures maden layes,
Rymeyed in hir firste Briton tonge;
Whiche layes with hir instruments they songe,
Or elles redden hem for hir plesaunce;
And oon of hem have I in remembraunce,
Which I shal seyn with good wyl as I kan.

But, sires, bycause I am a burel man,
At my bigynnyng first I yow biseche,
Have me excused of my rude speche.
I lerned nevere rethorik certeyn;
Thyng that I speke, it moot be bare and pleyn.
I sleep nevere on the Mount of Pernaso,
Ne lerned Marcus Tullius Cithero.
Colours ne knowe I none, withouten drede,
But swiche colours as growen in the mede,
Or elles swiche as men dye or peynte.
Colours of rethoryk been me to queynte;
My spirit feeleth noght of swich mateere,
But if yow list, my tale shul ye heere.

HEERE BIGYNNETH THE FRANKELEYNS TALE

IN ARMORIK, that called is Britayne,
Ther was a knyght that loved and dide his payne
To serve a lady in his beste wise;
And many a labour, many a greet emprise
He for his lady wroghte, er she were wonne;
For she was oon, the faireste under sonne,
And eek therto come of so heigh kynrede,
That wel unnethes dorste this knyght, for drede,
Telle hire his wo, his peyne, & his distresse.
But atte laste, she, for his worthynesse,
And namely for his meke obeysaunce,
Hath swich a pitee caught of his penaunce,
That pryvely she fil of his accord,
To take hym for hir housbonde and hir lord,
Of swich lordshipe as men han over hir wyves;
And for to lede the moore in blisse hir lyves,
Of his free wyl he swoor hire as a knyght,
That nevere in al his lyf he, day ne nyght,
Ne sholde upon hym take no maistrie
Agayn hir wyl, ne kithe hire jalousie;
But hire obeye, and folwe hir wyl in al,
As any lovere to his lady shal;
Save that the name of soveraynetee,
That wolde he have, for shame of his degree.

SHE thanked hym, and with ful greet humblesse,
She seyde, Sire, sith of youre gentillesse
Ye profre me to have so large a reyne,
Ne wolde nevere God bitwixe us tweyne,
As in my gilt, were outher werre or stryf.
Sire, I wol be youre humble trewe wyf;
Have heer my trouthe, til that myn herte breste.
Thus been they bothe in quiete & in reste.

FOR o thyng, sires, saufly dar I seye,
That freendes everych oother moot obeye,
If they wol longe holden compaignye.
Love wol nat been constreyned by maistrye;
Whan maistrie comth, the god of love anon
Beteth his wynges, and farewel! he is gon!
Love is a thyng as any spirit free;
Wommen of kynde desiren libertee,
And nat to been constreyned as a thral;
And so doon men, if I sooth seyen shal.
Looke, who that is moost pacient in love,
He is at his avantage al above.
Pacience is an heigh vertu certeyn;
For it venquysseth, as thise clerkes seyn,
Thynges that rigour sholde nevere atteyne.
For every word men may nat chide or pleyne.
Lerneth to suffre, or elles so moot I goon,
Ye shul it lerne, wherso ye wole or noon;
For in this world, certein, ther no wight is
That he ne dooth or seith somtyme amys.
Ire, siknesse, or constellacioun,
Wyn, wo, or chaungynge of complexioun,
Causeth ful ofte to doon amys or speken.
On every wrong a man may nat be wreken;
After the tyme moste be temperaunce
To every wight that kan on governaunce.
And therfore hath this wise worthy knyght,
To lyve in ese, suffrance hire bihight,
And she to hym ful wisly gan to swere
That nevere sholde ther be defaute in here.

HEERE may men seen an humble wys accord;
Thus hath she take hir servant and hir lord,
Servant in love, and lord in mariage,

Plate 27: The Franklin's Tale (p. 290)

Since he is gone, the foul fiend take him so!
For I will never more have thing to do
With him, for pence or pound, I promise you.
And he that brought me first into that game,
May he, before he die, have woe and shame!
Earnest it is to me – no game, in faith;
I feel that well, whatever any saith.
And yet for all my grief and all my trouble,
My suffering, my labor more than double,
I never had the strength to part with it!
I would to God I had sufficient wit
To tell of all pertaining to that art!
But none the less I shall reveal a part;
Since he is gone I will not scrimp or spare,
But everything I know, I will declare."

Here ends the Prologue of the Canon's Yeoman's Tale

Here the Canon's Yeoman begins his Tale

I DWELT beside this canon seven year,
But never toward his knowledge drew more near.
All that I ever had I have lost thereby,
And God knows, so have many more than I.
And where I used to go all fresh and gay,
In clothing and in other good array,
Now I must wear a stocking on my head;
And where my color once was fresh and red,
Now it is pale and of a leaden hue!
Who tries that craft does something he shall rue!
Also, the wool is pulled across my eyes;
These are the gains of one that multiplies.
That slippery art has stripped me all so bare,
That any way I turn, nothing is there.
And yet I stand so much in debt for gold
Borrowed for this, that, if the truth be told,
All my life long I cannot pay it – never.
Let every man be warned by me for ever!
Whoever tries that art, if he persist,
Farewell success for him, for I insist,
God help me, that he shall not win from it

More than an empty purse, and weaker wit.
And when, grown mad and foolish, he has tossed
His own wealth on the hazard, and has lost,
He will excite full many another one
To lose his goods, as he himself has done.
For rogues get joy and comfort when they see
Their fellows suffer pain and misery.
This is a thing I learned once of a clerk.
No matter – I will speak now of our work.
When we assemble where we exercise
Our elfish craft, we all seem wondrous wise,
Our language sounds so bookish and so quaint;
I blow the fire until I almost faint.
    Why should I tell you each proportionate part
Of what we work with when we ply our art –
As, ounces – five or six, it well might be
Of silver – or some other quantity;
Or what the names of each ingredient, –
As, iron sheets, burnt bones, or orpiment,
All ground to powder very fine and small?
How in an earthen pot we put it all,
And put in salt, and pepper with it, too,
Before these powders I have named for you,
And with a plate of glass cover it fair –
And many other things we practice there?
And how the glass is sealed fast with cement
Above the pot, that air shall have no vent
For passing forth; and of the fire made slow
Or hot, and all the trouble and the woe
We have in sublimating everything,
Also calcining and amalgaming
Our quicksilver, called Mercury. Indeed,
For all our shifts, we never can succeed.
Orpiment, sublimated Mercury,
Litharge ground smooth on slab of porphyry –
Ounces of each, allotted to the grain –
Nothing will help; our labor is in vain.
Nor any of our vapors upward flying,
Nor the fixed substance at the bottom lying,
Are of avail to make our work more sure.
Our preparation and expenditure

And all our labor that we give to make it
Successful – all are lost, the devil take it!

And there is many another thing remaining
To tell, as to this art of ours pertaining.
And though in order I cannot relate them,
Nor yet according to their natures state them,
Being unlearned in matters of this kind,
Yet I will tell them as they come to mind –
As, borax, clay Armenian, verdigris,
Vessels of earth and glass along with these,
And our descensories and urinals,
Our flasks and vials and our crucibles,
Our vessels that we use in sublimation,
And more, of not a farthing's valuation.
There is no need now to run through them all –
Water for reddening, brimstone, and bull's gall,
Or sal ammoniac, arsenic, or any
Herbs that we used – and I could tell you many –
As agrimony, valerian, and moonwort,
And – if I wished to stop – more of the sort;
And lamps that we keep burning day and night
To reach the end we seek with all our might.
Also our furnace used for calcination,
Waters subjected to albification,
Chalk, unslaked lime, and powders in array,
Ashes, and white of egg, urine and clay,
Waxed bags, saltpetre, dung, and vitriol,
And various fires made of wood and coal,
Alkali, tartar salt, sal preparate,
Matters combusted and coagulate,
Alum, clay made with man's or horse's hair,
Glass, oil of tartar, unfermented beer,
Yeast and crude tartar and red orpiment;
And how we mix, and how we use cement,
Of silver citronized, and fermentation,
And vessels for assays, conglomeration
Of moulds, and many another matter, too.

And, as was taught me, I will say for you
In order, just as many a time and more
I heard my master, all the spirits four
And bodies seven. The first of spirits reckoned

Is quicksilver, and orpiment is second,
The third is sal-ammoniac, and brimstone
The fourth. The seven bodies, one by one:
The sun is gold, the moon we take to be
Silver; and Mars is iron; Mercury
Quicksilver; Saturn, lead; Jupiter, tin,
And Venus copper, by my father's kin.

Who lets this cursèd craft of ours entice him,
The wealth he has in no case will suffice him,
For all the gold or goods that he lays out
Shall be his loss – of that I have no doubt.
He who would give his folly demonstration,
Let him come forth and study transmutation,
And every man with money in his chest
Come, and be born philosopher with the best!
This craft, ye think, is easy to acquire?
Nay, nay, God knows, for be he monk or friar,
Canon or priest or other man, I say,
And sit and read his book both night and day,
This elfish, foolish learning to rehearse,
All of his work is vain, by God, and worse!
To teach an ignorant man such subtlety –
Fie! Do not speak of it, it cannot be!
But men with bookish knowledge or with none –
It is the same result – for all is one;
The ignorant or the wise, by my salvation,
Will reach an end, sirs, in this transmutation,
Equally good when both of them are through –
That is to say, they fail alike, the two!

Yet of corrosive waters I forgot
To make rehearsal for you, did I not?
Of iron filings, and the mollification
Of bodies, also of their induration;
Of oils, ablutions, metals fusible,
Which all in all would make as much to tell
As any bible; and so of all this lore
I think it best that I should say no more.
For, I believe, I must have told enough
To raise a fiend, let him look never so rough.

No, let it be! The rare philosopher's stone,
Elixir called, we seek it hard, each one,

For if we found it, then our luck were rare!
But unto God that sits in heaven I swear
When we have done our best, for all our skill
And all our tricks, the thing eludes us still.
It makes us spend much gold, yea, all we have,
And this at times would almost make us rave,
Did not the good hope in us always spring,
And whisper that, despite our suffering,
We should be eased at last with our reward.
This hope and whisper, they are sharp and hard;
The search, I warn you well, will never end.
That future tense has lured men on to spend
All that they ever had, in trust of it.
Yet once they know that art they never quit,
For they will always find it bitter-sweet;
Yea, so it seems, for give them just a sheet
With which to wrap themselves in of a night,
And a rough cloak for walking by daylight,
And for this craft of theirs they sell and spend,
Nor stop till they have nothing in the end.
And always, anywhere that they may be,
The smell of brimstone marks them certainly;
They stink for all the world like any goat.
So hot and rammish does that odor float
That though a man should be a mile away
The smell will taint him, trust ye what I say.
Thus by their threadbare clothing and their smell
Any that wished could know these people well.
And if a man should ask them privately
Why they are clothed as if in poverty,
Then they will quickly whisper in his ear
That if they let their true estate appear
Men for their science would be sure to slay them –
The innocent thus let these men betray them!

   But let this go: now to my tale I get.
Before the pot upon the fire is set,
My lord compounds his metals – none but he –
With some alloys, a certain quantity –
Now he is gone, this I can boldly tell –
For, as men say, such craft he handles well;
At any rate, they give him such a name;

Yet often he appears to be to blame.
And know ye how? Sometimes it comes to pass
The kettle bursts, and all is gone, alas!
These metals are so violent when we brew them
No wall can ever make resistance to them
Unless it should be built of stone and lime –
They have such force they pierce it every time.
And some of them fly deep into the ground –
Thus on occasions lose we many a pound –
And some around the floor are strewn about,
And some fly through the roof, without a doubt,
And though the devil never shows his face
I know well he is with us in that place.
There is no more of rancor, woe, or ire
In hell, where he is set as lord and sire.
For when the pot is broken, as I have told,
Each feels abused, and then they rage and scold.
One blames the way the fire was set to going,
And one says Nay, the fault was in the blowing
(That was my task, and I am full of fear).
"Pshaw!" says a third. "What fools and babblers here!
I say ye did not mix it properly."
"Nay, stop now," cries the fourth. "Listen to me –
Because our fire was not with beech wood made,
That was the only cause, God be mine aid!"
What all the trouble was I cannot tell,
But there was great debate, I know it well.
"What!" cried my lord, "there's nothing to be done.
But I shall watch these dangers, every one;
The pot we used was cracked, sirs, I am sure.
In any case, feel no discomfiture.
After our custom, let us sweep the floor.
Pluck up your hearts – be glad and gay once more!"
   Quickly we swept the rubbish in a pile.
Above a canvas, in a little while,
We threw it in a sieve, and often lifted
And picked this rubbish over, and re-sifted.
   "Some of our metal," one began to call,
"Is here, by God, although indeed not all.
Although the thing has failed in this essay,
It may go well enough another day.

We have to venture, though 'tis hazardous.
By God, a merchant, sirs, must fare like us;
He cannot always have prosperity.
Sometimes his merchandise goes down at sea,
And sometimes comes in safety to the shore."

"Peace!" said my lord, "for when we try once more
I'll make another ending to our game;
Unless I do, sirs, let me take the blame.
There was an error made, I doubt it not!"

Another declared the fire had been too hot;
But, be it hot or cold, this much is true –
We end amiss, whatever we may do.
We always fail to get what we are craving,
And this forever sets us madly raving.
Yet when we walk together, every one,
Each of us seems a very Solomon.
But everything that glittereth like gold
Is not gold, as I've often heard it told,
Nor all the apples that may please the eye
Good ones, whatever men may shout or cry;
And so with us – just so – the thing will fall.
By Jesus, he that seems most wise of all
May prove the greatest fool, and come to grief,
And he that seemed the truest be a thief!
That ye shall know before I part with you,
Ere with the tale I tell you I am through.

Part II

THERE is a canon wears a holy gown
Among us, that would well infect a town,
Though great as Nineveh the place might be,
Or Rome, or Troy, or any other three.
His infinite falseness and the tricks he knows
No man could write in full, I should suppose,
Even if he lived a thousand years, for none
Could match his falseness – no, not anyone.
The terms he used were so involved and wily,
And he could speak his cunning words so slyly
In converse with a man, whoever he be,
That soon this priest would fool him utterly,

Unless it were a fiend, such as he is!
Many good men has he deceived ere this,
And will yet, if he live a little while.
Yet men would walk or gallop many a mile
To know him and to have his company,
Never suspecting his duplicity.
And this, if ye will deign to lend an ear,
I will relate now in your presence here.

But ye good canons, think not what I say
A slander on your house in any way,
Though of a canon I shall tell my tale.
By God, what order is there that can fail
To have a rogue within it? God forbid
That all should pay for what one rascal did!
To slander you is nowise in my mind,
But to correct what evils I may find.
Nor is this story told for you alone,
But others also. It is widely known
That of the twelve apostles, less or greater,
Judas Iscariot was the only traitor.
Then why should all the others bear the blame
That had no guilt? To you I say the same.
Save this – if ye will listen unto me –
If any Judas in your convent be,
Remove him, I advise you, in good season,
If there is fear of loss or shame by treason.
And bear me no displeasure now, I pray,
But listen in this case to what I say.

In London once a priest his life had led
For years, by singing annuals for the dead;
He was so useful, and such joy afforded
To the good lady at whose house he boarded,
That not a penny would she let him pay
For board or clothing, go he never so gay;
And he had all the silver he could need.
But let that go – for I will now proceed
My tale about the canon to relate
Who brought this priest to his unhappy fate.

Upon a day this treacherous canon made
A visit at the priest's room, where he stayed,
And begged a certain sum of gold, which he

Would soon repay him, of a certainty.
"Lend me a mark for just three days, I pray;
I will repay it promptly on my day;
And if thou find me false in this," he said,
"Next time I ask thee, have me hanged instead!"

The priest at once gave him a mark, and he
Many times gave him thanks, and presently
He took his leave, and went upon his way,
And brought the money back on the third day,
And promptly paid the priest the gold he had,
And he was pleased at this, and wondrous glad.

"Surely," he said, "it nowise vexes me
To lend a man a noble, or two or three,
Or anything, indeed, that I possess,
When he behaves with such punctiliousness
That in no manner will he break his day.
To such a man I never can say Nay."

"What!" cried the canon. "Should I be untrue?
Nay, such a thing with me were something new!
Truth is a thing that I will always keep,
Down to that very day when I shall creep
Into my grave, or God forbid, indeed!
Believe this thing as surely as your creed.
I thank God, and can promptly say that never
Have I offended any man whatever
That any gold or silver to me lent,
Or harbored in my heart a false intent.
And, sir," he said, "since ye have shown to me
Such goodness and such great nobility,
To pay you for your kindness, or in part,
I now will show you something of my art,
And, if indeed ye have a wish to learn,
So teach you that ye plainly can discern
How I can labor with philosophy.
Take heed, and those two eyes of yours shall see
That I will work a wonder ere I go."

"Yes," said the priest. "Yes, sir, and will ye so?
Mary! I pray you heartily to do it."

"Certainly, sir, if ye command me to it,
Otherwise God forbid!" the canon stated.

Lo! how this thief his tricks insinuated!

And it is true, as olden sages tell,
Such service always has an odious smell,
And that I soon shall prove and verify
In this vile canon, root of treachery,
That with delight would always play the part –
Such fiendish thoughts would press upon his heart –
Of bringing Christ's own folk to ruination.
God keep us from his false dissimulation !

This priest knew not at all with whom he dwelt,
Nor anything of coming evil felt.
O foolish priest! O foolish simple-minded!
With avarice too soon shalt thou be blinded!
O luckless one, how blind and unaware
Thou art! Thou seest not the deceitful snare
Which has been baited by this fox for thee.
Thou canst not shun his wily trickery!
Therefore, to go at once to my conclusion,
Which has to do, alas! with thy confusion,
Unhappy man, I hasten now, to tell
Thy folly and thine ignorant mind as well,
And as completely as my powers can,
The falseness of that other vicious man.

This canon was my lord, ye may suppose?
Sir Host, in faith, the queen of heaven knows
It was another canon, and not he,
That knew a hundred times more subtlety.
My master has betrayed men many a time;
Of his false ways it wearies me to rhyme;
For always, of his falseness let me speak,
And then for shame the red will mount my cheek –
At any rate, my cheeks begin to glow,
For redness have I none, as well I know,
In my complection, for the fumes of all
The various metals whose names ye heard me call
Have wasted and consumed my ruddiness.
Take heed now of this canon's cursedness.

"Sir," said he to the priest, "now let your man
Get quicksilver, as promptly as he can;
And let him bring two ounces here, or three;
And when he has returned, soon shall ye see
A wonder that ye never yet espied."

"Surely, it shall be done," the priest replied.
He bade the servant fetch this thing to hand,
And he was ready there at his command,
And out he went; and soon he came back duly
With this quicksilver, if I tell you truly,
And to the canon took these ounces three,
Who laid them by him fair and carefully;
And after that for coals the servant sent,
With which to further his experiment.

    The coals were quickly fetched, and, truth to tell,
This canon straightway took a crucible
Out of his bosom and showed it to the priest.
"This instrument," he told him, "which thou seest,
Take in thy hand, and thyself put therein
An ounce of this quicksilver, and begin
In the name of Christ, to be philosopher.
Few are the men on whom I would confer,
By demonstration, so much of my science.
For ye shall see here how, by this appliance,
I shall this quicksilver so mortify
Right in your sight, if I shall tell no lie,
That it will turn to silver, just as fine
And good as any in your purse or mine,
Or elsewhere; and shall make it malleable;
Otherwise hold me false, I pray you well,
And ever more unworthy to appear
Among mankind. I have a powder here
Shall do all this; for to its power is due
All of my skill that I shall show to you.
Send forth your man, and let him stay outside,
And shut the door, while we are occupied
About our secret practices, for fear
That while we labor, men might watch us there."

    All was arranged as he had specified.
This servant on the instant went outside,
His master shut the door at once, and so
Unto their labor with dispatch they go.

    Now at the canon's bidding and desire
The priest soon set this thing upon the fire,
And blew the fire, and labored hard and fast;
And in the crucible the canon cast

A powder; but I know not what it was –
Something compounded out of chalk or glass,
Or other stuff that was not worth a fly,
To blind the priest. He bade him to be spry
And rake the coals together well above
The crucible. "In token of the love
I bear thee, thy two hands shall do," said he,
"All things accomplished here by thee and me."

    "*Graunt merci*," said the priest, and he was glad;
And raked the coals up as the canon bade.
This fiend-like canon, false and treacherous,
(May the fiend take him!) while the priest toiled thus,
Out of his bosom took a beechen coal,
In which with cunning he had made a hole;
And silver filings he had secretly
Put there, an ounce, and stopped the cavity
With wax, to hold the filings, as he planned.
This false contrivance, ye will understand,
Was not made there, but it was made before;
And I shall tell you later on of more
Such things that he along with him had brought,
For to deceive this priest was all his thought,
And so he did before they separated;
He could not rest till this was consummated!
It wearies me to speak of him. I would
Avenge me for his falseness if I could,
Gladly – but he is always here and there;
He is so shifty he abides nowhere.

    But now, sirs, pay attention, for God's love!
He took this coal of which I spoke above,
And in his hand he held it secretly.
And while this priest was raking busily
Among the coals, as I explained ere this,
The canon told him: "Friend, ye work amiss;
This is not raked here as it ought to be!
But I shall quickly make it right," said he.
"Give me a chance to see what I can do;
For by Saint Giles, I truly pity you.
Ye grow all hot – I see that ye are wet;
Here – take a cloth and wipe away the sweat."
And then this canon, may God curse his soul!

While the priest mopped his face, slipped out the coal
And laid it on the glowing crucible,
Right in the middle, and afterwards blew well
Until the coals burned merrily and red.

"Now let us have a drink," the canon said.
"All will be well soon – nothing can miscarry;
Let us sit down a moment and make merry."
And when in time the canon's beechen coal
Had been consumed, the filings in the hole
Fell in the crucible in little season,
And so they must, for this was only reason,
Since they were placed so carefully above it.
But this, alas! – the priest knew nothing of it!
He thought that all the coals alike were good,
For nothing of this trick he understood.
And when this alchemist his time espied:
"Rise up, Sir Priest, and stand here by my side,
And since I know ye have no molds about,
Go bring a chalk stone for us – come, go out –
For I will make one of the shape," said he,
"That a mold has, if I have luck with me.
And bring a bowl or pan of water, too;
Then shall ye see it clearly proved to you
By test how we have prospered with our mission.
And yet, that ye shall harbor no suspicion
Of me, nor let false apprehension grieve you
While ye are absent – see, I will not leave you,
But go with you, and with you come once more."
And so, in brief, they opened the chamber door,
And shut it after them, and speedily
Went as they planned, and with them took the key,
And came back to the room without delay.
Why should I talk of this the live-long day?
He took the chalk, and straightway like a mold
He gave it shape, as ye shall soon be told.

I say, from out his sleeve he took a plate
Of silver (may he win an evil fate!)
Which was in weight only an ounce. Now see
The way of his accursed trickery.
The mold in length and breadth he hollowed out
To take this silver plate, ye need not doubt,

So slyly that the priest might not perceive,
And hid the plate again within his sleeve;
And from the fire, with merry air and bold,
He took his matters, and put them in the mold;
And when it pleased him, he deposited
All in the water, and to the priest he said:
"See what is there – put in thy hand and grope;
There shalt thou find some silver, as I hope.
What, devil in hell, but silver should it be?
A sliver of silver is silver, certainly!"
The priest put in his hand, and seized a plate
Of silver, and was happy and elate
In every vein to see that this was true.
"God's blessing on thee, and His mother's, too,
And all the saints within the universe,
Sir Canon! And may I receive their curse
Unless, if ye should deign to teach to me
This noble craft and all this subtlety,
In all ways possible I be your man!"

He said: "Still, I will do this if I can
A second time, that ye may take good heed,
And be expert in this, and at your need
When I am absent, make a demonstration
Of this high art and skilful occupation.
Now take another ounce," he added then,
"Of this quicksilver, and perform again
All that ye did before, for ye know how,
With the other ounce, turned into silver now."

This priest works hard in all ways that he can
To do just as the canon – cursèd man –
Commanded him, and blew hard at the fire
Thus to achieve the end of his desire.
Meanwhile this canon, most accursed of men,
Was all prepared to fool the priest again;
And in his hand, for show, he carried there
A hollow stick (observe this, and beware)
That in its end had just an ounce – no more –
Of silver filings hidden, as before
They were within the coal, stopped with a thin
Coating of wax to keep the filings in.
And while the priest was busy at his blowing,

The canon came, and stood beside the glowing
Coals with his stick, and cast the powder in
Just as before (The devil from his skin
Pluck him for falseness, unto God I pray;
His thoughts and acts were false in every way),
And with this stick that he had fitted well
With its false end, above the crucible
He stirred the coals, until the wax began
To melt above the fire, as every man,
Unless a fool, knows that it must, no doubt;
And all the filings in the stick ran out,
And in the crucible fell all this stuff.

    Good sirs, what would ye more than well enough?
When the priest thus had been once more deceived,
And, to be sure, nothing but good believed,
He was so glad that I cannot express
In any way his mirth and happiness;
And to the canon offered once again
Body and goods. "Yea," said the canon then,
"Though I am poor, I tell thee thou shalt find
That I am skilful. There is more behind.
Is there some copper in this place?" said he.
"Yes," said the priest, "I think, sir, there should be."
"If not, go quickly now and buy us some.
Now go thy way, good sir, and hasten! Come!"

    He went, and with the copper came again.
The canon in his hands received it then,
And weighed an ounce out from it, and no more.
My tongue is too unskilful to deplore,
As my wit's agent, the duplicity
This canon showed, root of all treachery.
To those who did not know him he seemed friendly,
Yet both in heart and thought the man was fiendly.
It wearies me to tell his cursedness.
And yet I will describe it, none the less,
With purpose – and no other reason, truly –
That from his falseness men take warning duly.

    He put his copper in the crucible,
And on the fire soon had it heating well,
And put in powder, and set the priest to blow;
And soon he, as before, was bending low

Over his work. All, as ye may suppose,
Was just a trick. He fooled him as he chose.
And next the matter in the mold he cast,
And in the pan of water then at last
He set it, and he put in his own hand.
And in his sleeve (as ye will understand
From what I told) he had a silver plate.
He slipped it out, the cursèd reprobate,
The priest not dreaming of this artful plan,
And left it in the bottom of the pan,
And in the water made to stir about,
And with a wondrous secrecy took out
The copper plate, though the priest never guessed.
He hid it, and he caught him by the breast,
And spoke to him, crying out sportively:
"Ye are to blame, by God! Stoop down," said he,
"Help me, as I helped you. Put in your hand –
See what is there!" The priest at his command
Out of the mold soon took the silver plate.
The canon said: "Let us no longer wait,
But take these sheets of metal we have wrought
To some goldsmith, and learn if they are aught.
For I, in faith, would wager my own hood
That they are silver, and are fine and good;
And that shall now be tested presently."

    Unto a goldsmith, carrying the three,
They went, and put these plates to the assay
By fire and hammer; and none could say them Nay
That they in all were as they ought to be.

    This stupid priest, who was more glad than he?
Never was bird more glad to greet the day,
And never was there, in the month of May,
A nightingale that had more joy to sing,
Nor lady lustier in caroling,
Or in the speech of love and womanhood,
Nor knight-at-arms to do brave deed and good
His well belovèd lady's grace to earn,
Than was this priest this sorry craft to learn.
And to the canon thus he spoke and cried:
"For love of God, that for us all hath died,
Tell me, say now – what costs this recipe?

Thanne was he bothe in lordship and servage;
Servage? nay, but in lordshipe above,
Sith he hath bothe his lady and his love;
His lady, certes, and his wyf also,
The which that lawe of love acordeth to.
And whan he was in this prosperitee,
Hoom with his wyf he gooth to his contree,
Nat fer fro Penmark, ther his dwellyng was,
Wheras he lyveth in blisse and in solas.

WHO koude telle, but he hadde wedded be,
The joye, the ese, and the prosperitee
That is bitwixe an housbonde & his wyf?

A YEER & moore lasted this blisful lyf,
Til that the knyght of which I speke of
thus,
That of Kayrrud was cleped Arveragus,
Shoop hym to goon & dwelle a yeer or tweyne
In Engelond, that cleped was eek Briteyne,
To seke, in armes worship and honour,
For al his lust he sette in swich labour;
And dwelled there two yeer, the book seith thus.

NOW wol I stynte of this Arveragus,
And speken I wole of Dorigene
his wyf,
That loveth hire housbonde as
hire hertes lyf.

for his absence wepeth she and siketh,
As doon thise noble wyves whan hem liketh.
She moorneth, waketh, wayleth, fasteth,
pleyneth;
Desir of his presence hire so distreyneth,
That al this wyde world she sette at noght.
Hire freendes, whiche that knewe hir hevy
thoght,
Conforten hire in al that ever they may;
They prechen hire, they telle hire nyght
and day,
That causelees she sleeth hirself, allas!
And every confort possible in this cas
They doon to hire with al hire bisynesse,
Al for to make hire leve hire hevynesse.

BY proces, as ye knowen everichoon,
Men may so longe graven in a stoon
Til som figure therinne emprented be.
So longe han they conforted hire, til she
Receyved hath, by hope and by resoun,
The emprentyng of hire consolacioun,
Thurgh which hir grete sorwe gan aswage;
She may nat alwey duren in swich rage.

AND eek Arveragus, in al this care,
Hath sent hire lettres hoom of his
welfare,
And that he wol come hastily agayn;

Plate 28: The Franklin's Tale (p. 291)

If I deserve that ye should give it me."

  "By our lady," said the canon, "it is dear;
For, save a friar and I, I warn you here,
No man in England can perform the same."
"No matter," he replied. "Sir, in God's name,
What shall I pay you? Tell me now, I pray."

  "Surely," he said. "The thing comes dear, I say.
Sir, in a word, if thou wouldst have it whole,
Thou must pay forty pounds, God save my soul.
And, but for that good act ye did for me,
In friendship, it were dearer, certainly."

  This priest soon got the sum of forty pound
In nobles, and he took them all around
Unto the canon, for that recipe.
Yet all of this was fraud and treachery.

  "Sir Priest, I wish to have no praise," he said,
"For skill, but rather keep it dark instead;
And as ye love me, guard it ever more.
For, did men fully know my secret lore,
By God, I tell you they would envy me
So much, because of my philosophy,
I should be dead, sir, and no other way."

  The priest said: "God forbid! What do ye say?
For I would rather spend all that I had
In property (else may I soon go mad)
Than see you fall upon an end so ill!"

  "Good luck be with you, sir, for your good will,"
This canon said, "and farewell, *graunt merci!*"
He went; and from that day the priest could see
No more of him. And when on any day
That he might choose, this priest would make assay
With this receipt – farewell! it would not be.
So was he gulled. And in this manner he –
This canon – falsely would insinuate
Himself with men, and bring them to their fate.

  Consider, sirs, how sharp in every station,
Men against gold, there runs the altercation
Till the gold goes, and there is hardly any!
This transmutation, sirs, blindeth so many
That in good faith I think that it must be
The greatest cause of such a scarcity.

And in this art philosophers discourse
So mistily, that men's wits lack the force
To understand its workings nowadays.
Yea, they may chatter like so many jays,
And polish up their words with a great air
And trouble, but their purpose gets nowhere.
Yet easy may one learn, if he have aught,
To multiply, and bring his wealth to naught!

  Lo now! This lusty sport such lucre hath
That it will turn a man's mirth into wrath,
And also empty great and heavy purses,
And buy for those who ply it bitter curses
From those who lent their wealth to have it turned!
O fie, for shame! They that have once been burned,
Can they not flee the hot tongue of the flame?
I warn you, leave it – ye that play this game,
Lest ye lose all, for better late than never.
It were too long to work unpaid forever.
Though ye keep prowling, nothing shall ye find.
Ye are as bold as Bayard is, the blind,
That scorning peril, blunders from his manger.
To run against a stone seems no more danger
Than to avoid and pass it on the way.
So then with you that multiply, I say,
If with your eyes ye cannot see aright,
Look that your mind shall still retain its sight.
However far ye look, how hard ye stare,
In that vile traffic ye shall get nowhere,
But lose all ye can steal or beg or borrow;
Remove the fire lest too hot, to your sorrow,
It burn – no more play with that art, I mean;
Else all your profit will be wiped out clean.
And now, sirs, I will tell you in a moment
What the philosophers say of it in comment.

  Lo, thus says Arnold, sirs, of the New Town,
As in his Rosary it is written down;
He says exactly thus – I tell no lie:
"There is no man can Mercury mortify
Unless he do so with its brother's aid;"
And tells us how the first that this thing said
Was Hermes, father of philosophy.

He said that any dragon, certainly,
Unless its brother slay it, would not die;
Which is to say, he understood thereby
That Mercury was the dragon, and no other,
And brimstone was the symbol for its brother,
That out of *sol* and *luna* had been drawn.
"And therefore heed my proverb," he went on,
"Let no man for this art indulge his leaning
Unless he understand the speech and meaning
Of the philosophers. Unless he can,
Any that tries it is an ignorant man.
This knowledge and this skill, by God, they be
Secret among the secret things," said he.

    There was with Plato a disciple, too,
That on a time unto his master drew,
As in his book *Senioris* ye can see,
And this was his demand in verity:
"Tell me the name of the secret stone," he pled.
    And Plato in a moment to him said:
"Take thou the stone that Titanos men name."
    "And what is that?" "Magnesia is the same,"
Said Plato. "Yea, sir, goes the matter thus?
This is *ignotum per ignotius*.
What is Magnesia, then, good sir, I pray?"
    "It is a water that is made, I say,

Out of four elements," said Plato then.
    "Tell me the principle," he begged again,
"Of that same water, if it please you well."
    "Nay, nay," said Plato, "that I will not tell.
Philosophers were sworn, yea, every one,
That this they would reveal or show to none,
Nor ever let it in a book appear;
So precious Christ regards it, and so dear,
That He permits of no discovery
Except as it may please His deity
To inspire man, and to forbid as well
Whomever He will. There is no more to tell."

    Then I conclude thus: that since God on high
Likes not philosophers to testify
How any man may come to have that stone –
I counsel for the best, let it alone.
For he who makes of God his adversary
By doing anything that stands contrary
Unto His will divine, shall not succeed,
Though all his life he multiply, indeed.
And here I stop, for I have told my tale.
God send all honest men weal for their bale.
Amen.

Here ends the Canon's Yeoman's Tale

The Manciple's Tale

THE MANCIPLE IS an officer who works in a monastery, in charge of buying provisions. He tells the tale of Phœbus and the crow, adapted from Ovid but drawing on a long tradition of stories about birds that tell tales and are punished. The story, which rejects story-telling, makes a suitable ending to the narrative part of *The Canterbury Tales*, though it is not clear whether Chaucer actually intended it to be the last of the stories before the Parson's sermon-like exposition.

THE MANCIPLE'S TALE

*Here follows the Prologue
to the Manciple's Tale*

DO ye not know where stands a little town
Below Blean Forest, called Bob-up-and-Down,
Which ye must pass on Canterbury Way?
Right there our Host began to joke and play,
And said, "What, sirs! The dun is in the mire!
Is there no man of you, for love or hire,
Will wake our comrade here that lags behind?
A thief could rob him easily, and bind.
Look how he nods! By cock's bones, turn and see;
He'll tumble from his saddle presently!
Curse him, is this a cook of London town?
Make him come up; his penance is well known,
For he shall tell a tale for us, I say,
Though it should not be worth a bunch of hay!
Wake up, thou Cook! God give thee grief," cried he;
"Morning – and thou asleep! What aileth thee?
Drunk art thou? Or hadst fleas in bed to fight?
Or hast thou labored with some wench all night
That thou canst hardly more than lift thine head?"

This Cook, whose pale face showed no trace of red,
Said to our Host: "As God my soul may bless,
There hangs upon me such a heaviness –
I know not why – that I had rather sleep
Than drink a stoup of wine, the best in Cheap."

"Well," said the Manciple, "if it bring some ease
To thee, sir Cook, and shall no man displease
That rides among us in this company,
And if our Host grant me his courtesy,

This time I will excuse thee from thy tale;
For, in good faith, thy face is very pale,
And thine eyes dull and glazed, it seems to me,
And well I know, thy breath stinks sourly,
Which shows thee ill-disposed, beyond a doubt.
I will not flatter thee, thou drunken lout!
Lo, see him yawning there, the sodden dunce –
Mile-wide, as if to swallow us at once!
What! Shut thy mouth, man! Close it up, this minute!
The devil from Hell will put his foot within it!
Thy putrid breath will taint us all, I say.
Fie, stinking swine! Bad luck to thee today!
Sirs, give attention to this lusty man!
Sweet fellow, wilt thou joust now at the fan?
Thou art in splendid shape for that, I think;
Ape-wine indeed thou must have had to drink,
That makes men ripe to frolic with a straw."
Hearing these words the Cook grew wroth and raw,
And could not speak, but nodded hard and fast
For rage, and pitched down from his horse at last,
And lay there, till they lifted him and shook –
That was a master-horseman of a cook!
Alas! Why did he ever leave his ladle?
Before he sat again within the saddle
There was a deal of shoving to and fro
In lifting him, and much of care and woe,
So hard to handle was this pallid ghost.
Then to the Manciple spoke up our Host:
"Since drink appears to have full domination
Over this man, I think, by my salvation,
That he would tell a rude and ignorant tale.
For whether it's wine or old or new-brewed ale
That he hath drunk, he speaketh through his nose,
And seems to have a cold, and puffs and blows!
Also I think he has enough to do
To keep his nag and him out of the slough;
And if the fellow tumbles off again
All of us will be more than busy then
Lifting his carcass up, the drunken sot!
Tell on thy tale, for I regard him not.

"And yet, Manciple, thou art in faith too nice

Thus openly to reprove him for his vice.
The fellow on another day, for sure,
May yet reclaim thee, bring thee to the lure.
I mean, he may refer to little things –
As, cast an eye upon thy reckonings –
Those not quite honest, if the proof were had."

   "No!" cried the Manciple. "That would be too bad!
How neatly he could take me in the snare!
Yet I had rather pay him for the mare
He rides upon, than fight with him or strive.
I would not anger him, as I may thrive.
Nay, what I said was just a joke of mine.
And know ye what? I have a draught of wine
Here in a gourd, a ripe grape and the best;
And ye shall soon enjoy a merry jest;
For he shall drink it, if I have my way;
I stake my life he will not say me Nay!"

   And certainly, to tell what came to pass,
Out of this gourd the Cook drank deep, alas!
What need? – for he had drunk enough that morn.
And having blown his blast upon this horn,
He then returned the gourd; and wondrous glad
This Cook was of the drink that he had had,
And gave what thanks he could before the crowd.

   Our Host began to laugh out wondrous loud,
And said: "I see well, it is necessary
That as we ride, we have good drink to carry,
For that will turn all strife and agitation
To love and peace, and smooth away vexation!
O thou great Bacchus, blessèd be thy name
That changest thus the solemn into game!
Honor and thanks to thy divinity!
But now ye get no more of that from me.
Tell on thy tale, sir Manciple, I pray."

   "Sir, it is well. Hear now what I shall say."

Here the Manciple's Prologue ends

Here begins the Manciple's Tale of the Crow

WHEN Phœbus dwelt upon the earth below,
As it is told in olden books we know,
He was the lustiest young knight and true
In all the world, and the best archer, too;
He slew the serpent Python as he lay
In slumber in the sunshine on a day,
And many another noble, worthy deed
Accomplished with his bow, as men may read.

   And he could play on every instrument;
And when his clear voice up in song he sent
It was melodious to hear it ring.
Not Amphion, indeed, the Theban king
That walled that city with a singing spell
Made any song that sounded half so well.
He was, besides, the best-appearing man
That is or has been since the world began.
But why describe his features to you here?
In all the world his fairness had no peer.
And Nature, too, had filled him generously
With honor, faith, and true nobility.

   This Phœbus, that was flower of all young knights
In generous ways and all chivalric rites,
For pleasure, and in symbol of the glory
He won from Python's death, as goes the story,
Carried by custom in his hand a bow.

   Now in his house this Phœbus had a crow
Which he had caged, and fostered many a day,
And taught to speak, as men will teach a jay.
This crow was white as any snow-white swan,
And he could mock the speech of any man
When he would talk; and, as they tell the tale,
In all the world there was no nightingale
Could sing a thousandth part so merrily
And wondrous clear and sweetly as could he.

   Now Phœbus kept within his house a wife,
And her he loved more than he loved his life,
And night and day was ever diligent
To do her pleasure, and be reverent;
But he was jealous, if the truth is said,
And gladly would have kept her closeted,
Lest she should fool him, as a woman can;

And so in such a case is every man,
Though it is vain and useless, for a fact.
A good wife, that is pure in thought and act,
Deserves no jealous watching, it is plain.
And truly, it is labor spent in vain
To guard a bad – for that cannot be done.
It is a foolish thing for anyone
To pen a wife up – this old writers show
That wrote in books about it long ago.

But to the end for which I first began:
This worthy Phœbus labors all he can
To please her, thinking if he gave her pleasure,
And played the man, and governed her in measure,
That none could ever rob him of her love.
And yet no man, as knoweth God above,
Can ever hope to stop a thing that Nature
Has naturally implanted in a creature.

Take any bird, and put it in a cage,
And let your mind and heart alike engage
To serve it tenderly with meat and drink –
All dainty things of which a man can think –
And keep it clean besides in every way;
Although its cage with gold be never so gay,
Yet it would rather, twenty thousand fold,
Live in a forest that is rude and cold,
And feed on worms and other wretched stuff.
For such a bird can never do enough
To get free from its cage, if that may be.
Always it longs to have its liberty.

Or take a cat, and rear him well on milk
And tender meat, and make his bed of silk;
And let him see a mouse along the wall,
And he abandons milk and meat and all,
Yea, every dainty that is in that house,
Such appetite he has to eat a mouse!
Lo, here desire has utter domination,
And appetite subdues discrimination.

A she-wolf, too, is low in character;
The basest wolf of all that come to her,
Whose reputation has the lowest rating
Will be her choice when she is ripe for mating!

These instances I give you – every one
Refers to men, for women I have none;
For men possess a lecherous appetite,
To take with lower creatures their delight
Rather than with their wives, though these are fair
And true and meek indeed beyond compare.
Flesh, devil take it! loves its novelty,
And we can never know a constancy
In pleasure that with virtue is combined.

Phœbus, with no suspicion in his mind,
Was fooled, for all his goodness. For his wife
Led with another love a secret life –
A man that had but little reputation,
Nothing when set by Phœbus' worth and station.
The greater harm! It often happens so,
Such things will cause great injury and woe.

And so one time when Phœbus went away,
His wife sent for her leman on a day;
Her leman? Nay, what knavish words I teach you!
Forgive me that I said it, I beseech you!

Plato the wise says well, as ye may read,
The word must be harmonious with the deed;
And if a story gives us satisfaction,
The word must be the cousin of the action.
I am a plain, rude man, and I must say
No difference can exist in any way
Between a wife that holds a lofty station,
If she submit herself to defamation,
And a poor wench, unless it may be this –
If, as it happens, both should go amiss –
The one that in position stands above
The other, is his lady in such love,
While for her poverty the other woman
Is known to be his wench, or else his leman.
And yet God knows the truth is this, dear brother:
Men drag the one as low as lies the other.

So with a tyrant that usurps a crown
And some wild thief that wanders up and down:
I say there is no difference save position.
King Alexander heard this definition:
That, since a tyrant has the greater power,

With armies strong to slay, that in an hour
Can make of house and home a smoking plain,
He has the name of captain. And again,
The outlaw, with his little company,
That cannot do so great a harm as he,
Or bring a country to such hurt and grief,
Is only called an outlaw or a thief.
But, since I am no bookish man, indeed,
I will not talk of books now, but proceed
As I began, to tell my tale, for sure.
After this wife sent for her paramour,
The two in wanton lust were soon engaged.

    The white crow, hanging there above them, caged,
Saw all their work, but never said a word.
But later, Phœbus coming home, his lord,
"Cuckoo! Cuckoo! Cuckoo!" this crow sang now.

    "What, bird!" cried Phœbus. "What song singest
        thou?
Wert thou not wont to sing so merrily
That all my heart was glad as it could be
To hear thy voice? Alas! What song is this?"

    "By God," he said, "I do not sing amiss.
Phœbus," he said to him, "for all thy worth,
And all thy beauty and thy noble birth,
And all thy songs that charm the very skies,
A hand hath pulled the wool across thine eyes –
The hand of one of little reputation,
Compared with thee not worth in parts or station
More than a gnat, or may I thrive no more!
Here on thy bed he made thy wife his whore!"

    What will ye more than that? Soon, by this bird's
Clear tokens shown, and his emphatic words,
Phœbus knew all about her lechery
And wrong to him, and shameful treachery.
The crow swore he had seen it with his eyes.
This Phœbus turned away with fearful sighs;
He thought his heart would burst that very minute;
He strung his bow and set an arrow in it,
And in his anger put his wife away.
This was his deed; what more is there to say?
Then all his instruments he broke in sharp

And bitter grief, his gittern, lute, and harp;
And then he broke his arrows and his bow.
And after that, he spoke thus to the crow:

    "Traitor, with tongue of scorpion," cried he,
"Thus hast thou brought me my catastrophe!
Alas! that I was made! Would I were dead!
O dear wife, jewel of all delight," he said,
"Whose faith and truth and virtue could not fail,
Now liest thou dead, thy face all wan and pale,
And surely thou art guiltless, I will swear!
O rash hand, that so foul a wrong would dare,
O turgid wit, O reckless anger bent
So heedlessly to slay the innocent!
O false suspicion, O distrust all blind,
Where were thy wisdom and foreseeing mind?
O let all men beware of headless action,
Demand strong proof ere seeking satisfaction,
Nor strike before the cause is plain to tell!
Think soberly, consider more than well
Before ye give your anger an effect,
Seeking revenge for something ye suspect!
Alas! A thousand men for heedless ire
Have found disaster, sinking in the mire!
Alas! Now will I slay myself for grief!"

    And to the crow he cried again: "False thief!
I will repay thee for thy lying tales!
Thy singing, that was like a nightingale's,
Thou thief, shall for this baseness disappear;
And so shall all thy feathers white and clear;
Nor shalt thou speak again all thy life long.
Thus shall a traitor suffer for his wrong.
Thou and thine offspring shall be black forever,
And from your throat sweet sounds shall echo never,
But ye shall cry when tempests rise, or rain,
In token that through thee my wife was slain!"

    And then he leapt and seized him with the word,
And plucked his fine white feathers from the bird,
And made him black; and made it that no more
He sing or speak; and threw him from the door
Unto the devil, and there I let him lie.
So now all crows are black, and this is why!

Now from this instance, lordings all, I pray
That ye beware, and heed well what I say;
Nor ever tell a man in all your life
Of how some other man has taken his wife,
For he will hate you with a mortal hate.
Lord Solomon, as learnèd scholars state,
Says one should keep a close tongue in his head;
But I am nowise bookish, as I said.
But none the less, my mother taught me so:
"My son, in God's name, keep in mind the crow;
Keep well thy tongue, son, lest thy friend be weaned;
A wicked tongue is worse than any fiend.
Men cross themselves, my son, to win protection
Against a fiend. God in his wise direction
Walled in a tongue with teeth and lips and cheeks
So that a man should think before he speaks.
Often, my son, a man for too much speech
Has met disaster, as our writers teach;
But for a little speech no man will be
Injured, if he will speak judiciously.
My son, to curb thy tongue is only sense
At all times, save for doing diligence
To speak of God, in honor and in prayer.
Thy first of actions, son, and thy chief care
Should be to wisely guard and curb thy tongue.
Teach this to children when they still are young.
My son, from too much speaking, ill-advised,
When fewer words had just as well sufficed,

There comes much harm, thus I was taught and told.
Amid much speech sin always finds a hold.
Knowst thou the way a rash tongue operates?
Just as a sword carves off and mutilates
An arm, dear son – just so a tongue will do:
A tongue will cut a friendship clean in two.
A chatterer is high God's abomination,
Says Solomon, with his wise penetration;
Thus David's Psalms and Seneca have said.
Speak not, my son; nod only with thine head.
Pretend that thou art deaf if thou hear chatter
Of prating tongues about some dangerous matter.
The Flemings say – and learn it, if thou please –
That little gossip brings a man much ease.
My son, if no ill word thou hast essayed,
Thou shalt not need to fear to be betrayed;
But he who speaks amiss, I dare to say,
Cannot bring back his words in any way.
That which is said, is said; the world will get it,
Whether the speaker like it or regret it.
He is the slave of him that heard his story,
Though having told it, he may well be sorry.
My son, beware; be not the author new
Of any tidings, whether false or true.
Wherever thou go'st, among the high or low,
Keep a close tongue; remember Phœbus' crow."

Here ends the Manciple's Tale of the Crow

The Parson's Tale

THE PARSON DOES not tell a tale, as such, but presents a long tract on the topic of penance. His review of the Seven Deadly Sins recalls some of the behaviour we have seen in the pilgrims, and he answers some of the questions the foregoing tales have raised by reference to Christian doctrine.

THE PARSON'S TALE

Here follows the Prologue of the Parson's Tale

WHEN the Manciple's tale was wholly ended,
From the south line the broad sun had descended
So low that he appeared now, to my sight,
Not more than twenty-nine degrees in height.
And it was four o'clock, as I should guess,
For eleven feet, or somewhat more or less,
My shadow at that time appeared to be,
Of such feet as, proportioned equally,
Would fix my height at six, by calculation.
And the moon also, in his exaltation,
Libra I mean, continued to ascend,
As we were entering a hamlet's end.
Therefore our Host, as in such cases he
Was used to guide our merry company,
Spoke in this fashion: "Lordings every one,
One tale is left to tell and we are done!
My judgment is fulfilled and my decree;
And we have heard from folk of each degree.
My plan is all but carried out. I pray
That God will throw a lucky chance his way
That tells this one tale to us lustily.
Sir Priest, art thou a vicar?" questioned he,
"Or art a parson? Tell the truth, I say!
But be thou what thou be – spoil not our play!
For every man has told his tale save thou.
Open thy bag; show what is in it now;
For truly, by thy look it would appear

That thou shouldst knit up some great matter here.
By cock's bones, then, tell us a tale at once!"
    The Parson on the instant made response:
"No fabulous story shalt thou have from me;
For Paul, when writing unto Timothy,
Reproves all those that from the truth digress
By telling fables and such wretchedness.
Why should my hand sow chaff for you," he said,
"That, at my will, can sow you wheat instead?
And therefore, if ye have an inclination
To moral things and virtuous dissertation,
And have a will to give me audience,
Then I will gladly give, in reverence
Of Christ, such lawful pleasure as I can.
But know this well: I am a Southern man;
I chant no legends – rum, ram, ruf, by letter,
And rhyme, God knows, I hold but little better,
And therefore, if it please you, will not gloze.
But I will tell a virtuous tale in prose
To wind this revel up, and make an end.
I pray that Jesus of His grace will send
The wit to me to show you stage by stage
That glorious and perfect pilgrimage
Known as Jerusalem the heavenly.
And soon, if ye will grant your leave to me,
I will begin my tale. And so I pray,
Tell me your wish: I have no more to say.
But none the less, I put this meditation
Under correction and examination
By clerks; for texts I have small skill or leaning;
Believe me, I take nothing but the meaning.
And therefore I protest that in subjection
To them I stand, and welcome all correction.
    On this word we were soon agreed, each one.
It was, we thought, a good thing to be done –
To give him time and opportunity
And end thus with some virtuous homily;
And asked our Host to say that without fail
We one and all prayed him tell his tale.
    Our Host had words for all of us. He said:

"Sir Priest, good fortune fall upon your head!
Say what ye please; ye shall be gladly heard;"
Then in this fashion added to that word:
"Tell us," he said, "your meditation, yet
Be quick about it, for the sun will set;
Be fruitful, yet be brief in what ye tell;
And God send grace that ye may do it well."

Explicit prohemium

Here Begins the Parson's Tale

Jer. 6°: *State super vias et videte et interrogate de viis antiquis, que sit via bona; et ambulate in ea, et inuenietis refrigerium animabus vestris, etc.*

OUR sweet Lord God of Heaven, who wishes no man to perish, but rather that we should all come to the knowledge of Him, and the blessed life that is imperishable, admonisheth us through the Prophet Jeremiah, who speaks in this manner: "Stand ye in the ways, and look, and ask for the old paths (that is to say, of old wisdom), where is the good way; and walk in that way, and ye shall find sustenance for your souls," &c. Many are the spiritual ways that lead men to our Lord Jesus Christ, and to the Kingdom of Glory. Of which ways there is a most notable and fitting one that cannot fail any man or woman, that through sin hath gone astray from the right road to celestial Jerusalem; and that way is called Penitence, concerning which a man should gladly listen, and about which he should inquire with all his heart; to know what Penitence is, and why it is called Penitence, and of how many kinds are the actions or workings of Penitence and how many species there are of Penitence, and what things pertain to and are behooving to Penitence, and what things interfere with Penitence.

Saint Ambrose says that "Penitence is the lamenting of a man for the wrong that he hath done,

and his desire to do no more anything for which he ought to lament." And some doctor says: "Penitence is the wailing of a man that sorrows for his sin and bitterly repents because he has erred." Penitence in certain circumstances is the true repentance of a man that feels sorrow and other pain on account of his guilt. And in order that he shall be truly penitent, he shall first bewail the sins that he has done, and steadfastly purpose in his heart to have shrift by mouth, and to make atonement, and never again to do anything for which he should again bewail or lament, and to continue in good works: or else his repentance cannot be of avail. For as Saint Isidore says: "He is a gabbler and a noisy fellow, and not truly repentant that soon does again a thing for which he ought to be repentant." Merely weeping, and not ceasing to do a sin, cannot avail. But none the less, men shall hope that every time a man falls, be it never so often, he can rise through Penitence, if he have grace: but certainly there is great doubt as to this. For as Saint Gregory says: "He is scarcely able to rise out of sin, that is burdened with the burden of evil habit." And therefore repentant men that stop all sin and forsake sin before sin forsakes them, Holy Church holds to be sure of their salvation. And he that sins, but is truly repentant in his last moments, Holy Church hopes may have salvation, by the great mercy of our Lord Jesus Christ, because of his repentance. But take the safe way.

And now, since I have explained to you what Penitence is, ye shall understand that there are three steps in Penitence. The first is that a man be baptized after he has sinned. Saint Augustine says: "Unless a man is penitent on account of his old sinful life, he cannot begin a new, clean life." For indeed, if he is baptized without penitence for his old error, he receives the mark of baptism but not the grace nor the remission of his sins, until he feels true repentance. Another fault is this, that men commit deadly sins after they have received baptism. The third fault is, that men fall into venial sins after their baptism, from day to day. Concerning this Saint Augustine says that "the penitence of good and humble men is daily penitence."

There are three kinds of Penitence. One is public, another is ordinary, and the third is secret. Public penance is of two kinds; such as to be put out of Holy Church in Lent, for the killing of children, and such things. Another is when a man has sinned openly, and his sin is known and spoken of throughout the country; and then Holy Church by judgment compels him to do public penance. Ordinary penance is that which priests enjoin upon men commonly in certain cases; as, perhaps, to go naked on pilgrimage, or barefoot. Secret penance is that which men do from day to day for secret sins, for which we shrive ourselves secretly and receive secret penance.

Now thou shalt understand what is behooving and necessary to true, perfect Penitence. And this consists of three things: Contrition of Heart, Confession by Mouth, and Atonement. And on this account Saint John Chrysostom says: "Penitence compels a man to accept in good spirit every punishment that is enjoined upon him, with Contrition of Heart and shrift by mouth, with Atonement; and with behavior in every way humble." And this is fruitful Penitence against three things in which we anger our Lord Jesus Christ: that is to say, by pleasure in our thoughts, by recklessness in speaking, and by wicked, sinful action. And opposed to these wicked sins stands Penitence, that may be likened unto a tree.

The root of this tree is Contrition, that buries itself in the heart of a man that is truly repentant, just as the root of a tree buries itself in the earth. From the Root of Contrition there springs a trunk that bears branches and leaves of Confession, and fruit of Atonement. And on this account Christ says in His Gospel: "Bring forth worthy fruits of Repentance;" for by this fruit men may know this tree, and not by the root that is hidden in the heart of man, nor by the branches and by the leaves of Confession. And therefore our Lord Jesus Christ says thus: "By their fruits ye shall know them." From this root there springs also a seed of grace, and this seed is the mother of security, and it is keen and fervent. The grace of this seed springs from God, through remembrance of the Day of Judgment and the pains of hell. On this matter Solomon says that "in the fear of God man abandons his sins." The fervency of this seed is the love of God and the desire for imperishable joy. This fervency draws the heart of a man to God, and causes him to hate his sin. For truly there is nothing that tastes so well to a child as the milk of his nurse, nor anything which tastes as abominable to him as that milk when it is corrupted with other food. Just so to the sinful man that loves his sin, it seems to him the sweetest of all things; but from that time that he loves earnestly our Lord Jesus Christ, and desires imperishable life, there is nothing more abominable to him. For indeed, the law of God is the love of God; and for this reason David the Prophet says: "I have loved Thy law and hated wickedness and hate"; he that loves God keeps His law and His word. This tree the prophet Daniel saw in spirit, at the time of the vision of King Nebuchadnezzar when he counselled him to be penitent. Penance is the tree of life to such as receive it, and he that keeps himself in true penitence is blessed, according to the opinion of Solomon.

In this Penitence or Contrition a man shall understand four things: that is to say, what Contrition is, and what are the causes that move a man to Contrition: and how he should be contrite: and of what avail Contrition is to the soul. Then the way of it is this: that Contrition is the true sorrow that a man receives into his heart because of his sins, with earnest purpose to shrive himself and to do penance, and nevermore to sin again. And this sorrow should be of this nature, as Saint Bernard says: "It shall be heavy and grievous, and very sharp and poignant in the heart." And this is so, first, because man has sinned against his Lord and his Creator; and more sharp and poignant because he has sinned against his Celestial Father, and yet more sharp and poignant, because he has angered and sinned against Him that redeemed him; Who with His precious Blood has delivered us from the bonds of sin, and from the cruelty of the devil and from the pains of hell.

The reasons that should move a man to Contrition are six. First, a man should recall his sins; but beware that in such remembrance he should not feel delight in any way, but great shame and sorrow for his guilt, for Job says: "Sinful men do works needing Confession." And therefore Hezekiah says: "I will remember all the years of my life in bitterness of heart." And God says in the Apocalypse: "Remember from whence ye are fallen"; for before the time when ye sinned, ye were the children of God, and members of the Kingdom of God; but because of your sin ye have become slaves and foul, and servants of the devil, the hate of angels, the scandal of Holy Church, food for the false serpent, and eternal matter for the fire of hell. And yet ye are the more foul and abominable because ye trespass so often as does the hound that returns to eat what he has spewed up. And again ye are the more foul for your long continuance in sin, and your sinful habits, on account of which ye are filthy in your sin as a beast in his dung. Such kind of thoughts make a man feel shame for his sin, and no delight, as God says through the Prophet Ezekiel: "Ye shall remember your ways and they shall displease you." Truly, sins are the ways that lead men to hell.

The second reason that should make a man disdain sin is this: that, as Saint Peter says, "Whoever commits sin is the thrall of sin"; and sin puts a man into great slavery. And therefore says the Prophet Ezekiel: "I went sorrowful in disdain of myself." And

truly, a man should have disdain of sin, and withdraw himself from that slavery and evil. And see what Seneca says concerning this matter. He says this: "Though I were sure that neither God nor man would ever know it, yet I would disdain to sin." And the same Seneca says also: "I am born to greater things than to be the slave of my body, or to make my body a slave." Nor can a man or a woman make a more foul slave of his body than to give it to sin. Although it were the foulest churl or the foulest woman that lives, and the least in value, yet is he then more foul and more enslaved. And the higher the position a man falls from, the more is he a slave, and the more vile and abominable to God and to the world. O good God, well should man have disdain of sin, since through sin where he was free he is now enslaved. And therefore says Saint Augustine: "If thou despise thy servant because he is guilty or commits a sin, then despise thyself for sinning." Take regard of thy worth, that thou be not foul to thyself. Alas! well should they disdain to be servants or thralls to sin, and sorely should they be ashamed of themselves, whom God in His endless goodness hath set in high positions or given wit, strength of body, health, beauty, prosperity, and redeemed from death with His heart's blood, that they so unnaturally against his nobleness repay Him so viciously as to slaughter their own souls. O good God, ye women that are of such great beauty, remember the proverb of Solomon, that says: "A fair woman that is a fool with her body is like a ring of gold in the snout of a sow." For just as a sow rooteth in every heap of ordure, so does she root her body in the stinking ordure of sin.

The third cause that should move a man to Contrition, is the dread of the Day of Judgment and of the horrible pains of hell. For as Saint Jerome says: "Every time that I remember the Day of Judgment I tremble, for when I eat or drink, or whatever I do, ever it seems to me that the trumpet

It may wel be he looked on hir face
In swich a wise, as man that asketh grace;
But nothyng wiste she of his entente.
Nathelees, it happed, er they thennes wente,
Bycause that he was hire neighebour,
And was a man of worship and honour,
And hadde yknowen hym of tyme yoore,
They fille in speche; and forth moore and
moore
Unto his purpos drough Aurelius,
And whan he saugh his tyme, he sayde thus:

MADAME, quod he, by God that this
world made,
    So that I wiste it myghte youre herte
glade,
I wolde, that day that youre Arveragus
Wente over the see, that I, Aurelius,
Hadde went ther nevere I sholde have come
agayn;
for wel I woot my servyce is in vayn.
My guerdoun is but brestyng of myn herte;
Madame, reweth upon my peynes smerte;
for with a word ye may me sleen or save,
Heere at youre feet God wolde that I were
grave!
I ne have as now no leyser moore to seye;
Have mercy, sweete, or ye wol do me deye!

SHE gan to looke upon Aurelius:
    Is this your wyl, quod she, and sey ye
    thus?
Nevere erst, quod she, ne wiste I what ye
mente;
But now, Aurelie, I knowe youre entente,
By thilke God that yaf me soule and lyf,
Ne shal I nevere been untrewe wyf
In word ne werk; as fer as I have wit,
I wol been his to whom that I am knyt!
Taak this for fynal answere as of me.
But after that in pley thus seyde she:
Aurelie, quod she, by heighe God above!
Yet wolde I graunte yow to been youre love,
Syn I yow se so pitously complayne;
Looke what day that, endelong Britayne,
Ye remoeve alle the rokkes, stoon by stoon,
That they ne lette ship ne boot to goon,
I seye, whan ye han maad the coost so clene
Of rokkes, that ther nys no stoon ysene,
Thanne wol I love yow best of any man;
Have heer my trouthe in al that evere I kan!

IS ther noon oother grace in yow? quod
he.
    No, by that Lord, quod she, that
maked me!
for wel I woot that it shal never bityde.

Plate 29: The Franklin's Tale (p. 293)

sounds in my ear, 'Rise up, ye that are dead, and come to judgment.'" O good God, much should a man dread such a judgment, "where we shall all," as Saint Paul says, "be before the throne of our Lord Jesus Christ;" where He shall make a general congregation, from which no man can be absent. For indeed there shall avail no excuse or explanation. And not only shall our defects be judged, but all our works shall openly be known. And as Saint Bernard says: "No pleading shall avail there, nor no trickery. We shall give reckoning for every idle word." There shall we have a judge that cannot be deceived or corrupted. And why? Because, in truth, all our thoughts have been made plain to Him; nor for any prayer or reward shall He be corrupted. And therefore says Solomon: "The wrath of God shall spare no person neither for prayer nor for gift;" and therefore at the day of judgment none can hope to escape. Therefore, as says Saint Anselm: "Very great anguish shall sinful folk have at that time; there shall be the stern and angry Judge sitting above, and under Him the horrible pit of hell opened to destroy him that must declare his sins, which sins are openly shown to God and to every creature. And on the left side, more devils than the heart may think of, to harry and draw the sinful souls to the torment of hell. And within the hearts of people shall be biting conscience, and without shall be a world of conflagration. Whither then shall the wretched sinful man flee to hide himself? Indeed, he cannot hide; he must come forth and show himself." For indeed, as says Saint Jerome: "The earth shall cast him forth, and the sea also; and the air, that shall be full of thunder-claps and lightnings." Now truly whoever firmly remembers these things, I think that his sin will not turn him towards delight, but towards great sorrow, for fear of the torment of hell. And therefore says Job to God: "Permit, Lord, that I may wail and weep a while, ere I go without returning to the dark land, covered with the darkness of death; to

the land of misery and darkness where is the shadow of death; where there is no order or rule, but grisly dread that shall last for evermore." Lo, here may ye see that Job prayed respite a while to weep and bewail his trespasses; for truly one day of respite is better than all the treasure of the world. And inasmuch as a man may acquit himself before God by penitence in this world, and not by wealth, therefore he should pray to God to give him respite a while to weep and bewail his evil-doing. For truly, all the sorrow that a man might know from the beginning of the world is but a little thing in comparison with the sorrow of hell. This is the reason that Job calls hell the land of darkness; he calls it "land" or earth, because it is stable and shall never fail; "dark," because he that is in hell has a lack of the things that are light. For in truth, the dark light, that shall come out of the ever-burning fire, shall put him wholly in the torment of hell; for it shows him to the horrible devils that torment him. "Covered with the darkness of death:" that is to say, that he that is in hell shall have no sight of God; for indeed, the sight of God is imperishable life. "The darkness of death" means the sins that the wretched man has committed, which prevent him from seeing the face of God, just like a dark cloud that lies between us and the sun. "Land of discomfort:" because there are three kinds of deprivations as opposed to three things which people of this world have in this present life, that is to say, honors, pleasures, and riches. As opposed to honor, they have in hell shame and confusion. For well I know that men call "honor" the reverence that man does to man; but in hell there is no honor nor reverence. For truly, no more reverence shall be done there to a king than to a knave. On this account God says through the Prophet Jeremiah: "Those that despise Me shall be in despite." "Honor" is also called great lordship; but there no man shall serve another, except with harm and torment. "Honor" is also called great dignity and elevation; but in hell all shall be trodden under foot by devils. And God says: "Horrible devils shall go and come upon the heads of them that are damned." And this is also true, that the higher they were in their present life, the more shall they be degraded and defouled in hell. As opposed to the riches of this world, they shall have the misery of poverty; and this poverty shall consist of four things: the lack of wealth, of which David says: "Rich men that embraced and united all their hearts to treasures of this world, shall sleep the sleep of death; and they shall find nothing in their hands of all their treasure." And furthermore, the discomfort of hell shall consist in the lack of meat and drink. For God says thus through Moses: "They shall be wasted with hunger and the birds of hell shall devour them with bitter death, and the gall of the dragon shall be their drink, and the venom of the dragon shall be their morsels of food." And more than this, their misery shall consist in a lack of clothing; for they shall be naked in body as regards clothing, save for the fire in which they burn, and other corruption; and they shall be naked of soul, of all kinds of virtue, which is the clothing of the soul. Where then are the gay habits, and the soft sheets, and the delicate shirts? Lo, what says God of this through the Prophet Isaiah? "Under them moths shall be strewn, and their covering shall be worms of hell." And more than this, their misery shall consist in the lack of friends; for he is not poor that has good friends, but there in Hell there are no friends; for neither God nor any creature shall be friend to them, and each of them shall hate the other with deadly hate. "Sons and daughters shall rebel against father and mother, and kindred against kindred, and chide and despise one another," both day and night, as God says through the Prophet Micah. And loving children, that formerly so humanly loved each other, would each eat the other if he could. For how should they love each other in the torments of hell when they hated each other in the prosperity of this life? For

trust well, their fleshly love was deadly hate, as the Prophet David says: "Whoever loves wickedness hates his own soul." And whoever hates his own soul, he indeed can love no other person in any manner. And therefore in hell there is no comfort or friendship, but the more fleshly kindred that are together in hell, the more cursing, the more chiding and the more deadly hate there is among them. Furthermore, they shall have lack of all kinds of pleasure; for indeed, pleasures are according to the appetites of the five senses, such as sight, hearing, smell, taste, and touch. But in hell their sight shall be full of darkness and smoke, and therefore full of tears; and their hearing full of lamentation and of grinding of teeth, as says Jesus Christ. Their nostrils shall be full of stinking odor, and as Isaiah the Prophet says: "Their taste shall be full of bitter gall." And with regard to all their bodies, they shall be covered with "fire that never shall be quenched and with worms that shall never die," as God says by the mouth of Isaiah. And insomuch as any may believe that they can die through torment, and by their death flee from torment, they should understand the word of Job who says: "In that place is the shadow of death." Truly a shadow is the likeness of the thing of which it is a shadow, but shadow is not the same thing as that of which it is shadow. Just so it is with the pain of hell; it is like death, for it is horrible anguish, and why? Because it torments men always as though they should die; but certainly they shall not die. For as Saint Gregory says: "For the wretched ones shall there be a death without death, an end without an end, and a want that shall never cease. For their death shall live always, and their end shall ever more begin, and their lack shall never pass." And therefore Saint John the Evangelist says: "They shall pursue death and they shall not find him. And they shall desire to die, and death shall flee from them." And also Job says: "In hell is there no order or rule." And although it is true that God has created all things in a proper order, and nothing without order, and all things are ordained and numbered; yet nevertheless they that are damned are no wise in an order, nor do they keep any order. For the earth shall bear them no fruit. As the Prophet David says: "God shall destroy the fruit of the earth insofar as it comes from them;" nor shall water give them any moisture, nor air any refreshment, nor fire any light. For as Saint Basil says: "God shall give the burning of fire in this world to those that are damned in hell; but the light and the clearness shall be given in heaven to His children;" just as the good man gives meat to his children, and bones to his dogs. And because they shall have no hope of escape, so Saint Job declares finally: "There shall horror and grisly fear persist without end." Horror is always the fear of harm that is to come, and this fear shall evermore dwell in the hearts of them that are damned. And therefore have they lost all their hope, for seven causes. First, because God that is their Judge shall be without mercy for them; nor can they please Him nor any within His halls; nor can they give anything for their ransom; nor have they any voice with which to speak to Him; nor can they flee from pain; nor have they any goodness in them that they can show, to deliver them from pain. And therefore Solomon says: "The wicked man dies, and when he is dead he shall have no hope of escape from pain." Whoever then would understand those pains well and consider that he has deserved those pains for his sins, surely he would have more disposition to sigh and weep than to sing and play. For as Solomon says: "Whoever has knowledge of the pains that are established and ordained for sin would make sorrow." "That knowledge," as says Saint Augustine, "makes a man lament in his heart."

The fourth point that should make a man have contrition, is the sorrowful remembrance of the good that he has left undone here on earth and also the good that he has lost. Truly, the good works that

he has left, either they are good works that he did before he fell into sin, or else good works that he did while he lay in sin. Indeed, the good works that he did before he fell into sin are all mortified and paralyzed and diminished by frequent sinning. The other good works, that he did while he was in deadly sin, they are clearly dead as regards imperishable life in heaven. Then those good works that are destroyed by frequent sinning, which he did while he was in favor with God, may never again come to life without true penitence. And of these God says, by the mouth of Ezekiel: "If the good man turn against his goodness and work wickedness, shall he live?" No; for all the good works that he has wrought shall not be remembered; for he shall die in his sin. And upon that subject Saint Gregory says this: "We shall understand this principally, that when we do deadly sin, it is all for nothing then to rehearse and call to memory the good works that we did previously." For truly, having done deadly sin, we can put no trust in any good work that we did beforehand; that is, hoping on that account to have imperishable life in heaven. And none the less, good works quicken again and come again and help to bring imperishable life in heaven when we have contrition. But truly, the good works that men do while they are in deadly sin, inasmuch as they were done in deadly sin, may never again come to life. For indeed, a thing that never had life, may never recover life; and none the less, although they are not of avail to gain the life imperishable, yet they do avail to shorten the torments of Hell, or to get temporal wealth, or because through them God will the sooner illumine and lighten the heart of the sinful man to repent. But also they are of avail to accustom a man to do good works, that the fiend may have the less power over his soul. And thus the courteous Lord Jesus Christ wills that no good work be lost; for to some extent it shall be of avail. But inasmuch as the good works that men do while they are living a good life are entirely destroyed by sin that follows, and also since all the good works that men do while they are in deadly sin are clearly dead as regards the life imperishable, well may that man that does not do good works sing that new French song: "*J'ai tout perdu mon temps et mon labour.*" For truly, sin bereaves a man both of goodness of nature and of goodness of grace. For the grace of the Holy Ghost behaves like fire, that cannot be idle; for fire fails as soon as it leaves off its working, and just so grace fails at once when it leaves off working. Then the sinful man loses the goodness of glory that is only promised to good men that labor and work. Well may he be sorry, then, that owes all his life to God as long as he has lived and as long as he shall live, that he has no goodness with which to pay his debt to God to Whom he owes his entire life. For trust well, "he shall give account," as Saint Bernard says, "of all the good things that have been given to him in this present life, and how he has used them; to such a degree there shall not perish a hair of his head, nor a moment of an hour of his time that he shall not give reckoning of it."

The fifth thing that should move a man to contrition is the remembrance of the passion that our Lord Jesus Christ suffered for our sins. For as Saint Bernard says: "While I live I shall have remembrance of the travail that our Lord Christ suffered in preaching; His weariness in His work, His temptations when He fasted, His long wakeful hours when He prayed, His tears when He wept in pity for good people; the woe and the shame, and the spittle that men spat in His face, the blows that men gave Him, the foul grievances and the reproofs that men spoke to Him; the nails with which He was nailed to the cross, and the remainder of His passion that He suffered for my sins and in no way on account of His own guilt." And ye shall understand that in man's sin every kind of order or ordinance is turned upside down. For it is true that God, and reason, and sensuality, and the body of man are so

ordained that each of these four things should have lordship over the other as thus: God shall have lordship over the reason, the reason over sensuality, and sensuality over the body of man. But indeed, when a man sins, all this order or ordinance is turned upside down. And therefore then, because the reason of man will not be subject nor obedient to God, that is his Lord by right, therefore it loses the lordship that it should have over sensuality, and also over the body of man. And why? Because sensuality rebels then against reason, and in that way reason loses the lordship over sensuality and over the body. For just as reason is rebel to God, just so is sensuality rebel both to reason and to the body also. And surely, this lack of order and this rebellion our Lord Jesus Christ paid for through His precious dear body, and listen in what manner. Inasmuch then as reason is rebel to God, therefore is man worthy to have woe and to be dead. This our Lord Jesus Christ suffered for man, after He had been betrayed by His disciples, and seized, and bound, "so that His blood burst out at every nail of His hands," as says Saint Augustine. And in addition, inasmuch as the reason of man will not control sensuality when it can, therefore man is worthy to be shamed; and this our Lord Jesus Christ suffered for man, when they spat in His face. And still further, inasmuch as the wretched body of man is rebel both to reason and to sensuality, therefore it is worthy of death. And this our Lord Jesus Christ suffered for man upon the cross, where there was no part of His body free from great pain and bitter suffering. And all this suffered Jesus Christ, who never did wrong. And therefore it may reasonably be said by Jesus in this way: "I am too greatly tormented for the things that I never deserved, and too much defouled for the shame that man is deserving to have." And therefore, the sinful man may well say as says Saint Bernard: "Cursed be the bitterness of my sin, for which there must be suffered so much bitterness." For surely, according to the various discords of our wickedness, the suffering of Jesus Christ was ordained in various things, as thus. Truly, man's sinful soul is betrayed by the devil through its coveting of temporal prosperity, and scorned by deceit when he chooses pleasures of the flesh; and yet it is tormented by the impatience of adversity, and spat upon by the slavery and subjection of sin; and in the end is slain. For this lack of order in sinful man, Jesus Christ was first betrayed, and after that He was bound, who came to unbind us from sin and torment. Then He was scorned who should only have been honored in and by all things. Then was His face that all men should desire to see and on which angels long to look, villainously spat upon. Then was he scourged who was guiltless, and finally He was crucified and slain. Then the word of Isaiah was accomplished: "He was wounded for our misdeeds and defouled for our violence." Now since Jesus Christ took upon Himself the pain of all our wickedness, sinful man ought greatly to weep and bewail, that for his sins God's Son in Heaven should endure all this torment.

The sixth thing that should move a man to contrition is the hope of three things; that is to say, forgiveness of sin, and the gift of grace to do well, and the glory of heaven, with which God shall reward a man for his good deeds. And inasmuch as Jesus Christ gives us these gifts in His generosity and in His sovereign goodness, therefore He is called *Jesus Nazarenus rex Judeorum.* "Jesus" is to say "Saviour" or "salvation," through Whom men shall hope to have forgiveness of sins, which is properly the salvation of sins. And therefore the angel said to Joseph: "Thou shalt call His name Jesus, that shall save His people from their sins." And of this Saint Peter says: "There is no name under heaven given to men by which a man may be saved but Jesus alone." *Nazarenus* is as much as to say "flourishing," through which a man shall hope that He who gives him remission of sins shall also give him grace to do good. For in the flower is hope of fruit in time to come; and in forgiveness of sins hope of the grace to do good. "I was at the door of thy heart," says Jesus, "and knocked to enter; he that opens to me shall have forgiveness of sin. I will enter in to him through my grace and sup with him," by the good works that he shall do; which works are the food of God; "and he shall sup with me, by the great joys that I shall give him." Thus shall a man hope, through his works of penance, that God will give him His Kingdom as it is promised to him in the Gospel.

Now a man shall understand of what nature his contrition shall be. I say that it shall be universal and total; that is to say, a man shall be truly repentant for all the sins that he has done for the pleasure of his mind; for pleasure is very dangerous. For there are two kinds of consenting; one of them is called the consenting of the affection when a man is moved to do sin, and long delights to think on that sin; and his reason perceives well that it has sinned against the law of God, and yet his reason restrains not his foul delight or inclination, though he see well and openly that it is against the reverence of God; though his reason may not consent to do that sin in the act, yet say some doctors that such pleasure that dwells long is perilous, although it be never so little. And also a man should sorrow that he has ever desired to do anything against the law of God with the full consent of his reason; for as to that there is no doubt that there is deadly sin in such consent. For indeed, there was never a deadly sin that was not beforehand in a man's thought, and after that in his pleasure, and so forth into consenting and into the deed. Therefore I say that many men never repent of such thoughts and pleasures and never shrive themselves of them, but only of the deed of great outward sin. Wherefore I say that such wicked delights and thoughts are subtle beguilers of them that shall be damned. And more, a man ought to sorrow for his wicked words as well as for his wicked deeds; for surely the repentance of a particular sin and the failure to repent of all his other sins, or else to repent of all his other sins and not of a particular sin, cannot be of avail. For truly, God Almighty is entirely good: and therefore He forgives all or else nothing. And with regard to this Saint Augustine says: "I know certainly that God is the enemy of every sin;" and how then? He that observes one sin, shall he have forgiveness for the remainder of his sins? No. And furthermore, contrition should be wonderfully sorrowful and full of anguish, and for that God plainly gives the sinner His mercy. And therefore, when my soul was full of anguish within me, I remembered God, and that my prayer could reach Him. Furthermore, contrition must be continuous, and a man should have a steadfast purpose to shrive himself, and to improve his life. For truly, while contrition lasts, a man will always have hope of forgiveness; and from this there comes the hate of sin, that destroys sin both in himself and in other people, at his discretion. And on this account David says: "Ye that love God are haters of wickedness." For trust well that to love God is to love what He loves and hate what He hates.

The last thing that man shall understand in contrition is this; for what contrition is useful. I say that sometimes contrition delivers a man from sin; concerning which David says: "I say," said David, that is to say, "I had firm purpose to be shriven; and Thou, Lord, didst forgive my sin." And just as contrition is of no avail without serious purpose of being shriven if a man have opportunity, just so are shrift and atonement of little worth without contrition. And moreover, contrition destroys the prison of hell and makes weak and feeble all the strength of devils, and restores the gifts of the Holy Spirit and of all God's virtues. And it cleanses the soul of sin and delivers the soul from the torment of hell, and from the company of the devil, and from the slavery of sin, and restores it to all spiritual good, and to the company and communion of Holy Church. And furthermore it makes him that formerly was a son of wrath to be a son of grace: and all these things are proved by Holy Writ. And therefore he that would set his mind to these things is wise; for indeed he would then never have a disposition to sin in all his life, but give his body and all his heart to the service of Jesus Christ and through that give Him homage. For truly our sweet Lord Jesus Christ hath spared us so graciously in our faults that if He had not had pity on man's soul we might all sing a sorry song.

Explicit prima pars Penitentie; et sequitur secunda pars eiusdem

THE second part of Penitence is Confession, which is the sign of contrition. Now ye shall understand what Confession is and whether it ought to be done or not, and what things are suitable to true Confession.

First thou shalt understand that Confession is the true revealing of sins to the priest, that is to say, "true," for a man must confess concerning all the conditions that belong to his sin as clearly as he can. All must be told, and no thing excused or hidden or wrapped up, and he shall make no boast of his good works. And in addition, it is necessary to understand whence sins spring, and how they increase, and what they are.

Of the beginning of sins Saint Paul says in this manner: "Just as sin first entered into this world through a man, and through that sin came death, just so death entered into all men that sin." And this man was Adam; through him sin entered into this world when he broke the commandment of God. And therefore he that was first so mighty that he should never have died, became such a one that he needs must die whether he would or not, and all his progeny must die in this world, since they too sinned through that man. See how in the estate of innocence when Adam and Eve were naked in Paradise and had no shame in their nakedness, the serpent that was the most wily of all other beasts that God had made, said to the woman: "Why did God command you that ye should not eat of every tree in Paradise?" The woman answered: "With the fruit," said she, "of the trees in Paradise we feed us; but truly, the fruit of the tree that is in the middle of Paradise, God forbade us to eat or touch, lest perhaps we should die." The serpent said to the woman: "Nay, nay, ye shall not die by death; for truly, God knows that on the day that ye eat thereof your eyes shall open and ye shall be as gods, knowing good and evil." The woman then saw that the tree was good for eating, and fair to the eye, and pleasurable to the sight; she took of the fruit of the tree, and ate of it, and gave to her husband, and he ate; and soon the eyes of both of them opened. And when they knew that they were naked they sewed fig leaves into a kind of breeches to hide their limbs. There ye may see that deadly sin has its first suggestion from the devil, as represented here by the serpent. And afterwards, through the delight of the flesh as shown here by Eve, and after that by the consent of reason, as shown here by Adam, for trust well, although it was the fiend who tempted Eve, who is the flesh, and the flesh had pleasure in the beauty of the forbidden fruit, none the less until reason, that is to say, Adam, consented to the eating of the fruit, man stood until then in a state of innocence. From that Adam we come by original sin; for from him we are all descended in the flesh, and engendered of vile and corrupt matter. And when the soul is put into our body, original sin is at once contracted by it; and that which at first was only the torment of concupiscence is later both torment and sin. And therefore we would all be born sons of wrath and imperishable damnation, if it were not for the baptism that we receive which takes from us our guilt; but in truth, the torment dwells with us as a temptation, which torment is called concupiscence. When it is wrongfully disposed or ordered in a man, it makes him covetous by covetousness of flesh, by fleshly sin, by the sight of his eyes as to earthly things, and by covetousness of rank through the pride of the heart.

Now to speak of the first kind of covetousness, which is concupiscence, according to the law of our limbs, that were lawfully made by the rightful judgment of God; I say, that inasmuch as man is not obedient to God, that is his Lord, therefore the flesh is disobedient to Him through concupiscence, which again is called the nourishing of sin and the occasion of sin. Therefore all the time that a man hath in himself the torment of concupiscence, it is impossible that he shall not be tempted some time and moved in his flesh to sin. And this thing cannot fail as long as he lives; it may grow feeble and fail by virtue of baptism and by the grace of God through penitence, but it shall never die fully unless he should be all cooled down by sickness or by the evil practice of sorcery or by cold drinks. But see what Saint Paul says: "The flesh becomes covetous in opposition to the spirit, and the spirit to the flesh; they are so contrary and strive so that a man cannot always do as he would." The same Saint Paul after his great penance in water and on land (in water by night and by day, in great peril and in great pain; in land, by famine, by thirst, by cold, and through the lack of clothing, and once being stoned almost to death), yet he said: "Alas! I, wretched man, who shall deliver me from the prison of my wretched body?" And Saint Jerome, when he had long dwelt in the desert, where he had no company but that of wild beasts, and where he had no food but herbs and water for drinking, nor no bed but the naked earth, on which account his flesh was as black as an Ethiopian's from the heat, and well nigh destroyed with cold, yet he said: "The burning fire of lechery boiled through all my body." Therefore I know for certainty that they are deceived that say they are not tempted through their bodies. Witness Saint James the Apostle, who says: "Every person is tempted through his own concupiscence;" that is to say, every one of us has material and occasion to be tempted by the nourishing of the sin that is in his body. And therefore says Saint John the Evangelist: "If we say we are without sin we deceive ourselves, and the truth is not in us."

Now shall ye understand in what manner sin grows or increases in man. The first thing is the nourishing of sin of which I spoke before, that fleshly concupiscence. And after that comes the subjection of the devil. That is to say, the devil's belly with which he blows into man the fire of fleshly concupiscence. And after that a man considers whether he will or will not do the thing to which he is tempted. And then, if a man withstand and avoid the first enticing of his flesh and the devil, then it is no sin. And if it is so that he does not do so, then he soon feels a flame of delight. And then it is good to beware, and protect himself well, or else he will fall soon into consenting to sin; and then he will do it if he has the time and place. And concerning this matter Moses, speaking of the devil, declares: "The fiend says, I will chase and pursue a man by wicked suggestion and I will seize him by the moving or stirring of sin. I will single out my prize or my prey by deliberation, and my pleasure shall be accomplished by delight; I will draw my sword in his consenting." For surely, just as a sword severs a thing in two pieces, just so consenting drives God from man: "and then I will slay him with my hand in the act of sin;" thus says the fiend. For truly then, a man is entirely dead in soul. And this sin is accomplished by temptation, by pleasure, and by consent; and then the sin is called actual.

For in truth, sin is of two kinds, either it is venial or deadly. Surely, when man loves any creature more than Jesus Christ our Creator, then it is deadly sin.

And it is venial if a man loves Jesus Christ less than he should. Truly, the act of this venial sin is very dangerous, for it lessens the love that man should have more and more for God. And therefore, if a man charge himself with many such venial sins, certainly unless he should some time discharge himself of them by shrift, they might very easily lessen in him all the love that he has for Jesus Christ; and in this manner venial sin runs into deadly sin. For certainly, the more a man charges his soul with venial sin, the more he is inclined to fall into deadly sin. And therefore, let us not be negligent to discharge our venial sins. For the proverb says that many small things make a great. And listen to this example. A great wave of the sea comes sometimes with such a violence that it sinks a ship. And the same evil may sometimes be done by small drops of water that enter through a little crevice into the lowest part of the ship's hull into the bottom of the ship, if men are so negligent that they do not prevent it in time. And therefore, although there is a difference between these two causes of sinking, nevertheless the ship is sunk. And just so it goes sometimes with deadly sin and with annoying venial sins when they multiply in a man so greatly that those worldly things that he loves through which he sins venially become as great in his heart as the love of God, or greater. And therefore the love of everything that is not set in God or done principally for God's sake, even though a man love it less than God, is, nevertheless, a venial sin. And it is deadly sin, when the love of anything weighs in the heart of man as much as the love of God or more. "Deadly sin," as says Saint Augustine, "is when a man turns his heart from God, Who is true, sovereign goodness, that cannot change; and gives his heart to things that may change and pass." And surely that is everything except God in heaven. For it is true that if a man give his love, which he owes entirely to God with all his heart, to a creature, certainly, as much of his love as he gives to that creature, so much he takes from God; and therefore he does a sin. For he, who is debtor to God does not pay God his debt, that is to say, all the love in his heart.

Now since a man understands in general what venial sin is, it will be proper to tell particularly of things that many men may not regard as sins, and do not shrive themselves of, and yet nevertheless, they are sins. Truly, as scholars write, every time a man eats or drinks more than is necessary for the sustenance of his body, surely he does a sin. And also when he speaks more than is necessary, it is a sin. Also when he does not listen kindly to the complaints of the poor. And again when he is in good bodily health and will not fast when other folk fast, for no reasonable cause. Again, when he sleeps more than is necessary, and when he comes on that account too late to church, and to other charitable activities. Also when he uses his wife without the sovereign desire of engendering, to the honor of God, or with the purpose of paying to his wife the debt of his body. Also, when he will not visit the sick and prisoners, if that is possible. Also, if he loves wife or child, or any other worldly thing, more than reason requires. Also, if he flatters or praises more than is necessary. Also, if he lessens or takes away the alms of the poor. And again, if he has his meat prepared more deliciously than is necessary, or eats it too hastily in his gluttony. Also if he tells foolish things at church or at God's Service, or is a speaker of idle words or folly or evil; for he shall render an account for it at the Day of Judgment. Also when he promises or gives assurance that he will do things which he cannot perform. Also when by lightness or folly, he misrepresents or scorns his neighbor. Also when he has any wicked suspicion of anything concerning which he has no true knowledge. These things and more without number are sins, as says Saint Augustine.

Now men shall understand that although no earthly man can put aside all venial sins, yet through the burning love that he has for our Lord Jesus Christ, and through prayers and confessions and other good works, he may so refrain from them that there shall be but little harm. For as Saint Augustine says: "If a man loves God in such a way that all that he does is done in love of God, and for the love of God truly, for he burns with the love of God, see – as much as a drop of water falling in a furnace full of fire troubles or disturbs, so much a venial sin troubles a man that is perfect in the love of Jesus Christ." Men may also reject venial sin by partaking worthily of the precious Body of Jesus Christ; by partaking also of holy water; by giving alms; by general confession of *Confiteor* at mass and at compline; and through the blessing of Bishops and Priests, and by other good works.

Explicit secunda pars Penitentie

Sequitur de Septem Peccatis Mortalibus et eorum dependenciis circumstanciis et speciebus

NOW it is a fitting thing to tell what are the deadly sins, that is to say, the chieftains among sins. They run all in one leash, but in different ways. Now they are called chieftains inasmuch as they lead and are the begetters of all other sins. The root of these seven sins then is Pride, the general root of all evils; for from this root spring certain branches, as Anger, Envy, Laziness or Sloth, Avarice or Covetousness (in the common understanding), Gluttony and Lechery. And every one of these chief sins has his branches and twigs, as shall be set forth in chapters upon them that follow.

De Superbia

AND though no man can plainly tell the number of twigs and of the evils that come from Pride, yet I will show some of them, as ye shall perceive. There is Disobedience, Boasting, Hypocrisy, Malice, Arrogance, Impudence, Swelling of Heart, Insolence, Elation, Impatience, Strife, Contumely, Presumption, Irreverence, Pertinacity, Vain-glory, and many another twig that I cannot declare. He is disobedient that disobeys in malice the commandments of God and his sovereigns, and those of his spiritual father. He is a boaster that boasts of the harm or the good that he has done. He is a hypocrite that conceals that which he is, and pretends to be that which he is not. He is malicious that has disdain of his neighbors, that is to say, of his fellow Christians, or scorns to do what he ought to do. He is arrogant that thinks he has those good things in him which he does not possess, or believes that he should have them according to his deserts; or else he believes that he is that which he is not. He is impudent that in his pride has no shame for his sins. When a man rejoices in the harm that he has done, then may he be said to have a swelling of the heart. He is insolent that despises in his judgment all other people with respect to his own value, and of his intelligence, and of his speaking, and of his bearing. That man shows elation who cannot submit to have a master or an equal. He is impudent that will not be taught nor instructed concerning his faults, and by strife makes war knowingly upon truth, and defends his folly. He is contumacious that because of his indignation is against every authority or power among those that are his sovereigns. A man is presumptuous when he undertakes an enterprise which he ought not to undertake, or one that he ought not do, and that is called vain-confidence. A man is irreverent when he does not give honor where he ought to give it, and waits to be reverenced. A man is pertinacious when he defends his folly and trusts too greatly in his own wit. When a man makes show of and takes delight in his temporal elevation and glorifies himself in this world's estate, that is

vain-glory. Babbling is when men speak too much before others and clatter as does a mill, and take no heed of what they say.

And yet there is a secret kind of Pride through which a man waits to be greeted before he will give greeting, although he is of less worth than the other is, perhaps; and also he waits or desires to sit, or else to go before him on the road, or to give the kiss of peace, or to offer incense, or to bring an offering in before his neighbor, and such things. And this may be against his duty, perhaps, except that he has set his heart and his purpose on a proud desire to be magnified and honored before men.

Now there are two kinds of Pride. One of them is within the heart of man, and the other is without. And the things of which I have spoken and many more of which I have not spoken pertain to pride that is in the heart of man; and other kinds of pride are outside it. But nevertheless, one of these kinds of pride is a sign of the other, just as the gay bush outside the tavern is the sign of the wine that is in the cellar. And this appears in many things; such as in the speech and expression of countenance, and in clothing excessively ornate. For indeed, if there had been no sin in clothing, Christ would not have noted and spoken of the clothing of the rich man in the Gospel. And, as Saint Gregory says, costly clothing is responsible for the dearth of clothing, and for soft living, and for strangeness of manner and elaborate ornamentation, and for superfluity, or for great honor. Alas! Can man not see in our days the sinful, costly array of clothing, and especially in too great superfluity or else in too great scantiness?

As to the first sin, superfluity of clothing, this makes apparel costly, to the great harm of the people. There is not only the cost of embroidery, the elaborate indenting or adorning with bars, the use of waved lines, or upright stripes, twisting or curving, and the like waste of cloth in vanity; but there is also costly furring in their gowns, so much punching of holes with chisels, so much cutting with shears; and also the unnecessary length of the aforesaid gowns, trailing in the dung and in the mire, on horseback and also on foot, as well for men as for women. And all this trailing is truly wasted and consumed, threadbare and rotten with dung, while the cloth should rather be given to the poor, who suffer great loss for want of it. And this happens in various ways, that is to say, the more that cloth is wasted, the more it costs people because of its scarcity. And furthermore, if they would give such punched or tagged clothing to the poor people, it is not suitable for them to wear in their station, nor sufficient to serve their necessity, nor keep them from the intemperance of the skies. On the other hand, we may speak of the horrible and unseemly scantiness of clothing, such as these loose garments or short jackets, that on account of their shortness do not cover the shameful members of men, and with a wicked purpose. Alas! Some of them show the curves of their shape and their horrible swollen members, that have the appearance of hernia, in the wrapping of their hose. And also their buttocks look like the hind part of a she-ape in the full of the moon. And moreover, the wretched, swollen members that show through the elaborate ornamentation, where their stockings are separated in white and red, make it seem that half their secret organs are exposed. And if it be that they divide their stockings in other colors, such as white and black, or white and blue, or black and red, etc., then it appears in the variety of color that the half part of their private members were corrupted by the fire of Saint Anthony, or by cancer, or by some other affliction. As to the hind part of their buttocks, these are horrible to see. For indeed, in that part of their body where they purge themselves of their stinking ordure, they show that part proudly to the people in scorn of modesty, which modesty Jesus Christ and His friends sought to show in their lives. Now as to the costly dress of

women, God knows that though the faces of some of them seem chaste and pretty, yet by their manner of attire they give notification of lecherousness and pride. I say not that a neatness in the clothing of men or women is unfitting, but certainly excess or inordinate scantiness of clothing is reprovable. Also the sin of adornment or dress appears in things that pertain to riding, as in too many fine horses kept for pleasure, that are fair, fat, and costly; also the too many vicious fellows that are kept because of them. And again it shows in curious harness, as saddles, croupers, breastbands, and bridles, covered with precious and rich ornament, bars, and plates of gold and silver. On this account God says through Zechariah the Prophet: "I will confound the riders of such horses." These people pay little regard to the manner of riding of the Son of God in Heaven, and of His equipment when He rode upon the ass, and He had no other equipment but the poor clothes of His disciples; and we do not read that he ever rode on any other beast. I say this concerning the sin of excess and not with regard to a sufficient amount of clothing for modesty's sake, when reason requires it. And furthermore, Pride is greatly indicated in the keeping of so many people when they are of little real use, or of no use at all. And especially is this so when such a following is mischievous and offensive to the people on account of the boldness of great lordship or on account of pride of office. For indeed, such lords sell their lordship to the devil in hell when they sustain the wickedness of their followers. Or else when people of low station, such as those that keep hostelries, back up or permit thieving by their hostlers, and that is in many kinds of trickery. Such kinds of people are the flies that follow the honey, or else the dogs that go after dead meat. Such people spiritually strangle their authority; on account of which David the Prophet says: "Wicked death must come upon that authority, and may God grant that they descend deep into hell; for in their houses are

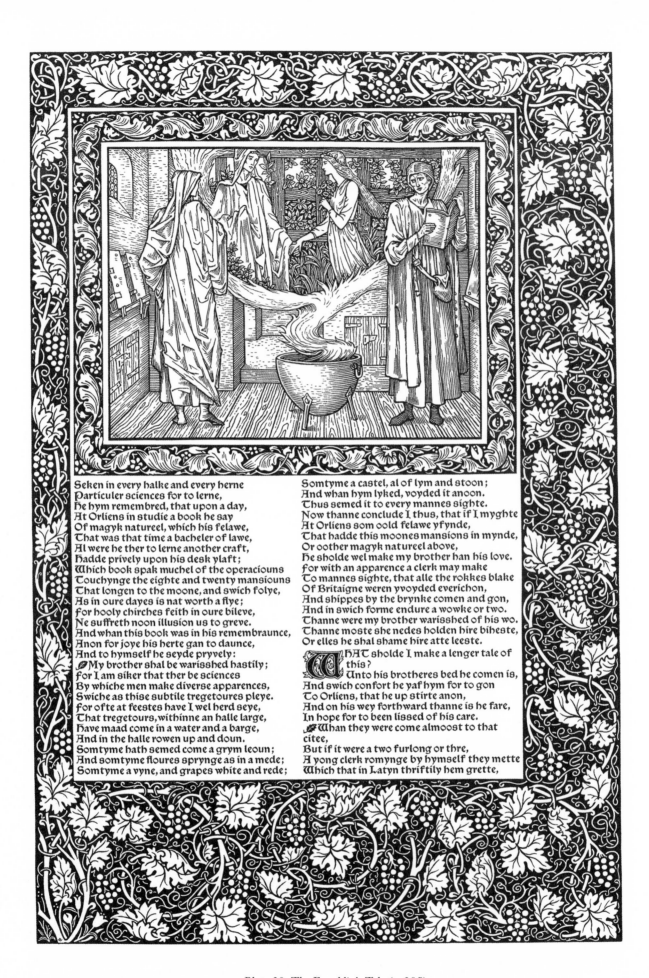

Seken in every halke and every herne
Particuler sciences for to lerne,
He hym remembred, that upon a day,
At Orliens in studie a book he say
Of magyk natureel, which his felawe,
That was that time a bacheler of lawe,
Al were he ther to lerne another craft,
Hadde prively upon his desk ylaft;
Which book spak muchel of the operaciouns
Touchynge the eighte and twenty mansiouns
That longen to the moone, and swich folye,
As in oure dayes is nat worth a flye;
For hooly chirches feith in oure bileve,
Ne suffreth noon illusion us to greve.
And whan this book was in his remembraunce,
Anon for joye his herte gan to daunce,
And to hymself he seyde pryvely:
My brother shal be warisshed hastily;
For I am siker that ther be sciences
By whiche men make diverse apparences,
Swiche as thise subtile tregetoures pleye.
For ofte at feestes have I wel herd seye,
That tregetours, withinne an halle large,
Have maad come in a water and a barge,
And in the halle rowen up and doun.
Somtyme hath semed come a grym leoun;
And somtyme floures sprynge as in a mede;
Somtyme a vyne, and grapes white and rede;

Somtyme a castel, al of lym and stoon;
And whan hym lyked, voyded it anoon.
Thus semed it to every mannes sighte.
Now thanne conclude I thus, that if I myghte
At Orliens som oold felawe yfynde,
That hadde this moones mansions in mynde,
Or oother magyk natureel above,
He sholde wel make my brother han his love.
For with an apparence a clerk may make
To mannes sighte, that alle the rokkes blake
Of Britaigne weren yvoyded everichon,
And shippes by the brynke comen and gon,
And in swich forme endure a wowke or two.
Thanne were my brother warisshed of his wo.
Thanne moste she nedes holden hire biheste,
Or elles he shal shame hire atte leeste.
WHAT sholde I make a lenger tale of
this?
Unto his brotheres bed he comen is,
And swich confort he yaf hym for to gon
To Orliens, that he up stirte anon,
And on his wey forthward thanne is he fare,
In hope for to been lissed of his care.
Whan they were come almoost to that citee,
But if it were a two furlong or thre,
A yong clerk romynge by hymself they mette
Which that in Latyn thriftily hem grette,

Plate 30: The Franklin's Tale (p. 295)

iniquities and wicked deeds," and not God in heaven. And truly, unless they correct this, just as God gave His blessing to Laban in the service of Jacob, and to Pharaoh in the service of Joseph, just so will God bring ill to such authority as disdains the wickedness of its servants, unless it reform itself. And pride as to table appears often also; for truly, rich men are called to feasts, and poor men are turned away and rebuked. Also in excess of various meats and drinks, and particularly such kinds of baked meats and meats in dishes burning with fire and painted and castled with paper and the likewise; so that it is a shameful thing to think of it. And also in too great costliness of vessels and elaborateness of minstrelsy, through which men are stirred the more to the delights of luxury – if, indeed, they set their hearts the less upon our Lord Jesus Christ, certainly this is a sin. And indeed the enjoyments might be so great in this case that one might easily fall through them into deadly sin. The kinds of sin that arise from pride, truly, when they arise from malice imagined, considered and fore-determined, or else from habit, are deadly sins, there is no doubt. And when they arise from sudden frailty, without consideration, and suddenly disappear again, although they are grievous sins, it is my guess that they are not deadly. Now men might ask from what pride springs and arises, and I say, sometimes it springs from the good things of nature and sometimes from the good things of fortune, and sometimes from the good things of grace. Truly, the good things of nature consist either in the good things of the body or in the good things of the soul. The good things of the body are health of body, such as strength, dexterity, beauty, noble blood, and freedom. The good things of nature, of the spirit, are good wit, sharp understanding, subtle skill, natural virtue and a good memory. The good things of fortune are wealth, high degrees of lordship, and the praise of people. The goods of grace are knowledge, power to suffer travail of spirit, goodness, virtuous

contemplation, the withstanding of temptation, and like things. Of which aforesaid good things, it is indeed a great folly in a man to pride himself on any of them. To speak of the good things of nature, God knows that sometimes we have them by nature as much to our damage as to our profit. As with health of body; certainly it disappears easily, and also it is often the cause of the sickness of our soul; for God knows the flesh is a very great enemy of the soul; and therefore the more the body is whole, the more we are in peril of falling. Also it is a high folly for a man to pride himself on his strength of body, for certainly the flesh envies the spirit, and the stronger the flesh is, the sorrier the soul may be. And, in addition to all this, strength of body and worldly boldness often brings many a man to peril and misfortune. Also for a man to pride himself on his noble birth is a great folly, for oftentimes the noble blood of the body takes away the nobility of the soul. And also we are all of one father and one mother, and we are all by nature corrupt and vicious, both rich and poor. In truth, only one kind of nobility is to be praised, that which adorns man's spirit with virtue and morality and makes him the child of Christ. For believe well that when sin has mastery over a man, he is the very servant of sin.

Now there are certain general tokens of nobility, such as the avoidance of vice and ribaldry, and thralldom to sin, in a word, work and continence; and the use of virtue, courtesy and clean living, and to be generous, that is to say, with moderation; for whatever is out of proportion is folly and sin. And another sign of nobility is for a man to remember the goodness that he has received from others. Another is to be kind to his good subjects; concerning which Seneca says: "There is nothing more fitting to a man of high station than kindness and pity. And therefore these flies that men call bees, when they make their king, choose one that has no stinger with which he can sting." Another token of nobility is that a man has a noble heart and a diligent one, and seeks to attain to high and virtuous things. Now certainly, for a man to pride himself on the good things of grace is also an outrageous folly; for these gifts of grace that should have turned him to goodness and healing, turn him to poison and confusion, as says Saint Gregory. Truly, whoever also prides himself on the goods of fortune is a great fool; for sometimes a man is a great lord in the morning and a churl and wretch before it is night. And sometimes the wealth of a man is the cause of his death. Sometimes the pleasures of a man are the cause of grievous sickness through which he perishes. Sometimes the commendation of people is a very false and brittle thing to trust. This day they praise, tomorrow they blame. God knows desire to have the praise of people has brought death to many a busy man.

Remedium contra peccatum Superbie

NOW since ye have understood what Pride is and what are the various kinds of Pride and whence Pride arises and springs, ye shall now understand what is the remedy for the sin of Pride, and this is humility or meekness. That is a virtue through which a man has true knowledge of himself and takes no pleasure and sets no value with regard to his deserts, always remembering his weakness. Now there are three kinds of humility – humility of heart, and humility of mouth, and the third is humility of action. Humility of the heart is of four kinds. One is when a man holds himself as worth nothing in the sight of God in heaven. Another is when he does not despise any other man. The third is when he does not care though men hold him of no worth. The fourth is when he does not grieve over his humiliation. Also, the humility of the mouth consists in four things: in temperate speech, in humbleness of speech, and when a man acknowledges with his own mouth that he is such as he believes himself in his heart to be.

Another is when he praises the goodness of another man, and in no way detracts from it. Humility of action is also of four kinds. The first is when a man puts other men before himself. The second is when he chooses the lowest place of all. The third is when he gladly agrees to good advice. The fourth is when he gladly accepts the word of his sovereigns or of one that is of higher station; certainly this is a great act of humility.

Sequitur de Inuidia

AFTER Pride I will speak of the foul sin of Envy which is, according to the word of the philosopher, sorrow for other men's prosperity; and, according to the word of Saint Augustine, the sorrow for other men's weal and joy in other men's harm. This foul sin is plainly against the Holy Ghost. Although every sin is against the Holy Ghost, yet inasmuch as goodness pertains especially to the Holy Ghost, and envy comes especially of malice, therefore it is especially against the goodness of the Holy Ghost. Now malice is of two kinds, that is to say, hardness of heart in wickedness or blindness on the part of the flesh in a man, so that he considers that he does not sin, or does not care that he sins; which is the cruelty of the devil. The other kind of malice is when a man attacks truth when he knows that it is truth. And also when he attacks the grace that God has given to his neighbor; and all this is in envy. Certainly, then, is envy the worst sin that there is. For truly, all other sins are at times only against one special virtue, but indeed, envy is against all virtues and against all goodness, for it is the regret for all the blessings of one's neighbor, and in this matter it is different from all other sins. For there is hardly any sin that does not have some pleasure in itself save only envy, that always has anguish and sorrow because of itself. The kinds of envy are these; there is first the regret for other men's goodness and prosperity; and prosperity is by nature a matter for joy; then is envy a sin against nature. The second kind of envy is a rejoicing in other men's ill fortune; and that appropriately resembles the devil, that ever rejoices in evil suffered by men. From these two kinds of envy comes back-biting; and this sin of back-biting or detraction has, in turn, certain varieties. Sometimes a man praises his neighbor with a wicked purpose; for he makes always a wicked knot at the end of what he says. Always he adds a "but" at the end, that is worthy of more blame than the value of all the praise he has given. The second variety is that if a man is good and does or says a thing from a good purpose, the detractor will turn all that good upside down, to his wicked purpose. The third kind of envy is to lessen the goodness of his neighbor. The fourth species of detraction is this, that if men speak goodness of a man then the detractor says, "In faith, such a man is nevertheless better than he;" in the disparagement of the man that men praise. The fifth variety is this: to consent gladly and listen gladly to the ill that men speak of other people. This sin is very great and always increases with the wicked purpose of the detractor. After detraction comes grudging or murmuring; sometimes it springs from impatience against God, and sometimes against man. It is against God when a man complains against the pains of hell, or against poverty, or loss of goods, or against rain or storm; or else complains that the wicked have prosperity, or because good men encounter adversity. And all these things men should endure patiently, for they come through the rightful judgment and rule of God. Sometimes complaining comes as a result of avarice; for instance, Judas complained against the Magdalene, when she anointed the head of our Lord Jesus Christ with her precious ointment. This kind of complaining is such as when one complains of the good deeds that he himself does, or that other people do with their possessions. Sometimes complaining arises from pride; as when Simon the Pharisee complained against the Magdalene when she approached Jesus Christ and wept at His feet for her sins. And sometimes complaining arises from Envy; when men reveal a secret harm that a man has endured, or swear to him that a thing is false. Complaining also often exists among servants, when their masters bid them do fitting things; for they dare not openly resist the commandments of their masters, yet they will say evil and complain and murmur secretly for very spite. And such words men call the devil's *Pater Noster*. Though the devil never had a *Pater Noster*, nevertheless ignorant people give it such a name. Sometimes murmuring comes from anger or secret hate that nourishes a rancor in the heart, as afterwards I shall explain. Then comes also bitterness of heart, and through this bitterness every good deed of his neighbor seems to a man bitter and unsavory. Then comes discord that sunders all kinds of friendship. Then comes scorn, as when a man seeks occasion to annoy his neighbor, though he is behaving never so well. Then comes accusation, as when a man seeks occasion to injure his neighbor, which resembles the craft of the devil that waits night and day to accuse all of us. Then comes malignity, through which a man hurts his neighbor secretly, if he can. And if he cannot, nevertheless his wicked will is not wanting, as for example, to burn his house secretly, or poison or kill his stock, and similar things.

Remedium contra peccatum Inuidie

NOW I will speak of the remedy against this foul sin of Envy. First, the love of God is the principal remedy, and the loving of one's neighbor as one's self; for indeed, the one cannot exist without the other. And trust well, that in the word "neighbor" thou shalt understand thy brothers; for truly, all of us have one fleshly father, and one mother, that is to say, Adam and Eve; and also one Spiritual Father, and that is God in Heaven. Thou art bound to love thy neighbor and wish him all goodness, and therefore God says, "Love thy neighbor as thyself," that is to say, to the saving of both his body and his soul. And moreover, thou shalt love him by word, and by friendly admonishing and chastisement; and comfort him in his injuries, and pray for him with all thine heart. And indeed, thou shalt love him in such a way that thou shalt in charity do to him as thou wouldst to thine own person. And therefore thou shalt do him no damage by wicked word, nor any harm to his body, nor to his goods, nor to his soul, by the enticement of wicked example. Thou shalt not desire his wife, nor any of his possessions. Understand also, that the word neighbor comprehends a man's enemy. A man shall, indeed, love his enemy by the commandment of God, and truly, thou shalt love thy friend in God. I say, thou shalt love thine enemy for God's sake, by His commandment, for if it were reason that a man should hate his enemy, God indeed would not receive into His love us that have been His enemies. Against three kinds of wrongs that his enemy may do to him, a man shall do three things, as follows: Against hate and rancor of heart he shall love him in his heart. Against scolding and wicked words he shall pray for his enemy. And in recompense for the wicked deed of his enemy he shall do good to him. For Christ says, "Love your enemies, and pray for them that speak harm of you; and also for them that harry and pursue you, and do good to them that hate you." Lo, thus Lord Jesus Christ commanded us to do to our enemies. For truly, nature drives us to love our friends, and by our faith, our enemies have more need of love than our friends; and they that have the greater need, certainly to them shall men do good; and truly, in such a deed we keep remembrance of the love of Jesus Christ, that died for His enemies. And insofar as that love is the more difficult to perform, just so much greater is its merit; and

therefore the loving of our enemies confounds the venom of the devil. For just as the devil is discomfited by humility, so also is he wounded to death by our love for our enemies. Certainly, then, love is the medicine that casts out the venom of Envy from men's hearts. The kinds of this quality shall be explained more fully in its following chapters.

Sequitur de Ira

AFTER Envy, I will describe the sin of Anger. For truly, whoever has envy of his neighbor will soon, in general, find an occasion for wrath, in word or in deed, against him towards whom he bears the envy. And Anger comes from Pride as well as from Envy; for truly, he that is proud or envious is easily made angry.

This sin of Anger, according to the description of Saint Augustine, is a wicked will to be avenged by word or by deed. Anger, according to the philosopher, is the fervent blood of man quickened in his heart, through which he desires to harm him that he hates. For indeed, the heart of man by the heating and moving of his blood becomes so troubled that he is out of all use of reason. But ye shall understand that Anger is of two kinds, the one of them is good and the other is wicked. The good Anger is from jealousy of goodness, through which a man is angry with wickedness and against wickedness; and therefore says a wise man that "Anger is better than play." This Anger is characterized by gentleness, and it is anger without bitterness; not anger against the man, but Anger with the misdeed of the man, as says the Prophet David, "*Irascimini et nolite peccare.*" And now understand that wicked Anger is of two kinds. One of these is sudden or hasty Anger, without the counsel and agreement of reason. The meaning and the sense of this is that the reason of man does not agree to this sudden Anger, and thus it is venial.

Another Anger is very wicked, that comes of felony of heart considered and determined upon beforehand; that wicked will to do vengeance to which the reason consents; and truly, this is a deadly sin. This Anger is so displeasing to God, that it troubles his house and chaseth the Holy Ghost out of man's soul, and wastes and destroys the likeness of God, that is to say, the virtue that is in man's soul, and puts him into the likeness of the devil, and steals the man from God that is his rightful Lord. This Anger is a very great pleasure to the devil, for it is the devil's furnace that is heated in the fires of hell. For indeed, just as fire is more mighty to destroy earthly things than is any other element, just so Anger is mighty to destroy all spiritual things. See how the fire of small coals, that are almost dead under ashes, will become alive again when they are touched with brimstone. In the same manner Anger will ever more revive again when it is touched by the Pride that is covered in man's heart. For surely, fire cannot come out of something unless it were first in the thing naturally, just as fire is drawn out of the flint by steel. And just as Pride is oftentimes material for Anger, just so is rancor the nurse and preserver of Anger. There is a kind of tree, as says Saint Isidore, that when men make fire of that tree and cover the coals with ashes, the fire will last indeed all of a year or more. And just so it goes with rancor when it is once conceived in the hearts of some men, certainly it will last perhaps from one Easter Day to another Easter Day and more. But indeed, that man is full far from the mercy of God all that while.

In this devil's furnace there are forged three evils. Pride is one of them, that always bloweth and increases the fire by scolding and wicked words. Then comes Envy and holds the hot irons against the heart of man with a pair of long tongs of enduring rancor. And then there comes the sin of Contumely, or striving and wrangling, and it batters and forges by villainous reproaches. Indeed,

this cursed sin injures both the man himself and his neighbor. For truly, almost all the harm that any man does to his neighbor comes from Anger. For surely, outrageous wrath does all that ever the devil commands it; for it spares neither Christ nor His sweet Mother. And in his outrageous wrath and anger, alas! alas! full many a one at that time feels in his heart wickedly both towards Christ and towards all His Saints. Is not this a cursed vice? Yes, certainly. Alas! it takes from man his wit and reason and all his fine spiritual life that should keep his soul. Certainly it takes away also God's due Lordship that is over man's soul, and the love of his neighbors. It striveth also always against truth. It disturbs the quiet of his heart and subverteth his soul.

From Anger come three stinking things: hate, that is ancient wrath; discord, through which a man forsakes his old friend that he has loved a long time; and war and every kind of wrong that man does to his neighbor, in body or to his property. From this cursed sin of Anger manslaughter comes also. And understand well that homicide, that is manslaughter, has various forms. Some kinds of homicide are spiritual and some bodily. Spiritual manslaughter is of six kinds. The first, by hate; as Saint John says, "He that hateth his brother is a homicide." Homicide comes also through backbiting; to these backbiters Solomon says: "They have two swords with which they slay their neighbors." For truly, it is as wicked to take away a good man's name as to take his life. Homicide also consists in the giving of wicked and fraudulent counsel; such as to give counsel to levy wrongful custom duties and taxes. Concerning this Solomon says: "A lion roaring and a hungry bear are like cruel lordships," that is, in withholding or injuring the sheep (or the shepherd), or the wages of servants, or else in usury or in withholding alms from poor people. On this account the wise man says: "Feed him that is almost dying of hunger;" for truly, unless thou feed him, thou slayest him. And all these are deadly sins. Bodily manslaughter occurs when thou slayest with thy tongue in another manner; as when thou commandest that a man should be slain, or else givest counsel to the slaying of a man. Manslaughter, in act, is of four kinds. One is under the law, just as a Justice condemns him that is guilty to his death. But let the Justice beware that he does it rightfully, and that he does it not for a delight in the spilling of blood, but for the preservation of righteousness. Another kind of homicide is that which is done for necessity, as when one man slays another in self-defence, when he cannot otherwise escape death himself. And certainly, if he can escape without the killing of his adversary and yet slays him, he commits sin and he shall bear penance as for a deadly sin. Also, if a man by accident or chance shoot an arrow or cast a stone with which he kills a man, he is a homicide. Also if a woman by negligence lies upon her child as she sleeps, it is a homicide and a deadly sin. Also, when a man interferes with the conception of a child, and makes a woman either barren by drinking venomous herbs, by means of which she may be prevented from conceiving, or willfully slays a child by drinks, or else puts some material things in her private parts to slay the child, or else does unnatural sin by which the man or woman discharge his seed in a manner or in a place where a child may not be conceived, or else if a woman have conceived and hurt herself and hurt the child, still it is homicide. What shall we say also of women that murder their children for fear of worldly shame? Certainly, it is a horrible homicide. It is homicide also if a man approaches a woman by lecherous desire, through which the child that she bears within her dies, or else strikes a woman knowingly, through which she loses her child. All these are homicides and horrible, deadly sins. There are in addition many more sins of Anger, as well in word as in thought and

deed; as he that accuses God, or blames God, of things of which he himself is guilty, or scorns God and all His Saints, as do these accursed gamblers in various countries. This cursed sin they do when they feel wickedly in their hearts towards God and His Saints. Also, when they treat irreverently the Sacrament of the Altar, that is a sin so great that it can hardly be forgiven, except that the mercy of God passes to His works, it is so great and so benign. Then from Anger comes a venomous rage, when a man is sharply admonished in his confession to abandon his sin, and becomes angry and answers scornfully and wrathfully, and defends or excuses his sin by the instability of his flesh, or because he did it to keep company with his fellows, or else he says the fiend enticed him; or else he did it on account of his youth, or else his nature is so high spirited that he cannot control it, or else it is his destiny, as he says, up to a certain age, or else he says it comes to him by reason of the nobility of his ancestors, and similar things. All this kind of people so wrap themselves in their sins that they will not deliver themselves, for truly, no person that excuses himself willfully in his sin can be freed of it until he humbly acknowledges it. After this, then comes swearing, which is expressly against the commandment of God; and this comes often from Anger and from Ire. God says: "Thou shalt not take the name of the Lord Thy God in vain." Also our Lord Jesus Christ says through the words of Saint Matthew: "*Nolite iurare omnino*: do not swear in any way, neither by the heaven, for it is God's throne, nor by the earth, for it is the bench for His feet; nor by Jerusalem, for it is the city of the great king; nor by thine head, for thou canst not make a hair white or black. But speak by your word, 'yea, yea,' and 'nay, nay.' And what is more than that is evil," says Christ. For Christ's sake do not swear so sinfully, dismembering Christ by soul, heart, bones, and body. For indeed, it would seem that ye think that the cursed Jews have not dismembered enough the sacred person of Christ, so that ye will dismember Him more. And if it be that the law compelled you to swear, then rule yourself according to the law of God, as says Saint Jeremy *quarto capitulo*, *"Iurabis in veritate, in iudicio et in iusticia:* thou shalt swear in truth, in judgment, and in righteousness." This is to say, thou shalt swear truth; for every lie is against Christ. For Christ is indeed truth. And bear this well in mind, that every great swearer who is not compelled lawfully to swear shall not have harm depart from his house while he affects such unlawful swearing. Thou shalt swear also in judgment, when thou art constrained by thy judge to witness the truth. Also thou shalt not swear on account of envy, nor for favor, nor for reward, but for righteousness, and in order to declare it to the worship of God and the help of thy fellow Christians. And therefore every man that takes God's name in vain, or swears villainously with his mouth, or else takes upon him the name of Christ, cannot be called a Christian man, and lives against Christ's living and teaching; all of these take God's name in vain. See also what Saint Peter says, *Actuum quarto capitulo,* *"Non est aliud nomen sub celo,"* etc. "There is no other name," says Saint Peter, "given to men under heaven through which they can be saved;" that is to say, except the name of Jesus Christ. Take heed also how the precious name of Christ as Saint Paul says *ad Philipenses secundo,* *"In nomine Jesu,* etc.; that in the name of Jesus every knee of heavenly creature or earthly or those of hell should bow." For it is so high and worthy of honor that the cursed fiend in hell should tremble to hear it pronounced. Then it seems that men that swear so horribly by His blessed name despise Him more outrightly than did the cursed Jews, or even the devil that trembles when he hears His name.

Now indeed, since swearing, unless it is lawfully done, is so highly forbidden, much worse is false forswearing, especially when it is needless.

What say we also of those that delight in swearing, and hold it a manly deed or a matter of nobleness to swear great oaths? And what of those that by their habit do not cease to swear great oaths, although the occasion is not worth a straw? Certainly this is a horrible sin. Swearing suddenly without considertion is also a sin. But let us go now to that horrible swearing of adjuration and conjuring, as false enchanters or necromancers do over basins full of water, or on a bright sword, or in a circle, or over a fire, or on the shoulder-bone of a sheep. I can say nothing but that they act accursedly and abominably against Christ, and all the faith of Holy Church. What shall we say of those that believe in divinations, as by the flight or sound of birds, or of beasts, or by lot, or by figures made upon the earth, or by dreams, or by the creaking of doors, or by the cracking of houses, or the gnawing of rats, and such kinds of wretchedness? Certainly all such things are forbidden by God and by Holy Church. On this account those that set their belief in such rubbish are cursed, until they reform. Charms for wounds or sickness of men, or of beasts, if they take any effect, do so perhaps because God permits it, that people should give the more faith and reverence to His name.

Now I will speak of Lying, which generally is a false use of words through which a man has the intent to deceive his fellow Christian. Some Lying is of a kind from which there comes no advantage to any person, and some Lying turns to the pleasure or profit of one man, and to the discomfort and damage of another. Another form of Lying is done by a man to save his life or his property. Another comes from the delight in Lying, in which delight some will forge long tales, and paint them with all kinds of circumstances, when the entire base of the tale is false. Some Lying occurs because a man wishes to sustain his word; and some lying comes of recklessness without consideration, and other similar things.

Now let us touch upon the vice of such Flattery, which does not come spontaneously, but from fear, or from covetousness. Flattery is in general wrongful praise. Flatterers are the devil's nurses that nurse his children with the milk of false praise. For in truth, Solomon says that "flattery is worse than detraction." For sometimes detraction makes a haughty man more humble, because he dreads detraction; but indeed flattery makes a man swell in his heart and in his visage. Flatterers are the devil's enchanters, for they make a man think he is like that which he is not like. They resemble Judas who betrayed God, and these flatterers betray a man to sell him to his enemy, that is, to the devil. Flatterers are the devil's disciples that sing ever *Placebo*. I consider Flattery as among the vices of Anger; for oftentimes if one man is angry with another then he will flatter some person to sustain him in his quarrel.

Now let us speak of such Cursing as comes from an angry heart. Cursing generally may be said to have every kind of power or harm. Such Cursing tears man from the Kingdom of God, as Saint Paul says. And oftentimes such Cursing wrongfully returns again to him that curses, as a bird returns again to his own nest. And above all things men ought to avoid cursing their children and giving to the devil their progeny, as much as they can. Certainly it is a great danger and a great sin. Let us then speak of scolding and reproach, which are great wounds in men's heart; for they unsew the seams of friendship in man's heart. For truly, a man can hardly be at harmony with one that has openly reviled and reproved him with slander. This is a horrible sin, as Christ says in the Gospel. And take warning now that he that reproaches his neighbor either reproaches him by some painful injury that he has on his body, as "leper," or "crooked rascal," or by referring to some sin that he does. Now if he reproach him by harm or pain, then the reproach turns upon Jesus Christ; for pain is sent by righteous decision of God, and by His sufferance, be it leprosy or crippling, or sickness. And if he reproach him uncharitably for sin, as "thou adulterer," "thou drunken rascal," etc., then this makes for the rejoicing of the devil, that always has joy when men sin. And certainly reproaching cannot come except from a wicked heart. For according to the fullness of the heart the mouth often speaks. And ye shall understand that when any man shall chastise another, he should beware of chiding or reproaching. For truly, unless he beware, he may easily awaken the fire of anger or wrath, which he should quench, and perhaps slay him whom he might chastise with goodness. For as Solomon says, "the kindly tongue is the tree of life," that is to say, of spiritual life. And truly, a foul tongue slays the spirit of him that reproaches and him that is reproached. Lo, what says Saint Augustine? "There is nothing so like the devil's child as one that often scolds." Saint Paul says also: "It is not fitting that I, the servant of God, should scold." And although chiding is a villainous thing between all kinds of people, yet it is certainly most unsuitable between a man and his wife; for in that case there is never rest. And therefore Solomon says: "A house that is uncovered and falling, and a scolding wife are alike." A man who is in a house which is falling in many places, though he avoid the falling of beams in one place, yet he is struck when in another place; so it goes with a scolding wife. If she does not chide him on one matter, she will chide him on another. And therefore "better a morsel of bread with joy than a house full of delight with chiding," says Solomon. Saint Paul says: "O ye women, be subjects to your husbands as is fitting in God; and ye men, love your wives." *Ad Colossenses, tertio.*

After this let us speak of Scorn which is a wicked sin; and especially when one scorns a man for his good works. For indeed, such scorners are like the foul toad, that cannot endure to smell the sweet savour of the fine vine when it flourishes. These scorners are fellow-partakers with the devil; for they have joy when the devil wins, and sorrow when he loses. They are the adversaries of Jesus Christ, for they hate what He loves, that is to say, the salvation of the soul.

Now let us speak of wicked advice, for he that gives wicked advice is a traitor, since he deceives him that trusts in him, *ut Achitofel ad Absolonem*. But none the less, his wicked counsel first strikes against himself. For as the wise man says, every false person living has this characteristic in himself, that in seeking to injure another man he first injures himself. And men shall understand that a man shall not take his counsel from false people, nor from angry people, nor from aggrieved people, nor from people that love too greatly their own profit, nor from people that are too worldly, especially in counsel affecting their souls.

Now comes the sin of those that sow and make discord among people, which is a sin that Christ especially hates, and no wonder. For He died to make harmony. And makers of discord do more shame to Christ than did they who crucified Him; for God loves friendship among people better than He loves His own Body, which He gave to promote unity. Therefore they are like unto the devil that always goes about to make discord.

Now comes the sin of the double tongue; such as speaking fairly before people and wickedly behind their backs; or else making an appearance as though they spoke with good intention, or else in sport and play, and yet speaking with a wicked intent.

Now comes the betrayal of counsel, through which a man is defamed. Indeed, he can scarcely restore the damage he occasions.

Now comes Threat, which is an open folly, for he that threatens often, many times threatens more than he can perform.

Now come Idle Words that are without profit to him that speaks the words, and also to him that listens to them. Or else idle words are those that are needless or without purpose of any natural profit. And although idle words sometimes make a venial sin, yet men should distrust them; for we must give account of them to God.

Now comes Idle Disputing, that cannot be without sin. And as Solomon says: "It is a sin of manifest folly." And therefore a philosopher said when men asked him how men should please the people: "Do many good works, and do little disputing."

After this comes the sin of Jesting, for jesters are the devil's apes, making folk laugh at their jesting as people do at the antics of an ape. Saint Paul forbids such folly. See how virtuous and holy words comfort those that suffer in the service of Christ; just so villainous words and tricks of jesting comfort them that labor in the service of the devil. These are the sins that come from the tongue, that come from Anger, and other offenses besides.

Sequitur remedium contra peccatum Ire

THE remedy against Anger is a virtue that men call Meekness, which is Gentleness; and also another virtue that men call Patience, or Sufferance.

Gentleness controls and subdues the impulses and actions of man's spirit in such a manner that they do not skip out through anger or wrath. Sufferance endures sweetly all the annoyances and wrongs that man does to man. Saint Jerome speaks thus of Gentleness: "It does no harm to any person, nor speaks any; nor for any harm that man can do or say will it become heated against reason." This virtue is sometimes natural; for, as says the philosopher: "A man is a living thing, by nature gentle and amenable to goodness, but when Gentleness is impregnated with Grace then it is of greater worth."

_Allas! quod she, that evere I was born!
Thus have I seyd, quod she, thus have I sworn._
And toold hym al as ye han herd bifore;
It nedeth nat reherce it yow namoore.
This housbonde, with glad chiere, in freendly wyse,
Answerde and seyde as I shal yow devyse:
_Is ther oght elles, Dorigen, but this?
_Nay, nay, quod she, God help me so, as wys!
This is to muche, and it were Goddes wille.
_Ye, wyf, quod he, lat sleepen that is stille;
It may be wel, paraventure, yet today.
Ye shul youre trouthe holden, by my fay!
For God so wisly have mercy upon me,
I hadde wel levere ystiked for to be,
For verray love which that I to yow have,
But if ye sholde youre trouthe kepe and save!
Trouthe is the hyeste thyng that man may kepe:
BUT with that word he brast anon to wepe,
And seyde, I yow forbede, up peyne of deeth,
That nevere, whil thee lasteth lyf ne breeth,
To no wight tel thou of this aventure.

As I may best, I wol my wo endure,
Ne make no contenance of hevynesse,
That folk of yow may demen harm or gesse.
AND forth he cleped a squier & a mayde:
Gooth forth anon with Dorigen, he sayde,
And bryngeth hire to swich a place anon.
_They take hir leve, and on hir wey they gon;
But they ne wiste why she thider wente.
He nolde no wight tellen his entente.
PARAVENTURE an heep of yow, ywis,
Wol holden hym a lewed man in this,
That he wol putte his wyf in jupartie;
Herkneth the tale, er ye upon hir crie.
She may have bettre fortune than yow semeth;
And whan that ye han herd the tale, demeth.
THIS squier, which that highte Aurelius,
On Dorigen that was so amorous,
Of aventure happed hire to meete
Amydde the toun, right in the quykkest strete,
As she was bown to goon the wey forthright
Toward the gardyn theras she had hight;
And he was to the gardynward also;
For wel he spyed, whan she wolde go
Out of hir hous to any maner place.

Plate 31: The Franklin's Tale (p. 300)

Patience which is another remedy against Anger, is a virtue by which a man suffers sweetly every man's goodness, and is not angered by any harm that is done to him. The philosopher says: "Patience is that virtue which suffers gently all the outrages of adversity and every wicked word." This virtue makes a man like to God, and makes him God's own dear child, as says Christ. This virtue discomfits thine enemy, and therefore the wise man says: "If thou wilt vanquish thine enemy, learn to endure." And thou shalt understand that men endure four kinds of grievances in outward things against which they may have four kinds of patiences.

The first grievance is for wicked words. These Jesus Christ suffered very patiently without murmuring, when the Jews despised and reproached Him often. Suffer thou, therefore, patiently; for the wise man says: "If thou strive with a fool, though the fool be angry, or though he laugh, in any case thou shalt have no peace." The other grievance, plainly, is to suffer damage to thy goods. Christ suffered this patiently when He was despoiled of all that He had in this life, which was nothing except His clothes. The third grievance is for a man to suffer harm in his body. Christ endured this patiently through all His passion. The fourth grievance is unreasonable suffering in work. Therefore I say that people that make their servants labor too grievously, or out of season, as on holidays, do in truth a great sin. Christ endured this patiently, and taught us patience when He bore upon His blessed shoulders the Cross upon which He suffered a shameful death. Here men may learn to be patient; for surely not only Christian men are patient for the love of Jesus Christ and for the reward of the blessed life that is imperishable; but indeed, the old Pagans, that were never Christian, commanded and used the virtue of Patience. A philosopher, once upon a time, that would have beaten his disciple for a great trespass, over which he was greatly perturbed, brought a rod with which to scourge the child. And when this child saw the rod, he said to his master: "What think ye to do?" "I will beat thee," said the master, "in order to correct thee." "Forsooth," said the child, "ye should first correct yourself, that have lost your patience over the guilt of a child." "Indeed," said the master, weeping, "thou sayst truly; take thou the rod, my dear son, and correct me for my impatience." From Patience Obedience comes, through which a man is obedient to Christ, and to all those to whom he ought to be obedient in Christ. And understand that Obedience is perfect when a man does gladly and quickly and entirely with a good heart, all that he should do. Obedience generally is to perform the instructions of God and of a man's sovereigns to whom he should in all righteousness be obedient.

Sequitur de Accidia

HAVING spoken of the sins of Envy and Anger, I will now speak of the sin of Sloth. For Envy blinds the heart of a man and Anger disturbs a man, and sloth makes him heavy, moody, and angry. Envy and Anger make bitterness of heart, which bitterness is the mother of Sloth, and takes from a man all his love of goodness. Then Sloth is the anguish of a troubled heart; and Saint Augustine says: "It is the injurer of goodness and the joy of evil." Certainly this is a damnable sin; for it does wrong to Jesus Christ inasmuch as it takes away the service that men should do to Christ with all their effort, as says Solomon. But Sloth makes no such effort; he does all things with annoyance, and with resentment, slackness and excuses, and with idleness and lack of spirit; and on this account the Book says: "Accursed is he that does service to God carelessly." Then Sloth is enemy to every condition of man; for certainly the condition of man is of three kinds. Either it is a condition of innocence, such as was the condition of Adam before he fell into sin, in which condition he was constrained to work, as in praising and adoring God. Another condition is the condition of sinful man in which men are compelled to labor in praising God for the correction of their sins, and that He will grant them to rise above their sins. Another condition is that of grace, in which a man is constrained to works of penitence. And indeed to all these things Sloth is an enemy and opposite, for he loves no activity at all. Now certainly this foul sin, Sloth, is also a great enemy to the livelihood of the body, for it has no provision against temporal necessity; since it strives and slays and destroys all temporal goods by carelessness. The fourth thing is that Sloth is like those that are in the pain of hell because of their Sloth and heaviness; for they that are damned are so bound that they can neither do well nor think well. Because of Sloth it comes first that a man is injured and prevented from doing any goodness, and on this account God has an abomination of such slothfulness, as says Saint John.

Now comes Sloth that will not suffer any hardship or do any penance, for truly, Sloth is so tender and so delicate, as Solomon says, that he will not suffer any hardness or penance, and therefore he shames everything that he does. Against this rotten-hearted sin of Sloth men should practice doing good works, and in a manly and virtuous fashion get the spirit to do well, remembering that our Lord Jesus Christ repays every good deed, be it never so little. The practice of labor is a great thing, for it makes, as says Saint Bernard, the laborer to have strong arms and hard sinews, and Sloth makes them feeble and tender. Then comes fear to begin to work any good works. For indeed, to him that is inclined to sin it seems so great an enterprise to undertake works of goodness that he tells himself in his heart that the circumstances of goodness are too grievous and too difficult to suffer, and that he will not undertake good works, as says Saint Gregory.

Now comes Despair, that is, Despair of the mercy of God, that comes sometimes from too much violent sorrow, and sometimes from too much fear, a man imagining that he has done so much sin that it will be of no avail to him though he should repent and forsake sin. And through the despair or dread that he feels he abandons all his heart to every kind of sin, as says Saint Augustine. This abominable sin, if it continue unto his death, is called sinning against the Holy Ghost. This horrible sin is so dangerous that the despairing man finds no felony or sin that he hesitates to do; as shown well by the case of Judas. Certainly above all sins, this then, is the sin most displeasing to Christ, and most hostile to Him. Truly, he that despairs of himself is like the coward recreant champion that needlessly acknowledges defeat. Alas! alas! Unnecessarily is he recreant and without cause does he despair. Certainly the mercy of God is ever ready for every penitent, and is above all God's works. Alas! Can not a man remember the Gospel of Saint Luke, 15, where Christ says that there shall be as much joy in heaven over a sinful man that is penitent, as over ninety and nine good men that need no penitence? Look further into the same Gospel, at the joy and feast of the good man when the son he had lost returned to him repentant. Can he not recall also, as Saint Luke says: *xxiii° capitulo*, how the thief that was hanging beside Jesus Christ said: "Lord, wilt Thou remember me when Thou comest into Thy Kingdom?" "In truth," said Christ, "I say to thee tomorrow shalt thou be with Me in Paradise." Truly, there is no sin of man so horrible that it cannot in his life be destroyed by penitence through virtue of the suffering and death of Christ. Alas! Why should a man, then, need to be in despair since mercy is so ready and so generous? Ask and have. Then comes Somnolence, which is heavy slumbering, and makes a man heavy and dull in body and soul; and this sin comes from Sloth. And indeed, the time when in reason a man should not sleep is in the morning, unless there is a reasonable cause, for indeed, the morning is the most suitable time for a man to say his prayers and to think upon God and to honor God and to give alms to the poor that come first in the name of Christ. Lo, what says Solomon: "Whoever will awake in the morning and seek me, he shall find me." Then comes Negligence, or Carelessness, that recks of nothing. And just as Ignorance is mother of all evil, so certainly Negligence is the nurse. Negligence takes no pains, in doing a thing, whether he does it well or badly.

Concerning the remedy for these two sins the wise man says that "he that fears God does not neglect to do what he should." And he that loves God will make an effort to please God by his actions, and give himself in all his strength to do well. Then comes Idleness that is the gate to all evils. An idle man is like a place without walls; the devil may enter on every side and shoot at him from any point through temptation, when he is unprotected. This idleness is the sink of all iniquity, and villainous thoughts, and noises, trifles, and filth. Truly, heaven is given to them that will labor, and not to idle people. Also David says that "they are not put to the labors of men, nor shall they be whipped with men," that is, in purgatory. Indeed, then, it seems that they shall be tormented by the devil in hell, unless they do penance.

Then comes the sin that men call *Tarditas*, as when a man is too late, or tarries too greatly, before he turns to God; and truly, that is a great folly. He is like one that falls into a ditch and will not arise. And this sin comes from a false hope, that he thinks he shall live long; but that hope often fails.

Then comes Indolence. And a man has indolence when he begins any good work, and soon leaves off and stops it; as they do that have any person to direct, and cease to regard him as soon as they encounter any opposition or injury. These are the new shepherds, that knowingly let their sheep run to the wolf in the briars, or take no pains to rule themselves. Poverty and destruction come from this, both in spiritual and temporal things. Then there comes a kind of coldness, that freezes all the heart of man. Then comes a lack of devotion, through which a man is so blinded, as Saint Bernard says, and has such languor of soul, that he can neither read nor sing in holy church, nor hear nor think of any devotion, nor work with his hands at any good work, without its being distasteful and vapid to him. Then he grows slow and sleepy, and is quickly roused to anger, and easily inclined to hate and envy. Then comes the sin of worldly sorrow, which is called *tristicia*, that, as Saint Paul says, slays a man. For indeed, such sorrow works toward the death of the soul and the body as well, since because of it a man grows weary of his own life. Therefore such sorrow often shortens the life of a man before his natural time has come.

Remedium contra peccatum Accidie

AGAINST this horrible sin of Sloth, and the branches of the same, there is a virtue that is called *Fortitudo* or Strength; that is, a devotion through which a man despises harmful things. This virtue is so mighty and so vigorous that it can strongly withstand and wisely protect itself from wicked perils, and strive against the assaults of the devil. For it raises and fortifies the soul, just as Sloth lowers it and makes it feeble. For this *Fortitudo* can endure by long patience such sufferings as are fitting.

This virtue is of many kinds, and the first is called Magnanimity, that is to say, greatness of spirit. For truly, a great spirit is needful against Sloth, lest it swallow the soul by the sin of sorrow, and destroy it by despair. This virtue makes men undertake hard and difficult things, of their own will, wisely and reasonably. And inasmuch as the devil fights against a man more by art and trickery than by strength, therefore men should withstand him through wit and reason and discretion. Then there are the virtues of faith, and hope in God and His saints, to achieve and accomplish the good works in which he firmly purposes to continue. Then comes surety or safeness, and that occurs when a man distrusts no future labor connected with the good works he has begun. Then comes Great-Well-Doing, that is to say, when a man does and performs great works of goodness that he has begun. And that is the end for which men should do good works, for in the accomplishing of great good works lies the great reward. Then there is Constancy, that is, stability of spirit. And this should be in the heart by steadfast faith, and in mouth, and in bearing, and in mood and in act. Also there are more particular remedies against Sloth, consisting of various works, and in the consideration of the pains of hell and the joys of heaven, and in a trust in the grace of the Holy Ghost, that will give a man power to carry out his good intentions.

Sequitur de Auaricia

AFTER Sloth, I will speak of Avarice and Covetousness, of which sin Saint Paul says that "Covetousness is the root of all evils": *Ad Timotheum, sexto capitulo*. For indeed, when the heart of a man is confused and troubled within, and the soul has lost the comfort of God, then a man seeks idle solace in worldly things.

Avarice, according to the description of Saint Augustine, is lecherousness of the heart for earthly things. Some others say that Avarice means the acquiring of many earthly things, and the giving of nothing to those that are needy. And understand, that Avarice relates not only to land and goods, but sometimes to knowledge and glory, and in every kind of excessive thing lie Avarice and Covetousness. And the difference between Avarice and Covetousness is

this. Covetousness means the coveting of such things as thou hast not, and Avarice means the withholding and keeping of such as thou hast, without rightful need. Truly, Avarice is a most damnable sin; for all Holy Writ curses it, and speaks against that vice, for it wrongs Jesus Christ. For it bereaves Him of the love that men owe Him, and turns it backward against all reason. And it causes the avaricious man to have more hope in his goods than in Jesus Christ, and pay more regard to the keeping of his treasure than to the service of Jesus Christ. And therefore Saint Paul says, *ad Ephesios, quinto*, that "an avaricious man is in the bondage of idolatry."

What difference is there between an avaricious man and an idolater, except that the idolater, perhaps, has but one idol or two, and the avaricious man has many? For truly, every florin in his coffer is his idol. And indeed, the sin of idolatry is the first thing God prohibited in the Ten Commandments, as *Exodi, capitulo xx°*, will bear witness. "Thou shalt have no false gods before me, nor shalt thou make unto thee any graven thing." Thus an avaricious man that loves his treasure before God is an idolater, through this cursed sin of Avarice. From Covetousness come hard lordships, under which men are taxed beyond due or reason by head taxes, customs, and tolls. And also such lords lay upon their bondsmen fines, which might more reasonably be called extortions. And concerning such fines and ransomings of vassals, the stewards of some lords say that it is rightful, inasmuch as a churl has no temporal thing that is not his lord's, as they say. But certainly those lordships do wrong that take from their bond-folk things that they never gave them: *Augustinus de Civitate, libro nono*. The truth is, that the state of thralldom and the first cause of thralldom lie in sin; *Genesis, quinto*.

Thus ye may see that sin establishes thralldom, but not Nature. Therefore these lords should not greatly glorify themselves in their lordships, since by nature they are not lords of thralls, but thralldom comes in the first place as the penalty of sin. And furthermore, while the law says that the temporal goods of bond-folk are the goods of their lords, that is to be understood thus: that they are the goods of the emperor to be defended in their proper ownership, but not to be robbed or taken away. And therefore Seneca says: "Thy discretion should live kindly with thy servants." Those that thou callest thy servants are God's people, for the humble are the friends of Christ; they live in friendliness with the Lord.

Remember also, that of such seed as churls spring from, lords spring also. The churl can be saved as well as the lord. The same death that takes the churl takes the lord. Therefore I advise thee, do right by thy churl, as thou wouldst that thy lord did by thee if thou wert in his place. Every sinful man is a churl to sin. I admonish thee, indeed, that thou, lord, behave toward thy churls in such a way that they will love rather than fear thee. I know well that there is station above station, as is reasonable; and it is reason that men pay their duty where it is due; but truly extortions and injury put upon your inferiors are damnable.

And further, understand well that conquerors or tyrants often make thralls of those that are born of as royal a blood as are they, the tyrants, who conquer them. The name of bondage was never known until Noah said that his son Canaan should be thrall to his brothers because of his sin. What then shall we say of those that pillage and lay extortions upon Holy Church? Truly, the sword, that men give when a man is first dubbed knight, signifies that he should defend Holy Church, and not rob or pillage it; and he that does is traitor to Christ. And, as says Saint Augustine, "They are the devil's wolves, that strangle the sheep of Jesus Christ;" and do worse than wolves. For truly, when the wolf has filled his belly, he ceases to trouble the sheep. But surely the pillagers and destroyers of God's Holy Church do not, for they never cease their pillaging. Now, as I have said that sin was the first cause of bondage, then this is true: that at the time when all the world was in sin, all of it was in thralldom and subjection. But truly, after the time of grace came, God ordained that some men should be higher in station and some lower, and that each should be served in his rank and station. And therefore, in some countries where they buy thralls, when the thralls receive the faith, the masters release them from bondage. And therefore, certainly, the lord owes to his man what the man owes to his lord. The Pope calls himself the servant of the servants of God, but inasmuch as the condition of Holy Church might not have been, nor common profit have been kept, nor peace and quiet upon the earth, unless God had ordained that some men should have a higher degree and some a lower, therefore sovereignty was established to keep and maintain and defend their inferiors or subjects within reason, as much as it lies in their power, and not to destroy or ruin them. Wherefore I say that those lords that are like wolves that devour the possessions or cattle of poor people wrongfully, without measure or mercy, shall receive, in just the degree that they have extended it to the poor, the mercy of Jesus Christ, unless they amend their ways. Now comes deceit between merchant and merchant. And thou shalt understand that merchandise is of two kinds, the one material and the other spiritual. The one is honest and permissible, and the other dishonest and forbidden. Of the material merchandise, which is permissible and honest, is this to be said: that, when God has ordained that a realm or a country is sufficient unto itself, therefore it is lawful and honest that from the abundance of that country men should help another country that is more needy. And therefore there may rightly be merchants to bring their merchandise from one country to another. The other kind of merchandise, which men invest with fraud and treachery and deceit, with falsehoods and false oaths, is accursed and damnable. Spiritual merchandise is really Simony – that is, an eager desire to buy spiritual things – things that pertain to God's holiness and the salvation of souls. This desire, if a man attempt to achieve it, even though his desire have no effect, is a deadly sin, and if he be a member of an order, he is irregular. Simony, indeed, is called after Simon Magnus, who would have bought with temporal goods the gift that God had given through the Holy Ghost to Saint Peter and the apostles. And therefore understand, that both he that sells and he that buys spiritual things are called Simonists, whether they buy with goods, or with influence, or through the fleshly prayer of friends, whether fleshly friends or spiritual friends. Fleshly – that is to say, in two ways: by kindred or by other friends. Truly, if they pray for one that is not worthy and deserving, it is Simony if he take the benefice; and if he is worthy and deserving, there is no Simony. The other way is when a man or woman prays for people in order to advance them, and only because of the wicked fleshly love they have for a person. That is foul Simony. But surely, in service for which men give spiritual things to their servants, it must be understood that the service must be right; otherwise they should not do it; and also that it must be without bargaining, and that the person must be deserving. For, as Saint Damasus says, "All the sins of the world, compared with this sin, are as nothing;" for it is the greatest sin that can be, after the sins of Lucifer and Antichrist. For by this sin God loses the Church and the soul that He redeemed with His precious blood, through those that give churches to the unworthy. For they put in thieves, that steal the souls of Jesus Christ and destroy his patrimony. On account of such unworthy priests and curates, ignorant men have the less reverence for the sacraments of Holy Church, and such givers of churches put out the children of Christ, and put the devil's own son into the church. They sell the souls that should remain lambs to the wolf that devours them. And therefore they shall never share the pasture of lambs, that is, the bliss of heaven. Now comes gambling with its appurtenances, such as backgammon and raffles, from which come deceit, false oaths, reproaches, and all kinds of theft, blaspheming and denying of God, and hate of one's neighbors, waste of goods, the misspending of time, and at times manslaughter. Certainly gamblers cannot help but have great sin while they follow that activity. From avarice also come lying, theft, false witness, and false oaths. And ye shall understand that these are great sins, and expressly against the commandment of God, as I have said. False witness can be both by word and deed. By word, when thou dost steal thy neighbor's good name from him by false swearing, or rob him of his goods or heritage by the same means. Also, when thou on account of anger, or for a bribe, or for envy, bearest false witness, or accusest him or excusest him by thy false witness, or else excusest thyself falsely. Take heed, notaries and jurymen. Certainly because of false witness Susanna fell into great sorrow and pain, and many another besides her. The sin of theft is also expressly against God's commandment, and in two ways, corporal and spiritual. In the corporal sense, as to take thy neighbor's goods against his will, whether by force or by trickery, or by false measure. And again, by framing false indictments against him stealthily, and by borrowing of thy neighbor's goods with the intention never to pay him back, and like things. Spiritual theft is Sacrilege, that is to say, the injuring of holy things, or of things sacred to Christ, in two ways. One of these has to do with the holiness of the place, such as churches or church yards, for every wicked sin that men commit in such places may be called sacrilege, or every violent act in like places. Another form of sacrilege is the false withdrawing of rights that belong to Holy Church. And plainly and in general, sacrilege is to take a holy thing from a holy place, or something not sacred from a holy place, or a holy thing from a place that is not sacred.

Relevacio contra peccatum Avaricie

NOW ye shall understand that the remedy for Avarice is mercy, and pity generously taken. And men might ask, why are mercy and pity the remedies for Avarice? Certainly, the avaricious man shows no mercy or pity to the needy one; for his delight is to keep his treasure, and not to rescue or relieve his fellow Christians. And therefore I speak first of mercy. Mercy, as the philosopher says, is a virtue by which the heart of man is stirred by the suffering of one that suffers. And after mercy follows pity, in performing charitable works of a merciful kind. And truly, these things move a man to sympathy for Jesus Christ: that He gave Himself because of our sins, and suffered death in His mercy, and forgave us our original sins, and thereby released us from the pains of hell, and lessened the pains of purgatory by penitence, and gave us the grace to do well, and, finally, the bliss of heaven. The kinds of mercy are, to give and to forgive and release, and to have pity in one's heart, and compassion for the suffering of fellow Christians, and also to give punishment where there is need for it. Another remedy for Avarice is reasonable liberality. But here, truly, it is fitting that a man consider the grace of Jesus Christ, and his temporal wealth and also the imperishable wealth that Christ gave us; and he should remember also the death that he shall meet, he knows not when, where, or how; and also that he shall in the end give up all he has, save only what he has expended in good works.

But inasmuch as some people are immoderate, men ought to avoid foolish liberality, that men call waste. Surely he that is foolishly liberal does not give his property but rather loses it. Truly, whatever he gives for vainglory, as to minstrels and in order that men should spread his renown in the world, constitutes a sin, and no alms. Certainly he foully loses his property who in giving it seeks nothing but sin. He is like a horse that seeks to drink dirty or troubled water rather than water from a clear well. And because they give where they should not give, the curse that Christ shall pronounce on the day of judgment to those that shall be damned belongs to them.

Sequitur de Gula

AFTER Avarice comes Gluttony, which is also expressly against the command of God. Gluttony is an immoderate desire to eat and drink, or else to minister to the immoderate appetite and inordinate craving to eat or drink. This sin corrupted all this world, as is clearly shown in the sin of Adam and Eve. See also what Saint Paul says of Gluttony. "Many," said Saint Paul, "go about, of whom I have often told you, and now I say weeping that they are the enemies of the cross of Christ; and their end is Death, and Belly is their god, and their delight is in the ruin of them that thus care for earthly things." He that is addicted to this sin of Gluttony can withstand no sin. He must be in subjection to all vices, for it is in the devil's treasure-house that he hides and rests himself. This sin has many varieties. The first is drunkenness, which is the horrible burying of man's reason; and therefore, when a man is drunk, he has lost his reason; and this is a deadly sin. But truly, when a man is not accustomed to strong drink, and perhaps knows not the strength of the drink, or has a weakness in his head, or has labored, which makes him drink the more – though he may thus be suddenly snared by drink, the sin is not deadly, but venial. The second kind of Gluttony is that by which the spirit of man grows all fouled;

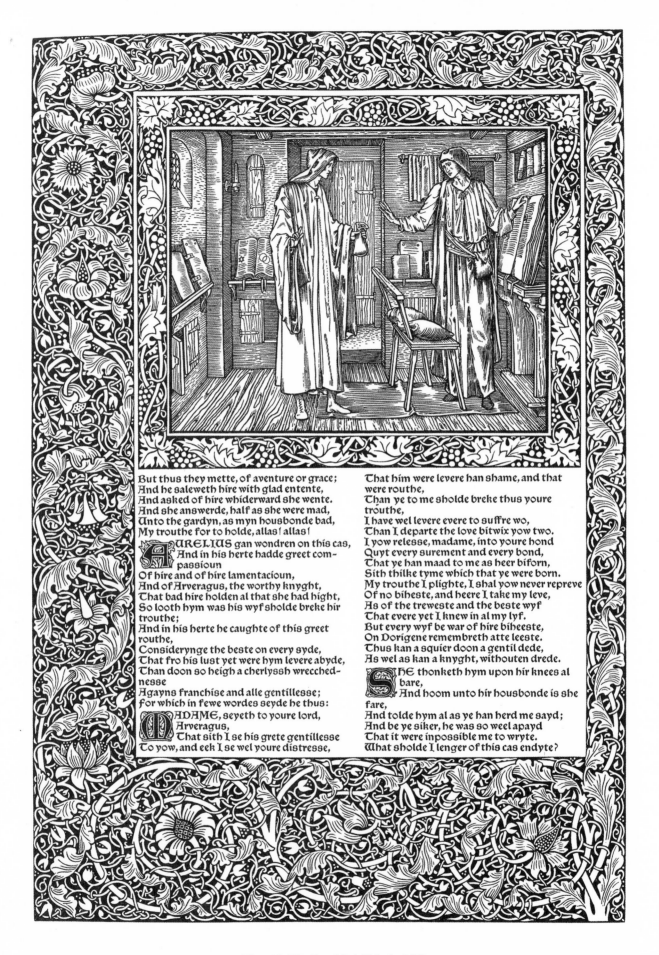

But thus they mette, of aventure or grace;
And he saleweth hire with glad entente,
And asked of hire whiderward she wente.
And she answerde, half as she were mad,
Unto the gardyn, as myn housbonde bad,
My trouthe for to holde, allas! allas!

AURELIUS gan wondren on this cas,
And in his herte hadde greet com-
passioun
Of hire and of hire lamentacioun,
And of Arveragus, the worthy knyght,
That bad hire holden al that she had hight,
So looth hym was his wyf sholde breke hir
trouthe;
And in his herte he caughte of this greet
routhe,
Considerynge the beste on every syde,
That fro his lust yet were hym levere abyde,
Than doon so heigh a cherlyssh wrecched-
nesse
Agayns franchise and alle gentillesse;
For which in fewe wordes seyde he thus:

MADAME, seyeth to youre lord,
Arveragus,
That sith I se his grete gentillesse
To yow, and eek I se wel youre distresse,

That him were levere han shame, and that
were routhe,
Than ye to me sholde breke thus youre
trouthe,
I have wel levere evere to suffre wo,
Than I departe the love bitwix yow two.
I yow relesse, madame, into youre hond
Quyt every surement and every bond,
That ye han maad to me as heer biforn,
Sith thilke tyme which that ye were born.
My trouthe I plighte, I shal yow never repreve
Of no biheste, and heere I take my leve,
As of the treweste and the beste wyf
That evere yet I knew in al my lyf.
But every wyf be war of hire biheeste,
On Dorigene remembreth atte leeste.
Thus kan a squier doon a gentil dede,
As wel as kan a knyght, withouten drede.

SHE thonketh hym upon hir knees al
bare,
And hoom unto hir housbonde is she
fare,
And tolde hym al as ye han herd me sayd;
And be ye siker, he was so weel apayd
That it were inpossible me to wryte.
What sholde I lenger of this cas endyte?

Plate 32: The Franklin's Tale (p. 300)

for drunkenness steals from him the just use of his mind. The third kind of Gluttony occurs when a man devours his food, and has no proper moderation in eating. The fourth is when, through the great quantity of his food, the humors of his body are distempered. The fifth is forgetfulness through great drinking; because of which a man sometimes forgets before morning what he did at even or on the night before.

In other ways the kinds of Gluttony can be distinguished, according to Saint Gregory. The first is, eating before the proper time. The second is, when a man procures himself too delicate food and drink. The third is, when a man is immoderate. The fourth is fastidiousness, with a great desire to dress up his food. The fifth is, to eat too greedily. These are the five fingers of the devil's hand, by which he draws men to sin.

Remedium contra Peccatum Gule

THE remedy for Gluttony is abstinence, as Galen says. But I do not hold that to be meritorious if a man practise it only for the healing of his body. Saint Augustine desires that Abstinence should be done for virtue's sake, and with patience. Abstinence, he says, is of little account, unless there is good will with it, and unless it is fortified by patience and charity, and unless men do it for God's sake, in hope to win the bliss of heaven.

The associates of Abstinence are Temperance, that keeps a mean in all things; also Shame, that avoids all unseemliness; Sufficiency, that seeks no rich foods or drinks, and has no regard for excessive dressing of food. Moderation also, that restrains by reason the enslaved appetite for eating; Soberness, that restrains the excess of drink; Sparing, that curbs the fastidious delight of sitting long and luxuriously at table; and for this last cause, some of their own will, stand up when they eat, that they may use the less leisure.

Sequitur de Luxuria

AFTER Gluttony, comes Lechery, for these two are such near cousins, that oftentimes they will not separate. God knows that this sin is very displeasing to Him, for He said Himself, "Do no lechery." And therefore He set great penalties for this sin in the old law. If a woman thrall were taken in this sin, she should be beaten to death with staves. And if she were a gentlewoman, she should be slain with stones. And if she were a bishop's daughter, she should be burned, by God's commandment. Furthermore, for the sin of Lechery God drowned all the world at the time of the deluge. After that, He burned five cities with thunder-light, and sank them into hell.

Now let us speak of the stinking sin of Lechery that men call Adultery for wedded folk, that is to say, if one of them is wedded, or both. Saint John says that adulterers shall be sunk in hell in a lake burning with fire and brimstone; in fire, for the lechery; in brimstone, for the stink of their rottenness. Truly, the breaking of this sacrament is an horrible thing; it was made by God himself in Paradise and confirmed by Jesus Christ, as Saint Matthew witnesses in his Gospel: "A man shall leave father and mother, and take him to his wife, and they shall be two in one flesh." This sacrament betokens the knitting together of Christ and his Holy Church. And not only does God forbid adultery by deed, but He commands also that thou shouldst not covet thy neighbor's wife. In this command, says Saint Augustine, is forbidden all kinds of desire to do lechery. Lo, what does Saint Matthew say in the gospel: that "whoso looketh upon a woman in lust, he hath done lechery with her in his heart"? Here may ye see that not only the act of this sin is forbidden, but also the desire to do that sin. This cursed sin harms grievously those that practise it. First, their souls; for it constrains them to sin and to the pain of everlasting death. And it harms the body grievously also; for it drains and wastes and shames it, and it makes a sacrifice of a man's blood to the fiend of hell. It wastes his goods and substance. And surely, if it be a foul thing for a man to waste his wealth on women, it is still more foul when for such filthiness women spend upon men their property and substance. This sin, as the prophet says, bereaves men and women of their good fame, and all their honor; and it is most pleasant to the devil; for through it he wins the greater part of this world. And just as a merchant enjoys most that business from which he has the greatest advantage, just so the fiend delights in this filth.

This is the other hand of the devil, with five fingers, to trap people into his wickedness. The first finger is the silly gazing of the foolish woman and the foolish man, and it slays, just as the basilisk slays people by the venom of his glance; for the coveting of eyes follows the coveting of the heart. The second finger is the vile touching in a wicked manner, and therefore Solomon says that whoever touches and handles a woman is like one that handles the scorpion that stings and suddenly slays through his poison, just as whoever touches warm pitch, it smirches his fingers. The third is foul words, that go like a fire that soon burns the heart. The fourth finger is kissing; and truly he would be a great fool that would kiss the mouth of a burning oven or of a furnace. And they are greater fools that kiss in wickedness, for that mouth is the mouth of hell. And especially these old dotard fornicators are fools, yet they kiss, though they can do nothing, and take a smattering. Truly, they are like dogs. For a dog, when he comes to a rosebush or some other shrub, though he cannot urinate, yet he will lift up his leg and make a pretense of doing so. And since many men believe that they cannot sin through any lechery they do with their wives, truly, that belief is a false one. God knows that a man can slay himself with his own knife, and make himself drunk from his own cask. Truly, be it wife, or child, or any worldly thing that he loves before God, it is his idol, and he is an idolater. A man should love his wife with discretion, patiently and temperately, and then she is as though she were his sister. The fifth finger of the devil's hand is the stinking act of Lechery. Truly, the five fingers of Gluttony the fiend puts into the belly of a man, and with his five fingers of Lechery he seizes him by the loins to throw him into the furnace of hell, where men shall have the fire and the worms that shall last forever, and weeping and wailing, sharp hunger and thirst, and horror of devils that shall trample them under foot without respite or end. From lechery, as I have said, arise various species, such as fornication, that takes place between men and women that are not married; and that is a deadly sin, and against nature. All that is the enemy and destruction of nature is against nature. By my faith, the reason of a man tells him it is a deadly sin, inasmuch as God forbade Lechery. And Saint Paul gives him the rule that applies to none but to those that do deadly sin. Another sin of Lechery is to bereave a maiden of her maidenhead; for he that does so, truly he casts a maiden from the highest station that is in this present life, and bereaves her of the precious fruit that the Book calls "the hundred fruit." I can say it in no other way in English, but in Latin it is called *Centesimus fructus*. Indeed, he that does this causes many harms and villainies, more than any man can count; just as he that breaks the hedge or enclosure is sometimes the cause of all the damage beasts do in the fields, through which he destroys what cannot be repaired. For in truth, maidenhead can no more be restored than an arm that has been smitten from thebody can return to it again, and grow. A woman thus abused can win mercy, that I know well, if she is penitent, but she can never make it that she has not been defiled. And although I have spoken somewhat of Adultery, it is good to show more perils that belong to it, in order that that foul sin may be avoided. Adultery in Latin means, the approaching of another man's bed, through which those that were formerly of one flesh abandon their bodies to other persons. From this sin, as the wise man says, there follow many evils. First, the breaking of faith; and truly, in faith lies the key of Christendom. And when that faith is broken and lost, truly Christendom stands vain and without fruit. This sin is also a theft; for theft commonly is to take from a person his possessions against his will. Truly, this is the foulest theft that can be, when a woman steals her body from her husband and gives it to her lecher to defoul; and steals her soul from Christ and gives it to the devil. This is a more foul theft than to break into a church and steal the chalice; for these adulterers break into the temple of God spiritually, and steal the vessel of grace, that is, the body and the soul, for which Christ shall destroy them, as says Saint Paul. Certainly Joseph greatly feared this theft when his lord's wife asked evil of him, and he said: "Lo, my lady, see how my lord has given to me to guard all that he has in this world; nor are any of these things out of my power, save only you that are his wife. And how then should I do this wickedness, sinning so horribly against God, and against my lord? God forbid it!" Alas! all too little is such faith found nowadays. The third evil is the filth through which they break the commandment of God, and defoul Christ, the author of matrimony. For truly, inasmuch as the sacrament of marriage is so noble and worthy, so much the greater is the sin of breaking it; for God made marriage in paradise, in the state of Innocence, that mankind might be multiplied for the service of God. And therefore is the breaking of it the more wicked. From such a breaking there often come false heirs, that wrongfully occupy men's heritages. And therefore Christ will put them out of the Kingdom of Heaven, that is the heritage of the good. From this violation it often happens also that men wed or do sin with

their own kindred; and particularly those scoundrels that haunt the brothels of these foolish women, that can be likened to a common privy where men purge themselves of their ordure. What, too, can we say of those pimps that live by the horrible sin of procuring, and force women to yield them a certain rent from the pimping of their bodies – yea, sometimes from their own wives or children, as these bawds do? Indeed, these are cursèd sins. Understand also that Adultery is fitly set in the ten commandments between Theft and Manslaughter; for it is the greatest theft that can be, for it is a theft both of the body and the soul. And it is like homicide; for it cuts and breaks in two those that were made one flesh, and therefore, by the ancient law of God, those that commit it should be slain. But none the less, by the law of Jesus Christ, which is the law of pity, He said to the woman taken in Adultery, who according to the will of the Jews should have been slain by stones, for this was their law: "Go," said Jesus Christ, "and have no more will to sin," or "will no more to do sin." Truly, the vengeance upon Adultery is given over to the pains of hell, unless that is hindered by penitence. There are still many more species of this cursèd sin – as when one that commits it is religious, or both of them; or in the case of people that have entered an order, such as deacons or subdeacons, or priests, or hospitalers. And the higher in an order a man is, the greater is the sin. The thing that greatly aggravates their sin is the breaking of the vow of chastity, when they received the order. And further, it is true that a holy order is the chief thing in all the treasury of God, and his special sign and mark of chastity, to show that they are joined in chastity, which is the most precious of lives. And these folk in orders are specially dedicated to God, and are of the special army of God; and therefore, when they commit a deadly sin, they are particularly the traitors to God and to His people. For they live off the people, to pray for the people, and while they are such traitors their prayers are of no avail to the people. Priests are angels, by the dignity of their ministry; but in truth Saint Paul says that "Satan transforms himself into an angel of light." Truly, the priests that practise deadly sin can be likened to the angel of darkness transformed into the angel of light; he appears to be an angel of light, but is really an angel of darkness. Such priests are the sons of Eli, as is shown in the book of *Kings*, who were the sons of Belial – that is, the devil. Belial means "without judge," and so it is with them; they think they are free, and have no judge, no more than a free bull has that takes any cow in the town that attracts him. So it goes with them as to women. For just as a free bull is enough for all the town, just so is a wicked priest sufficient corruption for an entire parish, or for a country. These priests, as the Book says, do not understand the ministry of priesthood to the people, and they do not know God. They were not satisfied, as the Book says, with the boiled flesh that was offered to them, but took by force the uncooked flesh. Truly, just so these wicked ones are not satisfied with roasted and boiled meat, with which people feed them with great reverence, but they will have the raw meat of men's wives and daughters. And truly, these women that consent to harlotry do great wrong to Christ and to Holy Church and to all the saints, and to all souls, for they steal from all these one that should worship Christ and Holy Church, and pray for Christian souls. And therefore such priests, and also their lemans that consent to their lechery, have the curse of all the house of Christ, until they reform. The third kind of Adultery is sometimes beween a man and his wife; and that is when they take no regard to their union, but only to their fleshly delight, as says Saint Jerome; and care for nothing except to be united; because they are married all is well enough, as it seems to them. But in such people the devil has power, as the angel Raphael said to Tobias; for in their union they put Jesus Christ out of their hearts, and give themselves to all kinds of filth. The fourth kind is, the union of those that are kindred, or of those that are of one relationship, or a union where the father of the one has sinned the sin of lechery with the other. This sin makes them like dogs, that have no regard for relationship. And truly, kinship is of two kinds, either spiritual or bodily; and it is spiritual sin to sin with one's god-parents. For just as he that engenders a child is its fleshly father, just so is the godfather its spiritual one. And on that account a woman sins no less in uniting with her god-parent than with her own fleshly brother. The fifth variety is that abominable sin of which any man can scarcely speak or write, none the less it is plainly set down in Holy Writ. This wickedness men and women do with various purpose and in different ways; but although Holy Writ speaks of horrible sins, truly, Holy Writ cannot be defouled, no more than the sun can be that shines on the dung hill. Another sin pertains to lechery, that comes in sleep, and this sin often comes to those that are pure, and also to those that are corrupt; and this sin men call pollution, and it comes in four ways. Sometimes from the weakness of the body, because the humors are too rank and abundant in the body of man. Sometimes from infirmity, because of the feebleness of the inhibitory virtue, as treatises on medicine mention. Sometimes, from a surfeit of meat and drink. And sometimes because of wicked thoughts, that are enclosed in a man's mind when he goes to sleep, which cannot be without sin. On which account men must conduct themselves wisely, or else they may sin most grievously.

Remedium contra peccatum Luxurie

NOW comes the remedy against Lechery, and that is generally Chastity and Continence, that restrain all the inordinate impulses that come of fleshly inclinations. And he shall have the greater merit that the more restrains the wicked inflammation of the filth of this sin. And this is done in two ways, that is, chastity in marriage, and chastity in widowhood. Now thou shalt understand that matrimony is the permissible union of man and woman, that receive, by virtue of the sacrament, the bond by which they cannot be divided during their lives, that is to say, while they both live. This, as the Book says, is a great sacrament indeed. God made it, as I have said, in Paradise, and Himself chose to be born in marriage. And to hallow marriage, he attended a wedding, where he turned water into wine, which was the first miracle he wrought on the earth in the presence of his disciples. The true results of marriage are that it cleanses fornication and replenishes Holy Church with servants, for that is the purpose of marriage. And it changes deadly sin into venial sin between those that are wedded, and makes one the hearts of those that are wedded, as well as the bodies. This is true marriage, that was established by God before sin began, when natural law was in its proper place in Paradise; and it was ordained that one man should have but one woman, and one woman but one man, as says Saint Augustine, for many reasons.

First, because marriage is signified between Christ and Holy Church. And another is, that a man is the leader of a woman; at any rate, it should by law be so. For if a woman had more men than one, then would she have more heads than one, and that would be a horrible thing before God; and also, a woman might not please too many at once. And also, there would never be peace or rest among them, for each one would demand his own will. And further, no man would know his own progeny, nor who should have his heritage; and the woman would be the less beloved from the time she lived conjointly with many men.

Now comes the matter of how a man should behave toward his wife, and particularly, with respect to two things, that is, patience and reverence, as Christ showed when He first made woman. For He did not make her from the head of Adam, lest she should claim too much lordship. For where the woman has the mastery she makes too much confusion; no examples need be given of this. Day by day experience should suffice. Also, indeed, God did not make woman from the foot of Adam, lest she should be held too low; for she cannot patiently suffer. But God made woman of the rib of Adam, so that woman should be the companion of man. Man should conduct himself toward his wife in faith, in truth, and in love, as says Saint Paul: "a man should love his wife as Christ loved Holy Church, who loved it so well that He died for it." So should a man for his wife, if there were need.

Now as to how a woman should be subject to her husband, on that point Saint Peter informs us. First, in obedience. And also, as the law says, a woman that is a wife, as long as she is one, has no authority to swear or bear witness without the permission of her husband, who is her lord; at any rate, he should in reason be so. Also, she should serve with all womanly virtue, and be moderate in her clothing. I know well that women should set their purpose to please their husbands, but not by the extravagance of their dress. Saint Jerome says that wives who are apparelled in silk and precious purple cannot clothe themselves in Jesus Christ. What also says Saint John on this matter? Saint Gregory also says that no person seeks costly clothing except for vainglory, to be honored the more before people. It is a great folly for a woman to have a fair appearance outwardly and to be foul inwardly. A wife should also be moderate in looking and in her bearing and in her laughter, and discreet in all her words and deeds. And she should love her husband with all her heart above all worldly things, and be true to him with her body; so also should a husband be to his wife. For since all her body is her husband's, so should her heart be, or else there is between those two, in that respect, no perfect marriage. Then men shall understand that a man and his wife shall come together for union for one of three reasons. The first is with the purpose of engendering children for the service of God, for truly that is the final cause of matrimony. Another cause is, for each to give to the other the debt of his body, for neither has power over his own body. The third is, to avoid lechery and wickedness. The fourth is in truth deadly sin! As to the first, it is meritorious, the second also; for, as the law says, she has the merit of chastity that yields to her husband the debt of her body, yea, though it be against her liking and the pleasure of her heart. The third way is venial sin, and truly, scarcely any of these can be without venial sin, because of the corruption and the pleasure of them. The fourth way may be defined as a union merely for amorous love, and for none of the aforesaid causes, being wholly to achieve that burning delight, they care not how often – and truly, that is deadly sin; and yet, bad luck to them! some people will try to do more than is sufficient for their appetite.

The second kind of Chastity is to be a clean widow, and avoid the embraces of men, and desire those of Jesus Christ. These widows are those that have given up their husbands, and also women that have done lechery and been relieved by Penitence. And truly, if a wife could keep herself wholly chaste by permission of her husband, so that she should never give an occasion for him to sin, it were a great merit in her. These women that observe chastity must be clean in heart as well as in body and in thought, and moderate in clothing and countenance, and abstinent in eating, drinking, speaking, and action. They are the vessel or box of the blessed Magdalene, that fills the church with a good odor. The third kind of Chastity is virginity, and it is fitting that she who practises it should be devout of heart and clean in body; then is she the spouse of Jesus Christ, and she is the life of the angels. She is the glory of this world, and she is on an equality with the martyrs; she has that in her which tongue cannot tell nor heart conceive. From Virginity came our Lord Jesus Christ, and He Himself was pure.

Another remedy against Lechery is the avoidance by a man or woman of the company of those by whom he fears to be tempted, for even if the act itself is resisted, yet there is great temptation. Indeed, a white wall, though it burn not fully when touched with a candle, yet the wall is blackened by the light. Often I have read that no man should trust in his own perfection, unless he is stronger than Samson, and holier than Daniel, and wiser than Solomon.

Now after explaining to you, as I have, the seven deadly sins, and some of their branches and remedies, truly, if I could I would tell you the ten commandments. But so high a doctrine I leave to divines. None the less, I hope to God they are touched upon in this treatise, every one of them.

De Confessione

NOW inasmuch as the second part of Penitence consists of Confession of Mouth, as I began in the first chapter, I say, Saint Augustine says that sin is every word and every deed, and all that men covet against the law of Christ, and this is to sin in heart, in mouth, and in act, and by thy five senses that are sight, hearing, smelling, tasting or savoring, and feeling. Now it is good to understand that which greatly aggravateth every sin. Thou shalt consider what thou art that dost the sin, whether thou art male or female, young or old, noble or enthralled, free or servant, well or sick, wedded or single, a member of an order or not, wise or foolish, cleric or secular; if she be of thy kindred, bodily or spiritually, or no; if any of thy kindred have sinned with her or not, and many other things.

Another consideration is this: whether it be done in fornication or adultery, or not; incest, or not; with a maiden, or not; in the form of homicide, or not;

whether horrible great sins or small ones; and how long thou hast continued to sin. The third thing to be considered is the place where thou hast done thy sin; whether in other men's houses or in thine own, whether in the open or in a church, or in a church yard; in a dedicated church or not. For if the church is hallowed, and man or woman spill his seed within that place by way of sin, or through wicked temptation, then the church is interdicted until it is re-consecrated by the bishop. And the priest that did such a wicked deed should not sing mass again all his life, and if he should, he would commit a deadly sin every time he sang mass. The fourth consideration is, by what go-betweens or messengers was the enticement to sin offered, or the consent to bear company with sinners; for many a wretch, for bearing evil men company, will go to the devil in hell. Therefore they that incite or agree to the sin are partners in the sin, and in the damnation of the sinner. The fifth consideration is, how many times has he sinned, if it be in his mind, and how many times has he fallen. For he that falls often into sin despises the mercy of God, and increases his sin, and is hostile to Christ; and he grows the feebler to withstand sin, and sins the more easily, and is slower to rise from sin, and the more averse to be shrived, particularly by him that is his confessor. And so people falling into their old follies again either abandon their old confessors definitely, or else they divide their shriving in a number of places; but truly, such divided shriving deserves no mercy of God for the sins involved. The sixth consideration is, why a man sins, and by what temptation; and if he himself provoke that temptation, or the incitement of others; or if he sin with a woman by force, or by her own consent; or if the woman, in spite of all she can do, has been forced, or not; this she shall tell; and whether it was for covetousness or on account of poverty, and if it was of her seeking, or not, and such kind of procedure. The seventh consideration is, in

what manner a man has done his sin, or, if a woman, how she has permitted that it be done to her. And the man shall tell this plainly, with all circumstances, and whether he has sinned with a common brothel woman, or not; or has done his sin at holy times, or not; in fasting times, or not; or before his shrift, or later after his shrift; and has therefore, perhaps, broken the penance enjoined; and by whose aid and advice he has sinned; or whether by sorcery or craft; all must be told. All these things, according to their degree, affect the conscience of a man. And also, the priest that is thy judge may be the better advised in prescribing thy penance, after thou hast shown contrition. For understand well, that after a man has defouled his baptism by sin, if he then wishes to win salvation, there is no other way but by penitence and shrift and atonement; and particularly by the two, if there is a confessor to whom he can confess, and by the third, if he live to make it.

Then a man shall consider that if he wishes to make a true and effective confession, he must meet four conditions. First, his confession must be made in sorrowful bitterness of heart, as said King Hezekiah to God: "I will remember me all the years of my life in bitterness of my heart." This condition of bitterness has five characteristics. The first is, that confession must be made in shame, and not to cover or hide his sin, for he has been guilty before his God and has defouled his soul. And concerning this Saint Augustine says: "The heart suffers for shame of its sin." For he that has great shame is worthy of great mercy from God. Such was the confession of the publican, who would not raise his eyes to heaven, since he had offended the God of heaven; and because of this sense of shame he shortly won the mercy of God. And of this Saint Augustine says that such shamefast souls are nearest to forgiveness and remission. Another characteristic is humility in confession, concerning which Saint Peter says: "Humble yourself beneath the power of God." The hand of God is mighty in confession, for through confession God forgives thee thy sins, for He alone has the power to do so. And this humility must be in the heart, and in outward behavior, for just as a man has humility toward God in his heart, just so should he humble his body outwardly before the priest that sits in God's place. And therefore, since Christ is sovereign and the priest the mean and mediator between Christ and the sinner, and the sinner is in reason the least among these, he should not sit as high as his confessor, but kneel before him or at his feet, unless sickness prevent him. For he shall not regard who sits there, but in Whose place he sits. A man that has trespassed against a lord, and comes to ask mercy and make his peace, and at once sits down beside the lord will be regarded by men as excessively bold, and not worthy so soon to have forgiveness or mercy. The third characteristic is, that thy shrift should be full of tears, if possible; and if a man cannot weep with his body's eyes, let him weep at heart. Such was the confession of Saint Peter; for after he had forsaken Jesus Christ he went out and wept bitterly. The fourth characteristic is, that he shall not be in anyway hindered by shame in his confession. Such was the confession of the Magdalene, that did not refrain for any sense of shame in the presence of those that feasted, to go to our Lord Jesus Christ and make her sins known to Him. The fifth characteristic is, that a man or a woman should be obedient in receiving the penance enjoined upon him for his sins; for surely Jesus Christ, suffering for the sins of men, was obedient to the death.

The second condition of true confession is, that it should be made speedily; for indeed, if a man had a deadly wound, the longer he delayed healing himself, the more it would corrupt, and hasten him toward his death; and also the wound would be more difficult to heal. And just so it goes with sin that stays a long time unrevealed in a man. Truly, a man ought to show his sins quickly for many reasons – such as the fear of death, for death often occurs suddenly, and is in no way certain as to what time it shall be, or in what place. And also the prolonging of one sin draws in another; and also the longer that a man tarries the farther he is from Christ. And if he wait until his last day, he can scarcely be shrived or remember his sins, or repent him of them, because of the grievous sickness of death. And inasmuch as in his life he has not listened to Jesus Christ when He has spoken, he shall cry to Jesus Christ on his last day, and scarcely shall He listen to him. And understand that this condition of speed must have four qualities. Thy shrift must be thought over beforehand, because there is no profit in wicked haste, and because a man must be able to shrive himself of his sins with all regard to the kind of sin and the circumstances, be it pride, or envy, and so forth. And he must rightly have understood the number and greatness of his sins, and how long he has lain in sin. And also he must be contrite because of his sins, and of a steadfast purpose, by the grace of God, never afterwards to fall into sin. And he must also fear and keep watch over himself, that he avoid occasion for the sin to which he is inclined. Also thou shalt shrive thee of all thy sins to one man, and not a part to one and a part to another with the purpose of dividing thy confession for shame or fear; for this is only strangling thy soul. For truly, Jesus Christ is entirely good; in Him is no imperfection; and therefore He forgives everything perfectly, or forgives not at all. I do not say that if thou art assigned to a confessor for penance because of a certain sin that thou art bound to reveal to him all the rest of thy sins of which thou hast been shriven by thy curate, unless in thy humility it please thee to do so; but there is no dividing shrift. Nor do I say, with regard to the dividing up of confession, that if thou hast license from thy curate to be shriven by a discreet and honorable priest in whatever respect thou choosest, that thou must be shriven there of all thy sins. But let no blot remain; let no sin be untold, in so far as thou hast remembrance. And when thou art shriven by thy curate, tell him also all the sins thou hast committed since thou wert last shriven. This is no wicked intention to divide thy shrift.

Also true shrift must have certain conditions. First, that thou shrive thyself of thy free will, with no constraint, nor because of the shame people may make thee feel, nor on account of sickness, or such causes; for it is only reason that he who trespasses of his free will, should confess his trespass of his free will; and no other man tell his sin, but only he himself tell it; and that he should not withhold or deny his sin, nor be angry with the priest for admonishing him to leave sin. The second condition is, that thy shrift be lawful; that is, that thou who art shriven, and also the priest who hears thy confession, are truly in the faith of Holy Church, and that a man shall not be in despair of the mercy of Jesus Christ, like Cain or Judas. And also a man must accuse himself of his own trespass, and not another; and he shall blame and reproach himself and the malice of his own sin, and no other. But none the less, if another man has been the occasion or provoker of his sin, or the condition of a person through whom his sin was aggravated should be such, or else that he cannot clearly shrive himself unless he tell the person with whom he sinned, then he may tell, so that his intention is not to back-bite the person concerned, but only to make his confession.

And thou shalt tell no lies in thy confession; even in humility, perhaps, saying that thou hast committed sins of which thou wert never guilty. For Saint Augustine says that if because of humility thou tell lies about thyself, even though thou wert not in sin before, yet because of thy lies thou shalt then be in sin. Thou must also reveal thy sin by thine own mouth, unless thou shalt become dumb, and not by any letter, for thou that hast done the sin must endure the shame of it. Also, thou shalt not paint thy confession with fair, subtle words, the more to conceal thy sin; for then thou dost deceive thyself and not the priest; thou must tell it plainly, be it never so foul or horrible. Thou shalt also shrive thyself to a priest that is discreet to give thee counsel, and also thou shalt not shrive thyself for vainglory, or hypocrisy, or for any cause except the fear of Jesus Christ and the health of thy soul. Also, thou shalt not run suddenly to the priest, to tell him lightly of thy sin, as one tells a jest or a story, but thou shalt go advisedly and with great devotion. And in general, shrive thyself often. If thou fallest often, thou shalt arise often through confession. And though thou mayst shrive thyself more than once of a sin, that is the greater merit. And, as Saint Augustine says, thou shalt the more easily have deliverance and grace from God, both from sin and suffering. And certainly, once a year at least it is lawful to receive communion, for once a year all things renew themselves.

Explicit secunda pars Penitencie; et sequitur pars eiusdem, de Satisfaccione

NOW have I told you of true Confession, which is the second part of Penitence.

The third part of Penitence is Atonement; and that consists most generally in alms and bodily pain. Now there are three kinds of alms: contrition of heart, in which a man offers himself to God; another, pity for the faults of his neighbors; and the third, the giving of good counsel spiritual and bodily, where men have need, and particularly the sustenance of man's food. And observe that a man has need of these things generally; he has need of food, he has need of clothing, and shelter; he has need of charitable counsel, and of being visited in prison and in sickness, and for the burial of his dead body. And if thou canst not visit the needful in person, visit him through thy messages and thy gifts. These are in general the alms or works of charity of those that have temporal riches or discretion in counselling. Of these works thou shalt hear at the Day of Judgment.

Thou shalt give thine alms from thine own possessions, and promptly, and privately if thou canst; but nevertheless, if thou canst not do it privately, thou shalt not forbear to give alms even though men see it, so long as it is not done for worldly credit, but only for the approval of Jesus Christ. For as Saint Matthew testifies, *capitulo quinto*, "A city that is set on a mountain cannot be hid; nor do men light a lantern and put it under a bushel; but men set it on a candle-stick, to give light to the people in the house. Just so shall your light shine before men; that they may see your good works, and glorify your father which is in heaven."

Now to speak of bodily pain, it consists in prayers, in vigils, in fasting, and in the virtuous exposition of prayers. And ye shall understand that by orisons or prayers is meant a piteous desire of the heart, that purifies itself in God and expresses itself by outward word, to remove evils and win things spiritual and durable, and sometimes to win temporal things. And among these prayers, truly, in the prayer of the *Pater-noster* Jesus Christ has included most things. Surely it is privileged in three things; its worth, on account of which it is more worthy than any other prayer: because Jesus Christ made it; and because it is short, so that it can be learned the more easily, and can the more easily be kept in mind, and a man can help himself oftener with this prayer, and be the less weary of saying it, and cannot excuse himself for not learning it, it is so short and easy; and because it comprehends in itself all good prayers. The explanation of this holy prayer, that is so excellent and worthy, I leave to masters of theology; except that I will say this much: that when thou prayest that God will forgive thee thy sins as thou forgive those that sin against thee, be sure that

thou art not out of favor with God. This holy prayer also lessens venial sin; and therefore pertains especially to penitence.

This prayer must be truly said, and in true faith, and men must pray to God in an orderly fashion, and discreetly and devoutly; and a man shall always make his will subject to the will of God. This orison must also be said with great humility and purity; and decently and not to the annoyance of any man or woman. It must also be supplemented with works of charity. It is of avail also against the sins of the soul; for, as says Saint Jerome: "By fasting the sins of the flesh are avoided, and by prayer the sins of the soul."

And following this, thou shalt understand that bodily pain consists in watching; for Jesus Christ said: "Watch, and pray that ye do not enter into wicked temptation." Ye shall understand also that fasting consists in three things: in abstinence from bodily meat and drink, and in abstinence from worldly merriment, and in abstinence from deadly sin; that is, that a man shall keep from deadly sin with all his might.

And thou shalt understand also, that God ordained fasting, and that four things pertain to it. These are: generosity to the poor, spiritual gladness of heart, not to be vexed or angry, nor grumble because one fasts; and also reasonable hours so that one eats in moderation; that is to say, a man shall not eat out of season, nor sit longer eating at his table because of his fasting.

Then thou shalt understand that bodily pain consists in discipline or teaching, by word or by writing; or in example. Also in the wearing of hair shirts or shirts of rough cloth, or of coats of mail on the naked flesh, for Christ's sake, and such kinds of penance. But take good care that such kinds of penance inflicted on thy flesh do not make thy heart bitter or angry or annoyed with thyself; for it is better to cast aside thine hair shirt than to cast aside the safety of Jesus Christ. And therefore Saint Paul says: "Clothe yourselves, as they that have been chosen by God, in hearts of mercy, goodness, sufferance, and such kinds of clothing;" by which Jesus Christ is more pleased than by hair shirts and coats of mail.

There is also discipline in beating thy breast, in scourging with rods, in kneeling, in bearing tribulations, in suffering patiently wrongs that are done to thee, and also in the patient endurance of maladies, or the losing of worldly goods, or of one's wife, or of a child, or of friends.

Then thou shalt understand what things interfere with penance; and they are four kinds, that is, fear, shame, hope, and despair. And to speak of fear first, by which a man comes to believe that he cannot endure penance, the remedy against that is to think that bodily penance is but short and little when compared with the pain of hell, which is so cruel and long, that it lasts ever, without an end.

Now again the shame that a man has at the idea of shriving himself, and especially these hypocrites who would be thought so perfect that they have no need to shrive themselves – against that shame a man should think that, in reason, he that was not ashamed to do foul things ought certainly not to be ashamed to do fair things, that is, confessions. A man should also think that God sees and knows all his thoughts and works; nothing may be hid or covered from Him. Men should also remember the shame that will come at the Day of Judgment, to those that are not penitent and shriven in this present life. For all the creatures in earth and hell see openly all that they hide in this world.

Now to speak of the hope of those that are negligent and slow to shrive themselves – this consists of two kinds. One kind is, hoping to live long and acquire much riches for his delight, and then to be shrived; and so a man with this hope will say, it seems timely enough to come to shrift then. Another is over-confidence in Christ's mercy.

Against the first vice, a man shall think that our life has no safety, and also that all the riches in the world are in the hands of Fortune, and pass like a shadow on the wall. And, as Saint Gregory says, it pertains to the great righteousness of God that the pain of those that would never withdraw themselves of their own will from sin, but always continue to sin, shall never cease; for that perpetual will to commit sin they shall have perpetual pain.

Despair is of two kinds; the first despair is of the mercy of Christ; the other is that men think that they could not long persevere in goodness. The first despair comes when a man considers that he has sinned so greatly and so often, and lain so long in sin that he cannot be saved. Truly, in opposition to that cursèd despair he should think that the suffering of Jesus Christ is stronger to unbind than sin is to bind. Against the second kind of despair, he shall think that as often as he falls he shall rise again by penitence. And although he may have lain in sin never so long, the mercy of Christ is always ready to receive him. Against the despair in which he thinks that he would not long persevere in goodness, he should think that the weakness of the devil could do nothing unless men would permit him to, and also that he will have the strength of the help of God, and of all Holy Church, and of the protection of the angels, if he wishes.

Then men shall understand what the fruit of penance is; and according to the word of Jesus Christ, it is the endless bliss of heaven, where joy has no opposition of woe or grievance, where all evils of this present life are passed, where there is security from the pain of hell; where there is the blissful company that give themselves to rejoicing evermore, each one glad of the other's joy; where the body of man, that was formerly foul and dark, is more clear than the sun; where the body that before was sick, frail, feeble, and mortal, is immortal, and so strong and whole that nothing can harm it; where there is neither hunger, thirst, nor cold, but every soul is replenished with the sight of the perfect knowing of God. This blissful realm men can purchase by spiritual poverty, and the glory by lowliness; the plenty of joy by hunger and thirst, and the rest by labor, and the life thereby death and the mortification of sin.

Here the Maker of this Book takes his Leave

NOW I pray all who listen to this little treatise or read it, that if there is in it anything that pleases them, they thank our Lord Jesus Christ for that from whom all wit and all goodness proceed. And if there is anything that displeases them, I pray also that they set it to the fault of my lack of skill, and not to my intention, which would gladly have expressed it better if only I had the skill to do. For our Book says: "All that is written is written for our instruction;" and to write thus is my purpose. And therefore I beseech you meekly for the mercy of God that ye pray for me, that Christ shall have mercy upon me and forgive me my sins, and particularly, my translations and writings of worldly vanities, things which I withdraw, such as The Book of Troilus, The Book of Fame also; The Book of the Nineteen Ladies; The Book of the Duchess; The Book of Saint Valentine's Day of the Parliament of Birds; The Canterbury Tales, those that make for sin; The Book of the Lion, and many other books, if I could remember them; and many songs and lecherous lays; I pray that Christ in his great mercy will forgive me the sin of making them. But for the translation of Boethius' *De Consolatione*, and other books dealing with legends of saints, and homilies, and morality, and devotion, I thank our Lord Jesus Christ and his blissful mother and all the saints of heaven, beseeching them that henceforth to the end of my life they send me grace to bewail my sins, and study for the salvation of my soul, and grant me the grace of true penitence, and make confession and atonement in this present life, through the good grace of Him that is King of Kings and Priest over all priests, that redeemed us with the precious blood of His heart, so that at the Day of Judgment I may be one of those that shall be saved: *Qui cum patre*, etc.

Here ends the Book of the Tales of Canterbury compiled by Geoffrey Chaucer on whose Soul may Jesus Christ have Mercy
Amen

Geoffrey Chaucer,
c. 1345-1400

Chaucer's life spanned a time of extreme turmoil and social upheaval. In 1348-9, when Chaucer would have been a small child, the Black Death killed around a third of the population of Europe. The resulting shortage of manual labourers, particularly on the farms, contributed to massive social changes. Chaucer lived through the Peasants' Revolt of 1381, part of the extended Hundred Years' War with France (1337-1453), and the overthrow of King Richard II by John of Gaunt's son Henry of Lancaster who became Henry IV.

Chaucer was born in the early or mid-1340s to a wealthy family in London. The exact year of his birth is unknown. His father was a vintner – a wholesale wine merchant – and worked in the customs service. Little is known of Chaucer's early life, and the first records are of him working in the London household of the Countess of Ulster, a daughter-in-law of King Edward III. Chaucer seems to have followed the Countess's husband, Prince Lionel, into the army and served in the forces invading France in 1359. In 1360 he was captured and ransomed. Nothing is known of his life between 1360 and 1366, but in 1366 he married and in 1367 he joined the royal household as an esquire. His work would have taken him on trips in England and mainland Europe and could have involved military service. He certainly visited France, Flanders (Belgium) and Italy in the 1360s and 1370s and may have met Boccaccio and Petrarch on a visit to Florence in 1373. He may have studied law, Latin and French at the Inns of Court during the 1360s, too.

In 1374 Chaucer was appointed controller of export taxes on wool, sheepskin and leather; later wine was added to his responsibilities. It was a senior position, and he handled taxes of £24,000 a year. By comparison, his own salary was £10 a year. Chaucer continued to work as a royal envoy travelling abroad, including going on 'secret business of the king' in 1377. He was also writing poetry in the evenings. Chaucer finally left the customhouse some time in the 1380s and apparently moved to Kent, south west of London. In 1385 he became a justice of the peace and in 1386 a Member of Parliament, one of two members of the House of Commons for Kent. In 1387, his wife apparently died and he made his last trip abroad. Between 1386 and 1389 he worked on the *General Prologue* to the *Canterbury Tales* and some of the tales themselves. In 1389 he was appointed clerk of the King's works, a job that gave him responsibility for constructing and maintaining royal residences including Westminster Palace and the Tower of London. He gave up the position in 1391 and may have moved to Somerset in the west of England, as he became forester of the royal forest of North Petherton there. He died in 1400 and was buried in Westminster Abbey. His tomb became the first in what is now 'Poet's Corner' where many of England's greatest literary figures are buried.

CHAUCER'S WORKS

Chaucer's first major poem, *The Book of the Duchess*, is an elegy for Blanche, Duchess of Lancaster and wife of John of Gaunt, who died in 1368. He may have translated many poems from French and written a large number of short poems early in his career, too. Following in the tradition of poem claiming to be based on a dream, he wrote *The Parliament of Fowls* and *The House of Fame* in the late 1370s and early 1380s. He wrote *Troilus and Criseyde*, a classical tale set during the siege of Troy and often acclaimed his greatest complete work, in 1382-6. He worked on *The Canterbury Tales*, first as individual tales and later as a structured collection, from the 1370s until the end of his life.